BRAXTON CAMPUS MYSTERIES COLLECTION

BOOKS 1-4

JAMES J. CUDNEY

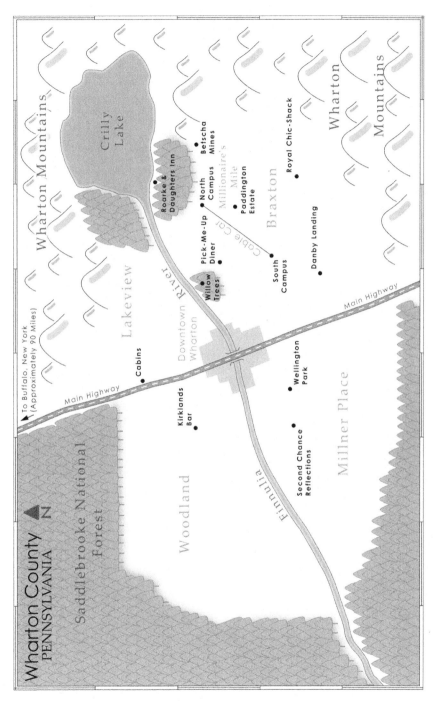

Welcome to Braxton, Wharton County (Map drawn by Timothy J. R. Rains, Cartographer)

ACADEMIC CURVEBALL

BRAXTON CAMPUS MYSTERIES BOOK 1

ACKNOWLEDGMENTS

Writing a book is not an achievement an individual person can do on his or her own. There are always people who contribute in a multitude of ways, sometimes unwittingly, throughout the journey from discovering the idea to drafting the last word. *Academic Curveball: A Braxton Campus Mystery* has had many supporters since its inception in June 2018, but before the concept even sparked in my mind, others nurtured my passion for writing.

First thanks go to my parents, Jim and Pat, for always believing in me as a writer, as well as teaching me how to become the person I am today. Their unconditional love and support have been the primary reason I'm accomplishing my goals. Through the guidance of my extended family and friends, who consistently encouraged me to pursue my passion, I found the confidence to take chances in life. With Winston and Baxter by my side, I was granted the opportunity to make my dreams come true by publishing this novel. I'm grateful to everyone for pushing me every day to complete this third book.

Academic Curveball was cultivated through the interaction, feedback, and input of several beta readers. I'd like to thank Shalini G, Lisa M. Berman, Didi Oviatt, Misty Swafford, Tyler Colins, Nina D. Silva, and Noriko for providing insight and perspective during the development of the story, setting, and character arcs. A special call-out goes to Shalini for countless conversations, helping me to fine-tune every aspect of the setting, characters, and plot. She read every version and offered a tremendous amount of her time to help advise me on this book over several months.

I'd also like to thank my editor, Nicki Kuzn at Booktique Editing, for helping fix all the things I missed along the way. She's been a wonderful addition to the team and has been very focused on making this book a success. Between coaching and suggesting areas for improvement, she's guided me in all the right directions.

Thank you to Next Chapter for publishing *Academic Curveball* and helping pave the road for more books to come. I look forward to our continued partnership.

WHO'S WHO IN BRAXTON?

AYRWICK FAMILY

- *Kellan*: Main Character, Braxton professor, amateur sleuth
- *Wesley*: Kellan's father, Braxton's retiring president
- *Violet*: Kellan's mother, Braxton's admissions director
- *Emma*: Kellan's daughter with Francesca
- *Eleanor*: Kellan's younger sister, manages Pick-Me-Up Diner
- *Nana D*: Kellan's grandmother, also known as Seraphina Danby
- *Francesca Castigliano*: Kellan's deceased wife
- *Vincenzo & Cecilia Castigliano*: Francesca's parents

BRAXTON CAMPUS

- *Myriam Castle*: Professor
- *Fern Terry*: Dean of Student Affairs
- *Connor Hawkins*: Director of Security, Kellan's best friend
- *Maggie Roarke*: Head Librarian, Kellan's ex-girlfriend
- *Jordan Ballantine*: Student
- *Carla Grey*: Student
- *Craig 'Striker' Magee*: Student
- *Bridget Colton*: Student
- *Coach Oliver*: Athletics Director
- *Abby Monroe*: Professor
- *Lorraine Candito*: Wesley's Assistant
- *Siobhan Walsh*: Communications Department Assistant

WHARTON COUNTY RESIDENTS

- *Ursula Power*: Friends with Myriam
- *Eustacia Paddington*: Nana D's frenemy
- *Alton Monroe*: Abby's Brother
- *April Montague*: Wharton County Sheriff
- *Marcus Stanton*: Braxton Town Councilman
- *Officer Flatman*: Police Officer

OTHER VISITORS

- *Derek*: Kellan's Boss in Los Angeles
- *Mrs. Ackerton*: Abby's Neighbor

OVERVIEW

When I decided to write a cozy mystery series, I adhered to all the main rules (light investigations, minimal violence or foul language, no sexual content, murder happens off-screen, protagonist is an amateur sleuth, and set in a quiet, small town). Some authors push the boundaries with variations, and in the Braxton Campus Mysteries, I followed the same route... just differently. Kellan, my protagonist, is a thirtyish single father, whereas traditionally a woman is the main character. Children aren't often seen in most series, but Kellan's family is important to the story. Kellan is also witty and snarky, but intended in a lovable and charming way, just like his eccentric grandmother, Nana D. Both are friendly, happy, and eager to help others, and they have a sarcastic or sassy way of interacting and building relationships... hopefully adding to the humor and tone of the books.

Cozy mysteries are different from hard-boiled investigations, thrillers, and suspense novels; the side stories, surrounding town, and background characters are equally important to building a vibrant world in which readers can escape. I hope you enjoy my alternative take on this classic sub-genre.

CHAPTER 1

I've never been comfortable flying. My suspicious nature assumed the magic suspending airplanes in the sky would cease to exist at some master planner's whim. Listening to the whirr of a jet propeller change speeds—or experiencing those jolting, mysterious *pockets of rough air*—equaled imminent death in an aluminum contraption destined for trouble. I spent the entire flight with my jaw clenched, hands clutching the armrests, and eyes glued to the seatback in front of me, impatiently hoping the diligent crypt keeper didn't claim another victim. Despite my uncanny knack for grasping anything mechanical and Nana D always calling me brilliant, I was entirely too doubtful of this mode of transportation. My gut promised I'd be safer plummeting over Niagara Falls naked and in a barrel.

After landing at the Buffalo Niagara International Airport on a miserable mid-February afternoon, I rented a Jeep to trek another ninety miles south into Pennsylvania. Several inches of densely packed snow and veiled black ice covered the only highway leading to my secluded childhood hometown. Braxton, one of four charming villages surrounded by the Wharton Mountains and the Saddlebrooke National Forest, felt impenetrable from outside forces.

As I changed lanes to avoid a slippery patch, my sister's number lit up the cell screen. I paused *Maroon 5* on my Spotify playlist, clicked accept, and moaned. "Remind me why I'm here again?"

"Guilt? Love? Boredom?" Eleanor chuckled.

"Stupidity?" Craving something of substance to squelch the angry noises radiating from my stomach, I grabbed a chocolate chip cookie from a bag on the passenger seat. The extra-tall, salted caramel mocha—free, courtesy of a pretty red-haired barista who'd shamelessly flirted with me—wouldn't suffice on its own. "Please save me from this torture!"

"Not gonna happen, Kellan. You should've heard Mom when I suggested you might not make it. '*He's always inventing excuses not to return home more often. This family needs him here!*' Don't worry! I calmed her down," shouted Eleanor over several dishes and glasses clanging in the background.

"Did she already forget I was here at Christmas?" Another cookie found its way into my mouth. I was powerless to desserts—also known as my kryptonite—hence why I'd always thought they should be a major food group. "Two trips home within six weeks is one too many by my count."

"How did our darling siblings invent acceptable excuses to skip the *biggest social event* of the season?" Eleanor said.

"I gave up competing with them years ago. It's easy to get away with things when they're not disappointing our parents like the rest of us."

"Hey! Don't take me down because you can't escape the awkward middle-child syndrome." Eleanor placed me on hold to deal with a customer complaint.

My younger sister unhappily turned thirty last month, given she *still hadn't met the right man*. She also insisted she wasn't morphing into our mother, despite every hour of every day steamrolling those figments of her imagination into oblivion. Truth be told, Eleanor was the spitting image of Violet Ayrwick, and everyone saw it but them. *Twinsies*, as Nana D always taunted with the cutest lilt to her voice. Eleanor would definitely be at our father's retirement party, as there wasn't a snowball's chance in you-know-where of me going to that boondoggle by myself. The man of the hour had been the president of Braxton College for the last eight years, but upon turning sixty-five, Wesley Ayrwick stepped down from the coveted role.

Eleanor jumped back on the line. "Was Emma okay with you visiting by yourself this time?"

"Yeah, she's staying with Francesca's parents. I couldn't sign her out of school again, but we'll *Facetime* every day I'm gone."

"You're an amazing father. I don't know how you do it on your own," Eleanor replied. "So, who's the woman you plan to meet while gracing us with your presence this weekend?"

"Abby Monroe completed a bunch of research for my boss, Derek," I said, cursing the slimy, party-going executive producer of our award-winning television show, *Dark Reality*. Upon informing Derek that I needed to return home for a family obligation, he generously suggested adding extra days to relax before everything exploded at the network, then assigned me to interview his latest source. "Ever heard the name?"

"Sounds familiar, but I can't place it," Eleanor replied in between yelling orders to the cook and urging him to hurry. "What's your next storyline?"

Dark Reality, an exposé-style show adding splashy drama to real-life crimes, aired weekly episodes full of cliffhangers like reality television and soap operas. The first season highlighted two serial killers, Jack the Ripper and The Human Vampire, causing it to top the charts as a series debut. "I've got season two's massive show bible to read this weekend... ghost-hunting and witch-burning in seventeenth-century American culture. I really need to get a new job. Or kill my boss."

"Prison stripes wouldn't look good on you." Eleanor teased me frequently.

"Don't forget, I'm too handsome."

"I'm not gonna touch that one. Let Nana D weigh in before I crush you for saying something so pathetic. Maybe Abby will be normal?"

"With my luck, she'll be another bitter, scorned victim rightfully intent on justice for whatever colossal trauma Derek's inflicted," I replied with a sigh. "I vote she's another loose cannon."

"When are you gonna interrogate her?"

I'd meant to schedule a lunch to get the basic lowdown on Abby, but I barely made the flight cutoff at the gate in the last-minute rigmarole. "Hopefully tomorrow, if she isn't too far away. Derek confirmed she lives in central Pennsylvania. He has no concept of space or distance."

"It's getting busy here. Gotta go. Can't make dinner tonight, but I'll see you tomorrow. Don't commit any murders until we chat again. Hugs and kisses."

"Only if you don't poison any patrons." I disconnected the phone, begging the gods to transport me back to Los Angeles. I couldn't take the stress anymore and devoured the last two remaining cookies. Given my obsession with desserts, the gym had never *not* been an option. Exercise happened daily unless I was sick or on vacation, which this trip didn't count as. There would be no beaches, cabanas, or mojitos. Therefore, I wouldn't enjoy myself.

I navigated the winding highway drive with the heater set to die-from-sauna max and the wiper blades on maniacal passive-aggressive mode to keep the windshield clear of heavy sleet and snow. It was the dead of winter, and my entire body shivered—not a good thing when my feet needed to brake for deer or elk. Yes, they were common in these parts. No, I hadn't hit any. Yet.

No time like the present to suggest a meeting to Abby. When she answered, I wasn't surprised at her naivety regarding my boss's underhanded approach.

"Derek said nothing about meeting anyone else. You got a last name, Kellan?" Abby whined after I'd already explained who I was in the first minute of the call.

"Ayrwick. I'm Kellan Ayrwick, an assistant director on the second season of *Dark Reality*. I thought we could review the research you prepared and discuss your experience working in the television industry."

A few seconds of silence lingered. "Ayrwick? As in... well... don't a few work at Braxton?"

I was momentarily stunned how a groupie girl would know anything about Braxton. Then I speculated she currently attended the college or previously went to school with one of my siblings. "Let's have lunch tomorrow. One o'clock?"

"Not really. I wasn't prepared to chat this weekend. I thought I'd fly out to Derek in the next few days. The timing is off."

"Can't we meet for a brief introduction?" Derek sure knew how to pick the dramatic ones. I could picture her twirling her hair and blinking her empty eyes despite not knowing what she looked like.

"I'm in the middle of an exclusive exposé about a crime in Wharton

9

County. Might be something to pitch to Derek for... well, it's too early to say anything." Her voice went limp. She'd probably forgotten how to use the phone or accidentally muted me.

"Is this what you proposed to him for a future season of *Dark Reality*? I'm more interested in true crimes and investigative reporting. Maybe I could help with this scoop." Once I realized she was in the same county as me, I tried all angles to snare a meeting.

"Are you Wesley's son? He's got a whole slew of kids."

My mouth dropped two inches. Nana D would've counted the flies as they swarmed in, given how long it remained open. Who was this girl? "I don't see how that's relevant, but yes, he's my father. Do you attend Braxton, Abby?"

"Attend Braxton? No, you've got a few things to learn if we're going to work together." She laughed hysterically, reaching full-on snort level.

"Great, so we can meet tomorrow?" The woman's tone annoyed me, but perhaps I'd misjudged her based on Derek's normal taste in women. "Even thirty minutes to build a working relationship. Are you familiar with the Pick-Me-Up Diner?" Eleanor ran the joint, so I'd have an excuse to step away if Abby became too much to handle. My sister could arrange for a waiter to dump a bowl of soup on Abby, then lock her in the bathroom while I escaped. There was nothing more I disliked than foolish, clueless, or vapid people. I'd had enough of them while dating my way through a sorority years ago. If I ran into one more *LA valley girl*, I'd let Francesca's family, the Castiglianos, take control of the situation. Scratch that, I never said those words out loud.

"No, sorry. I'm gonna be tied up, investigating all the nonsense going on around here. I'll see you on campus tomorrow night."

I shook my head in frustration and confusion. I clearly heard her stifling an obnoxious laugh again. If she weren't a student, why would she be on campus? "What do you mean *tomorrow night*?"

"The party celebrating your father's retirement."

Derek would owe me big-time for this ordeal. If he didn't watch himself, I'd give her his real cell number and not the fake one he initially dispensed.

"How do you know my—" A harsh tone beeped when she disconnected.

I continued on the main road into the heart of Braxton, tooting the horn as I passed Danby Landing, Nana D's organic orchard and farm. I was especially close with Nana D, also known as my grandmother, Seraphina, who'd turn seventy-five later this year. She kept threatening to bend our town's council-man, Marcus Stanton, over her lap, *slap his bottom silly,* and teach the ninny how things ought to be done in a modern world. It's my second job to keep her in check after the incident where she was *supposedly* locked up in jail overnight. Lacking any official records, she could continue to deny it, but I knew better given I was the one who had to convince Sheriff Montague to release Nana D. I hoped never again to spar toe-to-toe with our county's ever-so-charming head law enforcer, even if it's necessary to save Nana D from prison. I felt certain *that* had been a onetime card I could play.

The sun disappeared as I parked the Jeep at my parents' house and scampered toward the trunk to get my bags. Given the temperature had slipped to the single digits, and the icy snow wildly pelted my body, I hurried to the front door. Unfortunately, fate opted for revenge over some past indiscretion and struck back with the vengeance of a thousand plagues. Before long, I skated across a sheet of ice like an awkward ballerina wearing clown shoes and fell flat on my back.

I snapped a selfie while laughing on the frosty ground, to let Nana D know I'd arrived in Braxton. She loved getting pictures and witnessing me make a fool of myself. I couldn't decipher her reply, given my glasses had fogged over, and my vision was equivalent to Mr. Magoo's. I searched for a piece of a flannel shirt untouched by the falling sleet or the embarrassing crash to the ground and wiped them dry. A glance at the picture I'd sent caused the most absurd guffaw to erupt from my throat. My usually clean-cut dark-blond hair was littered with leaves, and the four days of stubble on my cheeks and chin was blanketed in mounds of snow. I dusted myself off and rushed under the protection of a covered porch to read her text.

Nana D: *Is that a dirty wet mop on your head? You're dressed like a hooligan. Put on a coat. It's cold out. I miss you!*
Me: *Thanks, Captain Obvious. I fell on the walkway. You think I'm normally this much of a disaster?*
Nana D: *And you're supposed to be the brilliant one? Have you given up on life, or did it give up on you?*
Me: *Keep it up, and I won't visit this weekend. You're supposed to be a sweet grandma.*
Nana D: *If that's what you want, go down to the old folks' home and rent yourself a little biddy. Maybe you two can share some smashed peas, green Jell-O, and a tasty glass of Ovaltine. I'll even pay.*

After ignoring Nana D's sass, I ran a pair of chilled hands through my hair and entered the foyer. Though the original shell of the house was a wood-framed cabin, my parents had added many rooms, including a west and an east wing bookending the massive structure. The ceilings were vaulted at least twelve feet high and covered in endless cedar planks with knots in all the right places. A pretty hunter-green paint coated three of the walls where the entranceway opened into a gigantic living room. It was anchored by a flagstone fireplace and adorned with hand-crafted antique furniture my parents had traveled all over the state to procure. My father was passionate about keeping the authenticity of a traditional log cabin while my mom required all the modern conveniences. If only the *Property Brothers* could see the results of their combined styles. Eleanor and I referred to it as the *Royal Chic-Shack*.

I dropped my bags to the floor and called out, "Anyone home?" My body jumped as the door to my father's study creaked open, and his head popped through the crack. Perhaps I had the paranormal and occult on my mind, knowing *Dark Reality's* next season was unfortunately in my foreseeable future.

"It's just me. Welcome back," replied my father, waiting for me to approach the study. "Your mother's still at Braxton, closing on the final admissions list for the prospective class."

"How's the jolly retiree doing?" I strolled down the hall toward him.

"I'm not retired yet," my father countered with a sneer. "I finished writing my speech for the party tomorrow evening. Interested in an early preview?"

Saying *no* would make me a bad son. Eleanor and I had promised one another at Christmas we'd try harder. I really wanted to be a bad son today—just kidding! "Sure, it must be exciting. You've had a bountiful career, Dad. It's undoubtedly the perfect example of oratory excellence." He loved when I stretched my vocabulary skills to align with his. I shuddered thinking about the spelling bees of long ago.

"Yes, I believe it is." My father squinted his eyes and scratched at his chin. No doubt he was judging my borderline unkempt appearance. I'd forgotten to shave and taken that classic nose-dive on the ground. Sometimes I preferred the messy look. Apparently, so did that airport barista!

I ambled to his desk, studying the frown lines forming around his lips. "Everything okay, Dad? You look a little peaked."

"Yes... a few things on my mind. Nothing to trouble you with, Kellan." He nodded and shook my hand—standard, male Ayrwick greeting. At six feet, my father stood only three inches taller than me, but the dominant Ayrwick genes made him look gargantuan. Lanky and wiry, he hadn't worked out a day in his life, but he also never needed to. His metabolism was more active than a thoroughbred, and he ate only the healthiest of foods. I was *lucky enough* to inherit the recessive Danby genes, but more on those cruel legacies another time.

"I'm a good listener, Dad. Tell me what's going on." I felt his bony hand pull away and watched his body settle into the worn, mustard-yellow leather chair in front of the bookcase. It was his only possession my mother hadn't yet replaced—purely because he'd threatened divorce. "It's been a while since we've talked."

My father stared out the window. I waited for his right eyebrow to twitch, signaling the onslaught of a battle, but the high arch never came. "We're having some problems at Braxton with a blogster. A bunch of articles or post-its, whatever you call them these days... trash is what I'd like to say." He closed his eyes and leaned back into the chair. "This isn't the way I pictured my pre-retirement weeks."

I stifled a laugh, hoping not to drive another decisive wedge between us. He'd opened up a little more than usual, and it didn't matter if he used the wrong terms to explain whatever fake news propaganda had developed at Braxton. "What's the blogger saying?"

"Someone has an ax to grind about the way I've supported parts of the college. He claims I'm favoring the athletics department by giving them more money this term." My father crossed his legs and cupped his hands together. His navy-blue corduroys and brown loafers seemed out of place.

Was he taking retirement seriously? I'd normally seen him in suits, or occasionally a pair of Dockers and a short-sleeve polo when he'd meet friends at the country club for a round of golf. I hoped it didn't mean he'd be wearing jeans soon. The shock of suddenly embraced normalcy might bury me in an early grave before that doomed airplane.

"Is the blogger going after you specifically or Braxton administration in general?"

My father quickly typed a few words on the iPad's keypad and handed the device to me. "That's the third message in two weeks. The links for the rest are at the bottom."

It's unlike my father to worry about this type of nonsense, but he'd become more sensitive about people's opinions as he grew older. It seemed the opposite of what I thought ordinarily happened as one aged. Nana D was the first to spill whatever was on her mind or laugh when others said anything negative about her. She almost delighted in their criticisms of her behavior. I couldn't wait to get old and say anything I want the way she did!

I scrolled through the recent post. The explicit focus on my father alarmed me the most.

Wesley Ayrwick, in his archaic and selfish ways, has struck another blow in eradicating the true purpose for Braxton's existence. His continued support for a failing athletics department while neglecting the proper education of our beloved student population has made it impossible for me to stand down. A recent six-figure donation was carelessly handed over to Grey Sports Complex for improving the technology infrastructure of the athletic facility, returfing the baseball field, and securing a modern bus for the players traveling to opposing teams. At the same time, the communications, humanities, and music departments suffer with minimal software programs, deteriorating equipment, and lack of innovative venue spaces for live performances. When asked about the decision to split the anonymous donation ninety percent to ten percent in favor of the athletics teams, President Ayrwick claimed they'd been waiting longer and were in danger of not being able to compete in the upcoming sports season. This is the third occurrence of his favoritism in the last two months, which clearly explains why the petition to remove Ayrwick from office sooner than the end of this semester is gaining momentum. Let's hope we can say goodbye to this crooked figurehead before Braxton's ship has sailed too far adrift from its proper course. Retirement must already be on the old coot's brain, or perhaps he's just one of the worst presidents we've ever had. My fondest wish is for Wesley Ayrwick's memory to be buried and long forgotten by the end of this term.

"What do you make of it?" he hesitantly asked.

A quick perusal of the earlier posts revealed similar sentiments, all fixated on my father for some perceived sense of unfair balance with the generous donations bestowed upon Braxton. The last line read like a death threat, but that might've been my imagination running wild since learning the startling truth about the Castigliano side of my family. "Who's the anonymous donor? Are you responsible for choosing where to allocate the funds?"

My father wrinkled his nose and raised his eyebrow. "No, you know better. When it's anonymous, even I'm not supposed to know. Sometimes the bene-factor has a specific request on where to distribute the money. I can offer my insight and suggestions, but the Board of Trustees and its budget committee ultimately decide where the funds go."

"I meant you have some influence." I stepped into the hallway to drop off my keys and wallet on a nearby bench. "Should it have gone to the athletics department?"

My father's scowl indicated his annoyance over my lack of unconditional support. "Yes. While I agree the purpose of a college education is to prepare for life in the real world, to study and learn a trade or a skill, it's also about devel-oping interpersonal relationships and opening one's eyes and mind to more than amassing facts." He crossed to the window, shaking his head back and forth, clearly distracted by something. "Sports build camaraderie, teamwork, and friendships. It provides opportunities for the college and the town to unite in support of their students. Leads to a stronger foundation and future."

I couldn't argue with his logic and pondered the past as I kicked off my shoes. "You've put that rather well. I believe you, Dad. Not to change topics, but I had a question about Abby Monroe. She mentioned attending—"

He never heard me as the door to his study slammed shut. I'd been home for ten minutes and already stuck my foot in my mouth. Between our off-the-charts intelligence and arrogant, stubborn streaks, neither of us could back down nor develop a normal relationship. I'd never learn how to bond with the indomitable Wesley Ayrwick. At least I could count on my quick wit and devilishly hand-some face to make things seem better!

I dragged the luggage to my old bedroom, which my mother had once fretted over, harboring some foolish notion I might move back home. Did she really think a thirty-two-year-old would want to sleep in a room still wallpa-pered with *Jurassic Park* and *Terminator* paraphernalia? Before settling in to digest Derek's show materials, I scurried downstairs for a light meal. The inci-dent in the study had left me zero desire to eat dinner with my parents. I'd just turned the corner when I heard my father's voice on the house phone.

"Yes, I read the latest post. I'm aware of our predicament, but we've already discussed it. Terminating the employee isn't an option."

It seemed the posts were causing major troubles, but my father had previ-ously acted like he didn't know who was behind the blog.

"I understand, but I've no intention of revealing this secret. I'm only keeping quiet because of the benefit to Braxton. If they discover the truth, we'll figure out the best solution. For now, I can handle a little hot water. You need to calm down," my father advised.

It sounded like the blogger was telling the truth about underhanded

14

chicanery. Was my father involved in a potentially illegal or unethical situation?

"You should've thought about it before taking a foolish approach to... now wait a minute... no, you listen to me... don't threaten me, or it'll be the last thing you do," he shouted angrily.

When he hung up, I ducked into the kitchen. Between the elusive Abby Monroe's connections to Braxton, the ruthless blogger publicly denouncing my father, and the hostile call I'd just overheard, this weekend might turn out more eventful than expected.

CHAPTER 2

When I stirred on Saturday morning, thick paste coated the insides of my mouth. The room was dark, and a low-rattling noise emanated from the far corner. I sat straight up in bed, smacked my head into a wood beam, and freaked out that I'd gone blind and a possum had snuck into the walls. I soon determined the obnoxious sound was the hissing of the radiators delivering much-needed warmth to the room.

Once the initial shock of my surroundings wore off, I stretched and grunted at the crunch in my lower spine from sleeping on the firmest mattress known to man. Between jet lag from the red-eye and the time difference, I'd dozed off early but woken up several times throughout the night. I checked my phone only to learn it was a few minutes shy of noon. That's also when I saw a message from my father chastising me for not bringing Emma home. Based on the time-stamp, it'd come in the previous night shortly after I'd overheard his argument. Did he know I'd been listening outside his office?

Wesley Ayrwick was not a frequent complainer, and if he elected to vent, it was only on important topics. The last time I'd pressed him for thoughts on something vital, he revealed how much he'd disliked my wife, Francesca. This had occurred when I asked for his help to plan her funeral after she'd been hit by a drunk driver in West Hollywood two years ago. Francesca and I had left her parents' house on Thanksgiving in separate cars, as she'd been staying with them while I was working on an out-of-town film project. I'd always be thankful Francesca's mother, Cecilia Castigliano, had strapped Emma into my car's safety seat that night. Thinking about the alternative scenario consistently brought me to tears. I wasn't anywhere ready to talk about losing my wife at such a young age, nor being a single parent, so let's allow that to sleep longer.

After brushing my teeth, I called to check on Emma, but she was swimming in the neighbor's pool. Her grandparents would contact me as soon as she returned home. I'd only been away for twenty-four hours, yet it felt as if a part of me was lost whenever we were apart. The connection felt fuzzy, as though the distance prevented me from truly knowing whether my six-year-old daughter was okay. I'd give up a lot of desserts to swing her in my arms right now. Or watch her dance to some silly cartoon on her iPad. My heart melted at the pure innocence of her smile.

Before summoning the courage to start the day, I tossed on some clothes and descended the staircase two steps at a time. Walking around the house in only my snug black boxer briefs wasn't an option. I trotted into the kitchen and brewed a pot of coffee, noticing my mother preparing lunch. I still needed to ferret out the detailed agenda for tonight's retirement party.

"How's the best mother in the world doing?" I embraced her the way only a son could remind his momma she's loved. Her shoulder-length auburn hair was pinned back with the jade butterfly clip Eleanor had given her for Christmas, and her face looked like she'd started applying makeup on one side but had forgotten the other half. I'd bet money on today's slipshod appearance resulting from something Nana D had done.

"Oh, Kellan! I wanted to come home early last night, but... the rehearsal for the party... talking to the planner about the seating chart... a near disaster. Do you know she had Nana D sitting next to Councilman Stanton at a table in the back row? I've told that planner ten times if I told her once... Marcus will make an important speech and needs to sit at the main table with your father. Nana D can't be anywhere near him based on their last public argument when she called him a—"

I interrupted before my mother prattled on for hours, bless her soul. "Got it. Makes total sense. You did the right thing, but I thought Nana D declined your invitation?" I suddenly remembered reading a text before falling asleep where Nana D clarified she'd rather spend an afternoon with her mouth crammed full of lemon wedges, her fingers pricked by a thousand tiny needles, and her feet glued inside a bumblebee's nest than attend another Braxton event for my father. "And what's with the crazy portrait-of-a-lady-with-two-faces look?" I cocked my head to the side, reached for the fruit bowl at the end of the island, and stepped a few inches away, certain she'd swat at me for that comment.

My mother, somewhere in her mid-fifties, had feverishly obsessed over her appearance for as long as I could remember. Despite my father telling her she's beautiful, or how he had to prevent all his friends from hitting on her, she put herself down. Even when my father explained how all his golf buddies called him a cradle robber because of my parents' ten-year age gap, she still went on a two-week hunt around the world for the latest wrinkle prevention products and anti-aging miracle cures.

"Whaaat? That woman is gonna be the death of me. She called while I was putting on my face and wanted to know if your father had changed his mind about retiring. She'd heard some rumor about his real intentions, then asked who wrote the scathing blog post. Any idea what she's talking about?" She ducked into the half-bath and applied a colorful powder to her right eyelid.

"We'll chat when you're done. Beauty first," I quipped, changing the topic and preparing a sandwich. "So, Nana D's not going? That's gonna make this party a lot less interesting."

My mother's lack of awareness surrounding the blog posts surprised me. She read everything about Braxton she could get her hands on—it was important to know what's being written about her college to prepare for questions from prospective or current students. Then again, she could've been craftily testing me to see what I knew and wasn't confessing. Often the little charade of trickery we played in the Ayrwick family got complicated—somewhere between a game of *Who's on First?* and *Russian Roulette.*

My mother smacked her lips together like a blowfish. "What did you say, Kellan?"

"Nothing. I'm glad to be home." Eleanor would have to agree that I'm being such a good son.

She retreated into the bathroom while I devoured the sandwich. When she reappeared, her face sparkled. Eleanor better watch herself, or people might ask questions like *who's the older sister* between the pair of them. Maybe I'd even start that rumor. It'd been an ice age since I stung Eleanor with a perfect zinger.

"What's the plan for tonight?" I blurted out while swallowing the last crumb of my sandwich.

"We'll greet early arrivals for the five o'clock cocktail hour. Then we present your father with a service award, and a few folks make speeches between six and seven. They'll serve dinner between seven and eight. Everyone can mingle afterward for an hour before it ends." She collected her breath, then popped a strawberry in her mouth. "I need to take lunch to your father. Please get there early. He wants to introduce you to people."

"Eleanor and I plan to arrive exactly at five. Cross one less worry off your list." I had to motivate her sometimes, or she'd fret over the tiniest things. "We'll be on our best behavior."

My mother kissed my cheek before ascending the stairs to deliver my father's meal. "I'll always worry about my children. Even Gabriel, despite not hearing from him for over seven years. Hugs and kisses!"

As she exited, I caught my reflection in the window and rolled my eyes at her lipstick marks. If I survived the night, I'd exact revenge on Nana D for avoiding it all. I sent her a text to remind her she'd promised to bake me a cherry pie for brunch tomorrow. There was no better dessert, especially the way Nana D prepared them with the cherries on top and the crust only on the bottom. She'd attach little pastry donuts on the side, so we could pull them off and dip them into the cherry filling. Mmm, delicious. Don't get me started on pie.

Nana D: *Arrive by 10. Have fun without me tonight. Please piss off your father for me.*

Wow! She had it in for him. I returned to my bedroom and dove into the show bible sitting on the night table. The next page was Abby's email to Derek from a week earlier. It read:

I'm so glad you selected me to provide the research on Dark Reality's *next season. I received the contract and will send back a signed copy next week. When do we meet again? I had so much fun drinking cocktails with you last month. You're adorable in that recent picture you sent from Tahiti.*
I have tons to share re the birth of witch covens in Pennsylvania and the Beguiling Curse of 1689. Should I book a flight to Hollywood soon? Will the network cover first-class tickets? This is the beginning of a lasting partnership. I've also stumbled upon something controversial going on in my hometown. It's worthy of a future season for our TV show, but I've got more research to do. I'll keep you posted.
How come I keep getting your voicemail? Can you please try to reach me tonight? I'll be home waiting for you to respond. In case you need my cell number, it's...

Derek had gotten himself into trouble again. Ever the talented rascal, Derek was known for dumping his crazy groupies on colleagues and getting everyone else to do his job for him. The last girl he'd assured a walk-on part on the set of *Dark Reality* hopped a series of red-carpet ropes during a season-one screening party, claiming Derek had promised her a front-row seat. When security called him over, my boss looked her right in the eyes and said, "*Never met this woman. Kick her out.*" I was there. I saw the confusion plastered on her face. I also noticed him blink twice, then his lip quivered. Derek had a *tell* I'd pegged from the first day we met.

Between yesterday's call and this email, a decisive picture of Abby Monroe popped into my head—twenty-six, blonde, hourglass shape, perky, and bubbly. She hadn't even known Derek blew her off and put me in the middle of this explosive atom bomb. I scrolled through the call log for Derek's number and patiently waited to connect. What was I walking into with Abby Monroe? Although I'd done most of the work on the first season, my name wasn't listed in the credits, nor were my contributions recognized by anyone at the network. Since I was way more experienced and intelligent—or maybe the better word was *talented*—than Derek, I'd learn everything I needed to earn my own award and escape his drama.

"Wussup? You should see the waves at this hour. Primo!" shouted Derek.

I'd forgotten he was in Hawaii and quickly converted the time before realizing the sun was just rising over countless breathtaking beaches. For some reason, I'd been gifted with the ability to retain way too much useless knowledge. "Oh, I hope I'm not waking you up."

"I haven't gone to bed yet, Kel-baby. We're about to rent surfboards. You should be here, man."

Any traces of guilt I had about rousing him from a blissful slumber disappeared, knowing he's the one who'd sent me on this foolish diversion. "No can do, Derek. Trying to pin down your source is proving to be difficult. How is Abby Monroe connected to Braxton?"

The waves intensely crashed against the sand as he mumbled about paying for rental surfboards. Someday I'd learn to extricate myself from these situations, but until then, it was best not to get on his nasty side. The last time we'd had creative differences, he hired my replacement to trail me all day, threatening to cut me loose if I didn't acknowledge his authority.

"She's a piece of work, ain't she? Never would have guessed Abby looked like that. You meet her yet? Thanks for dealing with this one, Kel-baby." He ignored the question about Braxton.

"It's Kellan." I'd told him before not to call me Kel-baby. It reminded me of a high school girlfriend who'd forced me to watch every episode of *Saved by the Bell* one summer, trying to perfect her acting skills. I'd had enough of the *Kelly Kelly Duo* and never again would someone mistakenly call me *Kel* or *Kelly* as a nickname. "What's Abby look like? Is this another awful Tinder date I should know about?"

"Dude, I'm innocent, I swear. She's hot for an older babe. And it's about time you got some—"

"Stop right there. My personal life is off limits," I said, knowing he irritated the most patient of people. "How much do you know about Abby?"

"I was going to say *attention*. You're acting holier-than-thou lately, and it's time you took off that faulty halo and engaged in some fun. Seriously, man. Let loose and take some risks while the network's paying for your trip. I gotta jet. My date's getting antsy, and these waves are fierce."

"Wait! Answer my question about Abby."

"I barely know her. We met at a conference in New York City last month. I gave her my number and email address. Didn't you read the show bible with all the open questions? Abby needs to fill in those blanks. I'm counting on you, Kel-baby. Later."

"You mean you gave her your fake number, right?" Various methods of revenge formulated in my head. I wanted to remind *Derek-baby* what people said about payback, but halfway through my witty comeback, he hung up.

Derek was the second person since I'd arrived in Braxton who'd chosen that route. Was I doing something wrong? What happened to proper manners? There were rules. One person initiated a goodbye sequence, and the other held it up to share remaining thoughts. There's an awkward moment how to end the call, and then you both said goodbye at the same time before the actual disconnect. Either I was getting old, or other people were getting crazier. I mentally added it to the list of things to ask Nana D the next time I saw her. Despite her age, she had all the answers about the new etiquette system of my generation's people.

Hoping to shake off the conversation and alleviate the knots in my back, I went for an hour-long run in Braxton's fresh mountain air. Many parts of the town—topping out at about three-thousand citizens—offered natural, untouched beauty everyone had protected for three hundred years. Shortly before Pennsylvania had become a state, my ancestors developed the sheltered land where the Finnulia River emptied into Crilly Lake at the base of the Wharton Mountains. Though the landscape was intoxicating, I had little time left before the party. I returned home, showered, and dressed for the event.

Promptly at four thirty, I stood outside Memorial Library, assuming Eleanor would be late. Inevitably, there would be some crisis at the diner—a lost car key or a last-minute wardrobe change. It's lucky my sister's saving grace had always been she's the most intelligent, loyal, and caring person in my life. If not, her constant tardiness and indecisiveness would drive me batty and send me running in the opposite direction.

The Paddington family originally erected Memorial Library. A fire damaged the first floor in the late 1960s during a Vietnam War protest that had gone off the deep end. The powers-that-be in charge of the campus at the time had rebelled against old-world charm and preserving history. The result was a cheap repair of the antiquated structure and an institutional, utilitarian-looking addition reminding everyone of a grammar school cafeteria gone wrong. It needed to be demolished and redesigned more than our town's government.

While waiting for Eleanor, a woman on a cell phone wandered past me. She was explaining how she'd already finished marking the exam and was on her way to enter the results in her grade book. It sounded like an unhappy student was trying to change the professor's mind about his or her grade. The last line I caught before she was out of range made me laugh, thinking about how far someone would go to demand a better mark. *"Yes, come to my office at eight thirty. But trust me, you won't alter my decision. Nada. Zilch. You're killing me with this persistent pressure and the multiple diversion tactics,"* she chastised.

My gaze switched to several students milling in and out of Memorial Library, surprising me how popular it was on a Saturday evening. Although I'd been a decent student during my time at Braxton, I had reserved weekends for fraternity parties, off-campus troublemaking excursions, and strenuous visits with my family. Saturday nights at a library were uncool a decade ago. It seemed much had changed.

I considered following a student inside to gander at the dreary interior décor, but stopped when two snowballs slammed into my shoulder. Not one to back down from a challenge, I ducked to the ground to gather a handful of snow and steadied myself to throw a powerful curveball. Had an immature student taken advantage of my distraction, or was the professor using me to express her frustration with the caller?

"So, he *can* clean himself up for the proper occasion," taunted my sister, throwing another snowball. "I'd have placed a bet you'd wear the usual jeans and a gray t-shirt tonight."

Nope, my expensive black suit and herringbone topcoat looked quite dapper. I rolled both eyes in her direction several times with enough emphasis that they almost got stuck on the final lap. "Funny! I'd have placed a bet you wouldn't be here until five thirty, so you could tell Mom it was my fault we were late."

Eleanor meandered over and gave me the biggest hug I'd received since the last time I was in town. "I miss you so much. Why do you leave me here in this boring arctic tundra alone with our parents? Can't you work from Braxton part of... oh, fine, I'll stop. The stars are telling me not to pester you anymore tonight."

I agreed about the arctic part. I'd never get used to it, especially after gazing at palm trees and listening to ocean waves in Los Angeles. When we separated, I scanned her shocking and brilliant transformation. Her curly, dirty-blond hair was pinned to one side of her head with a bright crimson bow matching the color of her dress. She wore heels, which I hardly ever saw her in for two reasons—one, she was a tad clumsy, and two, she claimed it made her tower over potential male suitors. We were the same height, but in the sparkling Christian Louboutin stilettos she'd chosen, I couldn't reach her on the tips of my toes.

I only knew the brand and type of shoes because Francesca had trained me well. We spent many Sunday afternoons window shopping up and down Rodeo Drive, guessing the prices of everything she loved but for which she refused to pay full cost. Despite being raised with money, my wife had loved a good bargain.

"You could always move to the West Coast if you can't hack it here." I smiled at how grown-up my baby sister looked in her red-sequined gown. She possessed a unique fashion sense, imposing her own spin on each outfit. Today, it was the dark-gray sash worn across her hips. Eleanor had always been sensitive about inheriting the Danby bone structure and found ways to either accentuate or hide it—whichever improved her look, depending on the garb and the position of the moon that day. She was a fanatic about horoscopes, astrology, and numerology. "Or consult that crystal ball of yours to see what's in store for your future."

"Oh, shut your trap door. Someday we'll live closer together. The cards have already decided so. Tell me, who do you think will be there tonight besides the usual stuffy colleagues and friends? I've had a premonition about something dark happening. Not sure who's in trouble, but someone's aura is dust!"

As she said her last line, thunder struck in the nearby Wharton Mountains. We both jumped. Our eyes bulged with indeterminate shock. "Yeah, let's get to the party before you invoke some sort of ancient curse on us. You've got the worst luck lately."

CHAPTER 3

Eleanor grabbed my hand, leading us toward Braxton's main entrance gate. As we walked, I summarized the incendiary blog posts and our father's mysterious phone conversation.

"I hope the blogger does nothing to embarrass Dad tonight," Eleanor said.

"He can take care of himself." We agreed not to confront him since it wasn't our business.

Braxton's campus was spread out across two parts of town and connected by a charming, antique cable car service covering the one-mile distance in between. The trendy transportation system functioned like an airport trolley between terminals—leaving North Campus every thirty minutes to make the return trip back and forth to South Campus. When the weather cooperated, it was a brisk fifteen-minute walk to reach either end. Quaint shops, the occasional college bar, and student rental housing lined the streets.

"Even though most of the primary academic buildings and student dorms are on North Campus, I've always found South Campus more idyllic." Besides hosting the executive offices and the campus coffeehouse, The Big Beanery, South Campus also housed the music, humanities, and communications departments. Paddington's Play House and Stanton Concert Hall were the big entertainment attractions keeping me from being bored as a student.

"True. I'm looking forward to seeing Mom's artisanal handiwork. She thought it would be a fun twist to rearrange all the tables in Stanton Concert Hall to face the center of the room. Even brought in a temporary dance floor and a raised platform for the speeches." As the cable car arrived, Eleanor filled me in on her exciting day at the Pick-Me-Up Diner. Braxton's baseball team had caused a big ruckus at their impromptu lunch. "It was odd when the cheerleading squad showed up too. They should've been discussing strategies to win the opening game."

"Aww, were you jealous? Did it stop you from flirting with the players?" I was on fire today.

"Bite me, Kellan. Even Coach Oliver couldn't control them when he handed out the team's newest college jackets. The burgundy and navy-blue colors looked like a cool design."

I quipped, "We both know the real reason the team's onset annoyed you is because cash-limited students are notorious for leaving no tips."

When all the passengers disembarked, Eleanor and I squeezed into a two-seater near the back plastered with characters from Marvel comics. Each year, the graduating class presented a gift to the college to redesign the cable car as their outgoing mark on Braxton.

"Bring back any memories, *gladiator-man?*" asked Eleanor.

I'm ashamed to admit my class had chosen a Spartan theme since the movie 300 had just hit theaters. At the unveiling ceremony, they forced me to wear an extremely short, body-hugging tunic while wielding a plastic shield and spear. I'd almost died of embarrassment when the fabric split open as I kneeled for a picture. I hadn't looked as handsome back then as I did now. Yep, you gotta get used to this humor!

We arrived at Stanton Concert Hall, aptly named for Lavinia Stanton, an elderly spinster ancestor of Marcus Stanton's who'd left her entire life savings to Braxton in the early twentieth century. A lippy security attendant greeted me, snapped my picture, and typed in a few commands on a keypad. Thirty seconds later, he returned a badge with a bunch of codes and symbols.

"Can you make the machine explode when you create Eleanor's ID?" I asked the attendant, who unfortunately didn't find me hilarious. The process completed flawlessly.

The guest list topped out at two hundred colleagues, family members, and friends. I skimmed the expanse of the room with a fleeting thought that I could pick out Abby, but no one matched the imagined description.

My mother had outdone herself. She transformed the hall into a full-on party atmosphere complete with authentic, old-fashioned lampposts retrofitted as conversation tables where we could eat endless amounts of hors d'oeuvres; ornate beverage carts rolled around by penguin-clad waiters serving a fizzy blue cocktail; and a fine mist spraying jasmine from the ceiling. Eleanor went in search of our parents while I tested the aqua concoction. A bit tart for me, but I saw the appeal.

While mingling, I caught up with my former art professor and shook hands with Councilman Marcus Stanton—his palm was so clammy I'd never wipe off the pungent pool of sweat. The handshake was also too weak for a real politician. No wonder Nana D had it in for him.

When an incoming text vibrated, I hoped it was Abby, but it was from my daughter, Emma. She was back from the neighbors and wanted to tell me she missed me and loved me. I sent a video of a papa bear cuddling with his baby bear—our way of sharing a hug when we weren't in the same place together.

She was intelligent and intuitive for her age and loved our quirky relationship. Six going on sixteen!

Before putting away the phone, I texted my father's assistant. Lorraine Candito had served as my father's right-hand woman for twenty years, including following him from his prior position at Woodland College across the river. I was certain she was the only reason I'd gotten birthday cards or frequent packages from my father. My mother was too busy and had her own way of showing how much she cared, but Lorraine was like a favorite aunt you could always count on. My phone buzzed with her response:

Let's connect after dinner. Need to get your gift. I left it on my desk.

Curiosity brewed, then I remembered something from Christmastime. She'd probably bought me a present with the new Braxton logo. I texted back a confirmation and caught sight of my father approaching from the dance floor.

"Let me introduce you to someone, Kellan," he began. A woman with short, spiky gray hair followed nearby. Her natural black shade had faded and rather than dye it, she'd accepted the graceful aging process. I commended her. If my hair color ever began to change, I'd be the first in line at the salon. I could be a bit vain about these things. Although her hair was striking, her pursed lips and icy stare stole my attention's focus.

I reached my hand to her, hoping the councilman's sweat had dissipated, or she'd be in for her own unpleasant shock. "Pleased to meet you... Mrs.... Miss...?"

My father continued talking when she failed to engage. "This is Dr. Myriam Castle. She's a professor in our communications department and has been at Braxton for... what, three years now?"

As she nodded, the temperature of the air between us distinctly dropped. It wasn't just the crisp, stark power suit molded against her thin frame. The deep and pointed collar of her pink dress shirt covered her entire neck and had a small opal and silver broach clasped over the top button. The lines on the shoulders, sleeves, and pant legs were as sharp as a knife blade, but the sensible black pumps convinced me she was a no-nonsense gal.

"Yes, three at the beginning of this last term. Are you enjoying the party the college has so thoughtfully thrown? It must have cost quite a small fortune to put on this show, but you are beloved around here for your... *generosity*," she replied with a tartness one only experienced when tasting something exorbitantly sour. "*Men's evil manners live in brass; their virtues we write in water.*"

I glanced from her to my father, anticipating an insightful and punishing retort. She'd quoted Shakespeare's *Henry VIII* in her petulant dig about virtues. Could she be the blogger? The acerbic tone of her words matched the profile of the anonymous villain.

"Oh, Myriam, ever the clever one. I'd love to chat, but I must prepare for my speech. I hope you'll have a splendid time despite it coming so unnaturally to you," my father replied.

As he walked away, a snicker formed on his lips. Maybe I *would* have some fun at this party. "I see you have quite the banter. I trust it's in good humor."

"Wesley Ayrwick and I have an understanding. He is aware of my contributions to the college. I am aware he'll be replaced imminently." As a server passed, Dr. Castle dropped her empty glass on a tray and grabbed a fresh one. "So, how do you know our fine president? Do you work at the college?"

Ah, she didn't know I was his son. I thought I'd leave out that fact to see what else I might learn. "I can't remember when we first met. Years ago, but it's all a little fuzzy. To answer your last question... no, I live in Los Angeles and am back in Braxton for a few days." I considered my options for extending the conversation about her opinions of my father, then realized I should take advantage of my opportunities. I had little time left before the speeches started. "Dr. Castle, are you familiar with Abby Monroe?"

My new friend cleared her throat and slid her glasses down the bridge of her nose. "My night keeps improving. Is that why you've attended this party? A guest of Monroe's?"

"On the contrary. I've never met the woman. Might you point her out?" I could tell Dr. Myriam Castle was an expressive woman. All her gestures were over-exaggerated, and her words offered two, maybe even three levels to them. "If you know what she looks like, that is."

"I've had the unwelcome privilege to meet Monroe many times. I'm not one to push my opinions on other people, Mister...?"

She hoped I'd fill in my surname, but it was more fun leaving her with the short end of the stick. "Oh, but I'd love to hear your thoughts. Please, feel comfortable sharing whatever's on your mind." I noticed a moment where Dr. Castle considered my words, then saw my father step to the podium.

"Monroe thinks the world of herself and has made it clear to everyone at Braxton how she got her job. An intelligent, savvy young man should easily recognize the elevator does not go all the way to the top floor in that woman's head." As she pivoted to leave, the boom of the microphone resounded.

I found it funny the way she called the woman *Monroe*. "It was a pleasure meeting you, Dr. Castle. I look forward to chatting again soon, but we need to gather around the center floor." I extended my hand in the stage's direction and watched her head lift higher and her nose wrinkle as though something odorous wafted by.

"Trust me. Stay clear of her. While you're in town, also be careful not to associate too closely with the Ayrwicks. They might be on top right now, but it won't be for long, I'm confident."

I shrugged and stepped in the opposite direction. Wait until I told Eleanor and Nana D all about Dr. Myriam Castle. Would they know any gossip about the woman? I needed to find out what this feud was all about. I sent a text to Abby asking when we could meet. She confirmed quickly, suggesting *nine in the foyer*, when the party ended.

My father's speech was better than I'd expected, as was Councilman Stanton's brief but remarkable words. Perhaps I could overlook the flimsy handshake if his verbal skills were a strong counterbalance. Dinner was relatively tasty—chicken cordon bleu, rice pilaf, and steamed asparagus. I saw a vegetarian dish at a few tables too. Kudos to my mother for remembering other people's needs and preferences. Ever since she'd developed a shellfish allergy, she became much more attentive to food choices.

I'd already sampled one fizzy blue drink and one glass of champagne earlier and was now standing near a portable bar cart, contemplating a third, when my sister approached. "Guess whom I ran into?" she sang in an awkward, jovial tone. "Don't turn around. I'll give you three chances."

I thought I'd met everyone at the party given how often I introduced myself in the last few hours, except of course for Abby, the one person I wanted to come across. Could my luck be changing? "Ummm... The Queen? Meryl Streep?" She's my favorite actress. A guy could dream, right? "Pink?" I had a crush on her for years, yet it was highly unlikely she'd show up for a retirement party. Now that I'd exhausted my three guesses, the silly game could end, and I could turn around.

"Wrong! It's Maggie Roarke. You remember her, right?" Eleanor teased while hopping up and down like an overzealous Easter bunny.

The room stood still, and I was transported back a decade. Even the song playing in the background felt like I'd leaped through time and was sitting on a giant comfy couch at The Big Beanery, listening to Michael Bublé croon while Maggie and I sipped cappuccinos and ate biscotti. I hadn't seen my best friend and former girlfriend since we'd broken up at our college graduation. "Maggie, I can't believe I didn't notice you earlier. You look... you look...." I wanted to say fantastic and gorgeous, but after ten years, it didn't seem appropriate.

"I look marvelous, Kellan. It's okay, you can say it." Her luscious straight brown hair was pulled back across one shoulder. There was a radiant shine making her more attractive today than when we were in our early twenties. She looked confident and decisive, traits she'd always envied but struggled to find in the past. "You're as handsome as ever."

When I leaned in to embrace her, instinct took over. I kissed her cheek, and my body flooded with an unusual yet familiar warmth. Alabaster skin shined, and deep brown eyes peered back at me, almost making her look like a frozen statue or an elegant piece of porcelain. "I'm sorry. It was a surprise to see you. A welcome surprise."

Eleanor chimed in, sensing she should give us a moment alone. "Oh, there's Mom. I've been looking for her. I'll be back." As she stepped away, a quick pinch at my waist confirmed she'd planned the setup. Retaliation for my earlier comments about her crystal ball search for the future. Score one for Eleanor tonight. At least she joined the playing field.

"I agree," Maggie replied. "You must be so excited your father is retiring. Will your mother leave next? They should travel the world after working so hard for Braxton. I'll miss seeing them."

Maggie and I had separated when we attended different graduate schools. We tried to maintain a friendship, but we were both secretly upset with the

27

other for not trying to make a long-distance relationship work. We'd emailed that summer, yet once she left for Boston, all communication stopped. It suddenly occurred to me what she'd said about missing my parents. "Great seeing you, but what brings you to the party, Maggie?"

"Oh, you don't know? I started working at Braxton this semester as the new head librarian. I moved back from Boston after the job fell into my lap. Do you remember Mrs. O'Malley?" Maggie announced it was too loud near the rest of the crowd, so we stepped to the far corner.

Mrs. O'Malley had been the head librarian for over thirty years when we'd attended Braxton—a fixture who knew everything and everyone on campus. She'd once caught Maggie and I making out behind the ancient microfiche machine and rather than scold us for getting intimate in a public place, she embarrassed us for picking the oldest piece of equipment in the building as our romantic hiding place. She told us even she had the intelligence to take Mr. Nickels, the cable car's engineer, to the downstairs reference section where no one had ever gone. Imagine a sixty-something lovesick woman shaking her finger at two college seniors over that.

"I haven't thought about her in forever. I guess she retired." I wasn't a granny chaser, but I'd felt a weird attraction to Mrs. O'Malley after she'd told us about her illicit affair.

"Last fall. I'd gotten the strangest call. We'd kept in touch over the years, and she wanted me to know about her plans to leave Braxton. Mrs. O'Malley was the primary reason I earned my advanced degrees in library studies. She invited me back to talk about the changes happening at Memorial Library, then had me meet with your father to discuss the position. Three weeks later, I gave notice to my job in Boston."

I couldn't believe how much Maggie had changed. Gone was the little mouse I used to know and adore. I always wondered what would've happened if Maggie and I had decided differently that day.

"That's awesome. I'm thrilled and also a trifle shocked my father never mentioned it."

"Or your mother. She and I meet for coffee when I can take a break from the library, or when she needs to get away from prospective students pressuring her for an acceptance decision." Maggie brushed several bangs from her soft and stunning features. "You know nothing about our weekly walk from South to North Campus along Millionaire's Mile?"

Behind the main road between campuses were larger estates where families like the Stantons, Greys, and Paddingtons lived. We had nicknamed it Millionaire's Mile long ago, and it was a key attraction in Braxton for visitors and new students who wanted to learn about the history of the town's wealth.

I shook my head. "I'll find out later. Now that I know you're back in Braxton, let's grab a coffee. I'll be in town for a week, maybe more." We chatted about the last decade, and I discovered her husband had tragically died of a brain aneurysm several years ago. My heart broke for her at having to go through the devastating loss of a spouse, but it was also a moment where our connection flourished like when we'd dated in college. It was in that instant I felt a sense of security about the future, as though reestablishing a friendship with Maggie might help me move forward.

I glanced toward the hall's entrance, where my father's assistant dashed into the room. Even at this distance, something looked off. Lorraine's blue dress was slightly askew, and her eyes darted erratically. She was clearly agitated and looking for someone. In the distraction, I failed to hear Maggie's response.

"Kellan, where did you go?" Maggie tapped my shoulder. "I'd love to meet at The Big Beanery to catch up on life post-college. Emma sounds delightful."

My gaze returned to Maggie. "We should do it. Definitely," I countered and rattled off my cell phone number. "Do you know my father's assistant, Lorraine?"

"Yes, such a sweet woman. I wonder if she's retiring now that your father will leave Braxton this semester."

It hadn't occurred to me, nor could I remember my father saying anything. "She's walking this way and looks quite unraveled. I hope the food's not making people sick."

Maggie and I turned toward the entrance and waited for her arrival. I spoke first. "Lorraine, it's so wonderful to see you. Everything okay?"

"Your father... dead body...." Lorraine struggled to respond, then slumped to the floor.

CHAPTER 4

While I reached for Lorraine's left arm, Maggie propped her against a table. "What's wrong? Are you ill?" I worried she was having a stroke or heart attack. She looked practically catatonic.

"I'm afraid your father... have you seennn hhhim?" Her breathing labored, and a look of terror possessed her face. Though her skin was usually quite pale, she looked nearly translucent.

What did she mean by *a dead body*? She'd aged ten years in those moments. I pulled out my phone and pressed the button to dial his cell. "What's going on, Lorraine?" Maggie briefly slipped away and returned with a glass of water. People had begun to leave the party. My phone verified it was exactly nine o'clock. The call went to voicemail. I didn't leave a message, as I had no idea what to say.

"I saw... ummm... someone needs to... check on... now!" She pointed out the window and covered her mouth. Exaggerated expressions produced unfortunate wrinkles on her forehead. "I'm sorry... such a shock."

"What?" I grew fearful over what she might have seen. "Did something happen to my father?"

Maggie rubbed Lorraine's back to comfort the panicked woman. "Talk to us."

Lorraine finished drinking her water. "I went back to the office to get your Christmas present. It was so lovely, and... but then I...."

I nodded. "That was thoughtful, thank you. But surely that's not what has you so upset." I had no clue what caused her to approach hyperventilation mode. "What about my father?"

"I couldn't find him, that's why I came to you. Went to the back door... closer to my desk... working there temporarily... finish all the construction."

Lorraine paused and let out a deep breath. Her hazel eyes shifted and filled with wild anxiety. "I got the key to unlock it... saw it was partially open."

I wasn't sure what she'd meant by temporarily working elsewhere, but I didn't want to interrupt her baffling train of thought. "Okay. Did you go inside?"

"No, I couldn't. I tried to push the door open... wouldn't budge. It only moved an inch... crack wasn't wide enough to stick my head through. That's when I ran around to the front of the building... used the main entrance."

"Keep talking, tell us everything." Maggie's gaze went broad with confusion.

Lorraine composed herself. "I walked through the hallway to the back of the building. I thought I could open the other door leading into the stairwell from the inside, but it wouldn't move either. Something was sitting on the platform, preventing both doors from opening."

"Right. It's such a tight space. Two people can't open the doors at the same time since they both open inward," Maggie responded. "Then what?"

Lorraine explained she'd gone up to the second floor to look down the stairwell and see what was on the other side of the doors. While she painfully told us everything—probably suffering from shock over what she'd seen—I wondered why my father had left the party. Had he gone to meet someone? Why wasn't he picking up my calls? Was there really a dead body?

"Somebody fell down the stairs. I could see blood. I thinkkk they hit their head. Might be deaddd," Lorraine stuttered with a wicked shiver.

Maggie stifled a scream. Her body twitched from the tension. She'd been leaning against me as we comforted Lorraine. "Who was it?"

Lorraine's eyes opened wider. "I was too afraid to go down. Will you checkkk the building next door?"

Maggie offered to stay and take care of Lorraine while I went to the other building. My stomach sank in fear something horrific had happened to my father.

"No, I have to come with you," Lorraine murmured. "I locked the front door after I left. I... I... didn't know what to do and just came running over here."

Lorraine had either drank too many fizzy blue concoctions or was imagining things in the dark, but intuition told me something real had genuinely frightened her. The three of us left the retirement party and scrambled toward the temporary office space. Meeting Abby would have to wait. I encouraged the ladies to run faster, eager to see what had happened to my father or someone else.

"I'm going as fast as I can," Lorraine noted.

Heaviness settled in my chest, and a sharp pain jabbed my gut. Please don't be my father. I wasn't ready for him to get sick or die. When Maggie, Lorraine, and I arrived at the building, it became clear she'd been referring to Diamond Hall, where I'd spent many hours attending literature, art, and media lectures.

It hadn't occurred to me when Lorraine said the building next door she'd meant *literally next door* to Stanton Concert Hall. My father's normal executive office building was farther away near the cable car station. Was the threatening call I'd overheard the previous night that serious?

Diamond Hall, an old colonial-style mansion, had been converted into a series of classrooms and departmental offices a few decades earlier. A limestone facade mined from local Betscha quarries in the 1870s covered all three stories of the impressive building. The well-manicured primary entrance contained a winding slate path, burgundy shutters adorning large, crisscross lattice windows, and giant rhododendron bushes growing in the front gardens. On the first floor were four large classrooms, each capable of seating at least thirty students, two single bathrooms, and a small supply closet. In the front entrance was a staircase set between two center walls taking visitors to the upper floors, and in the back was another small staircase—previously a servant's access passage—allowing professors direct access to their offices without having to go through the main classroom area.

"Show me exactly where you saw a body, Lorraine," I directed with increasing trepidation in my voice. "We should call 9-1-1, but I'd like to verify what you saw before we—"

"It's a body. I know what I saw, Kellan," Lorraine interjected with a much calmer voice than when she'd first informed us. "Follow me."

We ran up to the second floor where ten or twelve oddly shaped offices— typically the center of many vocal professors arguing about who deserved the biggest space—resided. While there was no staircase accessing the third floor from the back side of the building, a narrow one in the front led to a cozy library and common area for students working on a group project or a professor holding a special lecture session. Based on what Lorraine had told me on the walk over, my father recently commandeered the third floor during the renovations on his office. Since the top floor was only large enough for his furniture, given the peaks of the slanted roof and the built-in library shelves, Lorraine sat in a central open section on the second floor between the two staircases.

My stomach twisted in agony. There was a good chance my father could be at the bottom of the stairwell. All three of us crossed through the second floor past Lorraine's desk and looked at the swinging door to the back stairwell. "Did you leave it open?"

She shook her head. "I thought I'd closed it. Maybe I ran out and didn't pay attention. The body is inside. Step into the vestibule and look down to the right."

I'd seen a few dead bodies in the past. It had never bothered me until they called me to the morgue to verify Francesca's identity on Thanksgiving. I still remember the fear moments before they lifted the sheet. I ultimately couldn't do it and stepped out of the silent and frigid room, grateful to my father-in-law for taking on the responsibility. I had to be brave and determine if Lorraine were losing her mind or if there was any truth to what she'd seen. I tiptoed into the vestibule with my eyes closed, turned to the right, and felt my composure

fade. I slanted my head at the angle I thought would align with the bottom platform and opened my eyes.

The way the body laid on the floor all tangled up was the most horrid part.
Two legs were folded under the person's upper half, and his or her head was
trapped between twisted hands and arms. That's when I breathed a sigh of
relief. It wasn't my father. It was the woman I'd seen outside the library on the
phone while waiting for my sister.

I'd been quiet for too long, prompting Maggie to screech, "What's going on,
Kellan?"

I peeked my head around the corner of the wall and observed a shaky
Maggie and Lorraine holding hands. "Yes, someone's down there. I can't tell if
she's breathing."

"Please go check, Kellan. She could be hurt," begged Lorraine while
puttering with several pieces of costume jewelry on her wrist.

I shuffled down the steps. Something told me the victim was a goner. When
I reached the platform, there wasn't a lot of room to move around, but I
stretched my nervous hand to the woman's neck.

"Is she alive? Should I call 9-1-1?" Maggie asked.

"No, she's dead. There's no pulse, but we need to call them, anyway."

Lorraine yelled back at me. "I'm on my way down. I'm well enough to
assist."

Maggie dialed the emergency line and explained the situation on speakerphone. When Lorraine reached the last step and stood a few inches from me,
she grabbed my elbow. "Can you turn her head? I think I recognize her."

"Not a good idea. If she's just unconscious, we could cause spinal damage."
This wasn't the night I'd expected. I wanted something livelier than a boring
retirement party where I listened to dull speeches and met my father's insipid
friends and colleagues—not dealing with a dead body.

Lorraine leaned forward over my shoulders. I cautioned her to avoid the
patch of blood on the stairs. The woman must have smacked her skull hard
when she fell, to cause it to bleed like that. Just as I thought Lorraine was going
to back away, she gasped. "Oh, my word! I know her."

I wasn't in the mood to comfort someone else over death right now, especially if they were friendly with the person. I merely wanted to give a statement
and locate Eleanor. "Ummm... who is she, Lorraine?"

"Abby Monroe," squealed Lorraine with a series of "It can't be, it can't be"
wails.

Maggie bellowed to us from the top of the stairwell. "The ambulance is on
its way. The cops are coming too. I should call Connor."

When I first heard the name, my immediate thought shifted to my other
former best friend and fraternity brother, Connor Hawkins. He and I had
stopped chatting around the time we'd all graduated ten years ago too. "Hold
up, Maggie. Lorraine thinks she knows who this is." Tonight was becoming way
too creepy.

"I couldn't tell from way up top, but I saw her at the party earlier wearing this same outfit. Dean Terry remarked how well that sapphire blue empire-cut blouse matched her eyes. And that skirt... Abby always wears pencil skirts." Lorraine nervously pulled at her blond curls.

"Are you sure? I've been looking for Abby Monroe all evening," I said.

Lorraine wobbled her head. Based on the peculiar expression on her pale face, my news had confused her. "Why were you meeting her? Maybe we should wait for the cops upstairs. I feel a little weird standing so close to... you know... ummm—"

"The body?" I tossed both hands in the air. Things were not going well since I'd returned home to Braxton. "I'll explain another time why I was meeting her." As we both climbed the stairs to the second floor, Lorraine awkwardly grinned back at me.

When we arrived, Maggie rested her hand against her forehead. "Connor will be here any minute. He'd just gotten to the retirement party to wish your father well."

"Ummm... Connor who?" Given the number of times I'd been surprised already that night with Maggie returning to Braxton, finding Abby at the bottom of a stairwell, and meeting the peculiar Myriam Castle, I had an inkling Maggie's Connor would be our Connor from years ago.

"Connor Hawkins. Don't you remember anyone, Kellan?" shot her somewhat sassy response. The drama of finding a dead body was causing everyone to be irritable and short-tempered.

"Did I hear my name?" boomed a deep voice across the hall. A darker-skinned man a few inches taller than me walked past the central admin area and hugged Maggie. They whispered something and shared an intimate connection.

Yep, it was the same Connor. But it was also an extraordinarily different Connor. This Connor obviously spent his day working out at the gym or popping steroids. "Is that really you?" I asked in puzzlement, looking from him to the stairwell hiding Abby's lifeless body.

"Kellan, what are you doing here?" He wrinkled his brow and jolted his head sideways.

"Well, yeah, it seems kind of obvious being that it's my father's retirement party." I hadn't meant to sound like a jerk, but I was a bit off-kilter given everything happening that evening.

"I know... I meant at Diamond Hall," Connor said authoritatively.

A desperate sense of loss surrounded me. Connor, Maggie, and I had been inseparable all throughout college. When Maggie and I had broken up, he took her side and told me how stupid I was to let her go. What had happened to him after Braxton?

I responded, "Lorraine found the body and sought help. I was the nearest person she could find." Visions of Francesca's last moments plagued me. I couldn't think straight.

Connor moved uncomfortably in his light tan suit and striped Braxton tie, but it was a powerful offset to his cocoa-touched skin. His mother was from the Caribbean, and his father was a South African sailor on leave from the navy when they'd met. Connor had inherited the best features from both and was always considered charming and gorgeous by the girls who melted anytime they heard his accent. Back in school, he'd been in decent shape, but he could now pass for a twin to Adonis. "I can't believe you're here. And Abby is there. How did...?"

Maggie tapped her foot. "Although I'm sure you boys can't wait to catch up, maybe Braxton's crack security team could do a quick check on the body randomly hanging out at the bottom of the stairs?"

"It's Abby Monroe, the chair of the communications department," Lorraine insisted.

"I'll go check. Are you sure she's already dead?" Connor added with a pointed stare.

I nodded. "Pretty certain. You're a security guard now?"

"No, he's your father's *head* of security for the college. Do you not know about that either?" sniped Maggie. The shock was overwhelming all of us.

I swallowed my tongue and pride. My parents had some explaining to do. "Let's not get into that right now. Did she trip over something and hit her head?" Nobody responded. As Connor descended the steps, I turned to Lorraine. "Are you okay? Did you know Abby well?"

Before she could respond, two people strutted across the second-floor office space. A familiar, mid-thirties blonde in a pair of dark jeans, an ill-fitting tweed coat, and standard-issue beat-walking shoes announced, "I'm Sheriff Montague. There's been a report of someone falling down a flight of stairs?" She turned to her colleague, a male cop with a crew cut, an enormous nose that must have been broken several times, and a pair of furry earmuffs. "This is Officer Flatman."

"I'm down in the stairwell, Sheriff Montague," shouted Connor.

While the two newest arrivals followed Connor's voice to the body, I thought about what Abby's death would mean to Derek's plans for the second season of *Dark Reality*. I should have called him right away, but I had no information other than she'd died. I also tried to reach my father, but he didn't pick up again. I called my mother.

"Kellan, I've been looking for you for nearly an hour. Please don't tell me you left already," my mother said in a shrill voice. She should have been an actress instead of Braxton's admissions director.

"No, I'm... outside. Is Dad around? I need to talk with him about something... important." I didn't want to alarm my mother, given how easily agitated she'd become since my arrival.

"I was looking for him myself, but he got pulled into an urgent meeting and said he'd find me at some point tonight. You know your father, even in near-retirement, he still feels obligated to remain a workaholic."

I mumbled something to my mom, making it sound like I agreed with her, and told her I'd be back to the party as soon as possible. I turned to Maggie and Lorraine to verify what they were doing. Lorraine chatted on the phone with someone, but I couldn't determine his or her identity. Something about urgently returning a call that evening to discuss what she'd found.

Maggie sat on a guest chair opposite Lorraine's desk and fiddled with her earlobes. She'd always played with them when nervous or worried about something life changing. "It's awful to know she fell down the stairs, and no one was here to help her. I hope she didn't experience any pain."

I was about to reach out and wrap my arms around Maggie when Connor bounded into the room. "Okay, so Sheriff Montague asked me to tell you three not to leave. She has some questions about the order of events tonight, but she's still finishing a cursory review of the body. It's definitely Abby Monroe. I saw her leaving Stanton Concert Hall about a quarter after eight while I was doing my nightly walk through campus."

Lorraine perked up after finishing her call. "Is she really... dead?" A trail of mascara stained her cheek.

Connor nodded. "Yes, Mrs. Candito. The coroner will be here in a few minutes, but she's been dead for under an hour. I've seen this type of thing before."

Connor's response made me curious what he'd been up to the last ten years. What was going on between him and Maggie? My concentration broke when Lorraine burst into tears. Maggie comforted her.

Connor strode toward me. I didn't know whether to grab his fingers using our secret fraternity greeting or hover there in silence. I was grateful when he made the first move—a typical handshake, no double tuck and punch like the old days. "What a way to reconnect tonight, huh?"

"Yeah, feels like a nightmare. Over a professor falling down a flight of steps and dying."

Connor rubbed his temple. "Tragic, but it's far worse. She didn't just fall down the steps."

I thought I'd misheard my former best friend, but his panicked expression revealed I hadn't. "What do you mean? How can it be any worse than death?"

"It wasn't an accident." Connor stared at me, deliberating what he should and shouldn't reveal.

My eyes popped open like a deer caught in headlights. "Did she try to kill herself?" Though I felt both stupid and silly about the question, I barely knew anything about the woman. Anyone who hooked up with Derek was slightly off her rocker.

"No, that's not what I mean. Sheriff Montague wouldn't want me to say this, but the blood on the ground came from a deep gash behind Abby's ear. There were some metal flakes mixed throughout her hair in the middle of the wound."

"Wouldn't that be from when she hit the steps?" I scanned the room, filling with edginess over being around another dead body.

"Nope. She had a giant egg on the front of her head where she hit the steps. The wound on the back of her scalp was a much harder blow. Plus, there's nothing on the stairs or the floor that has any metal. It's all solid marble. We're looking at a murder tonight, Kellan."

CHAPTER 5

"Maybe your old man snapped his lid and killed that mischievous woman?" Nana D said as I scooped a forkful of cherry pie between my drooling lips. Given the cops had kept me on campus until two in the morning, I'd gotten minimal sleep. I was surprised to make it to Danby Landing on time.

"My father, Braxton's presidential killer! Wharton County News at eleven," I spat out between bites with a boisterous chuckle. Nana D's had it in for my father for as long as I can remember, but she's equally free with the barbs against my mother, her own daughter. "You're not supposed to know it was murder. I don't think Sheriff Montague wants that released."

"Listen here! I've got my finger on the pulse of this town. I knew before *you* it was murder," taunted my five-foot-tall nana while dropping another piece of pie on my plate. "Eat up."

"How's that possible?" Was she about to tell me she was psychic like Eleanor? All we needed was two of them in the family. Maybe they could get their own show like the *Long Island Medium*.

"I've got my ways. All part of my master plan. Keep up on the news, stay connected to hear all the gossip, and find out what's happening around town." Nana D slurped her coffee while fastening her nearly three-foot-long braid to the top of her head. She waffled between wearing her red tresses loose and tying them in a braid around the crown of her noggin—as she called it— depending on her activities for the day. It had to be dyed, but Eleanor's best guess was a henna rinse.

"Why did you call her a *mischievous woman?*" I recalled the conversation I'd overheard about a student's grades when Abby had been inches away from me the previous night.

"I never much cared for that tart. Sneaky type. Hassled with me over the price of a bushel of apples. I'm certain she filled her pockets with three extra grannies at the farmer's market last weekend."

"What else can you tell me about her?" I asked after updating Nana D on my reasons for trying to meet the late professor. "Anything bad enough for someone to want to murder her?"

Nana D loved her gossip and gave as good as she got when unearthing everyone's secrets. I didn't know how she did it or whom she bribed, but if there were information to be found, Nana D was the first in line. She's like the Mata Hari of the Americas, and I was even certain she knew the dance. Nana D had pushed her boundaries ever since my mother pressured her into semi-retirement from running Danby Landing on her own. In its heyday, the farm was the most productive, income-generating business in the entire county, but as the industry changed and the maintenance costs doubled, she sold off parts to a real estate company who built Willow Trees, a senior citizen's residential complex. With the new freedom, she'd taken on the role of community watchdog, ensuring she kept everyone in line. I swear she carried a stun gun just to watch people dance for her own pleasure sometimes.

"Murder's a funny thing, Kellan. Sometimes it's premeditated, but there's also the spur-of-the-moment killing when you can't control your emotions. I thought about murdering Grandpop a few times. Run him down with the tractor or stab him with the pitchfork while baling hay. Always too much of a mess to clean up, so I let him live." She snatched a piece of crust off the pie and dipped it into the cherry filling. "Mmm, I've surpassed myself again."

She'd never really thought about killing Grandpop. They'd been sweethearts since they'd fallen in love at thirteen at a drive-in movie theater. "That was kind of you not to kill him. I'd have missed spending all those summers with Grandpop if you offed him before he died of that heart attack."

"I miss that delicious man every day. The things he could do to my body just by winking at me. Did I ever tell you about the time he—"

"Stop, Nana D. I don't want to hear about it." I dropped my fork and covered my ears before they bled uncontrollably. "What about Abby?"

"That's what's wrong with you kids today... always so politically correct and sensitive about making love. Lost your emotions." Nana D washed our plates in the corner sink of her quaint kitchen.

"Focus, Nana D. I'm curious what you know about Abby or who might want her dead."

Nana D wrinkled her nose and squinted her eyes. "She was the type to piss off the dangerous people in this world by asking too many questions. Someone pushed her down the stairs to shut her up."

"I don't know how you know these things, but I trust your instincts," I consented, then grabbed a dish towel and began drying.

I filled her in on the events at the party before stumbling across Abby Monroe in the stairwell. Nana D planned to start a petition to have the councilman removed from office because of his sweaty hands. She'd try anything to get Marcus Stanton out of office ever since he'd served her with a summons for improper waste removal at the farm. Nana D might have dumped a bucket filled with manure from her tractor's front-loader over the fence into his back-yard last year, claiming the machine had malfunctioned. Unfortunately, it occurred during his family's Labor Day barbecue, and they'd been standing on the other side of the fence when it happened. I'm still unsure how or why their war ever started. "I've got to head downtown to the Wharton County Sheriff's Office to sign some statements. What are your plans today, Nana D? Harassing Councilman Stanton? Prank calling Ms. Paddington again?"

Nana D stuck out her tongue and made childish noises. "Didn't I tell you I started teaching music lessons again? Gotta fetch my old clarinet before she gets here." Nana D wrapped foil around the pie and placed it on the shelf in the refrigerator. "Keeps me young spending time with the college kids."

"Really? No, you hadn't mentioned it. I was thinking about teaching Emma to play the clarinet. She loves music and seems agile with her fingers. Maybe she'll follow in your footsteps."

"Well, you never could play worth a darn, could ya?" Nana D slapped my cheek until it hurt. "Talent might have skipped a few generations, but you sure got Grandpop's good looks. You probably drive all the girls crazy too." Nana D and Grandpop used to hold concerts at Danby Landing, entertaining the visitors and employees each weekend. Grandpop played the piano and guitar while Nana D sang and played the clarinet. She'd given it all up when he died, informing everyone it was *their thing to do together* and *all good things end, eventually.*

"Maybe so," I replied as the doorbell rang. "Want me to get that?"

"Yes, please, that would be Bridget. Go introduce yourself while I get the clarinet and make a call about a meeting I have later today," Nana D replied, winking and smirking.

"What are you up to now?" I narrowed my eyes and leaned my head in her direction. "More trouble?" I pictured news reporters showing up at my father's door and asking why he killed one of his professors, or a fake college student calling my mother to tell her he'd fallen in love with her and would do *anything* to attend Braxton. Nana D played way too many jokes on them in the past.

"Go get the door. Make yourself useful and quit being a party-pooper, love." Nana D disappeared down the hallway while I scurried through the living room and opened the front door.

Standing on the porch was a girl harboring an odd expression on her face—a cross between dumbstruck confusion and a pouty, angry elf. Not that I'd ever seen a real-life elf, but her ears were pointy, and she had these big, bright eyes that seemed to glow. I was afraid she might change shapes in front of me. "Hel-lo," I said curtly and cautiously.

"You're not Seraphina," questioned the elf. "Am I too early again?"

I shrugged as I didn't know what time she was supposed to be here. She wore striped red and white leggings and an oversized green parka. Granted, it was freezing outside, but the outfit truly reminded me of the Elf-on-a-Shelf appearing every Christmas in the Castigliano mansion for my daughter,

Emma. I wanted to ask why the elf couldn't use magic to answer her own question, but since I didn't know her, it might sound a tad obnoxious of me. Was she a good or a bad elf? I had enough crazy juju already and didn't need the vengeance of a nasty imp. Given Nana D expected someone for music lessons, there was a decent chance she was Bridget. "Not that I know. Come on in."

The elf stepped through the entryway and waited for me to say something else. "Ummm... so...?"

"Are you here for the Vespa driving lessons?" Perhaps I'd inherited too much of Nana D's wit. "We're bandaging up the last student, but don't worry... we put the bobcat back in its cage."

"If that's humor, I feel bad for you." The elf removed her coat. "I'm Bridget. Who are you?"

Bridget was a petite girl who seemed capable of holding her own. Besides her elf outfit, she had chestnut brown hair pulled back in a ponytail, emerald green eyes, and minimal makeup. It dawned on me this might be another romantic setup. Nana D had tried to match me up with a traveling horse groomer over the Christmas break until we learned not only had the woman already been married, but she was wanted in two other states for bigamy.

"Are you for real or is this part of Nana D's hoax?" I had to know if I was about to be played by my clever grandmother. It might've been early enough to convince Bridget, the elf, to join my team.

Bridget hung her coat on the rack, pushed past me into the living room, and dropped her backpack on the coffee table. "You're weird. You must be Kellan. Seraphina told me about you at last week's lesson."

So, the elf was smarter than she dressed. "Yes, I guess you must be normal if she's told you about me. How long have you been playing the clarinet?"

"I'm twenty-one. Started when I was nine. I'm sure you're capable of doing the math." As she sat on the couch across from me, she pulled out a couple of reeds and several sheets of music. "Are you gonna listen in and harass me today? Cause I didn't sign up for a super judgy audience."

I shook my head. I had places to be and needed to update Derek about Abby. With the retirement party over and no more source for season two, I could head back to Los Angeles early. Although the crime buff inside me wanted to do my own investigation into Abby's murder, it was secondary to escaping my parents. "Nope. Just visiting my nana. I'm leaving soon."

"So, I see you've met," Nana D announced, holding the clarinet behind us. "Behaving yourself, Kellan?"

I feigned a look of shock. "Of course, I always do."

Nana D glanced at Bridget, who responded, "He's been a perfect gentleman. I can see the resemblance between you two. He's got your humor and your nose. Like a little button." Bridget nervously laughed and reached for her bag.

"Well, I need to make a few calls, Nana D. I'll check in with you later. Anything with your *afternoon meetings* that I need to prepare for?" I questioned with a growing angst and curiosity.

"Not at all, dear. I'm not up to anything, at least nothing that your mother should worry about."

"Or Dad? I've heard he's a bit shaken about the... issue... from last night." I suddenly remembered I wasn't supposed to talk about it, per Sheriff Montague.

"Nothing for him to fret over either. Now skedaddle, please. I've got more important people to spend my time with." Nana D shoved me out the door before I could say goodbye to Bridget.

I drove to the sheriff's office and signed my official statement. In Wharton County, there was one sheriff and a few detectives to cover all the towns, including Braxton. Local police in each town ensured smaller crimes were addressed and minor ordinances were obeyed while the sheriff's office handled major crimes, specifically murder and grand larceny. The sheriff was out on an interview, but Officer Flatman who'd been on campus the night before was glad to assist. Stepping away from his desk, I saw a notation on a post-it about contact with an Alton Monroe. Next of kin? Something to follow up on.

Eleanor lured me over by offering to prepare an amazing meal. Ten minutes later, I sat at a corner booth at the Pick-Me-Up Diner and devoured my ham and cheese egg white omelet with avocado on the side. I needed something healthy to offset the two pieces of pie I'd already eaten for breakfast. Gone from last night was the relaxed sister who'd rocked a gorgeous dress, and in its place was a serious worker-bee in a pair of stained khakis, Keds, and a faded black polo shirt. Her hair was still pinned up, but she hardly had any makeup on today. Working in a diner would prevent a clean and spiffy appearance.

"Mom and Dad were meeting with Braxton's public relations director about the accident. Dad told me a bit about Abby. Poor woman, I can't believe she fell down the steps and died."

"Did Dad know her well?" I considered revealing what Connor had shared about it not being an accident. Bad enough Nana D had figured it out, I couldn't let it slip again.

"She'd been the chair of the communications department for many years, but they didn't get along well. After a few months, Dad decided she didn't properly represent Braxton. By then, they'd already granted tenure, which meant he had no simple way to get rid of Abby," Eleanor said.

A server cleared the plates, impressing her boss by wiping the table, asking how everything tasted, and suggesting different dessert options. I declined, knowing I'd already have to run twice as long that afternoon.

"What's the latest word on the over-achieving end of our family?" I asked Eleanor, who kept in contact with our older siblings much more than I did.

"Eh, Penelope seems happy, though there are days I wonder if she might not be looking for an excuse to have an early mid-life crisis," Eleanor replied.

"She has her hands full with the kids. But she loves it all, and I can't imagine she'd have given up any part of her life." I secretly knew Penelope was hoping to buy a larger stake in her real estate firm. "What about your brother?"

"Hampton's your brother too, no matter how much you two fight," she replied. "And with Gabriel refusing to talk to any of us, we can't ignore him."

"Yep, I should behave more brotherly to the Hampster." Don't even ask why I call him that, as it's been his nickname forever. Hampton, four years older than me, was a lawyer in Tulsa and married to an oil heiress who never let him go anywhere.

"He's coming to town soon to share news," Eleanor said. "I bet his wife's pregnant again."

I cringed at the thought of four kids under the age of six. "Speaking of Dad, did Mom say where he disappeared to last night? I tried to contact him. He never answered his phone." It was odd that he didn't even text me back, but I figured he got caught up in controlling the release of any information to the media. "Connor thought—"

"No, I left shortly after the party ended." Eleanor looked peculiar when her face flushed a deeper shade of red. Did she know something she wasn't telling me?

"I see. How about Connor working at Braxton? I was surprised to hear about that."

Eleanor shuffled across the booth. "Yeah, big changes, huh? Well, I need to check on a couple of things in the kitchen, which means you need to jet. I'll call you later. Hugs and kisses."

We said our goodbyes, which felt a little awkward given how abruptly she hightailed it out of the booth. I texted Maggie to see if she wanted to meet for dinner, but she had plans already. Instead, she suggested I stop by Memorial Library the next day. I confirmed, then bit the bullet to call Derek.

Astonishingly, he answered on the first ring. "How's the research going?"

"Not so well. There's been an incident," I said, angst rising inside my body. I couldn't tell him she'd been murdered, but it suddenly crossed my mind that he'd pawned her off on me. Could things have gone sour between them, and he was somehow involved in her death?

"Do tell. You know I'm counting on you to help put this background material to bed, so we can start this project as soon as possible, right?" replied Derek.

"Abby died last night." I pondered what kind of response I'd receive to my news. Would he be nervous? Relieved? Cool and collected?

Derek laughed hysterically. "That's a great one, Kel-baby. First time I've heard that excuse to get out of a work assignment. Awesome way to make me laugh, dude."

Not a reaction I'd considered. "Seriously, ummm... appears she fell down a flight of steps."

"Wait, you're not joking, are you?" he replied.

"No."

"That's insane. Didn't you talk to her yesterday?" He stopped laughing and listened to me.

"We were supposed to meet last night, but then I stumbled upon her dead body with a friend of mine on campus." I updated Derek about Abby working as a professor at the college, what Myriam Castle and Nana D had said about her, and the little I'd learned from visiting the sheriff's office that morning.

"Do whatever you can to get her research notes. I texted her earlier to give them to you." Derek didn't seem too phased about her death, but he also thought I'd have access to her personal things. "I guess I won't be getting a reply, huh?" He laughed again, but this time with a more sinister tone.

"And exactly how am I supposed to do that?" Perhaps I should ask *him* where he was last night.

"You're the wannabe investigative reporter, Kel-baby. Break into her office or tell the cops she left something behind for you about a project you were working on together. I need this to be your top priority. We have to film season two as soon as possible, dude."

Derek was the typical sleaze who made me doubt my career working in Hollywood over the last few months. "Listen, I know this is important. I'll see what I can do. I guess I'll be coming back to Los Angeles sooner than we planned."

Derek was unusually silent on the phone before finally responding. "Why don't you stick around for her funeral? Meet her contacts and find out who else she worked with. Take advantage of the situation. Get the scoop on her death too. Builds a good side story for the show. Research professor falls to her death while working on *Dark Reality*. Think of the ratings, Kel-baby!"

His last comment lit the proverbial fire under me to finish my time with him as quickly as possible. "Yeah, good plan. What hotel are you staying at? I'm thinking about visiting Hawaii next month." I had no intention of going to the tropical islands, but how much did I know about this man outside of work? Was he really where he said he was?

"Royal something, can't recall. Good chatting. Gotta run. Get that scoop. Your job depends on it!"

Before I responded, Derek hung up on me. What an idiot! I needed to quit, but I was close to getting my name on the credits for a full season, and this would be the exact bonus to staking a claim to my own show in the future. It wouldn't be difficult to check if Abby had any notes in her office. Attending the funeral with my family was a good show of faith.

Since Maggie was on my agenda the following day, I'd add in visiting Lorraine. She'd have information on Abby's funeral arrangements. I also wanted to touch base with Connor to determine what he'd been up to for the last ten years. Ever since Francesca's death, I'd pushed away all our friends in Los Angeles and spent my free time with Emma. I hadn't truly connected with a group of guys since my days in the fraternity. Abby's death reminded me too much of the lost man I'd become when my wife died two years ago. While in town, I could reconnect with some old buddies and solve a crime!

CHAPTER 6

After my five-mile run later that afternoon, I found my father sitting in his office drinking a glass of Macallan scotch and watching the sunset over the Wharton Mountains. It looked like the bottle I'd given him at Christmas was at least half empty, which meant for once he'd enjoyed one of my holiday gifts. I declined his offer since scotch after a run never settled well in my stomach. I was also starving and needed to eat something before I passed out. "Maybe next time. I'm gonna heat some party leftovers for dinner. Are you hungry?"

"I had an early meal with your mother before she went back to the campus. The final deadline is this week for notifying students who've been accepted for the next term. Not that I'll be the one welcoming them to Braxton," he replied in a somber tone while swallowing a mouthful of liquor. I could hear the melancholy oozing through the burn of the scotch.

It hadn't occurred to my overworked and distracted brain he'd be sad to retire. If I'd worked tirelessly for forty years, sitting on my rear end doing nothing for a few months would be a welcome change. *"That's the problem with this younger generation. Can't put in a full day's work without complaining,"* Nana D would likely chastise. "Chin up, Dad. You've got a lot to look forward to after the big day. The new president will want you to stick around to help settle in, right?"

He nodded. I waited for him to keep talking, but the scotch and the silence in the room overtook the possibility of him leading our conversation. "Any traction with the search for a new head honcho?"

"The Board finished all the interviews and asked me to meet with the final two candidates again this week. I'm not at liberty to provide details, but they've been considering internal and external options. I'm partial to one candidate. We're doing separate group panels with them both tomorrow before we make the final decision." He swung the chair away from the window and narrowed his eyes. "How long are you planning on staying this time, Kellan?"

I'd been theorizing when he'd ask that question. He'd suggested a few times over the Christmas break it'd be beneficial for Emma to be around both sets of grandparents. I thought for a moment he'd discovered my late wife's dirty family secrets, but if that were true, he'd not yet revealed it to me. "I'm trying to figure that out. I have work that might keep me here for the rest of the week."

"I see." He clicked his tongue against the roof of his mouth.

"So, I was trying to get hold of you last night after finding Abby's body at Diamond Hall."

My father cleared his throat. "The ringer was off, so I could enjoy the party in peace. I didn't realize you'd been desperately trying to find me," he replied in a bitter tone, pouring another scotch and opening his laptop.

Ouch! I wasn't sure what I'd said to deserve his scathing retort, but I'd obviously hit a nerve. "I wasn't desperate. Just curious about who killed Abby Monroe."

My father dismissed me through a combination of shrugging, lifting his eyebrows, and ignoring me as he typed away on the computer. I wanted to find out where he was and whom he'd threatened on the phone the night I arrived, but I took my cue and ate dinner in the kitchen by myself. Should I abandon the investigation or jump in deeper to protect someone I knew?

* * *

I'd fallen asleep in bed the night before while surfing the internet and reading the show bible for a second time, but at least I'd been able to ascertain several interesting facts about the late professor, or *Monroe,* as Myriam Castle referred to her. I'd researched that churlish woman too.

Abby had spent most of her life specializing in broadcasting and media studies, following a similar post-undergraduate degree path as me. As near as I could figure, Abby was at least fifteen years older than me. Although I'd made it to Hollywood, she'd worked in the academic world her entire adult career, hopping from college to college until settling at Braxton nearly ten years ago. She started right after I'd graduated and was promoted to chairman of the communications department when the incumbent retired. At Braxton, the communications department included media and broadcasting, literature, theater, writing, public relations, and art majors. Abby taught three courses this semester—Intro to Film, History of Television Production, and Broadcast Writing.

It surprised me to discover Myriam Castle was one of the professors who worked for Abby in the communications department. Her specialty was literature and theater productions, which made sense given her exaggerated facial expressions at the retirement party. On paper, Dr. Castle was clearly more qualified to be running the department, but Abby had been put in the role before Dr. Castle joined Braxton. No wonder there was tension between the women. It would be an interesting discussion with my father when he graciously stepped off his high horse and spoke to me again.

I'd also found a website where Abby referred to co-authoring articles in a widely published journal with her husband, Alton Monroe. The news filled in a blank from a scrap of paper I'd seen on Officer Flatman's desk at the sheriff's office. Could Alton be someone to provide a copy of Abby's *Dark Reality* notes? I cross-checked the names with online directories and located an address on the north side of the county. I made a note to swing by while on campus meeting Lorraine and Maggie later that day.

I braved the near-freezing temperature and dodged a few icicles dropping off the roofline as I hopped in the Jeep. Twenty minutes later, I found a lucky parking spot down the street from the Braxton Campus Security (BCS) office.

The last time I'd been there was after a rival fraternity, the Omega Delta Omicrons, complained we were having a loud party our senior year. I'd spent forty-five minutes trying to convince the previous security director not to report us to Fern Terry, the Dean of Student Affairs, but he wouldn't budge. I'd left his office after a few less-than-kind words that evening and found myself with a slap on the wrist the following morning when Dean Terry told me my childish word choices had disappointed her. Was she one of the two final candidates vying for Braxton's presidency? Maybe I should stop by the administration office to check if she still worked on campus. I hadn't seen her at the party, yet I assumed she would've shown up if she was employed at Braxton.

As I walked up the cobblestone pathway, I considered what kind of security director Connor would be. He was always the goody-two-shoes who cautioned not to let the fraternity get into trouble, but he'd protect me from taking the fall on my own when we'd been caught doing something wrong. Not that any wrongdoings happened often, but Connor was a dependable and honorable guy. In theory, it made sense that he went into security work, yet I had trouble imagining him sitting on the opposite side of college administration.

I stepped into the foyer of the single-story security building and gave it the once-over. Little had changed, possibly a coat of fresh paint and a series of new digital cameras and computer systems. Connor stepped out of his office, no longer looking uncomfortable in a tan suit and Braxton tie; now he busted out of his sports coat and jeans. "Kellan, I didn't expect to see you today. What's going on?"

"Got time for a cup of coffee? My treat." I hoped he'd take me up on the offer. When he nodded and told a student worker to call him promptly with any issues, I realized Connor had become an admirable and responsible adult.

He suggested The Big Beanery on South Campus. I was more than happy to visit our old stomping grounds. The car ride took less than five minutes because he was in a BCS vehicle, and everyone stopped to let him through the streets first. Must be good to have that kind of power—even come in handy one day if I needed his help.

When we arrived, Connor grabbed a table while I ordered two black coffees. I'd wanted creamer in mine, or even a cappuccino, but when he mumbled something about too much sugar, I followed suit and pulled up a chair across from him. "So, working in security at Braxton. That's quite a leap from what we used to do on campus ten years ago, huh?"

His laugh was hearty and deep. "Ten years is a long time. People mature. You've done some changing yourself. Seems like you even frequent the gym now."

"Well, no competing with you, man. You look like a brick wall!" I assumed he could throw me across the room. Not that I'd do anything to encourage it, but I'd be glad to have him on my side in any bar fight or street brawl. I had an urge to call him *Double-O-Seven*.

"I've always wondered what happened to you. We sort of lost touch, huh?" he asked after taking a giant sip of his coffee. His eyes continually scanned the room behind me as if he were looking for someone. It's probably a normal thing for the head of security to always check out his surroundings. "Gotta admit, it pissed me off when you left town that summer. I know you went off to grad school, but you were my best friend back then."

"Yeah, I felt bad about it. Life has this funny way of making decisions you don't understand at the time. When I look back, I had some growing up to do, didn't I?" I suspected Connor carried a grudge over the past. I might have a harder time trying to reestablish a friendship than expected.

A few students waved at him. It looked like a girl was trying to flirt. If he noticed, he ignored her. We reminisced about our last decade. Connor had spent a year living in Anguilla with his mother's family to rebuild after a series of devastating hurricanes took its toll on the people living on nearby islands. He'd also worked as a police officer in Philadelphia for several years, then left the force after dealing with too many violent gang fights and deaths. It was a year ago when he'd heard about the opening at Braxton.

"Married, kids?"

"A daughter." I always hated that question. It's never easy telling someone you lost your wife to a drunk driver. They inevitably felt uncomfortable about asking, then you felt weird for delivering the awful news. No one should feel bad except the idiot who stepped into his car after drinking a six-pack and thinking he was totally fine to drive. To this day, they hadn't caught the hit-and-run driver.

We covered more basics. He was still single, dated on and off through the years, but nothing serious. I got the distinct impression when Maggie came up that he'd been smitten with her since she'd returned from Boston. While I was in no frame of mind to consider anything more than rebuilding a friendship with Maggie, somehow the thought of her being with someone else didn't sit well. I changed the topic to Abby's death.

"I'm not sure I'd have the latest. Murder is the authority of Wharton County. Sheriff Montague's been in contact to discuss protocol, but we haven't established all the boundaries." Connor confirmed they were still searching for signs of a struggle other than the gash in Abby's head.

"True. I just meant how were you handling it from Braxton's perspective." I signaled to the young waitress clearing a table nearby that we wanted two more cups of coffee. If Connor would share any information, I knew from experience, he needed caffeine.

"Sheriff Montague wants everyone to think it was an accident. Braxton's public relations department was quite pleased to take that approach." Connor slurped the remnants of his coffee.

"Murder won't help the upcoming admissions cycle," I said with a laugh. "Did you know her?"

"Met at a few college functions. She stopped in to discuss things from time to time. Abby had it in her head that because I was from the Caribbean, my family practiced voodoo. She wanted me to hook her up with my shaman. What a kook! I don't even know what a shaman is."

The waitress dropped off the coffee refills and asked, "Who do you think will end up leading Saturday's big game, Director Hawkins? Striker our man? Or is Jordan gonna overtake him?"

I'd not been sure which sport they were talking about until remembering Eleanor's story at the Pick-Me-Up Diner about the baseball team. "Those the two choices for pitcher?" I tossed out my question, though her gaze barely left Connor's lips.

Connor replied, "Yep. Striker was last season's star, but his teammate, Jordan, suddenly jumped into the race based on his new curveball in the pre-season games. It's a close match."

When I went to hand her a ten-dollar bill, she waved me off. "Nah, we don't charge Director Hawkins. He checks on us from time to time to make sure we're doing okay." She backed away, nearly tripping over her own feet because she couldn't peel her focus off Connor.

"Someone thinks you're cute, huh?"

"Drop it, Kellan. She's a kid."

"I know. Seems like you're *king of the hill* around here these days. I'm happy for you."

"Yeah, I didn't ask for it. Just doing my job. I should head back soon. You need a lift?"

I declined. I planned to find Abby's house, and the access road to her neighborhood was closer to South Campus. "Before you go, do you think there's any chance I could look in Abby's office? It sounds funny, but I was supposed to meet her about some information for my boss, and I didn't get to before she died. We think it's somewhere buried on her desk." I felt awful asking for a favor from Connor after all these years, but I wasn't doing anything overtly wrong. Abby did the research for us, so we were getting back something owed to the network. I couldn't convince myself I wasn't stretching my justification, especially since the contract had never been signed.

"I don't have a problem as long as Sheriff Montague clears it. She might want an officer to be present." Connor stood, then smiled as someone walked to the table. "Speak of the devil."

"Devil? Something you care to explain, Connor?" Sheriff Montague's arms were crossed against her chest with the look of a woman ready to pounce. Whether it was to kiss or chastise him, I couldn't tell. Based on appearance, she was only two or three years older than us.

Connor excused himself, indicating I could fill in the blanks. As I pointed a hand to the open seat across from me, Sheriff Montague sat and said, "That is one fine man there."

I spat out a mouthful of coffee, then apologized and made excuses about it being too hot. "What Connor meant, Sheriff Montague, is I need to collect some papers from Abby's office regarding a project we were working on together. May I get in there?"

The sheriff had only moved to Braxton two years ago. I never got to know her. Did she remember me from the one time I bailed out Nana D? It didn't seem like she'd made the connection, but I'd think someone in her position as county sheriff wouldn't forget too many faces, especially not one associated with the frequently vocal Seraphina Danby. I got my answer rather quickly, after soaking up the spilled coffee and stopping myself from commenting on her motorcycle helmet hair.

"Your family might have some control in Braxton, Little Ayrwick, but let me assure you, I won't be pressured into any special circumstances or favors. I've got a murder investigation to lead, and I will run down anyone who gets in my way." When she finished, she stared at me like I might be dinner that night. I wasn't sure whether to wet my pants or put up a fight.

"You don't mince words, sheriff. I'm sorry if I came across the wrong way. When it became clear this wasn't just an accident, I worried it might have something to do with research Abby Monroe was handling on my television show, *Dark Reality*. Are you familiar with it?"

Surprisingly, that loosened her attitude. "That's your show? I watched the whole first season. My girlfriends and I can't get enough of it!" she replied in a syrupy tone as her eyes bulged wider.

Wow, I'd lucked out in that department. If I played my cards right, I could make an ally out of Sheriff Montague. "Yeah, definitely, I could get you a couple of tickets—"

"Cut the beeswax, Little Ayrwick. I don't watch the show. I've got better things to do than burn my eyes to their core from reality TV garbage. No offense since that's your thing."

Ouch, did I misjudge that one! "You got me there," I replied with my tail between my legs. "Seriously, I'll help the investigation however I can. Do you have any suspects?"

"A few. I'm not here to give you a tough time. I'll take all the help I can get, but you're a private citizen. We're not usually in the business of giving out that kind of information." She cupped her hands together and cracked both sets of knuckles, considering my offer as she stood. "We're focusing on a few people who had the means and the opportunity. We're still searching for the motive. I'm meeting with a witness who overheard a fight between Lorraine Candito and the victim."

I couldn't hold back my shock. "Lorraine? She wouldn't hurt a fly. I've known her for years, and I can vouch for her. Gentler than a Girl Scout or a newborn puppy. She might nibble from time to time, but there must be some misunderstanding."

Sheriff Montague shook her head vigorously. "A student worker Connor met this morning claimed to overhear the words *'over your dead body'* coming from Lorraine Candito's lips."

I'd been certain the fear on Lorraine's face was genuine. Could it have been guilt? "I'm meeting with Lorraine this afternoon. I can ask her about it if you'd like a second opinion."

"Leave the investigation to us, Little Ayrwick. I'll be in touch about access to Abby Monroe's office. Have yourself a good day." She adjusted one of her sleeves, glared at me a second time with laser eyes to ensure I got the message, then idled toward the counter to order something to go. Her sturdy gait and minimalist approach to dressing or wearing any makeup clearly showed she'd cared little about her appearance. Would it be wrong of me to ask Eleanor to give her a makeover in the hopes she'd win Connor's affection? I could think of no one else better to put a smile on the sheriff's face.

I wanted to warn Lorraine, but it wouldn't put me in good standing with the sheriff. It seemed most advantageous to give April Montague time to meet with the student worker and Lorraine before I dug any further. I'd pissed off enough people since returning to Braxton. It was time to let my spectacular curb appeal charm the rest before I found myself on the wrong side of town and living in a doghouse. In ten years, I'd foolishly forgotten what went on in a remote village.

CHAPTER 7

Abby's house was only a twenty-minute walk if I stuck to the path along the waterfront. Although still mighty cold, any snow on the ground had melted away, and since I wasn't likely to get to a gym that afternoon, the extra cardio was more than welcome. When I arrived at her street, I made a right and ambled past the first few houses before finally finding one with a number. Most of the homes in the immediate vicinity were three-bedroom ranches on small parcels with fenced-in front and backyards for children and dogs to play, less any worry about balls rolling into the street or wild animals roaming in from the mountains. The occasional bobcat had been sighted years ago, but as the area became more urbanized, the wildlife retreated further into the Wharton Mountains.

Abby's place was the second to last one on the left, a charming brick-fronted home with green shutters and a white door. As I neared the entrance, a four-door blue sedan crept down the driveway. I dropped to the ground to make it look like I'd been tying my boot laces. The driver reached into the mailbox, rifled through a few envelopes and a magazine, then took off down the street. He'd left the mail in the box. Had he been in the house?

I placed him in his mid-to-late forties, balding, and toying with facial hair. It was mostly grown in, a mixture of brown and gray surrounding his mouth and chin. Perhaps the goatee was making a comeback, or maybe he was hoping to lead the pack. Brother? Roommate? Could this be the husband, Alton? I hadn't seen a picture of Abby's spouse, but I'd gotten a good visual while this man was checking the mail.

If the *Dark Reality* notes weren't at her office, it was possible they'd be at her home. It wasn't like I was the kind of guy who'd break into the place to find them. Sheriff Montague would undoubtedly haul me to jail just for her laughs and revenge. When I was certain the blue sedan turned the corner, I stood and casually brushed off my pants. I was about to check for anything of interest in the backyard when someone startled me.

"May I help you?" asked a heavyset woman in a raspy voice and a peach-colored house dress. It was a little cold to be outside without a coat, but more power to her for being brave.

My eyes darted to the piece of mail in her hand, and I attempted to read the name. Even with my glasses, I could only decipher a few letters. "You must be Mrs. Ackerman, the neighbor my friend Abby talks about all the time."

She pulled back, slightly confused, then smiled. "Abby talks about me? How sweet of her! It's Mrs. Ackerton, handsome. And who might you be?" She pursed her lips and straightened her shoulders.

Wow! I was grateful for my quick thinking and stroke of luck. "Oh, I'm Justin. We work together at the college. I was just stopping by to check the mail for her while she's away."

Mrs. Ackerton shook her head and made a tsk-tsk sound with her tongue. "That explains why I haven't seen her lately. It worried me, especially when I saw that police car here yesterday. There wasn't a robbery, was there?" Mrs. Ackerton closed the lid on her mailbox and adjusted a hair curler. "Sorry, I'm not all fancied up for you at the moment."

"No robberies I've been told about." It seemed she wasn't aware Abby had died over the weekend, but she was awake enough to flirt with me. "I saw a car drive away while I was fixing my laces and thought maybe I'd missed her or her husband," I replied, ignoring the broccoli in her teeth.

"No, her husband don't live here no more. Noticed the car a few times, but I'm not sure I've ever gotten a good look at the person to say that's who's been sleeping here. If I see Abby, I'll mention you stopped by, Justin." She reached out her hand and grabbed my bicep. "I love a strong man."

"Do you think he was a friend of Abby's?" I asked, fishing for information. "She didn't tell me anyone else would stop by while she was away. I kinda thought I was the only—"

"Oh, I don't know if it was anything romantic. Don't reckon I'll ever understand relationships these days. I suppose playing the field is part of the game, eh? I hope she wasn't stepping out on you, Justin." She elbowed me a few times before heading back up her walkway.

Did she think I'd date someone like Abby? We said our goodbyes, and I began my excursion back to campus to meet with Lorraine. Along the path, I thought about whether Abby's death was a lover's quarrel gone wrong. Had her husband found out she was having an affair, or did her boyfriend get angry she wouldn't leave her husband? That's when I realized I still didn't know the exact cause of death. Connor had told me about the gash on her head, but it couldn't have been from hitting the steps. There was some other object that had knocked her out first. Maybe I could convince the sheriff to tell me what they'd discovered onsite.

Before I knew it, I found myself about to ascend the front entrance of Diamond Hall. My mother was exiting the building and waved at me.

"Hey, Mom. Fancy seeing you here. Were you visiting Dad?" I asked, noting how cute it was they'd still spend part of their day together on campus. She'd miss him when he retired.

"I thought Lorraine could tell me where he was, so I could surprise him for lunch, but apparently Sheriff Montague asked him to return to the precinct again. They have a lot of questions about his relationship with Abby Monroe."

"Did you ever find out where he went at the end of the retirement party?" I hoped she could fill in the information my father had conveniently left out.

My mother paused before offering an awkward, non-committal answer. "You know your father. He doesn't think to tell me where he goes. I'm worried about him lately. Something's not quite settled."

"What do you mean? Something to do with his retirement?" I thought about the phone call too.

"Well, not exactly," she replied, visibly drained and in need of a break. "He and Abby didn't have the best of relations. Your father tried unsuccessfully to remove her as department chair. I'm afraid Sheriff Montague thinks your father has something to do with her death." After glancing upward to the building's side windows, she covered her mouth as if she'd been shocked to say something out loud about the incident.

"Dad's hard to take sometimes, but he'd never hurt someone physically. He's more a master of verbal insults." I thought about his behavior the last few days. He'd become more strange, pensive, and closed-off despite my first chat with him. "Did Sheriff Montague accuse him of something, or are you reading between the lines?"

"Talk to him, Kellan. I can't make sense of it." My mother tilted her head to the side and began welling.

"Oh, don't cry, Mom. Everything will be okay." I pulled her in for a hug and patted her back. It was a rare moment to see my mother collapse.

"You were supposed to meet Abby, right? You could do a little investigating. See what she'd been doing recently or find someone else that detective could harass."

"April Montague is not a detective, Mom. She's the Wharton County sheriff. I'm sure she knows how to do her job. Asking Dad more questions could simply be to help find other suspects," I said, uncertain whether I believed my own words. Sheriff Montague had it out for my family in the past.

"Please, Kellan. I ask little of you. I know I keep begging you to come back home, but the least you could do while you're here is poke around. Isn't that what you do for a living? Research? Figure out what happened in a crime and then write a show all about it?"

While it was a cursory explanation of my job, she had a point. "Sure, I'll see what I can learn by asking some questions... starting with Lorraine. I'm on my way to see her. Was she particularly busy?"

My mother shivered from the wind. "Yes, a little frazzled. I got the impression she knew something but wasn't comfortable telling me just now. I'm sure you can get her to talk. Lorraine always had a soft spot for you."

"Is there anything you remember about the night of the party that might identify whom Abby was meeting at Diamond Hall?" She'd delayed chatting with me until nine, I presumed to give her time for her mysterious eight thirty meeting about a student's grades.

"I don't know if it has anything to do with Abby's death, but I saw someone walking around the side of the building. I'd stepped outside to find your father when I noticed Coach Oliver."

It was the second time I'd heard that name. "Who's Coach Oliver?"

"Our athletic director. He oversees the school's sports teams, practice fields, venues, and Grey Sports Complex, our main athletic facility. He's a nice guy, but that man seems a little obsessed with winning all the games rather than keeping the students focused on their studies."

"What time did you see him?"

My mother tapped her foot against the concrete steps. I could see the wheels turning inside her head as she thought about the night's events. "About eight thirty. I waved to him, but he was on his phone. He seemed distracted. I'm certain he planned to stop by the party, but he never showed up."

"Point out exactly where you saw him," I instructed her. She noted the far corner near the oak tree and bench on the narrow path toward Glass Hall. Coach Oliver had been near the back entrance of Diamond Hall, where the lighting was dim.

"Surely, you don't think he had anything to do with Abby's death, do you?" A grim expression overtook my mother's face while she moaned in an overstated fashion.

"I'm not certain. The woman I was supposed to meet with is dead. You're worried the sheriff assumes it involves Dad. Now you tell me you saw someone near where Abby died under mysterious circumstances. Did you inform Sheriff Montague?"

A blank and disconnected look told me she hadn't. "No, I didn't think to. Should I call her?"

I shook my head. There didn't seem to be any reason to share the news. I'd see if it were anything important before putting another family member in front of the persistent sheriff. Upon recovering from her worries, my mother walked toward the cable car to return to North Campus.

Exactly what I needed, another reason to put myself in the line of fire with the sheriff. I grew curious whether coach Oliver had authored the blog post or was the call I'd overheard in my father's study.

I climbed the steps and entered Diamond Hall. A string of yellow plastic tape blocked the entrance to the second-floor staircase. A sign indicated all classes were moved to Memorial Library. Lorraine called to me from the other side of the hallway. "Kellan, I'm over here."

Lorraine explained Sheriff Montague had quarantined the second and third floors for the balance of the week. Although they'd removed Abby's body and the cleaning crew had finished sanitizing the stairwell, the sheriff didn't want anyone in the building's top two floors while they searched for evidence. No students were allowed except a few workers who helped Lorraine with the daily administration in the communications department.

"So, there's no news yet?"

Lorraine leaned in and whispered, "Sheriff Montague is going through Abby's office. They're not telling me anything. It's awful."

I guessed I wouldn't be offered the chance to see Abby's belongings. I didn't expect the sheriff to take me up on my proposal, despite it making things much easier. "What's being said to students?"

"Full cooperation with local law enforcement to understand how Abby Monroe tragically fell to her death. We're expediting the investigation, and the building is off-limits until next weekend." Lorraine advised that she was given office space on the second floor of Diamond Hall because the communications department's office manager had gone on maternity leave earlier that year. Rather than fill the vacancy for the three months Siobhan would be away, Lorraine was asked to support my father and the professors since she'd temporarily be working in Diamond Hall. Knowing my father's impending retirement meant less work, Lorraine had agreed to handle the additional responsibilities and work from Siobhan's desk.

"I'm sorry you got stuck with all that. Holding up okay with the sheriff?" I asked.

"I've never found a dead body before. I'm so glad you were there to help me, Kellan. I haven't been able to sleep much." Her hands clasped together while rubbing her palms with nervous fingers.

"Lorraine, someone mentioned overhearing a conversation you had recently with Abby. Something about you issuing a veiled threat against her. I'm not entirely sure what that meant, but I wanted to ask you directly."

Lorraine sighed loudly. "Foolish of me. It was nothing. Honestly, the student worker simply misunderstood what I'd said."

"What do you mean?" I had to extract the explanation from her.

"I guess you'll find out, anyway. It wasn't common knowledge, but I knew Abby Monroe outside of Braxton. We were disagreeing about something... personal. It had nothing to do with her death. I could never hurt anyone." She glanced to the side and fiddled with a few papers.

"Does Sheriff Montague think you did something to Abby?" My mother seemed to be under the impression my father was a suspect. Could Lorraine be one too? "How did you know Abby?"

"My brother, Alton, had served her with divorce papers, but she wouldn't sign them for an entire year. Abby was a vindictive woman."

Lorraine filled me in on their history. Abby and Alton had been married for five years when he'd gotten fed up with her selfish attitude. He tried to mend the relationship, and even Lorraine had talked to Abby about the issues. In the end, Alton determined it was best to split up. The argument Lorraine had with Abby the prior week was about the divorce. Abby had threatened to ask for a larger amount of alimony if Alton wouldn't give her the rights to an upcoming book they'd planned to co-author.

"Someone overheard me saying *'It'll be over your dead body that I let you take anything else away from Alton.'* But I didn't mean it literally, Kellan. You've got to help me figure out what happened to Abby." Her hollow cheeks flushed, and she slammed her head against the desk.

There was something in the tone of Lorraine's voice, the imminent fear over what would happen if the cops couldn't find Abby's actual killer. She might always be suspected of the crime. As far as I knew, she had no children or a husband. Someone needed to protect her from any accusations cast in her direction. "I don't know the specific time Abby died, but surely Sheriff Montague understands you only slipped away from the party for a few minutes to stop by the office."

"Someone killed Abby between a quarter after eight and a quarter to nine. She'd only been dead a brief time when I'd first found her body. I can't find anyone who saw me at the party after eight o'clock."

"It'll be harder to prove you didn't do it, that's true. Do you know what they're hunting for upstairs?" The murder weapon had to be part of the search. I really wanted to know what it was.

"An officer said they'd swept the whole place but couldn't find anything. I still don't understand what they're looking for. I thought someone pushed her down the stairs."

Lorraine wasn't aware the gash on the back of Abby's head had come from a brutal blow. Either she was playing dumb or genuinely didn't know someone had hit Abby before she fell. I didn't think it was my responsibility to tell her, so I changed topics. "Is your brother holding up well enough?"

"Alton's my half-brother, we only share a mother. That's why we have different last names. I haven't been able to get in touch with him. He left last week for a remote research trip. No cell connection," Lorraine replied, dabbing her swollen eyes with a tissue. "I'm not sure he knows Abby is dead."

If Alton was away, then he couldn't be responsible for Abby's death. The sheriff would check his alibi, to be certain. The guy near Abby's house popped back into my head. "Was Abby seeing anyone new recently? If she was divorcing Alton, maybe there was a new man in the picture."

Lorraine shook her head. "I didn't keep tabs on her love life. Alton didn't care either, he just wanted out. They tried maintaining a friendship, but she was too egotistical."

I told Lorraine to think positively and cooperate as much as possible with the sheriff during the investigation. The truth had to come out at some point, and Sheriff Montague would realize Lorraine had nothing to do with Abby's death. I couldn't picture her as the killer. Unfortunately, that meant the sheriff might still suspect my father.

I checked the time and realized I still hadn't visited Maggie or eaten lunch. After stopping at the campus cafeteria, I would head to Memorial Library. I needed to learn what Maggie knew about the athletic director, theorizing she could figure out a way to introduce me to Coach Oliver.

CHAPTER 8

I caught the cable car back to North Campus. Students shared pics and tweets on their phone, arguing about which pitcher should start that Saturday. I'd been a baseball freak for years, but living in Los Angeles was difficult for a Phillies fan. Eventually, I'd given up quarreling over baseball and instead picked up football as my sport of choice. As the cable car pulled in, a light bulb went off in my head about how I could introduce myself to Coach Oliver.

I exited the cable car and took the shortest path to the cafeteria in the student union building. Lunch was winding down, so I got in and out quickly with two chicken salad croissants and a bag of salt and vinegar potato chips, Maggie's favorite.

No one at the library's reception desk stopped me from entering the building. Student workers busily studied or looked up naughty things on the reference computers. I made a right at the history section and found Maggie sitting behind her desk in the corner office. She smiled and pointed at the adjacent chair. The décor was truly in need of an update.

"I brought snacks, if you're hungry?"

"You're a savior! The staff meeting ran longer than expected, and I forgot to bring lunch. Please tell me those are potato chips?"

"It'll cost you," I said with a beaming smile. "My fees have gone up since senior year."

"I've never forgotten your silly games, Kellan. You always knew how to make me relax when the day had worn me out." She shifted a few books to the side of her desk and cleared a place for us to eat. "What's the price today? Study guides for an exam? Write an essay for you?"

"Inflation, baby. We're looking at a hundred-dollar bottle of champagne, or at the very least, an advanced copy of the latest Follett novel. I know you have connections as a librarian."

"As if I'd share it with you before I read it. I hardly think a bag of salt and vinegar potato chips is worth that much effort." Her eyes twinkled at me, and for a moment, I thought she caught me staring at her.

"True, I jumped the shark with that request, didn't I? Okay, today's a freebie, but next time, watch out. I won't be as easy with you."

We chatted about her new role at Memorial Library. She'd throw a magnificent costume ball later that semester for residents of Braxton, to receive more donations for the renovations. Although her predecessor was a fantastic librarian, Mrs. O'Malley hadn't embraced the technology curve as much as she should have. The college severely lacked access to the latest library hardware and software.

As we finished eating, Maggie surprised me by bringing up Abby's death. "Connor tells me they're announcing later today that they're close to identifying the killer. I guess they must reveal it was murder at that point, huh?"

I don't know whether I was more concerned they might apprehend someone I knew, or that Maggie had further demonstrated how close she and Connor had become in the last few weeks. "Really? I talked to him this morning. He mentioned nothing about an arrest."

"He called a few minutes ago. I'm glad we connected this year," she said with a rising glow.

A student worker popped in to ask if he could leave fifteen minutes early for an unplanned baseball practice. Maggie let him go and wished him luck on Saturday's game.

"So, what exactly are you and Connor these days?" Better to know than feel like I'd been left in the dark.

Maggie coughed and took a big swig of water. "Connor and... ummm... we are... well, what makes you ask, Kellan?" I'd seen that look on her face before, although in the past it was much more innocent.

"Yeah, I mean, you both lost touch like we did. Are you friends again? Are you colleagues who chat from time to time? You know what I mean." I didn't want to ask outright. I'd been clear enough with an open-ended question, but Maggie wasn't sure or didn't feel comfortable discussing it.

"I'd say we're friends. Good friends. He's been a big comfort since I returned. Connor's helped me figure out how to move on without my husband anymore." Maggie fiddled with the books on the desk, then stood. "I should get back to work. I'm so glad you came by today."

Ouch! I was being kicked out again, but Maggie's directness impressed me. "We must do this again soon. I should get going too. I need to swing by Grey Sports Complex to talk with Coach Oliver."

Maggie shifted her head sideways. "What's that about?"

"My mother thought I should meet him. That's all," I lied. Not that I didn't trust Maggie, but I wasn't sure it would amount to anything given the awkward moments we'd just shared. "What do you think of him?"

"He's a solid coach. Loves his job, but not a big supporter of the whole educational purpose for student enrollment at Braxton. That's why I let that pitcher leave early. If Jordan showed up late, Coach Oliver would penalize him in front of the entire team."

"That's cruel." No wonder I stayed away from playing sports back in college. I wouldn't have accepted it and gotten myself into trouble. I had a minor issue with authority figures in my teens and early twenties—the downside of being too clever for your own good.

"A bit, but he's trying to instill some discipline in the team. They had a rough year, and he wants to get a few of them into the minor or major leagues after graduation."

"I don't agree with his approach, but perhaps his heart's in the right place," I said.

"Listen, Kellan, it'd be nice to have dinner before you leave town. Call me when you have a free night?" When she grabbed my hand, a shock ran through my system.

I smiled my biggest smile since arriving back in Braxton. "Definitely. I'll call you soon, Maggie."

"I never could resist those baby blue eyes of yours." she said with a wink, giving me the shivers.

Ten minutes later, I stood outside Grey Sports Complex, a giant series of three-story buildings connected by a common, central entranceway. Above the front reception doors on the second floor, an enclosed courtyard with a ten-foot-tall statue of the college's founder, Heathcliff Braxton, loomed larger than life. Although you could see the top of the statue from the ground, the peaceful garden surrounding it—used by students in the spring and fall for outdoor physical education lectures—was only accessible from the second floor.

I rehearsed my planned conversation with Coach Oliver. *I'm a professional, I can do this*, I convinced myself while entering reception. There were two couches and a table, three doors besides the one I came in, and a television screen on the wall showing various camera positions throughout the building. I saw the baseball field, a swimming pool, what appeared to either be a tennis or volleyball court—the camera had a weird angle—and the fitness center. I looked around the reception area to determine where to go, but someone stopped me in my tracks. "May I help you?"

I heard the voice but couldn't find the corresponding body. I searched all around me in the small room, but I was alone. "Ummm... I'd love to introduce myself, but where exactly are you?"

"Please state your name and whom you are here to see."

Someone was way ruder than she needed to be. "Kellan Ayrwick. I am here to see Coach Oliver. Seriously, where are you hiding?"

"Notifying Coach Oliver. Please hold." The girl wasn't anywhere in the room, leading me to question my sanity.

Annoyed she wouldn't reveal herself, I tried all three of the doors. They were locked. Two minutes later, the middle door opened. After I walked twenty feet down the hall, another voice said, "May I help you?"

Oh, not this again. I was about to use some foul language, but then it occurred to me I heard a *male* voice this time. Maybe he could help me find Coach Oliver. When I reached the steps, a familiar man approached—the same guy in the blue sedan outside Abby Monroe's house. All my worlds were colliding in that one moment.

After the initial shock wore off, my entire plan to meet the athletic director flew out the window. I tried the first approach I could think of. "There was a voice that spoke to me in reception. I'm not crazy, or at least I don't think I am, but I told the girl I was looking for Coach Oliver."

The man laughed and extended his hand. "You've come to the right place. That would be me."

Luck must be on my side today, but that only connected a few of the dots for me. "Oh, terrific. Then I'm heading in the right direction. I'm Kellan Ayrwick. Could you explain what happened back there?"

"Ah, we're testing out some technology. Rather than pay a student to sit out front all day and check identification cards for who can enter the building, we've installed new facial recognition software. It didn't know who you were, so the system asked you to identify yourself. When I heard you state your name, I released the door to let you in." Coach Oliver told me to follow him to the third floor.

I remembered the blogger had mentioned something about technology for the athletics department. "Is this for sports teams? I saw something similar at my father's party the other night."

Coach Oliver responded, "Ah, you're their son. Your mother volunteered to use it to track entry at the retirement party. We're eventually hoping to use it around the college but initially at the sports games to help with access control and improved security."

While what he said made sense, I still didn't grasp fully how it functioned. "So, does that mean I was speaking to some robot or computer back in reception?"

"Yes, a camera snaps a photo when someone enters the building. We match it against the system to grant access. Eventually, we'll record your movement throughout the facility, but for now, the facial recognition software is only installed in the reception area." We'd reached the third floor, and he made a left down the hall. "Our new fitness center is down the other hall to the right."

"What else have you installed so far?"

"We have one camera near the fitness center and several around Grey Field. They're currently fitting voice-activated controls for the lighting on the third floor in my office and nearby conference room. Just the minimum until we finish testing it next week. The system isn't yet fully functional."

"Cool stuff," I replied, unconvinced of its potential value on campus. "Braxton seems like such a small school to need all these advanced systems."

"It's a way to move toward the twenty-first century. We need to look like we're at the front of the curve if we want the right people to notice us," he replied hesitantly and breathing more heavily.

"Happy with it?" I wondered who was expected to notice them. Potential students?

"Everyone forgets their identification cards. Facial recognition has helped our operations, although a few people have gotten in without proper access. We're working out the kinks. I only use the system's features for tracking player performance and interacting with potential team sponsors and sports management companies."

"How did you get the financial support for such an expensive technology?" I became the blogger taking aim at anyone supporting the athletics department.

"Not sure. I guess the Board of Trustees ultimately found the funds." Coach Oliver started sweating once we reached his office. Was it the two flights of stairs or the questions about the money?

"Those anonymous donations must have helped with the improvements to the playing fields." While Coach Oliver considered my words, the bags under his eyes indicated he hadn't slept in a few nights.

"No clue who donated the money, nor can I say much about the security side of it. Our security director can fill you in on that. How can I help today?" He absentmindedly scratched his balding head.

Oh, true. I had a reason to meet him before I'd realized he was the same guy I'd seen at Abby's place. "I'm in town for a few days and sorely missing the gym, but there aren't any true fitness centers in the area. Could I use the college's facilities while I'm in Braxton? I wouldn't ask but—"

"Ah, yes, that would be totally fine. Your parents are good people, I'd do anything to help them. Your father's a big supporter of the athletics department. I'll add access to your identification card and account, so you can use the fitness center. We're open twenty-four hours a day, seven days a week." He pulled out his phone and typed a few commands while leading me toward the fitness center down the hall. "Are you attending our opening game this Saturday? Expecting a full crowd." The excitement in his words leaped from his mouth. For someone who potentially killed Abby or just lost his friend, it was curious. Either he was a great actor or something else was going on behind the scenes in this mystery.

"I heard about a big rivalry between two pitchers. What was it, Striker and Jimmy?" I kept my tone simple, looking disinterested and as though I were making normal conversation.

"Jordan Ballantine, last year's relief pitcher. I used to bring him in, in the seventh or eighth inning whenever Striker tired out or gave up too many hits. I spent a lot of time with Jordan over the summer. His new curveball came out of nowhere. That kid might come close to a hundred miles per hour. He's got a chance of making the major leagues, but Striker's the current top dog."

"Sounds like a healthy competition. Decided who will start?"

"Got one more practice this week, then I'll make a big announcement on Friday at the pep rally," Coach Oliver replied, noting he had to finish working on a few things. "Come by the fitness center anytime. Top-notch facility here, just bought a few new pieces of equipment that'll work wonders for those delts of yours." He slapped the back of my shoulder with heavy force.

I couldn't let him go that easily. "I appreciate it. My mom thought you'd be able to help. She was upset over missing you at the party. Thought she saw you walking that night, but you were looking the other way or something. I guess you never made it, huh?"

Coach Oliver startled like a fox caught in the henhouse. "Saw me? Really? Hmmm... I got to the party and met your sister, Eleanor, in the lobby... on her way out."

I let him squirm. When he didn't seem to recall or offer anything further, I triggered his memory. "I think she said you might have been right outside Diamond Hall."

"Ah, yeah," Coach Oliver said with a slightly higher pitch to his voice. "I just remembered. I was late dropping off the schedule for the upcoming week. President Ayrwick, I mean your father, likes a hand-delivered copy of the weekly sporting event schedule each Friday, so he can plan accordingly. I ran into his assistant, and she offered to drop it off for me."

Lorraine hadn't mentioned this to me, which seemed odd. Surely, Coach Oliver wouldn't lie about something I could easily disprove. I didn't want to alienate him, so I nodded and smoothed over the conversation. Maybe he'd admit to knowing Abby. "Oh, that makes sense. My father is particular about his schedule. Such a shame about what happened to that professor."

"Definitely. It's always hard to hear someone's died, but to know they had an accident at such a young age, that's worse. She had a lot of life left in her."

Given he opened the door, I stepped further inside. "I take it you knew her well?"

"No, I wouldn't say that. I bumped into her occasionally. She'd attended an event or two. Staff functions. That's all I remember. I need to run, Kellan. I hope you'll join us for the game on Saturday."

"Thanks again," I said as he scampered down the hallway. I'd made him edgy and caught him in at least one, maybe two lies. I poked my head in the fitness center and quickly determined the newer machines had cost major money. I had to agree with the blogger that something was unusual about the anonymous donations and their distribution to Grey Sports Complex.

I texted Nana D to ask if she wanted company.

Nana D: *I'm busy. I've got a life. Unlike some people. Hugs and kisses.*
Me: *Why don't we schedule a meal?*
Nana D: *Go find a cow to tip or a pile of bricks to rearrange if you're bored. Or call Bridget.*
Me: *Perhaps you're pushing things a little too quickly?*
Nana D: *Don't ignore me. Move on at some point. I say that with love. Yes, to brunch soon.*

Was everyone sarcastic? And why did Nana D feel the need to keep setting me up with weird women? How about a normal one for a change... like Maggie... wait, was I even ready to date again?

CHAPTER 9

On Tuesday, I woke early and pushed myself to visit Grey Sports Complex for my first workout in five days. Jordan, the student employee who worked at Memorial Library—and Striker's new competition—ran on a treadmill. A pretty blonde raced furiously on the stationary bicycle. When I walked past both, I heard Jordan call out, "You're gonna beat your record, hot stuff!" She smiled at him, and they both focused on their workouts.

Rather than address a specific body part or group, I tested several of the new machines and acclimated to the equipment. Although I wouldn't stay in Braxton long, it would be helpful to take advantage of the opportunity.

When I arrived home, I scarfed down an early lunch—chocolate whey protein shake with almond milk, peanut butter, strawberries, and flaxseed. *'Don't knock it til you try it,'* I remembered the juice-maker telling me back at my home gym. Ever since that introduction, it'd become my new standard lunch on workout days. I unlocked my iPad, opened the *FaceTime* app, and contacted my daughter. As expected, she accepted the call without her grandmother's help and waved hello to me.

"Hello, my precious girl. Good morning to you."

"Daddy! Where are you?" Although Emma knew how to hold the device properly, so the camera caught her face, she couldn't stop from bouncing up and down on the couch in excitement.

"Slow down, baby. I'm gonna get seasick."

"Sorry. But if you bounced too, maybe we'd both look like we were super still."

I found little fault with her logic about not getting seasick. Maybe she was onto something. "What did you eat for breakfast?" I noticed blueberry stains on her lips. She loved to eat fruit and didn't seem to care for desserts. I often questioned if she were truly my daughter.

"*Bear Berries*. Ummm... Grandma said we could go to the zoo. They have a new baby giraffe."

Emma was in her *obsessed-with-animals* phase and wanted to go to the zoo every weekend. I suggested other sites like the planetarium or the beach, but nothing had taken the zoo's place in months. At some point, you had to give in if you wanted to maintain your sanity as a parent.

I told Emma about Nana D playing the clarinet years ago. She asked to take lessons after the next zoo trip. When her cartoons came on, she tossed the iPad to her grandmother. Cecilia waved hello and asked when I'd be back. Not another person adding to my list of aggravations.

While Francesca's parents were fantastic grandparents, they were horrendous in-laws. Were they still in-laws if I wasn't married to their daughter anymore? My point—they were amazing to Emma when Francesca died. But a few months after the burial, once life somehow got normal again—as normal as it could be for a thirty-year-old widower with a four-year-old daughter—I started seeing unfortunate changes. Vincenzo and Cecilia Castigliano showed up uninvited at my house with a request to keep Emma overnight, claiming they missed their daughter and wanted to feel close to her. One afternoon, Happy Tots Day Care called to say Emma's grandparents wanted to sign her out for the afternoon. I tried to keep an open mind about the Castigliano behavioral changes, but on the one-year anniversary of Francesca's death, Vincenzo snuck into my office to inform me he and Cecilia had decided it would be better if Emma moved in with them. I'd always known Vincenzo brokered shady business deals, but I never knew the extent until that night when Francesca's sister revealed their father was part of a Los Angeles mob. I started asking around, and a colleague pointed out the Castigliano family weren't just *part* of a Los Angeles mob. They were the main family who *ran* the Los Angeles mob.

Although I was non-confrontational, I needed their help since I was a single parent and wasn't planning to move back to Pennsylvania. I made it clear Emma was never to be placed in any dangerous situations given the *family business*. Vincenzo had shrugged and grunted, then said, "*I don't know what you talk about. We run a lovely import-export business. Very quiet and safe.*" We'd come to an agreement, but if they ever stepped out of line, I wouldn't be afraid to do something more drastic.

After I hung up, I dropped my head to the counter and closed my eyes. I was weary and needed a moment of silence. Too bad that wouldn't happen.

"Good afternoon, Kellan. It's about time you woke up," my father commented as he stood over me with a glass of water and a plate full of scattered whole wheat toast crumbs.

"I've been up since at least eight. Don't forget that's like five to me with the time difference. I haven't yet adjusted." I wish I knew whether he was serious or simply enjoyed pushing my buttons.

"You're young enough it shouldn't matter. At your age, I already had—"

"What are you doing home, anyway?" I couldn't compare our lives anymore. He'd always win. "Has retirement already begun?"

"As your mother and Lorraine told you yesterday, I can't return to my office until the sheriff finishes searching the building. It's easier to get most of my work done at home in the mornings, then go on campus for meetings in the afternoon. I won't be using the temporary office anymore and asked the facilities department to put my furniture in storage until they complete the renovations."

"Does Lorraine report everything she tells me back to you?" I'd have to be careful how much I spoke my mind in front of her. "She's concerned about what Sheriff Montague wants from you."

"Nothing you need to worry about, Kellan. The sheriff and I are on good terms with this whole debacle. I'm confident they'll do the right thing soon," he replied. "While you're here, I need to speak with you about something."

Oh, great. If he asked how long I'd be staying again, I'd pack my bags that afternoon and hop the next flight no matter the cost or location, even if Derek fired me. Speaking of Derek, I owed him a status update. "What's on your mind? I have some questions for you too, Dad."

"Go ahead. You first." My father perched on a stool at the kitchen island and glared at me.

"Where did you go the night of the retirement party? Mom's worried about you. Something's weird around here." I didn't want to bring up the call I'd overheard yet.

"Well, since you've put that so eloquently, Kellan, I was doing my job. Not all of us have the freedom to come and go or choose what projects we work on. I had an impromptu conversation with the Board of Trustees about something urgent near the end of their meeting."

"They meet on Saturday night. Who does that?"

"If you must know, they were discussing their final recommendations on the new president before the panel interviews. Their meeting was held after they all stopped by my party." He turned his hands over, so both palms faced upwards, then pulled them back to his body and crossed them in his lap.

I had the sudden urge to mock him. I didn't, as it wouldn't win me any favors. "Anything new from the blogger? I couldn't remember the site name to check myself."

"Yes, there was another post on Sunday talking about the opulence of my retirement party." His color faded as he spoke, making me debate if he were more human than I'd given him credit for. "Your mother and I paid for that party out of our pockets. The Board wanted to cover all costs, but we insisted they'd already bought me a wonderful going away present." He handed me his phone to read the post:

If you weren't in attendance at Saturday night's grand ceremony, you missed a soirée fit for royalty. Between the exotic scents and rare foods dripping in excess, I found everyone's admiration for Wesley Ayrwick to be so sickening, I couldn't force myself to stay exceptionally long. I'd hoped to share photos, but a security attendant who treated us like criminals stopped any camera or video recordings.

Are we supposed to bow to our king? He should've spoken less about the baseball team's new uniforms and more about the questionable source of the anonymous donations frivolously spent in all the wrong places. Stop by Grey Sports Complex to test the ridiculous new systems that were integrated into our curiously modernized athletic facility. I managed to overhear quite a conversation about an upcoming special visitor to campus, and a well-known community citizen might shake in their boots once I reveal what's been going on behind our backs. Look for my next post to disclose all the details of these shady shenanigans.

When I asked my father if there was any truth to the post, he changed the subject. He noted how students found the blogger to be a funny distraction but gave his or her messages little consideration. I recalled the conversation where Myriam accused him of spending the college's money in ways he shouldn't have. He'd let her believe Braxton covered the costs of the party and never attempted to defend himself. Was he learning how to be less combative with other people, just not me? "Do you think Myriam Castle is leading this crusade against you?"

"Doubtful. Myriam and I spar from time to time, and she doesn't particularly like me, but she's not someone to hide behind her words. She directly indicts me of wrongdoing."

He had a good point about why she'd blog under an anonymous name yet accuse him of similar things in a public setting, where anyone could have overheard the conversation. "What about the new technology at Grey Sports Complex? How did that get funded?"

"I don't know all the details going on behind the scenes at Braxton. The Board of Trustees decided. You should touch base with Councilman Stanton. He's on the Board," he replied. "That all?"

Nana D would be a perfect person to grill the councilman. Since I couldn't bring up the mysterious phone call, I jumped to other topics. "Why didn't you tell me that Maggie and Connor were working at Braxton? I was just here in December, and you could have said something. Or picked up the phone."

"I didn't think it was important. You haven't mentioned either in a decade. I'd assumed you lost touch and cared little about what had happened to them. You've never been one to rehash the past."

Ouch. The digs were back in full force. "That's a little unfair, Dad. I may have lost touch, but Mom's having weekly coffee dates with Maggie. Connor works as your director of security."

"I thought you'd be happy I hired your friends. Some might call that nepotism."

Why did he always know what to say to shut me up? And why did I always feel like I was five years old around him? Since throwing a tantrum wasn't an option, I reined in my frustrations and leapt into the big topic. "Who do you think murdered Abby Monroe?"

"That's a matter for Sheriff Montague. I can tell you that neither I nor

Lorraine had anything to do with it. What the sheriff does next, I don't know, but hopefully, she listens to me on the topic."

"Which means... what?" Seriously, did everyone have this much trouble with their parents?

"We had a complicated relationship. I liked Abby as a person, but she wasn't qualified for her position. The Board of Trustees was too worried about potential lawsuits if we tried to fire her. Instead, we kept her power in check," he said while crossing his arms and scowling. "I have it on good authority she'd been job hunting before Saturday's incident. The woman made enemies and was going through a nasty divorce. The sheriff plans to investigate those angles and put an end to this entire affair. Can I now discuss what I wanted to talk to you about?"

Abby was the person my father had been talking about failing to terminate on the call I'd overheard. I considered all his news and rationalized he had a solid theory about the investigation. "Yes, go ahead, Dad. I'm listening." I assumed it had something to do with Emma or my mother.

"Abby's death has left a hole in the communications department. There's only one other professor with experience in media studies, but she's covering Abby's administrative responsibilities for Dean Mulligan. We don't have anyone who can teach her classes for a few weeks until we find a suitable replacement." He paused to see if I had any reactions. If I remembered correctly, Dean Mulligan, Abby's boss, oversaw all the academic departments.

I suspected where he was going with the conversation but wanted him to ask me directly, before I put my foot in my mouth. "I imagine it's quite a predicament. You've solved bigger problems before."

"True, I most certainly have. I'm also supposed to announce the new president next week, transition my responsibilities, help the sheriff and Connor minimize the impact of this tragedy on the rest of the campus, and accept all these changes in my life. I'm not getting any younger, Kellan, and although it may seem like I can do everything all at once, I cannot."

Wow. I didn't think I'd ever hear my father admit a potential weakness. "You're strong and persistent."

"While that may be true, it's time to let someone else step into that role for this family. As a starting point, I'd like you to takeover Abby's classes until Dean Mulligan can decide how to handle potential reorganization of the department and hire her replacement."

After a fifteen-second void occupied all notions of life inside my head, I found the courage to respond. "I can appreciate your faith in me, Dad, and I'm honestly touched you would—"

"I'm not done. Just let me get this out," he replied, retreating from the counter toward the back window. "You're tired of everyone asking how long you plan to stay or when you'll move back. You've mentioned missing your friends. Your mother wants to spend more time with Emma. As do I. You've kept yourself distant from this family for a reason, and I've let this go on long enough."

"Dad, please don't say any more. I don't want to have this conversation." I knew where he was going. He'd tried this once before. We had a horrible fight when I left Christmas night two years ago, after accusing him of driving away all his children.

"Kellan, I'm not saying you're right or wrong. I'm saying you've done it your way ever since Francesca died. I wasn't there for you when it happened. I admitted I never cared much for her. But she was your wife, and Emma's mother, and I should have been a better father." He rested his hand on my shoulder. I hadn't even heard him walk toward me in those few confidence-shaking seconds. "All I'm asking from you, is three weeks to a month."

I told my father I needed the rest of the week to think about his proposal and would let him know my decision on the weekend. I abandoned him in the kitchen and raced out to the garage. I didn't know whom to turn to at that moment, but his words hit way too close to my heart.

I spent the rest of the day driving around Braxton and reminiscing about all the great times I had in the past with college friends and family, including when Francesca and Emma came home with me on a few trips. Taking the temporary job meant risking any opportunity I had of getting my own television show, to escape Derek and achieve something I'd been dreaming about for years. I had a lot more thinking to do before I could make any definitive decisions.

No longer interested in worsening my mood by talking to the sheriff, I pushed that task off until the following day. I also needed to let Connor know Coach Oliver had lied to me about how well he knew Abby. Regardless of their relationship, he'd been going through her mail when I was standing in the drive-way. If he was lying to me, he was lying to the sheriff too. I first needed to get some sleep, then I'd deal with all the concerns tomorrow.

CHAPTER 10

When Wednesday descended, I felt stronger and more alive. Going to the fitness center the prior day helped motivate me. I returned in the hopes I could work off some frustration and anger. It was even quieter than it'd been the day before. Only one other person was working on chest exercises, as if the weight amounted to nothing more than a pillow.

I approached the lat machine to his right, adjusted the seat height, and chose the amount of weight I hoped I could handle. I was about to get started when the other guy called out to me.

"Hey, would you mind spotting me on the bench press? No one's been in here all morning." He wore a baseball cap and a long-sleeve college jersey with the number three.

I wasn't sure I could lift the same amount of weight he could, but I'd try. "No problem. Are you on the baseball team?" I took his grunt while lifting for a yes, then asked more questions in between sets.

His dark hair was clipped short, and he hadn't shaved in a few days. "Yep, name's Craig Magee, but everyone calls me Striker. I'm the team's pitcher. You a student here?"

The famous Striker. Did he know who was pitching in the game on Saturday? Coach Oliver said he wouldn't reveal the decision until Friday to the public. "Me? Former student, but thanks for the ego boost, man." I enjoyed knowing I could sometimes still pass for my twenties. "I'm Kellan. I've heard a bit about you before. What does the three stand for?"

"Number of pitches it takes for me to knock down all the batters. Three strikes in a row and they're always out," he said with a huge grin.

"Clever. Ready for Saturday's game?"

"That's why I'm here today. Final pre-season practice tomorrow and then the coach decides the starting lineup." Additional reps failed to wind him.

"I'm sure all the extra focus will be helpful," I replied as Striker finished his third set, increasing the weight by ten each time. I would soon reach my limit on how much I could spot, but I didn't want to stop his momentum. I could push myself to hold more if necessary.

"Yep. I think I've got this in the bag, but it's not just the upcoming practice. I'm waiting on a few grades to confirm I'll be allowed to play. Dean Mulligan put me on academic probation and threatened to take away my scholarship because my GPA dropped below a 3.0 at the end of last semester."

"How do you plan to fix that?" I asked, recalling the conversation Abby had with someone on her phone in front of Memorial Library. Was she talking about meeting Striker that night at eight thirty?

"I was right on the border, but the dean said I could play as long as I kept up a 'B+' all semester long. Waiting on two grades from my biology class and Professor Monroe."

"Isn't Monroe the professor who had an accident last weekend?" I played dumb to see what else he'd reveal. I hadn't realized my coming to the fitness center would be an enlightening connection this morning. Kudos to me for doing the right thing. Nana D was right—I was brilliant.

"Yep," he replied before wiping himself off with a towel. "I'm confident I did well on a biology paper. I should know this morning. We haven't heard if Professor Monroe turned in the grades before... well, you know." He made a *BOOM* sound and dropped his head to the side.

I was dealing with someone just as mature as I'd once been. "Do you think Professor Monroe gave you a passing grade?"

"Doubt it. She didn't like me very much last semester. She's the one who failed me. That's why I'm back in her Intro to Film class again this semester. It fills one of my elective courses and unfortunately was the only other one that matched my schedule between baseball, my job, and other classes." Striker tagged me in to do my own set of chest presses.

"If you need any help with the class, I could tutor you. I was a communications major here a few years ago, and I'm well-versed in the broadcast curriculum."

"Seriously, you'd help? I barely know you." His friendliness and smile were contagious.

"You seem like a good guy. Besides, I met Coach Oliver yesterday. He's counting on you to take the team to the championship this year, even get you to the majors." I didn't want to inflate Striker's hopes, but he might have the scoop on Coach Oliver and Abby. Or he could have been the person who knocked Abby on her head and pushed her down the stairs.

When we finished working out, I handed him my cell number and advised him I'd be around for a few days. He mentioned he'd let me know after he found out his latest grade.

"Was Coach Oliver friendly with Professor Monroe? I wondered if he tried to talk with her about getting you some help with the class." It seemed unusual that those two had some sort of relationship while one of the star baseball students was stuck in the middle. I also remembered my mother mentioning changes to the policy of fraternization between certain departments, citing a scandal a year ago involving a staff member accused of harassing someone. Was Coach Oliver to blame back then?

"Wouldn't know. I tried to stay away from Professor Monroe as much as possible. Coach Oliver told me he'd help however he could, but I don't know if he did anything once she failed me last semester." Striker drank some water from the fountain, then wiped the bench with a wet towel. "I'm gonna hit the showers. Got class in thirty minutes. Thanks for spotting today."

"No worries. Good luck, Striker."

After he left, I finished my workout and reflected on our conversation. Had Sheriff Montague learned the same information and decided how the Jenga puzzle mysteriously collapsed in murder?

When I pulled out my phone to call her, I saw a new email from Derek with the name of the hotel and a copy of his check-in registration. He'd checked out the day before, which meant he was back in Los Angeles. I dialed the number for registration and pretended to be him inquiring about my final bill. While I listened to a lovely but ironic minute-long version of Michael Jackson's *Smooth Criminal*, I walked to the locker room to change into a towel before showering. The clerk came back on the line and confirmed the purchases I'd made in the room last Saturday and Sunday, as well as the additional damage fee for the state I'd left the room in. She mentioned it was the first time they'd ever had to replace a mattress due to guest misuse. *"Oops, my bad,"* I said, trying to sound like Derek but feeling a sense of fake guilt for something he'd done.

Unless Derek had sent someone to Hawaii in his place, enabling him to show up in Braxton, he likely hadn't killed Abby. I felt better knowing I didn't work for a murderer, but I still had to call the creep. After showering and noticing the marked improvement in my muscle definition, I pinged him on *FaceTime*, so I could see if his *tell* gave him away. Just to put the final check mark on his alibi, I asked if he knew any good mattress stores, claiming I was in the market to find a new one.

"Dude, I don't know but call and ask that hotel. Somehow my date and I broke the springs. They had the audacity to charge me an extra fee!" He didn't blink, nor did his lip quiver. He had told the truth.

With the alibi now confirmed and my stomach near revolt, I updated him on Abby's death formally being considered a murder. He responded, "Kel-baby, you've got quite a story. We could reposition season two to focus on her murder. Find out everything. This is your top priority. Do whatever you have to do."

"Yep, I'm on it." This time I hung up on him, feeling a sense of pride and accomplishment. Now I had many compelling reasons to say involved in the case.

I called the precinct to verify Sheriff Montague was in her office, but Officer Flatman told me she'd driven to Braxton to meet with Connor. Perfect, I could talk to them both after I stopped off at The Big Beanery to pick up a bribe —I meant thoughtful and kind gesture.

Twenty minutes later, I parked in the guest lot and dashed to the BCS Office. When I arrived, I saw the frown forming on Sheriff Montague's face from the outside walkway.

"Good afternoon," I announced through the screen door and entered the foyer. "I thought I'd visit my old friend, Connor. Fancy running into you here." I set the three coffees and donuts on the counter. "I have an extra cup if you're interested, sheriff."

"Little Ayrwick, you're pushing me... Flatman already texted that you were looking for me. What do you want?" She had the classic annoyed detective appearance again—hands on her hips, tweed blazer too tight across her back and pushing her shoulders up in the air, lips pursed, and frankly, that same look Nana D got when she'd consumed too many prunes.

"You might want to hear a few things I learned this week. Maybe you could give me an update on access to Abby's office or on anything happening with the case?" I stepped back in case she swung at me, but either she held out for one giant wallop, or she was considering my offer.

"Something tells me you won't go away until I entertain whatever you feel the hernia-popping need to divulge. If you have helpful information to share, maybe I'll feel obliged to return the favor. What's got those purple lacy panties crawling halfway up your—"

Connor spit out his coffee this time. "Dude, she's got your number. You better watch yourself."

His interruption had at least stopped her from finishing her thoughts. As much as her attitude annoyed me, I enjoyed being abused in a humorous sort of way. Little did she know I once had to wear a pair of purple lacy panties after losing a bet with Connor during our junior year. Could April Montague and I be friends in some alternate universe? When I thought about having to look at that dreadful tweed blazer over drinks or at a football game, I had the obvious answer. I stopped myself from retching.

"I went to Abby's house to see if she had a roommate or husband that might let me in to check, but when I got there...." I reiterated everything I'd learned to date. "It might have been a coincidence, or the meeting the night of Abby's murder might have changed times. Just felt it my responsibility to share the news."

Sheriff Montague smirked. "Not bad for an inexperienced, nosy pain in the butt. You discovered a few things my detectives haven't come up with yet. They'll suffer, thanks. We knew about her neighbor and that Abby was seen around with someone, but not about it being Coach Oliver. I appreciate the academic tips, but we're already looking into her cell records. Next time... one, don't dillydally before telling me, and two, stay out of my case. You've been warned not to interfere."

"Wait a minute! I have it on good authority you've nearly completed your search of Abby's office, yet there's been no phone call telling me when and where to show up." What could she do with Connor standing there as a witness?

"All accurate information except I didn't promise you. I said I'd take it under advisement. And I did. I also chose to follow proper protocol. Something with which you have difficulty." She manhandled two of the donuts and the remaining cup of coffee, enabling me to confirm she wore no wedding ring. "Thanks for the snacks, Little Ayrwick. I'll be in touch if I need additional assistance from Seraphina Danby's errand boy and savior, or if I learn which of you two won the award for Braxton's latest interfering washerwoman who likes to gab." She turned to Connor. "I know you have no control over him, and I direct none of this at you. I value your help as Braxton's security director."

I ignored the huge grin on Connor's face. He clearly hadn't picked up on the sheriff's crush. Nana D and I did not deserve that comment about gabbing. "Wait, didn't you say you'd share something as long as I provided useful information? Come on, Connor, you heard it too? How about the murder weapon? Any clues yet?"

I swear little hearts shot out from the sheriff's eyes in Connor's direction. "You kinda said that," he replied. "But I could have heard it wrong."

"Boys, and I mean boys for one of you, this is not a game we're playing. Let me wash, rinse, and repeat for those of you who own stock in all the hair gel companies. Murder is not a game. I can appreciate that you want to do your part. I don't think you have any ill intentions, Little Ayrwick. I need to protect the evidence and paper trails in the case, so we can clearly put our criminal behind bars. Keep your dirty paws to yourself. I'll only ask nicely once."

I nodded since she had a good point. "I'm not looking to receive any special favors this time. Maybe you could keep me in the loop. I'll immediately share anything I learn and stay out of your way. Honest!"

"We're still running tests to identify the shape and size of the murder weapon. I haven't given you access to Abby Monroe's office because I haven't been cleared to do so. I need approval from her next of kin and from Braxton staff. I just finished chatting with your father. I'm meeting momentarily with the other." She saluted us both and headed to the door. "Expect a call tomorrow, Little Ayrwick."

As she left, I turned to hit Connor in the shoulder with as much power as I could muster after having been deflated and emasculated by Sheriff Montague. "You could have stood up for me, dude."

Connor laughed. "I work with that woman all the time. I don't want to be on her nasty side."

"Oh, is there another side of her you want to be on?" I teased, forgetting how diesel he'd gotten and how easily I could end up on the floor from one punch. I'd never learn my lessons, would I?

"I'll ignore that. But I'll also point out you missed a key revelation there, Deputy Clueless. Besides her not liking your hair, pretty boy." The sheriff's comment was obviously meant for me given I had the long and wavy curls. Connor's buzz cut seemed off limits to her.

I shook my head. What clue did I miss? "I'm not sure what you... oooh!" If the sheriff was meeting with Abby's next of kin, then Alton Monroe had been located. "The husband's back in town!"

"Always the first one to figure it out, eh, Kellan? Listen, I need to finish some work before I meet up with Maggie. Take it easy, man," Connor replied while shoving a donut in his mouth.

He disappeared into his office, leaving me standing alone and disgruntled. What was he meeting Maggie for? I reached into the bag to grab a donut, but there were none left. "Bollocks! You got the better of me too many times today, Connor. Don't make me start a war."

I spent the rest of Wednesday working on urgent items that Derek needed me to handle for *Dark Reality*. Promo schedules, contract negotiations with supporting actors, and script edits to introduce Abby Monroe into season two's scope. Although we didn't have a full story, he wanted to show the updated plan to his boss at the network. I quickly pulled together revised outlines and some taglines, feeling a little unnerved about using Abby's death as a marketing ploy.

CHAPTER 11

With my immediate deadlines addressed, I went for a run Thursday morning and intentionally stopped at the Pick-Me-Up Diner to touch base with Eleanor. As I entered, Eustacia Paddington grabbed my arm and shook her head wildly. "You gotta do something about that wicked grandmother of yours, Kellan. She's outta control!" Wisps of gray hair shot out in all directions underneath a furry blue hat three-sizes too big on her frail and wrinkled head.

Eustacia Paddington had gone to high school with my nana. They'd been frenemies ever since. Whatever Ms. Paddington did, my nana had to go one step further in their quest to annoy one another. On the last count, Nana D rallied six volunteers to rotate weeks for shoveling snow at Willow Trees, a nearby senior citizen's community where Eustacia Paddington resided. Somehow all the volunteers were under the impression they could drop the mounds of shoveled snow on the corner lot. Eustacia's lot. Which Nana D had told everyone was empty for the winter while the tenant was in Florida. But she wasn't away, which meant Ms. Paddington couldn't get out of her home for a week.

I wasn't looking forward to hearing the latest battle. "Good to see you, Ms. Paddington. That color blue makes your eyes shine. How are you doing?"

"I know when I'm being worked. Don't even try the *you-catch-more-with-honey-than-vinegar* game with me. Your nana is the fly in this flaming puddle of hemorrhoid ointment, sonny." She stomped her wooden cane on the ground and caused a picture frame to fall off the wall. "She's trying to steal Lindsey Endicott. Everyone at Willow Trees knows we've been dating for months. You tell her—"

"I don't think she's trying to steal him away from you, Ms. Paddington. Nana D seems hardly interested in dating," I began, but was interrupted before I could finish my thoughts. Could Nana D really be putting herself on the market again? After that last debacle with Eustacia Paddington's brother, Nana D pitched such a fit I thought she was going to take a vow of chastity and join the nunnery.

"That woman is out to get me. You tell her not to start something she won't be able to finish!" As she left, all I could see was the blurry image of her giant pink parka waving in the parking lot like one of those tall, inflatable tube machines people put outside stores when holding sales and trying to capture shopper's attention. She looked like Gumby's ancient grandmother in need of an oxygen boost.

"You know Nana D probably flirted with him." Eleanor pushed the cash drawer shut. "She was in here earlier talking about pulling the wool over someone's eyes."

My sister was right. I didn't doubt it, but I couldn't let Eustacia know I was on to my nana's tricks. "Speaking of sly ones, what's up with you avoiding me yesterday?"

Eleanor lifted the countertop and passed through to the main waiting area. At least she'd swapped out the condiment-stained outfit from two days ago with a clean pair of pants and a brighter top. "Just busy. You take everything so personally sometimes, Kellan. If I didn't know better, I'd think my big brother got his wee feelings hurt." She kissed my cheek and placed two menus back in the cubby on the entrance wall while humming a tune from some psychic medium show.

I rolled my eyes at her. "What do your Tarot cards say?"

"Touché," she teased. "I'm sorry I ran off the other day. It's been a busy few weeks. Everyone's a little jumpy with the professor's death." Eleanor had a habit of shutting down whenever something was bothering her instead of opening up to me or anyone else. I assumed my mother had said or done something to annoy her again. *Twinsies* gone rogue!

"Tell me about it. I've been home for less than a week, and everything's changed." I followed her to the back office. "Hey, have you noticed anything going on between Connor and Maggie? I'm not sure if I picked up a weird vibe or if—"

"No, why?" she replied abruptly.

"I think she's seen him twice already since I've been home. Whenever I notice them together, they're making googly eyes—" I couldn't finish my thoughts again. People enjoyed interrupting me. Did I need to be more assertive?

"I'm sure they're just being friendly since they both work together at Braxton now." As she sat in her office chair, the phone rang, and I listened to her argue with a supplier about a late delivery.

Eleanor had squashed my theory about anything going on between Connor and Maggie. Still, I asked myself, why did I care? I had more pressing things to worry about. I scanned for email on my phone, but nothing from Derek. I was flipping through my calendar when Eleanor hung up.

"There's nothing between them. I'm sure of it," she replied. "Sorry about that, I'm having trouble with a supplier."

Something told me there was more going on than Eleanor was willing to reveal at that point. Since I wasn't ready to get into it with her, I dropped the Maggie and Connor discussion. "Maybe you could swap suppliers. Perhaps the place Mom used to help with Dad's party could provide an alternative option."

"I'm capable of figuring it out on my own, Kellan. Did you need something or were you just swinging by to perform today's good deed?" She rose, giving me the distinct impression it was time for me to leave. All the color had drained from her face.

"Well, I guess I should go," I replied, leaning in to offer a comforting hug. "I love you, Eleanor, and when you want to talk, I'll drop everything for you." I exited her office and headed to the Jeep. Before I started the engine, she texted me.

Eleanor: *I'm sorry. Let's get dinner Saturday, and we'll talk.*

I knew something was up, and now I needed to be patient until she revealed the source of her grief. When I arrived at Diamond Hall, things were no longer cordoned off, yet a sign still indicated classes were held elsewhere. I climbed the stairs, assuming someone might stop me but making it all the way to the second floor with no interruption. I called out on my way to Abby's office. "Hello, anyone there?" Was Sheriff Montague inside? I wasn't prepared for a battle of well-timed quips and her brutal one-liners.

A mid-forties, curly blond with a recent sunburn stood behind the desk. He was dressed casually and didn't appear to be a member of the Braxton police force. "Good afternoon. May I help you?"

"Kellan Ayrwick. I'm reviewing Professor Monroe's classes. I thought I'd drop by to see if...." I should have prepared better. I couldn't waltz into the office and rifle through drawers without questions being asked. Worrying about the sheriff had thrown me off my game.

"Oh, Kellan. I'm supposed to call you this afternoon. It's good to meet you. I'm Alton Monroe." He gestured at me to join him. "Sheriff Montague mentioned you wanted a quick peek at Abby's files."

So, this was the soon-to-be ex-husband and Lorraine's half-brother. I saw a slight resemblance between Lorraine and Alton, in their pinned-back ears, hair color, and narrow jawlines. He didn't look dangerous. I supposed I retained little worry over being alone with him in Abby's office. I was grateful I could finally poke around Abby's things, despite Sheriff Montague failing to notify me herself. I shook his hand and leaned against the doorframe. "I appreciate it. I believe you just got in from out of town, somewhere visiting...?" I paused, hoping he'd fill in the blank.

"A remote village near the border of Alaska and Russia. I go on occasional nature treks for an online magazine to write about animals going extinct." He prattled on about some bird whose population had been slowly declining in the last decade, allowing me a chance to scan the office.

As the department head, Abby had occupied one of the bigger offices on the floor. Two small wooden chairs sat across from an enormous mahogany desk. I idled near one of them, and what I assumed was Alton Monroe's briefcase borrowed the other one. Dozens of bookshelves lined the walls. On the open wall space were Abby's diplomas, confirming the schools I'd seen in her profile during my research. A few scattered papers cluttered the desk, the garbage pail had recently been emptied, and what looked like a grade book sat on the corner table near a reading lamp. Striker would love to get his hands on that. I was curious if he'd found out his grade and would be cleared to play in Saturday's game. The room was organized but devoid of any actual personality other than books. Abby liked a plain workspace.

It suddenly dawned on me Alton had stopped talking. I hoped he hadn't asked me a question as I'd lost interest in his story while scanning the room. Not that I didn't care about the plight of the short-tailed albatross, but I had more immediate problems to solve. "Very interesting. Sounds like a good trip. I heard you didn't have any wireless access. Hearing the news about your wife must have been a shock."

"Soon-to-be ex-wife," he replied smugly. "Although, that's not important anymore. Abby and I were trying to salvage a friendship, but I'm afraid things went south many months ago."

"I wasn't aware. So sorry to hear," I fibbed again. I wasn't in the habit of lying, but if it procured fresh information out of a potential source, I could comfortably blur the lines. Mostly, I was an honest and direct guy. Ask Eleanor. "They'll hold her funeral early next week. I expect I'll see you there?"

"Abby had no other family. I feel obligated to attend, perhaps a final goodbye."

"I imagine so. That's good of you." I paused, hoping he'd volunteer more information. In past interviews, it always seemed people of his nature were uncomfortable with silence, suddenly sharing things they might not normally say until the solitude nudged them over the edge.

"Sheriff Montague mentioned you wanted to look for some papers. I've been here for twenty minutes doing the same thing. She was planning to sign over a few rights, but her death might change the divorce, huh?" It was said too matter-of-factly for my taste. Alton noted that he'd found the grade book trapped between the desk and the wall. I assumed it'd either fallen there accidentally or been knocked down during a struggle at the eight thirty meeting.

"Have you figured out what happens to her assets? Did she leave a will?" I wasn't sure he'd answer, but there weren't any reasons not to inquire.

"Not that I'm aware of. I changed mine a year ago when we separated. As I said, she had no other family. I suppose that means it all comes to me... if she even had anything of value." Alton lifted the papers on her desk, then pointed to the far table. "There are also a few course materials. Your father mentioned you may need those."

Had my father already told strangers that I would take over Abby's classes, even though I hadn't given him a decision? My harried brow must have clued in Alton.

"He and I briefly met when I borrowed the key from his assistant. Your father also expressed his condolences. He mentioned you might stop by for the coursework."

A voice coming up the stairs startled us. When I turned around, Lorraine walked through the hallway toward me. "Kellan, it's wonderful to see you. Did my brother leave already?"

"No, he's right inside." I stepped sideways to allow Lorraine access.

Alton's cheeks reddened when he realized I knew about his connection to Lorraine. I grew curious how solid his alibi was and mentally noted ways to follow up. Abby's sudden death provided too many valuable gains for him.

"Are you about ready to head out?" she asked her brother, then turned to me. "Alton and I have a few things to talk about, Kellan. I'm thinking about getting a lawyer. Sheriff Montague keeps returning with more questions about the night of the accident." She nibbled on her lip in frustration.

"She's covering all her bases. I'm looking into a few angles myself. I gave the sheriff some useful information earlier about Abby's connection to others on campus."

Lorraine attempted to smile. "Oh, that's good news. I hope they figure this out soon. It's draining your father. Poor Alton can't move forward on her estate. I'd like to be out of the line of fire." She shivered and wrapped her arms around herself. "We should get going, Alton."

After Alton and Lorraine trotted off, I searched Abby's office. The book on her corner table was her current grade keeper. Subjecting myself to Dr. Castle's presence to decipher it offered little comfort or warm, fuzzy feelings. *Out damn spot, dearest Lady Macbeth.*

All I found of potential interest in the drawer was an oddly shaped key, the unsigned contract between Derek and Abby, and the folders with *Dark Reality*'s research notes. Derek would finally get what he was looking for. I packed them in an empty box I found in the corner, then perused several titles on the bookshelves. Mostly theater, media, and academic books stood out. Abby was also undeniably a fan of reality television shows and the paranormal.

When a large book with a red cover and no title or author captured my interest, I pulled it off the shelf. Though partially hollow, it had something hidden inside. Given the sheer volume of books, checking everything on the shelves couldn't have been part of the sheriff's sweep. Was Sheriff Montague not as skilled as Braxton needed her to be? I enjoyed thinking about how to best use the mistake against her in the future. Would her failure be my win? Time to put that sheriff in checkmate!

A locked, leather-bound journal lurked beneath the fake red book cover. I grabbed the key I'd found in the drawer and matched it up. The lock opened, and I suddenly had access to Abby Monroe's personal thoughts. Could I invade her privacy? I permitted myself to scan the pages for any current entries. When

I found a few, I dropped the journal in the storage box, deciding to ponder how comfortable I'd feel crossing such a line. I added her grade book and several printed copies of her current class syllabi to the box too. I had some reading to do that evening. How much would I learn about Abby's secret or not-so-secret life?

Prior to heading home, I connected my phone to the hands-free device in the Jeep and dialed Nana D. She picked up after the second ring. "Where've you been the last few days? I thought you'd have come by for more pie or to talk about Bridget Colton."

So, the elf had a last name. Nana D bringing her up again definitely concerned me this was a setup. "I ran into your bestie this morning. Ms. Paddington had some interesting information to share with me. It's time you and I had afternoon tea." I was sure she could hear the sarcasm dripping from my words, but then again, she'd ignore it even if she had.

"Pish! That woman speaks nonsense. She's worse than her brother, and after what he did to me, I have no time for those Paddingtons anymore. Troublemakers, I'm telling you," she chided. "I can't do tea today... maybe tomorrow? Why don't you come over around three? I should be home from the farmer's market and ready to hear some gossip."

"No, Nana D. I don't have any gossip. It's your turn to share." I had to be stern with her, otherwise she'd cross the line every time.

"What's that? Sorry, fuzzy connection," she replied, squawking loudly. I distinctly heard her making static sounds before she stopped to hack up what sounded like a hairball in the middle of her routine.

"Fine. I'll come by tomorrow." I played along with her charade, then asked if she knew anything about Marcus Stanton's role on the Board of Trustees. "What might you know about the anonymous donations to Braxton and who authorized all the new spending in the athletics department?"

"I'm meeting with Councilman Stanton tomorrow. I'll see what I can find out. We've got a few things to settle, and that man's gonna listen to me this time if it's the last thing I do." She harrumphed in the background before drinking a swig of something that caused her to shout, "That did the trick!"

"What does he need to listen to you about?" I raised the heat in the Jeep.

"Stanton's using Wharton County funds in all the wrong places. I intend to prove he's clueless."

I was surprised at how up to speed Nana D was on things going on with the county's fiduciary decisions. Then again, she always was sharp with insignificant details. "I wonder if Stanton has any kids at Braxton," I asked, suddenly remembering they would probably be about that age. "I didn't know he was on the Board of Trustees until Dad told me."

"Yep, that star pitcher, Craig Magee. You've probably heard of Striker. Can't wait to see the game on Saturday. This town needs a boost."

"Wait, what did you say about Striker? They have different last names." I was confused.

"Striker is his stepson. He married Striker's mother years ago when the kid was young. She died from cancer around the same time Francesca died. Good woman too."

"You need someone to go with you on Saturday?" I wondered whether the councilman had been Abby's eight thirty discussion that night. I'd need to recall when he'd left the party, but it was probably at the same time as my father for that impromptu board meeting.

Nana D and I confirmed our plans for tea the next day. She also noted she'd get back to me on the game as she might attend with someone else, but she wouldn't say whom. I suspected Nana's potential alternative date would not thrill Eustacia if his name was Lindsey Endicott.

I drove the long way to my parents' house and considered my next steps. I needed to go through Abby's papers and journal. Not that it was a fair thing to read her personal thoughts. I could either give them to Sheriff Montague, or I could casually check a few pages to verify whether any reason existed to share them. I wouldn't hide vital clues, but it wasn't fair to waste taxpayer money by forcing the sheriff to read the journal if it amounted to nothing, right?

CHAPTER 12

After hanging up with Nana D, I scheduled a time for dinner with Eleanor after the big baseball game. She usually took off Saturday nights, so there was at least one weekend evening as an option for potential dates. Unfortunately, the guy she'd hoped would ask her out this Saturday failed to extend an offer, which meant she was looking for company. I spent the rest of the night reading through the *Dark Reality* materials I'd collected from Abby's, so I could get Derek off my back on Abby's research before diving into anything else.

I chatted with Emma before bed, then caught up on some much-needed rest. When I awoke on Friday, I concentrated on reading all the pages of Abby's grade book, which clarified how the late professor documented student records. While the prior semesters had been well organized, as evidenced by Abby's weekly notes, the current semester was mostly empty. The lack of content didn't seem to add up properly at first, but I theorized if she'd been more focused on connecting with Derek for season two of *Dark Reality*, Abby might have let her normal standards slip.

I flipped to the current semester to check the grades and learned the other pitcher, Jordan Ballantine, had earned a 'B+' on the first exam. I turned a few more pages and came across an 'A+' for Carla Grey, wondering if she were related to the ruthless county judge whom I'd crossed paths with once before. I located Striker's page and at first thought he had zero entries, but when I looked closer, he had an 'F' that was partially erased or smudged. I held it up to the light by my bedside table and saw the definite markings of a failing grade. While an 'F' didn't look good for Striker playing in the upcoming game, the fact that it was partially erased made me worry this was why Abby had been killed.

Since Lorraine had run the department this semester while the previous office manager, Siobhan, took maternity leave, she might have some idea what was going on with grading processes. I was also interested in talking with

Lorraine about Abby's classes in case I accepted my father's request to assume their responsibility for a few weeks. Lorraine agreed to meet at noon, so I arranged my morning such that I could get in a workout at the fitness center before heading to Diamond Hall.

When I arrived, Lorraine was making copies of class materials. I joined her near the machine and inquired about her brother. "How's Alton handling Abby's death?"

Lorraine shrugged. "He feels bad about it, and although he never would have wished for anything to happen to her, Alton's better off. I don't mean to sound cold, but that woman really made life difficult for the poor man."

"He didn't seem shaken yesterday. Has he been back long from his out-of-town trip?" I was hoping to find out the details of his alibi and return home.

"Just a day or so. When the sheriff finally got a lead on his last credit card receipt, she was able to track down a local officer in Alaska who got word to him." Lorraine turned the photocopier off and walked toward her desk. "You're extremely interested in Alton. You don't think he had anything to do with it, do you? He has an alibi, Kellan."

Alton didn't seem like a killer based on our ten-minute conversation; however, both Nana D and Connor thought this was a spur-of-the-moment crime. "Nah, just trying to pull all the pieces together. I could use your help, Lorraine." Sensing Alton's alibi was airtight, I pulled out the grade book and asked Lorraine if she recognized it.

"Standard issue. We've mostly stopped using them, but some professors keep track manually before uploading any grades to the online system. Where did you find that one?" Lorraine had already sat at the desk to arrange the photocopies in a folder marked *Monday Coursework.*

"Belonged to Abby Monroe. Alton and I found it yesterday. I took it with me to learn more about her classes. You know my father suggested I—"

"Take them over? Yes, he asked what I thought you'd decide." She clasped her hands together. "If you take the job, this folder is for you. What are you going to do?"

Lorraine had thought ahead and prepared materials for me. I'd already decided it was too valuable of an opportunity, given Derek wanted me to stick around longer to find more content for the show. "I'm going to the baseball game tomorrow to observe some students. See if I fit in."

"It's important to your father." Lorraine's eyes were withdrawn and hollowed, and her lips were dry and cracked.

Lorraine wanted to say something, but I wasn't sure how to pull it out. "Is that the only thing on your mind?"

"You've always been so perceptive, Kellan. I seem to be at the center of this crazy situation."

That's when I remembered Coach Oliver's event schedule. Maybe he could prove her alibi. "Didn't you say no one saw you after eight that evening? Coach Oliver mentioned handing you a schedule outside Diamond Hall." I scanned her face for any reactions, curious why she'd failed to mention anything.

"Oh, that's right, I forgot." Lorraine shifted positions, and her gaze bored holes in the floor. "The entire exchange happened so quickly, just a few seconds after I'd left the retirement party. It wouldn't have helped prove much."

"Mention it to Sheriff Montague. My mother saw Coach Oliver. There's a chance he also noticed something or someone without realizing it." I rested my hand on her shoulder.

"Your mother saw the coach? I'll tell the sheriff." She smoothed out wrinkles in her blouse.

I would bet money Lorraine hid something. I'd have to wait until she was comfortable enough to tell me the rest. "You went to get something for me, right? Did you ever find it?" I wasn't worried unless the gift could help prove her alibi.

"No, that's part of what's bothering me. I can't find your present anywhere. I could have sworn I left it on my desk. I meant to wrap it before I left on Friday but got too busy." Lorraine wouldn't give me any details other than mentioning I'd been upset the prior fall, and she wanted to do something special for me.

I couldn't recall the specifics, but I'd find out soon enough. "Where could it be?"

"I wish I knew. That's not the only thing vanishing. A student reported something lost this week. I also can't find the new... ugh, never mind." She threw her hands in the air. "Three different things don't just get up and walk away by themselves, Kellan."

That caused some niggles. "Is Sheriff Montague aware of the thefts?"

"It didn't come up when we spoke."

"Will you inform Connor? Someone should know about them," I said.

"To be honest, I thought maybe with everything going on among the temporary office move, the extra work with Siobhan being out, and the retirement party plans, I must have misplaced your present. I'm still looking around for the other two missing items, but I'm gonna check your father's desk. It might have gotten put in a drawer accidentally before they sent it to storage." She clicked a few keys on her keyboard, then said, "Looks like I have a meeting coming up soon. Anything else I can help you with?"

I couldn't help wondering if the missing items related to Abby's death. With only a few minutes left, I asked Lorraine to describe the grading process. I also mentioned the scratch marks I'd found near Striker's name in Abby's book.

"That's bizarre. When the semester started, I asked each professor how they wanted me to assist with day-to-day operations while Siobhan was on leave. Almost everyone said they'd love it if I could handle all the computer work for them."

"Really, even Abby? What about the last few days, was anything different?" Had I latched on to something potentially important?

"Most professors would grade the papers or exams, then give me the printed documents with their notes to scan and upload before returning to the students. Some professors recorded the grades in their books in case students asked before I loaded the details into the computer. Abby didn't want any help with putting hers online. She told me specifically to stay out of her way. I'd assumed she was old school and didn't like me given everything going on with Alton and the divorce."

"Lorraine, this is helpful. Do you have any idea where I can find the students' exams from Abby's classes this semester?" A picture formulated in my mind. If Abby were somehow involved with Coach Oliver, could she have changed Striker's grades to ensure he played in the upcoming game? That would clarify how those two were connected, but not why Abby was murdered. Unless she changed her mind, and Coach Oliver, Stanton, or Striker killed her in revenge. I needed to focus on Striker's grades and the decision on which pitcher would play in the game. That felt like a place for a motive to lurk.

"No, as I said, Abby kept everything to herself. The only tasks she asked me to do was sort her mail and schedule any student appointments."

Once Lorraine exited the office, I sat at the top of the stairs to process all I'd just learned. I needed to get access to the computer system to find out if Abby had entered grades for any of the students. I decided to ask my father before approaching anyone else about my concerns with the grades. I called his cell when I couldn't reach him at home. No answer. I left a voicemail and followed it up with a text message saying I needed to see him as soon as possible. I took the cable car back to North Campus, excited to stumble on something that could identify Abby's murderer.

On the walk back toward my Jeep, I skimmed the last two months of journal entries. An entry in the week before she was killed expressed her hope that Derek would call soon about the *Dark Reality* contract. There was an entry in early January about an exciting night out with W. A. I flipped a few more pages only to learn things with W. A. had gotten complicated—she had feelings for him even though she knew how wrong it was. Still no full name or obvious clues. Then I read how Abby wanted to get revenge and expose W. A. for what he'd done to her. That must have been the exclusive story she was talking about in the email to Derek and on the call with me.

Stumped over the identity of the mysterious W. A., I was about to give up until a nauseating idea popped into my head. W. A., Wesley Ayrwick. My father had been acting strange lately. He had several nights where he wouldn't mention where he was going or what he was doing. He said his relationship with Abby was complicated. Was my father having an affair? Cheating on my mother with Abby? I sat on the bench for another twenty minutes, trying to convince myself there had to be some other explanation. Why wasn't my father calling me back?

A few students rushed by, yelling they were late for class, which reminded me I needed to get to Danby Landing. I tossed my backpack on the passenger seat and drove across town in a bit of a fog, debating if I should bring up the journal entry. I parked in Nana D's driveway, waved to the farm's operations manager who was unloading a wheelbarrow in the compost pile near the orchard, and entered through the side door into her kitchen. "I'm here, Nana D. What's going on with you this afternoon?"

Nana D hung up the phone. She still had an old-fashioned, buttercup-yellow handset with a curly cord installed next to the refrigerator. I always loved thinking about her standing in the kitchen, twirling it as we chatted on the phone while I was home in Los Angeles. She had cordless extensions in other parts of the home and her cell phone, but she preferred her kitchen have a touch of the past.

"Welcome back, my brilliant grandson. I was just on the phone with your mother. She's gone off the deep end again." Nana D rambled while brewing the tea. "Glad to see you can still read a clock."

"Of course. You didn't think I'd be late, did you? What's Mom's problem?"

"Oh, a little of this and that. That daughter of mine never could handle stress." Nana D uncovered a plate of desserts sitting on the counter. "I made us shortbread with lemon icing and mini pecan pies." She was dressed to the nines in a fitted gray skirt, stylish blouse, and black suit jacket.

The pies looked delicious. I'd enjoy a few of those, most definitely. She'd made at least three dozen bite-sized concoctions small enough to toss between my lips, big enough to force my mouth closed and not to say something I shouldn't. "Mom seems to be doing okay with everything going on as far as I can tell. Just some minor agitation. What happened today?"

"A fight with Eleanor about her job at the diner. Your father seems to have done something she wasn't too happy about last night. I think she had a hang-nail too." Nana D shrugged, finished pouring the tea, and carried the tray to the table—a beautiful old slab of oak my Grandpop had cut down from a tree on their farm. He shaped, sanded, and varnished it himself, even leaving some burnt edges scalloped and slanted to lend it an old-world charm. I made Nana D promise not to give it to anyone else in the future. She accused me of wishing her off to an early grave, but I assured her I only meant *if* she no longer had a reason to keep it. I assumed that got me out of hot water, but you never knew with Nana D, Braxton's longest holder of senseless grudges.

"Any idea what Dad did?" I worried my latest theory might be true. I ate my first mini-pecan pie. No one baked better than my nana. The level of gooey-ness in the filling and crunch in the crust... to die for! "Eleanor's been a little cranky lately too. I can see that bothering Mom."

"I'm staying out of it. *Twinsies* can solve their own problems. Did you set Eustacia straight about me not trying to date her fella? I ain't going to the base-ball game with Lindsey Endicott anymore, so you'll be my escort. The entire town's gone crazy thinking I'm always after them." Nana D plated some desserts for herself and took a seat next to me. "Eat up, I have another meeting shortly."

In between three more pecan pies and two lemon shortbreads, I downed a few cups of tea and inquired about Nana D's meeting with Marcus Stanton. "By the way, how did your discussion go earlier with our fine councilman?" I braced myself for a litany of his latest *crimes* and *misdemeanors*.

"Oh, I'm on to his skullduggery. The con artist claims he has no clue who donated the money. He said the entire board wanted it to benefit the athletic facility. He's hiding something, but I can't figure it out. He also had nothing nice to mention about Abby Monroe," Nana D said as she checked all the notes from her discussion with him. "Stanton thought she purposely failed Striker. Maybe he killed her!"

"I can't imagine the councilman would murder a professor over a disagreement about his stepson's grades." From what I could recall, Marcus only left Stanton Concert Hall the night of the party to attend that board meeting, but I couldn't be certain of his every move. The motive for this crime made little sense based on what I knew so far.

"Have you heard the rumor about a Major League Baseball scout coming to the game?" Nana D shocked me with that one.

"That's a reason someone might be desperate enough to kill!" As much as I loved the place, Braxton wasn't a top-tier school or known for its sports programs. Why would a Major League Baseball scout come here?

Nana D said she'd keep after the councilman to find out anything she could. I updated her on my progression on the Abby Monroe investigation, excluding any fears about my father or the actual initials. She was most intrigued by Lorraine's three missing objects, one of which could be the murder weapon. "It seems to me you need to sit Coach Oliver down, then talk to Sheriff Montague again. I don't like how Coach Oliver acts around women. I wouldn't put it past him to apply some pressure on Abby about the grades. Before I fancy him as the killer, we need to learn more about his little rendezvous at the woman's house. All seems a little too Tanya Harding versus Nancy Kerrigan to me."

Nana D was correct—we didn't know what the relationship was between Coach Oliver and Abby. If Abby were dating W. A., would she also be romantically involved with the coach? "You might be right about Sheriff Montague, although she's none too happy when I try to insert myself in the case."

"You pay her salary, Kellan. She should be happy to get some free help. That woman always had a mean streak to her, especially after—"

"I don't live in Braxton, Nana D. You might pay her salary, but I don't." I realized too late that was exactly the topic of conversation Nana D was bringing up.

"Speaking of where you live, how about you take me up on that offer to come live here at the farm? I could use someone else to talk to during the day." Nana D filled the tray with our empty teacups and dessert plates, then walked to the sink to wash them. "It'll be fun to gab all night!"

Maybe the sheriff was right about Nana D. I packaged the remaining cakes and pies, sneaking two into my pocket for the ride back home, then joined her at the sink. "I might have news to share with you about staying in Braxton when I pick you up for the game. Does twelve sound good?"

"Make it eleven. I need to see some folks before the first pitch. I hope you cleaned up the crumbs you dropped on the floor when those two cakes accidentally fell into your pocket, Kellan." Nana D began singing Kenny Rogers' *The Gambler* as she turned off the faucet, then danced her way across the kitchen.

89

"I would slap your bottom silly if I didn't let you get away with everything, brilliant one."

I shook my head at her. There would be no way to control my nana. I hugged her goodbye and drove back home, wondering whom she was meeting with that evening. Then I realized it was time to plan several interviews of my own to make traction in finding Abby's killer. It'd become a personal quest to solve the case before the sheriff. Perhaps to get Derek off my back too.

As I pulled into the driveway at my parents' house, my father stepped down the path toward his car. "I can't talk now, Kellan. I'm meeting your mother for an early dinner."

I wasn't letting him avoid me anymore. "Nope, we need to chat tonight, Dad," I said through the window, then parked and jogged over to his car, but he'd already slammed the driver's door closed. To his credit, he rolled down the window. "It's close to freezing out here, son. Make it quick."

"Listen, Dad. I think you need to know what I learned about Abby today."

"I understand, but I can't be late to meet your mother. She's not herself these days, ever since I started planning for my retirement. I am trying to do whatever I can to make her happy," he replied before hitting the button to roll up the window.

I grunted. "Breakfast. Tomorrow. Nine o'clock. Don't miss it!"

He smirked and backed out of the driveway. Something strange was going on in my family and at Braxton. The more everyone tried to hide it, the more I wanted to dig deeper.

Next, Derek and I exchanged a brief text conversation.

Kellan: *Got into Abby's office. I found her research notes in the folders. Going through them again this weekend.*
Derek: *Awesome. My boss is reviewing the revised materials you sent over. Didn't have time to tell him they were yours, but I'll be sure he knows how hard you worked.*

Ugh! I needed to call Emma to share the news she'd be coming back to Braxton for a few weeks. I also wanted to map out everything I'd discovered in the investigation. Then I planned to open a bottle of wine. Those were the only three things I thought might improve my night. Plus, the rest of Nana D's baked goods—those were the extent of my only evening plans.

CHAPTER 13

My mom left for a spa day with her girlfriends early in the morning. I brewed a pot of coffee, defrosted Nana D's blueberry scones, and tossed some turkey sausages in the frying pan. If my father were on time, he'd arrive any moment for the breakfast I'd *suggested* he attend the day before. As I began plating the food, the grandfather clock in the living room confirmed it was nine o'clock. My father pushed open the swinging door into the kitchen. That man had impeccable timing.

"Good day, Kellan. I believe you made a demand for my presence this morning."

Was he attempting to be funny? "We have things to discuss. Are you going to the game today?" I eased into the topic to avoid creating any tension.

"Indeed. I'm still head of the college, and it's the first baseball game. I'm looking forward to Striker kicking off the season." He carried his plate to the corner breakfast nook and sat on the bench closest to the back door. A quick escape route?

"Does that mean Coach Oliver decided the starting lineup?" In all the commotion, I'd forgotten about the pep rally. I joined him at the table and took a bite of Nana D's scone. The blueberry flavoring was so intense I closed my eyes to thoroughly enjoy the experience.

"I guess that answers my question about you taking over some classes. If you were interested in helping, you'd have followed the college's biggest news this week," my father said, savoring his breakfast, which meant I hadn't lost him yet.

"No, that's not exactly true. Is baseball Braxton's biggest news this week?" I shook my head in amazement at how easily he could dismiss a murder just to focus on the Striker-versus-Jordan rivalry. "We'll get to the job offer. First, something came up last night. I didn't check on Coach Oliver's pitching selection. Second, I'm going to today's game with Nana D."

He grunted and dropped his knife. The brash clang of metal against china made our silence more awkward. "I should have known it was Doomsday."

"Really, Dad? You need to stop this war with Nana D. I think you have bigger things to worry about based on our last conversation." I finished two scones and all the sausages during his silent treatment, then changed the topic again. "Any more blog postings?"

"Nothing. The last one was the day after the party."

Myriam was behind it all. I was certain she wanted Abby fired too. What was Myriam achieving with all these crafty illusions and distractions? "I have some questions about Abby for you."

"Go ahead. I'm listening." My father's eyebrow twitched.

"I found a few materials in Abby's office to help me understand the syllabi for her classes. I peeked at her grade book, and a couple of things didn't add up."

The sour expression on my father's face relaxed, but his shoulders still stiffened. "I see this as a good sign if you're researching her classes."

I explained what I'd seen, denoting no specific names. He couldn't offer much background about the process. He'd left the details of how a student's grades were finalized to each department chair and Dean Mulligan. "I rarely take active notice in any specific student's performance unless there's an issue of suspension or a major award. Myriam should help you with the particulars once you decide if you'll come on board."

"I understand. We'll get to that momentarily. Were you getting updates on Striker's grades?" I'd bet money he'd paid attention for a Major League Baseball opportunity.

"Yes." Wesley Ayrwick proved he wasn't a man of many words.

"Would you know what changed to permit Striker to play today? Unless he earned a 'B+' in Abby's class, his suspension from the team's upcoming games would still apply."

"Why the sudden obsession with a baseball player's academic standing, Kellan?" He stood from the breakfast nook to refill our coffee cups.

I was glad to hear Striker could play. I'd liked him when we met at the fitness center, but the 'F' I'd seen in Abby's grade book had set off some alarm bells. It was too coincidental to accept he'd failed the course last semester, and she'd marked an 'F' for his first exam this year. Then suddenly everything was back on track for him to pitch today. "Something fishy is going on with the way Abby graded her students."

"Talk to Myriam. She verified Abby's exam results were loaded into the system earlier this week. It takes a day for them to be approved, then students can check online."

"Okay. To answer your question, I'll stick around to handle Abby's classes for four weeks. I need to clear it with my boss, but he's already given me some signals indicating he'll be happy I'm in Braxton right now," I replied, preparing for my next point. "I have some conditions."

My father's smile brightened over my news. "That's terrific. I'm glad you're keeping an open mind." His bushy eyebrows raised inquisitively.

I explained to him I wanted to keep it quiet—he could only inform those who needed to know I'd be handling Abby's workload for the time being. I could see the news getting out and people thinking I've halfway moved back home already. I also asked him to explain everything he knew about Abby's personal life.

"I'd spent more time with her than I'd have liked. She'd asked for too many days off, been more argumentative with me than usual, and caused some trouble with Lorraine on campus."

"Is that whom you were talking about in your study the night I got home? I overheard your call, and it sounded—"

"Were you eavesdropping? I taught you better than that, Kellan." My father gathered his wallet and keys, mumbling to himself about the downward spiral of society's future.

"No, I came down to use the phone and heard part of the conversation. Who was on the call?"

"None of your business, Kellan." He was very calm and collected, but obviously dismayed.

I couldn't push my luck any further if I still wanted to ask the tough question. "How well did you know Abby? Were you socializing with her after work?"

"What? No, we met at her house a few times, so we could have an honest conversation about her future. That's how I knew she'd intended to leave Braxton in the new term."

He had to be the W. A. in her journal. Alton's initials were A. M. Coach Oliver's initials would've had an 'O' in them. The neighbor had seen a car at her house. Could I ask if he'd been having an affair with her?

"Dad, how are things between you and Mom? She seems worried about you, and Eleanor thought you guys were fighting."

"Your mother is under a lot of stress. You know this is her busiest time of the year." He placed his empty mug in the sink and rinsed his hands. "I appreciate you doing this favor for me. I'll call Myriam shortly to verify you've accepted and to help you get situated. I need to meet up with the guys. Judge Grey's probably on the fourth hole by now."

My father grabbed his jacket from the closet and walked toward the garage. As he pressed the remote to open the door, I stopped him. "Did Mom discover something going on between you and Abby? I don't mean to pry, but I found Abby's journal, and an entry said—"

"How dare you think I'd do something like that to your mother? I thought we were turning a corner with your decision today. Won't you ever grow up?" he shouted before slamming the kitchen door.

My first thought was he didn't answer the question. My second was how would I fix the situation. I didn't mean to aggravate the man, but my father knew something he wasn't telling me. I decided to give him some breathing room for the weekend.

An hour later, I picked up Nana D from Danby Landing. She'd decked herself out in a Braxton Bear's jersey, a pair of dark gray tights, and a baseball cap. The Bears were the team's mascot and most assuredly described the way the team normally played. In the first few innings, they'd always seem sleepy. By the third inning, they'd burst out of hibernation and score. I was optimistic for today's game, but Nana D lacked confidence.

"Striker's a good kid, but he's not prepared. I saw him at the pep rally last night. Definitely psyched to be chosen, but he looked worried about something." Nana D switched the radio station to her favorite country station and forced me to listen to her music.

"He passed Abby's last exam. That should make him happy." I turned into Grey Field's parking lot. We were an hour early, but Nana D wanted to check out the tailgate party. I hadn't been to one in years and guessed she made regular appearances based on her instructions about where to park, what to bring, and who would be in attendance.

"Yep. He was happy, but he mentioned a girl giving him a rough time." Nana D smirked at me. "I assume it was his girlfriend, but he said little. Chicks, sheesh!"

Why would college kids talk to Nana D about their personal lives? "You're everywhere these days."

"I'll be back in thirty minutes. I need to be seen." She gave me the thumbs-up sign as we parked the car, then jumped out quickly before I could ask about the meeting before the pep rally.

She had a more active social life than I did. While Nana D wandered away, I walked to the baseball stadium and watched the pitchers practice. When Striker finished in the bullpen, he crossed by the player's dugout, where Coach Oliver motivated the other team members. "Kellan, that you?"

"Congratulations. It looks like everything worked out with the grade. You must be excited to meet the scout today." I noticed a haze shadowing his eyes and hoped he had nothing to do with Abby's murder. Nana D was right.

"Yes, I passed. Coach Oliver called to tell me. Jordan didn't take it too well, but I think he understood he'd have a turn later this season." Striker tucked his glove under his right arm and fixed the sleeve on his uniform. As he twisted, a large scratch near his elbow appeared.

"Looks like that hurts." I hadn't seen it while working out, but he'd worn a longer shirt that day. Surely, the sheriff would've found his DNA on Abby's body if it had come from a struggle.

"Oh, that, yeah... I don't remember. Wanna meet my girlfriend?" he said as a pretty blue-eyed, blond cheerleader walked in our direction. "This is Carla Grey. She's supporting me today."

Carla smiled and dropped her pompoms on the dugout roof. "Hi. Ready for a great game? Who's your good-looking friend, Striker?" Her bright makeup and a very low-cut uniform with a short skirt stood out.

Striker clarified how we'd met. While I enjoyed compliments, I was distracted trying to recall where I'd seen her before and grew curious about her last name. "Are you related to Judge Grey?"

Carla nodded nervously. "Yeah, ummm... he's my grandfather. Do you know him?"

I did. My father played golf with him all the time. He'd also been the county judge for thirty years. Everyone was afraid of him. I suddenly felt bad for the poor girl. "I've not had the pleasure to directly meet Judge Grey before, but his reputation precedes him."

Carla snatched her pompoms. "I should go. Gotta pump the crowd soon, right? See you around, Kellan." When Striker went to kiss her goodbye, she turned her cheek. "Don't ruin the makeup!"

Carla exited, and Striker's mood worsened. I said, "Everything okay? You seem disconnected. I'd think you'd be thrilled to meet the scout."

"It's cool. Chick problems. Stepdad on my case. I just hope I do well." Striker returned to his warm-up when the coach called him over.

I went back to find Nana D, who was on her second hotdog at that point. She was entertaining several of the ladies from the local chamber of commerce with stories about her and Grandpop's golden days.

As we took our seats, she leaned against me and pointed. "You see that harlot. Eustacia might think she's got one over on me by convincing Lindsey to take her to the game. I'll fix that woman! Can you believe that get-up she's squeezed herself into? Honestly, a woman her age putting on the team's baseball uniform simply to impress a man."

As far as I could tell, Ms. Paddington and my nana were similarly dressed. "Ummm... aren't you and her about the same age, Nana D?"

I felt the pinch on the back of my arm before she'd even begun to verbally assault me. "I am three months younger than that jezebel, and you have no idea what you're talking about. You didn't even wear a single color to support our team today, and if I didn't know better, I'd think you were on Eustacia's side. No grandson of mine would ever do that to me, you little—"

The announcer interrupted her mini tirade to ask everyone to stand for the national anthem. I smiled at Nana D, but it didn't help my case. "No pie for you for two weeks, Kellan."

The rest of the game was a nail-biter like my temporary truce with Nana D, who agreed to forget my comment, claiming she didn't want any tension in the air to interrupt the Braxton Bear's mojo. I was shocked at how much school spirit the woman had. At one point, she tried to high kick with the cheerleaders, but after nearly falling into Dean Terry, Nana D calmed down.

The Braxton Bears led the game four to three when the seventh inning stretch started. Striker had done well, but I could tell he was tiring once he'd given up the last two runs before the break. Coach Oliver warmed up Jordan Ballantine in the bullpen. I worried about both players' chances with the scout.

While Nana D scrounged up a few more hotdogs, I caught up with Fern Terry, the same woman who'd been the dean when I attended Braxton. Fern was extremely tall with a steel-gray, pixie-style haircut. It hadn't changed since I'd known her, nor had her broad shoulders and puffy face. I'd always thought she'd look better with a longer hairdo, but then again, what did I know? She remembered me and the many times I'd defended my fraternity in her office. "I hear they're close to picking a new Braxton president. Still can't believe my father's retiring this year." I hoped to catch a clue if she was one of the two final candidates.

"Yes, Monday or Tuesday is the big day. I've got it on good authority they'll notify the candidate of the Board's decision," she said with an intimidating tone. When Dean Terry glanced at the dugout, a snarl erased her smile as she zoomed in on Coach Oliver.

"I imagine they picked two people who have served the college faithfully for years and truly know how to make Braxton excel like my father has for the last eight years." I smirked at her as if I were the cat who'd caught a little mouse.

"Most definitely. I'm sure that's the case." Dean Terry nodded, then walked down the bleachers toward the field. "I need to speak with Coach Oliver. Please excuse me."

I thought it odd she was at the game given sports were never something high on her list of interests in the past. Something was brewing between those two, but I was also certain she was one of the two presidential candidates, which meant someone else external was being considered. I racked my brain trying to figure out who could be in the running. Unless it was someone from the Paddington, Stanton, or Grey families, I was clueless.

Nana D returned. "Got you a turkey burger with avocado on an alfalfa sprout bun. Try it."

"Ummm... I've had them before, and since when do they serve health food at a baseball game?" I scrunched my face like the world had ended. I often ate healthy. Not that she realized it.

"When's the last time you went to a baseball game?"

I reflected for a few seconds, which were too long for Nana D. "I thought so. Just eat it, or I won't lift that two-week pie ban." Nana D elbowed me, then laughed. "I ran into Bridget just now."

I knew Nana D was intent on stirring trouble again. "How's my little elf doing?"

Nana D shushed me. "You *are* weird. Just thought you might like to know she was here. You could say hello after the game. Bridget doesn't know many people in town."

I was not dealing with Nana D's romantic set-ups. "Oh, look, the game's starting."

"Yep, seems Striker's out, poor kid. Marcus will grind him over that."

Striker threw his glove at the fence. Councilman Stanton and Coach Oliver argued about something, but I was too far away to guess the crux. Dean Terry walked away with a perplexed expression on her face. "Jordan just took the pitcher's mound. Guess you were right."

"When am I not right?" Nana D tilted her head and lowered her sunglasses. "About Bridget...?"

I shrugged her off, told her to focus on the game, and promised I'd come by the following morning for brunch if she'd leave the topic alone. Nana D was content I'd at least agreed to visit again.

Jordan pitched the remaining innings and only gave up one run when the Woodland Beavers tied the score. Luckily, the Braxton Bears hit a triple in the final inning and won the game seven to four. The crowd went wild when the players took to the parking lot to celebrate, thrilled they'd won the first game of the season. It meant Braxton might have a fighting chance to join this year's championships.

Nana D left as soon as the game concluded, noting she'd bum a ride home with one of her friends. I mingled among the fans and took in the college atmosphere. When I'd attended graduate school and earned my doctorate from the University of Southern California, I didn't live on campus. I'd also worked full time and gotten married, and Emma had been born shortly afterward. It had been a decade since I felt that electrifying school spirit. It was fantastic to see the entire town banding together to support the Braxton Bears.

On the drive home, I confirmed plans to meet with Dr. Castle the following Monday morning. She'd been curt on the phone and didn't want to discuss the classes until we met in person. At least I'd gotten that meeting coordinated, and I could find out more about Braxton's grading process, maybe even see the date and time stamp of when Striker's grades had been uploaded.

CHAPTER 14

By early evening, I'd gone for my daily run, choosing Millionaire's Mile for viewing pleasure. All the houses were grand and loomed high between Main Street and the Wharton Mountains in the background. The impressive sight for any newcomers to Braxton always encouraged me to recognize my hometown's beauty. I set my alarm and took a catnap before meeting Eleanor for dinner. Watching the game in the chilly, fresh air had tuckered me out.

When I awoke, I remembered failing to share with Connor my news about Abby's journal entries mentioning W. A. Since I was running late, it would have to be a Sunday activity. I found my favorite pair of dark jeans, added a light gray button-down shirt and a black sports jacket to the outfit, and eased my feet into a pair of black boots. A bit of snow had stuck to the ground once the typical evening flurries descended upon us.

I met Eleanor at an Italian restaurant near the Finnulia River waterfront. A few cool places had opened in the last year, but I'd only sampled one when I returned home at Christmas. She'd made the reservations and secured us a table in the back section overlooking the gorgeous, moonlit sandy banks.

"I know the owner. We once trained together at another restaurant." Eleanor had dressed a little more stylish than her normal work outfits, but nowhere near as fancy as the retirement party. I was glad to see she stayed in the warmer color families as her eyes and hair shined best when she wore red and yellow. Just like mine!

"I'm happy you came to your senses the other day and suggested dinner." I wouldn't tiptoe around her chilly attitude earlier in the week. "Thanks for dropping the cold front, *Anna Wintour*."

"I'm sorry about that, *Sherlock Holmes*. I didn't know how to react to something you said." She perused the menu, then recommended shareable appetizers.

I ordered two glasses of champagne to make the night more relaxing. I racked my brain trying to guess what sensitive topic I'd brought up. "Can you clue me in? I'm rubbish at remembering right now."

"Connor."

I hadn't seen that one coming. "He's grated on my nerves lately too. What's he done to you?"

Eleanor tapped her fingers on the white tablecloth and fidgeted with her flatware. "Ummm... well... it's not an easy topic for me to bring up around you."

I'd begun synthesizing what she was about to say before the words came tumbling from her mouth. Connor and my sister? I was torn between rage that he'd considered going out with Eleanor without asking me first and recognizing it also meant there might be nothing going on between him and Maggie. "Has something happened between you two before?"

"Not really."

"That's a crock of dirty rotten horse manure, to quote Nana D. Have you two gone out before?"

"Once. Maybe twice. But nothing's happened, I swear." Eleanor's cheeks flushed brighter than her blouse. "We came here for dinner two months ago."

In between the waitress delivering our cocktails and the appetizers, I learned Connor had stopped by the Pick-Me-Up Diner the prior fall before I'd come home for winter break. Eleanor hadn't seen him in years but was intrigued by his dramatic makeover when they'd run into each other again. They'd met for drinks at the end of her shift, and she thought there was a connection but couldn't be certain. Then he'd asked her to dinner, where they had a fantastic time. A few weeks before Christmas they'd met for lunch, but he'd gone cold in the last six weeks. She was too nervous to ask him what had changed.

"I'd have appreciated someone telling me sooner. Everyone forgets to inform me what's going on." I unleashed an aggravated tone somewhere between a hangry bear and a scorned lover.

"It's not like you've ever asked questions about my dates before. I didn't know what to do, but then you mentioned how close he and Maggie seemed to be, and well...."

I'd pieced together the concern. "You think he dropped you to date Maggie?"

Eleanor nodded. "I don't know what else it could be."

I gave some consideration to the facts. Connor and my sister had gone on several dates. Then he started snuggling up to Maggie, helping her acclimate at Braxton and surrender the memories with her late husband. "By any chance, did you ever talk about me with Connor?" I asked for a specific reason, but I also wanted to know whether he'd been upset about losing our friendship too.

"As if! Why would I chat about you when we were on a date?" Eleanor chided with disdain. "I'm sure I mentioned you were coming home for Christmas, but we didn't actually talk about you."

"How did he react when you said my name?" While Eleanor gave it proper reflection, I chugged my glass of champagne and asked the waitress to bring us more water. I'd already drunk enough liquor during the week, given how my jeans felt at that moment. It couldn't be the desserts.

"Come to think of it, he got quiet. When he dropped me off, it felt very chilly." She cocked her head to the side and wiped her lips with a napkin. "Any thoughts?"

"I was wondering whether he felt a smidge weird about going on a date with you, being my sister and all, right after you'd mentioned me coming home. And then, he probably heard I was coming back again for Dad's retirement party." Connor felt guilty. I knew it.

"He called once, and we talked about getting together again. Nothing ever materialized."

Eleanor and I played three rounds of *Rock, Paper, Scissors* to confirm who had to buckle up and ask them the next time.

"Ha! I always beat you, Kellan." Eleanor jabbed me with her fork. "You're done for the night!"

And she was right. Exhaustion prompted me to beg for the check. While we waited to pay our bill, we talked about everything I'd learned on the murder investigation. Eleanor was certain the W. A. in Abby's journal was not our father. She thought Connor would know other options and encouraged me to ask him about it when I brought up Maggie.

"Don't tell him you know we went on two dates!" she shouted as I closed her car door.

* * *

I slept way later than I intended the following morning and was going to be late to Nana D's. I didn't want to get in trouble or be penalized for any reason, so I exceeded the speed limit on a couple of streets to arrive on time. It was Sunday, and most people would be at church at that hour. As I rounded the corner to reach the dirt pathway to Danby Landing, sirens blasted. If I didn't have bad luck that morning, I wouldn't have had any kind at all.

I pulled to the side of the road and waited for the officer. "And what possessed you to drive fifty in a thirty-mile-per hour zone?" a familiar voice said.

I looked up and noticed my newest good buddy staring back. He must not have any older siblings as I'd never heard of or met anyone in his family before. "Officer Flatman, I'm so sorry. I wasn't thinking. Totally my fault. I didn't want to be late to my nana's place."

"Oh, it's you," he replied with a hint of a smile. His pudgy arms waved around mechanically. "You should know better. How would Mrs. Danby feel about her grandson earning a speeding ticket?"

I studied the crafty look on Officer Flatman's face. He was about to serve me an ironic piece of humble pie, the only pie I didn't like, or he was letting me know he understood my predicament. "I don't suppose you could look the other way."

Officer Flatman asked for my license and registration, then told me to sit tight. While he vanished, I thought about how to ask him if he knew the latest on Abby's murder investigation. He might be so thrilled to give me a ticket, he'd surrender vital information. I organized my approach before he walked back and handed me my paperwork.

"I think we can let this one slide, Mr. Ayrwick. But if I see you as much as a mile over the limit, or failing to come to a full stop, there won't be any second chances. You got me?" he said, holding back a snicker.

"Promise. I'm eternally grateful, Officer Flatman. You must be busy with the investigation. The sheriff speaks highly of your work collecting the evidence. This paperwork shouldn't be anything to get in your way," I replied with grave sincerity. *"Kill 'em with kindness,"* Nana D always preached.

"Did she say that? Wow, I wondered if Sheriff Montague valued my input. Especially when I found the hole in Fern Terry's alibi," he replied with glee as his face brightened.

Oh, it was working. "Definitely. You were such an immense help. And who knew you were such a methodical guy. You'll make detective someday soon, huh?"

"That's my greatest hope. *Detective* Flatman before I turn thirty. I've got a few years left, but—"

I needed to interrupt him if I would catch him off-guard. "Dean Terry's alibi... yeah... heard about that. I hadn't even known she was a suspect." I had no idea how Dean Terry could be connected to Abby's murder. It was a shock to hear her name. "Imagine her being—"

"Fern was seen leaving the retirement party at eight but claimed she left at nine," boasted Officer Flatman. "Eleanor watched the woman leave much earlier right after Myriam left too."

"Did you ever find out what happened?" If Myriam had left before Fern, the Shakespeare fanatic couldn't verify my sister's account of the events. Could anyone else have seen her?

"Nope, I guess Fern must have been wrong about the time. I'm waiting to find out if Sheriff Montague learned what happened between the time she left the party and the time she got home at a quarter to ten." Officer Flatman smiled, then blanched when he realized he said too much.

I couldn't recall seeing her at all, but much of my time had been focused on Maggie in that last hour. "I appreciate you not giving me a tough time today. I should head out to Nana D's."

"Absolutely, Mr. Ayrwick. You have yourself a good day." As he walked away, he giggled hysterically. Odd, given I was the one who got out of the ticket.

Not one to tempt fate, I thanked the powers-that-be for showing mercy on me and ensured the speedometer never passed twenty-nine as I drove down the dirt pathway to Nana D's farm. When I pulled up, she was swinging in a rocking chair on the porch. "Three minutes late, Kellan. You're lucky I had a phone call that kept me from finishing the breakfast preparations on time."

My luck was changing today—two in a row. "So sorry, I ran into a bit of...

traffic on the road." She didn't need to know it was just one car standing in my way of arriving here on time. The wind whipped up behind me, reminding me it may have been warmer than usual today, but it was still not decent enough to hang around outside. "Let's head in?"

Nana D continued rocking back and forth. Her braid was pulled apart today, and she looked quite pleased with herself. "Certainly. Aren't you gonna ask me who kept me so long on the phone?"

She was going to bring up Bridget again. "I'm sure it was important. Let's eat that delicious breakfast you've been cooking. What is it, bacon and eggs? Homemade biscuits?" I rubbed my stomach as the hunger pains grew. If she had fresh orange marmalade, I'd kiss the ground at her feet.

"I'll follow you in. I'm grateful Officer Flatman was kind enough to tell me all about your traffic jam." As the door banged shut behind her, she let out a roaring cackle worthy of Fran Drescher.

I turned bright red. It wasn't Bridget on the phone. Flatman had the last laugh. That pig! "You didn't?"

"I did. If there had been any so-called debt between you and me over a past trip to the county jail, it's surely been repaid by now."

All I could do was nod. Repeatedly. Thirty minutes later, I continued to swallow my pride as she chastised me for being late and getting pulled over. "I can't be having people say negative things about my family. We've already got some tarnish because of this murder your father let happen. Don't you follow in his footsteps and add another black eye. It's not gonna help me in the future."

"Help you with what?" I mumbled while shoveling half a biscuit into my mouth.

"Doesn't matter. You know what I mean." She stepped away from the table.

Knowing how much she loved gossip, I traded a few secrets to get myself out of trouble. Nana D wanted to be the one to ask Connor if they'd been dating, but I persuaded her to leave the situation alone.

"Convince Lorraine to report those missing items to Connor. Find out about the grades from Myriam. I'm going around Marcus Stanton and asking a friend on the Board of Trustees. No one's doing much about solving this debacle. I need a crime-free town. This doesn't look good for us right now."

"I'm on it. Why is it so important—" The doorbell interrupted me from finishing. "I'll get it."

"Thank you, Kellan. I'm sure glad you haven't lost your manners."

When I opened the door, I had a case of déjà vu. The elf was back! "What are you doing here?"

Bridget stepped inside and unbuttoned her coat—at least the neon green parka was gone, given the warmer weather. "Didn't we cover this last week? I take lessons from Seraphina on Sunday mornings. Today is Sunday. Any idea why I'm back?"

It appeared my little elfish friend liked to banter. Nana D had well trained her It was then I realized why Nana D was so willing to drop the conversation at the baseball game about finding Bridget at the tailgate party. When I'd volunteered to come for breakfast today, Nana D knew Bridget would be here for clarinet lessons. She was a devil, not an innocent grandmother.

"Music lessons. I'm back in the game, no worries," I replied, feeling glad she'd worn a different outfit this time—an actual normal one. Bridget had chosen a white cable-knit sweater and a pair of skinny jeans that looked modern and chic. "Speaking of games... I hear you were at Grey Field yesterday."

"Yes, I'm a major fan. I support the school teams whenever I can, but I've always had a strong connection with baseball. My pops instilled it in me when I was a young girl," she replied.

"Do you attend Braxton or know any of the guys on the team?" I couldn't remember if she'd said which college last time.

Bridget shrugged. "Yeah, I've met a few of them. I know Craig from stopping by the communications department last semester. I'm in a biology course with him and Carla Grey this year. Everyone else calls him Striker, but I'm not into that whole nickname thing."

While Nana D remained conspicuously absent, I learned Bridget had been orphaned at an early age and raised in foster care. When she'd turned eighteen, she received a scholarship to Braxton and had been there the last four years, which meant she'd graduate in a few months. She was studying to become a teacher with a double focus in English literature and music education. Bridget seemed like a nice girl, but what was my nana doing by setting me up with someone at least ten years younger than me? It may have worked for my parents, but I didn't see it working for me.

It was toward the end of our brief get-to-know-each-other session when I realized she'd mentioned Striker visiting the communications department. "How did you know Craig Magee would go to Diamond Hall so frequently?"

Bridget laughed. "Oh, I work there. I'm one of the student employees. It pays for my supplies and books, so I don't have any extra out-of-pocket expenses."

"Didn't a student overhear Lorraine and Abby fighting? Was that you or a different worker?"

Bridget fidgeted in her seat and unlocked the clarinet case. She looked past me, probably hoping Nana D would enter the room. "It was me, but I didn't mean to get anyone in trouble. That sheriff interviewed me because I worked in the building. She wanted to know if I'd seen anything in the past."

"I'm sorry. I didn't mean to make you uncomfortable. I heard it was a loud argument, and I was curious how it started." I felt guilty she was trying to do the right thing and had probably caused a slight rift in the department. "I'm sure Lorraine knows you only stated what you'd heard. She's an understanding woman."

"Yeah, it's been a little awkward, but I'm sure it will get better. I didn't think Lorraine had it in her, but she was rude to Professor Monroe on a couple of occasions. I saw her grab Professor Monroe's wrist that day and shake her wildly. It had something to do with some legal document. I didn't hear the entire conversation." As Bridget finished speaking, Nana D sauntered into the room as though she hadn't been playing matchmaker in the background.

"I'm so sorry to keep you two waiting. I had to put all that food away. Can I get you anything, Bridget?" Nana D asked sweetly.

"I should go." I cast an unforgiving glare in Nana D's direction. "It was great talking with you, Bridget. Perhaps if my daughter is visiting soon, you could teach her how to play the clarinet. It could be a little extra spending money in your pocket." I had two reasons for making the offer besides genuinely wanting Emma to get more involved with musical instruments. I needed an opportunity to find out how things worked in the communications department. I also wanted Nana D to think her plan to push Bridget and me together was working. Then she'd leave it alone. There might've also been a small part of me that relished in taking away Nana D's opportunity to teach Emma how to play the clarinet. Knowing how much she would love to spend time with her great-granddaughter, I had to engineer small ways to get back at Nana D for always beating me in our little games. We enjoyed teasing each other.

"What a lovely idea," Nana D said. "I'm sure you three would make quite an afternoon out of it."

"Excellent. I hope you'll lend Emma your clarinet, Nana D. I wouldn't want to buy one until I knew if it was something she'd use."

Nana D turned to Bridget. "Did you find your missing clarinet? I'd like to give mine to Kellan."

Bridget shook her head. "Not yet. I found my clarinet case, but the actual clarinet was missing. I'm annoyed about it too. I'm not made of money!"

I learned Bridget had forgotten her clarinet at Diamond Hall the prior weekend, but when she went back to retrieve it, after the cops let her into the building several days later, the case was empty. She reported it, which made sense based on Lorraine telling me there were several items missing. I'd have to ask about the third one. Was the clarinet still missing because someone had used it to hit Abby on the head? I made a note to ask Connor if that could be the murder weapon. I didn't want Bridget to think something of hers had killed Abby when students still thought Abby's fall was an accident. I had to admit it seemed peculiar that a thief would only take the clarinet or that a murderer wouldn't discard both the case and the clarinet used to kill someone.

CHAPTER 15

Mother Nature blessed Braxton overnight by sending boatloads of powdery white dust to blanket the Saddlebrooke National Forest. The giant fir trees looked gorgeous with their robust green branches covered in bright snowflakes. I pulled into The Big Beanery parking lot to meet Myriam for an early breakfast on Monday morning. After hemming and hawing about what to do, it seemed more appropriate to call her Myriam rather than Dr. Castle since we would be colleagues for the next month.

Myriam had chosen a chestnut brown pantsuit with a vibrant orange, open-collared blouse. Rather than add a tie or broach, she wrapped an elegant silk scarf around her neck. She looked impeccable, and I couldn't argue with her taste in clothes. Her hair, however, hadn't changed since the last time I'd seen her, causing me to wonder if she'd owned a collection of identical wigs. Not a single strand pointed in any different direction than last time. Working in television and research, my mind functioned like a photographic memory—too many nights spent verifying continuity between episodes. I controlled the desire to peel back a section of Myriam's hair to see if it said *Monday* somewhere. She *was* a professor in the theater department.

While Myriam selected a cup of herbal tea and a fruit salad, I ordered a double espresso and a slice of coffee cake, needing the extra boost. "I appreciate you carving out some time for me to get situated with Abby's classes. I taught some undergrad courses when I was getting my doctorate in—"

"Mr. Ayrwick," she interrupted. "I'm more than glad to do my part for Braxton to ensure the students aren't impacted any further than they've been already. However, your father slipped you in under the radar. He could have told me at the retirement party you were his son. What is it Brutus said in Julius Caesar? *'The abuse of greatness is when it disjoins remorse from power,'* I believe."

Her quote was correct, but she must have also felt guilt over the derogatory remarks about my father. "Perhaps. He has tunnel vision in those circumstances and does the minimum to get—"

"Not that it would have changed anything I said. I stand by my words, and this is another case of Wesley Ayrwick thinking he can play God." Myriam sipped her tea, dabbed a cotton handkerchief from her coat pocket against her lips, and sat taller on the seat.

"Well, rather than get caught up on the past, how about we focus on the classes I'm taking over this morning?" I had finished reading all the materials the previous night and was excited to revisit the introductory content I'd long forgotten.

"I'm willing to assume you can handle this coursework. I reviewed your qualifications, and while I'm appalled at the way your father ushered you into Braxton, I'm pleased you've way more experience than Monroe. Where you lack specific roles as a college professor, you probably make up for it with all you've accomplished in your career." She stuck her fork in a piece of grapefruit I swore winced as it entered her mouth. "And that's not a compliment. Just an observation and comparison. I expect when we hire a full-time professor, we will be more judicious in our candidate search."

This was going to be an uphill battle worthy of Attila the Hun. Myriam and I spent an hour discussing everything she'd known about Abby's current courses and upcoming deliverables from the students. In between discrete barbs and jabs, I mentioned the grading process.

"Monroe didn't upload the grades on that first exam. I did. There was a mix-up in all the commotion when the sheriff was going through things last weekend." Myriam tossed her bowl in the trash bin. "When I received access to the building, I found the folder with all the exams in my office mailbox. The woman had graded everything already, but the marks still needed to be keyed into the system."

"You didn't give the folder to anyone else?" It was odd she found them in the first place.

"I'd normally give them to the office manager, but given the lateness, I entered this round myself to prevent further delay of the results to the students. I approved them on Wednesday evening."

A few Braxton students took seats at nearby tables. I nodded at Connor while he ordered his morning caffeine boost, then turned back to Myriam. "Did you come across Striker's exam?"

Myriam wrinkled her nose. "I'm not familiar with that name."

Was she serious? Everyone knew about the baseball rivalry last week. "Craig Magee struggled in Abby's class last year. This was his second chance."

"Yes, your father specifically asked me to look at that exam. It would seem he's gotten private tutoring or focused on his studies more than his sports career. I don't understand why your father allows that athletic director to pull so much weight around—"

It was my opportunity to interrupt this time. "Do you know Coach Oliver?

Was he a regular visitor to the communications department?" I'd been convinced he had something to do with the grade being changed on Striker's exam. I was certain Striker had gotten an 'F' based on the entry in Abby's book. Someone must have swapped his exam to ensure he passed well enough to play for the game.

"I barely know the Neanderthal. As I said, the point of the athletics programs at Braxton is meaningless to me. I'm still shocked at how many donations go their way." Myriam swigged the last of her tea.

"Are you familiar with the blog that's had a lot to say about the allocation of Braxton's donations?" I hoped to make her slightly uncomfortable and to confirm my suspicions.

Myriam huffed and stood from the table. "I've been made aware of it. I rarely read anonymous blogs, but this one has hit the nail on the head, wouldn't you say, Mr. Ayrwick?" She gathered and secured her notes in her briefcase. "I'll stop by later today to see how your first day of classes went. If you need me, I'll be in my office making final stage blocking decisions on our upcoming production of *King Lear*. I thought it was a perfect selection for the change in leadership this year."

As Connor saddled up to the table, Myriam exited. If I had time to respond, I'd have reminded her Lear was a beloved character in the play's conclusion, as well as asked her on which of Lear's daughters she'd modeled herself. I certainly had my vote etched in stone.

"Kellan, today's your first day," Connor stated rather than asked.

I assumed he had to update my campus security clearances, which explained why he knew I was working at Braxton. "Yes. On my way to Diamond Hall now that we have access to use the classrooms again."

He joined me on the walk to the classroom. "I'm sure you'll do well. Sheriff Montague cleared everything last night. She's ready to make an arrest tomorrow."

I was sure they found enough evidence if there was a major break about to occur in the case. "Has she checked the phone records to see whom Abby was meeting? Any chance you know specifically what was used to kill Abby? Perhaps a clarinet?"

"They've completed testing a few objects and have verified the general size and shape of the weapon. The call you overheard came from someone in Grey Sports Complex. I'm working with the technology group for the exact location. Things aren't looking too good for Lorraine." Connor checked his phone and responded to an incoming message he'd be at the security office in ten minutes.

Based on his explanation, Lorraine must have reported the missing items. I also hoped Lorraine had updated Sheriff Montague on meeting Coach Oliver on campus that evening too. "There's no way she could have done it, Connor. I'm certain this has something to do with grades being changed to ensure a certain member of the baseball team could play in the big game. Lorraine has no motive for who pitched last Saturday."

"I think Sheriff Montague is smart enough not to arrest Lorraine without proper evidence. You know Lorraine was angry about Abby's treatment of her brother, Alton."

"What about Dean Terry's lack of an alibi?"

Connor's lips pursed. "Does she have a motive?"

His question was important. Other than a few odd looks at Coach Oliver during the game, I couldn't produce anything peculiar enough. "But she misled the sheriff over her whereabouts."

"Lots of people don't remember their exact movements that night, Kellan. I've had to help interview everyone, and there are still some people who don't have an alibi during the thirty-minute window when Abby was killed." His face squished together tightly with annoyance.

Although he had a point, I wasn't ready to give up. I remembered to ask Connor about the initials from the journal. "That may be true, but Abby was seeing someone named W. A. Might you know anyone on campus with whom she could have been involved?"

Connor gave it a few seconds of thought. "Besides your father?"

"Yes. Anyone else?" I hoped thoughts of Abby and my father together didn't sidetrack him. It'd already made me sick. "Also, do you have access to review the student system's security logs?" I repeated what Myriam told me about the day and time for uploading the grades.

"Kellan, you need to stay out of this investigation. You've got way too many theories going on in your head. The sheriff knows what she's doing. You can't sneak back into Braxton and insert yourself into everything just because you want to." Excessive frustration peaked in his voice.

I began to think his attitude went beyond my interest in Abby Monroe's death. "I appreciate the advice. Fine, I'll let it go for the moment. Seen Maggie lately?" Since he wasn't being open-minded about the investigation, I changed topics. I hadn't meant to be so blunt, though.

Connor halted and grabbed my shoulder. For a second, I worried about his next move, but then he stepped backward and took a deep breath. "Maggie and I have gone out on a few dates. I'm not sure where it's going, but there's chemistry. There's always been chemistry." Connor pivoted away from me and stared at his phone.

"Always been?"

"Yeah. I never told you this before, but it's time you knew."

Twelve years ago, when we were all friends at Braxton in our sophomore year, Connor had a crush on Maggie. He'd asked her out the same day I had, but she told him she needed to think about it. He never understood why until a few days later when I'd announced she and I were a couple.

"Why didn't you say something? I never realized you had such deep feelings for her." A rush of guilt blossomed inside me. "You never seemed upset when we went out without you."

"Trust me, I was angry. But we were all best friends. I didn't want to lose either of you, so I swallowed my pride and focused on school." Connor searched for the car keys in his pocket. "That's why I lost touch after graduation. When you broke up with her, it nearly killed me. I should have fought for her back then, especially if you were gonna ditch her for the first opportunity to leave Braxton."

I noticed the volatile frustration building inside him. Everything became more obvious as I thought back to the last conversation he and I had on campus that day. "So, is that what led to this dramatic change in what you look like?"

Connor nodded. "I needed to forget everything and to focus on my future. I threw myself into working out and the security field... it felt like the best place to concentrate my efforts."

"But when you and Maggie ended up working together at Braxton, you decided to—"

"Give it a chance," he added. "She's an amazing woman. I didn't want to screw up twice."

I had to ask, even if the answer would hurt. "Is that why you stopped calling Eleanor?"

"What? No." Connor looked at his phone again. "I gotta go. Sometimes you can be a real jerk."

As Connor strode toward the BCS vehicle, the jabbing pains in my side eased up, finally accepting there was something between him and Maggie. I wasn't happy about it, but at least it wasn't hidden anymore. Then I worried about how serious it was and whether it meant Eleanor would be in for heartbreak. Unfortunately, I had classes to teach and couldn't wallow in my concerns.

I ascended the back stairs, ignoring the cold sensation overtaking my body as I stepped through the vestibule where we'd found Abby's body. I dropped off my briefcase in her office—my temporary workspace—and shuffled to the main area on the floor to catch Lorraine. She was on the phone but waved and said she'd find me after the first class.

A few students were already hanging out and talking when I slipped back downstairs and sat at the corner desk in the classroom near the front entrance of the building. I said hello and that I'd be with them in a few minutes, then recognized Jordan Ballantine texting on his cell phone. While preparing my introductory remarks, a few stragglers walked in, including Striker and his girlfriend, Carla.

"Couldn't hack it on Saturday, Striker?" When Jordan lifted his head, deep brown eyes focused on his competition. With his shoulders squared and his chest puffed out, he looked menacing. Jordan was confident in his talent and voice and clearly not afraid to stand up for himself.

"What did you say?" Striker replied. "I'm pretty sure Coach Oliver only took me out of the game to give you an opportunity to be seen by the scout. He felt bad for picking me over you."

"That's not how it happened," yelled Jordan. "Your grades magically—"

"Guys, come on. You're supposed to be friends, stop this silliness," added Carla. "Be happy you both had the chance. And we won! That's what counts." Her lips were full and pouty.

It was then I remembered where I'd seen Carla before. She was the girl smiling at Jordan in the fitness center while cycling. I wasn't sure whether the conversation with Connor had impacted my judgment, but it seemed like there was a hidden agenda playing out in the classroom.

"Yep, we won because I saved the game. Striker shouldn't have been playing. He's on academic probation." Jordan shoved the phone into the pocket of his designer jeans and snickered. "I guess something must have changed, huh?"

Carla's face brightened quickly. "Yeah, maybe he studied hard and passed. Leave him alone."

"Exactly," Striker replied. "Coach Oliver wouldn't have let me play if I didn't ace that exam."

"Or something like that," Jordan said. "All seems kinda funny to me how quickly things improved once Professor Monroe died. I was supposed to start!"

When Striker stood and reached a fist in Jordan's direction, I raised my voice. "Welcome back to Diamond Hall, everyone. I'm sure you're curious who I am...."

I delivered my intro speech, which settled the room even if it didn't calm me. If the students gossiped about the peculiarity of Striker's grades changing so quickly, there was substance behind my intuition. I'd return to digging into it once I finished teaching classes for the day.

The first lecture went well. I covered a generic timeline of how the film industry evolved in the late 1800s and the first quarter of the twentieth century. When I dismissed the class, Carla ran out after Striker, followed by a few other students. I introduced myself to Jordan while he packed up to leave.

"Good meeting you, Professor Ayrwick. Would you be related to the president?"

I confirmed, then asked him what had happened before class began. "I noticed a little tension between you and a few other students. Anything I need to worry about?"

Jordan sniffed. "We're all friends, just like giving each other a tough time. Striker and I are cool."

"I saw you pitching last Saturday. You've got a fantastic curveball. I'm sure it impressed the Major League Baseball scout." And it was true, Jordan had definitely saved the season opener.

"Thanks, sir. I appreciate it." He clasped a button on his checkered shirt that had come loose.

Sir? He called me sir. Not even Derek called me sir. "Professor Ayrwick will do. I heard you share some concerns about how the grades were determined. Is there something you'd like to discuss?"

Jordan shifted his weight and tossed his head back and forth. "Nah. If he passed the exam, I'm sure it was legit, I mean, unless maybe Striker did something... never mind, it's just, you know—"

"No, Jordan, I don't know. I'm new here, so if you have information to share, I'd appreciate your candor," I could tell he was nervous, though he seemed to want to say more.

"I'm gonna be late for my next class." He made a mad dash toward the cable car station.

I had an hour before my next class, so I briefly called the sheriff. It had been a few days, and I needed to thank her for letting me obtain access to Abby's office. Officer Flatman answered. "Mr. Ayrwick, how was the visit with your grandmother yesterday?"

"It's always a pleasure to see her. I appreciate you letting me go so easily," I replied, unwilling to let him know I'd known that he'd known he'd gotten the better of me. "She cooked a delicious brunch. Any chance the sheriff is available?"

"Excellent. I'm happy I ran into you yesterday. I can't say for sure why, but my day improved afterward," he spouted before putting me on hold. Was that a southern accent I heard?

A few seconds later, Sheriff Montague picked up the call. "What do you want now?"

"Just to extend my hearty thanks for granting access to Abby Monroe's office. It made teaching her classes today a lot easier." While explaining my new temporary job, I made a list of things to mention about the case should she try to hang up quickly. It'd been a recurring theme in my life lately.

"Seems you wormed your way into things, Little Ayrwick," the sheriff replied. "I've got an arrest to make shortly. Just waiting on the analysis of some fiber samples we found under the deceased's fingernails. Make this quick, please." If there were fibers, it meant there was a struggle before Abby had been hit on the head with the mysterious and missing murder weapon.

"Absolutely. I hear Lorraine Candito notified you about the lost gift she'd intended to give me, as well as the other items stolen from Diamond Hall. Have you found anything? I'm keen to learn what she got me." I crossed the floor toward the staircase.

"We've not located that particular item, but should we stumble across your little trinket, you'll be the first to know. If that's all—" Her caustic tone left little room to debate, but it wasn't stopping me.

"No, actually, sheriff, I have a few other things," I confirmed while worrying she wasn't taking Lorraine's news about the thefts seriously. "I came across Abby's personal journal while sorting through her office."

The childish sarcasm dripping from the sheriff's tone was borderline obnoxious. If it hadn't been directed at me, I might have found her funny in a ridiculous sort of way. "And you called to tell me she had a crush on some movie star? How sweet! But I'm in the middle of a—"

"If only that were the case. Abby mentioned having a relationship with someone. I was curious if you might know the person's identity." I didn't want to reveal the initials yet.

"Nope, I'll send someone to get the journal. I followed up on your lead about Coach Oliver being near the crime scene. Lorraine confirmed his story, but it still leaves time for either to kill Abby during the death window. While I appreciate you letting me know these little pieces of random news—"

"Got it. Unless you want to share the results of Abby's phone call from someone in Grey Sports Complex, I guess we're done here," I replied, realizing she wouldn't be of any help. I'm not sure who hung up first, as I was already thinking about my next move. I received no answer about the phone call.

While ascending the stairs to find Lorraine, I emailed the technology department and asked them to confirm whether there were any logs on the student grading system indicating record changes. Sometimes it wasn't about directly finding the culprit but eliminating all your suspects until left with just one. As I reached the top, Lorraine smiled back at me from behind the desk. I opened my mouth to say hello, but my phone vibrated. Why wouldn't people leave me alone to investigate this crime? I retrieved it and read a text message from Eleanor.

Eleanor: *Talked to Connor yet? This is taking too long.*
Me: *In progress. Will update you soon.*
Eleanor: *Hurry, please. I'd like to know if he's still interested. I'm not very patient lately.*
Me: *Classes today. I'll come to the diner for lunch tomorrow.*
Eleanor: *The position of tonight's moon is not in my favor, but tomorrow looks great.*

Eleanor wouldn't be happy about the news I'd learned. I was hoping to chat with Connor before our lunch the next day, to understand what happened between him and my sister. The stress creeped back in, and I desperately craved one or four of Nana D's double fudge brownies.

CHAPTER 16

Lorraine and I walked around South Campus. I couldn't wander too far with another class starting in thirty minutes. She looked worn down, almost ready to yield to the pressure swirling around her.

"I'm so sorry you have to go through all this drama. I wish I could convince Sheriff Montague to focus on someone else besides you." I loosely placed my arm around her waist as a show of support. "Maybe you could help me decipher something I came across while reading Abby's journal."

"I'll try," Lorraine said when we stopped at a nearby bench. "I'm pretty useless these days. Alton thinks I should take a vacation, but I've been told not to leave town."

"I'm hoping to find the truth soon," I added, taking a seat next to her. "Do the initials W. A. mean anything to you? Abby mentioned going on a few dates with someone."

While running her fingers through her hair and pulling the bangs away from her forehead, Lorraine considered my question. "There's your father, of course. My mother was a W. A. before she married my daddy, but I doubt that Abby would write about her since she's been long gone."

"Anyone on campus? A faculty member, maybe a student Abby knew? After I saw Coach Oliver at her house, I thought I had the initials confused, but I double-checked."

Lorraine shook her head, then a look of fear materialized. Her eyes opened wide, and she gritted her teeth. She quickly transitioned from loving puppy to vicious beast. "It can't be! That louse."

"What? Do you know the person's identity?" I watched her eyes fill with tears and pulled her in for a hug. "Talk to me, Lorraine. Maybe this will help prove your innocence."

"The coach's full name is W. A. Oliver. His parents weren't very bright and

113

incorrectly filled in the first and middle names on his birth certificate with only his initials, W. A. He was embarrassed as a child that he never had an official name and told everyone to call him Oliver. When he started coaching, it became Coach Oliver, and that's how most people refer to him now."

"How did Abby know? And what do they stand for?" I pondered several guesses.

"I'm not sure. He won't tell anyone what his name was supposed to be. I heard Abby call him W. A. in the cafeteria once," Lorraine replied. "I think he's the person she was referring to in her journal."

"It makes sense given I saw him at her house last week, but how would you know about his nickname?" I noticed Lorraine's expression change from sad to angry, almost enraged. "What's wrong?"

"Oh, Kellan. I've been keeping a secret from everyone, but I can't do it anymore if that scoundrel was two-timing me." Lorraine dried her tears and beat her fists against the bench.

Lorraine explained that she and Coach Oliver had been dating the last few months. He begged her to keep the relationship just between the two of them because it was against school policy for colleagues to date without informing the college. After a lawsuit Coach Oliver had been in the middle of, the chief of staff issued an internal memo notifying everyone if they initiated a relationship with a colleague who met a few of the criteria in the revised policy, there was an obligation to ensure it was formally acknowledged by the school to protect everyone involved. Coach Oliver was insistent no one could know he and Lorraine were dating, fearing he'd be fired on the spot again because of the prior lawsuit. I thought the whole thing was an invasion of privacy, but it would make the situation between Maggie and Connor much more difficult if they'd continued any further in their relationship.

"Lorraine, you can do so much better than Coach Oliver. You're a major catch, and he's just... well, he's not worth your time." I wanted to console her, but if what she'd revealed was true, it would tie a perfect little bow on Sheriff Montague's case against her.

"I need to speak with him right now," she yelled, crunching her fists together. "I'll kill him."

I was alarmed but knew my news had blindsided her. "You best choose your words more carefully. Given everything going on, that's not something others should hear."

"When I get through with him, he'll wish we'd never met. I'm sorry to rush off, but I have to settle this right now." Lorraine thanked me for sharing the info and stomped away.

That's when I realized I'd forgotten to ask about the three missing items she'd shared with the sheriff. I desperately wanted to stop her from doing anything she'd regret, but my next class started shortly. I couldn't afford to annoy both my father and Myriam on my first day. I headed back to Diamond Hall and prepared for Abby's second lecture. I knew none of the students in the History of Television Production class, but it was an easy one to teach. I talked a lot about the recent focus on colorizing older shows like *I Love Lucy,* but when half the class looked at me like I'd just arrived from another planet, my temporary high evaporated.

In need of a boost once the lecture ended, I ordered a double macchiato and butterscotch Rice Krispies treat at The Big Beanery. After leaving and rounding the corner, I noticed Dean Terry talking with Jordan Ballantine outside Paddington's Play House. Although it wouldn't have seemed odd normally, learning Dean Terry had an open alibi and was disgruntled with Coach Oliver, then hearing Jordan complain about Striker still playing despite his previous academic probation, I couldn't help but be suspicious. As I approached, their conversation ended. Both walked off toward the cable car station.

Since following them wasn't an option, I used my break time to update my father. I hadn't heard from him after accusing him of cheating on my mother. I left a voicemail indicating the first two classes had gone effortlessly, and I was about to start the third one. I checked my email and found the location of Abby's funeral service. I texted my mother that I missed her, and she immediately wrote back how proud she was of me for following in her and my father's footsteps by working at Braxton. Seriously, it was only three weeks. She turned every little molehill into a mountain!

When I reached Diamond Hall again, my phone vibrated with two alerts. The package I'd sent Emma had arrived. I couldn't wait to see the gratitude on her face when she found the stuffed Braxton bears I'd mailed her. There were three in the set—a ballerina, a baseball player, and a doctor. She needed as many options as she could find in choosing her future career. I secretly hoped it wasn't the doctor as the thought of her looking after me in my old age or me having to pay for medical school was not appealing. Lorraine also texted that Coach Oliver would be back in his office after his offsite meetings. She she'd confront him at four thirty.

Connor joined me as I scrambled up the pathway back to the classrooms. "Hey, I was looking for you. To apologize for my behavior earlier today."

I tossed out my hand in a friendly gesture. "Apology accepted, but at the risk of ruining the world's shortest truce, can I ask you a question about my sister?"

"That's why I'm here. You deserve an explanation," Connor said.

A few students walked past us. "I only have ten minutes."

"I should have said something to Eleanor sooner. When she mentioned you were coming back for Christmas, I felt foolish about the whole thing and pulled away from her."

"Are you saying you were interested in... ummm... taking her on another... or that you had feelings...." I stumbled with my words. "I'm not sure how to say this. She's my sister."

"Yes. When we ran into one another, I felt some sparks. I thought we had a chance to get to know one another again without you in the middle," he replied.

It was the first time I'd seen Connor hesitant and anxious. It somehow made me feel better about the total mess. "Bottom line, are you still interested in my sister?" I cringed, not wanting to hear the answer but also feeling a need to protect Eleanor. "She's confused about what's going on between you two. And now she's under the impression you're dating Maggie. As am I."

"Ugh! Why couldn't you stay away, Kellan? Then, this whole thing would be ten-thousand times easier!" Connor's body tensed as he leaned against a column holding up the awning.

I worried he might knock the whole thing down. "I don't think that's the question you should be asking. Regardless of whether I came home, you can't date them both, can you? You need to figure out what you want, man."

"I'll give it some thought before I do anything drastic, Kellan. If you're telling me you wouldn't completely hate the idea of me going out with your sister, I'll call her to talk things out."

"I think that's a good first step." Finding out the truth was helpful, but it still meant the four of us were caught up in something complex. I'd only be in town for a few more weeks.

Connor agreed. "By the way, they're trying to match some fibers under Abby's fingernails against a few people and objects from the office. If they find any DNA, they'll move forward against someone."

"Thanks for the status. Can you share what the missing objects were?"

"I only know about the clarinet. Sheriff Montague's not ready to reveal all the details. Sorry," Connor said. "She doesn't tell me everything."

"Okay, thanks. I need to go, but Lorraine told me something I think you should know."

"Sure, what's up?"

I updated him on her revelation about W. A. and how she had been secretly dating Coach Oliver. "I know this makes her seem even guiltier, but if you saw the ire on her face when she realized he was two-timing her with Abby Monroe, she could have—"

"Killed someone?" Connor interrupted with a heavy sigh.

"Well, yeah, but that tells me she didn't know about it beforehand. It's not the reason Abby died. Lorraine is innocent." I felt compelled to stand up for my father's assistant and the woman who'd been so kind to me over the years.

"I'm sure you feel that way, but people can do the strangest of things under difficult circumstances. You understand Sheriff Montague needs to be informed about this, right?" Connor said. When I nodded, he continued. "Let me. The sheriff trusts nothing coming from you right now. I can share the news without her immediately arresting Lorraine. She's a good woman."

"Lorraine or April?" I asked in jest. Then, I realized if Connor recognized the sheriff had a crush on him, the entire Maggie versus my sister problem could go away.

"Both. And check your email. I located the system logs on those grades you mentioned."

"Thanks. Let's catch up later. I need to teach my final class for the day."

Connor had come through for me. I felt positive about rebuilding our friendship again.

Connor took off, and I taught three hours on Broadcast Writing. Rather than hold the class for an hour three times per week, Abby had opted for one longer lecture where they could watch various television programs and compare writing styles and format. It was a fun and easy session with mostly creative types looking to polish their communication skills before graduating and searching for jobs.

After the class ended at four thirty, Officer Flatman arrived to bag and tag Abby's journal. When I got back to my office, I jumped online and perused the logs Connor had sent. They confirmed Myriam had uploaded the grades herself last Wednesday evening. There were no previous entries or changes since her upload, which meant if Abby had originally marked Striker's exam as an 'F,' someone had done something to the physical copy between the time Abby had graded the test on the Friday before she was killed and when the exams mysteriously showed up in the folder in Myriam's mailbox. Myriam had found a version with a 'B+' and agreed with the person who'd marked Striker's test with that grade.

I popped my head into Myriam's office, where she mentioned sticking around that evening for a self-defense course at Grey Sports Complex. "I hope you have an exciting time at class. Always good to keep both the mind and the body in a healthy place, eh?"

"*The evil that men do lives after them; the good is oft interred with their bones,*" she replied with a sinister-looking sneer. "Except I much prefer the company of the genuine women at Braxton to that of its weak men who seem so substandard in every sense of the word."

Not having any response other than to ignore her, I left the offices realizing I hadn't eaten lunch. I grabbed a ham and Swiss cheese sandwich from The Big Beanery and headed home to map everything I'd learned about the case to date. I'd just started the drive at five thirty when my cell rang. It was from an exchange used only at the college, but I didn't recognize the number. "You've reached Kellan."

"It's Lorraine. I need to speak with you urgently." Her voice was breathy and panicked.

"Ummm... sure. I just left South Campus and am on the road. Everything okay? I'm worried about you."

"I told Coach Oliver I couldn't be with a cheater, but he swore he never dated Abby."

"Men lie, Lorraine," I said.

"I know, that's why I dumped him. But I need to see you about something else."

"Okay, I can meet you outside Grey Sports Complex." I pulled to the side of the road.

"No, it's fine. I'm coming back to Diamond Hall to finish a few things. I'll grab the cable car in a couple of minutes and meet you at The Big Beanery at six."

"Sure." I wanted to contemplate all my suspicions about the people involved in Abby's death, but this was a higher priority. "Any chance you learned something to find Abby's killer?"

"I might have. When Coach Oliver and I were done, he left his office first. I needed a few minutes to collect myself. I went to the women's locker room in the other hallway to wash my face, but on my way back, I saw someone leaving his office. I thought I recognized the person, but it made little sense. I went back, so I could call you with an update. That's when I found a note on his desk. You need to read it."

"Bring it with you to South Campus. We need to discuss those three missing objects too."

"Okay, I might be able to connect a few dots to several problems on campus."

"Does this have anything to do with Striker's latest grades?" I asked.

"Bingo! I'll give you all the details when I see you in a bit."

I warned Lorraine to be careful, then returned to South Campus, excited to hear her news. By the time I arrived at The Big Beanery at a quarter to six, the daytime crowd had dissipated. Most students were eating dinner in the cafeteria or hanging out with their friends somewhere else on campus. I'd heard something about a mega snowboarding event on the western peak of the Wharton Mountains. I ordered a lemonade as I'd already drunk way too much coffee during the day and grabbed a tall table near the front entrance to catch Lorraine as soon as she came through the door.

I thought back to the crime Abby had mentioned on the phone when we first connected. It made sense that either Coach Oliver was the culprit, or he knew the person's identity. I couldn't figure out why Abby wrote in her journal that her feelings had changed for him, but now that I had confirmation he was W. A., I could ask Coach Oliver myself why he lied to me about his relationship with Abby. What a man is willing to tell his girlfriend versus what he tells another guy were often two vastly different things. If I had any hope of getting Coach Oliver to spill the truth, I'd need to make it sound like I was on his side.

While I waited, my father returned my call. "It went smoothly for most of the day, Dad. I like the students, and Myriam was helpful. She's got a venomous tongue, but if you ignore that part of her, she's somewhat tolerable." I checked my watch and assumed Lorraine would arrive any minute.

"Myriam is keen to share her opinion. I enjoy our discourse most of the time, but occasionally, her words cut deep," my father replied.

For a fleeting moment, I unnaturally thought we were having a normal conversation. "She's annoyed at how you brought me on board to Braxton even though I—"

"Let it go. Just don't annoy her, and you'll succeed in this trial period."

Trial period? What was he talking about? "Ummm... you should be worried about her annoying me and posting those blogs about you. She quoted another line today about *weak men* as I was leaving."

"Let's continue this discussion when you get home tonight, Kellan. Your mother is eager to hear for herself how the day went." After he disconnected the call, I groaned and repeated to myself out loud several times... *I am not a child living at home with my parents again.*

The amber sun slowly set, highlighting the passing of time. My phone said a quarter after six, yet Lorraine was still a no-show. I called and texted but received no responses. I warily rang Connor.

"Did the logs I sent confirm what Dr. Castle told you earlier?" he said.

"Yes, they did. I appreciate it, but that's not why I'm calling."

"What's up? You sound anxious."

I conveyed everything that'd happened. He instructed me to take the cable car back to North Campus to meet him at Grey Sports Complex. He thought I might run into her if I wasn't driving. When I reached North Campus at a quarter to seven, several students were lined up to board the cable car. Carla huddled close to Jordan at the end of the queue. I would've interrupted them, but I needed to get to Grey Sports Complex. While jogging over, I recalled this was the second time I'd seen them together without Striker. Jordan had mentioned they were all friends, but it seemed like those two spent more time together than I'd be comfortable with if she were my girlfriend. Was that what Nana D meant when she'd told me Striker was having girl troubles?

Once arriving at Grey Sports Complex, I entered reception and checked the digital monitors on the walls opposite me. The third-floor fitness center was packed with a large group of students. I tried to locate Lorraine among the crowd, but I only recognized Striker doing intense pull-ups.

After showing my face to the camera, I entered through the middle door in search of Coach Oliver's office. When I arrived, the door was open, and the lights were on, but no one was inside. As I turned to walk down the hallway toward the fitness center, Connor called my name.

"I can't seem to find her anywhere. I checked the entire first floor. Could she be stuck in transit?" Connor's furrowed brow concerned me. "Unless you seriously believe something happened to her."

Lorraine wasn't the type to exaggerate or make someone wait. If she had something important to tell me, she'd have made it to The Big Beanery on time, answered my call, or reached out to explain her delay. "Something's definitely wrong. Let's check the rest of the building, and if we can't find her, then we need to locate Coach Oliver. Lorraine was with him before she contacted me."

Connor sprinted downstairs to check the second floor in case Lorraine was hiding in one of the empty rooms. I remained on the third floor and rushed to the other hallway to check if she was in the fitness center but hidden from the camera's view. No Lorraine. Striker waved to me while preparing for his next set of exercises. Either I was sweating from running around, or the building's heat was too high.

I exited the fitness center and crossed back to the hall housing Coach Oliver's office and the conference room. I doubted Lorraine lingered there, but a window overlooking the front of the building would provide an unobstructed view of the cable car station. Was Lorraine finally boarding the next car to South Campus? It was now seven o'clock.

I opened the door and stepped into a dark conference room, instantly feeling a chilly breeze blowing in my direction. Someone had left the window open, or the heat had stopped functioning. I felt along the wall for the light switch but couldn't find it. Remembering Coach Oliver had said they were installing a new voice-activated system, I shouted, *"Light on."* Two seconds later, the glow from three recessed bulbs flooded the room.

Two shutters banged against the exterior wall near a large open window. When Connor entered the room behind me, I jumped two feet off the floor. He said, "I didn't find Lorraine downstairs. How about you?"

I swiveled around, breathing deeply to regain my wits. "No. But look at all these overturned chairs." I walked to the window, noticing someone had pushed it to the ceiling. The opening was about four feet wide by six feet tall. I stuck my head outside to look in the enclosed front courtyard.

"Anything?" Connor approached my right side. His woodsy cologne over-powered me.

Several students meandered on the ground in front of the building. No Lorraine. It was hard to focus in the darkness. Then I noticed something odd at the base of the statue in the courtyard. "Do you have a flashlight?" When he nodded, I showed him where to shine the beam.

Connor confirmed my suspicions using a cold, matter-of-fact tone they'd taught him in the police academy. "That's a body on the ground near the statue, isn't it?"

CHAPTER 17

I gulped and closed my eyes, wishing I hadn't seen what I'd seen. We ran out of the conference room toward the nearest stairwell. Connor called Sheriff Montague as we exited on the second floor near the courtyard entrance.

He instructed me to wait while holding me at bay. After I followed his request, he cautiously approached the statue. I watched him kneel to check Lorraine's pulse. When he turned back toward me, a morose expression confirmed the devastating news.

"She's dead?" The weight of my entire body sank quickly.

"Yes, her neck broke when she hit the statue after the fall from the window," Connor replied.

"It's gotta be Coach Oliver. Lorraine surmised he was up to something illegal." My blood boiled as I shuffled toward the statue. My eyes filled with tears. How could this happen?

"Did she use those words? I'm not saying it doesn't look suspicious, but we have to be clear on the facts."

"Not exactly," I replied, calming myself down. "When I asked what she thought was going on, Lorraine confirmed it was connected with Coach Oliver and Striker's grades."

After the sheriff arrived, Connor recapped what I'd already confessed. I waited for them to evaluate the situation. Paramedics arrived and verified there was nothing they could do to help. Sheriff Montague directed her team to bring the coroner onsite while Connor called my father to inform him of tragedy. I wasn't ready to deliver the news, and the sheriff wanted to hear Lorraine's words directly from me.

"Did she sound like she might harm herself?" asked Sheriff Montague.

"What? No, that's crazy! She was frightened and wanted to meet me at The Big Beanery. There's no way she jumped from the window. Lorraine wouldn't do that!" I was irate over the way the sheriff had suggested Lorraine might have lost the will to live. "Plus, she saw someone unexpected. An assailant who killed her just like they killed Abby."

"Relax. I'm trying to ascertain the facts. This will be simpler if you trust me." She commandeered the seat next to me on the bench. "There was a note near Lorraine."

Easier said than done. Sheriff Montague hadn't given me any reason to assume she was on my side in the past. "What did the note say?"

"I can't get to it without moving her arm. I want the team to finish their initial analysis before we touch the body," noted Sheriff Montague, gently resting her hand on my forearm. "We'll find out what happened, I promise. Is there anyone both she and Abby fought with recently?"

I considered whom I'd encountered at Diamond Hall and shared the names. It was a concise list, but there also could have been several people before I'd returned home to Braxton. I wouldn't know their identities. I finished relaying my final account of the entire afternoon as Connor confirmed he'd contacted my father. "President Ayrwick is on his way, sheriff."

I knew how much my father relied on Lorraine, and as standoffish as he could be, her death would devastate him. It had devastated me. Connor and the sheriff stepped away to discuss something. As much as I wanted to pin the crimes on Coach Oliver, it didn't make complete sense. Why would he kill both the women he was dating? Dean Terry's behavior had also been puzzling me. Jordan and Carla's presence together on the cable car queue was suspicious, but any guilt I recognized on their faces might have resulted from someone catching them in a close embrace. Did they have alibis for the night of Abby's murder? Too many clues to follow up on. And it wasn't my job!

My mind had entered overdrive once I doubted if Connor could be responsible. Although I'd found Lorraine's body, the entire setup might have been part of his grand plan to cover up what he'd done. I shook the troubling thoughts from my head, confident my former best friend was not a double killer. I needed to drive home to get sleep and deal with the aftermath.

Sheriff Montague returned to the bench. "Holding up okay? I can't imagine finding two bodies within such a brief period is a normal thing for you."

"No, it's not," I replied, focusing my gaze on the pavement. "I'd like to get out of here."

"You are free to go, but you've figured out the drill by now." Sheriff Montague suggested a time to meet the following day to review a written statement. As I stepped away, she called out my name. "I can't tell you what the note said, but I'll confirm it wasn't a suicide message. I haven't made heads or tails of it yet. We can discuss it tomorrow."

"You mentioned earlier there were fibers under Abby's fingernails. Can you share anything?"

"No DNA. It looks like the fibers match the baseball team's newest jackets. But we haven't finished running all the tests, so please keep this to yourself."

I ambled toward the cable car to access South Campus, find my Jeep, and drive home. I should have stayed to support my father, but I needed to be alone. Lorraine had confronted Coach Oliver because I asked her about the W. A. in Abby's journal. Had I somehow sent Lorraine to her death?

* * *

I must've crashed when I got home because I barely remembered climbing into bed. I tossed and turned most of the night while mourning the loss of Lorraine, but when I woke up on Tuesday, the desire to punish the killer was at the center of my thoughts. I went for a run, then caught up with my mother, who was heading to Braxton at the same time. My father had departed much earlier to talk with the Board of Trustees about last night's incident, so she shared a ride with me to the campus. Sometimes you needed your mother to arrange things in perspective.

"Kellan, we'll all miss her very much," she said as I pulled out of the driveway. "I can't understand why she'd jump to certain death at Grey Sports Complex, but if she suffered from that much pain, I only hope she's in a better place now. Do you suspect she killed Abby?"

My mother knew nothing about Lorraine's relationship with Coach Oliver. While I was certain Lorraine hadn't committed suicide, my mother felt otherwise based on whatever my father had said the previous night. "I think someone pushed her, Mom. Maybe because of something she knew about Abby's death. They must be connected."

"We've never had murders at Braxton. Between those two awful events and this maniacal blogger, your poor father's retirement is causing him so much stress." My mother gripped the small handle on the roof of the Jeep when I took the curve near the river too quickly. My heart breaks for both women's families.

"Has he said anything recently about the blogs? I suspect Myriam," I replied.

"He knows who's behind them. He can't tell me, but we talked about it yesterday. I'm certain Connor is on top of it. There have been no posts since the one after the party."

I dropped off my mom at the admissions building on North Campus, then drove to South Campus to start my day. When I entered Diamond Hall, Lorraine's boxes in the first-floor hallway encouraged the pain to flood my body all over again. She'd have been moving back to the newly renovated executive offices during the upcoming weekend. I slipped to the second floor to steal a few minutes of solitude and map out a plan of attack for the day. Instead, I found a woman with bright red hair dressed in jeans and an oversized Braxton Bears baseball sweatshirt sitting at Lorraine's desk.

"Can I ask what you're doing in here?" Given both murders, I needed to talk to Connor about how well campus security operated if random people wandered into the building and rifled through someone's desk.

When she lifted her head, the wrinkled brow and the volume of makeup she had painted on her face made her look like a clown. "I could ask you the same question. Who are you?"

I wasn't accustomed to being questioned in such a manner when I was clearly in the right. "I'm Kellan Ayrwick. I work here, and this desk belongs to someone else. How about you?"

The woman stepped away and smiled pleasantly. "Oh, it's nice to meet you. I'm sorry I was rude. I didn't expect anyone to come in while I prepared things ready for the department. I'm Siobhan."

I knew the name, but I couldn't place it. "Are you a temp?"

"No, I've been on maternity leave for the last two months. The chief of staff called me last night and asked if I could stop in today to help organize. There was an accident, and Lorraine Candito won't be in the rest of the week." A thick Irish accent accompanied her words.

That's right! Siobhan was the office manager whose responsibilities Lorraine had been covering. "I believe congratulations are in order. Boy or girl?"

"One of each, twins," she replied, retrieving her phone to show tons of pictures of the twins dressed in green outfits. Siobhan and I chatted for several minutes, during which I learned she'd worked at the college for five years and moved to Braxton after visiting a friend who'd attended a semester abroad at a college in Dublin, Siobhan's hometown. She'd undergone in vitro fertilization the year before, never expecting two eggs to be fertilized simultaneously. Being a single mom to twins wasn't as easy as she assumed.

I explained my temporary role teaching Abby's classes. Siobhan had little to say about the late professor, suggesting she preferred not to speak ill of the dead. "Would you know who has access to the student systems. Myriam provided an overview, but I'll need to input the grades for an upcoming paper my students will turn in next week."

"Professors only have access to their own courses. They can't view anything about their students other than contact information, and we keep that at a bare minimum. I have advanced privileges, but I can only enter and update grades for classes if the professor authorizes my access."

I thanked Siobhan for her help and walked toward my office. She followed, querying if I needed anything, but I had little chance to respond. Myriam angrily darted out of her office. "Siobhan, I see you've met Mr. Ayrwick, resident troublemaker."

Me? What had I done? "Good morning. Have I offended you?" I mustered as much of a smile as I could while stepping into Myriam's path. Siobhan retreated across the floor's main area. Either she'd experienced one of Myriam's tongue lashings before, or she didn't want to embarrass me while I received one of my own.

"You mean other than telling Sheriff Montague I'd fought with both Monroe and Lorraine to make *me* look guilty of something? Honestly, the nerve of you spreading gossip after only working here for one day," shouted Myriam as she dropped her bags to the ground. *"One's doubts are traitors and make us lose the good we oft might win by fearing to attempt."*

Not another weird quote. "The sheriff inquired about whom Abby and Lorraine had spent considerable time with on campus. I mentioned your name, but I didn't accuse you of anything." Disdain for the beleaguering woman percolated inside me. "Unless you count being the author of that nasty blog against my father." I didn't mean to announce the formal accusation aloud. I unquestionably suspected her, and the woman's constant Shakespeare references were getting on my nerves.

"I have nothing to do with it, I assure you. I can see you do not differ from your father, Kellan, and I'll be certain to inform the next president. We can't continue to allow pompous men to work on this campus," she growled while pushing me into the hallway.

"How dare you say something like—" I stopped speaking when I heard another voice.

"Maybe you two could keep it down? Students are arriving for classes below and can hear everything," Connor advised. "Perhaps we could behave like civil human beings and have a rational discussion?" He extended his hand toward Myriam's office, and we all piled inside. "What seems to be the problem here?"

"Mr. Ayrwick is under the impression that I'm a cold-blooded murderer, ruthless blogger, and I can't even imagine what else will come out of his mouth next," Myriam replied. "I'm going to report his behavior to the Board of Trustees, Director Hawkins. You're a witness to this unprovoked instigation on his part."

"I did nothing of the kind, Connor. You were there, you heard everything I said last night." I left out the part about accusing her of being the blogger, but the woman had it out for me. As I reeled in my frustrations, I took notice of Myriam's chosen outfit that day. I couldn't help but admire how polished and poised she looked in her navy-blue, classically tailored pinstripe pantsuit. It was the shiny gold camisole underneath that made the whole ensemble pop to my dismay. *Just let me at the wig to see if it reads Tuesday.*

"Dr. Castle, he's telling the truth. The sheriff asked for anything that came to mind. Kellan didn't throw you under the bus at all, however...." After waiting for Myriam to settle in her chair, Connor added, "Everyone's on high alert after two unexpected deaths on campus. Why don't we agree to let this go?"

"Fine!" Myriam adjusted the tortoise-shell glasses on her hostile face. "I'm willing to accept it wasn't intentional insubordination."

Insubordination? Did I work for her and if so, how had I missed that? I opened my mouth to object, but Connor interrupted. "Let's take a walk, Kellan. I've got a few theories to discuss with you."

Myriam ushered us both out of her office, then shut the door. I followed Connor down the back steps to avoid the crowd assembling on the first floor of Diamond Hall. When we reached the door, I mumbled under my breath, "Never should have come back here."

Connor laughed. "Man, she gets under your skin. Shake it off. I've got some news to share, which might cheer you up a bit. Although, it's not positive on the whole."

His words intrigued me, but I soon learned why the news was a mixed message. Sheriff Montague had authorized him to share a copy of the note under Lorraine's body. It read:

I hope you appreciate how much I've done to help the baseball team reach the championships this year. I understand how important it is to impress the Major League Baseball scout. I'll check next week's exam results too, so there's no chance of the star player missing out.

"That matches what Lorraine told me on the phone before she was killed. She had something to show me. She caught Coach Oliver or someone else writing the note to Striker."

Connor nodded. "This could be the reason she was pushed out the window. The sheriff doesn't think it's suicide anymore either," he replied with a hesitant break in his voice. "But why would Coach Oliver put something like this in writing? Don't you think he'd pull Striker aside and tell him he took care of it? And why would the coach put it in his own office?"

I considered the validity of Connor's input. When I added together everything I'd learned, I conjured another theory. "There's no doubt in my mind Coach Oliver is mixed up in this grade-changing scandal. What if someone is making it look like Striker is part of the scheme? I got the distinct impression from a conversation with Jordan yesterday that he hated Striker."

"So, you think he changed the grades with the hopes it would make Striker look guilty and get him kicked off the team?"

"Perhaps," I said. "I'm concerned Dean Terry is involved too. I saw her and Jordan speaking on campus yesterday in a secluded area."

"And now you suspect a college dean?" Connor huffed as we arrived at Grey Sports Complex. "Hasn't he been training both Jordan and Striker to be star pitchers?"

"You've got a point," I acknowledged. "None of this makes sense, but all of it looks suspicious and ties into what that blogger has been saying. I need to see how upset Coach Oliver is over Lorraine's death. Has Sheriff Montague questioned him yet?"

"Last night after you left. He came back to the building, claimed he'd been watching several practices at Grey Field after Lorraine stopped by his office. He returned only for a few minutes to get his briefcase and go home. He looked quite shaken up over Lorraine's death."

"He's a liar," I argued while preparing to leave. "I'll prove it right after I pay him a visit."

"I admit you were right about Lorraine not being Abby's killer, especially now that she's also dead. The sheriff believes what Lorraine told you about the confrontation with Coach Oliver, but she has no proof." Connor explained he needed to get to a meeting he couldn't skip, but he was working with the technology department to pull all the CCTV tapes and security access logs to Grey Sports Complex.

"I appreciate it. Maybe they'll find out from that know-it-all computer system exactly who was in the athletic facility," I replied, feeling some encouragement from his words.

"Just don't cause any more trouble. You've already annoyed one important member of the college in your attack on Myriam. Try not to get on everyone's bad side, Kellan."

I promised him I'd tread lightly with Coach Oliver. After ignoring the computer voice greeting me in reception, I made my way to the athletic director's office. The coach hung up the phone as I arrived.

"We need to talk," I uttered in my most serene voice, picturing Connor yammering in my head.

"Isn't the news horrible?" Coach Oliver waved me into his office and waited for me to sit in the chair opposite him. "Lorraine was an upstanding employee of this college."

"Don't distract me. Lorraine told me you two were dating for months. I know she confronted you last night." I rattled off my frustrations in list form, failing to tell him specifically what she'd said in the hopes he'd trip up and reveal something.

"Let's not be too hasty in our judgment. I didn't know Lorraine told you about us. We were supposed to inform the college since it'd been more than a few dates. I was protecting her." A harrowing sadness accompanied his voice as he closed his eyes and scratched at his goatee.

While Coach Oliver appeared genuinely upset over Lorraine's death, I wasn't onsite to comfort him, especially when he claimed to be protecting her. He's the one who'd gotten in trouble in the past for harassment. "What exactly was your relationship with Lorraine?"

"I'll tell you, but you have to believe this sounds a lot worse than it is," he replied, fidgeting with a pencil between his fingers. "Three months ago, your father called me to his office to chat about convincing a Major League Baseball scout to check out Braxton. Whenever I stopped by, Lorraine and I flirted a little."

"She mentioned the same thing to me, but that doesn't explain how Abby fits into the picture," I countered, feeling queasy over his confession. "Or why a baseball scout would be interested in Braxton."

"At the end of last semester, Abby and I discussed Striker's inferior performance in her class. She'd asked to meet me for a drink to advise that she would fail him," Coach Oliver said with remorse, shaking off a nervous jitter. "I tried convincing her to give Striker another chance. I wanted to help the kid myself, but I know nothing about communications or television history. I asked Abby to tutor him, but she wouldn't."

"Lorraine said you denied anything happened between you and Abby. I saw you sneaking around her driveway last week." When Coach Oliver looked away, I could tell he'd deceived Lorraine about the extent of his relationship with Abby.

"You know how it is. Things happen. She was an attractive woman," Coach Oliver said. "It was purely professional at first. We met twice to agree to keep Striker on the team. Abby hinted she'd consider going easy on Striker when he took her class again this semester if I, well...." he hesitated, then smiled and bobbed his head a few times. "You know what I mean. I'm sure you've been in that position before, Kellan."

"Yes," I said, lying through my teeth. I'd never been in that position, but I wanted answers and wasn't about to tell the man he was a disgusting fool. "How is it Abby came to write in her journal about her feelings changing for you?" I wasn't sure if he knew about the entries but wanted to catch him off guard. I also didn't want to reveal her plan to expose him.

Coach Oliver stiffened with a shocked gasp. "Huh? It was just a fun time. Nothing serious. I really do like Lorraine," he said after releasing another heavy sigh. "I guess... I mean... *did* like Lorraine."

Although his demeanor grew melancholic, as if he'd finally accepted Lorraine's death, I had to press on. "Was Abby holding something over you?"

"Abby knew I was dating Lorraine. She'd been listening outside my door and heard part of a conversation about Lorraine and I going away together in a couple of weeks. Sometimes she ignored me, other times she put pressure on me to spend more time with her and tell her all about the new technology and perks the athletic facility had received. It was only a few weeks where anything actually happened between us." Coach Oliver kept changing positions and shifting his body weight. I was certain he hid vital information. He'd also avoided any explanation about why the scout selected Braxton.

"When was the last time you spoke to her before she died?"

"The previous Friday," he responded. Something about the way he said the words told me he still wasn't telling the truth. "Abby notified me that Striker failed his first exam again."

That explained why I found the 'F' in her grade book. "But ultimately, she passed him, right?"

"I assumed Abby made good on her promise," Coach Oliver replied with a sly grin.

As much as I wanted to pin both crimes on the pervert, I couldn't connect the dots. He was guilty of something, but it might not be murder. "I appreciate you sharing this version of the story with me. Do you have any idea who could have killed Abby or Lorraine? Could Striker be responsible?"

Coach Oliver shook his head. "No, Striker's a good kid. He may not pass his exams of his own accord, but he's an accomplished pitcher with a future destined for the big leagues. I can't come up with anyone else who had a motive. Maybe two different killers?"

"I doubt that. Neither Braxton nor Wharton County have ever had murders like this before. There's little chance of two deaths happening so close together without some connection. What about Braxton? Why is the scout here?"

"I guess we just got lucky. I'm not sure," he said hesitantly.

I stopped questioning Coach Oliver. My best next step was to dig into Striker's whereabouts when Abby and Lorraine had been murdered. But first it was time to meet my sister for lunch.

CHAPTER 18

"I'm so shocked," an exasperated Eleanor said while we chatted in her office at the Pick-Me-Up Diner. "Lorraine was such a caring person."

"She was truly a genuine soul. I have to find out who could do something so horrible."

"I understand." Eleanor thanked the server who dropped off two large dishes of a new beef stew recipe the chef was experimenting with for the upcoming weekend. "Does Sheriff Montague have any clue what happened?"

"I haven't talked to her today, but I'll head over to the precinct later. I spoke with Connor earlier. He'll go through all the security tapes and logs this afternoon." I swallowed a spoonful of the stew, then quickly grabbed a glass of water. It was way too hot to eat, but the brief taste I'd gotten before my tongue burned was flavorful. "A little heavy on the red wine, maybe?"

"Chef Manny likes to go the extra mile sometimes." She laughed and gestured like he enjoyed his liquor a little too much. "Speaking of Connor, any chance you talked to him?"

"Yes, Connor was worried about me coming home," I replied cautiously. I had to be honest with Eleanor, but I needed to be careful observing that fine line between revealing everything and saying just enough.

"So, you were right. Is he looking for your approval to go out with me?" asked Eleanor, sampling the stew and letting me know it had cooled off. "You won't stop this, right?"

I wasn't sure I had control. "There's more than me giving you two the all-clear."

Eleanor sank into the chair and pushed the plate away from the edge of her desk. "There's something going on with him and Maggie now. I'm too late, aren't I?" All the normal exuberance disappeared from her angelic face. I wanted to cast some magic spell and make the whole situation go away, but that wasn't likely. "The stars haven't shown me anything lately."

Just thinking about magic made me realize I hadn't talked to Derek about *Dark Reality's* second season. He'd be thrilled to hear about the latest murder. I reached across the desk for Eleanor's hand, but she was too far away. In an awkward moment of silence, we glanced at one another, and I relaxed back into my seat. "He's been out with Maggie a few times, but he has no idea where it's going. Connor wants to do the right thing. He adores you both."

"Really? You don't think he's letting me down easily," she said, perking up from her earlier wane.

I nodded. "Possibly. You're going to have to talk with him yourself, but I wouldn't count yourself out of the game. You're a total package. Who wouldn't want to go on a date with you?" I was in the wrong career. Should I be switching to life coach and matchmaker extraordinaire?

Eleanor's mood improved, and she promised to let the news linger for a few days, then she'd call Connor to suggest meeting for coffee one evening. "I think you should do the same with Maggie."

"I'm not ready to date. Nana D's already setting me up with one of her music students. Know anything about Bridget Colton?" I reminded myself to reach out to Bridget to see if she had anything else to tell me about the inner workings of the communications department. Maybe she saw something strange and didn't realize it was an important piece of the puzzle.

"No, Nana D hasn't mentioned her to me." Eleanor finished devouring the rest of her stew. "Add it to the menu or tell Chef Manny to try again?"

"It's a keeper," I confirmed as I handed the bowl to my sister. When Eleanor disappeared with the dishes, I checked my phone for any new messages.

Nana D had sent a text to find out when I'd come by for dinner. I suggested Thursday evening, which she agreed to as long as it was after seven because she had a meeting with the local miner's union and the head of the civic center. She was up to something, which I hoped wouldn't end in disaster. She was still talking to every member on the Board of Trustees about the anonymous donations.

Upon returning, Eleanor gagged like she was going to vomit. "Were we ever that young?"

"Define young. I thought we still were."

She waved at me to peek out the window in the hallway by the kitchen. "Check the far corner outside at the two lovebirds making out. I understand being in love, but to go at it like that in the parking lot of a decent restaurant. They could shut me down for lewd behavior."

The Pick-Me-Up Diner wouldn't be closed over two people kissing outside. I suspected it was how my sister had felt about anyone sharing a loving moment these days. Jealousy could be a big part of her frustration. When I peeped in the corner, I felt a pang of heartbreak for someone I'd come to know in the last few days. Poor Striker! Carla and Jordan were the two engaged in a passionate embrace. "Wow! Look at those two. I guess she and Striker are no longer dating." I returned to Eleanor's office.

"It's not the first time I've caught them in the act," my sister replied, pulling her hair back and sighing. "They've been sneaking back there a few times late at night."

"Really? I thought she was Striker's girlfriend, but I suspect something might be going on between her and Jordan."

"This has to be tied into Striker's grades and who played in the opening game, right?"

Eleanor and I discussed the different possibilities of how the three students could be involved in the scheme. There was a strong chance Abby had caught one of them and been killed, so she couldn't tell anyone. "All I know is that when Myriam got hold of Striker's exam a few days later, she agreed with the 'B+' before uploading it to the online system. Every student's grade in Abby's book matched except for Striker's. I checked them all myself," I replied, noticing the time. As I stood to leave, another option came to mind, and as much as it seemed silly, I had to mention it. "Unless Myriam is lying and fixed his results, so she could give him a 'B+.' Which I *highly doubt* is the case."

Eleanor laughed. "No chance. Dad says Myriam is a stickler about those things. Maybe the individual changing the grades isn't the same person who killed Abby and Lorraine. It could be unrelated, I suppose. You still don't know specifically what either woman knew about the discrepancies before they died."

Although Eleanor had a point, I was certain the two crimes were connected. I needed to check the exam Myriam graded when I was back on campus to verify that I'd also give it a 'B+' and not an 'F.' It was time to discuss the latest news with my father since it clearly showed something underhanded going on at Braxton. "I'd like to find out who wrote the note Lorraine had with her when she fell out the window. It could be many people based on the vague word choices." I hugged my sister for reminding me about the note and took off for the sheriff's office. "Sheriff Montague needs me to finalize a statement."

Thankfully, Officer Flatman was out on patrol. The sheriff escorted me to her office to cover the final details of last night's events. "How are you holding up, Little Ayrwick?" The tweed coat was back today, but this time she'd paired it with a pair of corduroys and cumbersome hiking boots.

"I'm okay, but I'd be a bit better if you called me, Kellan. I think we're past the formalities, April, and might look to build a friendship." I hoped it would go over well despite her unattractive hairdo.

"Sheriff Montague will do for now," she replied with tentative ease. "I prefer to keep a strict line between business and pleasure, and I don't believe I'd consider us *friends*."

I had no choice but to accept her decision. At least I knew to approach her carefully. I wouldn't get any answers if I pushed too much. "I'd be happy to read and sign the final statement. Any leads you can share? Lorraine Candito was a close family friend."

Sheriff Montague softened at least one level on the friendliness scale. "I'm sure it's been quite a shock. I trust Connor shared the contents of the note?" She continued after I nodded in confirmation. "He's going through the security logs and will update me within the hour. Once he finishes, we'll know more about who was in and out of Grey Sports Complex."

"Do you have an estimate of when someone pushed her out the window?"

"Between five forty and six fifteen," Sheriff Montague replied. "Minutes after your call with her ended. She died instantly after hitting the statue. There was little pain, if that helps."

"It does, thanks." I crossed my legs and relaxed into her office couch. I hoped we were having an open dialog but wasn't sure how much she'd reveal. "Have you given any thought to my grading concerns? I suspect a few students who are conveniently in the middle of what's happened to both women."

"I'm not at liberty to say what I've found out, but I'm learning to appreciate how you've picked up information we wouldn't normally come across." She leaned forward on the table and handed me a prepared statement. "I'm not saying you have any freedom to get involved in the investigation, but having someone like yourself on the inside has come in handy. It's led me to a few other discoveries."

I assumed that meant I could continue poking around in different areas. After glancing over the statement detailing what I'd seen last night—including making a few minor changes to correct Officer Flatman's inaccurate grammar—I signed off. "Thank you. I'm not trying to intervene. It's crystal clear how important it is not to muddy the collection of evidence or risk any issues with apprehending a suspect."

"I'm glad we're on the same page here," she said before standing. "If I learn anything of importance from Connor's security log research, and I believe you can provide further insight, I'll be in touch. For now, be cautious what you say to the students while teaching their classes. We might be dealing with some clever folks." At least she'd chosen to wear a more stylish pair of boots today.

I took her silence as my cue to leave, which I was more than happy to do since we'd brokered a potential understanding with one another. I still wasn't sure how much I believed her desire to separate anything personal from anything professional. Sheriff Montague's refusal to call me *Kellan* yet refer to my former best friend as *Connor* instead of *Director Hawkins* was not a prime example of her so-called strict line. Nor was that comment she'd made at The Big Beanery about *how fine a man* Connor was.

I wanted to hit the fitness center but had no desire to go back to the third floor of Grey Sports Complex given what had last happened there. I changed into a pair of jogging pants and a long-sleeve thermal shirt—it was still a bit chilly—and laced my running shoes. I felt like a kid again as I ducked in the back seat of the Jeep when someone walked by. I didn't need to be caught in my briefs or without a shirt, but I wasn't keen on asking Sheriff Montague if I could use the bathroom in the sheriff's office to change my outfit. As I navigated the roads near the base of the mountains and Crilly Lake, I compiled a list of ways I could check the alibis for Carla, Jordan, and Striker without outright asking them. If they were responsible, any direct questions would give them too much alarm. If they weren't involved in the murders, it would seem creepy for a professor to ask them where they were those nights.

Once the run was done, I pulled into my parents' driveway and slipped inside the house. I showered and dressed while my mother heated dinner, then headed downstairs to offer help. She'd finished following the housekeeper's instructions on how to warm the honey-roasted pork loin, butternut squash, and green beans. Luck was on my side as she'd already set the table. We all sat and talked about our days.

"Looks delicious, Mom. You've excelled in your chef skills tonight."

"It's not that hard to follow a few steps on a piece of paper," she giggled.

"You've totally come so far with this talent," I replied.

"I suppose I could win home cook of the year, eh?"

"Ahem. Are you ready for tomorrow's classes?" inquired my father, disinterested in engaging in our banter on my mother's lack of cooking skills.

"I have a few materials to read over tonight, but yes, everything looks to be in shape." The rosemary garlic sauce on the pork loin tasted phenomenal. I explained everything I'd discovered about Striker's grades to my father. I also told him I'd updated Sheriff Montague about all the students in question.

"It's alarming to think someone at Braxton is responsible for two murders. I don't want to admit we could have a killer lurking on campus," my father said. "I'll ask Myriam to compare Striker's exam results with prior exams and papers to determine if there's a reason to believe it wasn't his work."

"It is frightening, but hopefully Sheriff Montague solves it soon," my mother replied. "Thankfully, Kellan is helping her."

"I wouldn't go that far, Mom."

"I'll also update the Board of Trustees tonight. I think it's appropriate for our attorneys to get involved. Hopefully, Connor has an update to clear any wrongdoing by the college."

"What do you mean, Dad?"

"If there are inconsistencies with our grading processes or someone on our staff has been involved in anything illegal, it will not look good for us. The baseball scout will pick no one from Braxton, nor will we get the final approvals for the plans to... never mind. There's no need to get ahead of myself."

My father's concerns opened my eyes to something I'd missed. This might be larger than getting Striker off the team, so Jordan could play. What if this was about ensuring Braxton impressed the scout? I asked my father, but he said I'd need to talk with Coach Oliver about that angle—Coach Oliver, who was sketchy about his whereabouts during both murders.

My father added, "Coach Oliver might be a little rough around the edges, but he's not responsible for the murders. Sometimes people can't always tell you the specifics of their alibi."

I wanted to ask what the man had done in the past to cause the sexual harassment policy changes to be put in place, but I wasn't supposed to know about them. My mother interrupted as I cleared the table. "Sit down, Kellan," she said, then sternly looked at my father. "Don't you have something to discuss with our son, Wesley?"

As she left the room with the plates, my father spoke. "I suppose she means telling you where I was the night of Abby's murder." He took a swig of water to allow himself a moment to think.

I wasn't expecting this conversation tonight. "It's important to know where you went."

"You would say that," my father replied. "The Board of Trustees is concerned about me leaving Braxton, especially when they contemplated the development of an entirely new academic program."

"That sounds like a wonderful opportunity. I'm sure they could find someone to make that happen in your absence," I replied, hazarding a guess what new fields they might be considering.

"Did you ask him yet?" my mother said, carrying a peach cobbler to the table. "Nana D dropped this off for you earlier today."

I had the best nana out there, hands down. "Dad's started to tell me something, but I don't know what you mean about asking *me* anything."

"Lord, Violet, would you give me a few minutes? It's like this is an everyday occurrence." My father pushed his chair back a few inches. "Don't you need to make some coffee?"

"What's going on?" Unwilling to wait any longer, I sliced a giant slice of pie.

"We've been completing a study and working with generous donors in the background about the possibility of Braxton adding graduate courses. The Board of Trustees has given the final go-ahead to obtain approval to convert Braxton College into Braxton University. We'll be starting with three key fields of study, but the plan is to expand our academic offerings to include several MBA options and an extensive Ph.D. program within the medical fields. The third will be a complete rearchitecture of the communications department, enabling us to become the primary school of choice for students looking to build careers in the television industry."

My mother caught the look of surprise on my face. "That's not all. Tell him now, Wesley."

"You can't keep quiet, can you, Violet?" My father turned to me with a huge surprise about to burst from his lips. "I tentatively agreed to take leadership of the entire rebranding campaign and build-out of the new university while my successor runs the existing college. In time, I'll turn over the expanded curriculum to the new president, but it's too much for one person to handle all at once."

I knew he wouldn't retire. My father couldn't sit still if his life depended on it. "I guess congratulations are in order?"

"Well, I had one condition." My father glanced at my mother and covered her hand with his. "It involves you, Kellan."

I didn't like the sound of where things were going. "I see."

"I'll only take on this role if you agree to return home and accept an assistant professor position under the new department chair and president, as well as a role on the committee to assemble the new communications department within Braxton University. I'm talking about developing relationships with all the major television stations, the elite production teams in Hollywood, these digital or cable subscription services like Netflixy or whatever you call them."

I stuffed my mouth full of a massive chunk of pie and closed my eyes. *This can't be happening...*

CHAPTER 19

After the bombshell my parents had dropped on me at dinner, I excused myself to consider their news. Not only would it be a major life change, but my father needed an answer by the end of Friday, so he could work with the Board of Trustees to structure the announcement they'd make at Braxton about the new president. I went to sleep early and tried to forget all the drama and concerns. Early Wednesday morning, I pushed aside those gnawing fears, skipped my normal run, and showed up in time for classes.

I dumped my briefcase on the desk, retrieved the pop quiz I'd created to verify how well the students had paid attention to the previous lecture, and placed a copy face down on twenty desks. For a moment, I thought a little part of Myriam Castle's personality had invaded me for tossing the surprise quiz on the class, but it was only fleeting. I couldn't be that mean. When students assembled in the room, I asked them not to turn over the papers. Striker and Carla entered and sat together. I looked around the room and saw only two people missing. One student had informed me in advance that she wasn't feeling well, but the other absence belonged to Jordan.

I gave the students thirty minutes to complete the quiz. If they finished early, they were free to leave but had to turn in their overviews of an upcoming term paper due in two weeks, or they could stick around to write it during the remaining lecture time. Although most students dropped off their overviews and depart, Carla turned in her quiz and went back to her desk. I assumed she was writing her overview but couldn't see that far away. Maybe I needed new glasses. Age had nothing to do with it.

A few minutes later, Striker left his seat and handed me his quiz. "Could you look at it now? I'm curious how I did." A few drops of sweat pooled at his temples.

I told him to take a seat while I read his responses. It was a combination of multiple-choice questions and a few open-ended sections, giving the students a chance to dazzle me with whatever they remembered from Monday's lecture. Although he missed a few easy ones, he earned another 'B+' with this quiz. When I looked up, only Striker and Carla remained in the room.

I delivered the good news, happy there wouldn't be any worry over the grades on today's exam. "You should be proud. Look at what you can achieve if you focus."

Carla winked at me. "Maybe you're a more talented teacher."

"Flattery will get you everywhere, Miss Grey, but I was being serious. It's a shame what happened to Professor Monroe. Were you not a fan of hers?"

"I'd rather not say. She was... difficult," Carla noted before turning to Striker. "You ready?"

Striker stood. "Yeah, pretty awful she died, though. You found her, right, Professor Ayrwick?"

"It isn't one of my more favorable memories." I'd unearthed my route to ascertain their alibis. While Striker loaded his backpack, I seized my opportunity. "You know, they always say you remember exactly where you were when something bad happened. How about you both?"

Carla awkwardly smiled at Striker. "We were together. Hanging out at my dorm. Right, babe?"

He nodded. "I had a lot of homework, and Carla was helping me study for a few classes."

"On a Saturday?" Somehow, I didn't believe they studied in the dorms. "That's a different way of spending the weekend than I did when I was a student here."

Carla coughed, then shrugged. "Ugh! Yeah, I guess you got us. We were in his dorm, just the two of us, but there might have been a few drinks and less studying involved, ya know?"

"Sounds closer to my memory," I said.

"I guess we should've been honest from the beginning. I don't turn twenty-one for a few more weeks," Carla added. "But you'll keep our secret, right, professor?"

"We should run. I've got that appointment with Dean Mulligan." Striker grabbed Carla's hand and led her out of Diamond Hall. They were bunched together, whispering something as I watched through the window. When they reached the end of the walkway, Carla yanked her hand away and took off in the opposite direction of Striker.

With them gone, I looked up Jordan's contact information and called his dorm room. He picked up on the first ring.

"Yo, who's this?"

"Jordan? It's Professor Ayrwick," I replied, suddenly feeling ancient. Was I turning into that mean professor who called out his students for missing one class? "I was following up with everyone to see if they had questions on the upcoming term paper."

"Sorry, I missed class. I was with Coach Oliver talking about the Major

League Baseball scout. Looks like I'll be pitching this Saturday." Jordan excitedly shared his news.

"Oh, well, that's fantastic. Things come up, no worries. Missing one or two classes each semester is acceptable. You can make up the quiz anytime between now and Friday." Then I stalled, unable to produce a simple way to ask him about his alibis.

We agreed to a time for the redo and hung up. What had changed Coach Oliver's mind to lead with Jordan instead of Striker? I'd have to ask him when I saw him again. I pondered whether he would show up at Abby's funeral service that afternoon.

I peeked at my notes for my second lecture of the day, then had a bite to eat. Just as I finished, Connor called. "Kellan, I wanted to update you on what I learned from the security logs."

"Hit me with it. Is Coach Oliver guilty?"

"There are only a few cameras installed in Grey Sports Complex, but we had an excellent view of the fitness center entrance on the third floor." The sound of his flipping pages in the background filled the empty air. "Keep in mind there aren't any cameras near the conference room, so we can only tell who was spotted somewhere on the floor or in the building."

I pictured the layout as best I could from memory, recognizing this wouldn't be an exact confirmation of who had access. "There were a dozen people in the fitness center when we arrived."

"Yes, but Officer Flatman and I watched the video recording from four thirty to seven, which covers the full period for someone to leave, push Lorraine out the window to her death, and escape without being caught. Only two people I couldn't account for elsewhere entered or exited the fitness center. It doesn't mean someone else couldn't have hovered in the outside hall or approached the conference room, but at least we can eliminate those still inside the fitness center when it happened."

"Got it. Who slipped out?"

"Jordan Ballantine left about ten after five, but I don't see him anywhere else on the camera. Then there's Striker Magee. He showed at five, argued with Jordan, and exited five minutes later. He returned at six."

"Do you know where he was during that time?" I asked, curious why he'd leave in the middle of a workout. I'd seen him doing pull-ups when I got to the fitness center just before seven.

"I checked the other cameras in the building but didn't see him. He might have used the restroom or made a phone call between his workouts."

"Or he might have killed Lorraine. What about the self-defense class?"

"We don't have a camera view where the instructor was teaching it, but he provided the list of staff and confirmed there was only one no-show. No one left early, and he doesn't accept late arrivals. The class ran from five thirty to six thirty. I saw everyone leaving the building when I arrived."

"Who was the no-show?"

"Dean Terry, but she was seen on camera entering the building during the window Lorraine was killed. I'm going to speak with her today to find out why she skipped the self-defense course," Connor replied. "Looks suspicious."

"That's interesting. So where does that leave us?"

"I'm cross-checking the list of people captured by the front camera entering or exiting with anyone we can eliminate based on other camera angles or being in the fitness center or self-defense class. It'll leave us with about twenty people whose time we can't account for inside the building between four thirty when Lorraine showed up to confront Coach Oliver and seven thirty when the sheriff began a sweep for anyone still onsite. We'll document alibis over the weekend."

"That's helpful. Anything else you can add right now?" I asked.

"We can't verify Coach Oliver's whereabouts during the latter part of the period. He says he was at Grey Field for a practice volleyball game, but we have minimal camera coverage in that area. Jordan and Carla were also in Grey Sports Complex during that time, but you saw them at a quarter to seven when the cable car arrived at North Campus. Oddly enough, Alton Monroe met with his sister right outside the building before Lorraine confronted Coach Oliver at four thirty."

"Excellent progress. Thank you for letting me know." A sense of relief filled the empty space inside me. I still grieved for Lorraine, but at least we'd know soon. I was curious why her brother had shown up.

I disconnected and contacted Cecilia, Emma's grandmother. I needed an update on my baby girl, and hearing about her day at school would help me feel better. Then I delivered the news I wouldn't be back for a few weeks as I was doing a favor for my father. Cecilia was unhappy when I instructed her to put Emma on a plane to Braxton. She agreed to only when I accepted she'd be coming with my daughter too. Luckily, she'd only intended to stay long enough to drop her off, as she planned to visit New York City for a shopping trip with some friends.

I called Derek and left a message about the second murder. It was strange he didn't answer my call, but I had a wake to attend. After arriving at the funeral home, I switched off my cell and exited the Jeep. The last time I'd been in one was for Francesca's services. I hadn't wanted to attend today, but it was a necessary evil.

As I approached the front entrance, I almost collided with two women heading down the stairs. "Oh, I'm so sorry. My head's not quite right at these kinds of places." When I looked up, I felt even worse.

"I wondered whether you'd show," Myriam replied. "How did your second day of classes go?"

I nodded at my dreaded colleague. Even in mourning, she was as elegant as possible. It was also the first time I'd seen her in anything but a pantsuit. Her slate-gray winter coat hung open and revealed a floor-length black dress beneath its heavy fabric. A string of diamonds around her neck beamed at me rather than a smile. I supposed it was a funeral, but I recognized in the four or five times I'd met the woman, she always carried a bitter expression.

"Fine, thanks. I'm feeling well integrated and connecting with several of the students." I studied her companion, knowing I'd recognized her somewhere but not how or why. She was taller than Myriam and in her four-inch heels easily matched my height. Whereas Myriam had a sour expression and stark features, this woman projected an ethereal composure—that was the only description coming to mind. Her wavy, golden hair flowed endlessly down her back, and her almond-shaped green eyes sparkled. I thought she was a model, and I'd seen her on the cover of a magazine, but my brain wasn't capable of recalling details right now.

"This is Ursula Power." Myriam cocked her head in the other woman's direction. "She met Monroe a few times last semester during some on-campus events and wanted to pay her respects."

"Pleased to meet you, Kellan. Did you know Abby well?" the goddess replied.

The woman's stunning appearance mesmerized me, but it then occurred to me Myriam hadn't revealed my name when introducing us. How did she know me? "I hadn't met her in person. I was supposed to interview her the day she unfortunately died, but well—"

"*He that dies pays all debts,*" Myriam replied before I could finish. A self-righteous grimace waned as she said the words.

I might have been distracted and not interpreted her body language in the fairest manner, given my less-than-welcoming feelings toward the woman. I also had no idea what her quote meant, but I was more focused on how Ursula knew my identity. "Pardon me, but have we met before?"

"I don't believe so, but I've heard a lot about you."

What had Myriam told her? I had little time to ask any further questions once Coach Oliver interrupted us. Myriam glared at him.

"Hello. Such a tragic reason to bring us together," he noted before introducing himself to Ursula.

Myriam responded, "I suppose you received notice that I've asked Dean Mulligan and Dean Terry to suspend Craig Magee until the investigation into his grades from earlier this semester has concluded. After reviewing the last exam he took for Monroe, there's no way those were his test results. Someone else completed that test or switched his results with a different student's."

"Yes, that's exactly why I stopped to see you right now. Who do you think you are interfering in my baseball team's success? Professor Monroe gave him that 'B+' and you verified it was a passing grade. Striker was ready to lead the game this week. Jordan was only going to relieve him if needed. Now I've got to start the other way around and all because you've stuck your nose where it shouldn't be." Coach Oliver angrily shook his finger in Myriam's face. As his nostrils flared, I could barely contain my glee at two of my least favorite people arguing right before my eyes.

It suddenly made sense why Jordan told me he would be starting pitcher in the upcoming game. I watched Coach Oliver and Myriam go at each other until Ursula inserted herself into the conversation. "This isn't the time or place for you two to have this debate. Regardless of how either of you felt about

Abby Monroe or who should pitch on Saturday, this is a memorial service for a woman who was murdered in cold blood," she replied with sheer, impressive elegance. "I'd suggest saving your personal feelings for tomorrow when you can have a civilized conversation about the investigation into the student's grades."

Myriam stepped backward and calmed herself down. Ursula had certainly made an impression on Coach Oliver too. I added my two cents, not to feel left out of the conversation, but also to continue the theme of behaving in public. "I concur, Miss Power. This is definitely not the time or place." I looked sternly at Myriam, as it might have been the first opportunity I could push back on her with no retaliation.

"I think it's time to leave. Shall we, Ursula...." Myriam replied, trudging away. I was unsure if it was a question or a statement. Ursula indicated she looked forward to seeing me around. Both women dashed toward the parking lot. Then a dark-colored BMW angrily tore away from the funeral home. Myriam had been the driver.

"Ain't that Ursula one fine specimen!" Coach Oliver whistled and entered the building with the smug look of a man who needed the expression quickly wiped off his face.

Although I had more questions for Braxton's seedy athletic director, they'd have to wait. I followed him into the funeral home to pay my respects for Abby Monroe. After the customary nods and weak, uncomfortable half-smiles with a few students and faculty members I'd previously met, I searched for any member of my family or Alton Monroe, so I could use my time at the funeral parlor wisely. I set my sights on Alton when he stepped away from the casket and toward a few of the flower arrangements.

"Kellan, is it?" asked Alton, extending a hand in my direction. His expression clearly showed he wanted to escape the room full of people he barely knew. "It's kind of you to come when you never met Abby."

"Of course, it felt like the right thing to do. I'm deeply sorry for Lorraine's death." Despite his tenuous relationship with Abby, the grief on his face was apparent. Losing both his sister and his soon-to-be ex-wife had taken its toll. While I didn't think he could be responsible for the murders, I wasn't ready to cross him off my list and worried what I mistook for grief was guilt. Why he was at Grey Sports Complex at the same moment someone had pushed Lorraine through the window?

"I almost didn't come, but your father thought it would be beneficial to have a representative from Abby's family," he replied as we walked toward a quieter corner of the room.

My parents were embroiled in a conversation with Dean Terry and Dean Mulligan that looked way too uncomfortable. My mother quietly nodded at the deans while my father smirked. I'd have to ask him what it was about when I had a moment. I noticed Connor and Sheriff Montague step into the room as Alton began talking again.

"Braxton's finest," he quipped. "I spent a fair part of my morning with her discussing my whereabouts during my sister's unfortunate death. They are quite persistent about specific dates, times, and places, aren't they?"

Alton's words intensified my curiosity and opened the opportunity I'd been looking for. "I take it they questioned why you were on campus the day Lorraine was killed?"

"Exactly. I told them she called me to help calm her down about some louse cheating on her. I met up with her near the athletic facility to give her the courage she needed to dump him. I asked if she wanted me to stick around, but she told me she needed to confront the man herself. Why anyone would think I could hurt my sister is beyond me. It's appalling the way they interrogate you over the littlest things."

"I'm sure someone can verify your whereabouts, right? That should clarify your alibi."

He shook his head. "Lorraine and I talked for thirty minutes, but I left right at four thirty. I had spent little time on campus before, so I walked through the sports fields, then I got in my car at six thirty. Unfortunately, nothing will confirm where I was during the time in between."

Alton had an airtight alibi during Abby's murder. "What motive would they have to suspect you?"

"My sister invested in several stocks throughout her lifetime and made a windfall in last year's upturn. I was notified this morning she left two hundred thousand dollars to me," Alton replied, seemingly calm about the inheritance, which made me think he was even less guilty than I'd considered earlier.

"I would never have guessed by the way Lorraine acted or lived her life," I said. Although she always dressed well and drove a nice car, she had no air of wealth or attitude about her. "She was a wonderful friend to me over the years."

Alton nodded and indicated he concurred with me about Lorraine's generosity. "That sheriff seems convinced Abby's death is connected to something on campus, but she wouldn't give me a lot of details. Did you ever find what you were looking for in those files?"

"Yes, it wasn't a lot, but we have the last of her research for the television show. I also came across a few odd things in her grade book, which is why I agree with the sheriff that her death might be related to something underhanded at Braxton."

When Alton seemed interested, I explained the basics of Striker's grades and what Coach Oliver had said about Abby offering to change them if he agreed to give in to her demands. I unexpectedly learned a new piece of information from Alton.

"Abby might have bent the less important rules in life to access a story, but she would do nothing unethical or immoral with students' grades. She also had a severe distaste for college athletics usurping a student's time while preparing for future careers."

"I'm glad to know, but I can't figure out why Coach Oliver would lie."

"I might be able to explain now that you've filled in some blanks. Abby and I'd met up a few evenings to close on the divorce settlement. I don't know whether it was the wine or a momentary truce, but on those nights, it felt like old times. Abby had started dating someone and was glad she and I could settle things. She was ready to finalize our divorce. Then everything came crashing down. Abby realized the guy had only been taking her on dates in the hopes she'd change her mind about a student's grades. She'd caught an incorrect grade once before and originally thought she'd made a mistake, but when it happened again, she knew there was something sinister transpiring. She was going to expose something fraudulent."

Coach Oliver was looking much guiltier. Maybe Sheriff Montague was here to finally arrest him. "Abby mentioned something about a crime happening in Wharton County. Do you know what it was?"

"Regrettably, no. She and I had spoken little afterward. Besides taking out her anger on the guy, she also put the screws to me by reneging on the deal we'd made to sign the divorce papers." That news explained Abby's fight with Lorraine the day before she died.

Alton excused himself and offered his goodbyes to my father. I was on my way to see Connor and Sheriff Montague when Nana D called out my name. Somehow, this wouldn't end well.

CHAPTER 20

"What are you doing here, Nana D?" I crossed to the funeral parlor's Entrance.

"I had a few stops to make downtown today. Just thought since I was in the area, I should put in an appearance." Nana D wore her standard funeral outfit—a stylish, vintage dress cut just below the knees with a bit of white trim on the hem. "I also needed to talk to you about Bridget."

I couldn't believe her persistence about setting me up with the girl. It was fine to keep inventing ways to bring us together, but it was unacceptable to be so pushy at a funeral service. "Nana D, I think you—"

"Oh, slow your roll. I thought you should hear something she told me earlier today when I called to change the time for our lessons on Sunday."

She ceased talking to me as if I understood what she was implying. "Keep going, Nana D."

"Don't rush me." After helping herself to a few cookies and a cup of tea, she glared at me with a satisfied expression. "Okay, now I can finish my train of thought. I must be doing too much. Feeling like I'm getting a little more mature lately."

"Rest a minute if you need. I'm not going anywhere."

"But I am. I've got to see Marcus Stanton in twenty minutes. That man owes me his final decision, and if he doesn't back down, he won't know what hit him." Nana D slammed her fist on the arm of the chair, sending the tray of cookies way too close to the edge of the table. "Where were we?"

I stopped the tray from falling and waved off my mother when she looked ready to rush over. "What did you need to share?"

"Bridget had some interesting news. Apparently, she overheard a scandalous conversation on campus between someone and that baseball scout."

My imagination overloaded with curiosity. "What did she learn?"

"That scout said that he was doing his best and couldn't be stuck in the middle anymore. The decision was out of his hands."

"To whom did Bridget see the scout talking?"

"Pish! I didn't say she saw them. She overheard them," Nana D contradicted.

"Okay. Did Bridget know to whom he was talking?"

"One, what's with the formal speak? Two, would you let me finish telling the story, brilliant one?"

I kept my mouth shut and let Nana D relay her conversation. While Bridget had been eating lunch in the student union building, the scout sat at a nearby table talking on his phone. She recognized him from last week's pep rally and baseball game, but she wasn't sure who was on the other end of the device. The scout said he'd already made the recommendation for the position and that if all went well, there'd be a place in the Major League Baseball organization after the semester ended at Braxton. The scout also said he couldn't do anything else to help, then hung up.

"What do you think it's about?" I couldn't think of who else would be on the call but Coach Oliver. Was he looking for a job outside Braxton? Was that why he was so adamant about an optimal baseball season?

"Bridget didn't understand what the scout meant, but she thought it was peculiar. That's why she mentioned it to me. I might have inquired about what the students thought of Abby's and Lorraine's deaths."

"Why are you sticking yourself in the middle of this investigation?"

"Listen, pot. This kettle already told you I'm worried about the county. Since that school keeps this town running, it's important I pay attention." Nana D stood, insisting it was time to leave.

I couldn't argue with her since I'd also inserted myself into the search for the killer or killers. Nana D said she had one more meeting to uncover the anonymous donor's identity, then left. As I walked to the foyer, Connor approached me. "That grandmother of yours sure likes to make an entrance and exit. I think she might have pinched my bum as she walked by."

I felt my skin flush at the thought of Nana D doing that to Connor. I was going to ask how long she pinched him but thought better of it. "It must have been an accident. She was in a rush."

"Somehow I'm not sure I agree. I know she's not the sheriff's biggest fan, but that wouldn't win her any points," he replied with a smirk. "April is waiting on some test results. They picked up a few fibers under Lorraine's fingernails. She's hoping they might match the samples they found under Abby's too. I can't tell you anything else yet."

I temporarily ignored the fact that he called the sheriff by her first name. Connor was taking advantage of his admirers these days. I told myself I wasn't jealous, but the jury was still deliberating on that one. "That's good to hear. Hopefully, it will give them a big lead." I updated him on the news Alton and Nana D had shared with me earlier.

"Are you going to tell Sheriff Montague what you've learned?"

"I thought I might get a chance to speak with her here, but she left while I was talking to Nana D. I could stop by the sheriff's office on my way home." I considered my options yet found myself reluctant to be the guy always delivering the latest news. Both pieces of information had fallen into my lap. I never went in search of the clues. Didn't the responsibility belong to Alton and Bridget to tell Sheriff Montague? After all, *April* told me I was merely a private citizen and warned me to stay out of it.

After Connor headed back to Braxton to finish interviewing the people whom he'd seen on the CCTV tapes, I updated Derek. When I wrapped up, he mentioned relaying the details to the network executive the following morning. They'd called an impromptu meeting to talk about *Dark Reality*, but he wasn't sure why. He asked for my advice on how to handle the meeting, explaining he didn't have a good feeling. It was the first time I'd ever heard or seen him act nervous and ask for my opinion as opposed to instructing me to do something for him. Part of me wanted to assuage his worries, but just like sharing the updates with the sheriff wasn't Kel-baby's responsibility, I needed to let things happen without my interference in Derek's world too. I'd stood up for myself with my boss. Letting that twenty-four-year-old know-it-all learn a lesson on his own was a step in the right direction.

* * *

Thursday morning passed quickly given most of my time was focused on convincing Emma's first-grade teacher and school administrators why I had to pull her out of classes for three weeks. Then I struggled with my former mother-in-law to defend my position on why Emma needed to be with me until I finished my temporary teaching assignment. Once that was settled, we coordinated the flight arrangements for Cecilia and Emma to arrive in Braxton when my last class ended on Monday. Eleanor would meet Cecilia at our parents' house, ensuring my delay wouldn't interrupt her driver's schedule to arrive in Manhattan that evening for dinner with her best friends at a Michelin-starred restaurant. Oh, to be a Castigliano and have the world drop everything to impress you. Or ensure they didn't wipe your existence off the face of the earth.

After a run and a simple lunch, I set off for Braxton to prepare for the next day's classes and to administer both students' makeup exams. The first one showed up on time and finished the pop quiz in less than twenty minutes. When Jordan arrived, I got to know him better before making him complete the quiz.

"Getting ready for Saturday's game?"

"Yep. I spent most of my morning perfecting my curveball with Coach Oliver. The scout watched us for a few minutes too. I didn't know he was Coach Oliver's best friend."

While Jordan searched through his bag for a pen, I contained my shock about his news. No wonder Coach Oliver was so focused on ensuring the team

147

looked good. I filed that under a list of things to analyze later in the day when I had more time.

"How are you handling Tuesday's incident at Grey Sports Complex?" I asked, remembering that Jordan was on the building list when Lorraine had been pushed from the third-story window.

"Two accidents in the same month. That's scary, huh?" He slunk further into his seat and uncapped a pen. "I can't believe I'd just seen Mrs. Candito a few minutes before it happened."

"Really, I didn't know. You must have been one of the last people to see her alive." I was surprised he volunteered the information, but he must have been questioned by the sheriff or campus security. "Did you already talk to Director Hawkins?"

"Yeah, he grilled me a little while ago."

I removed the test from my folder and leaned against the main desk in the classroom. I didn't want Jordan to start, so I continued asking more questions. "Where did you see Mrs. Candito?"

"I wanted to talk about an issue that'd occurred during a workout with Striker, but Coach Oliver wasn't in his office. Mrs. Candito was on the phone talking to someone. I felt awful. I wish I'd stopped her from jumping out the window."

It seemed like news hadn't gotten out that it was murder. "What time was this?" Could he have seen the killer? Or was it him?

"Had to be just before a quarter to six. I was in a rush to meet my study group. I mentioned it to Director Hawkins, but I didn't actually speak with Mrs. Candito. She never saw me."

"What was the issue with Striker?" I assumed Jordan had almost interrupted Lorraine talking to me on the phone.

"Ummm... Striker had been working out while I was at the fitness center. We had some words. I didn't want to cause any more problems." Jordan wrinkled his brow and groaned loudly, then confirmed he'd shown up at four fifteen and worked out until five when Striker came in. After their disagreement, Striker left. Jordan finished his workout, then went to the locker room by five fifteen to shower and change.

"But I thought you mentioned you and Striker were friends the other day in class. What happened?"

"After class, Carla told Striker she wasn't sure about dating him anymore. He was angry and confronted me about it. I wanted to give him some breathing room, I guess," Jordan said.

"Why would he confront you?" While he was nattering, I took advantage of the opportunity to learn as much as I could about the three of them.

"I think Carla finally told him something occurred between her and me the night Professor Monroe fell down the stairs. Striker accused me of moving in on his girl, but that's not how it happened. Honest." Jordan sat back up and placed his hands on the desk. "Can I take my quiz now?"

I was about to hand Jordan the paper when I remembered that Striker and

Carla previously told me they'd spent that night together drinking in the dorms. Someone was lying. "Sure, in a minute. I don't mean to pry, but I've seen you and Carla together a few times. It looked little to me like you were completely innocent, Jordan."

"We went to the movies that night just as friends. Carla needed a break from all the work and drama with Striker and his stepfather freaking out over who would be the starting pitcher in the opening game. Halfway through the movie, she grabbed my hand, then asked if I wanted to leave early. On the walk home, she kissed me. I told her I wanted to see her again, but not until she broke up with Striker. I know what it looks like, but she came onto me, Professor Ayrwick."

"What time did you end up leaving the movies? Did you meet up with other friends or see anyone else?" I needed to find out if he had a legitimate alibi for the night of Abby's murder.

"I dropped off Carla at her dorm. She promised to think about what I said, then I went home. I guess it was somewhere between eight fifteen and nine. I hung out in my room by myself and caught the end of the Phillies first spring training game. Oh yeah, and my aunt stopped by to chat."

"What about Carla? Did you hear from her again?" If he spoke with his aunt, that could cement his alibi. I knew it was the Phillies first spring training day too. I'd caught a few news clips the next day. Either he was telling the truth, or he'd seriously rehearsed his explanation should anyone ask for his whereabouts.

"Striker called her while we were walking home. I guess she went to meet him. I didn't talk to either of them again until Monday in class. You've got a lot of questions, Professor Ayrwick. What's up with that?" Jordan was becoming irritated with my rapid-fire technique. His perceptive manner meant the inquisition needed to slow down.

"Oh, I'm just worried about this getting too far out of hand. I've been in your shoes before. It's hard when you have feelings for your buddy's girlfriend. I guess that was the only time something happened between you two, huh?" I remembered Eleanor also mentioned seeing them hooking up in the parking lot of the Pick-Me-Up Diner recently.

"No, we met a few times to talk about the chemistry between us. We kissed and well, you know how things happen." Jordan shrugged and reached his hand toward the quiz.

He sounded like a younger Coach Oliver. I couldn't keep harassing him without some pushback. I let him take his quiz and thought through everything he'd revealed. Carla and Striker's alibi didn't match Jordan's confession. Jordan also put himself on the suspect list by stating he was alone after eight fifteen unless his aunt could prove part of his alibi. Connor had to have security records from that night for all students entering the dorm room unless there were no cameras there either. Jordan finished the quiz and exited in a rush without asking to know the results. As I scooped up his exam to head back to my office, I fortuitously encountered another person with whom I needed to speak.

"Good afternoon, Myriam." I blocked her from heading downstairs. "I'm glad we ran into one another. Do you have a minute?"

"I have to teach a class. What can I do for you now?" Myriam seemed to forget I'd witnessed her unseemly argument with Coach Oliver at the funeral parlor, but it was crucial for me to bring it up.

"I'm curious about your decision to push for Craig Magee's suspension from the baseball team over his grades. Can you give me any background on what happened?"

"Why is it any of your business, Mr. Ayrwick?"

"The student is in a class I'm teaching. If there was an issue with past exam performance, I think it's important for me to know about it now. Don't you agree?"

Myriam hesitantly nodded, then took off her glasses. "After you expressed concerns about grading processes within the department, I studied copies of Magee's past exams. Not only was the handwriting different, but his sentence structure and word choices were dissimilar. There's little chance he actually took Monroe's last test, and I intend to find out what happened. In the meantime, until we know the truth, he shouldn't represent Braxton on the baseball team, nor should we have lifted his suspension."

"I agree with assuming something funny happened on that last exam." I suspected it would be one of the few things Myriam Castle and I would ever concur on. "Would you mind sharing with me who's looking into it right now?"

"Based on discussion with your father, Magee has been placed on suspension for one week while Dean Terry, Dean Mulligan, and I investigate other student papers and exams to see if this is an isolated incident or happening with multiple students in Abby's classes or others in the communications department." Myriam looked quite angry over the situation as she wandered away.

"I'd be happy to help in any way I can." On my walk toward the cable car station, I ran into Dean Terry. "What brings you to South Campus? It's rare I see you here."

"I'm meeting with your father, Kellan. We have a few issues to work out before Monday's announcement about the new president. He asked if I could join him this afternoon for a discussion with the Board of Trustees in the executive offices. And he's the *current* president, right?" she said with a curious smile and a slight bit of nervousness.

"I suppose there will be tremendous changes coming soon."

Dean Terry shook her head and sighed heavily. "You're telling me. At least we can take pride in the positive impacts the baseball players have brought to Braxton this year. We should all be thankful for whatever stroke of luck has blessed the team and the scout's presence on campus this year. The sports program has been a major source of comfort and excitement for the community despite the students' concerns over the two shocking deaths we've had recently."

Dean Terry excused herself for the meeting with my father while I hopped on the cable car toward North Campus. I'd never known her to be so interested in the school's athletics program. When I'd been a student, Dean Terry focused on the honor societies and student government rather than sports, sororities, and fraternities.

Since I'd remembered to bring gym clothes with me, I stopped by the fitness center to get in a workout before going home. Upon arriving, I averted my eyes from the second floor as it would bring too many memories of Lorraine lying helpless at the statue's feet. After stretching my muscles, I focused on strengthening my back and legs since the bed at my parents' house was destroying my posture. An hour later, I overheard a conversation between two students who'd just entered the fitness center and sat side by side on the rowing machines.

"Totes. My boss just came back from the executive building and kicked everyone out. She was royally pissed off."

"What did Dean Terry say?"

"She was angry about the selection of the new president."

"Yeah, weird. The cops were onsite interviewing students who were at Grey Sports Complex on Monday. I told you something funny happened to that professor and the president's assistant who bit the dust."

"Seriously, I thought they both fell."

"Don't be so dense. Two people falling and dying so close together can't be a coincidence. Even your boss was trying to cover it up when I asked her for a quote for the school's newspaper. I got the distinct impression she was hiding something. After I pushed her more, she warned me that people sometimes get hurt by asking too many questions."

When my cell phone rang, the girls looked in my direction. Since I didn't want them to know I'd been eavesdropping, nor did I want to interrupt anyone's workout, I stepped into the hallway to answer the call. I had little time left to get Emma's input on our possible permanent move to the East Coast.

CHAPTER 21

Emma had just gotten home from school and was excited to visit Braxton the following Monday. I promised her a trip to a local farm to see a few horses, sheep, and goats. By the time I finished explaining the potential job change I was considering, Emma's pure excitement became contagious. She astutely admitted while she would miss Nonna Cecilia, she hardly ever got to see my parents. Emma had reasoned out we should come back to Pennsylvania for six years since she'd lived six years in Los Angeles.

"That's fair, Daddy, right? Splitting my time between both sets of grandparents?" Emma asked with the assured confidence of a much older girl.

"Yes, honey. You're looking at things the proper way." When I hung up, I thanked the powers-that-be for blessing me with the most amazing daughter. Now that I had her opinion, I was ready to make my decision.

While showering and changing before the trip back to my parents' house, I processed the conversation I'd overheard in the fitness center. What had gotten Dean Terry so irate she kicked everyone out and threatened a student for asking so many questions? I was certain she'd gone to see my father about the presidency, but given the reaction, that didn't seem logical anymore. I tried to connect all the dots, but it was time to visit Nana D.

Between the new paella recipe she was testing out and the scrumptious coconut cream pie, I was in a food coma for most of the evening. "Nana D, I might need to crash here tonight. I don't think I'm capable of driving home the way I feel," I mentioned while rubbing my stomach and curling up with a blanket on her couch. As I wrapped myself in it, I fondly remembered spending cozy afternoons in the summer with her and Grandpop while they'd babysat us as young children.

"I've been telling you it's about time you came home and moved in with me. I'm not getting any younger, and that daughter of yours needs my guidance."

She dropped off a cup of tea on the end table next to me. "And this four-week teaching gig you committed to your father ain't gonna cut it, brilliant one."

"I know what you mean. There's something going on at Braxton that might be a reason for me to stick around longer. Dad doesn't want me to talk about it. I respect his need to keep the information quiet, but it's a hard decision, Nana D."

"You must be talking about those plans to expand the college, huh? Don't think I haven't already heard about them." Nana D sank into the recliner across from me. "Not that your parents ever thought to mention it to me. I've got my own ways to keep in the loo."

"I think you mean in the loop." It hurt to laugh at her confusion, but I pushed through it. "I should've assumed you picked up clues somewhere. I won't even ask how this time."

Nana D sipped from her teacup, exorbitantly satisfied with herself. "Good boy. What do you think you're gonna do about the new university? Is the offer big enough to convince you to stay?"

"I'm excited about the opportunity to build an entire college program that could put our town on the map one day. Then again, I'm not keen on working for my father. We've struggled to get along too much in the past." I'd been considering it in between all the activities keeping me focused on the murder investigation, but I consistently arrived at this causing a huge family rift.

"Set some ground rules with the man. Tell him what you will and will not do. If he doesn't agree to abide by 'em, then you know it won't work out. But if he says he will, you've got an opportunity most people never see fall into their lap. Tis could help launch your own career and get one of them television shows too," Nana D said.

I agreed with Nana D about the new role putting me in the spotlight with Hollywood. I could use those connections to find support and funding for my own true crime show. Maybe even center the first episode around what was happening at Braxton this semester. "I should sleep on it. I promised Dad I'd let him know tomorrow since the big announcement is next Monday about both the new college president and the expansion plans."

"In that case, tell me what's going on with the investigation. Figure out who murdered those two ladies yet? I asked the sheriff yesterday, but that woman's lips are sealed tighter than this new denture cream I'm trying out." Nana D clicked her jaw, then proved she couldn't easily remove them. She was on a roll this evening.

I said, "Sheriff Montague doesn't like to take risks. I can understand that, but I'm planning to see her tomorrow. Connor mentioned they'd have the results of the analysis on what they found under Lorraine's and Abby's fingernails."

"I finally got the lowdown from someone else on the Board of Trustees. She's confident that anonymous donation came from Marcus Stanton himself —that's why he's been so secretive. If he's the one pushing for all the improve-ments to the athletic facility and team, then he's the person the blogger has it out for. Not your father as much as I love seeing him get roasted," Nana D said.

Nana D and I chatted for another hour despite not coming to any specific conclusions. When we couldn't come up with any reason Marcus would want to hide his donation, we called it a night. Nana D had already made up one of the guest rooms, and I crashed within minutes of hitting the mattress. Her offer to live at Danby Landing made the whole prospect of moving home a lot more tolerable. Giving the same sort of experience I had as a child to Emma was a comforting thought.

* * *

After a solid night's sleep, I hightailed it to the office early on Friday to accomplish as much as possible. Once the quizzes were graded, I dropped them off with Siobhan, who'd stopped into the office for a few hours. She planned to scan and enter them into the student system for me, then return them to my desk, so I could deliver them to the class the following week.

Although I tried to talk to Striker after class, he was one of the first students out the door. I was stuck answering questions from a more talkative kid who wanted to tell me she'd watched *Dark Reality* reruns the night before and loved my episodes. I appreciated the compliments, but between my desire to corner Jordan and Carla and the need to avoid brown-nosers, I ended the conversation as soon as possible. By lunchtime, I desperately needed a break and something to eat. I'd only had a small piece of cake at Nana D's and was starving.

Maggie was in a staff meeting again. My mother was knee-deep in reviewing profiles of all the students to whom they'd finally settled on offering acceptance. She planned to verify all the state's guidelines had been met, so there was a fair balance of diversity among the prospective class. With no one else around, I visited Grey Sports Complex in case Coach Oliver hadn't eaten. I didn't relish the idea of sitting down to a meal with him, but it'd be an opportunity to elicit some facts. As I strolled down the hall on the third floor, I heard loud voices in Coach Oliver's office.

"I didn't do it. I swear. Believe me." Coach Oliver was adamantly defending himself from something, but I couldn't tell who was with him.

"If you won't cooperate with me, I'm happy to make a formal arrest in a more public setting. I am giving you a chance to willingly come downtown with me, but if you insist on screaming at me, I will detain you right here and now," Sheriff Montague calmly replied.

I turned the corner and found Officer Flatman and Connor standing outside the door. In the office, Coach Oliver pointed his finger at the sheriff and refused to leave. Everyone turned and looked at me.

"Just what we needed. An audience with a penchant for being the second coming of Miss Marple," said Sheriff Montague.

"I'd prefer to think of myself as Hercule Poirot if I need to be compared to a literary character from nearly a hundred years ago, *April.*" When she frowned at me, I shrugged and turned to Coach Oliver. "What's going on here?"

"Tell her I'm innocent, Kellan. I didn't kill Lorraine and Abby. I'm being framed."

Connor pulled me aside while Officer Flatman and the sheriff applied more pressure on Coach Oliver to stop resisting them. He explained the results of the fingernail analysis and a second test they'd run on Coach Oliver's car. I hadn't known about the last one. Then again, I suspected Sheriff Montague didn't feel compelled to tell me anything about the case. After the sheriff revealed what she'd learned from Abby's journal, validated Abby's call discussing an eight thirty meeting had come from Coach Oliver's office, considered Lorraine's call to me accusing Coach Oliver of something, and discovered the suspicious note in Lorraine's hands when she was killed, Coach Oliver admitted he'd been dating both women. He claimed that when Lorraine had confronted him, they argued, and she left. When the test results on the red fibers under Abby's fingernails definitively matched the baseball team's jackets, Sheriff Montague convinced Judge Grey to issue a warrant to search Coach Oliver's house and car given his connection to both women and potential presence at the scene of both crimes. That's when the sheriff found stronger evidence she couldn't ignore.

A few drops of blood on the passenger seat in Coach Oliver's blue sedan matched Abby's DNA. I had suspected Coach Oliver all along, yet while I wanted to pin the crime on him, I wasn't feeling confident we had the whole story—especially with the news about Marcus Stanton being the anonymous donor. Coach Oliver was assuredly part of the grade-changing scheme, but there was more going on than anyone knew at this point. I had to prove it.

"What about Lorraine? Any evidence he pushed her out the window?"

Connor smiled, then breathed loudly. "There were also fibers found under Lorraine's fingernails. I suspect both women tried to stop him and grabbed onto his jacket. Maybe there was a brief struggle in Abby's office where she grabbed the killer's jacket, then ran away toward the stairs. In Lorraine's case, she probably reached for the killer before he pushed her out the window. In the process, it transferred fibers. The sheriff also found fragments of skin under Lorraine's fingernails. If they turn out to be Coach Oliver's, the sheriff will arrest him tonight."

"Can't anyone buy those jackets in the school store?" They were mostly for the baseball team, but it wasn't as if they'd been custom or specially given to select individuals. I thought it might have been the gift Lorraine was searching for.

"That wasn't the gift, Kellan, but it was the third supposedly missing item from Diamond Hall. Coach Oliver swears he dropped off a new jacket for Lorraine the day of the party after he'd received the shipment, but she never saw it. These were the new ones just issued for the upcoming baseball season. Very few had been sold or given out," explained Connor. "Only Coach Oliver had possession of them, except for the players and cheerleaders. The sheriff is checking with anyone who received a jacket to see if those have a rip or any damage."

"So now what happens?" As I posed the question, Sheriff Montague led Coach Oliver away in handcuffs.

"I'm taking him into custody, so we can convince him to tell us everything. When I know more, I'll share it with you, Little Ayrwick. For now, I'd appreciate you keeping this quiet. I trust you can handle these instructions," the sheriff said with a pointed stare that gave me the chills.

"Yep, I understand," I replied to the sheriff, then turned to Connor and shared the details of the conversation Bridget had overheard with the scout.

"It lends more credence to why it was so important for the baseball team to do well this year. If Coach Oliver was holding out for a job at the Major League Baseball organization, he needed to look good when his best friend, the scout, was onsite. Coach Oliver was probably doing anything he could to keep Striker on the team, all the while working with Jordan as a backup." Connor stepped further into the office and checked on Officer Flatman's progress. "I will need a list of everything you find and take from the office. This might be a murder investigation, but this is still college property. There could be confidential information in here."

Officer Flatman acknowledged Connor's request. "We can start with this note I found under his desk."

I poked my head inside to hear what they were talking about. "A note?"

"Yes, Coach Oliver was holding it when I walked in, but when the sheriff placed the handcuffs on him, it fell to the floor. He kicked it under the desk."

When Connor asked to see the note, Officer Flatman handed it to him. He read it aloud.

You're an amazing baseball player who deserves to be the starting pitcher at this Saturday's game. I hope I can make this happen for you. I'm behind you all the way and won't let you down again. I believe in you and will do whatever it takes to help you take the lead spot.

Connor and I turned to one another. I was certain he had the same thoughts. "It's identical handwriting, isn't it?"

Connor pulled up the image he'd shown me on his phone earlier in the week. We compared the two notes and smiled. "Exactly the same."

"But what does it mean?" It made no sense why Coach Oliver had this note in his possession. It would be stupid of him to write a message to a student in such an open manner, which meant he was probably not the author. It also could have been about Striker or Jordan. Maybe the person who wrote the note was hoping to fix Striker's grades to get him permission to play again or to help Jordan by having Striker forced off the team permanently for cheating.

Connor instructed Officer Flatman to deliver the note to the sheriff as soon as possible. He turned to me and said, "Other than Striker himself, who's been angry about him not getting to play?"

"My first guess would be Marcus Stanton, but he was busy at the retirement party or board meeting when Abby was killed. Nana D confirmed he was in a council meeting when Lorraine was pushed out the window. Carla Grey has some explaining to do regarding her waffling support between Jordan and Striker," I replied. It was time I got to the bottom of whatever game she was playing.

"While we wait for the sheriff's team to catalog any additional evidence, do you have a sample of Carla's handwriting?" asked Connor.

"I might." I tried to remember what was in my possession. After recalling I'd left all my class materials in Diamond Hall, I told Connor I would check my office. We agreed to touch base later that evening to outline a game plan.

I took off on foot back to Diamond Hall. I shuffled through all the papers on my desk but couldn't find the recent pop quiz. Then I remembered dropping them off with Siobhan to photocopy, enter into the grading system, and return to me before classes next Monday. I thought it was odd and quickly scanned my email to see if she'd messaged me about them. And she had. Siobhan had taken the papers home with her to get the work finished on the weekend while the babies were sleeping. Since I didn't have her phone number, I replied to Siobhan's email asking her to upload Carla's quiz as soon as possible and to send me a copy. I also left an urgent message for Myriam to provide Siobhan's home number.

Two hours later, I was fully caught up for my classes but still had no updates from Siobhan or Myriam. Before leaving, I texted Connor with my current status. He was just departing Braxton for the night after the sheriff's crew had finished their search of Grey Sports Complex. The sheriff mentioned she wouldn't arrest Coach Oliver until they could review all the evidence over the weekend. Coach Oliver would be free to leave the precinct later that evening.

When I arrived home, I offered to cook dinner since my mother was running behind from visiting Eleanor. I made garlic bread and threw together a pasta dish with zucchini, tomatoes, orange peppers, and a white cream sauce. It was already getting late, and I didn't want to have a full stomach when I went to sleep. It would be important to get enough rest to prepare for tomorrow's game and hopeful discovery of the killer.

I mentioned the concerns to my father about what I'd overheard in the fitness center regarding students' fears over the recent deaths. He was grateful and understanding at the same time. After recalling I had heard nothing about the mysterious blogger, I said, "I haven't seen any new blog posts about you. I guess Dr. Castle is behaving herself?"

"As I mentioned previously, the blogger is not Myriam. In fact, we've solved the situation." My father reached for another piece of garlic bread and sampled a glass of the wine I'd poured with dinner. "There won't be any more blogs being written about me."

"Can you tell me who wrote them?" If it wasn't Myriam, I had no other suspects in mind unless that was the reason he'd called Dean Terry to his office.

Was she lying through her teeth to me about supporting the athletic program? Or tossing out confusion in various places?

"Not yet. After Monday, I can share the name with you. Sheriff Montague is convinced it has something to do with both deaths and has asked me not to discuss the person's identity with anyone."

"This is all getting too frightening," added my mother. "I'm wondering if Nana D has a point about this crime taking too long to solve."

"Your mother is a gossip, Violet. She's not content unless there's someone or something to complain about. This is just more fodder for her to sink her teeth into," my father replied.

"Nana D is right, Dad. Tomorrow is two weeks, and the sheriff hasn't made a lot of progress. Just today she dragged Coach Oliver back in for questions, but I've been telling her all along to dig deeper into his alibis for both nights."

"Kellan's right, Wesley. He's more on top of this than Sheriff Montague," my mother said.

"Let's agree to let this go for now. Murder's no topic for dinnertime," my father announced, pushing his plate away and changing subjects. "I'm able to move back into my regular office after tomorrow's baseball game. The movers will have my desk and belongings returned to the executive building. Things will finally be back to normal again."

"I'm sure moving back and forth was difficult, Dad." It's always about his inconveniences.

"Speaking of moving, I believe you owe me an answer."

"I believe you are correct. And I believe you gave me until the end of today, right?"

He nodded.

"Then I've got a few hours left."

My father stood, raised his finger as if he wanted to chastise me but thought better of it, and left the room mumbling to himself.

"Do you really think that's how to solve your problems, Kellan?" asked my mother while scraping food from his plate onto hers to carry them to the kitchen. "I don't see how you two will ever work together if you're both so similar and intent on aggravating one another all the time."

Similar? What was she talking about? I was in no way, shape, or form like my father. Was I? After retreating to my room, I stewed like a child who'd been reprimanded by his mommy for doing something bad. But I had done nothing wrong. They'd given me until the end of the day. It was only dinner time. I knew I needed to make my decision. When it was approaching midnight, and I still hadn't come to any conclusion, I admitted she was right.

CHAPTER 22

I continued to second-guess my decision regarding acceptance of the new role, despite tacking a note to the door on my father's study at precisely one minute before midnight. I spent most of the night listening to the wind rustle through the trees while I laid awake staring at the ceiling. After a quick breakfast, I verified my decision was no longer fastened to the door, which meant he'd read my pronouncement. I should've told him in person, but he'd been sleeping when I'd come to my conclusion, and I didn't want to talk about it anymore last night. I packed my gym bag and drove to Grey Sports Complex.

Upon arriving, I proceeded to Coach Oliver's office to determine if he'd returned from the precinct and was prepping for the afternoon game. With his head on the desk, the disgruntled man snarled at me. "Some help you were yesterday. I just got done a few minutes ago. Now I have to figure out how to motivate the team when I feel like I've been hit by an eighteen-wheeler." The dark circles under his eyes convinced me he'd been telling the truth about being up all night.

"It's time you leveled with me, Coach Oliver. There's something you've been hiding. Why not get it out in the open? You'll feel better." I had to go with my instincts. The sheriff wouldn't have released the man if he was the murderer. I felt safe alone in his office. "Let's start with why they didn't arrest you."

"My attorney has advised me not to discuss it with anyone." He shrugged and squarely set his jaw, then relented. "Fine, I guess I can tell you if you promise to help me." Coach Oliver waited for me to agree, which I did, knowing I could back out if it involved anything illegal. "My DNA wasn't a match against whatever they found under Lorraine's fingernails. The blood they discovered in my car was a match with Abby's, but her nosy neighbor verified she'd watched Abby cut herself in my car weeks ago. There wasn't enough to hold me any longer."

"I guess that's a good thing for your case, but you still don't have valid alibis for either murder, do you? I don't believe you about dropping the schedules off for my father the night Abby died. You were at Diamond Hall to see her, weren't you?"

"All right, yes. She agreed to chat at eight thirty to discuss Striker's grades." Coach Oliver explained he'd been about to enter the back of the building to meet Abby when Lorraine whispered his name. After Lorraine led him to a nearby bench, he handed her the schedule and talked for ten minutes. Once she walked back to the building, Coach Oliver took off and contacted Abby, but she never picked up the phone. He went to the retirement party, assuming Abby would call him back at some point, then ran into Eleanor at nine when it was about to end. My mother had seen him after Lorraine left him. "That sheriff has no clue what's going on and wants to close the case, so she doesn't look foolish," Coach Oliver noted.

I agreed with him, but taking a stance on Sheriff Montague's intelligence wouldn't help me. "I'm sure they're looking at other suspects besides you. What about the note under your desk?"

Coach Oliver's head jerked back in alarm. I'd caught him off guard and temporarily speechless. "Ah, I'm not exactly sure. I won't deny it. That cop saw me hide it."

"It's illegal to conceal evidence. I'm sure you're aware they could charge you with something for that," I added, hoping to scare him into talking more. "You must have told the sheriff something about it."

Coach Oliver explained how he'd been finding notes since the semester started from someone claiming Striker should be the starting pitcher. The person had previously left one for Striker, indicating they had ensured Striker's grades were good enough to lift the suspension. Coach Oliver had stolen the notes as he didn't want his star to worry or get in trouble. He hoped it was someone messing around. He grew alarmed when he got a second note and Striker's grades didn't match what Abby had earlier told him about an 'F.' He knew they'd been changed, but not how or why.

"I don't get it. Why was it so important for Striker to pitch?" I inquired while shaking my head. I went out on a limb to test a theory I'd been considering ever since Nana D conveyed the conversation Bridget overheard. "Does this have anything to do with the rumor about the scout helping somebody at Braxton get a job at the Major League Baseball organization? And that you happen to be the scout's best friend?"

Coach Oliver turned as white as a ghost. "How do you know about that?"

Bullseye! "Were you hoping that by ensuring Striker played in the game, you'd have a better chance of getting that job? Was it some sweet executive position? Access to all the major league teams?"

"No, you've got it all wrong," shouted Coach Oliver as he paced the room. "From the beginning, I wanted both Striker and Jordan to play. I care about the guys and want them to land a contract with one of the Major League Baseball teams after graduating from Braxton. That's why I privately coached both last semester and encouraged the competition between them. I needed my buddy to see how well they both played and draft them into the leagues."

"So, you're saying the league job isn't for you? This is entirely for the players?"

"Right, I don't want to leave Braxton. I love working here, but I was being blackmailed."

"I don't understand what you're saying." I pushed him to explain the complete story.

"Last fall, Marcus Stanton approached me, suggesting he knew I needed improvements in the athletic department. He offered to buy new gym equipment, returf the baseball field, and fund our technology."

"Isn't that a good thing?" I asked, suddenly arranging things together. It was Marcus Stanton threatening my father on that call I'd overheard. He didn't want anyone to know he'd made the anonymous donation, but I couldn't figure out why. It might've looked a little self-centered if he were donating money that helped his stepson, but that wasn't enough reason to be so secretive.

Coach Oliver explained how Marcus made an anonymous donation indicating a majority needed to be allocated to whatever Coach Oliver said was a priority for Grey Sports Complex. Marcus had only one condition. He wanted his stepson to be the only star—Coach Oliver had to convince his best friend, the Major League Baseball scout, to recommend Striker join a team after graduation. When Coach Oliver said he couldn't do that, Marcus Stanton revealed his knowledge of the secret relationship with Lorraine Candito. He planned to expose Coach Oliver if he didn't agree to the deal. Blackmail was a much better reason to remain anonymous with his donation, so it looked like two vastly different transactions.

"I cared so much for Lorraine and didn't want her to get hurt, plus I didn't want to get in trouble again. They'd fire me, and I'd be out of a job with no chance of being hired ever again. That stupid policy was put in place because of me, and I wasn't supposed to be dating anyone from the college at all. I finally agreed to force my buddy to recommend Striker to a major league team."

Coach Oliver explained once Striker failed his class last semester, Marcus demanded he fix Striker's grades. Coach Oliver tried to convince Abby not to fail him, but it didn't work. He later tried to wine and dine her, which started changing her mind. She considered being easier on Striker by using an academic Bell Curve grading style to help him pass, but when Abby found out about Lorraine and Coach Oliver, she realized he was just using her. When she threatened to report him to the Board of Trustees and my father, he revealed Councilman Stanton's blackmail scheme. Coach Oliver wanted to meet with Abby the night she died, to pass Striker and prevent her from exposing the entire situation.

I recognized the similarities between Coach Oliver's explanation and Alton's conversation with Abby before she died. She'd stumbled upon all this happening and thought she could write an exposé about small-town sports and politics. "I'm still not sure why he was so worried about donating in his name. He's also got alibis for both murders unless he hired someone else."

"Marcus didn't want to interfere with Judge Grey. He'd been the primary person to fund the athletic facility in the past, hence why it's named after his family. Stanton is also running for mayor in the next election. He wanted everything to look squeaky clean. He's not a killer. If people thought he was bribing the scout to get his stepson onto a Major League Baseball team, they'd never vote him into office," Coach Oliver said.

"They'd probably strip away his role as a councilman too. Is this absolutely everything you know? You've lied several times before." I scowled. As slippery as he'd been before, I believed him this time.

"Yes, Marcus can't hurt me anymore now that Abby and Lorraine are gone. I've got nothing to lose. He won't reveal anything as it would hurt him too." Coach Oliver ushered me toward the door. "I need to get ready. My buddy is coming by to watch Jordan play, since Myriam won't release Striker from his academic probation. At least I can give one of the players a chance. Maybe with Jordan finally earning his opportunity, Dean Terry won't give me any nasty glowers and interfere in today's game."

I stopped short in the hallway. "Wait! What did you say?"

"Dean Terry's been attending all the games this past year. She's always looked dismayed over my interactions with Jordan," Coach Oliver replied. "It's like she wants me to show favoritism because she's his aunt. I'm so tired of the games women play." When he finally closed the door, I stood in the hallway, more stunned than when I'd arrived.

If Dean Terry's nephew had a chance to be the team's starting pitcher and get noticed by the scout, how much would she manipulate behind the scenes to ensure no one took that opportunity away? Was Dean Terry trying to make it look like Striker was cheating or changing his grades, so he would get put on probation? I left Grey Sports Complex and shuffled to the BCS Office in search of Connor. I wanted him to be with me when I called Sheriff Montague, but he wasn't around. A student employee radioed Connor, who indicated he'd be done with his security checks on the field in an hour. I planned to meet him near the hotdog stand on the west side of the bleachers at eleven thirty.

I dashed to the cafeteria to buy a cup of coffee and logged into the student system to retrieve Carla's and Striker's contact information. I needed to meet with them both before the game started, to learn as much as I could about their actual activities the night of Abby's murder. Striker picked up my call and told me he was leaving his dorm room and on his way to the field to meet with Coach Oliver. Although he still wasn't allowed to play in the game, Striker had to support his teammates and warm up in the bullpen in case anything changed with his probation. I asked him to meet me at a quarter after eleven before his practice began. When he agreed and hung up, I tried to reach Carla, but she didn't pick up her dorm phone. I'd have to try again after I met Connor and Striker at the field.

I scrolled through my email but had nothing from Myriam or Siobhan, which meant I couldn't yet check Carla's handwriting against the note we'd found in Coach Oliver's office. I left the cafeteria and began my hike across North Campus toward the baseball field. I took the longer route as I had several minutes before it was time to meet Striker. After passing the last set of academic buildings, I heard my name being called. I turned and saw from a distance Dean Terry jogging toward me. I stood on the far side of the campus, not remotely near any other buildings. It was a half-mile walk to reach the parking lot for the sports field, which meant I would be alone with Dean Terry for too long. Although I could defend myself, two women had already been killed.

"Dean Terry, what brings you along this path? It's a little out of the way to get to Grey Field." I stepped several feet away. Everything I'd learned could be a coincidence, I reminded myself.

"Oh, I was getting ready to attend the game. It's gonna be an important one." Dean Terry was a bit winded from trying to catch up with me. She wrinkled her brow and pulled her bottom lip into her mouth. "Then I saw you walking by, and well, I had to follow you."

"Yes, big game. I would never have pegged you for an enthusiastic sports fan. Back when I was a student, that didn't seem to be one of your focal points." I danced around the topic to gauge her state of mind before asking any direct questions.

"I know, me neither," she said, then reached a hand to grab my elbow. "I think you and I should talk. Do you have a few minutes to come back to my office?"

"Ummm... not really. I told several people I'd meet them at Grey Field. I wouldn't want to cause them to wait unnecessarily for me." I tried stepping away, but her grip was too tight.

Dean Terry breathed deeply. "I know you're aware, Kellan. I need a few minutes of your time."

Was she about to confess? Or get me alone to silence me too? "I'm not sure what you're talking about. Maybe we could chat at the field once I'm done? Connor Hawkins is expecting me any minute." I thought mentioning his name would keep her at bay if she was going to try anything. I didn't like the annoyed and distant look she was giving me.

"We can chat more later, but there's no pussyfooting around it, Kellan. The Board of Trustees didn't choose me as your father's successor. Your father insisted I couldn't talk to anyone about it until after the announcement on Monday, except for the Board and you. I guess that means you're aware of the expansion plans too. They told me I should feel honored over being asked to take a larger role in the new Braxton University. Some consolation prize, huh?"

It was then I realized Dean Terry wasn't stopping me to discuss her role in the grade-changing scheme or either of the murders. "I didn't know they gave the presidency to the other candidate. I thought they would choose you." I wasn't exactly sure what had transpired, yet I felt like it was better to stay on her good side. "I'm so sorry. Do you know whom they selected?"

"I don't. They wouldn't tell me. Thanks for your understanding. Once I found out I was their second choice the other day, it annoyed me. When I ran into you, I genuinely thought they were going to offer me the job. I was a real witch when I got back to my office afterward. I have to apologize next week to everyone who saw me get heated."

The conversation I'd overheard with the students made sense now. I felt like I could ask some questions about Jordan without causing too much suspicion. "I heard your nephew will pitch today. You must be excited."

Dean Terry nodded. "I'm proud of how well he's done. I feel bad Striker is still on probation. I even tried convincing Myriam there was no proof Striker was involved in the grade changes. While we suspect his exam isn't his own work, Braxton doesn't have enough evidence to suspend him. She wouldn't budge. That woman is a piece of work."

"Are you saying you didn't want to put Striker on academic probation? I assumed you agreed with Myriam." I was glad she openly admitted Jordan was her nephew, but her support of Striker confused me.

"No, I urged the need to complete an investigation and thorough analysis, but this has gone on long enough," she replied. "Without Striker on the team, Coach Oliver is much harder on Jordan. I prefer when he can split his focus between them. The coach is trying to strengthen their confidence, but he's a monster with motivating and training them."

"That's why you've been issuing dirty scowls at Coach Oliver?"

Dean Terry explained she'd never thought Jordan could break into the big leagues when he was in high school. He was a cocky kid who had little discipline. In the last few years, she finally saw him prove his pitching prowess. That's when she took a bigger interest in his baseball career and changed her tune about the sports program at Braxton. Coach Oliver didn't like her getting involved on his turf and had misread her intentions for getting tangled in his department's operations.

"Wow, I wish I knew this sooner. I never realized you were his aunt. By the way... did you visit Jordan the night of my father's party? Jordan mentioned you'd stopped by."

"Yes, I'd forgotten I left the party to give him some encouragement. He'd only gotten home a few minutes before I showed up at nine. He'd been out on a date and just left the girl's dorm room," she replied. If that were true, then Carla and Dean Terry corroborated his alibi. Dean Terry might have had time to leave the party, kill Abby, then visit Jordan, but it seemed unlikely.

"How did your self-defense class go?" She wouldn't understand why I asked, but it might finalize the open issues with her alibi.

"Never made it. I got pulled into an urgent call with your father and showed up tardy. There was a sign on the door indicating no late arrivals, so I went back to the office." Knowing that cleared up the confusion and meant Dean Terry wasn't a murderer, I wished her success in her expanded role at Braxton. I sidestepped the conversation about why I'd known anything about the plans for the new university since she didn't need to know whether I was going to join the project. While her explanations left minor doubt over her guilt, casting her as the murderer had too many holes. I was missing something but couldn't prompt a breakthrough.

As I took off in the direction of the baseball field, breathing a sigh of relief I hadn't been a third victim, my phone rang. It was Myriam. "I'm not used to being summoned on a Saturday with another crucial college issue, Mr. Ayrwick. I'd have thought with your father identifying the blogger this morning, you would be busy figuring out what that was all about. Surely, you have a good reason to disturb me?" Myriam knew the blogger's identity.

"My father has mentioned no names yet. I will ask him again soon."

"It was Monroe. Apparently, she'd been pressuring him about the donations, but he hadn't put it all together until you started asking questions about who installed the new technology systems at Grey Sports Complex. She was a classic fool worthy of Shakespeare's court jesters."

"How did Abby post that last article after she died?" It didn't add up.

"It was the very last thing she did. She'd been writing the blog while walking around the retirement party, set it to post the following day, and then went back to her office. I checked the date and time stamps and validated it was last saved at eight o'clock."

"How do you know this?"

"When I received the materials from her office, I found her username and password for the blog. I tried to log on, and it worked. Once I confirmed it was her account, I saw all the posts. That's when I updated your father, Connor, and the sheriff." Myriam sounded too smug in her explanation.

Myriam's news timely explained why my father was so busy this morning. "I apologize. I only contacted you because of an urgent police matter. I need a copy of some exams that Siobhan took home to upload into the grading system."

"You're quite obsessed with grades. Were you a poor student when you attended Braxton? Is it a self-confidence booster to point out when someone has tampered with a student's grades?"

Given she brought up the subject, I requested a status on the analysis she held up. "Dean Terry said she's recommended closing the investigation and allowing Striker to play today."

"Mr. Ayrwick, I've turned over everything to Dean Mulligan. Everyone on the committee has weighed in as of an hour ago. There will be a decision on Monday. I'm sorry this means your little friend, Craig Magee, cannot play today. There's more to life than tossing a ball around for a few hours."

"I appreciate your candor. I'll keep it in mind," I said politely. "And Siobhan's number?"

"*All the infections that the sun sucks up. From bogs, fens, flats, on Prosper fall, and make him. By inch-meal a disease!*" Myriam growled in disgust.

"Surely you're not comparing me to an insect or an illness. Is that the most appropriate quote you could summon, Myriam?"

She rattled off the phone number and hung up without a goodbye.

CHAPTER 23

On the walk to the field, Siobhan returned my call. "I'm sorry I missed your email, Kellan. I've been so busy with the twins and scanning all the exams, I hadn't checked my account."

"No worries, I understand. If it weren't important, I wouldn't bother you over the weekend."

Siobhan confirmed she would log online when she got home that evening to email me a copy of her exam. When I asked what her schedule was for the next few weeks, she mentioned they'd hired a temp to fill in while everything was sorted out with the new chair of the department. "I'll be onsite three mornings a week to transition everything in the meantime. I'm also asking the student employees to work a few extra hours. I'm sure they can use the money since your father cleared the expense for the short term." Siobhan put me on hold when a baby cried.

I'd forgotten about the student workers in the communications department until Siobhan mentioned them. When she returned, I said, "I met one worker, Bridget. I don't believe I know the other one."

"Yes, I'm not surprised. Bridget's fantastic, very enthusiastic. I was none too pleased when they assigned the other girl to me last semester. She's always late and barely did any work."

"Why wouldn't you ask for a reassignment? Or fire her?" It seemed logical to me. I'd rather not have to deal with someone incompetent for the next few weeks while I taught Abby's classes.

"There's no firing Carla. Can you imagine Judge Grey's fury if I gave his granddaughter the heave-ho? That might cost me my job, Kellan." Siobhan laughed loudly before adding, "And with two little ones at home, that's not an option."

Wow! How did I miss that fact? I hung up with Siobhan, checked my watch, and rushed off to meet Striker. He was leaning against the dugout wall when I arrived at Grey Field's baseball stadium. Given he was dressed in his uniform, I didn't have the heart to tell him based on Myriam's latest status that he had no chance of playing in today's game. I felt awful holding that information from him, but knowing his current or former girlfriend might be the person who killed Abby and Lorraine seemed far worse.

"Hey Striker, how are warm-ups going?"

Striker tried to smile despite his face's refusal to comply. "I'm in decent shape. Part of me wants to head home, but the coach won't let me leave. He says I need to show the scout I'm a contender."

"He's right. The scout's seen students deal with academic probation before. He cares about your pitching consistency and attitude on the field. Not what the dean says about the results of one exam," I added, feeling the soft spot I had for the kid, reminding me to give him a boost. I hoped he wasn't the murderer.

"I don't understand what happened with that test. They won't show me the paper, but Dr. Castle says she believes the version she graded wasn't mine. How does that occur?"

I asked Striker to clarify exactly what he remembered transpiring around the time of the exam. He explained that Profess Monroe had promised to grade it over the weekend and let him know the following week before the next practice. Then he heard she'd fallen down the steps, and everyone was searching for the exams. Coach Oliver had called Striker last Friday afternoon to say he'd gotten a 'B+' which meant he could play in the game. At the pep rally, everyone was excited he could still play. Then Dean Mulligan called a meeting and told him there was suspicion over whether it was actually his test results.

I had no reason to suspect Dean Mulligan, but I should check his alibis. "Now what happens?"

"I meet with the dean again on Monday to review the exam they're saying isn't mine. My stepfather's gonna kill me if I don't make it to the major leagues."

"I'm sure they'll figure it out soon. I'll see if I can attend the meeting. Would that help?"

Striker nodded. "You've been really cool about this. I wish you'd been my professor all along."

Everyone wanted me at Braxton these days. "Striker, I have to ask you a sensitive question. I wouldn't ask if I didn't have a good reason, but I need to share something confidential with you. Can I trust you not to talk to anyone else about it?"

"Yep. You're the only person on my side. Of course, I'll answer anything you want."

I asked Striker why he'd left and returned to the fitness center on the day Lorraine died. He explained he didn't want to be around Jordan, then mentioned a few people saw him in the sauna and could confirm he was present until he finished working out. I'd verify it later. "Have you ever been given or found any notes about helping you pass your classes so you could play on the baseball team? Or has Coach Oliver ever told you about them?" I hesitated in revealing something the sheriff wouldn't want to be shared, but it might yield me valuable insight.

Striker jerked back with a shocked expression. "Notes? Like emails or text messages?"

"Not exactly. A piece of paper taped to your locker at Grey Sports Complex? Or something through the mail?"

"Nope. Got no clue what you're talking about, man. Did someone say I did?"

"Nobody's said you did anything, Striker. I'm trying to piece together a very peculiar puzzle. So, you do not know of anyone tampering with your grades, telling you they did anything, or sharing any sort of communication about you deserving to play in the baseball games?"

"Seriously, I'm clueless. This is turning out to be a horrible senior year. First, I can't play baseball. Then Carla dumps me. I just want to go home."

"What are you implying, Striker?" Alarm bells were going off, but I couldn't figure out why.

"I might as well tell you. She's the one who looks bad, not me." When Striker kicked the dirt, clouds of dust wafted by us. "Carla was just interested in me because of the scout. When she thought I had a chance of getting into the major leagues, she threw herself at me last semester. She and my stepfather kept pushing me to do better, so I could get a lucrative contract. But as soon as I got put on academic probation and the scout looked elsewhere, Carla distanced herself."

"I'm not surprised. I must admit I didn't get a positive vibe from her when I saw you two together at last week's game or in the classroom this week. She's very flirtatious with other guys."

"I was too distracted by everything. I didn't notice it. That's why I lied to you last week about where she and I were the night Professor Monroe died. Carla and I had a few drinks in the dorms, but it was much later than I said. I was at the fitness center most of the night. We met up at nine thirty."

"I don't understand why you couldn't say that when I asked," I complained, recognizing Carla was looking increasingly suspicious.

"I didn't want to contradict her in front of you since we were already fighting all the time. I figured if I agreed with her, she wouldn't start something again. She said we were together because everyone assumed the professor's death wasn't an accident. She didn't want anyone to think I killed the woman over my poor grades. I guess Carla was covering up that she was cheating on me with Jordan that night," Striker said.

"I think you're partially right. When did she break up with you?"

"When I was put on probation again and couldn't play for the scout, Carla told me she needed space to think about whether she could be involved with someone who was suspected of cheating."

Based on Striker's news, neither he nor Carla had a complete alibi during the window of time when Abby was killed. Striker explained that the scratch on his arm was from Carla when they had a fight about his return to academic probation. He was glad not to deal with Carla's frequent physical attacks whenever she didn't get her way. Once he left for the dugout, I walked to the hotdog stand near the west bleachers and located Connor. "Able to give the all-clear for today's game?"

"Yes, we're in solid shape. With two murders on campus, I'm more cautious than normal."

"I have to admit, security seems to be lacking around here. I don't mean any offense, but anyone can walk in and out of the academic buildings. Grey Sports Complex only has security cameras and card readers in a handful of places. Grades or exam results are being changed." I took the risk of antagonizing Connor, but it had to be said.

"You're absolutely right. That's part of the reason your father hired me. The previous director had gotten lax about protocols. There have also been significant changes in the national security requirements around colleges and universities given all the school shootings. We've got a two-year plan to bring everything up to standards."

"You've got your work cut out for you."

"I'm glad to have your help, Kellan. Just be careful how integrally involved you get. I've been in the middle of some nasty wars in the past. What did you need to talk to me about?"

I updated Connor on all my conversations. While he put a call into the sheriff, I scanned the stadium. Bridget was talking with Dean Terry in the stands on the third base line. She had on the giant green parka again today, but in her defense, the temperature had dropped quickly. The latest weather report mentioned another blizzard from the north in the coming days. I studied the crowd for anyone else I knew. Nana D hovered a few rows behind them, near Marcus Stanton. I watched them interact for a few minutes, and as the time passed, their discussion grew increasingly animated. By the time the game started, the councilman had thrown his tray of fries on the ground and stormed up the steps to the exit.

Then Derek called to tell me the results of his big meeting with the executives. They weren't happy with his season two plans. Instead of giving him another chance, they fired him. While Derek had already found himself another gig, he advised me to be ready for news from the network about my future.

Jordan pitched for all the innings while I forced myself to ignore Derek's news. Since we were the home team and ahead going into the ninth inning, when the Millner Coyotes failed to pick up any additional runs during the top half, the game was over. The Bears had won both of their games so far this season, and the crowd was intense with excitement. Dean Terry was cheering, Nana D was performing some a mock Moon Dance, and Jordan's teammates carried him off the pitching mound. It was exactly what the campus needed to keep its mind off the murder investigation.

With the event concluding and the fans heading back to the parking lot for post-game parties, Connor and I called the sheriff to reveal our latest news. We searched for a quiet area in the stadium and found a table under a covered awning.

"I appreciate your help, Connor. We spent another round here at the precinct going through the alibis for everyone who was recorded entering or leaving Grey Sports Complex. Officer Flatman will drop off a copy at your office tonight to do a final compare to see what doesn't add up."

"How about Carla Grey? Any chance you remember if she was included? Now that we know she was lying about her whereabouts the night Abby died, she's clearly at the top of the list," I said, unable to help myself. Connor had asked me not to speak, but I couldn't keep my mouth shut.

"Yes, she was on that list, Little Ayrwick, as were at least six other people who might not have alibis the night of Abby's murder. Cross-referencing every-thing is not as easy as it sounds. Nor do I intend to incur the wrath of Judge Grey or Councilman Stanton if we don't have an airtight case against either student."

Connor chimed in. "So, April, how do you want to handle talking to the suspect?"

"I think our best chance is to get Carla to meet with me. If she thinks it's about her last exam or something to do with class, she might slip when I ask questions about the nights of the murders." She was hiding something. I could feel it. Nana D would say it's a sixth sense unique to the Danbys, but I wasn't so certain. I was skilled at reading people who had something to conceal.

"I agree asking Carla about her dating life or what she does while working in the communications department would come across better from you. And she wouldn't run to her granddaddy because you asked to meet," Sheriff Montague replied.

"Exactly, which is why—"

"But," she continued, "verifying her alibi for both nights is something my office should handle. I'm willing to concede it's also something Director Hawkins could ask as part of a campus review on access control. I will make you a deal. While you two are talking to her, I want to be present. I will be sitting nearby listening in, so I can stop you if you're doing anything to ruin my case."

Connor attempted to speak, but I interrupted him. "Connor used to be a police officer. I'm sure he's qualified to keep my conversation with Carla from causing any detriment to your case."

"That's not my point. It's my butt on the line here. If anything goes wrong, I'll be held responsible for allowing you to do this," the sheriff argued. "I don't want to be accused of setting up a witness and then not being able to arrest her."

"Are you saying you don't trust me?"

"I wouldn't trust you if you were the last person on the planet and I needed your help to survive. I'd rather let the zombies eat my flesh alive than turn to you as a savior. I'm only giving this a chance because Connor will be present."

I distinctly heard the obnoxious guffaw of Officer Flatman in the background. Connor had the decency to stifle his outburst. I'd caught her referring to him as *Connor* again. That professionalism sure came and went like my aunt Deirdre's fake British accent. She'd moved to the UK years ago and was notorious for using it whenever it worked to her advantage, but it was sure gone when she drank.

After we all made our concessions, the plan was to invite Carla to The Big Beanery the following morning. While I was dialing her number, Connor received another call and stepped away. After Carla picked up, I mentioned I wanted to meet with her about the upcoming term paper. "My schedule is packed next week, and I know it's last-minute notice, Carla. I was hoping maybe you wouldn't mind getting together tomorrow."

"Sure, would ten work? I can only stay for thirty minutes. I usually meet my grandfather for brunch on Sundays, but he lives on Millionaire's Mile, which isn't too far away."

"That's fantastic. Bring any handwritten notes. It'll help us complete the full outline for your paper. I appreciate it."

"You're welcome. It's always hard to say no to a cute guy," she replied in a kittenish tone.

I'd only talked to her the one time outside of class, but I'd never picked up this type of direct flirtation with me before. Was she really acting that way toward her professor? I assumed I'd read into it and let it go for the moment.

"Excellent, Miss Grey. See you tomorrow." I hung up, eager to tell Connor about the call. When he returned to the table, I noticed his puzzled expression. "What's up?"

"You'll never believe who contacted me."

"Well, don't keep me in suspense. Out with it." If it were Nana D playing another game or my father trying to cause trouble, I would scream in frustration.

"The facilities crew was moving your father's desk out of storage. Since everyone was at the game today, they finished the relocation, so he could have his office back on Monday."

"Wow, scintillating. Who would have thought an office move would get you so worked up?"

"Cut the sarcasm, man. They accidentally bumped the desk into the handrail while walking up the steps. They couldn't hold on, and it went sliding down the staircase."

"Oh, no. Not his antique mahogany desk. The one he found at the historical auction years ago?"

"Yes." Connor shook his head back and forth, then reminded me that my father had asked for his desk to be moved to storage once the sheriff had placed a lockdown on access to Diamond Hall's upper floors. After the sheriff had done a quick check on the desk the next day, she cleared Braxton's facilities department to store the furniture. Today was the final move back to his post-renovation office.

171

"Ummm... okay... what's got you so unnerved?"

"Does your father play the clarinet as one of his hobbies, Kellan?"

I knew the answer was no. But I also remembered that Bridget's clarinet had gone missing two weeks ago. "Did it have blood on it?"

"That's what I'm about to go check out," Connor said.

CHAPTER 24

After Connor took off to meet the facilities crew, I returned to Diamond Hall to retrieve my briefcase and download Siobhan's emails. When I compared the photo of the note we'd found in Coach Oliver's office to the handwriting on Carla's pop quiz, some letters were almost identical. A couple on Carla's paper were much loopier and grander. I needed Connor's advanced security system to be certain, but he was busy checking out the potential murder weapon discovery. He sent me a text that while the clarinet had some damage, it could've been from the fall and not from hitting Abby. The sheriff's team had confiscated the instrument and would run tests overnight. He'd update me the next day before we met with Carla Grey.

I went home only to find my father locked in his study and not in a position to talk. Sheriff Montague was already in there. I didn't dare interrupt that conversation, no matter how much I wanted to be a fly on the wall. While I believed there had to be a reasonable explanation for the missing clarinet's presence in his desk, I knew my father was in no condition to be questioned once his beloved antique piece of furniture had been destroyed. Once I heard the sheriff leaving, I checked with my mother. She begged me to let it simmer overnight. I agreed and proceeded with other important tasks.

Cecilia verified that Emma was excitedly packing for her trip. I called Nana D to let her know the latest news and made plans to stop by the next day. We agreed on a late brunch, as she had something important to tell me about a decision she'd made. Was she going to finally retire from Danby Landing altogether? While most of the staff handled the day-to-day tasks, she still went to the daily farmer's market, decided on what to grow each year, and found ways to reuse and recycle everything she could on the land to help protect the earth. Her latest focus had been a study in composting, and while I applauded her efforts, the last time I'd been there I recommended she move the pile further away from the back door. It was not the most pleasant of odors, and no matter the deliciousness of her baking, it couldn't overpower overly sweet or rotten fruit.

I also found time to research and select a restaurant. I thought Simply Stoddard near the riverfront would be a perfect backdrop, so Maggie and I could have dinner on Tuesday evening. I confirmed a time with her and scheduled a reservation, still contemplating whether it should be for two or three. If I brought Emma, it might make the conversation much easier and lighter, but it would also mean Maggie and I would spend the time getting to know one another again rather than discussing Connor. As I pulled up the bedcovers, I closed my eyes and prepared for my conversation with Carla the following morning.

* * *

"Livid. That's the only word I can come up with right now," my father said while slamming his fists on something inside the kitchen on Sunday morning. "I will have to find a specialist to repair that desk, and it will take weeks if not months. Now what am I supposed to do, Violet?"

I'd been standing outside the door in the hallway listening to their increasingly tense disagreement for the last few minutes, debating whether to wander in and surprise them or make a decent amount of noise, so they knew I was about to enter.

I pretended to stub my toe on the kitchen door and made a splashy entrance as if I were in pain. It would make me feel better about interrupting their conversation and let them quickly cool down, so there was no embarrassment over their argument. As near as I could tell, my mother wanted my father to hire a lawyer, but he was insistent he had nothing to hide.

"Ouch! I can't do anything without coffee. Why am I always walking into things?" I whined and winced while entering the kitchen. The room was overly chilly when I hobbled to the counter to pour myself a cup.

"You need to be more careful, honey," my mother said, standing near the back door and staring into the backyard. "And wear some shoes. Then you won't hurt yourself."

I nodded. "How was everyone's night?"

"I'm leaving for Braxton. I need to see the damage myself and find out if there's any hope for a repair," my father said while exiting the room.

"He's a bit grumpy, huh?" I poked around the cupboard and looked for something to eat.

"Your father refuses to acknowledge Sheriff Montague is out to get him. And he doesn't want to cooperate with her on the investigation." My mother settled into the breakfast nook and sighed.

"What happened?" I spread Nana D's raspberry jam on a corn muffin and took a huge bite.

"Your father was tired of moving offices back and forth between the renovations and the eventual move when he retires from the presidency. He told them to put his desk in storage until he made a final decision. He was worried that something might happen to it once it became apparent how easy it was for a murderer to sneak around campus. Nothing sinister."

"And the clarinet?" I asked curtly. "I'm assuming few people knew about that secret panel?"

"Lorraine knew, but his best guess is someone playing games by hiding things. He doesn't know how they found out about it," my mother replied with increasing desperation. "This has to end, Kellan."

"I know, Mom. It's been a rough two weeks. I've got a little experiment prepared. It might help bring this to a close soon. I'm sure Dad's telling the truth. The sheriff will figure it out before long." I knew this morning's discussion with Carla would be fruitful, and I hoped everything would come together by the end of the day.

"I appreciate it. I've got to get ready for church." My mother kissed my cheek and shuffled out the kitchen with a heaviness that tweaked my heart.

An hour later, after a quick run and shower, I pulled into the parking lot at The Big Beanery. I located Connor, so we could compare notes.

"There wasn't any blood on the clarinet." The anguish in Connor's voice was concerning.

"I don't understand. Does it mean that's not the murder weapon? Is this all a coincidence?" There had to be a logical explanation, but it wasn't obvious to me.

"It could be many reasons. Maybe the killer wiped it clean and hid it there, thinking someone would discover the lost clarinet and assume it was a practical joke." Connor shook his head and inhaled deeply. "The sheriff hasn't told me everything yet."

"There were those thefts too. I suppose it could be unrelated to the murders," I added, then checked my watch. "Carla will be here in ten minutes. Where's April?"

"A slight change of plans. *Sheriff Montague* came across some additional evidence this morning and wanted to check it out. She's assigned Officer Flatman to monitor us." Connor pointed to the corner where a man with a snow hat and giant fuzzy sweater sat. "See him?"

It took a minute, but I finally recognized him in his disguise. Officer Flatman looked like an ordinary patron of The Big Beanery, enjoying a cup of coffee and reading the paper on a Sunday morning. "Okay. I guess it's a good sign she has confidence in us."

"She has confidence in me. I have specific instructions to shut you up if you cross any lines with Carla," Connor said authoritatively. "Don't make me use force on you if I have to."

I acknowledged his sarcasm and ushered Connor out of the café, so he could reenter after Carla arrived. I ordered a cup of coffee at the counter, then walked to the table near the corner behind Officer Flatman. "How's that article on cross-stitching?" I whispered as I sat.

"Shut it, Mr. Ayrwick. The suspect just walked in," he replied.

Carla waved hello and came by. As she peeled off a heavy winter coat, I told her to place an order at the register, and they'd deliver it with mine in a few minutes. While waiting, I assumed her conservative skirt and long-sleeve baby-blue sweater were par for the course when meeting her grandfather for brunch. The pearls gently bouncing around her neck as she walked back to the table were an even nicer touch. Maybe I didn't have it so bad in the Ayrwick family.

"Thanks for buying my coffee, Professor Ayrwick."

"It's the least I could do for asking you to meet on a Sunday morning," I replied as she sat across from me. "What did you think of yesterday's game? You must have been upset Striker wasn't pitching."

A hesitant smile formed on her lips. "Nah, Striker had his chance, but he screwed that up. I'm with Jordan now. He was awesome yesterday. I'm sure that scout's gonna find a place for him in the major leagues."

A trail of steam rose from her cup. As it dissipated near her cheek, I considered how to keep her talking about the baseball team until Connor arrived. She seemed relaxed for someone who might have committed two murders. "Oh, I misunderstood. I didn't realize things ended between you two. I'm sorry."

"Don't be. He wasn't the right guy for me. I want to be with someone who has a future. Someone who can impress my grandfather." Carla's hand reached part way across the table and closer to my coffee cup.

"I guess that explains why I saw you and Jordan together a few times this week at the... ummm... diner." It was an awkward way for a professor to mention noticing his students making out. Nor was it any of my business, but it would get her to tell me more. As I grabbed hold of my cup, Carla rested her hand on top of mine.

"Oh, that... yeah, we just started dating. You know how it is. Sometimes I think I should be with someone older, more established." Carla smiled at me and squeezed my hand.

I quickly pulled back and faked a yawn, so she wasn't touching me. She was clearly flirting with me at the same time as telling me she'd dumped Striker for Jordan. "You're so young. I imagine there are lots of things you want to explore one day. It must have been a shock when Striker was on probation again. I'm helping him next week when he meets with Dean Mulligan."

My phone vibrated. When I looked at the screen, it was Nana D. I couldn't take the call and sent it to voicemail. I'd feel the wrath later, but this was more important. She'd eventually understand.

"Someone needs to help him. I tried studying with him, but schoolwork's not his thing, ya know?" she said, tapping a finger against her temple. "But I can tell you are into—"

Luckily, Connor interrupted. "Kellan, Miss Grey, two of the people I've been searching for."

"Hi, Connor. What can we do for you?" I asked. Carla turned in his direction and smiled.

"I'm trying to complete the remaining interviews with anyone who was near

Grey Sports Complex the day of Lorraine Candito's accident. Could I ask you both a few questions? Should only take a few minutes." Connor was exceptionally smooth, making it obvious why he'd gone into the security field.

"Sure, we don't have a lot of time. Carla and I are going over her term paper, and she's meeting Judge Grey in a few minutes."

After he pulled up a chair, Connor studied Carla first. "I'll make it quick. So, you entered the building around a quarter to five from what the security camera recorded. Do you remember seeing Mrs. Candito? I'm trying to figure out if anyone knows what kind of mood she was in. Perhaps she was sad or upset, and it led to her drastic decision to jump."

Carla shook her head and widened her eyes. "It's so awful, but I heard it may not have been suicide. Is there any truth to that rumor?"

"I'm not sure what the sheriff thinks. I'm trying to confirm a timeline in case there was anything Braxton could've done. Can you clarify the times you were onsite? I take it you didn't see her?"

"Nope. Let's see... I ran the indoor track for an hour from five to six. Freshened up and went to the student union building to check my mail about six thirty, then met up with my boyfriend, Jordan. Didn't we see you at the cable car station around a quarter to seven, Professor Ayrwick?" Carla replied, sipping from her cup and sitting back in the chair.

"Yes, I thought I saw you. Couldn't stop since I'd been on my way to meet Lorraine. I guess you never saw her, huh?"

"I would have said hello and helped her if she was upset. I worked with her at Diamond Hall," Carla said, saddened by Lorraine's death and unlike someone who could have killed her.

My phone vibrated with another call from Nana D. I sent it to voicemail again. Hopefully, she would remember I had an important meeting this morning and stop calling soon. If not, I'd turn off the device until we finished.

Connor pretended to ask me a few questions, then said, "I appreciate it. That addresses two more people on my list. Anything else you might share, Miss Grey?"

"I don't think so. I should finish talking to Professor Ayrwick about my term paper." She pulled out a new copy from her bag and placed it on the table. "There are a few changes to discuss regarding Hitchcock's early movies."

It contained a bunch of handwritten notes in the margins. I looked up at a smiling Connor. "Oh, that's great. I had some ideas for you too."

Connor interjected. "Can I look? I'm a huge Hitchcock fan. What's your paper about?"

As Carla explained her theory, Connor pretended to check something on his phone. I knew he was bringing up the images of the notes we'd found. He looked at me and shook his head quickly. I couldn't be sure what he'd meant and lifted my eyes in confusion.

"It looks like you've got a great outline here," Connor advised, pocketing his phone. "I don't think it matched my expectations of what I thought you'd write about, but I'm sure you'll do well."

He was trying to tell me the handwriting didn't match. I worried she was clever enough to disguise her penmanship on the notes. "Well, I guess you've got everything you need, Connor? Anything else I can do to help you?"

My phone vibrated again. This time it was a text message from Nana D.

Please call me as soon as possible, or I'll slap you silly later. I found something. Crucial.

Nana D's urgency could be anything from a secret episode of *Myth Busters* to a new recipe for German chocolate cake. I would call her back as soon as I finished with Carla.

Since Connor was leaving, I could offer Carla a few tips on the paper and end this charade. We'd learned absolutely nothing except she wasn't guilty of murder. Probably guilty of leading Striker on and dumping him for a potentially better opportunity. Possibly guilty of flirting with every available man. But there was little reason for her to be involved in changing grades. She simply wanted to find a guy to impress her grandfather and was even considering me. Not that there was any chance of it happening.

"No, I'm going to let everyone know what I've found out today and head back to my office. I'll be in touch if I need anything else," Connor said before walking out the door.

Officer Flatman departed thirty seconds later to compare notes before they updated Sheriff Montague. I turned to Carla. "Well, that was weird. What were we talking about before he stopped by?"

"I was saying someone needed to help Striker learn how to study. And that I was glad to have your help on my paper." Carla reached for my hand again. Luckily, I was too quick and grabbed my coffee cup.

"I imagine Striker didn't take the news well about the break-up, huh?" I needed to stop her from flirting with me. If she talked about Striker, maybe she'd eventually feel guilty for what she'd done.

"He's a big boy. He can handle himself. I'm sure the girls will be lining up for him. Speaking of girls lining up for someone—"

If I didn't nip this in the bud, I was going to have a big problem. "Miss Grey, I need to make you aware that your attempt to flirt with me today is not something I can reciprocate. You are one of my students, and I make it a policy *never* to get involved in any personal relationships with them. It is also against Braxton's rules of conduct—"

"Oh, lighten up, Professor Ayrwick. I'm just playing. Girls flirt all the time. If you knew how often dozens of them tried to seduce Striker in the past. The obsession one of them had! So ridiculous."

"What do you mean?" I feared Connor and Officer Flatman had left too early.

"Ugh! This one girl has been in love with him forever. She goes to his games and stares at him all the time. It's creepy if you ask me." Carla shoved the term paper into her bag. "She came on to him at the game yesterday and didn't look happy with Striker's response. I saw them talking during the seventh inning stretch. He practically had to shake her away to get her to leave him alone."

"Do you know the girl's name?" I asked, desperate to find out what she knew. This was going to be the major break in the case I needed.

"Yeah, I work with her. She always acts like I don't exist and purposely forgets to tell me things to do for the professors. Listen, I need to meet my grandfather. Maybe we could chat again?"

"Hold up. You're not talking about Siobhan, are you?"

"No way! Bridget Colton is the fruit loop in love with Striker."

CHAPTER 25

My brain entered overdrive to assemble all the information I'd learned in the last few days. I couldn't believe how obvious it had been. "Tell me everything you know."

"She's always sneaking into his dorm to talk to him. She almost caught Jordan and me together when we got back from the movies the night Professor Monroe died."

"What do you mean? Where did you see her?" My heart raced as everything plunged into place.

"Jordan escorted me to my dorm and was about to kiss me goodbye. Bridget came running onto the floor, all freaked out. I thought she saw us as she dropped her clarinet case. I remember laughing when I noticed she was wearing one of the new baseball jackets. They wouldn't be put out for sale in the school bookstore until the following week for the new season, and already she'd bought one. That's one obsessed nutjob!"

Nana D rang my phone again and out of sheer shock, I hit the accept button. "I can't talk—"

"Kellan, I've been trying to reach you. Why didn't you pick up?" Nana D sounded exasperated.

"I'm with a student. Can I call you back?" I tried to stop Carla from putting on her coat.

"No. This is important. I found something," yelled Nana D.

Carla tossed her bookbag over her shoulder and waved to me. "Professor Ayrwick, I need to go. I'm gonna be late, and my grandfather will get angry."

"No, wait," I whispered to Carla.

"Nana D, hold on, please."

"Kellan, I was cleaning out the compost pile after you read me the riot act about the smell. I think I found the weapon used to kill Abby," said Nana D in a hushed voice. "Please get here as soon as possible."

Knowing it must have been Bridget all along, my stomach sank. She worked in the communications department. She had a crush on Striker. She claimed someone had stolen her clarinet. "Okay, Nana D, give me a few minutes. Don't hang up yet."

I turned to Carla. "I might call you in a little while. Will you answer the phone, please? I need to know if there's anything else you can remember about Bridget."

"That's all I can think of, but sure." As Carla scribbled her cell number on my free hand, my mind exploded with new connections.

After Carla left, Nana D rambled on before a gigantic crash occurred. "Bridget, what are you—"

"What's going on?" I shrieked in a panic.

A few seconds later, Nana D said, "Let's not be hasty, dear. We can talk this out."

Then a dial tone blasted through the phone. Bridget must have walked in and had seen what Nana D found in the compost pile.

I grabbed my jacket and dialed Connor to tell him what I'd learned. He would call the sheriff and meet us at Danby Landing. I drove as quickly as I could to save my nana. If anything happened to her, I wouldn't know what to do with myself. I loved my parents, but the bond and connection I'd built with Nana D would always be the one I felt the most. She'd showed up in Los Angeles a few weeks after Francesca's funeral, setting up camp in my small three-bedroom house to look out for Emma and me until we were ready to start a new life on our own. For the first few days, Nana D had entertained Emma and taught her how to cook. There were days I couldn't even leave the bedroom. The thought of Nana D being caught in Bridget's web of lies was too much to bear.

I slammed on my brakes and turned off the ignition in the Jeep. I didn't even bother to close the door and instead raced into Nana D's house. Upon arriving, I heard them arguing in the kitchen. I stopped short in the doorway when I noticed Bridget holding a knife on Nana D near the back counter.

"Please don't hurt her, Bridget. We can figure this out," I muttered with little remaining breath.

"I'm so sorry. I don't want to hurt her." Tears streamed down Bridget's cheeks, highlighting a genuine fear and concern for what she was doing. She must have known she was losing control.

"Why don't you tell us what happened? Nana D's a superb listener. She's always helped me figure things out." I needed to keep her talking until Connor or the sheriff arrived. The more people to stop her, the better.

"It just happened. I never meant to kill her. Believe me." Bridget tightened her grip around my grandmother's waist with one hand while her other pressed the knife against Nana D's throat.

"Are you talking about Professor Monroe or Lorraine?" I asked.

Bridget closed her eyes and bit her lip. "Professor Monroe caught me changing Striker's test results in her grade book. I was trying to help him. I loved him. I wanted him to play in the game, so the Major League Baseball scout would choose him."

"Tell us what happened, Bridget. Walk me through what you were thinking." I watched Nana D struggle a little, but she looked relatively calm for being held hostage.

"I was so angry when she failed him last semester. I'd changed his grade once before, but somehow Professor Monroe caught it and assumed she'd made the mistake. I thought if I could change his grade just one more time for that first exam, he'd be allowed to play in the opening game. I didn't think anyone would discover the switch until much later. By then, Striker would have impressed the scout, and it would all blow over." Bridget pulled Nana D closer, and the tip of the blade landed against the small indentation near my grandmother's windpipe.

"I saw the original 'F' in the grade book. What were you doing to make the changes?"

Bridget explained she'd stopped by on the evening of the retirement party to change the exam's grade but had gotten distracted by the jacket Coach Oliver had dropped off for Lorraine. She put it on, pretending Striker had given it to her as though she was his girlfriend. "I had a blank copy of the exam and copied over some of his answers, then I altered a few to ensure it looked like he had a 'B+' instead of the 'F.' I had already put the updated version back into the folder for Lorraine to enter into the student system. I was changing the mark in Professor Monroe's grade book when she found me in her office." Bridget swallowed deeply, internalizing the pain over reliving her crime.

She hadn't fully thought the scenario through. Even if Abby hadn't caught her that night, Abby would've eventually realized it when she entered the grades into the student system. Bridget didn't know Abby let no one else access her class materials or students' exams and papers.

"It's okay, honey," soothed Nana D. "You wanted to help your friend, Striker. Is that all?"

"Yes, he was always so nice to me in the beginning. I hated the way Carla Grey treated him. She's a mean girl. I thought he would realize it one day and dump her. Be happy I was helping him. I left him all those notes, but he told me yesterday he never got them."

Coach Oliver had purposely kept a couple of notes from Striker, so the kid couldn't ever be accused of knowing what was going on. I applauded the coach's efforts to protect the players, but if he'd told someone, none of this would have gotten out of hand. "What happened when Professor Monroe found you in her office?" As I stepped closer, Bridget gripped Nana D tighter around the waist.

"She was furious and accused me of working with Coach Oliver and Councilman Stanton to bribe the scout. I had no idea what she was talking about. Professor Monroe picked up the phone to call campus security. I freaked out. I didn't want to get in trouble and told her I wouldn't do it anymore. But she wouldn't listen to me. She said I needed to be punished, and that she would see to it."

"Is that when you did something to her?" I noticed out of the corner of my eye Sheriff Montague approaching the back door. She held her finger to her lips and nodded to the side. I assumed that meant she'd brought backup with her.

"Professor Monroe started dialing BCS. I pushed her away to stop. We struggled for a few minutes, and that's when she ripped the jacket I'd stolen from Lorraine. She must have been scared and tried to leave. I followed her to the hallway and begged her to give me another chance, but she wouldn't listen. As she was rushing down the back steps, something came over me," cried Bridget. "I don't have anyone else, and she was going to take the only thing I had left."

"What do you mean?" Nana D stretched for something behind her on the counter.

"My parents are dead. I have no real friends. I just had Striker and school. Professor Monroe would've blabbed about what I'd done. I'd be kicked out. I grabbed that stupid award from Lorraine's desk and ran after her. I hit her on the head, thinking I had to stop her. Then she fell down the stairs."

As Bridget broke down crying, Sheriff Montague snuck through the door. Nana D was able to reach a cherry pie she had cooled off on the counter. By the time Bridget realized what was happening, Nana D smashed the pie into her face. Sheriff Montague tackled them. I grabbed the knife from Bridget's hand during the commotion and backed away.

Officer Flatman sprinted through the front door and placed handcuffs on Bridget. Connor hurried through the back door. I hugged Nana D, finally able to breathe again.

Sheriff Montague said, "We have a full confession to Abby Monroe's murder. We just need to find out what occurred with Lorraine Candito."

"What happens next?" I felt bad knowing Bridget was desperate and had no one to support her. I was furious she'd killed someone I cared for very much, but it wouldn't bring Lorraine back.

"I'm going to take her in. She may not talk until her lawyer arrives. If she can't afford one, the county will appoint a public defender," the sheriff replied.

"There's no hope for me now. I thought Striker would give me a chance now that he and Carla are over. But he rejected me at the game yesterday. I might as well tell you everything," whispered Bridget. Officer Flatman had been leading her out the back door to read her Miranda rights when she stopped him.

"You should wait for an attorney," Nana D replied, still wanting to protect someone she'd grown fond of the last few weeks. "I'm disappointed in you, but don't get yourself into worse trouble, dear."

Bridget refused to wait for her lawyer to explain the details. Everything made sense once I heard the entire saga. After Abby fell down the stairs, Bridget panicked. She overheard Lorraine and Coach Oliver talking outside the door and rushed back up the stairs to hide the weapon. The first thing she could find was her clarinet case. She remembered seeing Lorraine hide a bottle of whiskey for my father behind a secret panel in his desk, so she went to the third floor and put her clarinet in its place. Then she put the award, which was similar in size and shape to the clarinet, inside the case and hid upstairs.

When Lorraine ran out after first discovering Abby's dead body, Bridget left with her clarinet case, assuming she could come back for the actual clarinet the next morning. She rushed across campus and back to her dorm room where she convinced herself everything would be okay and that everyone would think Professor Monroe had fallen down the steps and hit her head. She hadn't thought the award would leave a gash and pieces of metal on the body. The next morning, she went back to get her clarinet but saw all the police tape and couldn't access the building. She transferred the award to her backpack and went to her music lesson with Nana D, where she asked to borrow Nana D's clarinet. When lessons were done, she tossed the award at the bottom of the compost pile, thinking no one would find it, and if they ever did, it couldn't be linked back to her.

"And when you went back to retrieve the clarinet, you reported it lost?"

"I thought everyone would just assume someone had played a practical joke on me, or there was a thief taking a bunch of things from the building," noted Bridget.

After the sheriff had publicly deemed Professor Monroe's death an accident, Bridget thought she'd gotten away with it. Although she felt awful, there was nothing she could do but eventually find the clarinet and say someone had returned it to her.

Bridget then explained what had transpired with Lorraine. When Striker was put on academic probation after we discovered his exam was a fake, Bridget went to Grey Sports Complex to leave another note for him and Coach Oliver, confirming she'd fix it again. While Lorraine was in the locker room, Bridget placed the note on the desk and left his office. She was walking down the hallway when suddenly Lorraine had come back to the office.

"You hid in the conference room and overheard my conversation with Lorraine?" I realized Jordan had missed seeing Bridget by only a minute or two.

"I thought I'd been caught. It was so hot in there, I needed to open the window. I couldn't get the lights to turn on. That's when I bumped into the table and chairs. Lorraine must have heard the noises after she hung up with you and came into the room," Bridget said.

"Did you push her out the window?" I asked, hoping Bridget wasn't that cruel.

"No, it was an accident. Lorraine approached me while I was near the window. We struggled in the dark. When I shoved her to get away, she fell through the window. I didn't mean to kill her." Bridget wailed and tried to dry her tears, but Officer Flatman had her hands held tightly.

"Bridget was one of the last names on my list to investigate. I made a connection between the missing jacket, Bridget entering Grey Sports Complex just before the murder window, and her job in Diamond Hall. Then everything came together, especially after I spoke with Dr. Castle this morning. That's why I couldn't meet you at The Big Beanery," Sheriff Montague said.

"Myriam knew about Bridget's responsibility for both murders?"

"No, Bridget's name kept popping up in different conversations after Dr. Castle shared the fraudulent exam. Dr. Castle pulled some other papers from students in different classes and thought she'd found a match to the manipulated one. I don't think she suspected Bridget of anything more than changing a few grades from time to time."

Once most of her team left, Sheriff Montague approached me. "You did a fine job, Little Ayrwick. Officer Flatman let me know you followed all my rules earlier this morning. Thank you."

"You're welcome. I never expected Carla to reveal anything about Bridget flirting with Striker. Once Connor and Officer Flatman left, I thought we'd finish talking about her exam. I got lucky."

"What do you mean by that?" asked the sheriff.

"Carla started flirting with me. I called her out, and she made a comment about girls flirting all the time," I said, thinking about how Sheriff Montague had spoken to Connor recently.

"Not all girls behave like Carla Grey, Little Ayrwick. Some are much subtler when they're interested in a man." Sheriff Montague glanced at Connor, then turned back to me.

I don't think Connor picked up on it. If he did, he wasn't letting on. "I'd like to think so. When she mentioned a girl flirting with Striker, I asked more questions, and that's when it all fell into place."

"It's a good thing you were at the top of your game, Little Ayrwick. The Wharton County Sheriff's Office is grateful for your unsolicited help, but I'll remind you in the future to stay out of my investigations. As you can tell, I am more than capable of solving things on my own." Sheriff Montague asked Connor to walk her out, so they could cover a few things.

While the sheriff might have figured out it was Bridget in the same twenty-four hours I did, it wouldn't have been possible had I not pushed for alternative suspects and discovered the issue with the grades. But I'd never get credit for it again. I would have to be happy with her minor concession when stating the Wharton County Sheriff's Office was grateful for my services.

When I saw the murder weapon being bagged and tagged, my chest twanged. I recalled the conversation Lorraine had referred to earlier in the week. I'd forgotten how much I'd told Lorraine on the phone the day after I lost the award for my work on the first season of *Dark Reality*. I had called my father to reveal Derek won, figuring it would be easier to hear from me than anyone else. He wasn't available, and I'd vented to Lorraine about the whole thing around Thanksgiving. I'm usually not myself around that holiday and have a challenging time balancing my emotions. Lorraine was overly sweet on the phone. She told me I was the only reason she watched the show and deserved to beat that nasty Derek what's-his-name. It looked like she had a replica of the award custom-made, complete with my name. I appreciated the sentiment, knowing how much I'd miss the woman.

Nana D was fine, just a little shook up. She'd been brewing tea and defrosting cinnamon buns while the sheriff and I talked. "I guess we won't be able to eat the cherry pie I baked!" She laughed, knowing there would be more in my future. After everyone else walked out, Nana D said, "Flirting with college girls doesn't suit you, Kellan. I thought I brought you up better than that."

"What? You were the one trying to set me up with Bridget. Last time it was a two-time bigamist, now it's a two-time murderer," I whined. What leg did she have to stand on?

"Pish! I never once did that. I knew all along Bridget was trouble, and that's why I pushed you together. I thought you'd figure it out eventually, but you're still a little slow on the uptake there, brilliant one. Maybe next time." Nana D checked her cinnamon buns and deemed them ready.

I rolled my eyes at her. "For the record, I would never be interested in someone like Carla Grey."

"I sure hope not, Kellan. Things are already about to get ugly enough for our family." A devious smile formed on Nana D's face. "No more shady connections, please. We've got things to accomplish."

"What did you do now?"

"I heard a rumor Councilman Stanton is planning to announce he's running for mayor of Wharton County in the upcoming election," she replied. "His role in this crime was the final straw."

"Yeah, and what about it?" I could feel my insides trembling. She wouldn't.

"He's no good. Someone needs to stand up to that man."

"What exactly does that mean, Nana D?" She couldn't possibly.

"I've been polling a few folks around town, and well—"

"Nana D, you can't!"

"Oh, but I can. I've got a press conference scheduled one hour earlier than his tomorrow." She slapped her hip and started dancing. "Let's go. Come help me pick out something to wear for my big news! Mayor Seraphina Danby has a magnificent ring to it, doesn't it?"

CHAPTER 26

I spent the rest of Sunday afternoon answering questions for the sheriff, rehashing the entire experience with Eleanor, and preparing for the week's classes. We needed to tell everyone on campus the truth, but it would have to wait until the public relations department sorted all the details for their press release. I fell asleep early thinking I'd received enough shocking news since discovering Bridget was the killer and learning about Nana D's decision to run for mayor of Wharton County. Little had I known, Monday would be the day when the shocking revelations pushed me over the edge.

I finished teaching my first broadcasting course in the morning. I only agreed to a one-year contract with the potential to renegotiate again. I still couldn't be sure how well my father and I would do working together, but I was comfortable enough to give it a shot given the school wouldn't allow someone to work directly for their spouse or family member. I could only work for my father on the conversion to Braxton University because there would be someone between us once they hired more staff. And I desperately needed that middleman until I heard about my future on *Dark Reality* from the television network. The LA honchos said to wait two weeks while they decided my fate.

In between classes, I spoke with Alton Monroe to confirm the details for Lorraine's funeral later that week. We'd partnered together to assemble a special remembrance service for a woman we both would miss. Lorraine had been like an aunt to me, which made me realize how much I'd lost touch with my family in the last few years. I promised myself to do a better job and stay in frequent contact with everyone, even pull together a family reunion that summer.

The last time I checked, the Board of Trustees was meeting with the new president to determine whether there would be any formal action taken against Coach Oliver for his role in hiding information and misleading Braxton during discussions with the Major League Baseball scout. Unfortunately for Striker and Jordan, the unethical aspects of how the scout ended up on campus prevented them from being offered any contracts to join a team through the Major League Baseball organization. Carla dumped Jordan when that happened and was already in search of her next victim. Striker and Jordan both told me they were focusing on finishing the semester with their heads held high and a prayer to get accepted into the minor leagues.

Nana D's press conference revealed to the entire county her candidacy for Wharton County mayor. I noticed several people including Eustacia Paddington hooting and hollering on the television. I hoped that meant their war over Lindsey Endicott was on hold, or at the very least, they planned to behave like two civilized senior citizens competing for the man's attention. Nana D promised everyone if they elected her, there would be substantial changes. More jobs. Less red tape. No more shady business deals behind the scenes. And free ice cream in Wellington Park on Sundays. I couldn't for the life of me understand why, but her last promise got everyone the most excited.

I checked in with Connor to find out what was going to happen with Bridget Colton after her unique perspective on how to implement an academic curve within Braxton's student grading system.

"Sheriff Montague's charged her with both murders. Based on all the evidence and her public defender's request, Bridget will be detained in the psychiatric ward of Wharton County General Hospital for further analysis," he replied while the call was on speakerphone. Sheriff Montague was talking in the background, which meant she'd stopped by BCS to visit him.

"Thanks, Connor. I wouldn't have solved this without you," I replied loudly, hoping the sheriff would hear too. I couldn't help myself. Somehow, I would win over that sheriff with unequivocally adorable sarcasm. "It's a good thing we kept the Wharton Country Sheriff's Office in line, huh?"

"Listen, Little Ayrwick, one more comment like that, and I'll arrest you for—"

"For what, sheriff? Speaking the truth?" I replied with a rowdy laugh as I teased the woman.

"Try indecent exposure. Connor shared the story of a certain pair of purple lacy panties—"

"Okay, truce. I'm done!" I waved a white flag in defeat. No need to get into that conversation. I'd give Connor a piece of my mind for sharing with her the truth of that embarrassment.

After we hung up, I walked over to the Pick-Me-Up Diner to enjoy lunch with my sister. When I arrived, a big sign out front read *Now Under New Management*. A moment of worry crept inside me, wondering whether it meant Eleanor would be out of a job.

As I shut the door, the bell clanged above me, and she came running over. "We're closed for a few days this week... oh, it's you," shouted my sister.

If she was still there, it was a positive sign that Eleanor hadn't lost her job. "What's going on?"

Eleanor smiled at me. "Well, my former boss no longer wanted to be in the diner-running business after thirty years. He and his wife retired to Florida."

"Have you met the new owners?" Why hadn't she told me anything about it the last few times we'd chatted? The place was empty, and there was construction going on near the kitchen.

Maggie walked out of the kitchen wearing denim overalls and a bright yellow construction hat. A decent amount of sheetrock dusted her left arm and leg. "Kellan, what are you doing here?"

A flood of excitement surged inside me upon seeing Maggie dressed that way. It was the first physical reaction I had about another woman since Francesca was killed in the car accident.

"I guess there's no keeping it a secret anymore, Eleanor," Maggie replied.

After they finished laughing, my sister explained Maggie had stopped by the diner earlier that week to grab a bite to eat. One thing led to another, and they'd made two deals that afternoon. The owners had asked Eleanor if she wanted to buy the diner, but she couldn't afford to do it on her own. Maggie had always been fond of the place and thought it might be a fun adventure to take a risk on. Both had saved enough money to split the costs, talked to a local bank about a loan, and opted to go into business together. Eleanor would run the place day-to-day, and Maggie would be more of a silent partner helping when she had time away from Memorial Library. The other deal they made that day was about Connor. Eleanor and Maggie agreed they were friends first, and if Connor wanted to take them both on dates, they could accept it in the short term. Neither would interfere in the other's relationship, but once he made a choice, they would respect the decision.

That was a disaster waiting to happen! It's one thing to go into business with a friend. You might have a few fights, but usually there's a way to work through the tension. Add in the drama of both women dating the same man, and Braxton might become the center of World War III. I knew better than to talk them out of it, so I just congratulated them, confirmed Eleanor would still meet Cecilia and Emma, and listened to their renovation plans.

By the time they finished telling me about the new diner, I had to return to campus to teach my last class before the big announcement about the new president. On the walk back, I realized not only did it mean Maggie and Eleanor were both dating the same guy, but it also meant Connor and I were possibly dating the same girl. I still hadn't decided whether my dinner with Maggie would be an official date or a relaxing meal with a friend, but I knew my old feelings had been stirred up.

As if that weren't enough to ruin my afternoon, I also didn't get a free lunch out of my trip to the Pick-Me-Up Diner. I grabbed a bag of salt and vinegar potato chips from the snack machine and quickly shoveled them into my mouth. What had I done to myself? Whatever it was, I couldn't get sidetracked as the students settled in the classroom for my final lecture of the day. Three hours later, the entire school gathered in Paddington's Play House for the big announcement. My father had reserved a seat for me by the stage since they'd

189

be publicizing both his new role and mine. I looked around for my mother, but she was busy in a conversation with Dean Terry. I suspected my father asked her to keep the dean distracted since losing the Braxton presidency would upset her.

When I finally reached the front row, I ran into Myriam. She was dressed to the nines and had the silliest grin on her face. I honestly thought she might have just come from the plastic surgeon. I suddenly felt a tremor grow inside my stomach that she would be named the new president, but I was certain an outside candidate had ultimately been awarded the prominent position.

"Good day, Myriam. You look excited to be here," I said, hoping to keep the conversation civil. I'd had enough words with her the last few days to last a life-time. I also didn't want to bring up her discovery of Bridget's underhanded role in the grade changes.

"Kellan, I didn't expect to see you here today. I thought you were only sticking around for a few weeks. Since they've selected the new department chair, I'm certain we'll find a replacement for Abby in the next few days, and you can head back to Los Angeles." As Myriam finished speaking, the goddess I'd met at Abby's funeral joined her side.

"It's Kellan, right?" asked Ursula with a sparkle in her eyes.

I wasn't attracted to her as much as her elegance and poise impressed me. I was in awe of what I suspected might be as close to perfection as a person could get. "Yes, and you're Ursula Power. I met you at the funeral parlor this week. I'm a little surprised to see you here today." Unless she was our new department chair, which would make her both Myriam's and my boss. Interesting theory.

"Ursula is my wife, Kellan. I thought your father would have told you that already," Myriam replied. Her smile grew even larger. Not that I thought such a thing was remotely possible given the elasticity of a human being's mouth. Then again, she was part monster.

Wow! I would never have guessed Myriam and Ursula were a couple. A sourpuss and a goddess. If Ursula was Myriam's wife, there's no way she could also be the new chair of the department. I still didn't understand why she was present at my father's big meeting. Just as I was about to respond, someone on the stage asked everyone to take their seats, so the president could begin speaking. I leaned over to Myriam as we sat. "Do you know our new department chair's identity?"

"Yes."

"Are you going to share that news with me?" *It's wrong to hit a woman. Even Myriam Castle.*

"I'm your new *temporary* boss, Kellan," Myriam replied with a sinister look on her face.

I could do nothing but sink into my seat, wishing to disappear into its crack at the thought of my new queen bee. Not only would I have to obey my father for anything with the new Braxton University, but while I was teaching classes at the existing college, Myriam would have control over everything I did.

My father gripped the microphone and began his speech. After thanking us for attending, he informed everyone that the Board of Trustees had gone through a long and arduous search for a new president. He mentioned how it was a close race, and the runner-up was an amazing and brilliant candidate, but they'd chosen someone else to assume leadership as Braxton's next commander-in-chief. "It is my privilege to welcome our new president, Ursula Power, who...."

Now I understood why she was here. Not as Myriam's wife. Not as a new faculty member. But as the new head of the college. Even with Myriam being promoted to chair of the communications department, Myriam still reported to Dean Mulligan as the Dean of Academics, so it didn't violate any policies. Ultimately, the dean reported to the president and the Board of Trustees, which meant at that level, there were fewer concerns about people's relationships. I tuned out my father's speech while reflecting on all the repercussions of the changes going on in Braxton. When I found myself alert again, I caught wind of his change in topics on the stage.

"And it gives me immense pleasure to announce who will work with me to lead the new Braxton University. Please come to the stage, Professor Kellan Ayrwick and Dean Fern Terry," my father stated.

As I stood, Myriam's excruciatingly annoying grin finally receded. I found the strength to join Dean Terry, and together we marched up the stage steps and faced the crowd. All I could think about at that moment was that I'd gotten myself in way too deep with the stupid, ridiculous mistake of a move back home to Braxton. How could so much change in only two weeks? Dean Terry first took the microphone, sharing her excitement about Braxton's future direction. "Sometimes life throws you lemons. And then everyone tells you to make lemonade. But I don't like lemonade. Usually, it's too sweet. Other times it's too sour. When life throws me a lemon-size curveball, I throw it right back into the universe and forget about it. Kind of like our remarkable baseball team who's won all their games so far this year. Last year's failures are this year's wins. I have infinite plans for expanding our amazing institution, and nothing will stop us from achieving greatness."

I admired her ability to pick herself up by the bootstraps—not that she was wearing any mind you—and trudge forward despite initial setbacks. Should I look to her for how to handle my old, sourpuss spitfire lemon better known as Dr. Myriam Castle? Was Dean Terry motivating me to mix up some lemonade and douse it over my enemy-turned-boss? As I pictured the possibilities, she handed me the microphone. *Please don't let me screw this up!*

"I'm honored to be here. Before I say anything, let me get the obvious out of the way, right? You're probably thinking... *Not another stuffy Ayrwick running the show at Braxton. They're like pesky rabbits popping up all over the place...*" I caught both my parents staring at me with fear consuming their expressions. Then I heard laughter from the crowd."Or maybe you're worried I'm not quite committed to this new role? Let me assure you, I don't decide on a whim, and I never say *no* to a challenge. How else could I survive being the middle child of Wesley and Violet Ayrwick?"

My mother held my father back as he approached the center of the stage. I nodded at him and whispered, 'Trust me', which seemed to hold him at bay. "My parents gave me all their strengths, and I'm confident that I've learned from the best. I look forward to serving all of you as we take Dean Terry's lemons and kick them to the curb." The room erupted with a boisterous applause, and for a moment, I felt on top of the world despite everything that had happened or that I'd lost in the last few days.

Once the announcements were finished, I stepped backstage to steal a moment to myself. I wanted to stick around to talk to a few people, but Emma would arrive any minute, and she was exactly what I needed to make myself feel better and to find normalcy again. I heard my phone vibrate and retrieved it from my pocket. It was Eleanor.

"Hey, please tell me Emma is here, and all is right with the world again," I said.

"Yes, but we have a problem, Kellan."

"What's wrong? I worried Emma wasn't feeling well or Cecilia was being difficult about the extended stay in Braxton." I stepped into an offstage dressing room to better hear our conversation.

"I'm not exactly sure how to say this," Eleanor replied.

"Out with it. If this is about my daughter, don't keep me in suspense." Eleanor could be overly dramatic. I'd been through enough already today.

"She's not alone."

"What do you mean?" I contained a mounting annoyance with my sister.

"Francesca's here too. It seems your dead wife might not be so dead, after all."

BROKEN HEART ATTACK

BRAXTON CAMPUS MYSTERIES BOOK 2

ACKNOWLEDGMENTS

Writing a book is not an achievement an individual person can do on his or her own. There are always people who contribute in a multitude of ways, sometimes unwittingly, throughout the journey from discovering the idea to drafting the last word. *Broken Heart Attack: A Braxton Campus Mystery* has had many supporters since its inception in September 2018, but before the concept even sparked in my mind, my passion for writing was nurtured by others.

First thanks go to my parents, Jim and Pat, for always believing in me as a writer, as well as teaching me how to become the person I am today. Their unconditional love and support have been the primary reason I'm accomplishing my goals. Through the guidance of my extended family and friends, who consistently encouraged me to pursue my passion, I found the confidence to take chances in life. With Winston and Baxter by my side, I was granted the opportunity to make my dreams come true by publishing this novel. I'm grateful to everyone for pushing me every day to complete this second book.

Broken Heart Attack was cultivated through the interaction, feedback, and input of several beta readers. I'd like to thank Shalini G, Lisa M. Berman, Rekha Rao, Laura Albert, and Nina D. Silva for providing insight and perspective during the development of the story, setting, and character arcs.

- A special call-out goes to Shalini for countless conversations helping me to fine-tune every aspect of the setting, characters, and plot. She read every version and offered a tremendous amount of her time to advise me on this book over several weeks. All the medical points were reviewed with Shalini to be sure I covered them appropriately. I am beyond grateful for her help. Any mistakes are my own from misunderstanding our discussions.
- Nina also read all the versions and provided in-depth and varied feedback on character relationships, actions, and personality traits. She's a keen eye for knowing what will and won't work. She messaged back and forth for weeks to keep me focused and provide the motivation to challenge myself. Many thanks!
- Much appreciation for Lisa, who has become a fantastic friend and confidante in the last few years. I appreciate all her time and effort

into reading my books before launch. She always finds those items I miss, and I'm grateful more than I can say.

- A huge welcome to Laura for joining the team with this book. Laura provided lots of ideas for how to grow the characters, but she also found a few dozen proofreading issues, which made my life so much easier. I'm truly thrilled to be working with her this time around.
- A big welcome to Rekha for joining the team with this book. Rekha read and reviewed the entire novel over a weekend and provided helpful comments on scenes that worked well and some that needed more pop. Thank you!

Much gratitude to all my friends and mentors at Moravian College. Although no murders have ever taken place there, the setting of this series is loosely based on my former multi-campus school set in Pennsylvania. Most of the locations are completely fabricated, but Millionaire's Mile exists... I only made up the name and cable car system!

Thank you to Creativia / Next Chapter for publishing *Broken Heart Attack* and paving the road for more books to come. I look forward to our continued partnership.

WHO'S WHO IN BRAXTON?

AYRWICK FAMILY

- Kellan: Main Character, Braxton professor, amateur sleuth
- Wesley: Kellan's father, Braxton's retired president
- Violet: Kellan's mother, Braxton's admissions director
- Emma: Kellan's daughter with Francesca
- Eleanor: Kellan's younger sister, owns Pick-Me-Up Diner
- Hampton: Kellan's older brother
- Nana D: Kellan's grandmother, also known as Seraphina Danby
- Francesca Castigliano: Kellan's supposedly deceased wife
- Vincenzo & Cecilia Castigliano: Francesca's parents, run the mob
- Alexander Betscha: Nana D's cousin, doctor

BRAXTON CAMPUS

- Ursula Power: President of Braxton, Myriam's wife
- Myriam Castle: Chair of Communications Dept., Ursula's wife
- Fern Terry: Dean of Student Affairs
- Connor Hawkins: Director of Security, Kellan's best friend
- Maggie Roarke: Head Librarian, Kellan's ex-girlfriend
- Yuri Sato: Student, Dana's friend
- Craig 'Striker' Magee: Student
- Arthur Terry: Fern's son, works at Paddington's Play House

PADDINGTON HOUSEHOLD

- Millard Paddington: Brother to Eustacia
- Eustacia Paddington: Sister to Millard
- Gwendolyn Paddington: Sister-in-law to Eustacia and Millard
- Jennifer Paddington: Daughter of Gwendolyn
- Timothy Paddington: Son of Gwendolyn
- Ophelia Taft: Daughter of Gwendolyn, Married to Richard
- Richard Taft: Married to Ophelia
- Dana Taft: Ophelia and Richard's daughter
- Lilly Taft: Ophelia and Richard's daughter
- Sam Taft: Ophelia and Richard's son
- Brad Shope: Nurse
- Bertha Crawford: Housekeeper

WHARTON COUNTY RESIDENTS

- April Montague: Wharton County Sheriff
- Marcus Stanton: Braxton Town Councilman
- Officer Flatman: Police Officer
- Finnigan Masters: Attorney
- Buddy: Works at Second Chance Reflections
- Tiffany Nutberry: HR Employee
- Lindsey Endicott: Friend of Nana D & Paddingtons

OVERVIEW

When I decided to write a cozy mystery series, I adhered to all the main rules (light investigations, minimal violence or foul language, no sexual content, murder happens off-screen, protagonist is an amateur sleuth, and set in a quiet, small town). Some authors push the boundaries with variations, and in the Braxton Campus Mysteries, I followed the same route... just differently. Kellan, my protagonist, is a thirtyish single father, whereas traditionally a woman is the main character. Children aren't often seen in most series, but Kellan's family is important to the story. Kellan is also witty and snarky, but intended in a lovable and charming way, just like his eccentric grandmother, Nana D. Both are friendly, happy, and eager to help others, and they have a sarcastic or sassy way of interacting and building relationships... hopefully adding to the humor and tone of the books.

Cozy mysteries are different from hard-boiled investigations, thrillers, and suspense novels; the side stories, surrounding town, and background characters are equally important to building a vibrant world in which readers can escape. I hope you enjoy my alternative take on this classic sub-genre.

CHAPTER 1

March weather in Wharton County, Pennsylvania was as unpredictable as a cutting jeer from Nana D. Although bound to happen, the actual impact boasted an infinite range unlike any missile I'd ever seen launched. There might be a blizzard worthy of a Christmas snow globe furiously shaken by an over-eager child, or spring could test its feverish desire to burst through the frozen soil with an unparalleled zest for life. While thunder rolled above me in a murky gray sky, I read my nana's latest message for the third time, wondering if she realized the extent to which she could confuse people and make them want to cry—all in a single, random meandering text.

Nana D: *Can't stand these old whiners. Save me. You better not be late. Did you get a haircut yet? I've seen more attractive farm animals than you lately. Sometimes I can't believe we're related. Made you a special dessert. Why didn't you talk me out of this stupid race? I'm proud of you for coming back home. What's an emoji again? I need to find us both dates. Do I swipe right or left if I'm interested in a man? Hurry. Hugs and kisses.*

Since we enjoyed torturing one another in a loving yet competitive way, I ignored my grandmother's craziness, hoping it'd lead to a conniption fit in front of her friends. That wind-up Energizer bunny desperately needed a case of extra-strength Valium while I craved the warmer, drier weather as my drug of choice. Instead, I stared depressingly at an over-stuffed storm cloud threatening to torture us again. We'd already suffered through a nasty four-day bout of torrential rain that made everything feel like soggy bread. And in case it wasn't obvious, no one liked soggy bread. Truthfully, my entire week had felt like soggy bread mischievously sprinkled with a side of unrelenting and peculiar death.

Fresh off accepting a new job as a professor at Braxton and unravelling my first murder case, I was hopeful for some relaxation. Unfortunately, everything morphed into swiss cheese with holes the size of the Grand Canyon. No, I wasn't a police detective or private investigator. I got lucky solving the murder of two colleagues before our county's crabby sheriff finally nabbed the misguided culprit, yet that wasn't the most scandalous thing about my recent return home after a decade's absence.

When I told my in-laws that I was leaving Los Angeles and moving back to Pennsylvania, I learned through ordinary conversation that my supposedly dead wife, Francesca, wasn't really dead. Nearly two-and-a-half years ago, her family had led me to believe she'd perished in a car accident when a drunk driver plowed through a red light at a dangerous intersection. No longer true! *'Alive today, gone tomorrow. Hey, I'm back again. The afterlife wasn't too fun, so I changed my mind about dying. Just not for me!'* Maybe things happened like that in the menacing world of my in-laws, *The Castigliano Family*, but definitely not in mine.

Francesca's parents had staged the car accident after someone tried to kill my wife as revenge for a multitude of mob faux pas. My in-laws sat at the helm of a ruthless LA crime syndicate, and somehow Francesca—who never told me anything about this aspect of her life while she was *alive*—had gotten caught up in their web of deception. The only way for them to protect Francesca and our young daughter, Emma, was to fake Francesca's death.

My emotions had been incredibly erratic and raw for the last five days since learning the truth. I couldn't tell anyone except my sister, Eleanor, who'd been present when Francesca showed up. And just as easily as my no-longer-dead-wife had materialized, she vanished again under the dark iron curtain that was the protection of her parents. Was there a handbook for dealing with a wife who'd come back from the grave? Had a cult performing some maddening initiation rite kidnapped and brainwashed me? Seriously, what did I do in the past to be saddled with the mother of all gut punches? Sadly, I had no answers, but as far as priorities went, my presence was imminently required elsewhere for a different kind of brutal torture.

I was driving to visit my almost seventy-five-year-old grandmother, Nana D —known to everyone else as Seraphina Danby—who'd declared her intent to run for Mayor of Wharton County in a surprise press conference earlier that week. Five-foot-tall, less than a hundred pounds wet—mostly from her wild, henna-rinsed red hair taking up half her height—and full of boat loads more sarcasm than me, Nana D was preparing for her first major campaign activity. I'd promised to organize all her *old, whiny* volunteers for the mayoral race, since none of them knew where to begin.

Although a proper tea would be served at Nana D's, I popped into The Big Beanery, Braxton's charming and crowded South Campus student café, and ordered an extra-strong, extra-tall, salted caramel mocha to go. I drooled at the pastry counter despite knowing Nana D had baked something delicious I'd undoubtedly consume everything like a pig from a trough. I scanned the room, searching for any of my students who might've been hanging out with their friends or reviewing class materials in study group, but I only saw one person I recognized who was not a student by any means.

Why was Dean Terry on campus on a quiet Saturday? While waiting for my overly complex coffee and assuming she sat by herself, I moseyed over to the table to brighten her day. That's the kinda guy I was. Although I was a mere three inches shy of a full six feet, my colleague tipped the other side of the scale and unwisely kept her hair extremely short. Built like a quarterback who'd recently eaten way too much salt, the dean had been using her thick, towering presence to intimidate students for twenty-five years at Braxton. Once you got beyond the surface, she was truly a pussycat.

After getting used to the idea of being colleagues, I refrained from calling her Dean Terry and addressed her by her first name. With a smile, I said, "Good afternoon, Fern. Don't you ever take a break?" She'd almost been awarded the coveted presidency of our well-regarded institution last week. The Board of Trustees had surprisingly gone with someone else and instead offered her a leading role on the committee that would convert Braxton from a college into a university over the next two years. She was disappointed, but once we reconnected and realized we could make a vast difference together, Fern quickly got on board with the decision.

"Kellan, so nice to see you. I'm meeting my son for brunch. He's stepped outside to fix an issue with the school's *King Lear* production." Fern's tone had more verve than I was ready to handle at that time of day. Although I'd always known her academic and disciplinarian side, I'd recently connected with the dean on a more personal level, finding we had a lot in common. Between our mutual love of black-and-white films and traveling cross-country by train, we were destined to develop a stronger friendship. Where was that love when she'd raked me over the coals for something my frat had done while I was a student ten years ago?

As far as I recalled, Fern only had one son who'd graduated high school with me. Instead of going directly to college, he'd moved to New York City to become an actor before returning three years later to obtain his bachelor's degree. "How is Arthur? I haven't seen him in years." I pushed away wavy, unruly dirty-blond hair from my three-day unshaven face. Nana D had astutely remarked I was overdue for a haircut, but since I hadn't been to a barber in Wharton County in a decade, I had no idea where to go. Eleanor had tried to convince me to let her trim it, but that would never happen. A steady grip with a pair of scissors and erring on the side of caution were not her strong points.

"Arthur's directing Braxton's play this semester. Unfortunately, it means he's working for a tyrant, but he's dealt with far worse on Broadway, I'm sure." Fern shrugged, then offered me a seat. My mouth watered over the gooey cinnamon roll sitting on her plate inches away from my nimble fingers.

"No, I shouldn't. I have to be somewhere but thought I'd say hello." I prepared to leave while Arthur returned from his phone call and stormed up to the table.

Hints of a ferocious dog came to mind when his alarming expression and cold, dark pupils centered on his unsuspecting mother. "That woman is a miserable old cow, Mom. I don't know how you cope working with her every day," Arthur snarled. He was tall with round and puffy features like his mother but instead of a gray pixie-cut, thinning, sandy-colored hair was combed over in a failed attempt to hide what was inevitably going to happen relatively soon. Although he was thirty-two like me, early crow's feet and cavernous lines had already dominated his face. "Oh, wait... Kellan Ayrwick, is that you?"

I nodded. "I can only imagine you're speaking about my wonderful boss, Myriam Castle. I'd appreciate any tips you might have for dealing with that venomous barracuda!" It'd spilled from my lips before I could stop my verbal diarrhea. Myriam was one of my least favorite people. Ever. I'd barely known her for three weeks, but every interaction left me bristled and inflicted with a rash the size of Texas. Between her nasty, chirpy tone and inciting way of quoting Shakespeare, it often felt like a nails-on-chalkboard episode of *Twilight Zone* or a sinister case of *Candid Camera*. I waited for someone wearing a demon mask to jump out and yell surprise, but sadly, it never happened. I would've popped that charlatan right in the schnoz for messing with me.

"If only." Arthur sat forcefully on the chair, wiping wet hands across his jeans. He'd regrettably gotten caught in the deluge without an umbrella. "Run. That's all I can say when it comes to that—"

"Now, Arthur. We all know she can be difficult, but let's not say something you'll regret." Fern patted her son's forearm. "Remember, this is your opportunity to get into directing and away from acting. Isn't that what you said you wanted?" Fern fretted like a mother hen trying to calm her little chick. I'd rarely seen this side of her, but she handled her son with aplomb and tact.

"I know, Mom. Myriam's squashed the entire opening scene we'd been rehearsing for days. Now I have to reblock the stage before tomorrow's dress rehearsal." He grunted and took an aggressive bite out of his grilled cheese sandwich. His canine teeth resembled a ravenous vampire's fangs.

Arthur answered an incoming call from someone named Dana on his cell phone. Since he and Fern were busy and my coffee grew colder on the counter, I excused myself to leave. I pretended not to hear Fern gasp when Arthur told Dana he also wanted to kill some woman for what she'd said at the previous night's rehearsal. I felt bad for Arthur, who'd have to work with the corrosive woman, or she'd make his life miserable.

When Myriam had become the new chairperson of our department, I suddenly took direction from her since I was teaching a full course load on broadcasting writing, television production, and history of film. We'd held our first supervisory meeting this week where she'd made things exorbitantly clear —once my father officially retired as the president of Braxton College in the coming days, I no longer had anyone to protect me. I might've been granted a one-year contract, but Myriam articulately clarified the new president—her wife, Ursula Power—could override it.

I grabbed my coffee and took off for Nana D's. She owned and operated

Danby Landing, an organic orchard and farm in the southernmost section of Wharton County. At one point in the county's history, it had the largest acreage of any homestead, but Nana D had sold off a sizeable chunk after my grandpop passed away. As I turned onto the dirt path leading to her farmhouse, I quarantined thoughts of my back-from-the-dead wife and loony boss and focused on the next irrational mess I had to deal with.

When I pulled up at Danby Landing, my six-year-old daughter raced out of the house and jumped in my arms. I swung Emma from side to side and kissed her cheeks. She'd slept at Nana D's the previous night, so they could have a fancy slumber party—no boys invited, apparently.

"Daddy! We made s'mores. I got to ride the tractor with Nana D's farmhand this morning. He has a daughter my age. Can I play with her? When are we going to the zoo?" Emma asked, unable to control her glee. Her crimped dark-brown hair was pulled into pigtails, and she wore an adorable pair of denim overalls Nana D had sewed the previous week. Emma inherited her mother's olive-tinted skin, which made me unable to forget my wife's enchanting beauty.

"That sounds like fun, baby girl!" I placed her on the swinging bench next to me to spend a few minutes together before dealing with the old whiners. We played a few rounds of *Cat-in-the-Cradle* and discussed the sleepover, then Emma dragged me inside the house. While she poured herself a cup of juice and turned on a video, I trudged into the den to be terrorized.

There were four others in the room besides my nana, all of whom I'd met in the past. It was a meeting of the founding members of Braxton's Septuagenarian Club: Nana D, Eustacia Paddington, Gwendolyn Paddington, Millard Paddington, and Lindsey Endicott. They'd formed the group years ago upon turning seventy to celebrate a revival of their youth. They'd initiated at least forty new members and ran amok trying to reclaim any remaining independence from their family who'd locked them in nursing homes or taken away their driver's licenses. Nana D was the ringleader and caused the most disturbances around town. 'Not my monkey, not my circus,' I often reminded myself when anyone begged me to stop her from whatever trouble she'd brewed up.

"If it ain't the little bedwetter," taunted Lindsey Endicott, a seventy-six-year-old retired attorney whom Nana D and Eustacia Paddington were both dating. His bright pink polo was two sizes too small and revealed way too much of his rotund beer belly. As soon as he'd sold his law practice, he'd opened a microbrewery in one of the well-frequented downtown shopping areas. The only problem was that he was his best customer and had never learned when or how to cut himself off.

"Awww, he hasn't done that in years, right, Kellan?" Eustacia's electric-blue track suit fit properly, but she obviously wasn't wearing anything underneath it. I shook my head in disbelief at the multitude of oddly shaped age spots and diverted my sight anywhere but in her direction. She continued, "I remember when he had that awful problem. Poor Seraphina had to change the sheets whenever that boy stayed over."

Could we get any more embarrassing? I'd been three years old and had a nervous bladder. I'd gained full control of the situation for close to three decades at that point. "Cut it out, you two. I'll toss your little blue pills down the garbage disposal, Mr. Endicott. How do you like that?" His eyes opened wide, sending two giant, bushy eyebrows in every direction like ants in search of a morsel of food. "And you, Ms. Paddington... I'll slice several inches off your cane and see how you like hobbling around."

Millard Paddington, Eustacia's older brother—by less than a year, Irish twins as she often called them—blushed a shade of red I rarely saw anymore. He was the only truly gentle human being in the bunch. "Leave the boy alone, you rascals, or I'll swap Gwennie's high-blood pressure pills with Eustacia's gastrointestinal medication. Neither of you will know what hit you. Don't we have important business to attend to?" Millard was the tallest of the bunch, rail thin, and had lost his hair years ago. He'd grown a handlebar moustache and had almost perfected the curls, but the children at the library held a penchant for yanking on it when he'd read to them. Calling it *spotty* would be a generous description, yet he seemed to enjoy all the attention from the boisterous toddlers.

Gwendolyn, or Gwennie as her fellow club members called her, had been married to Eustacia's and Millard's brother, Charles, who'd passed away the prior year. She was exceedingly prim and proper and had a habit of being hasty and judgmental. I'd luckily rarely been on the receiving end of it, but Nana D had to put the woman in her place many times in the past. Gwendolyn remained silent with her upturned nose, looking as snooty as possible—old schoolmarm after tasting a rancid, sour grapefruit.

"As much as I'd love to keep getting roasted by the old timers' club, Mr. Paddington is correct. How can I help with Nana D's campaign?" I relaxed into the only remaining chair in the room, which left me practically sitting inside the roaring fireplace. "What have you prepared so far?"

Silence. No one said a word, just looked back and forth at each other, waiting for someone else to chime in. We continued like this for another five minutes until I finally encouraged them to produce a list of the top ten changes they wanted to see happen in Wharton County. I was pleasantly surprised to discover at least six of them were pragmatic ideas others could get behind. The remaining four were not—free massages in the park by 'the hot little number at the Willow Trees Retirement Complex' and a new dating app called 'Let's Get Lucky' for the over-seventy crowd seemed a tad unnecessary and inflammatory to me. Then again, I might want those things in forty years, too. Who was I to judge or put the kibosh on someone's late-in-life carnal desires? I won't even mention the other two ideas.

While I assigned everyone tasks, Gwendolyn excused herself to use the powder room. "I'm borrowing your cane, Eustacia. I'm not feeling too steady on my feet the last few days."

As Gwendolyn walked down the hall, Nana D teased, "I'm sorry I don't have a chamber pot, you old bat. Here we call it a restroom! No one says powder room anymore." Was Gwendolyn avoiding her responsibilities, or was the absence a coincidence? As if she were privy to the conversation going on in my head, Nana D turned and said, "She always does that. When she returns, Gwennie will rush out saying she has to deal with an emergency. Just like Millard whenever I asked him to sleep over. That's the reason things didn't work out between us. He was selfish when it came to intimate things like—"

"No, Nana D. Please stop. I can't listen to it," I begged once my insides cringed and turned to Jell-O. "We've talked about this many times. I don't want to hear anything about your love life. And in return, I won't bother you with anything about mine."

"Does that mean you have a love life to speak of? Because last time we chatted, your ability to flirt and any awkward sex appeal you still clung to had disappeared the way of the pony express." She then kissed her finger, touched her derriere, and made a sizzle sound. Her tiny noise erupted into a room full of irritable senior citizens hooting at my expense.

"I'm only here for a little while, Nana D. You need to use your time wisely, or I might not help you win the mayoral race." I filled Gwendolyn's box with campaign promotional flyers and walked out the front door to load them in Lindsey's car. He'd carted the gang over to Nana D's given he was the best driver in the entire group. When I got to the porch, I heard Gwendolyn on her phone as she shuffled to the far corner.

Gwendolyn said, "Well, if you can't make it, then I'll find someone else to take your ticket. It's not the first time you've disappointed me, and I'm sure it won't be the last. I've sponsored this production of *King Lear*. The whole family is supposed to be there to support our generous donations. Maybe you're not cut out to be a member of this clan anymore."

I watched the sourpuss expression deepen until it was her turn to speak again. When she did, even I got the chills from her icy tone and unexpected threat.

"You remember that when I'm no longer around. Family is supposed to look out for one another as they get older. Not throw them to the curb like trash. Maybe I need to make another trip to the lawyer to look over my will again." A few seconds later Gwendolyn shouted into the phone, "You've always been useless. I've got a good mind to take you down right now. We'll see how you like it when things don't turn out as you expected." Then she hung up and struggled with the clasp on her vintage 50s-style handbag. She finally got it open, flung her phone inside, and agitatedly clutched it to her side.

I'd already stepped onto the porch and couldn't sneak back inside without her noticing me. As she turned around, Gwendolyn sneered. "You eavesdropping on my call? What kind of manners did your nana teach you, Kellan? I've got a good mind to—"

"I'm sorry. I was bringing this box to the car and didn't know you were out here." I cautiously held up my free hand and balanced the box against my chest with the other. I felt bad for interrupting her privacy but was shocked at what she'd said on the phone. "Is everything okay?"

"No, my awful family keeps taking my money but refuses to do anything nice for me. I'm about to learn how dreadful one of them truly is. What are you doing tomorrow?" she asked in a raspy voice.

Other than preparing for classes and trying to contact Francesca, who'd left me no number to reach her when she absconded with her mother to New York, nothing was planned. "Spending time with my daughter and helping Nana D prepare for her upcoming debate with Councilman Stanton."

"Well, find yourself a babysitter. You're coming with me to Braxton's dress rehearsal for *King Lear*. One of my useless kinsfolks canceled and I have an extra ticket." Gwendolyn wiped a speck of dust from her eye. A woman like her never cried about family. She complained about them to anyone who'd listen. Or even those who didn't.

"I'm sure they love you. Maybe it's a misunderstanding," I suggested, sympathetic to her plight. Nana D had mentioned several times how Gwendolyn's kids had either abandoned her or gotten into trouble ever since their father had passed away. Her husband, Charles, had been the family's center of gravity while he'd been alive, but lately they all treated her like a burden or an ATM.

"That's certainly a load of petrified cow dung! They'd be happier if I kicked the bucket on the drive home tonight. I'm concerned one of them might try to kill me. Something ain't right with how I feel lately. Going to the doctor on Monday to find out." She steadied herself against the doorjamb and huffed loudly. "Stupid ungrateful beasts. If I find out one of them has been gaslighting me, I'll have them arrested. No two thoughts about it. We might be family, but they're all a bunch of vultures."

Gwendolyn plodded inside to corral the rest of the Septuagenarian Club. I rubbed my temples, loaded the box into Lindsey's car, and returned to the house. After everyone left, Nana D pulled me into the kitchen, away from Emma's curious ears. "Did I overhear Gwennie tell you someone in her family is trying to murder her?" Nana D asked with a peculiar twitch in her left cheek.

"Yes, I assumed she was upset about one of them not going to the show. I guess I'll be going with you now." I sighed as if the weight of the world rested on my shoulders. I loved my nana, but her friends were harder to handle than standing upside down catching a greasy pig in a mudslide.

"No, brilliant one. That's where you're wrong. Something is whackadoodle in that family. She's been acting strange for weeks. I wouldn't be surprised if one of those Paddingtons was trying to kill Gwennie. You're gonna help her figure out which crazy one it is before they succeed, right?"

CHAPTER 2

After leaving Nana D's farm, Emma and I went shopping at a local bookstore. An hour later and a hundred dollars deeper in debt, we exited the charming literary wonder set between the two Braxton campuses with our hands full of recycled bags stocked with books. I'd snagged a copy of the debut novel in a new mystery series that had caught my eye. Next stop, the Pick-Me-Up Diner for an early dinner and much-needed therapy session with my sister. Since she was the only person I could talk to about Francesca, Eleanor would have to suffer through endless conversations about what to do next.

When we arrived, I ordered Emma to wear a hard hat in case she bumped into any of the construction in the currently being renovated Pick-Me-Up Diner. Emma joined Manny, Eleanor's chef, who was in the kitchen testing new recipes even though the place wasn't accessible to the public. It still needed a final inspection on Wednesday morning before allowing in any paying customers.

"She seems to be adjusting well." Eleanor pulled her dirty-blonde, curly hair into a bun on the top of her head and wrapped a scrunchie around to hold it in place. While our older siblings had inherited our father's lanky body structure, Eleanor and I split the dominant Danby and Betscha traits in resemblance of our mother. Eleanor got saddled with wider hips and shorter arms than she'd liked, and I ungraciously accepted untamable hair and a tiny button nose that refused to properly balance my glasses. "Still haven't said anything to Emma, right?"

"No, I wouldn't know how or where to begin. I'm living in one of your daytime dramas lately." I teased my sister even though it hadn't felt like a laughing matter. I loved Francesca, and the day I buried my wife was the worst day of my life. I was having trouble believing her reappearance wasn't a dream.

"Tell me again exactly how the Castiglianos pulled this off?" When Eleanor had met my mother-in-law to pick up Emma, Cecilia sent my daughter upstairs in my parents' log cabin, aka *Royal Chic-Shack* as we all called it, while she informed Eleanor to wait in our father's study. A few minutes later, Cecilia snuck Francesca into the small, private office nestled in the far corner and locked the door. Eleanor shockingly learned that Francesca was alive, and I was summoned home immediately.

"I had less than one hour with her, then Cecilia whisked Francesca away to New York, refusing to provide any way to reach her. All communication must go through my controlling in-laws," I replied. It was like a Woody Allen movie playing out in front of me, not my own life. "I'm hoping to see her again when they return tomorrow."

"You're seriously telling me Francesca's been hiding out at the Castigliano mansion for over two years?" Eleanor asked with bright eyes and an exaggerated amount of air blown through her lips to push rogue bangs away from her forehead. "Diabolical!"

"Yes, the whole macabre series of events happened quietly and quickly. A few days before the fake car accident, a rival mob family, the Vargas gang, had kidnapped Francesca. I never knew about it because I'd been away on a film set. Her father's goons killed one of their men, and as retaliation, the Vargas mob captured Francesca. When he found out what'd happened, Vincenzo instructed his henchmen to do whatever it took to return his daughter."

"But how did she end up faking her death? You've never explained that part." Eleanor peered through the small window in the kitchen door to verify Emma was still helping Manny prepare dinner and not listening to our conversation.

"The only way Vincenzo could protect her was to stage an accident that looked like the Vargas family's newest driver had killed her. He bought off a local cop who poured alcohol all over the other guy's car and had the medics attempt to rescue Francesca. They never caught the driver because there never was one. When the police called to tell me about the accident, Francesca was in the room with them, trying to convince her father to find another solution."

"I can't believe she'd hurt you like this. Painful." Eleanor acted as if it were her wife who'd lied and disappeared. I knew she was empathetic, but no one could understand the impact to my world.

"I remember seeing a few random thugs checking out the accident. They must have been there to ensure Francesca looked dead and to report my reaction. Vincenzo eventually convinced the Vargas family that he'd suffered enough by losing his daughter. Everyone agreed to call off their turf war and carefully observe proper boundaries in the future."

"Does she have to stay dead forever? What kind of life is that?"

"I wish I knew. We only had time to agree on not telling Emma for now." It'd made me so happy to see my wife, but my body filled with an intense anger I'd never experienced before. "Francesca's been spying our daughter at the Castigliano mansion whenever Emma slept over. When I told the Castiglianos

I was moving back to Pennsylvania, Francesca freaked out. It meant she could no longer watch Emma from a safe, comfortable distance."

"That's why she came back from the dead *now*?" Eleanor said without blinking for a long time.

I nodded. Francesca tried to abide by her father's rules and stay hidden, but when the possibility of never seeing her daughter again became a reality, she snuck onto the plane with her new fake identity to convince me not to take Emma away. Francesca had worn a costume, dyed her hair, and sat far away in coach from Emma—Cecilia had undoubtedly flown first class. "I have no idea what to do next. I can't let this impact Emma, but if her mother's alive, shouldn't she get to be part of her life?"

"Only if it isn't dangerous. What about you? Are you thinking about getting a new identity and disappearing somewhere to rebuild a life together?" Eleanor looked disappointed and worried that I would leave town again.

In the forty-one minutes Francesca and I had together, all of which were supervised by my mother-in-law, we only discussed what to do about Emma. "I haven't thought about it. Right now, I just want to find out what she's been doing the last two-and-a-half years. I don't even know if we're technically still married, or how any of this works."

"Don't you still want to be married to her? You loved Francesca so much." Eleanor hugged me, then stepped away.

"I'm overwhelmed. I want to reclaim what we once had, but she lied to me. She ended something intimate and passionate. We were great together, and now, it feels strange to be around her." I paused to keep my emotions from exploding. "The new Francesca has short blonde hair, wears colored contact lenses, and speaks differently. I don't recognize my wife anymore, Eleanor."

My sister leaned in to kiss my cheek, but my ringing cell phone interrupted us. I looked at the screen and groaned. What did my boss want with me on a Saturday evening? I preferred to ignore her but needed a temporary break from thinking about Francesca's reappearance in my life.

"Good evening, Myriam. How's your weekend?" I asked in as calm a voice as I could muster. Eleanor patted my shoulder, then went into the kitchen to check on Emma and offer me some privacy.

"I've no time for small talk. I'm fixing gargantuan issues with our upcoming *King Lear* production. I suddenly remembered you were supposed to drop off your course recommendations for next semester. You seem fond of keeping me waiting for you to get your job done properly," Myriam said haughtily. Her normal appearance backed up the narcissistic attitude, too—she always wore immaculately cut power suits and kept her short, spiky gray hair perfectly styled. I'd suspected at one time it was a wig, and if I ever had the chance, I'd rip that sucker off to test my theory. It didn't matter that she could be old enough to be my mother. The viper needed to be taken down a notch or two.

While Myriam was correct about the deliverable, we'd agreed on Monday being the due date. It was only Saturday. I'd completed them that morning but hadn't planned to submit them until the last minute as retaliation for her giving me such a short deadline. It was the only way I could irritate my boss without crossing any overt boundaries. "Certainly. I thought we could discuss them in our weekly meeting next Tuesday. I'd be happy to email them to you tomorrow."

"That simply won't do. I need time to review before we meet, and I'm in rehearsals all day tomorrow. I distinctly asked you to get them to me in advance, but it seems you struggle with listening and punctuality. *'Better three hours too soon than a minute too late.'* Wouldn't you agree?" Myriam ordered me to hold on, then shouted at someone in the theater about annunciating properly.

"As you like it," I replied, naming the Shakespearean comedy from where her line came.

"Now you understand who's the boss. Drop it off in thirty minutes at Paddington's Play House. And don't dawdle. I'm sure it'll take me hours to revise and comment on it," Myriam growled before hanging up.

As I tapped my fingers on the diner's dusty table, I considered my options. If I stood my ground, Myriam would continue to itemize everything she'd felt was an influential enough reason to push me out of Braxton. If I let her obnoxious attitude roll off my shoulders like it meant nothing, she might eventually tire and bore of chiding me every moment of every day. Before I acted too severely, it'd be beneficial to have my first official meeting with Ursula to understand her perspective on the situation.

Eleanor agreed to drop Emma off at our parents' place on her way home since our mother was remaining in for the evening. Our father had an out-of-town golf game that weekend, which meant our mother planned to curl up with the latest regency romance novel from her favorite author—her sister, Deirdre.

A few minutes later, I pulled into the South Campus parking lot and grabbed the printed course outlines and film suggestions from my briefcase. As I entered Paddington's Play House, someone shouted terse stage directions at the actors and loudly dropped a prop. It sounded like something made of glass when I heard the earth-shaking shatter as it hit the stage. I ambled around the lobby, hoping whatever commotion was stirring up inside the theater would settle down.

Paddington's Play House had been built by Charles, Millard, and Eustacia's father in the late 1940s while his children were young. None of the other colleges had a theater program or entertainment venues, and the Paddingtons were determined to always be first in every endeavor. Built in the shape of a large octagon that resembled Shakespeare's Globe Theatre, it seated up to one-thousand guests. Unlike the original Globe Theatre, there was no standing room. A large cathedral ceiling with reclaimed wood beams, antique gilded and cushioned seats, and plastered walls painted an ivory white offered a charming and bespoke atmosphere. The college played four shows a year, one of which was always a Shakespearean production to properly celebrate the Bard.

I admired the inlaid, two-toned natural wood flooring as I descended into the seating area, hoping the ruckus had died down. Arthur and Myriam attempted to co-direct several reticent actors on stage. They both waved their hands furiously and stomped across the narrow expanse, demonstrating what the actors should've been doing. I was too far away to hear their words or see the expressions on their faces, but it was obvious they provided contradictory direction.

Two female voices startled me from the corner. A dark brunette in designer jeans and low-cut red blouse said, "He told me how pretty I looked earlier. I think maybe I have a chance."

"Get out. He's too old for you, Dana. Why would you be interested in him?" the thin, taller girl with a pasty complexion and nasal voice replied. She'd pulled her neon-green hair up under a baseball cap and was dressed in a pair of old, ratty sweats.

Dana said, "I know he's not exactly the hottest guy and he might be a little on the older side, but he's hilarious. And he knows so many famous people." She swooned as she spoke, then looked toward the stage. As her head turned, she caught sight of me.

I nodded in her direction. "Excuse me, would you know when they'll take a break? I need to drop something off for Myriam Castle."

"Ugh, you better wait until she's done. Dr. Castle doesn't like to be interrupted," Dana said.

"We're about ready to do a scene change. I'm the set designer... Yuri," the girl wearing the sweats replied. I understood why she looked more casual than the rest. "She's Dana. You are?"

I remembered seeing the name *Dana* on Arthur Terry's cell phone earlier. Could she have been talking about having a crush on Arthur? Dana could barely have been nineteen or twenty-years-old, and he was my age. "Kellan Ayrwick. I'm a professor here at Braxton."

"Awesome sauce. Let's head up together. They'll be done by the time we get to the front. Just wait in the front row until I climb on stage to change the set," Yuri said.

Dana followed. "I'm handling props for the show. I'm not an actress, but I love everything about the theater." Her bouncy walk and flashy grin demonstrated vast excitement of working on the show.

"You must be a student at Braxton?" I remembered Myriam had indicated everyone who worked on the play had to be a current or former Braxton attendee. They'd first cast any performers and hired all back-of-the-house roles from currently enrolled students. If there was a special need or talent not in existence at the school, they'd solicit help from alumni.

"Sophomore. Studying drama and psychology. I want to work on Broadway one day, but my parents forced me to take something practical as a back-up. It's not like I'll ever need to get an actual job. My family's loaded," Dana said, shrugging indifferently.

She looked familiar, but I couldn't place her. "What did you say your last name was?"

"Ummm... Taft, but my mother's family has the money. You must know the

Paddingtons. They own this place," Dana noted with a slew of pretentiousness that hadn't gone unnoticed by either of us.

That's why she looked familiar. She had the same patrician face and narrow jawline as Eustacia and Millard. "I've met a few of your family members. Which branch do you hail from?"

"Grandmother is Gwendolyn Paddington. Grandfather passed away last year, but my parents are still around. Do you know Richard and Ophelia Taft? The grand dame is named for Grandmother's favorite Shakespearean character." Dana leaned against the side wall while Yuri scattered toward the stage once the scene finished.

"I saw your grandmother earlier today. She was visiting my nana," I replied. If Dana was related to Gwendolyn, she might be one of the family members trying to do away with the difficult matriarch. "You must spend a lot of time with your grandmother, too?"

Dana rolled her eyes. She'd never be able to compete with me. I was king of that move. "Grandmother is hard to take. She cares more about what things look like than what's under the surface, you know what I mean?"

I shrugged. "Different generations, I suppose. They expect all the skeletons in our closets to stay hidden. I heard she's not been feeling too well lately." I wasn't convinced anyone had been trying to kill Gwendolyn, but it wouldn't hurt to poke around.

"She is kind of old. Ever since Grandfather passed away, she's gotten worse. Grandmother keeps reminding everyone she's paying for this entire show." Dana seemed like a typical college girl with a large chip on her shoulder. Kids her age thought anyone over forty was old. Wait until she saw the world without rose-colored glasses.

"Are you worried about something happening to her?" I asked.

"She's a tough old bird, but yesterday she could barely get through brunch. Everything tires her out quickly in the last few weeks." Dana adjusted the straps on her blouse and checked her reflection in a compact mirror. "Looks like they're done on stage."

As Dana marched up the stairs, Myriam waved me over. "Don't just stand around making me wait. Do you have the course outlines?"

After handing them to her, I said, "How's the show going?" Tomorrow's dress rehearsal would only be open to family and select faculty. Students were on Spring Break this week, but if they were involved in the theater, they had to stay on campus.

"Like a root canal with no pain relief. I never should have hired Arthur Terry, but like other people around here, he was forced upon me." Myriam slid her tortoise-shell glasses an inch down her nose, pointedly stared at me, then sighed. Even the ruffles on her royal-blue blouse seemed to fluster.

"Is Arthur a bad director? We went to high school together, you know." I ignored her dig about how I'd gotten my job at Braxton. She took every opportunity to belittle me or my family.

"He's new to the role. Actors often think they can easily transition from in front of the camera to behind the camera. His Broadway experience is lacklus-ter." Myriam walked away from me and descended the stairs. "Don't dally! Follow me."

I had a gnawing urge to mock her as I trailed behind, but decided to set a good example in case anyone was watching. As Myriam hovered in the front row, I noticed Dana cornering Arthur on the opposite side of the venue. She'd placed her hand on his right arm and rubbed his shoulder. The girl was on a mission, but Arthur didn't appear highly responsive or remotely interested.

"If you didn't hire Arthur, who did?" I asked.

"Gwendolyn Paddington insisted I offer him the opportunity. Some people don't understand the value of hard work and earning their positions." Myriam pulled a red marker from her briefcase and crossed out items on the outlines I'd given to her. "No, no. This won't do. You need to be more creative." As the ink bled on the paper like a murder scene, her forehead wrinkled in spades.

"Gwendolyn's always been active in the arts, like her father-in-law from what I understand. She assumed responsibility as the patron of Paddington's Play House when he died." She'd also been a savagely brutal and vocal art and theater critic before retiring several years earlier.

"She's one to put her nose where it doesn't belong." Myriam stared at me, waiting for a response. When I didn't share one, she said, "We're done. Expect feedback on Tuesday. You may leave."

I had little energy to argue with the monster and muttered a goodbye. As I strolled down the center aisle, a pale and disheveled Arthur joined me. "Ugh, those Paddingtons are truly going to drive me insane. I can't win with any of them. One day they'll be begging me to do something for them instead of the other way around." He pulled at his hair and sneered as we entered the lobby.

"It sounds like things aren't going so well with the show. I'm sorry to hear it." I hoped my empathy might calm him down.

"If it's not Dana playing her little games or Gwendolyn thinking she can control me, it's the confusion with that other one. And on top of it all, I can't find any way to win with that witch, Myriam. I should never have come back home," Arthur grunted.

I couldn't agree with him more about returning to Braxton if I'd tried. Which other Paddington was causing him trouble? "Myriam mentioned Gwen-dolyn insisted you take this job. I would've thought you were on good terms."

Arthur laughed wildly as he opened the door to step outside. "Maybe a long time ago, but not after what she did to me. I'm gonna take a cigarette break before I do something I regret. Is it dreadful that all I dream about is squeezing my hands around Gwendolyn Paddington's neck until her every breath has expired?"

CHAPTER 3

After my trip to Paddington's Play House, Emma and I ate dinner and settled in for a movie. Emma convinced my mother to give up reading—Aunt Deirdre's latest romance novel about Casanova and his voluptuous lover, Torrentia, who was dying of consumption—and instead, watch an animated film about dogs ruling the world. An hour later, I lost count of how many times Emma inquired if we could get a puppy. We only convinced her to stop asking us once my mother agreed to make ice cream sundaes. Emma wasn't a big dessert connoisseur like me, but she loved butterscotch crunch. After I tucked my best girl into bed, I fell asleep dreaming about giant dogs headlining an astoundingly different production of *King Lear*. Even Myriam was present in the strange oddity, barking and all, as a wrinkled Shar-Pei playing the Fool advising Gwendolyn's Dalmatian version of Lear.

On Sunday morning, while my mother took Emma to church, I went for a run at Grey Sports Complex, Braxton College's sprawling athletic facility. As I ran the third loop around the indoor track, I remembered that I'd forgotten to reschedule dinner with Maggie Roarke, my ex-girlfriend from college days. We had recently met up again, and we're supposed to get together last Tuesday, but once Francesca showed up, I'd canceled, citing the need for a couple more days to get Emma settled. Maggie asked me to call her this weekend to pick a new date. I hadn't done it yet, but I also no longer knew what I should do since Francesca was alive. Where was that handbook on dating protocols when you had a dead-not-so-dead spouse?

My mother-in-law and I had planned for Francesca to arrive this morning at ten o'clock. Since my mother would be at church and a subsequent banquet celebrating Lent, and my father wasn't coming home from his trip until late afternoon, it'd give us the entire house to ourselves to discuss the situation. I finished the run, showered, and arrived home as their limo pulled up. Cecilia and Francesca slipped through the back door and greeted me in the living room.

When Francesca and I had met in California, she had long, flowing jet-black hair and wore makeup in muted, natural colors. With her new appearance, she'd cut her hair into a short bob, dyed it an interesting platinum blonde, and wore brash pinks and reds on her face. Even her clothing was different. She truly was a whole new woman, but not one I found as attractive. I didn't mean strictly in terms of beauty and sex appeal. Francesca's attitude seemed colder, more distant.

"How was New York?" I reached for her hand as we sat on the couch.

"It was fun. I didn't get out much, but it felt good to see another city again." Francesca turned to her mother and asked nervously, "Can you give us a little time alone?"

Cecilia agreed. "We only have forty-five minutes before we need to leave for the airport. I'll make a cup of tea in the kitchen." As she left the room, her overly sweet perfume lingered in the air. I'd always hoped she'd explore something other than Chanel Number Five, but Cecilia Castigliano was a creature of habit worthy of Mario Puzo's Vito Corleone.

When Francesca smiled, memories of our past flooded back. "Did you miss me?"

What kind of question was that? I'd missed her for two years, three months, and fourteen days. Did she mean since I'd found out she was alive earlier that week? Since the day I saw what I thought was her dead body? Since I cradled our daughter and wiped away her tears every night for a month upon learning her mother had been killed?

"I don't know how to answer that question. Of course, I do, but where do we go from here?" I held myself back from saying too much too quickly. Staring at her nostalgic and hopeful face only made it hurt worse.

"I've apologized many times, Kellan. I had little choice in what my father did. If I resume my previous identity, they'll be too much collateral damage. Not only will the Vargas family kill me, but they'll go after you and Emma, my parents, and anyone I know as part of their revenge." Several tears cascaded down her withdrawn cheeks in painfully slow motion. As I stared into the new blue color of her weary eyes, I sighed. She asked, "Do you still love me?"

I had given so much thought to how I felt about her return, but as awful as it sounded, would it be better to continue pretending for Emma's sake that her mother had truly died? Francesca inched closer to me and tickled my forearm the way she'd do every night before bed to relax me. There was still an intense connection, but fear and apprehension enveloped it. Would I always need to look over my shoulder to protect myself from what the Castiglianos had done? "I will never stop loving you. But how do we make this work?"

After we discussed assorted options and talked about how much Emma had grown, Francesca said, "I have to fly back to LA today. I want you to come with me... we can figure out a solution... maybe run away together. Or we can live together in secret in my parents' house... when Emma's old enough, we can tell her the truth. My father has to end this war, so I can come out of hiding."

I started to respond, but Cecilia stepped back into the room. "You know that will never be an option, bella. There are still many members of the Vargas family who are alive and angry they couldn't exact revenge against us the way they wanted to. A few don't believe their driver accidentally killed you. They don't see your death as a proper balance to everything."

I stood from the couch and reflected on the six years I had with Francesca before our happy world ceased to exist. All the parties we'd attended with my Hollywood colleagues. The quiet nights at home watching Emma sleep in her crib. The romantic, moonlit walks to the beach. Then I recalled the sleepless nights after Francesca died. The dark night I spent trying to understand how a drunk could get behind the wheel of a car and kill another human being. Or the tears I kissed on Emma's face the first day of school when the teacher asked why her mommy wasn't dropping her off anymore.

"Francesca, I can't do this to Emma. She can't be forced to keep secrets and live a life in hiding." Emma was undoubtedly my priority in all this chaos.

"I can't give up seeing her again, Kellan. We have a perfect solution back in LA. I can watch her grow up, and maybe one day in the future, I'll be able to actually talk to her." When Francesca sobbed, it was Cecilia who comforted her. I wanted to hold my wife, but I held back.

"We should go. Let's give Kellan time to rightly decide. He'll return to LA, I'm certain of it. He's in shock, bella." Cecilia patted her daughter's back and offered me a cold, angry stare.

"I promise to give this some thought. How can I reach you, Francesca?" I asked, knowing I could never abandon my family. As much as they frustrated me, I couldn't say goodbye to Nana D, my parents, Eleanor, or other siblings, even if it meant I could be with Francesca again.

"You can't," Cecilia retorted sharply before ushering my wife toward the back door. "I expect you to return to LA soon, Kellan. You have two weeks to figure this out before I decide for you."

Before I could object, they snuck out the garage door and into the waiting limo. I could've stopped them, but I was too distressed thinking about all the pressure and the veiled threat of a decision being made for me. I paced the floor for at least ten minutes searching for a compromise, but nothing seemed plausible. In a moment of sheer frustration, I grabbed the door handle, ready to pull the entire door off its hinges, but Emma's voice stopped me.

"We're home, Daddy. I brought you a red velvet cupcake," she said while running up to hug me. I basked in her innocence and love before she bounded up the steps to her room, raving about a new cartoon someone had discovered at the church banquet.

I lifted my head and noticed my mother staring back at me. "You look like someone just stole your favorite blanket, my son." And with that, she pulled me against her, squeezed as hard as she could, and kissed my cheek. "I'm always here if you need to talk, Kellan. Even though I sense there's something weighing heavily on your mind, I know better than to push you."

Just a few words from my mother helped me realize despite some awful situations going on around me, I still had loads of love and support in my life. She offered to take Emma shopping for the afternoon to buy some new spring clothes, then encouraged me to attend the *King Lear* dress rehearsal with Nana D and the Paddington family. Although I wasn't in the mood for heavy drama, I changed into a suit and dashed to the theater in a daze.

The performance started at two o'clock which meant I had at least thirty minutes to find Nana D and Gwendolyn to get my ticket. When I entered the lobby, a sea of guests meandered aimlessly. Arthur entered the lobby and called approximately three-hundred patrons to attention by instructing everyone where to look on their tickets for the assigned seat number. As people filed into the venue, the noise level grew more tolerable and I could freely move around without feeling every nook and cranny of every weirdo in the joint. First up was texting Nana D to confirm where our seats. If she sat me next to some new Tinder blind date she'd coordinated...

Me: *Where are you? It's like a blue-haired Neil Diamond concert in here today.*
Nana D: *More like a wannabe Lady Gaga gig. Don't you know any current pop references?*
Me: *Given the number of septuagenarians, I assumed they wouldn't know who she was.*
Nana D: *You know what happens when you ASS-U-ME, don't you, Kellan?*
Me: *That was weak, even for you. Epic FAIL! Where's my ticket?*
Nana D: *I left it at the Box Office. Wasn't sure you'd show. Go get it. Now.*
Me: *Yes, chief. On my way. You're feisty today. Too much bran? Not enough veges?*
Nana D: *Pop a cork in it and get to your seat. You ain't seen nothing yet, brilliant one.*

I waved to Fern while passing by other colleagues whose names I failed to remember. As I approached the ticket window, Maggie looked up, smiled, and dropped a bag of programs to the floor. Her flawless alabaster skin was a perfect offset to rich brown hair and eyes that tempted everyone to fall in love with her.

"I didn't expect to see you here today." I debated whether to lean in and hug her. Maggie decided when she stepped forward and kissed my cheek.

"I volunteered to hold tickets for anyone picking them up at will call. Then I'm seeing the show with Connor. He's finishing at the office and should be here any minute," Maggie said while stepping away from me. The fresh lavender smell of her skin comforted and teased me.

Did she consider it a date? The last time Connor and I had talked, my former best friend told me he'd been in love with my former girlfriend for years and planned to get to know her better. I hadn't seen either in a decade, so I didn't feel comfortable stopping them from taking a chance. Maggie could date whomever she wanted. Okay, except Connor. There, I said it out loud.

"Oh, sounds fun. I believe you might be holding a ticket for me," I noted timidly, trying to keep myself from thinking about Maggie in any way other than as a friend.

"Oh, yes. Nana D dropped it off a few minutes ago. Come on back, it's inside the office." As I followed Maggie through the door, she asked me not to close it all the way. "It sometimes gets stuck, and you can only open it from the outside."

I found a small, wire wastepaper basket in the narrow hallway and wedged it between the door and its frame to prevent it from closing. "How've you been? I'm so sorry about canceling dinner last Tuesday."

Maggie smiled and placed her hand on top of mine. "Emma comes first. We have plenty of time to get to know each other again, right?"

Her warm touch reminded me of a finely spun silk scarf caressing my palm. Every cherished moment in our past together vied for control of my attention. A flood of heat surged through my torn body. I almost got lost in the moment, but a loud thud interrupted my thoughts. "What was that?" I turned around to check.

"Oh no, the door must've closed," Maggie moaned, rushing past me and kicking the rolling wastepaper basket out of her way. She tried opening the door, but it wouldn't budge. I looked at the clock and verified we had several minutes before the show began. My phone chimed.

Nana D: *A brilliant person once told me to use my time wisely. I think you should heed the same advice. I'll let you out when the show starts. Go get her, tiger.*

"I think we'll be fine. It appears fate in the form of a nosy old woman who will be properly punished has intervened." I wobbled my head shamefully.

"Nana D?"

"Yep."

"She saw me struggle with the door earlier. I might've said something about it being broken." Maggie winked.

Perhaps Nana D had a point, but what could one really do with such a short amount of time? All I could think about was that silly game we played in junior high school. As I remembered the name, Maggie said, "It's like we've been locked in the closet to play *Seven Minutes in Heaven*." When she walked by me to access the back-office area, her skin flushed a deep shade of crimson.

"Are you saying being locked in here with me is like heaven?" I felt cheesy using the line, but so much of our past connection revolved around humor and acting silly. "It must be a thoroughly different game at thirty-two than it was at twelve, right?"

Maggie giggled and handed me my ticket. "It's been a long time since we actually kissed. Do you remember that night we got locked in the library?"

I did. "It was the night we first said I love you to one another."

A huge part of me wanted to take a few steps closer to Maggie, to see if the touch of her lips against mine would ignite the same intensity it had years ago. It seemed like she was struggling with a similar longing and began leaning toward me.

When we met in the middle, we stood staring at one another for what felt like an eternity. Who would make the first move? I didn't think I was strong enough since I couldn't split my focus between her and Francesca. Foolishly, I asked, "Are you sure about this?"

The chemistry between us temporarily broke when the door busted open. I had just enough time to back two steps away before Connor saw us.

"Ah, did you get locked in again?" Connor queried in a hesitant voice while squinting with concern. His all-black suit, dark and stormy complexion, and striking facial features made us both do a double take. Maggie because of his general sexiness according to all women and half the male population, me because Connor had been a frequent weightlifter who could easily knock me out with a single punch.

I released a bunch of hot air from my mouth. "Yes, thank you. I needed to get my ticket. I'm meeting Nana D and her friends."

As I rushed past, Connor stopped me. A musky cologne consumed the remaining oxygen between us in the small passageway. "It's good to see you. We should grab a beer sometime soon now that you're living in Braxton." His thick, rich Caribbean accent was more noticeable than normal.

"I like the sound of that," I mumbled while giving him an awkward thumbs-up sign. Was I back in college again? As I scrambled toward the double doors opening into the venue, Nana D winked. "Sorry, kiddo, I tried. But that man is one desirable piece of beef we can't ignore. Pity I'm not ten years younger."

While we searched for our seats, I gagged over Nana D's comment. I also told myself Connor's interruption was a good thing. I couldn't get involved with Maggie until I knew what was going on with Francesca. Nor if Maggie and Connor were seriously interested in one another. They deserved a chance since I'd blown mine years ago.

I sat in the front center row between Nana D and Gwendolyn. To Gwendolyn's right was Eustacia, then Millard. Lindsey was on the other side of Nana D, which annoyed Eustacia since they were still involved in a quirky, repressed love triangle. I apparently took after Nana D way more than I wanted to admit.

Gwendolyn leaned over to me. "I'm glad you came to your senses and attended the show. My son-in-law, Richard, was the one who canceled. That's whom you overheard me talking with yesterday."

"I'm sorry he's missed out. I hope you two can patch things up," I replied, noticing Gwendolyn looked unwell. Her hands shook more than normal, and her breathing seemed labored.

"Richard's a pain in my ass. Always has been. I'll fix him one day, but right now, I'm more concerned about my son, Timothy," she spat out with a heavy sense of frustration and mixed-emotions.

"I guess we never stop worrying about our kids, huh?" Emma's future reaction to learning her mother was still alive frightened me to a point I'd never reached before as a parent.

"Timothy and I had a long talk last night. Important stuff. The relationship between parents and their children is never easy, Kellan. I've got a few pieces of dead fruit of my loins hanging around, and I intend to clear those limbs off the tree soon enough. Sometimes we don't know our family as well as we think we do. There's something everyone's hiding these days, even in your brood, too. I'm sure you'll find out soon enough." As Gwendolyn sat up straight with her back firmly pressed against the seat, I wondered what she'd meant by her last few comments. Was she talking about disinheriting them or evicting them from the house? And what did it have to do with my family?

I scanned the room to see whom else I knew. Dana and Arthur stood on the far corner of the stage, embroiled in an animated discussion. I could hear people behind me chattering about this being Dana's first significant role in a college production. I turned my head to the side and recognized whom I thought was likely her mother, Ophelia, whispering to someone directly behind me. I couldn't turn around further without it looking obvious, so I'd have to try again during the intermission. I heard Ophelia rant, "It's not like she has anything else going on in her life. She's certainly my laziest child."

Ophelia could give her mother, Gwendolyn, a run for her money when bad-mouthing her own children. Just as the other person behind me was about to respond, Myriam stepped to the stage, organized her notes on the podium, and introduced the debut performance of *King Lear*. The first half lasted about an hour and kept everyone entertained. Despite their differences, Arthur and Myriam pulled off an engaging performance full of wit, depth, and intelligence.

When intermission began, I stretched in such a way I could validate who was behind us. I was clearly able to tell Ophelia and Jennifer were sisters given their shoulder-length, chestnut-brown hair, sparkling green eyes, and golden-tan complexion. Ophelia was the older of the pair, early to mid fifties, evident only in a few fine lines developing around her mouth and on her forehead. She probably wore top-tier designer clothes only released on this year's fashion runway and had been to the salon moments before the show. To say she'd recently had a lengthy blow-out would be over-stating the obvious. How did hair triple to such an all-consuming degree?

Jennifer was less bold in her appearance. Instead of faint hints of aging, the contours of her face were smoother and softer with a penchant for dark, moody colors. She was an inch taller than her sister, putting her closer to my range, but she since wore heels we were practically the same height. Jennifer dressed more casually, covering up her svelte figure with a stylish black A-line dress and silver wrap.

When Nana D and her friends stepped into the aisle in search of the restroom, I listened in to Jennifer and Ophelia's conversation. Jennifer said, "Mother has been particularly difficult the last few weeks. Every time we have one of her brief chats, it's an inquisition. I'm forty-seven years old and do not need her relentless judgment."

Ophelia nodded in agreement. "Awful. I know we're supposed to love our parents, but it's time for her to get with the program or take her final bow."

"You said it. I wish she'd learn to be kinder and more open-minded. She's always miserable and never thinks about what's best for us. It's constantly what she wants," Jennifer sniped.

"That's why Timothy avoided it all today. He's the only one in the family who didn't show up," Ophelia said. Timothy was the middle brother, but I hardly knew anything about him, nor had I ever met the man as far as I could recall. While Timothy and Jennifer didn't have any kids, Ophelia had two others besides Dana. I'd just never been introduced to either of them.

"Except your husband. Where is Richard these days... off gallivanting again?" Jennifer accused with a gaze that seemed to penetrate through Ophelia's skin and scratch at her iron composure.

"He's meeting with clients. At least I can keep a husband around. Still waiting for mother's approval, are you?" Ophelia continued their vicious barbs against one another. "You know the only way to control her is to stand up to her. Mother doesn't like it when we all stick together or say *no* to her."

Jennifer stood as if to walk away, then chose not to. "Maybe we should all confront her and tell her it's time to let go of Father's money and give us our inheritances."

"Let's discuss it another time. I need to talk with Dana before the second half. Please get out of my way." Ophelia demanded while waving both hands furiously.

When Ophelia went searching for Dana, and Jennifer wandered closer to the stage, I strolled to the lobby to hunt for Nana D. I couldn't find her but noticed Gwendolyn talking to a man in his fifties. They looked like they were arguing. As I approached, it appeared like he grabbed hold of her wrist with intensity. Gwendolyn almost spilled her drink from the pressure. By the time I reached her, he'd already walked away.

"Are you okay, Mrs. Paddington? It looked like that man was harassing you." I scanned the room to see if he was still nearby.

"That was my son, Timothy. He needed to talk to me for a minute. Have you seen Brad around?" Gwendolyn inhaled as if she were taking a last breath.

"I don't know anyone named Brad," I responded as Nana D walked up with a younger guy.

"Brad is Gwennie's nurse. She can't find the travel bottle with her medicine in her purse. I called him earlier to drop it off." Nana D introduced me to Brad, a fit guy in his mid-twenties who wore skinny jeans and a heather gray sweater.

"I'm right here, Mrs. Paddington. Here's your medication." Brad handed her several pills.

"You must explain to me how we screwed this up earlier. I thought you put the bottle in my purse. But I don't have time to discuss it right now. I'm coming right home once the show ends." Gwendolyn tossed the pills into her mouth.

From my brief glimpse, there were three tablets ranging from small to large sizes and coated in different colors. Brad waited for her to swallow them, reminded her to take a sip of her iced tea to wash them down, and then disappeared, probably used to being dismissed as one of the servants who knew his place in the household.

"Should we take you home? I'm like your older brother. You should listen to me," Millard said.

"Nah, I'll be fine. Just lost my breath for a few minutes. Let's go sit down," Gwendolyn replied.

We all scrambled into the theater and took our seats. Jennifer and Ophelia had already returned and stood near one another but were clearly not speaking. While Eustacia held her sister-in-law's glass, Lindsey helped Gwendolyn get seated. Nana D introduced me to Ophelia's two other children, Sam, a senior at Braxton, and Lilly, who'd graduated two years earlier. Neither noticed their grandmother profusely sweating or her inability to get situated without nearly falling. The Paddingtons were a strange family. Everyone seemed to care enough to show up, but no one looked fond of one another.

When the lights blinked several times, Myriam stepped onto the stage to announce intermission was over and the show was about to begin. A few seconds later, the theater went dark. The actors portraying King Lear and the Fool appeared on stage for one of my favorite sets of witty and revealing dialogs. Midway into the scene, something bumped my right shoulder. I looked to the side only to notice Gwendolyn leaning into me. I whispered, "Is the performance that boring?" but she didn't answer.

I nudged her arm, thinking she'd fallen asleep, but that didn't rouse her either. I shook her more forcefully. Gwendolyn wouldn't respond. I activated the flashlight on my cell phone and shined it on her face. Gwendolyn had passed out after the lights went down. I pressed my fingers into her cool and moist neck, searching for her carotid artery. I couldn't find a pulse, nor could I find any sign of life. I leaned over to Nana D and said, "I think Gwendolyn just died in her seat!"

CHAPTER 4

Interrupting a live theater performance was not a simple task. While my stomach revolted over finding another dead body and having it physically leaning against me in the dark, I made use of my extensive grasp on the English language to delicately inform the actors we needed to stop the show. As Lear emphatically cursed the weather surrounding him, I'd been forced to shout over him from a few feet off center stage. First came the boos and sounds of people hushing my disturbance. Then the actor portraying Lear turned to me in full character questioning if I were the impetuous and virulent storm about to hit the stage. Thankfully, once the lighting director moved the spotlight to my seat, the entire troupe could see I was serious about someone needing medical attention.

Myriam assumed control of the stage and directed all the guests to quietly and orderly file into the main lobby. Nana D volunteered to call 9-1-1 as I thwarted Gwendolyn's family from rushing up to check on her. I knew the woman had passed away, and while I hadn't truly given credence to her suspicions about someone in her family trying to kill her, it was important to prevent what could be a crime scene from contamination. I'd learned that tenet many times over in the past from our county sheriff.

Eustacia moaned loudly and turned to Lindsey for comfort. Millard, her brother, stepped to the side aisle to provide some space. But I was too focused on Ophelia's daughters to listen to his conversation. A tear-stained Jennifer breathed in and out in an almost panicked mode, but soon gained control of her composure. Ophelia kept looking toward two of her children to judge their reactions, but she didn't appear to be shocked or devastated by her mother's passing. Dana was still back stage and probably hadn't known who'd fallen ill or what'd stopped the performance.

"The ambulance is on its way," Nana D said in a soothing but despondent voice. "My poor friend... Gwennie wasn't feeling well earlier, but I didn't know it was so serious."

I wrapped my arms around my grandmother, who'd leaned against me for comfort. "She did have a minor spell out in the lobby earlier. I'm wondering if she had a heart attack or a stroke."

Maggie idled closer to the stage, tilting her head in a way I knew she was telling me everything would be okay. I always could read her expressions as though I were inside her mind, too. Connor arrived within a few seconds, desperate to take control of the situation. As the head of the Braxton Campus Security Office, he'd be the first on the scene, even if he hadn't been on a date with Maggie. After checking Gwendolyn's pulse, Connor pulled Nana D and me aside. "She's definitely gone. I'm so sorry for her family," he said with sorrow while resting a hand on Nana D's shoulder.

"Connor, you need to check for evidence right away," whispered Nana D while tugging on his sport coat. "Gwennie told me someone was trying to hurt her in the last few weeks. She knew something was wrong. We should've done something sooner about it."

"Nana D, I'm sure the coroner will check for any sign of something unnatural happening." I didn't want to stir the pot when we were already in an awkward state.

Connor's gaze opened wide. "Are you saying you think someone tried to kill her today, Mrs. Danby?" He looked at me for confirmation, but I shrugged. I was distracted first by everything going on, then by Arthur's wide grin while talking on his cell phone near the stage steps.

Nana D explained that her friend had been feeling fine until the prior month, when she began having dizzy spells and shortness of breath. Gwendolyn initially thought it was a touch of the flu or a severe winter cold. After four weeks, Lindsey and Nana D had convinced Gwendolyn to listen to Brad, who'd wanted to schedule an appointment with her doctor. In the last two weeks, she'd vomited several times and her skin tone had grown paler each day. She'd even become disoriented in her own house, but blamed it on lack of being able to keep down any food or get a full night's sleep.

"Did she tell you she thought someone was trying to hurt her?" Connor asked.

I nodded. "She mentioned something funny was going on at the Paddington mansion and planned to address it with her family after the doctor's visit."

As the paramedics arrived, I stepped to the side to let them work. Connor returned to Maggie, who waited with him while he made a phone call. Nana D sat a few seats further away near Millard, Eustacia, and Lindsey. The Septuagenarian Club had lost one of their founding members and comforted one another in a way no one else could. While Nana D placed something inside her oversized purse, she nodded at me and pointed toward the stage.

Arthur ended his phone call, then spoke with Myriam, who appeared quite rattled. Arthur disappeared behind the curtain, prompting Myriam to approach me with a scowl plastered on her face.

"You seem to find yourself in the middle of everything these days, Kellan. Ever since you returned to Braxton, *'Death, that hath suck'd the honey of thy breath,'* follows you like a ghost to Hamlet's conscience," Myriam criticized before clearing her throat.

"Romeo said that while putting Paris in the tomb, I believe, didn't he? You're mixing the Bard's greatest tragedies." I wanted to ask Myriam what her outlandish fascination was with Shakespearean quotes, particularly at inappropriate times, but Ophelia interrupted me. I felt sufficiently satisfied about getting in at least one dig.

"I recognize that line. How fitting, my mother loved Romeo and Juliet. She died of a broken heart from missing my father the last year," Ophelia said with a faint smile, then sighed. She ran a few fingers through the many layers of her voluminous hair and adjusted a diamond earring. "Myriam, tell me, how has Dana's work been on the show thus far?"

I tuned out while they discussed Ophelia's youngest daughter's participation in *King Lear*. Was this the time to bring up such a topic? Ophelia had as much tact as Myriam had kindness in her bones. I glanced toward Ophelia's other two children, noticing Lilly, the eldest, listening as her brother Sam spoke to their Aunt Jennifer.

Lilly seemed disinterested in the conversation and kept leaning away to look at the paramedics as they attended to her grandmother. Perfectly styled, ruler-straight ebony hair cascaded down her back against a stuffy, jade-green silk blouse that belonged on someone older like Gwendolyn or Eustacia. It was pulled tightly across her ample chest and disappeared into high-waisted pants that forced her to walk erect like a model balancing a book on the top of her head. Angular features stood out against hollow cheeks. Widely set eyes furiously darted from side to side. It made her appear gaunt and sickly, but also as though she thought she was more important than the crowd surrounding her.

Other than once witnessing Lilly berate a barista at The Big Beanery over a weak café au lait, all I'd known about her was that she'd survived a skiing accident that had occurred years earlier while her college roommate hadn't been so lucky. During winter break in their junior year, they'd been competing on one of the more treacherous slopes in the Wharton Mountains. Lilly had fallen into her friend, who tumbled down the mountain and careened directly into a large fir tree. Lilly eventually stopped herself before she encountered the same fate but couldn't recall what had prompted her to fall. There had been another friend, a boy they'd both dated that year, who was supposed to ski with them but had gotten food poisoning the night before. I'd heard the story from Eleanor, who'd been a part-time ski instructor on the mountain. She always felt there was more to the event than what Lilly had told everyone.

Myriam excused herself to meet with the cast about the next rehearsal. Ophelia rushed off, citing a need to use the restroom, but it was clear she didn't want to be left alone to talk with me. I'd only met her moments before, yet knew enough to recognize a blow-off when I saw one. My gaze returned to Jennifer, who hugged Lilly and Sam before leaving the theater. Lilly walked toward her sister, Dana, and they both vanished into the lobby laughing, presumably about something funny one of them had just said. Dana wore a low-cut magenta top with her bare shoulders and midriff showing as though it were the middle of spring or summer. Though the room was heated, the chill in the air couldn't be ignored. Dana wore too little clothing for this event, in my opinion. Despite being a red-blooded American man, I believed there was a fine line between dressing sexy and inappropriately.

Sam disappeared in a corner several rows away from everyone. The distant, withdrawn look in his bright green eyes revealed intense pain over losing someone he loved. Nana D had often remarked how sweet and kind he'd always been to her in the past. *'Not like a typical pompous or irascible Paddington,'* she'd quip whenever visiting Gwendolyn and he'd been home. Sam's slight build and baby face made him appear younger than a college senior. His neatly combed, straw-colored blond hair and delicate features reminded me of a Norman Rockwell painting. There seemed to be a maturity and quietness about him unlike his siblings.

He smiled despite my interrupting his solitude. "I'm so sorry about your grandmother, Sam. I lost my grandpop several years ago. I still remember it like it was only yesterday."

"Thank you, I'm in a bit of shock," Sam replied, shifting back and forth on the heels of his feet. "We spent a lot of time together. We both loved the theater so much."

"Mrs. Paddington was a prominent supporter of the arts. I'm sure she will be missed. How's your family holding up?" I hoped to learn more from someone on the inside.

"Do I know you, I mean, have we met... never mind." Sam looked perplexed at my words, but responded in a gentle voice. "Mom's strong. She and Grandmother didn't get along very well, but I know she'll collapse at some point. Aunt Jennifer is a mess, even said she had to leave before everyone noticed how awful she looked. I wish I could go, but Lilly is my ride back home."

"Were your sisters close to her, too?"

"Not particularly. Grandmother could be difficult if you didn't know how to handle her. She respected honesty and directness. I learned that early on and tried to always remain on her good side." Sam looked weary and desperate to leave. "I'm sorry, I didn't get your name."

"I apologize," I responded, realizing I'd forgotten to introduce myself. Although I knew whom he was, he hadn't a clue why I still hung around. "I'm Kellan Ayrwick, Seraphina Danby's grandson. I was sitting next to Mrs. Paddington when she, ummm... fell ill. I'd met her many times through my grandmother. They've been best friends for over fifty years."

Sam smiled nervously, then pulled back as if he'd felt awkward having any moment of positivity given the circumstances. "Or frenemies from what I hear, too. Ayrwick, you said?" A look of confusion clouded his face as he processed our conversation.

I nodded. "Yes, they've had their trials in the past. I wonder if it was a heart attack or if anything else was going on with her health."

Sam pulled out his phone. "I should go. Nice to meet you. I appreciate you being there for her just now... you know... when..."

"I understand. You're welcome," I replied. Sam rushed away, leaving me concerned why his mood further soured near the end of our conversation. He exited into the lobby, then took off through the front doors by himself. So much for waiting for a ride from his sister, Lilly.

While none of the Paddingtons seemed like potential killers, they were all mysterious and disparate from one another. The family had enough money. I couldn't be sure about the younger generation's personal lives or spending habits. I'd have to ask Nana D, or maybe Millard and Eustacia could fill in the blanks. It wasn't any of my business, but if one of them had purposely caused Gwendolyn's death, I should let Sheriff Montague know.

The paramedics informed everyone they were going to remove the body soon. It was a polite way of indicating it was time for us to leave the building, since no one would want to see Gwendolyn being tucked into a black body bag. Nana D was watching everyone else get into Lindsey's car, holding her purse strangely so it wouldn't fall. As I unlocked my SUV's door, Sheriff Montague's motorcycle pulled up. She parked near the entrance and removed her helmet, then went inside. I'd never seen the woman wear anything fashionable before today. She'd had on designer black jeans and knee-high gray leather boots. Under her open form-fitting raincoat, a purple silk blouse and cream-colored scarf stared back at me. Perhaps she had a personal life like the rest of us and didn't live in a dark cave, despite my theory she was a hermit or a troll.

"Kellan, I need to speak with you," whispered Nana D before I pulled the SUV's door shut. Nana D ran around to the other side and snuck into the passenger seat. "Shhh, say nothing."

I had no idea what Nana D was trying to hide, but she opened her purse and pulled out a half-empty glass with a straw sticking out the top. She'd wrapped a piece of cloth over the top, so she wasn't touching anything. "What is that?" I asked, fearing the worst.

"Gwennie's iced tea. She hadn't finished it, and I was afraid the cleaning staff would throw it out." Nana D brimmed with excitement about why she'd kept the glass.

"I don't understand. What's that for?" I grabbed the glass, careful not to touch any surface with my fingers.

"Evidence. You need to have this tested to see if someone drugged Gwennie," Nana D said bluntly while slapping my arm with her free hand. "Do I have to do *everything*?"

"Even if someone put something in her drink, you've contaminated it. Why didn't you leave it there?" I slapped my forehead in disbelief with my free hand.

"Don't be absurd! I used my handkerchief and touched nothing. I told Connor it was a suspicious death, but I didn't know if he'd call that lazy sheriff."

"Well, April Montague is here now. What are you planning to do with the glass?"

Nana D pulled back. "Me? I can't be involved in this. I'm running for Wharton County Mayor. You need to take it from here. Someone's gotta protect Gwennie now that she's gone."

There are days I wish my nana was an eccentric old woman who liked to sit home and play Yahtzee or do needlepoint. Maybe talk to herself or twenty cats about the price of a bottle of unpasteurized milk prior to the Great War. But Nana D wouldn't let the barn cats indoors, and she had a lactose intolerance—neither of those things were possible. Nor was she ever the type to act her age. Instead, I had a super-charged nana who interfered in everyone's business and thrust herself into every kind of trouble. Is this what I'd turn into when I reached her age? I'd have to warn Emma to put me in a home far away from everyone.

"Nana D, I can't hand a glass of iced tea to the sheriff and demand she run lab tests on it. One, she already dislikes me. Two, it will make her angry that I took evidence away from a crime scene. Three, she'll accuse me of trying to go around her to solve another crime. Four, she'll—"

"That's what's wrong with you, Kellan. You think like you're stuck inside a box. Life's not about staying within four perfect walls or coloring within the lines." Nana D held her hands, making the shape of a square with her fingers, then zoomed it in and out of my face. "It's blurry, kinda like your vision, Magoo. I'm sure you're smart enough to realize that sometimes you can get away with anything you want by claiming you didn't know any better."

"That might work for a meddlesome member of the Septuagenarian Club, but I highly doubt Sheriff Montague would believe me if I said I didn't know any better when it came to contaminating evidence."

"Fine. If you don't want to help me, poor Gwennie's soul will roam around Braxton unable to properly pass over to the other side because she didn't know who killed her. *Tsk tsk.*" Nana D pursed her lips and shook her head. "Such a good woman. Stuck in between like those *Beetlejuice* characters. You don't want Eleanor to host a séance, do you, Kellan? Think of the dangers in doing that—"

"Are you guilting me into finding Gwendolyn's killer? She might not have been murdered. This could have been a natural death. Seriously, why don't you let the sheriff poke around and if something seems off, we can produce a better plan later on? They're going to have to do an autopsy, anyway."

"Kellan Michael Ayrwick! I am wiser and more experienced than you. I am your elder by a couple of years. I have a right to—"

"More than a couple years, if you're trying to be an honest candidate for mayor," I said, unable to stop myself. That's when Nana D gently slapped my cheek and almost caused me to bang the iced tea glass into the rearview mirror. "Ouch. Uncalled for!"

"Totally called for. My point is... you better do something about this, or I will disown you."

"No, you won't."

Nana D rolled her bright bug eyes. I knew where I'd gotten it from. She continued to taunt me, saying, "Fine, you're right. I won't disown you, but I will set you up with every available harebrained girl in this town. I'll have you fending off more cougars and petty criminals than that fool of a district attorney currently in office. She's next on my list as soon as you understand I'm right about testing this iced tea."

Nana D had it out for every branch of Wharton County's government. "Ugh, go away, Beelzebub," I said with a grimace while repositioning the glass, so I could keep it hidden under my coat. "I'll fix your mistake." While Nana D went back to her own car whining, *"I don't make mistakes,"* I walked toward the side entrance of Paddington's Play House.

As I scurried through the hallway in the backstage area, I noticed Dana talking to Arthur. I eavesdropped on their conversation.

"I can't believe she's gone," Dana said. "I know she's my grandmother, and I'm supposed to be upset, but she was always so cruel to me. It's better off this way. Now I'll finally get some of my own money and won't have to listen to my family anymore."

Arthur responded, "She was a royal pain, wasn't she? No offense, but the world's a much better place without Gwendolyn Paddington. She got what she deserved."

They stopped speaking, and in fear they might catch me listening, I kept moving. When I made it to the curtain, I looked down at the seating area. Only the paramedics were still around. I waited for them to roll the stretcher with the body through the main aisle before I snuck down the stage stairs. What had my days come to? I was helping my nana sneak evidence back into a potential crime scene, so the sheriff could find it on her own accord.

I quickly put the glass into the seat's cup holder and rushed up the stairs toward the stage. As I stepped behind the curtain and tucked the handkerchief in my pocket, I noticed the sheriff looking in my direction. I wasn't sure if April saw me, but I knew it wouldn't be ideal to get caught handling evidence. Connor pointed to the iced tea glass. Then the sheriff called to an officer standing at the side of the room. A few seconds later, she bagged and labeled the glass. I wasn't sure how I'd have gotten her to inspect the glass if they hadn't done it on their own, but luckily it wasn't a concern. Instead of returning to my car, I stopped next door at The Big Beanery for a cup of coffee and a pastry filled with as much sugary cream or jelly as I could find. I'd earned it. As I entered through the door, my phone beeped.

Connor: *I covered for you, but you better explain what was going on with that glass and why you sneaked it back into the theater.*

Me: *I owe you dinner. I promise, there's a valid explanation. Call me when you're done flirting with your girlfriend. Give the sheriff a hug from me.*

Connor: *Watch it, or I'll tell her the truth about you. She and I are not dating, Purple Panty Boy.*

Connor liked to use my dreaded nickname from college days, but I was too distracted dealing with another dead body. It brought me tumbling back to thinking about Francesca. As I settled into the corner table trying to keep myself from ordering a second dessert, Maggie walked into The Big Beanery. Why did thoughts of the two greatest loves of my life always come in pairs since I'd come back home?

CHAPTER 5

"Hey, stranger. Didn't I just see you a little while ago?" Maggie said in a coy tone with an enormous smile displaying bright white teeth.

"Yes, but that was before the drama. Although I feel bad for the Paddington family, I'm glad to see you again." Between the unexpected death and my determined attempt to avoid memories of Francesca, I'd originally thought being alone was the best thing for me. Sharing an afternoon cup of coffee with Maggie changed my mind.

"What happened?" she asked, signaling to a server for a large decaf. When it was delivered, I handed the kid a ten-dollar bill and told him to keep the change. I didn't want to be interrupted again.

"I'm not sure if there's any merit to Gwendolyn Paddington's fears, but if the sheriff or coroner find anything concerning, we might have another murder in Braxton. I'm starting to think it's all because I returned home."

Maggie cocked her head like I'd spoken some foreign language. "Perhaps you're being a little self-involved with that theory? You had nothing to do with the other deaths, and I'm fairly certain even if someone killed Gwendolyn, it wasn't because of you."

"I didn't mean it that way. I'm not saying people are dying because I came back, I just meant—"

Maggie playfully tapped my right hand. "I was teasing." Her fingers lingered, making me think back to what might have happened when we were stuck in the Box Office before Connor's interruption. "Gwendolyn was in her mid-seventies. There's every chance it could've been a heart attack or something else normal. Let's wait until we hear if this is anything suspicious."

"I know. I just got strange vibes from her family. Do you know much about them?"

Maggie shook her head. "Since I've only been back for the one semester, I never interacted with Lilly. I helped Sam find a book on some rare plants and flowers several weeks ago, but we barely spent much time together. Dana and I have had a few interesting encounters in the library."

"Really... such as?" I assumed it related to an intimate discussion with Arthur. "Do tell!"

"Dana is extremely boy crazy. When she gets a crush on someone, she goes to great lengths to capture his attention. Last month, she claimed to be in love with one of my student workers and snuck into the archive room. I still don't know how she got in with no one seeing, but she'd arranged a picnic lunch and was wearing minimal clothing."

"Was the student worker with her?"

"No, Jordan kept saying he was worried about an upcoming exam, so I finally advised him to quit bugging me and leave. He mentioned accidentally leaving the door to the archive room unlocked, which is how I found Dana crying and drinking from a nearly empty bottle of wine. I suspect Jordan was afraid to meet her, so he rushed out and forced me to be the one to find her."

"Dana sounds like she's a bit of a troublemaker," I said. Jordan Ballantine was a good kid I'd met earlier that month when he was a suspect on a murder investigation. He was also one of my students and Fern's nephew, which made him Arthur's cousin. Dana preferred to focus on guys in the same family!

"The next day, when I asked why he did that, Jordan claimed she was 'Jack Nicholson in *The Shining*' crazy. She'd been texting him to come find her and sending him compromising pictures. Apparently, she doesn't like to be told *no*." Maggie finished her coffee, then mentioned she was meeting Connor for dinner later that evening since their date at the theater had been preempted.

I thanked her for the information, suggested a day for our meal the upcoming week, and pretended to be happy she had a date with someone else. As I finished up my coffee, Connor called. Had his ears been burning? I explained what Nana D had done, and he promised to keep our actions quiet, assuming our fingerprints didn't show up on the glass despite our supposed intent to be careful.

"Next time inform Nana D that I listen when she tells me things. That grandmother of yours is going to outlast all of us," Connor jested.

"Did you learn any additional information after I left Paddington's Play House?" I asked, curious whether he believed anything suspicious had occurred.

"The sheriff ordered an autopsy given the death happened in a public place when the deceased had just taken pills that might have been misplaced earlier that day. She wanted to know the exact cause of death before proceeding with anything else. April was angry the paramedics cleared the body before her team could investigate, but since it occurred so quickly, she couldn't say much."

"What happens next?" I debated whether any delays were going to be an issue. If there was a killer, could they be hiding additional evidence at Gwendolyn's home?

"The coroner and lab will be done tonight with preliminary observations on cause of death. Both agreed to rush their analyses, so the sheriff could get warrants to search the house. She's also inquiring with the family to understand if anyone thinks there's reasonable cause for this amounting to anything other than natural causes."

"Because of what Nana D said?"

"That's part of it. April also overheard people talking about an argument Gwendolyn had with her son, Timothy, in the lobby during intermission. That's also how she knew about the issue with the misplaced pills when the nurse showed up."

"I heard it, too. Something seemed odd in Gwendolyn's discussion with the nurse about misplaced pills."

"Don't put yourself in the middle of an investigation again, Kellan, if there's even a need for one. Please let the Sheriff's Office do their work," Connor grunted before hanging up.

I walked back to my SUV, eager to get home for dinner with Emma and away from the devastation of the afternoon. Although it seemed morbid at first, I'd bought my new vehicle from the estate of a friend, Lorraine, who'd been killed several weeks earlier. Her brother's highly discounted offer helped me maintain a connection to someone I'd cared for. When I asked my sister, Eleanor, whether it was a good idea, she consulted her Tarot cards and quickly learned I was meant to stay connected with Lorraine even though she'd passed over to The Great Beyond. It's not that I didn't believe in spirits, but I'd never met one before and honestly, it wasn't my thing. I left the supernatural and horoscope stuff to Eleanor. And if Lorraine ever showed up as a ghost riding shotgun in her former vehicle, claiming she wanted to help solve Gwendolyn's murder, I'd sell the haunted SUV to the first interested party. As I started the engine, my phone chimed.

Nana D: *I forced Lindsey to tell me about Gwennie's will.*

Me: *Isn't that a violation of some law? Shouldn't he maintain her confidences?*

Nana D: *Lindsey's retired. He transferred the will with Gwennie's permission to another attorney a few years ago. Besides, we won't tell anyone else, will we?*

Me: *Most unbecoming for a mayoral candidate. What did it say?*

Nana D: *That hairdo of yours is unbecoming. At the time Lindsey worked on it, Gwennie and Charles had planned to leave everything to all three of their children, but something changed right around the time Charles died. Lindsey said Gwennie was keen on altering the will again.*

Me: *Who inherits now?*

Nana D: *Gwennie wouldn't tell Lindsey anything about the adjustment. Anyone could've killed her, thinking they were still included in the will and set to inherit.*

* * *

As soon as I arrived home, my mother left to meet my father for dinner since he'd been away all weekend. I spent the rest of Sunday evening eating and assembling a puzzle with Emma. She'd chosen a collage of zoo animals at the bookstore earlier in the week. We baked peanut butter cookies in the shape of cows and sheep while play-fighting over who got to work on all the puzzle corners. I let her find three out of four corners, but never them all. It was important she knew the value of being a good loser.

Since Spring Break began at Braxton on Monday, classes weren't in session for the next week. I planned to spend a few hours on campus each day, but I also wanted to help get Emma settled in second grade at her new school. The school's principal and Board of Education had agreed to let her skip forward a year based on past exam results and a successful interview the prior week. I stayed for thirty minutes to watch her interact with other kids before leaving for Braxton. If I hadn't known better, my precocious daughter was trying to push me out the door.

When I got to Memorial Library, I researched an upcoming digital project required as part of one course I taught. After securing enough hours with the librarians for the entire class, I finished grading my last few papers in one of the reading rooms rather than trek back to my office on South Campus. Ten minutes later, Fern waved to me and asked if she could sit for a moment. I assumed the Dean of Student Affairs also didn't have off this week and was using the time to catch up on administrative functions. "What brings you to the library today? I can't imagine you're saddled with grading papers like me!"

"I'm reviewing the proposals from this year's student committee assigned to the cable car upgrades. There are some doozies in here, Kellan." Every year, the graduating class proposed three ideas for redesigning the interior of the cable car that ran from North Campus to South Campus.

"What do you think will win?" I asked, recalling my own year's debacle over choosing a *Spartan 300* theme. A picture of me in a highly unflattering outfit still hung in the Alumni Office for all to see.

"Heaven help us, but the committee's favorite is an apocalypse caused by global warming and a cyber takeover," she sighed heavily. "What happened to the lighter sides of life? I'd even go for *Star Wars* again since it's become so popular."

"Good luck with that. How's Arthur doing since yesterday's incident?" I asked cautiously. After I'd overheard him backstage, I knew he was fine. It'd be eye opening to learn what his mother thought.

"Oh, he's surviving." Fern squished together her lips and nose, then covered her face with both hands. "It was awful. I cared little for Gwendolyn Paddington, but I felt bad for her family. At least her death occurred in one of her favorite places. That's a comfort if nothing else."

"I interacted with them in the theater while the paramedics were onsite. Did Arthur know them well?" I hoped Fern would innocently share something valuable.

"Gwendolyn got him the job. She was incredibly supportive back when he was in high school, but something changed in their relationship and she turned on him. He doesn't talk about it much anymore, but I know all about what she did to him afterward." Fern shook her head and made a *tsk tsk* sound.

My ears perked up. "I knew there was bad blood between them. Arthur mentioned it one day, but I didn't realize the feud had gone back so far."

"Well, he asked her to introduce him to her contacts in New York City when he moved there after graduating from high school. She'd been coaching the drama club back then and praised his talent, but she wanted him to get a degree at Braxton, so he was a step ahead of everyone before taking his chances on Broadway."

"And things fell apart?"

"There was some sort of disagreement. She'd offered to introduce him to a few of her friends, but he was foolish. He'd gotten full of himself and used her name too much. He inherited those traits from his father. I should've left the man sooner, but unfortunately, I tried to make it work. Anyway, Gwendolyn chastised him for overstepping a boundary and blackballed him across the industry. She could be vicious. That's why he came back to Braxton to get his degree a few years afterward."

It made sense. I'd only seen him around campus twice my senior year, but he'd become suddenly snobby and difficult. "If she was angry, why did she give him the job directing the *King Lear* play?"

"Well, there's the reason I know, and there's the reason I suspect." Fern smirked and made a funny noise in her throat like she was frustrated with the whole series of events.

I laughed. "That sounds... confusing. Or intriguing."

"Myriam was stuck last-minute when the woman she thought was going to direct the show had to bow out after getting a national tour for an up-and-coming comedy revival. I happened to be meeting with her and Gwendolyn to discuss the plans for the production. I suggested that Arthur could pitch in, knowing he hadn't been able to find a job for the last few months. The doting mom in me couldn't stop myself." A mixed look of pride and embarrassment overtook her calm and confident expression.

"So, what were the reasons she said yes?"

"Gwendolyn felt bad about how hard she was on Arthur and wanted to give him another chance. She also despised Myriam more than anyone I know." Before Fern spoke again, our eyes connected and part of me wondered whether Fern realized I might be the only one who disliked Myriam even more. "I suspect Gwendolyn wanted to witness Arthur and Myriam battle it out purely for her own entertainment. Not exactly mature, but she wasn't always the nicest of people."

"Based on what I know about her, she would do something like that," I responded. Could Gwendolyn have been wrong, thinking it was her family trying to hurt her? Perhaps Myriam or Arthur exacted revenge on the unsuspecting and tetchy septuagenarian.

"Both women had been giving him a challenging time while preparing for the show. Apparently, Myriam told Arthur this morning that she no longer needed his services and set him free with only two weeks' notice." Fern rubbed her fingers against the surface of the table while determining what to say next. "She's completely within her rights as the head of the drama department to decide. I'm not even sure who will represent the Paddington family anymore. I wondered if you might know whom I could speak with to convince Myriam not to push my son out."

Now I understood why Fern wanted to talk with me. "I don't know the Paddingtons all that well, but I suppose I could ask one of them." I wasn't exactly certain how it all came together. Gwendolyn was Braxton's patron for the art and theater program. She represented the Paddington family on all decisions regarding the Play House and its operations. Was it a formal position given to someone upon her death or a volunteer role within the family to look out for the campus and its creative endeavors?

I agreed to discuss it with Eustacia, knowing I was meeting her and Nana D at the Paddington mansion for lunch that afternoon. When Fern left, I finished grading my papers for the remaining classes. I felt bad giving two students an 'F,' but one had clearly plagiarized an online database of essays written by an esteemed college professor. The other failed to visit the writing center, which was a requirement for the assignment. I'd counted thirty-eight grammatical and spelling errors, many of which would have been caught by a word processing program's spellchecker. Despite my education and experience, I still made a few mistakes. But his paper was unreadable.

I drove to Millionaire's Mile, a mile-long street running parallel to the Braxton cable car system between the two campuses, where several enormous estates resided. The Paddington mansion was set between the Grey and Stanton properties and loomed over everything in the vicinity. The house had originally belonged to Eustacia and Millard's parents, but when they died, it was left to their son, Charles Paddington, even though he wasn't the oldest son. I never understood why and made a mental note to ask Nana D how that had all worked out years ago. Charles, Gwendolyn's late husband, had assumed responsibility for running the family businesses, Paddington Enterprises, for many years before turning it over to his son, Timothy. The conglomerate comprised several financial advisory firms, shipping warehouses and docks along the Finnulia River and Crilly Lake, and real estate investment and development holding companies.

Although I'd driven by the Paddington estate in the past, I was never invited through the gates to explore the crown jewel of all the homes in Braxton. The three-story estate had four separate wings and had been built in the early twentieth century using reclaimed materials from a Georgia manor house that was given up at auction. I parked in the small lot to the right of the principal building and ambled up the cedar-chipped path. A large baroque fountain with at least six shooting sprays of water dominated the circle driveway. Home to several species of fish and floating water lilies, the crystal-clear bubbles resembled bottles of overflowing champagne. Robust gardens with shrubbery and trees shaped into forest animals adorned both sides of the house, suggesting scenes of various famous paintings from the Gilded Age. A gentle stream of water filled with colorful flowers encircled them and sculpted rock collections.

I smiled at the beauty and obnoxious personality of the estate as I meandered the sprawling pathway and climbed the polished marble steps. Before I could knock or ring a bell, the door opened. An older, plump woman with gray curls, a pair of spectacles hung on a beaded chain, and a black-and-white uniform reminiscent of those I'd seen in early 1930s films introduced herself as Mrs. Crawford. "The Paddingtons are expecting you. Give me one moment to let them know you're here, Mr. Ayrwick." Even her charming accent had made the lucrative move from Georgia.

Before the woman could leave the large travertine-tiled foyer, Nana D stepped into the slippery space. It felt like an accident waiting to happen, especially for anyone using a cane. "Don't worry, Mrs. Crawford. I'll bring my grandson into the dining room. Isn't it time you took a break? I left you a peach crumble on the counter in the kitchen. Don't you be sharing that with anyone else! It's yours alone."

"That's generous of you, Mrs. Danby." Mrs. Crawford beamed with a smile that had probably never seen the light of day in the Paddington mansion.

"I've told you before, please call me Seraphina. None of my friends call me Mrs. *Anything*, so you shouldn't either." Nana D guided Mrs. Crawford down the west hall toward the kitchen.

"This place is enormous." I marched behind her through the central section of the house. When we entered the Great Hall, it felt like it was the first time I'd ever seen light. A giant conservatory occupied the middle of the room, offering so much brightness I could barely focus. I noticed dozens of exotic plants and trees scattered all around, many of which I was certain couldn't survive anywhere north of the equator. "Did we suddenly transport to the Amazon? Who's their gardener, Martha Stewart's South American doppelganger?"

Nana D grinned. "It is beautiful, but don't be juvenile. Millard has the green thumb. He's the designer and inspiration behind all of this. He hired lots of help over the years to maintain it, but there isn't a species in this room he didn't select himself from the original location."

Nana D had dated Millard for a few months while I'd lived in LA, but it didn't last long. I never understood exactly what'd caused her to break it off, but she often mentioned his inability to be generous or treat women equally to men. He was charming and intelligent, but some old-fashioned sense of men being the dominant gender prevailed in his mind. Nana D tried to teach him how to be a modern man, but he simply couldn't tolerate the new way of doing things.

"I could sit for hours and admire his imagination and creative genius. Does Millard live here, too?" I asked, not knowing which of the Paddingtons resided in the family home.

Nana D shook her head. "When Millard was passed over as the rightful heir, he moved out to allow Charles to occupy the family estate. His brother encouraged him to stay, but Millard felt their parents had decided and he had to abide by it."

"Where does he live?" I knew Eustacia had been invited to move in with Gwendolyn when it came time for in-residence assistance, but she never did. Eustacia was too proud to move back in with her brother's family and had bought a small upscale condo in the newly built Willow Trees senior living retirement facility. She was surrounded by other sixty-five-plus inhabitants who kept her youthful and full of spite.

"Millard has a few houses. He mostly stays in a cottage closer to the Wharton mountains. He prefers to be near nature, but he comes back every week to take care of this garden," Nana D noted. I wanted to ask why as the eldest he was never given the family estate, but it felt like too personal of a question. I'd barely been inside the palace and was already wondering who kicked out the rightful king. I blamed it on my love of English royalty and their order of succession.

"Does that mean only Gwendolyn's children and grandchildren live here?" I wandered around the immediate vicinity, admiring the vivacious colors and shiny green leaves on all the lush foliage.

"Some, but not all. Why don't we head to the dining room and discuss it over lunch with Eustacia? She's staying here temporarily to help with the funeral arrangements and keep things running on the estate."

I followed Nana D through the Great Hall and exited in the back, right down a long hallway covered in famous paintings and prints. I assumed they were copies, but I wasn't well trained in that particular art medium. Given the wealth all around me, I wouldn't have been surprised if one or two were originals. When we turned down the final hall, I said, "How's Eustacia doing?"

"Tired. She didn't sleep last night, and it's hard to keep everyone under control. Let her tell you all about it, Kellan. Sheriff Montague was here earlier today and shared some news which confirms Gwennie's concern someone had been trying to hurt her." Nana D looked back at me with a heaviness I'd not seen in a long time. She pushed open the door into the dining room. "Drugs from some dirty hoodlum on the street killed her. It's rather scandalous and disturbing."

CHAPTER 6

"Kellan's here. I'll let Mrs. Crawford know to serve lunch in a few minutes," Nana D noted before leaving the room again. I didn't know whether to hug Eustacia or take a seat near her at the table as if I were a subject of hers. We'd known each other for years, but I barely knew much about her as a person. Occasionally, I'd run into her around town where we'd have a quick conversation, or she'd chide me for something my nana had done, then direct me to get involved in sorting out the debacle. Eustacia and Nana D had a symbiotic relationship where they often couldn't stand to be around one another, but if ever two days went by without time for tea or gossip, the world might've ended.

"Did Seraphina tell you about the sheriff's conversation?" Eustacia pointed to a nearby chair.

I sat, then answered. "Not really. Just that it wasn't from natural causes."

"They found traces of street drugs in my sister-in-law's body. Gwennie's never taken any in her life!" She fanned herself with a cloth napkin she'd snatched from beside the table's fine china setting.

"So, she was right to be concerned," I said with despair in my voice. "I'm sorry. How do you think it got into her system?" Could Nana D have been right to swipe that iced tea glass?

"It's rather unusual. Apparently, she consumed such a large dose of it yesterday, her heart couldn't handle the intensity. Dr. Betscha hadn't received the entire report from the coroner, but that was the preliminary finding."

"Do they know exactly when it was ingested yesterday?" I asked tentatively. "Or what it was?"

"Not yet. It had to occur while she was at Paddington's Play House. She wasn't feeling well yesterday morning. Nothing more unusual than we'd seen in the last month. Seraphina told me you were integral to solving those two murders weeks ago. Is that true?" Hope materialized on Eustacia's face as she searched for answers. But I knew nothing about the situation.

"I suppose you could say that, but it differed greatly from what happened to your sister-in-law. In the last murder, my father was a suspect, and the victims were people I knew well or was supposed to be interviewing as part of my job. The sheriff should handle this one, Ms. Paddington."

"Nonsense. If Seraphina says you solved the last murder, then you're capable of solving this murder. There are few things I will concede to that troublesome nana of yours, but she is one of my dearest friends. When she believes in someone, I believe in them, too. I might not like all the things that ninny does, but it's none of your dang business nor pertinent to this conversation, sonny boy."

Sonny boy? I felt like a child again. I needed to say something that would show her otherwise. "You did make it my business when you wanted me to stop Nana D from dating Lindsey, right?" I shouldn't have used an accusatory tone while saying the words, but I was being tricked or about to fall into a trap. So much for obeying our elders!

"Don't you start with me about what I did or didn't do. This is different. I'm not trying to stop Seraphina this time. I want her involved in solving my sister-in-law's murder. Gwennie was like a sister to me all these years. When Charles passed, I only had Millard left. As much as I love my brother, he's not exactly sentimental and open-minded. I want justice for Gwennie even if it means learning someone in our family goes to the pokey."

Nana D returned with the cook to deliver lunch. She'd told Mrs. Crawford to remain on a break and leave us in the room for the afternoon. While we had a delicious feast of butternut squash soup, rosemary-herbed Cornish game hens, and roasted Brussel sprouts, I considered everything Eustacia had told me. In the con column, I truly wasn't qualified to dig into the murder. I wasn't a family member; I wasn't a suspect, and I barely knew the victim. I also would get my rear end kicked from here to Timbuktu by Sheriff Montague if I went anywhere near another case of hers. In the pro column, I was a major crime buff. I did find the body in a manner of speaking, I had already seen a few suspicious behaviors, and the thought of digging into the Paddington family secrets excited me. I also would get my rear end kicked from here to Mars by Nana D if I didn't solve the case.

Since Mars was a lot longer of a journey than Timbuktu, and I was more afraid of Nana D than the sheriff, I settled on a compromise. "What if I agree to help, but you two are my front line of support on anything where the sheriff is involved. I value my life and freedom, and while I'm not that afraid of her, she could make things miserable for me."

"Kellan, no grandson of mine would be scared to do the right thing. You're on the side of the law, and that nuisance of a sheriff needs to be more tolerant. If I'm elected mayor, she will learn to take direction from me." Nana slammed her fist on the table as further proof of her proclamation.

"Exactly. And Seraphina will be Wharton County's next mayor. Hey, that reminds me, don't we need to prepare for your debate with Councilman Silly Man on Thursday?" Eustacia teased.

"Nana D, the sheriff doesn't take direction solely from the mayor. It's an elected position in Wharton County, not appointed by the mayor. I'm sure there's a partnership in that relationship."

"What? I thought I could fire that woman!" she scowled. "Or that fickle-fish DA!"

"No. I think if you're gonna run for public office, we need to get you up to speed on how politics work in Wharton County." I shook my head for even trying to reason with the woman.

"Well, that's not good news. Okay, you're assigned to teach me how this county works, brilliant one. Let's pull our plan together this afternoon," Nana D said with a slight irritation to her voice.

Before I could reply, Mrs. Crawford knocked on the dining room door and asked if she could enter. All three of us responded, "Come in." We laughed when she arrived saying, "Well, that's a first. Usually Mrs. Paddington, that is, the last Mrs. Paddington, would tell me to go away the first three times I knocked. Pardon the intrusion, but there's someone here to see you, Ms. Paddington. New Mrs. Paddington, that is. Oh dear, this is complicated."

Eustacia smiled at Nana D. "Since Gwennie's not around anymore, God rest her soul, there's gonna be a few changes in this house... starting with an end to all the rudeness in this family." Eustacia turned to Mrs. Crawford. "First, you no longer have to knock when coming into the dining room. Second, what's your first name?" A bony finger wiggled in the maid's direction.

"Bertha, ma'am," Mrs. Crawford said hesitantly, nearly dropping a dish towel.

"Third, there's no more sir and ma'am while I'm in charge around here. I might not have control once we find the will and discover who inherits this place, but until then, I've got Gwennie's power-of-attorney, so things will be how I say things are gonna be. Got that, Bertha?"

"Yes, ma'am. I mean Ms. Paddington... wait... I'm not sure what to call you?" she said scratching her head.

I watched the entire conversation play out in front of me as though I were sitting at a tennis match. We had a murder to solve. We had a mayoral race to win. Bertha had said someone was here to see us. I attempted to interrupt the latest volley but got the look of death and a hand held up like a school crossing guard's stop signal from Eustacia.

"You can call me Eustacia. That's what everyone I know calls me except people who are trying to suck up to me for money." She looked in my direction, then quickly turned back to Bertha.

"When I call you Ms. Paddington, I'm not sucking—" I started to say but was stopped again.

Eustacia glared at me. "Didn't I give you the halt sign, Kellan? Learn your basics if you want to keep up with this crowd." Then she turned to Nana D with her thumb jabbing in my direction. "How do you tolerate the likes of that one? He's full of hot air, vinegar, and prissy fuss. Oh, never mind. It's almost like the two of you are cut from the same cloth, Seraphina."

Bertha's head jutted to the side as she took two steps backward. "Ummm, I'm sorry to interrupt, but I have Brad Shope here to see you."

"Isn't that Gwennie's live-in nurse? What's he want? Bring him in. He might help explain a few things," Eustacia demanded while pouring herself another glass of white wine. She spoke so quickly and assuredly. I wondered if she'd been a drill sergeant in the past.

There were days when I wanted to pack myself in a box and ship it anywhere but Braxton for another forty years. It was like once people turned seventy, they decided it's their right to do and say whatever they wanted. Since I'd agreed to help solve Gwendolyn's murder, I'd have to deal with not only one ornery septuagenarian but a second who from first glance might be far worse than my nana. Why couldn't I have stayed back in Los Angeles? Oh right, the Castiglianos!

Before Bertha brought Brad into the room, I asked Eustacia to explain his role in caring for Gwendolyn. He'd been hired the previous year after Gwendolyn's husband, Charles, died from pancreatic cancer. Weeks had gone by where Gwendolyn laid in bed all day, ate the bare minimum, and stopped taking her normal medications. Although Bertha had done everything she could to help, nothing had changed. Over the winter, while no one noticed, Gwendolyn finally forced herself out of bed and wandered the vast property all alone. She'd become disoriented, fallen into the stream, broken her leg, and suffered from hypothermia. Her family subsequently moved her to an outpatient facility rather than nurse her back to health themselves. Once she'd begun recovering from her injuries and the death of her husband, Gwendolyn moved back into the family estate. Brad followed suit as a private nurse she'd hired after meeting him through a friend who'd also been in recovery at the outpatient facility.

Brad stepped into the room and offered his condolences to Eustacia. He wore an untucked plaid shirt and mid-rise, stone wash jeans. His face was slightly rounded, as though he still had some baby fat to lose, while his dimples probably drove all the girls crazy. Mahogany brown hair was spiked at the top and shaved close to the skin on both sides of his head. I'd been considering a similar style for myself for whenever I found time to choose a new barber. "I apologize for interrupting your lunch, but I finished packing all my things. I thought I'd check in before leaving this afternoon," noted Brad in a quiet voice.

Nana D asked him to take a seat at the table across from her. "Have you eaten lunch?"

"Not yet. I've been cleaning up Mrs. Paddington's room to organize everything before I left. I assume I should review any final items with Bertha?" Brad had a gentle demeanor and good manners. Although on the shorter side, he looked capable of handling his role as a nurse and physical therapist.

Eustacia asked Bertha to bring an extra plate and insisted Brad have something to eat. "Do you have somewhere else to go? I'm not sure how your role works when a client passes away."

Brad explained that he'd only worked at clinics and rehabilitation facilities in the past. This was his first in-residence, private client. He'd surrendered his apartment the previous year when Gwendolyn hired him to move in and take care of her. I decided to ask him a few questions while the opportunity presented itself. After explaining myself, I said, "What type of services did you provide for Mrs. Paddington?"

Brad took a large bite, swallowed, and answered me. "It changed in the last few weeks. At first, I ensured she did her physical therapy each day to get her walking again. It's different being at home where things are spread out further and harder to reach. The rehabilitation facility does its best to duplicate home environments, but it's not usually enough."

"Especially in this place, right?" Nana D joked while adjusting the braid on top of her head. "I still get lost despite coming here for years."

"True. For one thing, we had to move her to a downstairs bedroom, so she didn't have to climb the steps. Once she was able to walk on her own, we moved her back, and I prepared a new routine to help keep her body active but carefully protected from the possibility of another fall. I managed her medication and doctor appointments. We went for walks each day to keep up her spirit and flexibility. I suppose I became more of a confidante in the last few weeks once she needed less medical care."

"What pills was she taking? I recall someone mentioning she had high blood pressure," I noted while glancing at Nana D. From her smile, I knew she was happy about my prying into the details of Gwendolyn's health.

"Yes, she'd been taking those before I started working here. After the accident, the doctor added more medication to address increasing hypertension and high cholesterol. I'd also suggested she consider an anti-depressant in the beginning to help get her mind in a better place. She was distraught over losing Mr. Paddington. And since her... well, never mind, that doesn't matter anymore."

Eustacia cleared her throat. "I'd appreciate you saying whatever's on your mind, Brad. My sister-in-law is gone, and I'm worried about how she was feeling these last few weeks. Did I miss any additional issues with her health?"

Brad shook his head. "No, I meant nothing... it's just... ummm, she was dismayed about her family and how they weren't bothering much with her anymore." He looked at the floor and went silent.

"It was good she had you to support her body and her mind. What can you tell me about your visit to the theater yesterday?" I said.

Nana D interjected. "I called him when Gwennie felt unwell. She was struggling to catch her breath."

"What pills did you give her when you showed up? Are you certain there wasn't a mix-up?" Eustacia asked abruptly.

Brad sat back with a nervous look on his face. His eyebrows raised and his lips stretched out thinly. "Did something else happen besides the heart attack? I gave her the normal afternoon medication, she'd just accidentally left them at home. She'd also been having a few panic attacks lately, which is why we were going to Dr. Betscha this week."

I glanced at Eustacia. "I'm sure her family is worried about how sudden this all seems to be. I'm helping them look into her last couple of weeks to ease their peace of mind." I knew Eustacia wanted answers, but she had to be more delicate in her approach.

"I understand. Mrs. Paddington was a special woman. I noticed a few things that didn't add up, but nothing too alarming. I don't mean any offense," he said, looking at Nana D and Eustacia, "But at her age we unfortunately see the body having trouble keeping up with everything."

"You're telling me," quipped Eustacia as she stood reaching for her cane. At the top, a brass lion's head stared at me with a set of ferocious teeth, as if to tell me to beware. "I take so many dang medications, I consider them my daily rainbow meal. Still looking for that leprechaun, though."

"Speak for yourself. I'm as healthy as a thoroughbred mare in the prime of her racing career," Nana D said with a chuckle. She was adamant about taking only herbal supplements and following holistic healthcare. At seventy-four, she *had* avoided every possible drug thus far.

If I let those two keep talking, we'd never get useful information. "Brad, can you provide a list of any medication she was taking? I think it would help the family feel a little better about her last few days. Also, if you don't have anywhere to move to, what are you planning to do?"

"Actually, I had those details written out already for when we went to the doctor. As for my living situation, I'm planning to rent a room at the Roarke & Daughters Inn for a few days." He shrugged and stood to leave. I'd recognized the name of the bed-and-breakfast he'd mentioned. Maggie's parents and her sisters ran the charming ten-room inn near Crilly Lake.

"Nonsense," Eustacia whined while leading him toward the door. "You will stay here until you find your next job and a place to live. I could use a little help myself. Would that work?"

Eustacia was a lot smarter than she let others realize. If the autopsy revealed someone had been drugging Gwendolyn all along, Brad might identify which member of the family had access to any medication or food where it could've been introduced. Or revealed if he was involved in trying to kill her. Having him onsite would be a helpful asset. Once Brad left, Nana D, Eustacia, and I focused on the upcoming mayoral debate.

For too long, Wharton County's current mayor, Bartleby Grosvalet, and Braxton's town councilman, Marcus Stanton, had been in office together running the show. In the last decade, the powerful duo had skated by in the polls, winning via a narrow margin. Very few ever dared run against them, but their loyalists ensured both men garnered enough votes to push forth their dreary agendas. Mayor Grosvalet was in his seventies, like Nana D, but he'd become a recluse since the last election and delegated many of his powers to Marcus. Nana D's biggest obstacles to winning would be her age and Stanton's experience as Grosvalet's right-hand man. The only way to gain support would be if she could reach the soul of the county by appealing to their need for change and growth in the future. We outlined Nana D's key points and scheduled practice-runs over the next couple of days.

I left to attend my first official meeting with Ursula Power. In my two previous interactions with the new president, I was extremely impressed with her candor and professionalism. I was a little concerned about being fired since my other job back in Los Angeles as an assistant director on the hit television show, *Dark Reality*, was in flux. The executive producer had recently canned my boss and informed me he needed a few weeks to decide whether I had a future at the network. I wasn't sure what I wanted to happen given everything else going on in my life, but directing my own television crime series was still at the top of the options list. When were they going to call with an update?

I pulled into an empty South Campus parking lot given students were on break and entered the executive office building. Although my father would still be the president for another couple of weeks, he and Ursula were meeting daily to provide a smooth transition to the campus. He'd graciously moved into a smaller office on the first floor of Prentiss Hall, so Ursula could settle in the second-floor corner suite. I swung by to say hello, but a student worker said outgoing president Wesley Ayrwick had already left the building.

Ursula hadn't yet hired a permanent assistant, but a cheerful temp notified her boss I'd arrived. While the temp went to the small kitchenette, Myriam walked out and glared at me. "This was all your doing, wasn't it, Kellan?" Myriam said in a fit of semi-controlled rage. "I feel compelled to share with you of a line from this semester's theater performance. *'Come not between the dragon and her wrath.'* It will do you some good to remember that!"

It was rare I could find a hole in Myriam's quotations, but when I did, I felt the need to ride it like a hurricane's feverish winds. "I do believe you mean *his* wrath. I can appreciate you changing the actual line to suit your intended message, but a true historian would always leave the original message intact." Lear's warning to Kent was a passage I'd overheard during rehearsal the previous weekend, otherwise I might not have noticed her slight alteration.

"That's preposterous! I changed only the gender and not the meaning of the line. I wouldn't expect someone like you to separate the trivial things from the important things. Obviously, you've less experience than I thought when it comes to grasping the semantics of the English language," Myriam sniped while turning toward the door to exit.

Ursula stepped out of her office, obviously disgruntled. I'd never been certain of her age but guessed somewhere in her mid-forties, a few years younger than her wife. Given the frown lines I'd just seen for the first time, perhaps I was off. "Myriam, I'll see you at home this evening. I can tell I made the right decision earlier about addressing the issue between you and Kellan," Ursula said, smiling like Cheshire cat, then directing me to follow her into the office. I suddenly had the urge to ask those same hurricane winds to sweep me far away.

CHAPTER 7

What decision was Ursula talking about? My stomach felt ten pounds heavier, and it wasn't the strawberry cheesecake I'd eaten at lunch. "How've your first few days been?" I sat in a tall wingback chair across from her desk. The room had been redecorated with a pale gray wallpaper depicting a variety of Japanese maple trees. The pop of pinks and reds on the branches were a significant contrast, but also blended well with the new lighter-colored furniture and wrought-iron sculptures near the bay window.

When I'd first met Ursula weeks earlier, she had an ethereal quality about her. She truly could've been a model, but what made her even more charismatic was her genuine humility and intelligence. She accepted the cup of tea from her temporary assistant and smiled at me. "Braxton is the type of campus I dreamed about as a teenager. Unfortunately, I couldn't afford to live on my campus and worked too many jobs to cover tuition. I never had that classic college experience where I bonded with dorm-mates, snuck off to parties, and swung lazily in a hammock while reading *Jane Eyre* or *A Tale of Two Cities.*"

I felt an incredibly warm sensation about Ursula's presence on campus. My father had been a strong president who brought in countless donations, elevating the school from a small community college to the best in the county. But he often forgot to focus on the softer side of a liberal arts education—friendships, bonds, and memories. Ursula would be the one to make it happen, I could tell already.

"I remember them fondly, though now we often see students reading *Harry Potter* and *The Secret History* under the canopy of those golden yellow, red, and orange autumn trees." My stomach began to settle given the way Ursula handled herself and the conversation. "I'm excited about the opportunity to be part of the Braxton University team. Have you plunged into the proposed curriculum?"

We talked for twenty minutes about all the areas of expansion, in particular the communications department's overhaul. She was impressed by my experience and agreed with both my father's and the Board's decision to include me on the planning committee. As our time concluded, I grew curious about what she and Myriam had been discussing before I walked in. I was keen to bring up the topic, but Ursula beat me to it.

"Kellan, I'm sure this might be awkward for you to answer, but I'd like to learn more about your relationship with Myriam. Please don't worry about her being my wife. I can easily separate work from personal, and I've known her for over twenty years. She has an advanced degree in quarreling and authored a thesis on button-pushing. I still don't know when to successfully pick my battles." She gently shook her head and pulled her long, wavy blonde hair toward one shoulder.

Considering Ursula asked me directly what I thought of Myriam, I felt honesty was the best policy. However, I was nothing without my humor. "Let's not forget her special honorary certificate in obtuse Shakespearean zingers."

Ursula laughed so loudly the temp poked her head into verify everything was okay. When she went back to her seat, Ursula said, "Apart from all that, where do you see things going with Myriam? You've a one-year contract, which I intend to honor. I make it a policy not to insert myself into professional relationships among colleagues. Unfortunately, there've been several incidents between the two of you, which are worrisome."

I nodded. "I agree with you. We aren't mixing well, but I assure you I intend to remedy our differences or keep them hidden. I suspect you have something in mind to assist with the current volatility." I was a tad nervous about what might come out of Ursula's mouth next, given the curious look on her face and the accusatory remarks Myriam had made upon my arrival.

"I respect when someone cuts to the chase, so I'll do the same, Kellan." Ursula handed me a folder full of papers. "I had a call from Eustacia Paddington early this morning. Even in mourning, she's on top of important transitions. Besides contacting me to congratulate me on the new position and asking me to attend her sister-in-law's funeral service later in the week, she's proposed that you be made the temporary representative for the Paddington family on all things related to the Play House."

Some unintelligible sound emanated from my mouth before I could collect my thoughts. "I don't understand. She said nothing to me."

"Let me clear up any confusion. Gwendolyn Paddington partnered with our drama department to determine what shows we performed in the theater, worked with sponsors to offset any costs for set design and costumes, marketed our shows across the county, and mentored students beginning their careers. Apparently, there isn't anyone else in the family qualified to assume the role, so Eustacia suggested that you fill it until we could decide the future together, as I settle into my new position at Braxton."

"Suggested or insisted?"

"I'm sure you can appreciate the fine line I need to walk. The Paddingtons donate a tremendous amount of money to Braxton. They have certain, shall we say, liberties to make decisions on the theater program and the Play House which has been named after them."

"What about Myriam? She oversees the drama department and operations at Paddington's Play House," I hesitantly said, realizing why my boss had been so angry at me. "Isn't she a better choice?"

"I was planning to find an activity for the two of you to co-lead in the hopes it would encourage you both to get along better. When Eustacia suggested for you to be the temporary patron, I struck a deal with her."

"But Myriam's the one with all the experience in theater. She has the Broadway connections and has been running everything for years." I sounded like I was whining but couldn't stop myself.

"And you have experience writing television scripts, directing shows, and working in Hollywood. You have a different but valid perspective, and you also have the ear of the Paddington family right now. As a team, I expect remarkable things from your partnership with Myriam."

"Is this a proposal, or are you telling me this is a requirement for my continued role at Braxton?" I kept my tone civil despite wanting to scream.

"I prefer to think of it as a mutually beneficial decision we've all made together with the best intentions for Braxton among our collective minds." Ursula stood, smiling and nodding. "I'm sure you see it the same way, too. Unfortunately, I have another meeting. I appreciate you making time for me."

Ursula indicated the papers in the folder outlined the Play House's budget, staffing, and general operations. I thanked the new president for her input, as Nana D taught me never to tease an animal until you knew how ferocious it could be. I'd initially put Ursula in the gentle teddy bear category, but it might've been fallacious. If she could hold her own against Myriam, there undoubtedly must be a powerful stamina worthy of the grizzlies wandering the nearby Saddlebrooke National Forest.

As I left Ursula's office, the temp handed me an envelope. "Your father stopped by while you were inside meeting with Ms. Power. He asked me to give you this and said he found it on the floor in his office last night when he got home from his trip. He also mentioned something about you needing to explain what it meant." She turned and scampered away with a smug grin.

"I appreciate it," I mumbled, wondering why my father wouldn't have given it to me when I got home. As I scurried to the parking lot, I perused the envelope. Written on the front in block print was: **TO MY DEAREST HUSBAND, KELLAN**. I understood why he had it delivered as soon as possible. Had he read Francesca's letter and known she was alive? I swiftly tore it open and read the contents.

In one week, it will be our eighth anniversary. Every night before I fall asleep, I think of how you looked when I walked down the aisle at the botanical gardens on our wedding day. You'd never been more handsome than you were that afternoon. The sun hit your face in such a way that you reminded me of an angel. I knew then I had to protect you from my family at any cost. I foolishly thought if you never knew their secrets, you'd never be in danger.

When the Vargas family kidnapped me, I honestly thought I wouldn't be rescued. I knew my father would do everything in his power to get revenge, but I said a silent, terrified goodbye to you and Emma as they locked me in a freezer filled with devices meant to torture me. Once my father's security team found me, I promised myself this would never happen again. I'm not telling you this because I want to hurt you or to make you feel guilty. I need you to understand that I decided to protect you and Emma above anything else.

My mother doesn't know I've written this note. I hope you find it hidden under the desk. I had only a few seconds to drop it in there as we were arriving. I am not giving up on us. I will find a solution to bring us back together. Don't give up on me. Remember the stars. We will always have a future.

I stared at Francesca's letter for what felt like an eternity but had only been a few seconds. I was pulled from my trance by a series of tears rolling across my cheeks onto the envelope and blurring out my name. She wanted me to remember the stars.

Francesca had referred to the night of our first anniversary. She'd asked me to meet her at the top of a mountain not too far from where we lived. When I arrived, she had a picnic set up with a late dinner. She told me to lie down on the blanket and stare up at the sky. She filled two glasses with sparkling cider, then handed me one. I glanced back at her with a confused look as she knew how much I loved champagne. Moments later, Francesca clinked my glass and told me she was going to have a baby. Then she encouraged me to look at the stars because one of them was our daughter waiting for us to love her. We must have pointed out dozens of stars that night talking about what kind of baby girl we wanted to have. In the end, Francesca told me she'd be happy no matter what the universe had given to us, as long as she was healthy and happy. It was the beginning of our family and our future.

Remember the stars. I remembered them every year on our anniversary. We celebrated near them on each of Emma's birthdays. And the night Francesca died, I slept under them because there was nowhere else I could be by myself for the first time. But she never died. I tossed my head against the back of the seat and concentrated with soul-crushing focus. What was I going to do about our future?

Unfortunately, I couldn't think about it any longer because it was time to pick Emma up from her first day at school. When I arrived, she bragged about how amazing it was and how she couldn't wait to go back. We had dinner with my mother since my father was working late with Ursula on an upcoming presentation. Emma went to sleep early, and I watched a few sitcom reruns to distract myself from thinking about the surrounding reality. I ended up calling Cecilia and begging her to let me speak with my wife, but she put Vincenzo on the line. He heavily encouraged me to find my way back to Los Angeles quickly. He noted he wasn't in agreement with Cecilia, who'd given me two weeks to decide how to proceed, but he would let his wife's decision stand only this one time.

* * *

I slept poorly that night, trying to decide what to do about Francesca. Early on Tuesday morning, I texted Eleanor to check on the diner renovations, but she couldn't speak. She had a doctor's appointment and needed to finish preparing for the final inspection the next day before she could officially reopen. We agreed that I would stop by for dinner that evening to get her thoughts on the situation with Francesca.

After dropping off Emma at school, I went for a run to clear my head. I chose the Finnulia River path as the weather was finally warming up in the high forties, which meant I could leave the thermal gym clothes at home. The air was also much cleaner and easier to breathe near the north end of town where the river emptied into Crilly Lake. Halfway through my return, I took a brief break to stretch and drink some water near Maggie's family's inn. As I prepared to finish the final lag, a runner I recognized came toward me. I called out, watching smoke from the crisp air funnel away from my lips. "You're Sam Paddington, right?"

He looked strangely at me on his approach, then stopped while still jogging in place. "It's Sam Taft. My mother was a Paddington. Not my father."

I hadn't forgotten, but I wanted to verify it with him. I knew his sister called herself Dana Taft, but I wasn't sure if they all shared the same father. Ophelia and Richard Taft had a complicated relationship from what Nana D had told me. "Oh, that's right. I forgot. Dana and Lilly Taft, your sisters. Now it makes sense."

He nodded. "Yes, we're all Tafts. You're Kellan, right?"

I asked him how his family was doing, and he noted they were all grieving in their own private ways. "I've spent a lot of time looking through photo albums and some videos we took years ago. I don't know what I'm gonna do without her." Sam wore a pair of navy-blue running shorts and a Nike t-shirt whose sweat stains clearly showed he'd been on the trail for a long time. Was he working off grief or guilt?

"It takes time. I still reminisce about my grandpop who's been gone close to ten years," I said, nostalgic for the past. "Looks like you know what you're doing out here."

"I'm a health nut. I've seen what poor diet and little exercise can do to people and don't want to throw away the future. I've got lots of hopes and dreams." Sam stopped jogging in place and checked his phone. He had something else in his pocket, but I couldn't tell what it was. I looked like a small cylinder or bottle filled with liquid. It almost reminded me of a tube of glue, which seemed odd for him to be carrying on a run. He smiled when his phone beeped, indicating he had a text message. I was too far away to see any of the words or name of the sender.

"Someone brightening your day?" I noticed the positive change in his demeanor. "Girlfriend, I presume?" I knew it was nosy of me, but I had to find out a little more about him.

"Ummm, not exactly. Listen, I gotta go. I'm meeting my mom to plan the funeral service. Take it easy," Sam replied. It was the second time he looked awkward or nervous talking to me. I watched him take off toward the more treacherous path at a speed I could not keep up with. Granted, he had ten years on me, but he was also most definitely at the top of his game.

Five minutes before I got home, my cell rang. "It's your grandmother. Get over to the Paddington estate pronto. That sheriff's crew is here with a warrant to search the house. Sheriff Montague is on her way here now," Nana D said in a clearly aggravated tone.

"Did you call a lawyer? What's she looking for?" I sped a little faster than I should've. I needed to shower before going to the estate.

"Eustacia called Lindsey. He may have retired years ago, but he'll know what to do. I can't read that mumbo jumbo legal speak. It could've said something about searching for a witch riding a broom in her pink polka-dot daisy dukes and sports brassiere for all I know, brilliant one."

"I'll be there in thirty minutes. Who's handling the Paddington legal affairs?" I pulled into the driveway and jogged up the back steps to the Royal Chic-Shack, laughing about her unique expressions.

Nana D explained she didn't know which attorney was working for them anymore. I suggested she call Finnigan Masters, who'd handled my parents' legal affairs over the last few years. I'd met him once before when I had to sign a document for them, but being back in Braxton meant I should reconnect with the man. I'd gone to school with his younger brother, who'd become a professional hockey player. After a shower and change of clothes, I hightailed it to the Paddington estate.

Given how unlucky I'd been lately, of course the first person I ran into in the small parking area outside the mansion was April Montague. Her nearly translucent skin, brassy blonde Viking helmet hair, as I liked to call it, and high cheekbones were so prominent, I couldn't help but stare. "Good morning, sheriff. How's everything going today?" I offered the fakest smile I could muster. It sounded like I had marbles in my mouth given how much I didn't want to speak with the insufferable woman.

"I might have guessed you'd show up, Little Ayrwick. Please tell me you're here to mow the lawn or scoop off the algae and pond scum?" April taunted me, wearing her favorite worn blazer and starched jeans—she was not one who should cast judgment.

"I'm visiting an old friend, that's all. Ms. Paddington and I have some business to discuss regarding the upcoming *King Lear* performance. You might not know this, but I'm their representative on anything connected to the drama department or the Play House." I considered reaching my hand in her direction despite her callous wisecrack about gardening responsibilities. "What brings you here?"

"You've exceeded my expectations, I must say. Back for only three weeks and clearly embedded with the Paddingtons and the Stantons as if you were their trained pet. I hear you were even present when Gwendolyn died of that unfortunate heart attack the other day," Sheriff Montague said with a half-smile and sneer. Her jaw was set so tightly I thought she might chip a cap.

"Surely, it couldn't have been a heart attack if you're at the estate with a warrant to search the premises. Anything I should be concerned about?" I pinched myself in excitement for proving my point.

"Other than getting back into your car and driving off the property, so I can do my job? Last I checked, you didn't pass the Pennsylvania bar exam. I see no reason for you to remain." She shut the passenger door to the sheriff's county vehicle. It was good to see her arriving in something other than her motorcycle. Although the thought of a woman riding a Harley excited me, picturing April Montague on it made me nauseous. Exorcist-level nauseous.

I tilted my head to the side and sighed. "I can't keep the Paddingtons waiting. Why don't we arrive together as a show of good faith? After you." I pointed toward the house like a flight attendant.

Once Bertha let us inside, we entered the foyer. "Kellan, it's so lovely to see you again."

After we hugged and exchanged thoughts about Nana D's peach crumble, Sheriff Montague interjected. "I always said you had a gift for gab, Little Ayrwick. Since you know the place so well, how about you navigate me toward my team?"

I declined, having little energy to continue our banter. As the sheriff went off with Bertha, I located Nana D. "What's going on?"

"They showed up an hour ago with a warrant to search the place. Lindsey just got here and said it's legal. They have reasonable cause that someone drugged Gwennie at the theater, but apparently they suspect something's been going on for weeks," Nana D said in a fury as we navigated the corridors toward the Great Hall. "I can't believe no one noticed what was happening."

"Lindsey knows one of the cops from past cases. He shared more than he should've, but I'm glad he did. There was something erratic or amiss with various counts and numbers in Gwennie's blood chemistry. Some whipper-snapper hootenanny talk, if you ask me. All I know is what Brad said makes sense—he was right to bring her to the doctor this week. If only he had the chance."

"What exactly happened at the theater to cause her to finally succumb?" I asked, filling with genuine concern for the entire family.

"An overdose of cocaine. Enormous amounts in her body from the preliminary results of the autopsy. I have a call into Alex to find out what he knows." Alex, better known as Dr. Alexander Betscha, was Nana D's forty-year-old distant cousin, who served as a physician for most of Braxton's inhabitants.

"Did you learn the family attorney's identity? Where's everyone?" I gazed back and forth.

"Nope. Ophelia's with Sam at the funeral parlor planning the services. I don't think Eustacia's called them yet. Dana lives on campus. Lilly comes and goes so much, no one ever knows where she is."

"What about Jennifer or Richard?" I asked.

"Richard's away. Jennifer doesn't live here. It was just Eustacia at home when the cops showed up. She rang me, and I rushed over. That's when I contacted you and told her to call Lindsey."

Eustacia hobbled down the hall, balancing on her cane and shouting at us. "Disaster. This entire town and family are a sheer disaster. Is that Kellan? What's he got to report? Did he figure out who killed Gwennie yet? What the devil is taking him so long?"

Unfortunately, Sheriff Montague was following Eustacia down the hall when she had her outburst. "Excuse me, Ms. Paddington. Can you explain why Kellan would figure out who killed Gwendolyn? First, he's not a member of the Wharton County Sheriff's Office. Second, how does he know it was murder when I haven't made it public knowledge. No one is to know anything about this crime until I say so."

It was at that moment I knew I'd be punished no matter if I behaved or misbehaved. The world liked to torture me, which meant I had to accept it and move on. "Well, you see, Sheriff Montague, it sorta goes like this..."

CHAPTER 8

"Close your mouth. I'm tired of you showing up everywhere I am," the sheriff shouted until another voice interrupted her tirade, leading us to all turn around at the same time and see from whom it'd come.

Millard stepped into the hallway and demanded that everyone calm down. He ushered us back into the Great Hall, where we all took seats near the palm trees and kidney-shaped pond. A submerged plant that looked like a Venus flytrap floated past me as I walked by. "What's that one?" I asked, wondering if it were about to snap at my fingers. How could I dunk the sheriff?

"Water wheel plant. Rare species, not usually in North America. I've been able to keep it alive through a proper feeding schedule," Millard noted. After what must have been a puzzled or concern expression appeared on my face, he continued, "They're carnivorous. I have to supply them with meat."

"How fitting," the sheriff added with a sinister glower in my direction. I also hear her mutter under her breath, "*Must be a friend of Little Ayrwick's.*" Yikes, we really had it out for each other.

"How about we try starting this conversation all over again, sheriff?" Millard said.

"Please explain what is going on, Little Ayrwick," the sheriff said, clearly frustrated and tired of my involvement in her cases and the vigor of the Paddington family.

"Gwendolyn told Nana D and I last Saturday she thought someone had been trying to hurt her. She wasn't feeling well and had some disputes with different family members. I didn't take it seriously at first, but when I went with them to the *King Lear* dress rehearsal the following day, I noticed a few peculiar behaviors and conversations. When she had the heart attack, it didn't feel right."

254

"I asked him to poke around and see if he could figure out what was going on. He's got my authority to be involved," Eustacia yelled in a cranky voice.

"And as the next mayor, I support it!" Nana rapped her knuckles on the wooden insert in the couch's arms as a misguided display of support.

"That's not how the law works, ladies," the sheriff replied in an authoritative tone. "Here's how this is going to proceed. All of you will be interviewed this afternoon. My team is collecting evidence around the estate. Your attorney will be notified of everything we take off property. If after these discussions I have any further questions, I will contact you directly. In return, not a single one of you will do anything to search for a potential killer nor discuss the case with anyone. At this point, we believe something suspicious led to Gwendolyn Paddington's death, but we have more tests to run, a full autopsy to complete, and an investigation to conclude."

"It might be important for you to know we've already started compiling a list of suspects who—" Nana D began but was told to be quiet.

"Can it, Mrs. Danby. All of you are to remain in this room until I call you into the front study for questions. Is that clear?" Sheriff Montague departed the room. A few seconds later, Officer Flatman, a young cop hoping to make detective one day—something I definitely did not see happening soon given my past interactions with him—called Millard into the room. Nana D, Eustacia, and I decided to review our list of suspects, next steps, and theories while we waited. Lindsey was allowed to leave since he wasn't a member of the household or the family, but he was staying put until Finnigan showed up.

I narrowed my gaze at Eustacia and Nana D. "I've agreed to help you with this only because you're forcing me to do so, but I am staying out of April Montague's path. You will interact with her if there are questions this time—not me. Is that clear?" Both nodded. "Okay. Who's tracking down the will to understand what motives might exist?"

Eustacia volunteered for that effort. "I've got power-of-attorney. Lindsey told me Finnigan Masters is the attorney he recommended to Charles years ago. Charles and Gwendolyn both had wills on file with him. All I need to do is chat with Finnigan later today when he comes by to discuss everything. He was in court and couldn't leave until three o'clock."

"Great, that will cover any motives for an inheritance. Who can converse with Bertha Crawford and Brad Shope to get a clearer picture of all of Gwendolyn's activities, meals, prescriptions and anything else the last few weeks?" I pointedly stared at Nana D. She'd already connected with both, since she'd been hanging around the house to support Eustacia during her sister-in-law's death.

Nana D confirmed. "I'll find out what they know. I'll also get the full details from my cousin, Alex, about the autopsy. I owe it to Gwennie to help figure out what happened. And I need to teach that sheriff a lesson she won't forget. No one tells Seraphina Danby to *can it*!"

I rolled my eyes. "I'd like to meet the entire family again. Can you arrange a lunch or tea for tomorrow when everyone can come by, so we can carefully inquire about anything they might know?"

Millard walked back in the room as I brought up the family meeting. "I'll handle that one. We have to discuss funeral arrangements with Ophelia anyway, so this will be a perfect opportunity to get everyone together." He indicated that Eustacia was next to meet with the sheriff. While she was gone, I informed Millard and Nana D that I'd chat with Arthur. He'd made a few disparaging remarks about Gwendolyn and had several run-ins with her in the past. As far as I was concerned, he should be on the suspect list.

By the time I finished documenting everyone's responsibilities, it was my time to see the sheriff. I luckily got away fairly unscathed but also had learned nothing new. She reminded me to stay out of the investigation, which I, of course, agreed to do while crossing my fingers behind my back. At three o'clock, I left to pick up Emma at school. I'd been hoping to have a few minutes with Finnigan, but he was running late from court. I'd have to follow up with him in the future.

Emma and I stopped to speedily consume a bowl of fruit. I also had a coffee. We discussed her day before she had to go to a gymnastics lesson. I'd arranged for a friend of Eleanor's who had a daughter the same age as Emma to split today's responsibilities for drop off and pick up at the gymnasium. While Emma and I drove to her friend's house, she asked questions about her mother.

"Nonna Cecilia says I should still talk about her all the time. It helps keep the memory alive. How come you never talk about her anymore, Daddy?" Emma asked with a curiosity I didn't want to hear.

"When did she say that?" I sincerely hoped Cecilia wasn't forcing her demented plans behind my back. Although everyone complained about their mother-in-law, I knew for a fact mine was the worst.

"She called yesterday to see if I liked my new school. Did you know I can touch my tongue to my nose?" Emma demonstrated it for me and asked if I could, too. I tried but failed miserably. I ended up with drool sliding off my lips and a six-year-old daughter cackling like a goose.

"Does Nonna Cecilia call you often?" I asked, preparing to block Cecilia's number from Emma's phone. I'd been against giving Emma her own phone at such a young age, but I realized she was a lot more mature than others. Since my daughter was often going back and forth between my house and her grandparents in LA, and the same was happening between Nana D, Eleanor, and my parents' house in Braxton, a phone would be useful to reach her easily.

"Almost every day. Except not today. She had a big meeting and couldn't use her phone where she was going." Emma changed the radio station as we pulled up to her friend's house. "We like rock music, Daddy."

"Okay, that's my favorite, too." While we waited for her friend, I told Emma that I missed her mother very much and hoped one day in the future to see her again.

"When you're in heaven?"

I nodded, not knowing what else to say. Luckily, the rear passenger door opened, and Emma's new best friend jumped inside. I worked out the details with the girl's mother on when and where to drop Emma off, then drove to the gymnasium. It was an enormous facility near the Betscha mines filled with authentic rock-climbing walls, rings hanging from the ceiling, balance beams, and tons of mats on the floor. I verified they were both in the beginner's class and only working on the mats today. I wanted to be present the first time Emma used any of the more intense or dangerous equipment. Thirty minutes later, I arrived at the diner to catch up with my sister.

"You look like you lost your best friend," Eleanor said while hugging me. "Your horoscopes this week keep warning about a devil consuming every ounce of energy you have left."

I couldn't agree more. But was the devil Cecilia? Francesca? Myriam? April? One of the Paddingtons? How was I supposed to know how to stop it from happening when I didn't know whom it was? "What should I be doing to prevent it?" I asked cautiously, fearing the worst.

Eleanor ordered me to cut the deck of Tarot cards, then she displayed several in front of me, sharing the story of my future. Or my past, I never knew what she was doing with all the numerology and astrology readings she forced on me. "Basically, you're screwed for the next two weeks. Someone's angry and you're going to feel the brunt of it," she said in a matter-of-fact tone.

"Tell me something I don't already know. That's just a fact of my life, sis."

We both guffawed, then talked about the renovations at the diner. She'd expanded the kitchen and closed one of the small party rooms in the back corner, explaining that no one had ever rented it. Rather than try to include more tables, she'd thought a larger kitchen with more state-of-the-art tools and appliances would help drive customers to keep coming back.

"The inspector comes tomorrow morning. If everything goes well, we have a few minor things to finish, then we can open next week."

"Not bad, only closed for two weeks. Are you and Maggie able to afford being offline this long?"

"We built it into the cost of the loan. I think we'll be okay, but we can't let any delays get in the way." Eleanor's face relaxed as she spoke, showing how much stronger she'd become in the last few years. There was a fair balance between confidence and humility that shined through.

I was proud of my sister. She'd been through countless discussions with my mother about why she hadn't settled down and gotten married. Eleanor explained she'd been trying, but things weren't looking promising in that area of her life. Until she met the right man, the diner would be her partner. I felt obliged to ask about Connor.

"Yes, Connor called earlier today. We're planning to talk soon about what's going on between us. He's still interested, but he doesn't want to rush anything."

"I assume that's code for *scared to be in the middle of you and Maggie?*"

"Wouldn't you be?" Eleanor used her *'I'm being serious'* tone and mean face.

"Only because you can be vicious when you go after something you desperately desire!"

"I'm a woman who knows what she wants and isn't afraid to go after it. I'm thirty-years-old and might not be married with kids, but I own a business and a small home. I'm on the board of the town community center, and I volunteer on several committees in Wharton County. Life's good, but there can always be more. Why not throw myself at something when I want it?" There was a twinkle in her eye when she told me how she felt about herself these days.

I was excited for her becoming a big business woman around town. "You're pretty awesome, Eleanor. I don't tell you that enough."

"You're the best big brother around. Speaking of brothers, have you heard from Hampton at all?" Hampton, the eldest of the five Ayrwick siblings, was a lawyer married to a snobby, rich oil heiress.

I said, "Nope. I figured he'd call Dad first, then we'd know whatever surprise he had in store. How about Gabriel or Penelope?" Penelope was our second oldest sibling at thirty-four, married to Jack with twin boys about to enter their teenage years and a trouble-making stepdaughter from Jack's first marriage—all of which I unabashedly hoped would wreak havoc with my sister's many OCDs.

"Penelope and I talked this morning. She made partner at that fancy New York City real estate firm. Gabriel is still a mystery," Eleanor said with a pang of sadness in her voice.

Nearly eight years ago, my youngest brother, Gabriel, announced he was transferring to Penn State to finish his degree, having only been at Braxton for two years. That's when our father accepted the presidency Braxton had been offering to him for years—especially once they upped the ante until it was too sweet. Even I might have passed on dessert for a taste of it. After Gabriel changed his mind on the transfer, he expected our father to withdraw from the job. Of course, he couldn't. Gabriel in his usual elegant manner left Braxton and decided never to come home again, claiming our father had stabbed him in the back. He was too proud to attend the same school where our father was the head honcho. I couldn't say they ever got along, but I still didn't know exactly what had kept him away for so long.

"I was thinking about hiring a detective to track down Gabriel. Maybe we could convince him to give Dad another chance," I said.

"Hire a detective? I thought that was your new job from what Nana D tells me about the search for Gwendolyn's killer. Aren't you running for sheriff, so you can be Nana D's sidekick when she wins the mayoral race?" Eleanor giggled like a schoolgirl before standing up to plate some dessert for us.

I might have made an inappropriate gesture at her. "No, I'm not running for sheriff. That's not until next year, but you have a point. I've picked up some more skills since returning home. I *could* track Gabriel down." Hmmm... could I also run for sheriff? No, I wasn't qualified. Yet.

"What's going on with the Paddington case?" Eleanor asked, as if I'd actually refer to them as cases. "I saw Jennifer today at the doctor's office. She's Gwendolyn's daughter, right?"

I nodded. "One of them, at least. Did you speak to her?"

"No, I've never met her before, but I recognized her from a few charity organizations we both worked on in the past. She was arguing with the receptionist." Eleanor scooped banana pudding between her lips, practically drooling over the taste.

"That good?" I said with a cheer before shoveling down my spoonful. "What was the disagreement about?"

"Money. She complained that some procedure was too expensive, and she'd lost her insurance when her last job ended. I'm not sure what it was about, but she seemed steamed no one had explained the costs to her before she saw the doctor."

At the risk of learning too much, I asked anyway. "What kind of doctor?" Fearing it was the gynecologist, I closed my eyes and covered my ears.

"You're such a baby! Yes, it was related to her lady parts. Honestly, Kellan. You're thirty-two-years-old and you have a daughter. You're gonna have to get used to talking about it someday." Eleanor dropped her spoon into the bowl and pushed it toward the end of the table. "Have you made any decisions about Francesca?"

Phew, I was glad she brought it up. I struggled to acknowledge out loud what was going in my life. "Thank you for asking. I'm still in shock. Cecilia's playing games, trying to manipulate Emma. And I found a letter Francesca left for me the day she came by."

"What did it say?" Eleanor reached out and patted my hand.

"She reminded me of wonderful times in our past. Just some personal things that made me realize I'll never stop loving her." My normally protected barriers had weakened. I rarely cried, but in the last few days, I'd felt like the waterworks were always near the surface. "How can this be happening?"

Eleanor dragged me to the kitchen to wash our dishes, thinking manual labor would be a suitable solution for improving my humdrum mood. We settled on not deciding until Cecilia's two-week deadline arrived, and even then, I would take control of the situation. Eleanor reminded me I held the cards—not them.

When Emma arrived, we turned on some music and had a lively dance party. We also helped Eleanor finish setting up the rest of the diner to prepare for the inspection the following day. Maggie stopped by to check on progress but made it clear she fully trusted Eleanor to make all the decisions. As the silent partner in their new business venture, Maggie let Eleanor take the lead until her job at the library settled down. After introducing Emma to Maggie, Eleanor took my daughter into the kitchen to view the new equipment. I knew she was trying to give Maggie and me a few moments alone.

"She's gorgeous, Kellan. And so smart and kind. You must be an amazing father," Maggie said while hugging me. "She's a lucky girl."

As Maggie pulled away, our favorite song came on the radio. An instrumental version of 'I'll Stand By You' by The Pretenders accompanied us as we stood in an embrace swaying back and forth like we had years ago. The street light poured in through the crackled window and illuminated her tender face.

For just a minute, I saw a different future than the one I'd thought would always be present with Francesca. Lost in thought, I hadn't immediately realized my phone was ringing.

"I guess you need to answer that," Maggie mumbled with disappointment.

I'd have let it go to voicemail for just about anyone, but I had to respond to Nana D's ring. I pulled the phone from my pocket as Maggie told me she needed to vamoose. When I watched her leave, my heart raced even faster. I forced myself to answer Nana D's call. "Hi. Everything okay?"

"No, Kellan, it's most definitely not. Finnigan told us what the cops found. We were right."

"What do you mean?" I was too distracted to think clearly.

"There wasn't anything in the iced tea. It's a good thing we saved that glass. It means the cocaine was introduced in the pills Brad gave to Gwennie. There was enough in there to kill a horse."

"That's awful. What else did you learn?" My head throbbed from overload of things taking up all my attention.

"Gwennie called last week to redraft her will again with Finnigan."

"Did he say what changes were made?"

"No, that's the issue. Finnigan wrote up the revisions, but she asked him to leave the names blank. She planned to fill them in and send it back to him. That was the night before she died."

"Where's the will now?" I contemplated whether that approach was even legal, but Finnigan wouldn't have allowed it to happen if he had concerns. I'd need to validate that at some point. Maybe my brother, Hampton, would know the specifics of this type of law. Did I dare call him?

"Finnigan doesn't know. She might have put it in the mail, or it might not have been finalized. We're as confused as a fart in a fan factory on a humid day."

What did she say? I couldn't permit myself to ask without conjuring up the most awful images and horrendous smells. I hung up with Nana D, realizing the possible existence of two wills made the investigation a lot more complicated. What did it all mean? And was the sheriff looking at Brad as the guilty party for giving her the pills laced with cocaine?

* * *

"I must've dropped it in your office, Dad. I was going through some paperwork to change my mailing address and found it," I fibbed at breakfast the following morning when my father grilled me about Francesca's letter. I'd gotten home too late the night before to explain anything and had come up with the excuse overnight.

"What were you doing in my study? And under the desk no less." my father said curtly while sitting in the kitchen, drinking coffee, and eating a bowl of granola. He'd already dressed in his power suit for a big meeting on campus with the Board of Trustees to review the budget for Braxton's conversion into a university. "It's not that I don't want you in there, but it was odd."

I stared at him as he methodically collected several grains and a raspberry on the same spoonful before swallowing it. He'd always advised it was important to achieve the right balance in weight and taste with each bite. "I'm not sure, I probably bent down to pick up some loose change that fell from my pants and knocked the letter under the file cabinet. I had the letter in my pocket when I was thinking about my upcoming anniversary with Francesca. It's several years old." My brow sweat despite not having completed my morning run.

We chatted idly about the weather and Emma's new school. I could tell he was suspicious, but he had no way of knowing how the letter had wound up on the floor. Unless he had installed a security camera in his study in the past. A drop of sweat from my forehead splashed into my coffee. My father looked over and scratched his head. "Are you feeling okay, son?"

I nodded and mumbled something about it being too warm in the room. He offered to drop Emma off at school for me, which was a tremendous help since I needed to run a few errands, get in a workout, and meet Eustacia's family at noon for the family meeting Millard had organized.

Once I kissed Emma goodbye and my father's car pulled down the driveway, I dashed into his study and combed every corner or crevice I could find. I waved in every direction to see if I heard a camera making any noise or moving to capture my picture. I made it appear like I was looking for a stamp. When I found one a few minutes later, I said out loud in case he was listening too, "Exactly what I needed to mail my change of address forms. I can always count on Dad to save the day." I even made a big show of holding out the stamp and admiring the latest design. Arthur or Myriam might cast me in their next production.

I found no cameras, but I wasn't as versed in the world of security as I needed to be. For all I knew, he could've hidden something in a pen or a clock. Maybe even one of Emma's old teddy bears, which sat on the shelf staring at me in judgment. I imagined it chastising me for lying to my family. For some reason, the bear sounded like Winnie The Pooh.

CHAPTER 9

Once all my tasks were completed, I pulled up in front of the Paddington estate at five minutes to noon. What does one wear when you plan to secretly grill the *loving* family of a woman who'd been murdered, but you aren't a detective? I'd settled on traditional clothing by choosing a pair of tan corduroys, a classic single-breasted blue blazer, and open-collared white dress shirt. If it weren't for the Paddingtons, I might have chosen something more comfortable like jeans and a t-shirt, but I wasn't completely clueless as to the need to impress a potential killer. Or should I have looked sloppy, so the perp ignored me? This new secret job of mine was more cumbersome and baffling than necessary.

Bertha led me to a new room I hadn't been in before. We turned left at the Great Hall and trundled past a grand library and a game room, both decorated in mauve and gold wallpaper. She dropped me off in what I assumed to be Gwendolyn's office, given it had a conference table and lavish desk in the corner. "The others will be in shortly," she said, pulling the door closed behind her.

The room felt inordinately stuffy. Everything had been dusted recently, as not a speck could be found. No personal items of any sort offered warmth or comfort. The lighting was minimal, and there was only one small window covered in heavy drapery. I organized my thoughts as the grandfather clock's minute hand ticked by, leaving me more unsettled with my approach. I reviewed the notes on my phone to ensure I had all the questions listed. I'd been intently reading when the door opened and spooked me back to reality.

Jennifer Paddington was the first to enter the room. Her slightly stooped posture and slow entrance felt awkward and unusual. Something darker had replaced her normal elegance and confidence. After a confused expression where she nervously scratched at the table's solid wood, Jennifer said, "Kellan, I didn't expect to see you in here. Uncle Millard told us we needed to discuss my mother's funeral plans. I'm sorry I'm late, did I miss that conversation?"

Hoping not to be caught off-guard as well, I shrugged and suggested she take a seat at the table. I also thought I'd be interviewing the entire family in one meeting, but it seemed Millard had other plans. "I'm sure they'll be along soon enough. Millard and Eustacia asked me to swing by, so I could find out if anyone had input on the Paddington family's role in overseeing the Play House at Braxton," I squeaked out as a cover. If she thought I was there to solicit ideas as I temporarily stepped into the role of patron, it might relax her.

"Oh, I forgot about that. Mother was so active with the theater. Sometimes she spent more time with that crowd than her own family," Jennifer remarked with slightly pursed lips, followed by a fake smile. I knew it was fake because she couldn't hold a gaze with me for more than a second at a time without blushing or coughing.

I considered her response, uncertain if she was being flippant or had seriously felt that way about her relationship with her mother. "She had a passion to support the arts. Were you close?"

"Mother wasn't someone you could easily be close to, Kellan. She loved us, sure, but we were often left to ourselves while she and Father kept busy running Paddington Enterprises, traveling to New York City for shows, and entertaining the more important people." Jennifer glanced around the room as if she were recalling previous times where her needs had been overshadowed by those of her parents. "I've never liked this room. It's cold. Empty. Don't you think?"

I sighed. "It's not an inviting space for cozy family time. I'm sorry things weren't so wonderful at home. I admired your mother's forthright approach, but I can see how it might be difficult being one of her children." I hoped there'd been a different, more private side to Gwendolyn, but it appeared that wasn't the case.

"There's nothing I can add of value to the Play House. It's not something I've ever been interested in. My nephew, Sam, and niece, Dana, were much more involved with Mother in that area. If that's all, I'm going to track down Uncle Millard. I don't have a lot of time today to—"

The door opened and in skulked Ophelia. "What's the purpose of calling us all together today? I'm handling Mother's funeral plans. There's nothing anyone else needs—" A knitted brow and an unflattering frown revealed her disgust before the words had even left her lips. She stopped short and adjusted the collar on her lavender silk blouse when she saw me sitting at the table. "Who are you?"

Jennifer moaned at the interruption. I attempted to reintroduce myself, but Ophelia turned away from me and focused on her sister. "Did you hear anything about Mother's will? I've called Finnigan Masters, but he hasn't returned my voicemail. It's quite irresponsible of him."

Eustacia walked in the room, leaning on her cane for support until she reached the table. "Sit down, the both of you. Finnigan has no responsibility to discuss the will with either of you. I have Gwendolyn's power-of-attorney. We're pulling everything together this week, so we can determine when to have the formal will reading."

Jennifer took a seat at the table. Ophelia waved her hand at her aunt dismissively. "I don't understand why she left you in charge. You're not even her sister."

Jennifer said, "Behave, Ophelia. You know they've been close ever since Father died."

"My name is Kellan Ayrwick, Mrs. Taft," I said, looking toward Ophelia. "We met the other day during the *King Lear* performance. I am a friend of your family—"

"Oh, yes, the guy Mother fell onto during the second half of the show. What are you doing here?" Her voice held enough contempt to rival any narcissist I'd met in the past, perhaps even Myriam.

"Kellan's here to discuss the Play House, but also to help me figure out which one of you drove poor Gwennie to her death." Eustacia sat taller in the chair, unaffected by her accusation against someone in the family. She chose to go directly for the kill instead of gradually introducing the conversation.

"One of us? Are you mad, Aunt Eustacia? Mother died of a heart attack," replied Ophelia with a shriek in her voice. "What the devil are you talking about?"

"Didn't you know the cops were here searching the house yesterday?" Jennifer said, shaking her head at her sister. "Maybe you shouldn't have gone off for a spa day in the middle of everything blowing up around us."

"No one cares what you think, Jennifer. You're one to talk. If anyone had it out for Mother, it's you. She's the one who pushed—"

"Why would you say that, Mrs. Taft?" I interrupted, hoping to learn something of importance. It wasn't exactly my place to insert myself, but there were clearly problems in the Paddington family.

"Jennifer only visited Mother to get money out of her. She's kept herself distant from the rest of us unless she needed something or Mother forced her to attend a family function," Ophelia chastised while pouring herself a glass of sherry from the antique bar cart in the room's corner.

Eustacia remained silent. I assumed she wanted me to witness the various antics and nasty behavior of her nieces. It was certainly an over-acted show reminiscent of a Kardashian family reunion.

"That's simply not true. You've been trying to get money out of her for years ever since that husband of yours disappeared," Jennifer reminded her sister while slapping her hand against the table.

"He hasn't disappeared. He goes out of town to do work for Paddington Enterprises. Besides, I have three children to take care of. You don't have anyone else!" Ophelia replied swiftly.

Jennifer looked away, offering no response. A bucket of rage flooded her face before she buried her focus on a family portrait behind the desk. It had been painted at least twenty years ago when Ophelia and Jennifer were in their late twenties or early thirties. I saw their brother standing between them, prompting me to ask a question. "What about Timothy? I noticed him at the show last weekend. I guess he was sitting elsewhere. How's he handling your mother's death?"

Jennifer shrugged. "I haven't heard from him."

"Neither have I," Ophelia added. "I doubt he attended the actual performance."

Eustacia cleared her throat. "The last I saw him was during the intermission. Has no one spoken to him? Surely he's aware what happened to Gwennie."

The room was silent when Millard entered. "I'm glad you started without me. I've been detained talking to Brad upstairs about a few things."

"Mr. Paddington, it's good to see you. Your family was just saying that no one's heard from Timothy since Gwendolyn passed away on Sunday. Were you able to get in touch with him?" I asked, finding it odd that no one knew anything. I also knew minimal information about the man and would need to ask more questions privately when I had a chance.

"No, I thought you did, Eustacia. I left him a voice mail to be here at noon today. Is he not around?" Millard walked toward Ophelia and handed her an envelope. I couldn't see what was written on it, but it looked like something you'd get from a bank.

"No one's heard from him in three days?" Eustacia shouted in exasperation. As she stood from the table, her cane fell to the floor. I jumped up to help her regain her balance and be able to walk without falling. I looked around, discovering no one else seemed to pay attention. This was not a family with an abundance of love. Gwendolyn's son was missing. Both her daughters were fighting about money. Millard was acting strangely given he'd agreed to set up the meeting today but showed up late and hadn't invited the whole family. What had he handed Ophelia?

"Where are Dana, Sam, and Lilly?" I asked.

Millard offered an apologetic look. "I should've mentioned it to you before. I didn't invite them. I thought it best for you to meet Gwennie's children first, then we can follow up with the others."

I would have preferred to know that in advance, but it wouldn't help me to admonish him. I was certain no one reprimanded a Paddington. Ophelia announced she had to leave. Millard followed her out the door, intent on discussing something before she left. Jennifer thanked me for stopping by, then exited. Eustacia and I looked at one another and snickered.

"How do you deal with them? I don't mean it offensively, but your family is more disruptive and bitter than mine," I said half-heartedly.

"It's always been like that, Kellan. My brother was the one person who kept everyone in line. When Charles passed away last year, Gwennie lost interest in controlling her children. Ophelia's husband is consistently in and out of the picture, I never know what's going on between them."

"They're still married?"

Eustacia nodded. "Ophelia claims Richard left her penniless, so she'd constantly ask her mother for money to cover expenses. Although, given she lives here and all the bills are paid for by the household budget, I'm uncertain how much she needs to survive."

"Jennifer seemed shaken when Ophelia dismissed her because she didn't have any children to support."

"Jennifer's had a hard life. She's been engaged twice. Both men broke it off. The first practically left her at the altar, poor thing. And the last time, well, that wasn't fair to her," Eustacia said wistfully while closing her eyes. "My dear niece had two miscarriages while they were engaged, and the louse walked away when he thought she couldn't bear him any children."

"That's terrible," I said, thinking about my sister. Though Eleanor had never been pregnant, wanting a child of her own had been a driving force in her life the last few years. "Is Jennifer still hoping to have a child?"

"I'm not the one to ask. We were close years ago, but after the last broken engagement, she moved out of the house and keeps to herself," Eustacia noted while shuffling toward the door. "Did you learn anything of importance today?"

I shook my head. "Perhaps a little. I think we need to track down Timothy. I find it concerning he had a public disagreement with his mother moments before she died. He might have had access to put cocaine in her pills at any point before Brad brought them to the theater."

"As did Ophelia and Jennifer, as well as any of her grandchildren or anyone who had access to her medication closet," Eustacia explained, pivoting back to the portrait above the desk with discerning focus. "We need to find out what was written in the will. Either someone killed Gwennie for the inheritance, or they were angry with her over something else. I can't think of another motive, can you?"

I confessed I couldn't. When Eustacia left, Bertha stepped inside to escort me to the front door. As we walked down the hallway, I asked, "Had you seen anything odd with Gwendolyn's behavior during the last few weeks?" I knew Nana D was going to talk with the staff, but since I was already there, I took advantage of the opportunity.

"Mrs. Paddington was distressed more than usual. She rarely said anything to me about them, mostly complained over their lack of consideration for her. But she did note something one afternoon," Bertha clarified as we reached the front door. When I asked for details, Bertha's face blanched. "That girl needs to be taught a lesson."

"Gwendolyn said that about whom?" I asked, not understanding the comment.

"I think it was Jennifer. Gwendolyn had just hung up the phone with her when I announced lunch. Mrs. Paddington kept repeating the line, then told me to call her attorney," Bertha explained before saying goodbye.

As I stepped down, shocked at the news, I pressed accept on my ringing phone. "How did the inspection go?"

Eleanor grunted. "I failed. He told me the electrical work didn't meet code and that I couldn't open next week. I need help, Kellan."

This wasn't good news. "Did he give you a write-up of what needs to be corrected?"

"Yes, and it's way more than I can afford based on what the inspector suggested should be done. Apparently, once I started construction by opening up walls and installing new appliances, I was responsible for bringing up the kitchen to current electrical code. I can't get this done with no money or time." Eleanor sounded infuriated. I couldn't blame her. I'd also be disheartened and worried if I'd sunk all my savings into a new business that wasn't starting off in a positive position.

"What does the contractor say?"

"He's gone already. He packed up yesterday when the work was done and told me to call him if I needed anything. When I tried just now, his phone was no longer in service."

I inquired how she'd located the contractor to begin with, but Eleanor mumbled something about the previous owners recommending him. Given the abbreviated time frame, she didn't bother with any additional quotes or references and foolishly trusted their judgment. Eleanor gave me the contractor's name, and I promised her I'd find out what I could.

On the drive to Braxton to visit my mother, I thought through all the people who might help Eleanor. I called the Play House to see if Arthur Terry was available. As the person responsible for running the *King Lear* production, he likely had an available carpenter or electrician who might spare an hour and provide a quote and options for Eleanor. He didn't pick up the phone, but Yuri, the girl working on the stage design, promised to deliver my urgent message as soon as Arthur returned. My day was getting entirely too busy for what was supposed to be Spring Break.

I parked the SUV in the North Campus lot and briskly strode to the admissions building to visit my mother. Her assistant mentioned my mother was almost done updating a family who was about to take a tour of the campus. I waited in the lobby outside her door, admiring the fancy new nameplate— Violet Ayrwick, Admissions Director. When she was done, my mother led me into her office, then closed the door. "Is there something you're keeping from your father and me, Kellan?"

I guess that meant my father had told my mother about the letter. "Not at all. Why do you ask?"

"Oh, just wondering... your father mentioned finding something. You've been hanging out with the Paddingtons lately. Nana D said you were running her campaign. Do you think that's a wise thing to do? She's almost seventy-five years old, honey. Nana D needs to rest," my mother reproached.

"Nana D's a lot sprier than you give her credit for, Mom."

"That's not what I'm worried about. I'm sure she can handle it, but do you think Wharton County will support her? She's not qualified to run for mayor. Marcus Stanton is going to destroy her reputation." My mother took a giant swig of water, then sighed heavily. "I wish my brother was home to help talk her out of it. He's been silent ever since he left on that year-long African safari."

"I understand, but when have you ever known Nana D to back down from a challenge? She's determined to fix Braxton while she still has enough energy and time." I'd already tried to convince Nana D not to take on the job, encouraging her to become a councilwoman when Marcus vacated his role to run for mayor. She wouldn't listen and promised to *slap his bottom silly*. That was her frequent method for teaching people lessons—she came from a different era.

"Just watch her closely, please. She listens to you," my mother begged. We laughed for a minute, knowing Nana D listened to no one but herself.

My mother brewed coffee while we talked. I asked her what she knew about the Paddington family. I remembered her telling me she'd gone to high school with Ophelia nearly forty years ago.

"Ophelia's ruthless and nasty, a terrible combination. Many people say she's just like her mother, but there's a subtle difference. Where Gwendolyn was ornery and stubborn, Ophelia brandishes much more than a mean streak. That woman likes to get revenge on anyone who hurts her."

"It sounds like you speak from experience, Mom." I pictured an epic battle between my mother and Ophelia, not knowing who'd win. While my mother was gentle, she had a competitive side and could be stealthy.

My mother pondered her past before responding. "Not really. We were never friends or enemies. We didn't hang out in the same crowd. I had to help run things on the farm at Danby Landing after school. Ophelia went to a variety of social clubs and had a nanny who looked out for her."

"Do you know her husband?" I realized I still needed to meet him.

"Richard Taft used to be friendly with your father, and occasionally we'd see them at charity or sporting events around campus. He took an out-of-town job over a year ago last Christmas. I heard he and Ophelia might consider separating, which makes sense since I haven't seen him around at all."

"Has Dad not heard from him either?"

"No, he tried a few times, but after a couple of months, your father assumed Richard didn't want to talk anymore. There were a few unfortunate, public arguments between him and Ophelia."

"Do you think Ophelia is capable of killing her mother? From what I understand, she had little money left and was recently pressuring Gwendolyn to lend her some." I didn't like the way the woman had treated me or her family earlier that day, but there's a fine line between being a menace and killing someone. I didn't have enough information to hazard a guess if she were dangerous or simply cruel.

"Oh, goodness. I don't know her that well now. I suppose under the right circumstances she could be vindictive enough. But surely someone wouldn't kill their own mother over money, Kellan." My mother looked at me with both judgment and concern.

"Don't worry, Mom. I'm not thinking about sending you to an early grave," I joked, then looked in the other direction while tapping my fingers together devilishly. "Besides, how else would I deal with Nana D if you weren't there to help me?"

My mother hooted and warned me to be careful. "I don't trust that family. I've never had any issues with them, but something's not right. Everyone seems out to hurt each other, even those older ones."

My mother told me that when their parents passed away, Charles, Millard, and Eustacia had a huge falling out over the distribution of assets. At the time and given the way things ran in the Paddington family, the eldest male inherited the bulk of the estate. For some reason, Millard was skipped, and everything had been given to Charles. Eustacia had pitched such a fit. Her siblings stopped speaking to her for a year. My mother had no idea about the source of the blow-up.

"What happened when Charles died?"

"His son, Timothy, had been running the company for the last decade after Charles retired, but shortly before Charles passed away, he convinced the Board of Directors to place his son on temporary leave. Timothy had a substance abuse problem he'd been struggling with and was making some horrendous business decisions. I believe Gwendolyn kept the house because she was still alive, but I'm uncertain of the other details or the current state of the family business," my mother indicated before telling me she had to prepare for a meeting.

CHAPTER 10

After I left the admissions building, the current state of Paddington Enterprises became my focus. Was Timothy still running the organization, or did he never come back from the forced leave of absence? I needed his help to fill in the missing pieces, but before I could do that, it was time to help Nana D prepare for her first debate with Marcus Stanton. I sent her a text indicating I'd stop by for dinner after finishing afternoon errands.

Nana D: *I want tacos. I'm feeling the need to have Mexican tonight.*
Me: *Are we cooking them ourselves, or am I bringing take out?*
Nana D: *Can't you make any decisions yourself, brilliant one?*
Me: *If I brought takeout, you'd tell me it was full of chemicals. If I bought all the ingredients, you'd tell me we had no time to cook since we're supposed to practice for your debate.*
Nana D: *Are you saying I never let you win? Margaritas, too.*
Me: *I think staying sober would be better for tomorrow.*
Nana D: *I wasn't asking your opinion. Don't be cheap. Get the good liquor. I'm out.*

I compromised by picking up tortilla chips, tacos, and burritos at our favorite Mexican restaurant, but I'd also buy all the ingredients to make our own guacamole. I'd developed a secret recipe with shallots, cumin, and bacon that couldn't be topped. As for the drinks, I knew I had no chance to stop her, so why bother? I'd make them as weak as possible or spill half of hers out when she wasn't looking.

* * *

I woke up Thursday morning with a hangover so painful my head had put out a foreclosure sign. My eyelids blinked several times in a row, trying to read the clock on the far wall. Where was I? Nana D's couch. I then heard someone speaking and tried to understand the conversation.

"He doesn't look so well, Nana D," Emma noted and poked my cheek.

"That's what happens when you try to pull the wool over Nana D's eyes, baby girl. Never forget that lesson," Nana D teased.

"Is he gonna throw up again? That was yucky," Emma shuddered.

"It's the only way to teach your Daddy who knows better. He likes to learn things the hard way. Always has, even at your age. Such a stubborn little boy." Nana D sighed relentlessly.

"I can hear you both." My left foot dropped to the ground with a thud. "Please explain to me what happened last night?"

Emma told me we were all having a good time eating dinner, but she didn't understand why I kept switching out Nana D's glass with a different one. When she asked Nana D about it, my grandmother told Emma that the rules needed to change. It was time to swap out her daddy's glass with a different one that Nana D had prepared. It seemed at the end of the night, my nana had two margaritas and I had eight of them. I knew why I had the hangover from that place I told Emma never to speak of.

Emma dashed to the kitchen to pour me a glass of water. "I'm the only person in the world whose nana purposely tried to get him drunk. Hardly seems fair, nor something you should teach Emma, Nana D," I said, feeling a dry pastiness in my mouth I hadn't felt in years.

"Pish! All Emma knows is that you drank so much you almost wet the couch. I explained that she should never drink that much liquid before bed, so honestly, it was a useful thing for her to learn, Kellan. I hope *you've* also realized something from last night." Nana D handed me two aspirin and a cold rag, followed by a glass of something that smelled like rotten tomatoes and looked like the salsa we'd eaten the night before.

"What's this?" The contents of my stomach rose and swirled over the smell in the glass.

"Your hangover cure. I couldn't leave you feeling this bad all day long. I need your support at the debate." Nana D smiled at me like a gentle and innocent grandmother who wanted only the best for me.

"You're a wicked woman. I get it. Don't mess with Nana D. It won't happen again." I swallowed a large gulp of her concoction and gagged.

"Excellent. Then we're off to a good start today. Also, Timothy still hasn't turned up. Eustacia called an hour ago to tell me no one's heard from him in nearly four days."

"I'll see what I can find out after the debate." I accepted the glass of water from Emma. I alternated between the water and Nana D's hangover cure until both drinks were gone. Soon enough, I felt like a new person. "You're a miracle worker." Thirty minutes later, after showering and shaving, I hurried downstairs, dressed and ready to depart. "Has anyone found out what's going on with either of the two wills?"

Nana D shook her head. "Eustacia was going to ask Bertha to go through the entire house to see if she could find anything. I, unfortunately, learned nothing from talking to her."

After dropping Emma off at school, we drove to the debate. As soon as we got back on the main road, my phone rang. Once we saw whom it was, Nana D put it on speaker, so we could both listen. Arthur called to offer the use of his stage contractor and an electrician who could stop by the Pick-Me-Up Diner on their break to give Eleanor a quote for the repairs. When I told him the name of Eleanor's contractor, he laughed wildly. "That man's a crook. I looked him up on a few websites when he applied at the Play House for a job. Steals from everyone, then doesn't finish the work. Eleanor should count herself lucky he accomplished what he did before vanishing!" Arthur suggested we should meet for coffee on Friday to catch up. We firmed up plans, then hung up.

As we entered the Wharton County Civic Center's parking lot, Nana D said, "I'm gonna crack down on these slipshod contractors and get them out of my county. By the way, might Arthur be a good catch for Eleanor? She could stand to get herself a date sometime soon. Between you and her, it's like an entire generation has given up on love."

I rolled my eyes for the umpteenth time at my grandmother. When I realized having her focus on setting up Eleanor would be a blessing in disguise, I gave in. "That's a possibility. Maybe you should try to help her out with a new romance?"

"Sounds like a deal. But don't think that gets you off the hook. You're still my primary focus right now. I've found a charming girl who works at the prison. Real chipper. Built like an ox, too. A security guard, I believe," Nana D casually mentioned as she popped open the door and raced into the building before I had a chance to reply. Was she serious?

While Nana D and Marcus prepared with the moderator, Lara Bouvier, on stage for the upcoming debate, I made a list of things to inquire about once it concluded. I needed to find out from the sheriff what she'd learned, not that she'd share easily. The debate kicked off with Lara introducing herself to the room. The local news station, WCLN, had planned to cover all three of the debates which meant the entire county could watch, even though the attendance for today's first one was kept to a few hundred citizens ranging from members of the civic center to local merchant groups. Lara, a mid-forties divorcee, was the political correspondent at Wharton County's local news station who covered both national and regional politics in the area. She'd once been married to one of Judge Grey's sons, but it hadn't lasted long. Rumor had it —via the Septuagenarian Club—Lara was getting hot and heavy with Marcus Stanton's younger brother, Niles, owner of Wharton County's prime real estate agency.

Marcus got the first question and dazzled the room by indicating his record for single-handedly reducing the percentage of crime every year for the last seven years. When Nana D countered, she went for the jugular. "Really? I may not have access to all the same metrics and phony details you've got, Stanton, but three weeks ago there were two murders in Braxton. Where were you when they were happening?" Nana D was skirting a dangerous line given they both had reason to keep the details of those incidents from being available to the public—Nana D and Marcus Stanton had interacted with the killer and never realized what was going on behind their backs the whole time.

After a few retorts, Lara pushed them both to the next question. She asked Nana D, "What are your top three initiatives?" Given we'd prepared for it, Nana D would nail this question.

"First, we're gonna rid this town of red tape, bully politicians, and false promises. I'm not one to point out the current regime's faults, but clearly these shenanigans need to stop. Wharton County needs a mayor committed to staying true to this land's history. We've got to focus on rebuilding our downtown area and that includes the Finnulia River waterfront and shores at Crilly Lake."

The audience cheered when Nana D told them she intended to ensure the county would bring in three enormous new business opportunities to create jobs. She then promised to recreate the family atmosphere in Wellington Park from when there were cherished afternoons eating delicious frozen treats, playing old-fashioned games with family, and relaxing in the beauty of the outdoors.

By the end of the debate, Marcus Stanton earned some wins when he pointed out Nana D's lack of experience and her age. It was ironic given he was in his early sixties and right on the cusp himself of being eligible to move to Willow Trees. He suggested forming a council of the community's elder population to advise him on how to help make Wharton County a better place. He even proposed Nana D step down from the mayoral race to be his right-hand woman running such a council. When the debate ended, Lara wouldn't declare anyone a winner but assured us she saw excellent points from both sides that day. As Marcus stepped off the stage, he snubbed Nana D and went into his private limo. I quickly pointed out his disgraceful attitude to the cameraman, who was grateful to capture it on video.

"I think I did well," Nana D exclaimed when she found me thirty minutes later.

"You got in a few curveballs, Nana D. I'm proud of you," I noted, embracing her as the cameras snapped some photos of us. It would be good for the campaign, if nothing else. Or maybe a silver-framed photo for her upcoming seventy-fifth birthday.

When I got back to Nana D's place, I noticed I had a voicemail from the executive producer at the network back in LA. After firing my boss a few weeks earlier, they'd told me they were planning to take the show in a different direction but weren't sure how or where I'd fit in. They'd recently finished their initial discussions with some investors and the top brass at the network, who had decided to put *Dark Reality*, our television series, on hiatus for one year.

During that time, I would be free to work for another television show, but in one year, when they were ready to start production on their next season, they'd be in contact with me to discuss potential roles. In one way, it was good. It meant I could try to convince them to take the show in a direction where I could focus on true crime instead of the mock-crime-made-for-reality-television-series my former boss had insisted on.

It was also bad because that meant I had no immediate reason to return to LA. I'd committed to staying in and teaching at Braxton for the next year, too. I guess it meant my professional life was settled for the short-term, but there was still a need to figure out the situation with Francesca. If I went back to LA as she wanted, I had no job. How could I afford to keep my house and raise Emma? The Castiglianos would surely foot the bill and be thoroughly thrilled if I moved in with them. It would mean they'd see Emma every day, and Francesca could be near us. But hiding with my in-laws and sneaking around to see my wife wasn't the life I wanted. I needed time to fully digest the news about my delayed contract at *Dark Reality*.

We got back to Nana D's house and enjoyed a late lunch. When we were finished, she called Dr. Betscha to find out more about Gwendolyn's death. I wasn't sure exactly how he and Nana D were related, but they both descended from the Betscha siblings who'd been founding members of Braxton and Wharton County over two hundred years earlier. Third cousins once removed by hopping branches and traversing leaves blowing in the wind via a stepladder and eighth remarriage. Who knew? I just called him a cousin.

"You might be family, Seraphina, but I can't give you too many details. This is tied to a police investigation, and you're not the next of kin," Dr. Betscha cautioned.

"Well, Eustacia is next of kin, and she informed me she told you it was okay to talk to us," Nana D demanded of her cousin. "I'm only trying to figure out what happened to my poor friend. Something doesn't add up, and I'm willing to bet you know why, Alex."

"I've turned over a final report to Sheriff Montague as of this morning. I'll tell you a few things, but please don't let it slip to the sheriff," he replied.

"You're a solid man. Momma always told me your daddy was good to her. I can see it runs in the family. When we're all done talking here, you need to come by for dinner, Alex. I still can't believe you haven't been scooped up, yet. Forty and not married. What's this world coming to?" Nana D teased.

"I'm a confirmed bachelor, Seraphina. I've gone on a few dates from time to time, but I haven't met the right woman. Someday it might happen. Until then, let's leave it alone, alright?"

Nana D agreed. I didn't say a word, feeling grateful I wasn't the focus of her attention for once. Although, I wondered whether I should set him up with Jennifer Paddington, who was trying to have a child. He might be a prime candidate. "What can you tell us, Dr. Betscha?"

"Give us details. How does this work?" Nana D said, unable to let him do the talking.

"Slow down, Seraphina. Gwendolyn was sick, probably sicker than she knew. She hadn't come in to see me in close to three months. A lot had changed during that time, and she wasn't a well woman. Her heart had begun to deteriorate, and she was developing clots. We could've controlled many of the symptoms, but given what I saw in her bloodstream, some recent infections, and the impact on her heart, the poor woman would've needed advanced medicine soon enough. The medication she'd been on already for years should've been keeping her system running a little better, but—"

"Are you saying she was going to die from something else?" I inquired, feeling a twinge in my chest. Had Gwendolyn known how sick she was?

"I'm afraid so," Dr. Betscha remarked in a sympathetic tone. "But there's one key thing to point out. The blood tests did not show a satisfactory level of the medications she was supposedly taking. I double checked it. If she were regularly following her prescribed medication plan, I would have seen it in the test results. Based on what I saw, either Gwendolyn stopped taking her medicine, or someone swapped a decent chunk of her pills with a placebo. I told the sheriff I suspected she'd been swallowing fake sugar pills based on adding up everything found in her bloodwork."

I gasped. The shock of someone's intentional wickedness unnerved me. "Is there anything you can tell us about the placebos? Or whether her nurse, Brad, should have recognized any symptoms?"

"Perhaps Brad should have put a few things together based on the symptoms you mentioned. It's not uncommon for someone in their seventies to experience these same signs and have it be advanced age and existing illness."

"You're saying she would've thought it was only a need to change the amount of her medication? At least until she came to you, and you ran tests picking up the missing medications in her bloodwork," I noted.

"Correct. The cocaine definitely killed her, but lack of any real medication would've led it to happen relatively soon, anyway."

When we hung up with Dr. Betscha, Nana D and I agreed it was time to have a detailed discussion with Gwendolyn's nurse, Brad. He would be able to shed light on how he managed her medication. He might also be someone who could've helped the killer plan Gwendolyn's death. Something must have changed in that last twenty-four hours to cause the killer to push his or her plan forward, so Gwendolyn was out of the picture much sooner.

* * *

"You're a lifesaver, big brother," Eleanor gleefully shouted into the phone the next morning. "I called the electrician Arthur suggested, and he's starting work today. He thinks he can get everything converted by Sunday. I might still open early next week."

I pulled the phone away from my ear and studied the time. Why did my sister feel the need to call me at six o'clock in the morning to share her good news? "That's awesome. Do you ever sleep? This is an uncivilized hour to call people, you know." Before she could respond, my phone beeped telling me I had another caller. This time it was Nana D. "Seriously? I need to learn how to shut my phone off at night. Can I call you back later, Eleanor?"

I switched back to the other line. "This better be important. I love you to pieces, Nana D, but I was dreaming about a sunny beach full of calming waves and palm trees."

"Get your patootie out of bed. The sun is on its way up, and you've got a nurse to grill. Honestly, Kellan, I don't know what kind of lesson you're teaching Emma by staying in bed so late when there are major priorities in need of your attention." Nana D's voice was like a foghorn blasting at full volume in the middle of a tiny room.

"Emma is still sleeping. She gets up at seven o'clock for breakfast and then I drop her off at school. We have a routine. I thought we were meeting at the Paddington estate at ten o'clock today to talk with Brad?" After we'd spoken with Dr. Betscha the previous night, she'd cooked me dinner as an apology for getting me drunk on margaritas. Subsequently, I'd gone home early, helped Emma complete her homework, and caught up on sleep, as I'd started feeling like I was coming down with a cold or had overworked my body during the last few days at the gym. I climbed out of my bed, threw on my robe, and checked Emma's room to confirm she was still sound asleep. "What changed?"

Nana D continued, "That's yesterday's news, kiddo. Finnigan Masters is coming by to review the will with Eustacia this morning at eight thirty. Meet me there, so we can find out who else has a motive."

"I'll do my best, but I can't promise I'll be there by—" I heard the phone click when she hung up. My grandmother didn't care about my own plans this morning. I trudged down the hall to the shower and turned the cold water on full blast. Within seconds, my body startled out of hibernation as I reached for the shampoo. As I got myself ready for the day, I waffled on whether Brad wasn't a proficient nurse, or he had something to do with the plot to kill her. There was a small chance he was innocent and had everything documented to review with Dr. Betscha, but the entire situation felt too suspicious.

CHAPTER 11

After dropping off Emma at school, I arrived at the Paddington estate shortly after eight thirty. Bertha greeted me and led me to the Great Hall where Nana D, Millard, Eustacia, and Finnigan were having coffee.

"I see you chose to attend," Nana D teased. "We've discussed punctuality before, brilliant one."

"It's a shame what's happening this generation. They've no appreciation for getting up early to put in a hard day's work," Eustacia continued, piling on the lectures. "Today's youth will be the downfall of this society."

I wanted to defend myself, but pride over being called a youth despite being in my early thirties won out. Instead, I turned to Finnigan. "I'm sorry I missed you the other day. So glad to hear how well you're doing with the practice these days."

Finnigan was two years older than me. His tawny brown hair had grayed at the temples, but he still maintained a youthful appearance. His family was English and had moved to Wharton County when we were children. Traces of his accent appeared at times, but mostly he'd been Americanized. Tall and thin, he and his brother, Liam, towered over me. Yet they always seemed to shrink their appearance to blend in with the crowd. He wore a striped blue suit with a colorful tie that reminded me of a Monet painting I'd seen in a hall around the Paddington estate.

"Thanks, Kellan. I'm excited you're back in Braxton. Liam's hoping to find a few days to stop home in between hockey games." Finnigan shared a picture of him and Liam at a recent game. I was glad to see they stayed close over the years. I wish I had that chance with my own brothers, but it hadn't worked out in the past.

"Shall we get started?" Millard queried with a hint of nervousness in his voice. He sipped from his coffee cup while pruning one of the nearby lemon trees. Each time he brushed against a branch, a whiff of fresh citrus wafted by us.

Finnigan cleared his throat. "I'll make this as easy as possible. When Charles and Gwendolyn Paddington first came to see my father, I was recently out of law school and interning in the family practice. Dad handled the Paddington affairs, but he transitioned them to me shortly before Charles passed away. I met with Gwendolyn when Charles was diagnosed with pancreatic cancer, then again once he was gone. I tried to be as caring and gentle as possible with her during that tough time to help prepare a new will."

Millard nodded. "Your father is an excellent attorney. He and Lindsey worked on many cases together in the past. Clever mind. He knew American law better than Lindsey did. I should call him to have tea soon."

"Yes, he insisted I study it even as a child. I still know extraordinarily little about the UK because of his pressure to learn everything about our new homeland."

Eustacia emphatically banged her cane on the tiled floor. "I don't mean to rush you, but could we forego the details of your education and focus on the will? This ain't a remake of *Romper Room*."

Nana D pressed her fingers into my forearm as if to tell me to remain quiet. I was there to listen; I understood the message.

Finnigan blushed. "My apologies, I know this is complicated given the circumstances. At the time, Charles and Gwendolyn had excluded their son, Timothy, from the will. I wasn't privy to all the detailed reasons, but Charles and Gwendolyn had split the estate among various charities and theater organizations, as well as with their daughters, Ophelia and Jennifer. It was a clean separation. Fifty percent was allocated as donations, and the remaining fifty percent was split equally between both women."

I watched Millard's expression as he turned toward us. He'd also been cut out of his parents' will in the past. His face became quite pale, almost translucent. I needed to understand what had prompted such a decision.

"What can you tell us about the new will she discussed with you?" Eustacia questioned bluntly.

"It was also split with an equal portion being given to various charities, but the other fifty percent was allocated to different individuals. Unfortunately, I do not know whom Gwendolyn selected. She contacted me the day before she died, telling me she'd had enough with all the drama in her family and needed to correct something that'd happened in the past."

"Have you found the new will?" I asked.

Finnigan shook his head. "We thoroughly checked her bedroom suite, but it's not in there. Neither Millard nor Eustacia had any knowledge of the revised will's location. I assume if it's finished, perhaps she mailed it to me. I'll give it a few more days before I unveil the current will to the rest of the family."

"Obviously, something happened between Gwendolyn and her daughters. If she was changing her will, one or both were going to be removed as beneficiaries," Nana D noted.

"Or they stayed in it and someone new was added," Finnigan suggested.

"Were Gwendolyn's children aware of this will? Did they know Timothy would inherit nothing? Or that both daughters would?" I inquired. It was important to understand who was privy to the details of the inheritances.

"Gwendolyn mentioned that she'd never shared the decision with her children. In fact, she'd forgotten the details in the original will when we first spoke as it had been a while and she wasn't highly alert after Charles had passed on. My guess is none of the children knew who would benefit from her death," Finnigan explained while packing up his briefcase.

"Was anyone else aware she planned to write a new will?" Millard inquired.

"I can't answer that question," Finnigan replied while putting on his winter coat. "All I can tell you is that something happened last Saturday to result in her need to make an urgent change. I've only told the four of you about the potential existence of a new will. Unless Gwendolyn told the person or persons who would be the new beneficiaries, no one else knows about it either." He left with Millard, who mentioned he had to get to the nursery to inspect some new arrivals. Nana D, Eustacia, and I continued talking as we weren't set to meet with Brad until he returned from running errands for Eustacia at ten o'clock.

"This is ludicrous," Eustacia whined and shook her head repeatedly. "How are we supposed to figure it out?"

Nana D said, "Don't give up, Eustacia. We've only just begun. Kellan will find Gwennie's killer. Let's go over the facts again."

"I'll do my best, but I have to agree with Eustacia. There are a lot of possibilities. It would help if you could tell me why Millard was left out of your parents' will." I wandered around the Great Hall, thinking about the dynamics among all the members of the Paddington family.

Eustacia explained that Millard had been groomed to assume responsibility for Paddington Enterprises. He'd earned an MBA at Columbia, worked in the family business for twenty years, and had become a vice-president under his father. When he turned fifty, Millard realized he'd thrown his entire life away to run a large corporation but had no wife or children to love. He resigned from his position and took a job at a gardening center. Their parents were so upset they threatened to stop speaking with him over the embarrassment of the situation. Around the same time, Millard had befriended a young maid at the mansion. The family disapproved of the friendship since the girl was far beneath expected standards for a Paddington.

"It's hard to believe your parents were so old-fashioned. It was the early 1990s, right?" I asked.

Eustacia nodded. "Understand, my parents were considered high society, as were their parents before them. Braxton's a small town, people talk. My brother, Charles, and Gwennie had just finished raising their three children. Jennifer had graduated from college, Ophelia and Richard had become engaged, and Timothy had started working at the family business. They were seen as the perfect family. Gwennie was running around New York City with

Broadway stars and the rich and famous. Millard threw it all away to grow flowers and trees. Our parents couldn't understand it."

"They disinherited Millard because he quit his job and had an affair with a maid?" I asked.

"There's more to the story. The maid was young, barely eighteen or nineteen. After a few months, it had become obvious to them she was pregnant. My parents were afraid of a scandal. They sent her away before anyone could find out. I thought I was the only one who'd learned the truth, but..." She seemed lost in thought and stopped speaking.

Eustacia's news shocked me. It wasn't like this took place a century ago. It'd been barely twenty-five years earlier. "What happened to the child? And why didn't Millard try to support the girl?"

"I don't think he or anyone else knew the maid was pregnant. Millard didn't care about the inheritance. He'd already made enough money working at the family company. That's when he traveled the world and focused on gardening." It was clear the past had haunted Eustacia, but I wasn't certain how it would have anything to do with Gwendolyn's death.

Nana D added, "Millard's been so happy since he left Paddington Enterprises. I know he regretted never having had any children. How did you find out?"

Eustacia explained that she only knew about the baby because her mother had mentioned it on her deathbed. Eustacia had never told Millard about the child. She felt guilty about keeping the secret even after their parents had passed away almost two decades earlier. Eustacia wanted to tell her brother many times but had no way to track down the girl or learn what had happened to her. She thought it would be a futile attempt that would only make Millard more upset to discover the truth.

"What was the maid's name?" I asked.

"We called her Hannah. That's all I remember about her," Eustacia said with a heavy sigh.

Nana D accompanied Eustacia to the restroom to help her splash some water on her face before we met with Brad. If Millard had a secret child, could that child have tried to get revenge on Gwendolyn if he or she discovered their true identity? If Gwendolyn had found out, could she have left money to this child to right her parents' wrong when they'd excluded Millard from their will? It was an excellent theory, but until I could figure out whom the child was, it felt too fuzzy.

Just as the thought popped into my head, Brad entered the Great Hall. I nodded at him, then froze. "Brad, how old are you?" I asked, suddenly feeling alarmed at the potential connection I was about to make. "I, uh, apologize. I didn't mean to be too personal. I was curious. You look so young to have finished nursing school and worked several jobs already." Phew! Epic save.

Brad was initially silent, then tilted his head. "No, you can ask. I don't mind. I turned twenty-five three weeks ago. Where is Ms. Paddington?"

"Eustacia will be along shortly, I'm sure." Maybe he'd tell me about his family thinking it was an innocent conversation. "You've got good genes, Brad. I guess you must have inherited them from your parents."

"My mother always looked young, too. I think it was pretty common on her side of the family," he said, rubbing a few leaves of a nearby shrub, looking away from me. "I'm happy to answer any questions you have about the list of Gwendolyn's medications I gave to everyone."

"How's the search for a job going?" I stalled until the others returned to the Great Hall.

"I have two interviews this afternoon. Eustacia set one up at Willow Trees, and the other is a private patient. I'm also waiting for a few calls back on apartments that looked promising." Brad sat on a bench near the pond. He looked tired and distracted by something weighing heavily on his mind.

I heard Eustacia's cane pounding the floor as she entered the room. "Pardon my absence. I see Brad's come down to meet with us. Have you started already, Kellan?" she asked. When I shook my head, Eustacia continued. "Brad, a few things have come to my attention regarding Gwennie's death. I should like to hear from you exactly what you—"

"If I may interrupt," he said, standing to attention. "I've already been by to discuss it with the sheriff earlier this morning. I was stunned, in fact. I can't believe someone would intentionally try to kill Mrs. Paddington. I assure you, I had no idea."

"Surely, you have more to say than that," Eustacia admonished with a hard glare in his direction. "You were solely responsible for my sister-in-law's medication and gave her those pills moments before she died in the theater. While I'm not directly accusing you of having something to do with her murder, I hope you can understand I need to hear a lot more than *can't believe someone would intentionally try to kill her* as your meager response."

Brad clasped his hands together. "The police took all of her medications and any glasses, cups, or utensils from her bedroom. I'm sure they plan to test them. If someone tampered with any of the medication I administered, we'll find out quickly. It didn't come from me if that's what you're implying." He seemed to take offense at her tone and quickly responded by defending himself.

I wish I had a few minutes alone with Eustacia, so I could tell her about his age lining up with the baby the Paddington maid had supposedly given birth to. Possibly Millard Paddington's child. When Eustacia and Nana D turned to me, I took control of the conversation.

"Brad, this is definitely an awkward discussion. Please understand we are not accusing you of anything directly, but we need your help to understand some facts. Gwendolyn was acting strangely the last few weeks. We now know she was slowly being made sicker without proper medication. A lethal dose of cocaine was ingested moments before she died in the theater," I said, pausing to make direct eye contact with him. He stared back with a chilled, blank look that made me want to squirm. "You've spent the most time with her, and you gave her the medication she'd forgotten to take with her earlier in the day. Any reasonable person would want to understand what you think happened."

"But I had no reason to want Mrs. Paddington dead. She was my employer and truthfully, a confidante in the last few weeks. I'd been having a few personal issues she helped me deal with. Don't you understand? I have no job and home now. Why would I kill her?" he said in frustration, then threw his hands in the air. "I'm not in the habit of killing my patients despite what anyone has said in the past."

Nana D interrupted to put her arm around Brad's shoulder as if she were trying to play good cop to Eustacia's or my bad cop. "Brad, you've been a wonderful support to my friend in the last year. Was there anyone other than you that handled her medication, or had you seen anyone in her room that maybe didn't belong there?"

Nana D had a good point in terms of who had the opportunity. We needed to know exactly what the sheriff had found during the search of Gwendolyn's bedroom to understand if the cocaine was in all her pills or just the one dosage she'd taken at the theater. "Let's start with how you managed your patient's medication, so we can determine how the cocaine got put into those pills."

Brad perked up and explained that Gwendolyn took her medication three times each day—morning, afternoon, and evening. Some were gel-based capsules filled with the ground up medication and others were solid tablets. Each dosage contained a combination of pills, but Brad would prepare a weekly pill box separating each day's allotment. If Gwendolyn were going out for the day, she used a travel bottle to hold the next dosage while she'd be gone from the house. "Earlier that morning, she took her regular pills. At the same time as I gave her the morning pills, she took out her travel bottle for the afternoon dosage. It was too early to take that next dosage at brunch, so she planned to take it while attending the theater. I used the pills from the regular pill box that I'd prepared earlier that week and that contained the pills she'd taken a few hours earlier. There was nothing different about them."

"They couldn't have been tampered with in the early morning batch as nothing happened to her then," I concluded. If the killer had only switched a few pills in the batch, it would have been too coincidental that Brad had randomly chosen those same cocaine-laced pills from the whole supply when he'd brought them to her at the theater that afternoon. That specific tainted dosage had to have been swapped after the travel bottle was prepared that morning. "When did you give her the travel bottle? And where was it from the point you gave it to her to the point you brought it to the theater?"

"I watched her put the filled travel bottle on her night table in the bedroom. It was sitting there while she showered and dressed. I suppose it was partially unattended while she was in the bathroom, but I was in my own room by then. At some point, she must have put the bottle in her purse and gone downstairs to the dining room to eat brunch with everyone. I don't know what happened during brunch until she sent Bertha to find me again," Brad explained.

"While we were eating brunch, we talked about going out for dinner with the entire family after the show ended. That's when she called Brad downstairs to ask him to have two travel dosages ready before she left for the theater,"

Eustacia noted. "Gwennie wanted us to all show up together for the first performance at the family theater. Jennifer and Millard were both at the house that morning. Ophelia and the kids, too. Richard was already out of town and couldn't make the *King Lear* performance. Timothy was nowhere to be found."

"I was there, too," Nana D interjected while snapping her fingers. "Brad said he would add the second dosage to her pills and put it back in her purse on the Edwardian console table in the hallway while everyone got ready to leave. He indicated he'd be done in less than fifteen minutes."

"Correct. So, I took the bottle out of her purse and placed it on the table next to her coat. I left it there while I went upstairs to get the pill box, so I could get the second dosage of all her medications," Brad said. "In retrospect, I should've taken the bottle with me, but I wasn't thinking straight."

"We sat for five minutes, then everyone went to the Great Hall to prepare to leave," Eustacia added before clearing her throat. "We were all in and out of that hallway using the restroom, getting our coats, and talking to each other. Anyone could've accessed the bottle to switch the pills."

"Jennifer left for the longest amount of time. Remember, someone joked about her always causing delays," Nana D mentioned.

While I wanted to explore Jennifer's extended absence, I had another important question. "I still don't understand how Gwendolyn left without the pills. Brad, you said you left the bottle on the table next to her purse when you went upstairs to get the additional pills. Then you returned and brought the additional dosage back down, right?" I questioned.

"When I got back to the hallway, her coat, purse, and pill bottle were gone," Brad said before biting his lip. "I thought we had a miscommunication... that she no longer needed the second travel dosage of medication."

"So, you knew something odd was going on that morning?" I suggested.

"Not really. I figured she changed her mind. It'd happened other times where she previously decided not to take an extra dosage of medication at the last minute."

"Didn't you try to find her to ask her?" Nana D said with an annoyed look.

"I asked Bertha where everyone went, but while I was upstairs, they'd left for Paddington's Play House," Brad explained. "I should've tracked her down, but I guess I made a mistake."

A potentially life-changing one. "What did you do then?" I asked.

"I put the extra dosage of pills back in the regular pill box, went for a long walk around the property, and did some laundry. Then I got Mrs. Danby's call that Mrs. Paddington wasn't feeling well and needed her pills. I was confused, so I went back downstairs to see if she'd accidentally left them somewhere else in the dining room. There they were on the table. I asked Bertha, who said she'd found them on the floor under the table when she was cleaning. She assumed it was an older bottle and planned to give it to me later that day." When Bertha told him how she'd found them, Brad assumed they'd accidentally fallen to the floor and that Gwendolyn must've thought he'd already put them back in her purse before she'd left. "Timothy was also in the kitchen talking to Bertha. He offered to bring the pills to his mother, but it was my job. I thought little of it at the time and rushed to the Play House to drop off the pills."

Nana D squeezed the bridge of her nose. "Someone must have changed the first travel dosage of pills after Brad had filled them that morning but before everyone left for Paddington's Play House."

"Would Gwendolyn have left without validating she had all her pills?" I asked.

Eustacia responded, "I can see it happening. Gwennie was behaving oddly that morning. If she were changing her will, she might not have been paying full attention and didn't verify whether he'd already added the second dosage to her travel bottle. In the rush, she probably grabbed everything she saw and left, assuming Brad had added the second dosage into the bottle and put it back in her purse."

Nana D added, "I vaguely remember hearing something fall to the floor when I returned from the bathroom, but I thought nothing of it at the time. I thought it had come from another room."

"I'm not sure we'll be able to figure out who slipped into the hallway or bedroom and switched the medication that morning. At least we know when it happened, but unfortunately everyone had access. I'm sure it's possible someone else could've snuck in and swapped them," I said, trying to figure out if there was any way to narrow down the list of suspects. "In theory, with no one watching, it only takes a minute to remove a few pills and drop in the cocaine-laced ones."

Brad agreed with me, then explained he had to get to an interview. After he left, I developed a headache. I'd eventually verify what he'd said with Bertha. I didn't think he was lying, but needed to confirm his explanation. Timothy's sudden appearance and Jennifer's lengthy disappearance seemed highly suspect. We were definitely missing something important.

CHAPTER 12

Eustacia asked Bertha to prepare a light lunch for Nana D and I. We devoured a Caesar salad with grilled chicken breast, battered prawns, and homemade croutons. In my mind I was expecting a grilled cheese sandwich or a bowl of tomato soup, but I would not complain about a free meal.

"I still don't agree with you for putting my brother's name on the list. He didn't have any reason to kill Gwennie." Eustacia's hands and arms waved about feverishly to make her point.

"I understand it doesn't seem logical to you, but if Millard found out he had a child and that Gwendolyn could have known something about it, he might have been too angry to stop himself," I explained as simply as I could.

"Kellan has a point. If that's his logic, we should also put Eustacia on the suspect list," Nana D suggested, looking serious and determined.

Eustacia gasped. "Me? Have you lost your mind, Seraphina? I had no reason to want my sister-in-law dead."

"Perhaps she discovered you'd kept the secret from Millard, and you killed her to keep it quiet," Nana D said with a flourish. "It's as plausible as Millard being the murderer. We've gotta look at this from every angle. I don't think you did it, but we should consider anyone who had the opportunity or the means. Although the motive might not be obvious right now, we can't rule out those with immediate access to Gwennie."

While Nana D and Eustacia engaged in a battle of wills, I absconded to Brad's room. I'd heard Bertha say goodbye to him a few moments earlier, which meant his room was unoccupied. She led me through one of the back hallways to the servants' quarters. While we walked, she corroborated his story about the pills falling under the table in the hallway. "That's his room on the far left, near the laundry facility," she said with a nod. "I must get back to the table to clean up."

Brad's door was unlocked when I turned the glass-covered knob. His living quarters were at least twelve by twelve and situated in the far corner of the wing. He had two pairs of double windows on the east and south walls, a queen-size bed with a muted blue comforter tucked neatly on both sides, and a small French country writing desk and chair set. I checked the desk drawers first, which like the room were spotless and organized. Other than a few current bills with minimal expenditures and a typical amount of debt for someone his age, nothing seemed out of the ordinary.

It was in the night table where I found something of interest. Hidden beneath a folder marked job opportunities and a crossword puzzle book was a framed photo of a little boy and a woman at the beach. I stared at the picture, deciding if the child was Brad from years ago, but I couldn't be certain. There was a strong likeness, but none of the clothing or furniture in the background suggested the time frame when the photo had been captured. I set it on the night table and took out my cell phone to take a picture for future reference. The velvet-covered cardboard flap holding the picture upright gave way and the entire frame fell to the floor.

When I picked up the picture, an obituary card slipped out. It read:

March 14, 2017, Hannah Shope

Hannah Shope, 45, of Boise, Idaho, passed away after a long battle with MS. Hannah had been active in the St. Francis Catholic Church until her diagnosis several years ago when she became unable to leave her house. She is survived by a loving son, Brad Shope, who took care of his mother in the last few years. Hannah was an only child who'd moved to the area twenty-five years ago from Pennsylvania, where she'd worked in domestic services. She will be missed by all her friends in the rosary group and at Sunday morning mass. May she eternally rest in peace.

I snapped a picture of both the photograph and the obituary card before quickly shutting the drawer and verifying everything was left exactly as I'd found it. I dashed back to the dining room where Nana D and Eustacia were still arguing about the potential suspects.

"What if it was the mail carrier? Maybe he snuck into Gwennie's bedroom every morning and swapped the pills. Honestly, Seraphina, you're pulling these ideas out of your crotchety old—"

"Ladies, I found something," I said with a zest of energy. "Didn't you say the maid's name was Hannah? Look at this." I handed my phone to Eustacia and Nana D, who huddled around the table's corner.

"I don't remember the name Shope, but that's definitely her. I now remember what she looked like and can't believe I didn't identify the resemblance with Brad."

"Do you know who introduced Brad to Gwendolyn at the rehabilitation facility?" I asked.

They both shook their heads. "I don't have the foggiest clue," Eustacia said, rubbing her fingers together. "But I'll call that whippersnapper Lydia Nutberry, she knows everyone."

I'd spent much longer at the Paddington mansion than planned and escaped to The Big Beanery. As I stood in line to order, I heard a pair of familiar voices talking in the nearby corner. I leaned in their direction and saw Connor speaking with Sheriff Montague. After picking up my dark roast coffee and a slice of coffee cake, I sidled up to their table and plopped down on an empty chair in an exaggerated fashion. "Top of the morning to you!" I said with a giant grin.

"Little Ayrwick, did you misunderstand our silence as an invitation to interrupt? I can only assume you've been drinking already and must be heavily impaired," Sheriff Montague chided while crumpling her napkin and tossing it into the garbage pail behind me.

"Kellan," Connor said with a quick nod of his head. "What can we do for you?"

"Well, it's what I can do for the sheriff, that is, if she's at all interested in discussing the Paddington case," I teased while gawking directly at April Montague. "Have I got some shocking information for you!"

"Let me guess. You've realized wearing tighty-whities cuts off all circulation to your brain and felt obligated to share your golden ticket discovery with every man or woman in the tri-state area? Or did you finally realize it is possible to walk and talk at the same time without forgetting to breathe?" The sheriff had a knack for delivering every word with such a disinterested and bland tone, I decided she'd make a good straight man in a comedy team.

"For your information, since you seem to be obsessed with my choice in underwear, I wear boxer briefs." For added delight, I stood up, peeled away the bottom section of my long-sleeve Henley and pulled up the black waistband of my underwear. "If you're so inclined to need further proof, I'm sure that can be arranged. Also, I've been walking and talking since I was two years old. Since you've already deemed me and my nana the biggest gabbers in all of Wharton County, be careful not to contradict yourself when trying to crack a joke at my expense. Emphasis on *trying*."

Connor's eyes opened wide. He obviously thought I was overstepping some invisible line that dictated I should be afraid of the sheriff. Given the abuse I'd already taken from her, I would not let it become the norm. "Dude, nice eight pack," he said, commenting on my increasingly defined ab muscles.

"Are you saying you don't find me funny?" the sheriff inquired while cocking her head to the left and smiling like a clown. "Because I think it'd be hilarious to slap a pair of handcuffs on your wrists and take you down to the station for a few hours."

"I've done nothing wrong. You can't arrest me, unless that's your way of trying to flirt with me. In which case, I'm compelled to remind you... emphasis on *trying*." I wasn't sure what had come over me. Maybe after having been home for close to a month as well as realizing I was making decent headway into another murder investigation, my confidence had grown stronger.

"We could banter all day and night. Sure, I could arrest you for something, but then I'd have to deal with the paperwork. You're not worth my time. I have five minutes and will listen with full attention if it means you'll go away faster." Sheriff Montague growled and slurped the muddy remnants at the bottom of her coffee cup.

"I've unexpectedly come across some information about the Paddington family's wills and a few instances where certain members have been left out. I also discovered someone who might have a connection to the Paddingtons, but I can't figure out if it has any bearing on Gwendolyn's death." I didn't want to give away all the information I'd learned and dropped enough hints to see what the sheriff responded to.

"If you're referring to Gwendolyn's will, I'm already in contact with Finnigan Masters to discuss when it will be available to read. As far as these clues you're dropping about other wills and connections, spill it." The sheriff pulled out a pad and begin writing a few notes.

I explained what I'd learned about Millard having been excluded from his parents' will, then Brad's arrival a few months after Charles died. I left out the missing new will just so I had leverage for later. "There must be a connection somewhere. Brad's mother, Hannah, died several days after Charles died. It could be a coincidence, yet that's when Brad went to work for Gwendolyn. What if Millard is Brad's father and one or both have some sort of diabolical plot to flee with the family money?"

"It's odd, I agree. Careful with your allegations. I'm not sure what that means, but doesn't Millard have his own money? He's a world-famous land-scaper and used to run the family company decades ago." Sheriff Montague cracked her knuckles and pushed her chair back from the table.

I nodded. "I couldn't make heads or tails of that myself. Any chance you've heard from Timothy? Eustacia has been trying to track him down for almost six days, but she can't find him. She'd like to hold the funeral service this weekend but hoped to find him. He was Gwendolyn's son."

"Timothy's been located and is currently a person of interest. As you're aware, he was seen arguing with his mother at the theater less than thirty minutes before she was murdered."

Connor said, "I've viewed the security camera footage in the lobby. The only two people who touched Gwendolyn's drink in the lobby were Brad and Timothy. I'm sure someone else had access inside the theater where we didn't have any cameras. And the cashier who poured the iced tea is a student who has impeccable references. No known connection to Gwendolyn."

The sheriff cleared her throat. "We've run tests on everything we pulled from the theater. There was no trace of any drugs in any beverages, containers, or any of the surfaces in the refreshment stand where she'd gotten the iced tea. It had to be introduced in the actual pills and not the glass that had been given to the victim. I'm waiting for the results on the rest of the pills from the house."

"Can you tell me where you found Timothy?" I asked.

"I'm not sure that's something he'd want the public to know. Besides, I expect within the next twenty-four hours, Timothy will no longer be there and will be in my custody," the sheriff said with a pointed stare.

"Are you saying he's your prime suspect?" I inquired. While everything pointed to Brad or Millard based on what I'd learned, not knowing where Timothy had been hiding out left me at a disadvantage. "What about the news I've just shared?"

"I'll be following up on it. In the meantime, if anything else pops up, be sure you alert me."

"And stay out of your murder investigation... yeah, yeah, got it. I understand," I said, lying through my teeth. I needed to find out where Timothy was hiding, but I was supposed to meet Arthur. I said goodbye to Connor and the sheriff, ordered a coffee to go, and skedaddled to Paddington's Play House. As I entered, my phone vibrated with a text message. It was uncanny how timely she could be.

Nana D: *We've found Timothy. You'll never guess where he is.*
Me: *At a hotel on a bender?*
Nana D: *Nope, the complete opposite.*

I had no idea what Nana D meant by her last comment and couldn't understand her cryptic clues. I looked up and saw Dana Taft waving at me.

Me: *Gotta go. Just tell me.*
Nana D: *You've got a lot to learn about being a detective.*
Me: *Fine, pretty please, with sugar on top. Can I know the secret, too?*
Nana D: *That's better. Timothy checked himself into rehab.*
Me: *For drug abuse?*
Nana D: *And gambling. He apparently went there right after his fight with Gwennie... at the show... before she died.*

Wow! What did that mean? I had no time to respond once Dana interrupted. "Hey. It's Kellan, right?" she asked while blinking a few times at me. "Arthur will be right over."

"How are you holding up?" I said.

"Oh, you know how it is. Trying to keep up with classes and the show."

"And losing your grandmother, I'm sure, has been painful." I winced at how quickly she seemed to forget or ignore Gwendolyn's death.

"We really weren't close," Dana noted. "No one liked her very much."

"I thought she and your brother, Sam, were very close," I countered.

"Oh, he fooled you, too, huh?" Dana obviously had something she wanted to share with me.

While I cared little about Dana given her attitude and the way she'd behaved with Arthur in the past, Sam didn't deserve his sister's reproach. "I may not know your family, Dana, but I'm an excellent judge of character. Sam was devastated the day she passed away."

"You're clueless! She and Sam had a tremendous fight the day before. I heard them arguing when I stopped back at the house to get something from my bedroom," Dana whined. "He tries so hard to look innocent, but he's hiding something from everyone."

"Is there something you're trying to tell me, Dana? Because to be honest, right now, it feels like you're acting a little jealous and immature." I wasn't sure whether it was the childish tone she spoke in or the dismissive gestures she'd made with each retort, but Dana's attitude angered me. I didn't know Sam from Adam, but his grandmother's death had genuinely devastated the kid.

"I don't need to listen to this. If you don't believe me, ask Sam yourself. I distinctly heard him tell Grandmother she was being a judgmental sourpuss. Then he slammed the door and told her he wouldn't back down. I have no idea what he meant, but he's been super-secretive for the last few months and refuses to talk to anyone about it." Dana demanded that I leave her alone and stomped off as Arthur walked up to us. She apparently enjoyed making a spectacle of herself.

"I've seen that look before. What did you do? Tell her you weren't interested?" Arthur teased.

"If only. It's a bit more complicated than that. How well do you know her?"

"I never met Dana before this show, but she's a wily one. If you don't push back, she tries to worm her way into every minute of your day," Arthur noted. "I hesitate to say this but be careful you're never alone with her. She's very hands on and easily misconstrues a situation."

"I appreciate the advice. Listen, thank you for sending us the name of your electrician. He saved the day for my sister and might help her open the Pick-Me-Up Diner on schedule," I said, shaking his hand. He'd done me a solid, and I owed him a favor in the future.

"That's what friends are for, Kellan. I know things got outta hand when I came back to Braxton years ago, but all that's under control now. I've got my life back in order again." Arthur's posture was more relaxed than the last time I'd seen him.

"How've things been around here the last week? I can't imagine it's been easy with the dress rehearsal's cancelation last Sunday."

"Myriam and I worked out some of our differences, but ultimately, the show must go on, right?" he said with a flourish and a bow. "The cops suspected I had something to do with Gwendolyn's death. Called me in for a *conference*, as that unctuous sheriff put it."

"Par for the course. I had to talk with them, too. Was it because of your past differences with Gwendolyn?" I asked.

Arthur nodded. "Someone told them I threatened to kill her last week. I don't remember saying it, and even if I did, I'm an actor. I say things I don't mean all the time," he quipped. Arthur could be putting on a performance for everyone's sake. I asked him to tell me more about his time working on Broadway, hoping to find any potential hole in his account of the past. I learned nothing of importance.

Arthur later explained he had little interaction other than once a week where Gwendolyn had met with all the staff at the Play House to discuss current and future projects. She'd also stopped in at rehearsals from time to time to provide direction to him and Myriam. It often resulted in tentative compromises or highly caustic arguments, but Gwendolyn always got what she wanted. He'd begun to learn that's how it was with the powerful woman. He'd been to the Paddington house once earlier that month when she invited the complete management team over for a brunch, but he knew the bare minimum about the estate. Arthur finished his coffee and returned to rehearsing the final act with the rest of the cast.

I'd made little progress other than conjecturing potential reasons for anyone to have been the killer. It was time to collect Emma from school, then transport her to the library for an after-school reading program. I dropped her off for the ninety-minute activity, then took advantage of the unallocated time to get in a run since I'd had no opportunity earlier that morning once Nana D demanded my presence. As I navigated the steep hills of the Wharton mountains, I continued to search for a solution to my problem with Francesca's reappearance.

Marriage was about living with both the good and the bad. Was I the kind of guy who could abandon my wife because I couldn't see myself hiding under cover for a few years? Instead of being grateful she hadn't died in the car accident, I was angry about being put into an impossible situation. It wasn't fair to keep Emma from seeing her mother, but if it put my daughter in any amount of danger, I reasoned out it was acceptable to stay far away from LA. I didn't see how I could rebuild the trust and love with Francesca if we lived nearly three-thousand miles apart. Others had made long-distance relationships work, but never with the added complication of death threats and mob interference.

Feeling satisfied with my decision not to return to LA, I knew I'd made Emma the priority in the whole sordid affair. Unfortunately, it would also make things much harder for me. Even if I forgot how much I loved Francesca, we'd always be married in the eyes of the law. There could never be another woman in my life as long as she was still out there somewhere. It was an impossible decision to force someone to make. I finished the last mile of the trail and pulled up outside of the library. Emma rushed from the lobby entrance when she saw me.

After hugging me, Emma said, "You smell like the dirty laundry basket, Daddy. I think you need to shower for a very long time tonight."

I took a quick sniff, then made a fake gagging sound for effect. "Oh, I'm worse than a wet dog who rolled around in the mud." Then I realized it was the wrong thing to say, as Emma would never let me forget it.

"When are we getting a puppy, Daddy? I think since you're making me sit in this car when you're so stinky, you owe me big time!" Emma buckled her belt in the back seat and grinned so widely I feared she'd split in half.

I tugged on the seatbelt to be sure it was properly connected, then waved my dirty towel in her direction. "You think I stink? Wait until you have to clean up after the puppy, baby girl!" As I started the engine and looked in the rearview mirror, I caught Emma rolling her eyes in exactly the same way I did.

"Nah! That's your job. I'm there to entertain the puppy. You have to keep it clean!"

If she were a little older, I might have said *touché*, but she needed a few more years before I could let her mimic my sarcasm.

CHAPTER 13

I woke up the following morning and continued my cozy time with Emma by shopping. Fighting traffic to get to the mall on a Saturday morning was never an issue in Wharton County. Emma and I parked the car—she insisted on choosing the exact spot and helping navigate from the back seat—and skipped all the way to the north entrance. We played a few games of *Frogger* and *Pac-Man*, both of which Emma said had very poor graphics—evidence of the downside to a child being brought up on iPads and other digital technology. She giggled as the ghosts captured me in a few corners and told me I must be getting old if I couldn't run away from a ghost floating as slow as molasses. Since children hardly know enough to sugarcoat anything related to an adult's age, I tousled her hair and told her she was precious.

"Maybe Nana D can teach you how to play better. She beat me at *Candy Crush* this week!" Emma cooed as we left the arcade and headed to pick out a new puzzle for the upcoming week. When I noticed the floor tiles were randomly covered with pastel-colored stickers for spring, I challenged her to only walk on ones with blue or pink, and I took orange and green. She was so excited I almost felt bad when she got stuck too far away from the toy store entrance with no tiles to step on. I waved to her from inside the store. "I guess I must choose the puzzle by myself, huh?" I teased.

Emma squinted at me, then gave me an evil eye that made her look so much like Nana D, I caught myself choking. I'd been so shocked I also hadn't heard someone call my name from further inside the store. Once I told Emma she'd won the game, she bee-lined it for the entrance. I caught her midair as she jumped in my arms. As I turned around, Jennifer Paddington walked toward me. After introductions, Emma asked if she could check out the puzzles in the back of the store. I let her go, knowing I could see her in the reflection of the giant mirror on the side wall.

"She looks like such a happy girl. Be proud," Jennifer noted while tossing two baby blankets over her left shoulder and kneeling on the ground near the shelf. "I didn't realize you had children. How long have you been back home?"

"Just Emma. We only moved back to Braxton a few weeks ago," I replied, remembering what Eustacia had told me about Jennifer's previous miscarriages. What'd brought her to the toy store?

"Children are a blessing. We've not had any babies in the family for a long time." A cloudy gaze descended upon Jennifer's spirit as she spoke. I couldn't imagine desperately longing for a child only to lose the pregnancy.

"Shopping for a gift?" I hoped to keep her from growing too distant or sad.

"Oh, sort of. I stop in the store every so often. I... I don't have any children of my own, but I'm anticipating someday soon," Jennifer said in a faint almost-whisper. She folded up one of the blankets and placed it back on the shelf next to the entrance.

"I hope it works out for you. My sister mentioned seeing you at a doctor's office the other day," I said praying it wasn't perceived as an invasion of privacy. If Jennifer had mentioned wanting to have a baby, it felt acceptable to bring up what Eleanor had seen at the gynecologist.

"Hmmm... I didn't see her. When was this?"

"A couple of days ago, I don't remember exactly. I think she was there for a check-up." After verifying Emma was still combing through the puzzles, I turned back to Jennifer. "I could be wrong."

"Well, I have been to the physician a lot, but the only one in the last few weeks was the in-vitro fertilization clinic. It wasn't my regular doctor," she explained. "It's not impossible to conceive on my own, but I need all the help I can get when fifty is much closer than forty these days." She tried to make light of the situation, but I could tell it was painful for her to discuss.

I nodded, feeling uncomfortable about asking too many personal questions. "That must be tough. Maybe something unexpected will work out for you."

"It's not looking too positive. All the procedures are expensive. I've got to put them on hold until I can find more money," Jennifer said as her eyes swelled and reddened.

"I don't mean to pry, but couldn't your family help with the financial aspect? The Paddingtons seem to have more than enough to go around." I felt my heartstrings twinge for the woman. I was curious how much her family knew about her current predicament.

"No, it's not like that in our family. My mother wasn't supportive of me trying to have a child on my own. I'm not very close with Timothy or Ophelia either. We just sort of tolerate one another the last few years." Jennifer folded the other blanket and shoved it on the lower shelf.

"Again, I'm sorry to hear that." Could Jennifer have been desperate enough to push her mother into an early grave, knowing she'd inherit enough money to pay for the procedures? "Maybe things will be different now. Have you spoken to your Aunt Eustacia about your mother's estate?"

"No," she said tersely. "Aunt Eustacia said we needed to hold the funeral service tomorrow, then we'd meet with the lawyers next week. Something about it taking time to verify the final version of the will." Jennifer retrieved her cell phone from her purse, then noted she needed to get going.

Eustacia was savvy in keeping the family on hold while Finnigan tried to track down the supposedly new will Gwendolyn might have finalized the night before she was killed. "Have you spoken to anyone about the specific cause of your mother's death?"

Jennifer pulled away. "She was old and had a heart condition. I assumed it was the heart attack that finally did her in. Why do you ask?"

Hmmm... I didn't want to be the one to tell her the truth. She looked genuinely surprised at my question, but I couldn't be sure if she was a talented actress. "Just curious. Sometimes it helps the grieving process to know what happened to a loved one," I said, remembering some questions I wanted to ask but never did when Francesca died. Or supposedly died.

Jennifer thanked me for the suggestion, and I wished her success in finding the money to schedule another in-vitro fertilization procedure. As she left, an enormous lump appeared in my throat. If Jennifer wasn't at her regular doctor when she saw Eleanor, it meant Eleanor had also been visiting the in-vitro fertilization clinic. Was she trying to have a baby on her own? I knew how important it was for my sister to have children, but she hadn't ever said she'd look to alternative methods. Could I ask her? Or was it just an initial conversation to understand her options? I'd have to think about the best way to approach the topic, ensuring I didn't alienate or upset Eleanor.

Emma returned to the front of the store with two puzzle options. I went with the *Frozen* theme, knowing she was obsessed with Disney as much as she was with getting a puppy. We paid for our purchase and took off for Grey Sports Field to attend Braxton's baseball game. After a quick tour of the campus, we bought hotdogs and French fries at the concession stand, then skipped to the center condiment stand to stock up on napkins and catsup. As we finished loading our trays, Emma waved at Nana D who stood a few feet from the restroom entrance talking to Marcus.

"Nana D looks a little busy, honey. Let's give her a minute to finish her discussion." Emma shoved a few fries into her mouth while I innocently listened to their conversation.

Nana D said, "No, I'm not ready to have our next debate on Tuesday. We agreed to all these dates in advance. You're not moving it up, Stanton!"

"Come on, Seraphina. I'm only asking to change it by three days. When we agreed, I had forgotten about my family's vacation beginning next week. I can't cancel it so close to the trip," Marcus replied. "Besides, I've already got the staff setting up the hall for us to discuss the campaign issues."

"What? We *also* agreed to hold the next debate at Wellington Park. Can't you keep any promises you make? That explains why the homeless shelter lost its funding this year," Nana D argued.

"That's baloney! They lost the money because the state reduced its contribution. I had nothing to do with it," Marcus challenged in a louder voice.

A few people stopped and listened to them fight. Nana D threw one hand to her hip and poked Marcus in his chest with the other. "You're a liar and a thief. We're having the debate on Friday as we previously agreed, and if you try to change it, I'll tell everyone what a fraud you are." Nana D continued to poke him extra times. She was a smart woman. By focusing on his attempt to change something they'd agreed to, it made him look far worse. At least fifteen people had crowded around.

I grabbed Emma's hand and walked in their direction, hoping to temper their argument. "Hello, Councilman, Nana D. It's gonna be an exciting game today. Why don't we go take our seats and watch the pitchers warm up?"

"Yeah, Nana D. I need to tell you all about how bad Daddy lost at *Packer-Man*," Emma teased while leading her great-grandmother toward the stands. Nana D winked at me as she walked away, deeply engaged in conversation with Emma.

I turned to Marcus. "Diffusing that situation seemed ideal."

"Hmmm, probably a good plan. That grandmother of yours is one ornery gal. She's determined to hold me accountable for every little thing we discuss. Sometimes changes are necessary," he said, trying to rationalize his behavior and pretending I wouldn't automatically support the family before him.

"You two have been at each other's throat for years. What started it all?" I asked, curious about the past. Nana D would never reveal what'd happened between them, which made me even more determined to discover their secrets.

"Nothing I'm going to discuss!" Marcus tightened both fists and shook them with gusto. "You would do well to mind your business when it comes to the past, Kellan."

"Well, if that's how you feel, I'll give it some consideration," I consented, knowing it wouldn't be the only way I could find out the truth. "I see Striker is pitching in today's game." Striker was his stepson, and he'd effectively raised the kid for most of his life when Striker's mother passed away.

Marcus had stopped paying attention to me and instead focused on a pair of twenty-something girls walking by us. I'd only caught them from behind, but I saw more of one girl's legs than I had of the strippers at my bachelor party. Although I'd tried to stop my colleagues from throwing me a posh shindig at a LA-based gentlemen's club, I'd eventually caved and behaved myself. This girl sashaying by the town councilman clearly thought dental floss was appropriate attire at a baseball game. Okay, it was more than dental floss, but Emma would never be allowed to dress like that!

"Excuse me, Kellan. I need to discuss something with Miss Taft," he said, waving me off.

I realized it was Lilly and her sister, Dana, who'd trotted by. Dana wore the risqué outfit while Lilly was much more conservative and pretentious in dress. "Wait, councilman. Lilly Taft? What do you have to discuss with her?"

"What business is that of yours?" Marcus cocked his head in my direction and held a sour expression with one raised eye.

"None, really. I've been getting to know the family. Now that I live in Braxton, it's important for me to connect with my roots, that's all." I hoped it was enough not to raise any suspicion, but I was curious about anything that had to do with the Paddingtons these days.

"Lilly graduated with my youngest daughter. I know her family well. She's been looking for investors for some new business she wants to open."

Interesting. What could she be trying to do? "Are you lending her money?"

"It seems I no longer have to," Marcus replied, stepping away from me.

"How did she get the money?" I asked, despite having no reason to interject myself into their business transaction. If she didn't need the money anymore, why was he trying to track her down?

"I don't have a clue. I told her I'd think about it the last time we discussed the opportunity, but then Lilly told my daughter this week she no longer needed my help." Marcus began walking away, then stopped and turned toward me. "Perhaps your time would be better spent if you'd focus on controlling that flaky grandmother of yours rather than obsessing over the daily activities of the Stantons and the Paddingtons. We're a little out of your family's league, Kellan," Marcus quipped as he rushed off in pursuit of Lilly.

I couldn't follow them without being noticed, nor did I have any idea where they were going. I ignored his derogatory remarks about my social status and pondered the information I'd learned. Lilly had either found an investor or thought she'd be coming into money. I needed to bring it up to Eustacia. Hopefully, she had knowledge of Lilly's entrepreneurial undertakings.

The announcer asked everyone to stand for the national anthem being sung by the college's choir. After its dazzling finish, I made my way to our seats and watched the game with Nana D and Emma. At the end of the game, Emma was so excited the Braxton Bears had won, she begged to go home with Nana D for a sleepover. When Nana D agreed, I accepted knowing it meant I could get a majority of the work done for my classes on Monday since Spring Break would be over. As Emma left with Nana D, I walked to the parking lot and turned down the row where I'd left the SUV. I noticed Sam Taft waving at someone who'd pulled out of the parking spot next to him.

"Hey, Sam. Showing some school spirit today?" I said.

"Kellan, oh... hi... did you just see... ummm... never mind. Yeah, I volunteer at the hospital." Sam looked alarmed and confused. He again refused to look directly at me.

"For what?" I imagined him conversing with various senior citizens.

"What do you mean?" he said, tossing his hands into his pockets and swallowing noisily.

"You said you volunteer. I was asking what you volunteered for," I explained. People had always felt relaxed around me. I'd never been known to worry about someone so much in the past. Sam was easily frightened, or he had something to hide from me.

"Right. I bring sick children from the Wharton County General Hospital to some of Braxton's sporting events. Helps get them out for a few hours, so they might forget how ill they are," he said, perking up a little.

"That's such a thoughtful thing to do," I replied. "It's good to see how generous you are with your time." Sam didn't behave like the rest of the Paddingtons or Tafts. There was a genuine down-to-earth quality about him. "I saw your sister, Lilly, a little earlier. She was meeting with Councilman Stanton."

Sam bit his lip. "Oh, really? Yeah, she's friends with his daughter." He started walking toward the driver's side door.

"The councilman mentioned something about investing in a business opportunity with your sister. Do you know anything about that?" I asked, hoping he'd share whatever he knew.

"Oh, that... yeah, she's trying to start up a digital advertising agency. Lilly's all about social media and marketing partnerships. I think it's going well, but we don't talk that much." When Sam pulled his hand from his pocket to open the door, something fell to the ground.

I walked closer to him and bent down to pick it up at the same time as him. "I'll get it."

"No, leave it." Sam reached first, then shoved it back in his pocket before I could figure out what it was.

"Ummm, is everything okay, Sam? You seem rattled." I noticed his face fluster and redden.

"Yes, I gotta go."

As Sam pulled away, I shook my head. He was private and closed-off from everyone, including me. I barely knew him, but it was easy to see even in the three or four times we'd crossed paths. Whether it was lack of confidence from being surrounded by the vultures in his family, or a potentially dangerous secret he was hiding based on Dana's theory, the kid was close to exploding soon. I needed to find out whom he trusted, hoping that person might clue me in as to what made Sam tick. As I drove home, I called Eustacia to see what she might know.

"I've no clue how Lilly could've produced the money to open her business. I only know she was trying to find investors because Brad mentioned it," Eustacia said after I told her what I'd discussed with Marcus.

"I wasn't aware Lilly and Brad knew each other well," I countered. Lilly lived at the Paddington estate, but she didn't seem to be the type of girl who'd hang around with the help. "What can you tell me about that relationship?"

"Beats me. I don't know what the kids are doing these days. Why don't you ask them? I saw them talking a few times in the hall this week whenever she made it home," Eustacia noted with disdain. "That girl comes and goes more than my hot flashes. Well, when I had hot flashes. Now I have lukewarm ones followed by these dang constant shakes. It's like my battery is dying or something."

If we couldn't track down any revised copies of Gwendolyn's will, then Eustacia and Finnigan would have to proceed with the one he had on file. Maybe Lilly thought she was getting the money from her mother, who would inherit a lot of cash upon Gwendolyn's death. I ignored Eustacia's random musings about her body temperature since I didn't want to have mind-damaging nightmares that evening. "How about Sam? Do you know much about him? He always seems flustered whenever I run into him," I asked Eustacia. "Even just now, he dropped something and acted odd when I tried to pick it up."

"Could it have been his web pen?" Eustacia asked. I could hear in the background Bertha advising that dinner was being served. "The kid can't eat anything without blowing up."

Web pen. Blowing up. What was she talking about? "Huh, is Sam sick?" I asked, remembering back to the first time I'd seen him holding something in his pocket. Did she mean an epi pen? Whatever he had that day would've been the same size and shape. Could he be carrying around medicine in case his body went into anaphylactic shock?

"I guess you could say that. He's allergic to a lot of things, so he's gotta carry that doohickey around to stab himself if he can't breathe or he passes out," Eustacia noted before telling me she had to hang up. "Sam's always been a nervous child. He's the gentlest and most respectful kid I've ever met, but he's secretive. He's vague whenever you ask him direct questions. I'm not sure what it's about, but it's probably because he was always afraid of getting sick."

CHAPTER 14

Several minutes after returning from a run the next morning, I found a note from my parents indicating they'd gone to Sunday mass and planned to meet some friends for brunch. I'd just peeled out of my sweaty gym clothes and turned the shower on when the house phone rang. I looked at the caller id, noticing my brother, Hampton, was calling. Other than a few summers and major holidays, we'd spent little time together as adults. He'd grown more conservative and closed-minded once he connected with his wife's oil tycoon father and focused on building his own empire.

"Howdy! How's my favorite hampster doing?" I teased, answering the phone. When we were young kids, my brother had brought home his class pet, Houdini, to care for it over a long holiday weekend, but the hamster went missing. While feeling sad and embarrassed at losing the school pet, my brother collected his laundry to give to the cleaning lady before we left for school. As she bent down to lift the basket, the furry creature popped his head out of the laundry pile, scaring the poor woman into quitting. Knowing Hampton was going to collect the laundry, I neglected to tell him I'd found his school pet and instead, I placed Houdini underneath the top layer of clothes a few minutes before the cleaning lady picked up the pile. To this day, Hampton still didn't know what I'd done. If I told him, I wouldn't be able to use his hated nickname, The Hampster, anymore.

"I see you're still as childish as ever, Kellan. I guess I couldn't expect you to grow up knowing you're still sponging off Mom and Dad by living at home," Hampton scoffed on the phone.

"I'm here temporarily while I decide what to do. I haven't sold my house in LA and am considering renting it for a year. I think that's a fairly astute thing to do, ya know?" I tried to appeal to his cheap side by highlighting an opportunity to be fiscally responsible.

"Let's have this conversation again in a few months to see if anything's changed," he replied. Hampton constantly told everyone about his 401Ks, pensions, IRAs, bonuses, summer home on the Maryland shore, and anything else that clearly demonstrated how well-off he was. "How's that teacher's salary working out for you?"

"I'm sure you'd be pleased to know I negotiated a nice package for myself. I'm really working two jobs by helping develop the program to expand Braxton," I noted, feeling proud of myself for simply stating the facts rather than going after him for his less-than-kind attitude.

"No doubt because of something Dad pulled to make that happen, I'm sure. Is he around?"

I wasn't sure why I even tried to impress my brother. It was a losing battle, no matter what path I took. "No, they're at brunch with friends. May I ask you a legal question?" I leaned against the bathroom wall, watching the steam build up around me, perhaps inside of me as well.

"I suppose I can give you one free consultation. Are you about to be arrested for something? I'm not as familiar with criminal law as I am corporate and business law." Hampton sighed, then laughed when he finished speaking.

"Estates and inheritances are what I need to know more about. I'm helping one of Nana D's friends who passed away recently. Do you remember Gwendolyn Paddington?"

"You're helping her? The Paddingtons are well off. I'm sure they have plenty of attorneys to handle it, Kellan. Why are you inserting yourself into a situation where you have zero qualifications? Mom could handle it better than you would. Or Nana D."

"Quit being so sarcastic. I haven't said a single thing to you on this call to deserve your ruthless jibes. Talk about never growing up, big brother."

"Fine. What do you need to know?" he asked. I couldn't be sure if he genuinely wanted to help or preferred to hang up as quickly as possible.

I explained the situation about the missing will and noted I was still uncertain if it even existed.

He replied, "It's completely legal if Finnigan drew up the will and a few names were handwritten in the proper places. Assuming it's been signed by two parties who aren't named as beneficiaries, and it's dated after the previously written will, the new one would be upheld in any court in Pennsylvania."

I made a throaty noise that indicated I agreed. "I'm concerned someone's holding on to it until the funeral is finished, then he or she will claim they mysteriously found it."

"Have you asked around? Maybe one of the staff members at the Paddington estate served as a witness. It's likely no one in the family acted as a witness, assuming Gwendolyn left her money to the family. Witnesses should be disinterested parties."

The Hampster made a solid point. The staff might not have thought it was their business to disclose anything, or they believed the will was being handled already with the lawyers. "Speaking of family, Eleanor and I were talking the other day. Neither of us have heard from Gabriel. Have you?"

"Nope. As far as I'm concerned, he abandoned this family when he took off years ago. If Gabriel doesn't want to stay in contact with us, then I've no desire to waste any time thinking about him."

Ah, the brother I knew had returned after letting down his guard for just a few minutes. "I heard you had some news recently. Are you ready to share it with me?" Eleanor was convinced his wife was pregnant again. I thought it was something bigger.

"That's why I was calling Dad. I suppose I can tell you, but please let me be the one to tell him when he returns my call. You will let him know that I called, right, Kellan?"

"Of course. What's going on?" I asked, hoping it was something positive. As much as I enjoyed teasing him, I wished only the best for my brother. We may not have much in common anymore, but with Gabriel gone and Penelope living in New York, we were losing siblings left and right.

"Natasha's expecting a fourth child this summer. We've also decided to move back home to Pennsylvania. Her father has located a new well up near the Betscha mines he thinks might be lucrative. He wants me to help him run the operations side of the business this time. I think he's considering leaving his companies to Natasha and me rather than his son, who doesn't seem interested. Or competent. It'd be almost as bad as if he'd given them to you."

After I hung up with Hampton, I finished showering and dressing for my third visit to a funeral home in the last several weeks. Nana D called as I climbed into the SUV to let me know she'd dropped Emma off with Eleanor at the Pick-Me-Up Diner. Eleanor had agreed to watch Emma as she needed to stay at the diner while the electrician finished all the work in her kitchen. She planned to have Emma help her decide the final menu with Chef Manny. They'd kept many of the original dishes, but Eleanor wanted the new diner to reflect her personality and the history of the beloved eatery. Knowing Eleanor's love of astrology, I pictured new dishes with names like "Random Luck Fish" and "Crystal Ball Pancakes."

I arrived at the Wharton Whispering Pines funeral home ten minutes later. There were only two funeral homes in all of Wharton County, and for some reason, all three recent funerals had been held at this one. I entered the building and greeted the director, Lydia Nutberry, a third-generation mortician, who recognized me. "Room three down the hall, same as last time, Kellan," she said.

Although Gwendolyn was well-known in Braxton, the family kept the service private. A separate memorial would be held the following week at Paddington Enterprises for any staff or colleagues who'd known Gwendolyn, and there would be a similar one for her at Paddington's Play House at the end of the *King Lear* production for any of her fellow theater comrades. I'd emailed Myriam suggesting we have a special dedication to Gwendolyn at the opening performance and was pleasantly surprised when she supported the idea.

Since today's service at the funeral parlor was an invitation-only event, Eustacia and the rest of the family had made a specific list of who could attend. Exceptions were cleared only through Ophelia, who'd deemed it her right to limit the guest list. While it seemed peculiar at first, Nana D pointed out that people in Braxton often went to funerals just to hear idle gossip and consume free coffee and desserts. Given there were two separate services being held to allow friends and others to properly grieve, I kept my mouth shut. It might also be easier for me to observe the family's movements and reactions to one another once they were all finally in a room together.

After a quick discussion with Lindsey, Millard, Eustacia, and Nana D, I scanned the room to get a feel for who'd already arrived. Dana spoke with her mother in a corner near the back of the room. There was an older man with them, but I didn't recognize him. It might have been Richard Taft, Ophelia's husband and Dana's father. He had his arm around Dana in a parental way. Gray hair was closely cropped to the sides and top of his head, and he wore a pair of silver wire-framed glasses. He wasn't particularly tall and had a few extra pounds in his gut area. He nodded at Lilly when she started walking away from Jennifer and toward me.

"You're Kellan, right?" she said with her nose held high in the air. She wore a respectable yet on-trend, dark gray dress with her shoulders and arms covered by poofy sleeves. Lilly's shiny black hair was tightly pulled across her scalp in a French braid and fastened against the back of her head. She crossed her arms together and said, "I hear you've been around the manse lately, asking a lot of q's about me. What gives?"

Who'd said that? I suppose Marcus Stanton could've mentioned I inquired about her. I doubted very much Eustacia or Millard had said anything. Perhaps Sam or Dana, maybe even Jennifer, had brought up my name. I didn't think I'd talked to Brad about her, but all the conversations were blurring together given the number of adversarial and unclear relationships among the Paddingtons.

"Oh, really? I must have indicated I hadn't found a chance to speak with you after your grandmother passed away. Please accept my condolences on her loss," I said with a brief dip of my head in her direction.

"Yeah, thanks. So, I'm used to people talking about me. I'm usually at the center of things. You've found me now. What is it you want to know?" Lilly shifted her weight as if she'd been compelled to listen to me for some miniscule amount of time but wanted to be anywhere else.

"I don't think there's anything specific I wanted to know. Since I'm spending so much time with your family and representing them at the Play House, it seemed appropriate to learn a little more about everyone," I noted while watching the man who'd been standing with Ophelia and Dana kiss them both on the cheek, then take off toward the exit. "Would you know whom that gentleman is?" I said, pointing toward the gray-haired man I suspected was Richard Taft.

"Shouldn't you have figured that out already? I mean, if you're going to be our representative at the Play House, whatever that actually includes, you need to get with the program, Kellan. I can't see what Aunt Eustacia sees in you if you're this unaware of the family members." Lilly huffed loudly and walked toward the table to pour herself a cup of tea.

I followed her. "I assume it's your father, but I've only been acquainted with your family for the last few days. He hasn't been around as far as I can tell, has he, Lilly?" I tried to be as polite as possible, so I didn't isolate a potential lead, but the girl spewed venom like her mother and grandmother. Nastiness or uncivil attitudes definitely ran in the family.

"Yes, that's Daddy. He travels for work, but not much longer. If you haven't heard, he's going to be the new head of the family company." Lilly looked pleased with herself, obviously a daddy's girl. Could this be where she thought she'd find the money to launch her new business?

"Oh, Eustacia hadn't mentioned it to me, yet. I suppose that's a good thing for your family. I had been under the impression your Uncle Timothy was only on a temporary leave of absence from Paddington Enterprises."

"That drugged-out loser? Ugh, please. Yesterday's news." When Lilly poured milk into her tea, it spilled on the table. Before walking away, she said to me, "Get that, will you, love?"

I wiped the mess, laughing to myself about her lack of manners and impertinent countenance. When I caught up with her, she was peeping around before zeroing in on Brad as he entered the room.

"I understand you and Brad are friendly," I said, hoping to stir a reaction.

"I'm not sure that's any of your business. If you've nothing else to ask me, then I think we're done here," Lilly said, waving her hand at me. Before she stepped away, she turned and handed me her paper cup. "That goes in the trash, if you don't mind, love."

I accepted the cup but gently held onto her wrist for a moment. "Oh, certainly. I don't mind at all, but we're clearly not finished, *love*. Tell me more about this little project you're trying to find investors for." I'd previously dealt with many girls like her in LA. If you let them walk all over you, they always did. Sometimes you had to push back, even if it meant risking the relationship or your opportunity to find answers.

"It's not a *little* project. I have a brilliant team ready to execute solid marketing plans and unique approaches to better sell products and services. I'm the queen of social media, and this is going to be huge when it gets rolling," Lilly replied, flicking my hand off her wrist. "I'll thank you not to paw at me."

"My apologies, I only intended to continue our conversation, not to make you feel uncomfortable. I'm fascinated by the science behind advertising data and research. I take it you've found some investors?" I said with a fake smile.

"Not exactly, but I'll either be coming into some money soon, or my father has offered to have Paddington Enterprises fund the entire launch. My mother was unwilling to help until he stepped back into our lives. She's quite useless when it comes to any sort of business matters. I know enough not to end up like her. I'm surprised she hadn't tried to knock off Grandmother before now." Lilly blinked several times, then walked away displaying unwarranted pride in herself.

I stood in silence, reflecting on Lilly's ill-mannered behavior when I was interrupted. "What did my daughter want with you?" a shrill voice said behind me. I grimaced when I turned around as Ophelia stared at me with panicked eyes and pursed lips. "And don't give me the run-around, I know all about the questions you've been asking the rest of the family. My son, Sam, mentioned you'd been harassing him several times throughout the last week."

"First, I certainly wasn't harassing your son. We ran into one another while out on a run near the Wharton mountains, then again in the Grey Sports Field parking lot. He was tense and upset over losing his grandmother. I shared my own history losing a loved one hoping to comfort the kid."

"I suggest you leave my family alone. I'm not sure why Aunt Eustacia insisted you be given full access to the estate and the Play House, but that will all change soon when the will is read and I'm responsible for things going forward," Ophelia noted looking more and more like Cruella de Vil. "In the meantime, if you have questions about my family, you can direct them to me. Leave Sam, Dana, and Lilly alone. They're quite young and don't clearly understand what's going on here. They don't know someone might have tampered with my mother's medication, nor do they need to know anything about it. Am I clear?"

What was with the Paddington family? They'd all made me their whipping boy instead of learning how to have a civil conversation with a normal person. "My only intention is to help Eustacia understand what happened to Gwendolyn in the last few weeks. She was getting sicker, and no one did anything to remedy it, nor did they realize what was going on in the background. But the fact remains, someone switched her heart medication with placebos, then overdosed her with cocaine."

"All you're doing is restating the supposed facts. I've had enough of it from that invasive sheriff," Ophelia replied while fixing a stray hair that had come loose from her perfectly styled coiffure.

"Pardon my saying so, Ophelia, but few people in the family seem concerned about who might have tinkered with your mother's medication. Everyone's more interested in having the will read and moving on from the entire ordeal. What if it's your sister or one of your children? Or do you already know whom it is?" I assumed it would be controversial to suggest such a theory, but at that point, the only way to combat the derisive lashings I'd been receiving was to return fire. I didn't like being cruel, but I'd been backed into a corner.

"How dare you! No one in this family murdered my mother. I'm sure there was a mix-up with her medication. As for the drug overdose, I can't explain it. Call the pharmacist! As I told the sheriff, leave this family alone to grieve. If you insist there was something shady, perhaps you should focus on that interfering nurse and that repugnant theater director who's had it in for my mother for over a decade." Ophelia shook her finger in my face but kept her voice low, not wanting to create a disturbance.

"I'm looking at those angles. If you're so certain your family is innocent, why did Lilly say she thought you might have killed your mother? Your daughter doesn't seem focused on protecting you."

Ophelia pulled back, then guffawed at me. "Lilly is angry because I won't give her any money to open that confounded business she wants to start. There's room for her in any of the family's corporations, she doesn't need to look elsewhere." Ophelia promptly turned in the opposite direction, looking for anyone else she knew, and stomped away from me.

Well, that was fun. It was as if I'd been tag-teamed by a mother and daughter looking to take their anger and vengeance out on anyone nearby. Rather than try to engage with Dana, Jennifer, or Sam, I gave up and left the funeral parlor, after stopping by Gwendolyn's closed casket to say my goodbye. When I slipped into the car, my phone indicated I had a message. Please don't let this be another Paddington or Taft screeching at me.

Nana D: *Looked like you had fun. Learn anything?*
Me: *Not really. We need to find out if there is another will. If not, my money's on Jennifer or Ophelia being the killer. They stood to collect the most.*
Nana D: *You're in luck. I spoke with Bertha. She never saw the details, but she was one of the two people who signed it. It definitely exists.*
Me: *That's great news. Who was the other witness? And where is the will now?*
Nana D: *She could only answer one of those questions.*
Me: *Which one? Out with it, Nana D. I'm tired of being dragged around and kept at bay today.*
Nana D: *You're the most impatient imp I've ever known. Brad was the second witness. Bertha wasn't sure where the new will end up.*
Me: *Brad??? Where did Bertha last see it?*
Nana D: *In the mailbox. Gwendolyn sent it to herself. Clever girl.*
Me: *It's been a week. It should've arrived already.*
Nana D: *Unless someone found it and destroyed it, so they wouldn't lose out on the inheritance.*

CHAPTER 15

Classes resumed on Monday morning. After dropping Emma off at school, I drove to campus and held my first lecture for the day. While the students talked in groups, the pregnant maid who disappeared from the Paddington estate years earlier flashed front and center in my mind. If Brad were Hannah's child, had the discovery of his father been why Gwendolyn had died? I needed to convince Eustacia that we had to tell Millard what we'd learned, even if it caused him any heartache. While I didn't think he could've killed his own sister-in-law, it was time for the truth to come out about Hannah giving birth to his child.

Once my second course was finished, I followed the students out of the classroom to grab another cup of coffee. I'd woken up too late and needed extra caffeine to push through the rest of the day. While I stood in line, Connor and Sheriff Montague stepped into The Big Beanery. I paid for my coffee and snatched a corner table, then waved them over once they'd finished collecting their orders.

"Kellan, good to see you," Connor said while sitting across from me. "The sheriff and I only have a minute, but we didn't want to be rude."

"I appreciate it. I'm sure you two have a lot to discuss about Gwendolyn's death. I understand you've located Timothy finally," I offered up as a way to focus the conversation. "I wanted to speak with him myself, but as far as I understood, he was refusing visitors at the rehabilitation facility."

"Yes, he's trying to get clean and fight his gambling addiction. Although I commend him for fighting his demons, it's certainly a convenient time to hide out," Sheriff Montague growled while stirring milk into her cup. When I handed her the tray of sugar packets, she raised her palm at me. "Connor's shown me the light about staying away from that stuff."

In the four or five times I'd seen the two of them together, I'd picked up on a growing crush. I don't think Connor was fully aware how often she stared at him or tried to casually flirt. I'd mentioned it once, but Connor, who's built like a brick wall, bluntly told me to keep my mouth shut. Not one to risk any unintended consequences, I'd heeded his advice and observed from afar April's behavior around him. There were at least two furtive glances and a clandestine brush against his arm when she sat at the table with us.

"What makes you think Timothy's decision to quit drugs and gambling is convenient?" I said.

"While his mother has a heart attack and drops dead in the middle of a theater performance from a cocaine overdose, he suddenly sees the light and checks himself into rehab? You see nothing coincidental about that, Little Ayrwick?" She cracked her knuckles, causing me to flinch when each successive pop reached my eardrums.

"I didn't see him at the funeral. You haven't arrested him, have you?" I asked, mostly believing the sheriff wouldn't have kept a son from visiting his mother one last time before the burial.

"Timothy has not been arrested. We've questioned him, hoping to understand more about his drug choices. It appears cocaine was also his downfall," Sheriff Montague said with a tone so shallow I could practically see what she was thinking. She thought Timothy had killed his own mother.

"Timothy was free to leave the rehab facility but apparently chose not to show up at the funeral parlor," Connor added. He placed both hands together on the table in front of him and began tapping. "Seems he didn't need to say a final goodbye."

"Maybe he found religion and made his peace with her death. Not everyone enjoys a funeral service." Personally, I found them tedious and frustrating. Most people showed up because they felt compelled to say goodbye to a body. While I had no clue where the spirit or the soul went after you died, I was much more comfortable talking to somebody I'd lost from the comfort of my own home or a quiet bench in the park's sanctity. "Did he explain what they fought about at the theater during the intermission?" I still didn't know why Timothy had chosen not to attend yet showed up, anyway.

"If you're so curious, why don't you go to the Second Chance Reflections rehabilitation facility yourself to ask him?" the sheriff directed.

I was glad she did since I hadn't known which one he'd checked himself into. Cha-ching! "Just curious. There are many people who thought they'd benefit from Gwendolyn's death."

Sheriff Montague said, "Well, one of them went to a great length to swap just one dosage of pills with vast amounts of cocaine to kill her. There was no trace of any additional cocaine anywhere other than those pills Gwendolyn took at the theater. None of the rest we found in her house were contaminated either."

At least I had confirmation the tainted pills were specifically swapped for that afternoon's dosage. "I guess until someone finds the new missing will, we can't determine who might be the culprit. I don't particularly like or trust anyone in that family."

"Excuse me, did you say a new will?" the sheriff said while her eyes brightened, and a sour expression developed. "I'm not aware of anyone searching for a missing will."

"Yes, Gwendolyn signed a new one the night before she died. No one's been able to locate it, but as I understand, there were two witnesses who signed it. I'm sure they can vouch for its existence, as can Finnigan Masters, Gwendolyn's attorney." I smiled as I responded to the sheriff, feeling smug that I'd known something she hadn't. It wasn't mature of me, but I accepted little wins from time to time.

"Okay, Little Ayrwick... let's backtrack a bit. Please explain whatever it is you know. I can tell by the nauseating grin on your face you like having your ego stroked. Share your investigative prowess with the poor, unfortunate sheriff who seems to be one step behind you this time." She cupped her hands together in prayer mode and faked as though she were begging me to assist.

Was she really admitting that I'd been able to find out more than she had? "What's in it for me?" I stared directly into her eyes as I replied. "I mean, it sounds like you're looking to work together on solving this peculiar puzzle."

"In exchange for you telling me what you know, I will happily not cart your pathetic rump to the county jail for withholding evidence and disrespecting law enforcement." As she stood, one hand reached for her hip where a gun had been safely locked in its holster. Was she trying to intimidate me?

"I'm trying to partner with you, April, but you block me at every turn. I think you need to be more open-minded and flexible. At the risk of annoying you any further, what's the harm in a little quid pro quo if it helps find a criminal? It's not like I'm broadcasting what you say on the news. I haven't once done anything on this case to get in your way, have I?"

Connor's shock and trepidation clearly told me to back down. "Kellan, I'm sure the sheriff appreciates your help, but why is this so important to you?"

"Honestly, at first it was because Nana D asked me to figure out if someone was trying to hurt Gwendolyn, but less than twenty-four hours later, the woman was murdered. Every single time I talk to someone in the Paddington family, they berate me or treat me like I'm not worth the dirt they step on. I want to see whoever killed the woman go to prison."

"You're annoying me even more than usual, but obviously, once again, you have an ability to get close to all the key players in this murder investigation. I won't pretend that having you on the inside isn't a benefit, but we need to establish some ground rules. I'd rather not have to put you in prison while that crazy grandmother of yours is in the lead to become the next mayor."

"I can respect rules if they're fair and mutually beneficial," I added. There had to be a way I could stay clear of causing any additional friction with the sheriff, yet also still help Eustacia learn who killed her sister-in-law.

After explaining everything I knew, the sheriff asked me to give her twenty-four hours to process the updates. "Don't give any information away to anyone in that family right now!" she bellowed before walking out the door.

"You need to tread a little more lightly, Kellan," Connor noted after she left. "You've always been nosy, but you seem to be getting a lot more confident and pushier than I remember."

I hadn't thought of it that way. I saw myself as capable of getting answers, and my intellect and curiosity were intrigued by investigating real life crimes. I'd always wanted my own show focused on historical cases, but the adrenaline rush over something current or connected to people I knew was exciting me. "I don't mean to act cocky. I just think I have natural talents in this area. Why should I let them go to waste if I can find the right balance between observing the laws and discovering the truth?"

"Until you get killed because the murderer is smarter and more prepared than you. Have you thought about how Emma would feel losing both parents at such a young age?" Connor sniped.

I closed my eyes to prevent myself from saying something I knew I couldn't. Or shouldn't. When I felt relieved enough to respond, I said, "I know you're right. I promise to be more careful."

"If you're committed to staying in Braxton, I'd like to suggest maybe we could rebuild our friendship. Get back to college days," Connor replied, punching me in the arm. "I've been on my own for too long and miss having a best friend."

"I do, too." I pushed down the emotional ball of stress trying to project itself from my gut. As much as Eleanor was helping me understand what I should do about Francesca, talking to Connor about it was something I desperately wanted to do for days.

"Let's get back to having drinks and dinner more often. Maybe we could go for a few runs together?" Connor stood and slapped my shoulder twice. "You've got a little catching up to do, buddy."

I laughed, knowing I could use the motivation. "Speaking of dinner, Eleanor mentioned you guys were going out tomorrow to talk about whatever happened between you last Christmas."

"Yep. I'm not saying it's gonna work out between her and me, and I'm still interested in Maggie, but I promised you I'd talk to Eleanor. She's an amazing woman. Who wouldn't want to date her?"

Although I knew he was right, she was my sister, and I still hadn't asked her about why she was at the fertility clinic. After Connor and I made plans to go running that weekend and said our goodbyes, I taught my three-hour lecture and reviewed my upcoming lesson plans. The sun was setting and though I wanted to get in a workout, I needed to find out from Brad what he knew about signing Gwendolyn's will. When I pulled out my phone to find the number for the Paddington estate, I noticed several missed messages from Eleanor.

I had forgotten today was the final meeting with the inspector to see if she could open for dinner service. I quickly checked in with her and learned she'd passed with flying colors. Eleanor was thrilled to finally have everything fall into place. I told her I would stop by in a couple of hours with Emma for a late dinner. My grandmother had also left a text message for me.

Nana D: *Emma is here with me. We're baking dessert since you had a rough weekend.*
Me: *You're the best. I'll be by at seven, so we can go to the Pick-Me-Up Diner's opening.*
Nana D: *Did you speak with Brad?*
Me: *On my way now, that's why I'm running late.*
Nana D: *Then stop bothering me and go accomplish something for a change.*
Me: *Speaking of getting things done, do you have the plan ready for Friday's debate?*
Nana D: *Did anyone ever tell you that you're a smug little devil?*
Me: *Yep. A crotchety woman I rather like being around, even if I don't admit it often enough. It goes to her head too easily. And we've all had enough of that experience for a lifetime.*
Nana D: *Does that mean you'll be moving in with me? Your parents need their privacy. They need to be empty nesters, so they have some space to get their groove on. You're cramping their style. I imagine they haven't made whoopie since you returned.*
Me: *We're done. Thanks for giving me an image I'll never erase from memory. If you understood emojis, I'd share a picture of a frog throwing up. Since you don't, I'll settle for saying BARF!*
Nana D: *You're so immature. I didn't raise you to be so weak.*

I shook my head to detach any images the conversation had conjured up. When I called the Paddington estate, Bertha informed me that Brad had left for an interview at the hospital. I ran through a list of contacts who might know where his interview was being held, then settled on a former high school classmate who worked in the Human Resources department at the Wharton County General Hospital. Ten minutes later, including a promise to take Lydia Nutberry's daughter, Tiffany, for coffee the next week, I knew the time, location, and contact whom Brad would meet with. I'm sure her revealing the information violated some law, but it was likely nothing Sheriff Montague could arrest me for. I promised the sheriff I'd stand down for twenty-four hours. Having an itty-bitty conversation with my new friend, Brad, about my old friend's will couldn't possibly lead to trouble.

Unfortunately, I hit a bunch of traffic while driving downtown during rush hour. By the time I arrived, I had three minutes to catch Brad before his interview started. I left my SUV on the third floor of the parking garage and rode the elevator to the administrative wing. Wharton Country General Hospital had been built twenty years earlier in the center of the county, so it was easily accessible from all four towns. With generous donations from the Grey family, it served the needs for most illnesses and injuries, but any major surgeries or risky

311

procedures were transferred to Philadelphia. Located near the sheriff's office and court buildings, the hospital stretched two blocks wide and two blocks long.

I rushed out of the stairwell—the elevator was taking too long—hoping the interview would start late and jogged down the final hall to the place Brad was supposed to be. I stopped outside the frosted glass door to catch my breath. Despite running several times per week, I must not have been used to racing up and down stairs as I thought I was having my own heart attack. When I entered the room, my throat seized up for an entirely different reason. Brad wasn't in the room. The sheriff was.

"Little Ayrwick, are you here to interview for a role as a nurse? I'd pay top dollar to see you in a pair of scrubs," she said with an enormous grin. "Surely, you couldn't be here to track down a potential person of interest in one of my murder investigations."

I could have lied. I could have said I was there for any other reason. Except nothing came to mind. Instead, my mouth hung open and a drop of drool oozed out of the corner of my lips. I took a deep breath, then said, "I'm awful. I don't know how to listen. I was trying to make your job easier. I thought if I could find out what Brad knew about the will, it would be one less person you had to find time to deal with. Is there any chance of me getting out of here with my—"

"Outside, now!" she shouted. As I slithered through the door, Tiffany whispered 'sorry' at me. I shrugged, preparing to accept whatever punishment she threw in my direction.

"Can you just overlook this one time? You don't even know exactly what—"

"Shut. Your. Mouth. Before. I. Shut. It. For. You," Sheriff Montague said with a distinct pause between each word. Is that how it sounded when I taught Emma how to pronounce big words? I waited in silence until we got to the end of the hall and sat in a tiny waiting area. If she was going to arrest me, she would've done it in public. Not a room where we were alone.

"Brad Shope signed the will at the same time as Bertha Crawford. Neither one of them were shown the specifics of who inherited anything upon Gwendolyn Paddington's death. He was under the impression Gwendolyn planned to give the will to her lawyer the following week. He assured me he didn't kill her, not that I'm inclined to believe him yet."

"Why are you telling me this and not kicking my—"

"I asked you to be quiet, Little Ayrwick. Are we going to do this the easy way or the hard way?" the sheriff announced obnoxiously. When I didn't respond, she said, "I asked you a question."

Was I supposed to respond or shut up? How did this keep happening to me? I decided to type my response on my cell phone's notepad. I could acknowledge that I preferred the simple way, but I didn't actually need to speak the words. When I finished typing, I handed her my phone.

April read my message and broke out in an unexpected chuckle. "You are the most sarcastic and obstinate man I've ever met!"

I typed on my phone in response: 'Can I speak now?' When she nodded, I said, "Did you ask about his mother's obituary or if he knew his father's identity?"

"No, I didn't. Since our earlier chat, I decided it would be better for you to handle that angle. I'm not sure it has anything to do with Gwendolyn's death. Brad will be coming by to see me in two days. I didn't want to inhibit his chances of getting the job he was interviewing for."

"Okay, so you want me to talk to Millard to find out if they are father and son?"

"Yep, call me as soon as possible, so we can discuss it. And do not think I've forgotten you disobeyed direct orders. I hope you will see this chivalrous act of kindness as the teeniest of olive branches. We shall discuss this further once you find out something useful."

I watched the sheriff walk toward the elevator and step inside the car after the doors opened. As they closed, she stared through the diminishing crack, holding two fingers first to her eyes, then pointed at me mouthing what I was pretty sure were the words 'I'm watching you closely, Little Ayrwick.'

CHAPTER 16

"Are you sure it was really the sheriff? Maybe there was an invasion of body snatchers earlier today. I smelled something funky in the air this afternoon," Nana D said in an exaggerated alien-sounding voice, causing Emma to laugh like a hyena. "What do you think, kiddo, did some nasty, green-colored four-eyed creature from outer space tell your father to keep investigating?"

Emma giggled again and slapped her forehead. "Aliens don't visit the Earth during the winter, Nana D. It's waaayyy too cold for them. They need hot air to breathe. Didn't you watch *Avatar*?"

"Oh, honey, I don't know what an avatar is or what it does, but if you met that sheriff, you'd know she's full of enough hot air she could support an entire space alien planet," replied Nana D, bugging her eyes out so fiercely she fell forward on the table from putting so much pressure behind them.

"Nana D, you're gonna give yourself an aneurysm. Quit it while you're ahead of the game," I said. We'd just sat down in a cozy booth Eleanor had reserved for us in the front corner of the Pick-Me-Up Diner. The grand reopening had sent the entire town out in droves. We were lucky to hold on to it despite Mayor Bartleby Grosvalet showing up last minute without a reserva-tion. Eleanor found a space for him at the bar and comped him several martinis. The mayor liked to drink heavily.

"What's an anarysm, Daddy?" Emma placed her menu back on the table and announced she was ordering steak Diane.

"Aneurysm. It's kinda like when you consume too much ice cream and you get a headache only a lot worse," I explained, then suggested she might not enjoy eating a woman named Diane.

"No, silly. Diane is the name of the goddess of hunting. I'm not going to eat anybody. My name's not Hannibal." She stuck her tongue out at Nana D who promptly returned the gesture, only it contained some childish noises in her attempt to up the ante. How did my daughter even know whom either of those people were? *She's only six years old,* I repeated several times inside my head.

"I'm not sure who's more mature between the two of you," I scolded. Judging by the competition currently occurring at the table, I was the most mature, and that wasn't saying very much. "As for the sheriff, I wasn't gonna press my luck to find out what led to her generosity. I hightailed it out of there and called Millard. He's meeting us here in twenty minutes."

My phone rang before anyone could respond. It was my mother-in-law, and I wasn't letting her go to voicemail. "Be back shortly," I muttered to Nana D and Emma, who were still making outrageous faces at one another.

I passed Eleanor walking near the kitchen and pointed to the phone. "The she-devil's calling me, I'm hiding out in your office." After I shut the door, I clicked accept to stop the theme song from Jaws ringing on an endless loop. "Hi, Cecilia. I'm at my sister's diner having dinner with Emma. I only picked up because we need to talk about this ridiculous mess. Can I call you back in a little while?"

"Time is almost up. Have you come to your senses?" she bellowed with no other greeting.

"I left several messages for you over the weekend. I need to speak with my wife," I said through gritted teeth, realizing she would not cooperate. I unclenched my jaw when thinking about being forced to see the dentist if I'd broken one. It was on my top five list of places never to go again unless necessary to prevent death.

"The Castiglianos do not answer to you, Kellan. I've clarified that you cannot speak with her. I also remind you that while this may be a secure line, please stop using her name." Cecilia had always been headstrong, but for many years, she knew Francesca wouldn't tolerate her parents treating me poorly. It seemed she had the upper hand and felt no need to hold back.

"Why are you doing this to us? Do you have any remorse over what pain you've caused Emma? Forget what it's done to me, but you and your husband's dirty businesses have robbed a precious girl from growing up with two loving parents." Emma had bounced back from her mother's death, but there would still be a permanent impact on her future. I'd never forgive them for what they'd done to her.

"I'm not going to rehash another conversation where you tell us we're terrible parents or we should be in prison. You've made your point. You do not respect our business, the decision we made, or the need to ensure our future safety. It's rather selfish of you, but I always told her you weren't good enough to marry." Cecilia huffed loudly, causing me to pull the phone away from my ears. If I hadn't been in a public place, I would've lost my cool and shouted back at her.

"Do you have any solutions other than living in some secret wing of your mansion? How do you see this working out long term, Cecilia?"

"I don't have all the answers. But what I do have is enough history and knowledge of the potential dangers involved if you don't return to LA. My daughter will not give up. She's been angry ever since this whole situation blew up in our faces years ago."

"I can't live in seclusion. Can't you get the police involved? How many members of the Vargas family are we expecting to still be angry years later?" I knew little about mob policies and etiquette. Were we talking about waiting for one ancient godfather-type to kick the bucket? Or were there hordes of irate Vargas relatives looking to stick dead horse heads in every member of my family's beds?

"It's not like that anymore. We run everything like a business. There's a fine line to keep status quo among all the different territories. If anyone found out we tricked the Vargas family, everyone would draw lines, form alliances, and execute retaliatory tactics," Cecilia replied in a demeaning tone. "I'm doing the best I can to help you both, Kellan. I don't want to see anyone hurt."

Fat chance! She practically threatened me when she was in Braxton the last time. "I've got a few more days, but I can tell you one thing for certain. I refuse to decide without talking to my wife again. If you think there's any chance of me listening to you, then you better cut me some slack here," I hissed. One half of my body burned as if fire coursed through my veins while the other half froze with a chill that might never regain normal temperature again. I stared at the cell phone screen, watching the call length increase. I couldn't take another second and hung up on Cecilia. For added effect, I also turned the whole device off, not wanting to talk to the woman anymore that evening.

I stomped back to the table at the same time Millard arrived. After introducing him to Emma, I asked her to find her Aunt Eleanor to help prepare our dinners. I didn't want Emma to overhear any part of the conversation with Millard.

"So, Kellan, what was so urgent that you had to meet with me tonight?" Millard asked while scratching at his moustache. Emma had found it so funny; she'd called him Yosemite Sam after one of her favorite cartoons.

"Mr. Paddington, I need to talk to you about something in your past. I don't know you all that well, so this might be a little tough. Are you the kinda guy who likes to slowly peel away a Band-Aid to avoid pain? Or are you a rip it off, scream once, and get it over with kinda guy?" Personally, I was a rip it off and scream *several* times kinda guy. I wasn't giving him that option and judging by the number of scratches on his forearm from pruning holly trees earlier that day, he would not scream, anyway.

Nana D's head cocked to the side. "Stop being a fusspot, Kellan. Just ask him if he knew Hannah Shope had his baby twenty-five years ago. He's a big boy, I think he can take it." Not usually known for her tact, Nana D threw both hands into the air between her and Millard, waiting for his response.

Millard stiffened against the booth's back padding. "I would have said rip the Band-Aid off, Kellan. Seraphina knows me well enough." He paused and dug deep into thought. While I waited for his response, I studied the distant look in his gaze, knowing he was remembering happier days of his past.

"Take your time, I'm sure this isn't easy," I added.

"If she had a baby twenty-five years ago, it sounds to me like you're saying she was pregnant when she left Braxton. More specifically, when she quit working at the Paddington estate," Millard said. His left hand shook with a few tremors before he rested it against the stable one on the table's surface.

"That's what I understand if I've done the math properly. I gather from your expression this is not something you were aware of. I'm sorry to be the one to tell you about your long-lost child. But I think I know his identity. As do you," I said slowly, hoping not to agitate Millard more than necessary.

"You've always wanted to be a father, Millard. I suppose this might give you an opportunity to make up for the past. He may be a fully grown adult, but there's still time to connect with him," Nana D responded as she cupped his hands with hers. Despite a relationship not working out between them in the past, her affection for a friend was evident.

A confused look settled on Millard's face. "You think I was the father of Hannah's child?"

Nana D and I looked at one another. "Of course. Weren't you the reason she was fired? I know your parents weren't tolerant of anyone getting involved with the staff."

"Oh, Seraphina, you might know my family well, but clearly you must think I'm just as bad as them." Millard shifted toward the end of the bench. "I couldn't have been that child's father."

I thought I'd heard him incorrectly. "I don't understand why not."

"Hannah and I were never intimate. We were friends. I needed someone to talk to about wanting to quit the family business and take up gardening. She helped keep me sane in that loony bin," Millard said with a chuckle. "I need a bit of fresh air if you don't mind. I think I'll take a rain check on dinner. Please extend my apologies to your daughter and your sister, Kellan."

As he rifled through his wallet and dropped cash on the table, Nana D spoke. I was too confused at what he'd just told us. "Millard, what do you mean? If you weren't the child's father, who was?" Nana D whispered. It was rare she kept her mouth quiet, but she seemed not to want anyone to overhear the question.

"In return for supporting me, I also lent my ears to Hannah those few months she worked at the mansion. She'd found herself attracted to someone in the house and had apparently developed sincere feelings for him. It wasn't exactly someone she should've been involved with either, but it certainly wasn't me. I merely counseled her to let it go if she wanted to keep her job and not incur the wrath of someone in my family." As he started walking away from the table, he turned back and looked at Nana D. "I can't believe you think I would have seduced a young girl. I could have been her father, Seraphina. We had a vastly different kind of relationship than what you've implied today."

I called out before he got too far away. "Mr. Paddington, is there anything you can tell us about who could've been the child's father? We're afraid it's the reason Gwendolyn was murdered."

"I can't. Hannah never told me whom she'd fallen for. I didn't want to know either. I needed to get away from my family. They also thought I was fooling around with that poor girl, which is why they let her go. I never had a chance to say goodbye. That same day I quit the family business, and she was fired, my father informed me I was cut out of the will for making the choices I did. I guess he thought it was a fair and just punishment."

As Millard left the diner, Nana D turned to me. "I can't believe you made such a huge mistake, Kellan. We need to make it up to that man."

Me? She should've told me he wasn't the type to do something like that. "I don't understand. If it wasn't him, was Millard saying it could've been his father, Timothy, or Charles?"

"Millard was over fifty at that point. I can't imagine it was his father. Old man Paddington was close to eighty! And not the kinda spry eighty I'll be one day. He was knocking on death's door."

We both shivered thinking about an eighty-year-old and an eighteen-year-old being intimate. "Do you think Charles could've cheated on Gwendolyn with a maid?"

"I don't know. But if Brad is actually a Paddington..." Nana D noted.

"It would have angered Timothy, Ophelia, and Jennifer who thought they were supposed to get all the money," I said feeling confident Brad's parentage had something to do with the reason Gwendolyn died. "Something still makes little sense. Brad couldn't have been left anything by Gwendolyn if he also signed the will as a witness. The Hampster had confirmed what Finnigan told us. Pennsylvania law might leave a bit of wiggle room for the beneficiary to also be a witness, but Finnigan clarified he told Gwendolyn to be sure she didn't do it."

Nana D reminded me that not everyone knows the specifics of those laws. Once Emma returned, we finished our meal, choosing to leave the murder investigation out of our discussions. Eleanor and Maggie stopped by to ensure our meals were good but couldn't stay to chat. They had hundreds of other guests to check with on their opening night.

As we finished saying our goodbyes and leaving a generous tip—our meal had been free since we knew the owners—Myriam arrived at the diner. I checked my watch and was surprised to learn it read nine thirty. I needed to get Emma home to bed. Hoping to sneak past Myriam without her noticing me, I pushed Emma and Nana D out first, so I could stand on the other side of them. After they exited, I attempted to leave too, but Myriam's penetrating gaze zeroed in on me.

"Kellan, I thought I'd stop by to sample the cuisine at the new Pick-Me-Up Diner. The *King Lear* performance ended a little while ago, and I was hungry," she said, lifting a single finger to let the waitress know she needed a table for one. The harried server asked Myriam to wait several minutes for a table to be cleared.

"I appreciate you throwing a little business my sister's way, thank you," I said walking through the doorway. I smiled, knowing she had to summon an ability to be patient before she could sit at a table, too. She hated to be kept waiting for any reason.

"You should know I didn't come by because she's your sister. I thought it was important to support my colleague, Maggie Roarke. I believe she's a co-owner here, correct? I didn't choose this place because of your family. I'd have thought you knew that already," Myriam grunted.

"Of course. I should have guessed. Please accept my humble apologies, but I need to catch up with my daughter." I was keenly aware Myriam severely disliked my family. But given the ultimatum Ursula had given us regarding working together, I thought she would have attempted to play better in the sandbox.

"Ursula has been detained by Braxton's Board of Trustees this evening, so I'm grabbing dinner alone. I'd like to schedule time with you in the next few days to discuss your role as the Paddington family member's voice at the Play House." Her nose wrinkled in irritation, clearly revealing how she felt about the entire situation.

"Certainly, perhaps tomorrow? I need to discuss your decision to terminate Arthur. If I understand correctly, you gave him two weeks' notice. Perhaps we could find a way to reconsider." I remembered that I'd promised Fern I'd try to help save her son's job.

"I'm usually open to discussion on many topics. That is not one of them. Engaging in lewd behavior in a dressing room on public property is assuredly not acceptable in my book. Arthur is lucky I didn't fire him on the spot with no additional pay." Myriam grabbed a menu from the wall cubby and lifted her glasses onto the bridge of her nose to begin reading.

What was she talking about? Arthur said he'd been avoiding Dana's overt flirtations the last few weeks. "Are you sure it was Arthur? Or for that matter... was it definitely two people engaging in—"

"You don't need to articulate any further descriptions. It most definitely was Arthur because I saw him leaving the dressing room twenty minutes later," Myriam replied, pursing her lips.

"May I ask when this was?"

"A month ago. Why is that important? Isn't the fact it happened enough to agree with me? I expected you to support me on this decision, but I can see your morals are nearly as impious as his."

"Honestly, I can't discuss this right now. I'll be happy to talk further tomor-row. If he and Dana were behaving inappropriately, then I can understand the decision to fire him," I said, reaching back for a mint from the countertop. I suddenly had a sour taste in my mouth.

"I positively didn't say it was Dana. I'm not sure who was inside the room with him, but I insisted it be fumigated by the janitor that evening. As for Dana, she's a smart girl. I doubt she'd get involved with that joker. She was the only person who could locate the fake medication we needed for this summer's next production." As Myriam finished speaking, the waitress told her the table was ready.

"Hold up. What did you say about fake medication?" My heart nearly stopped when she said the word *fake*. "Tell me exactly what that means."

Myriam explained that she'd been searching for various sorts of pills and medication bottles for a future hospital scene. Since Dana handled props, she'd been assigned the task. Within twenty-four hours, she had options for Myriam to choose from. Dana had stumbled upon the placebos on a website used by theaters and television shows to locate hard-to-find props. As Myriam left, she turned and said, "So *farewell to the little good you bear me. Farewell! A long farewell, to all my greatness!*"

If I remembered properly, that was from Henry VIII. Cardinal Wolsey, an ambitious and arrogant man, had delivered the lines. "Myriam, are you proud of the similarity you just exhibited to a man who supported one of the most abominable kings in English history?"

Myriam stopped short in her path and without turning around to face me directly, replied, "You always go for the obvious, Kellan, don't you? Perhaps you need to convince the tiny, little, miniscule, uneducated gray cells in your brain to look past the words being said and find the true meaning."

As she continued walking away, Eleanor appeared. "She's got a point, big brother. Sometimes you have tunnel vision."

"Why are you supporting her?" I asked, feeling my frustration levels increase.

Eleanor shrugged. "She's a paying guest. You're not. I know where my bread's buttered."

I closed my eyes, humming loudly to distract myself from exploding at the next person who said anything rude, mean, or negative to me. When I opened them, Emma stood in front of me. "Are you coming, Daddy? Nana D complained you always take too long. She sent me back inside and told me to tell you something."

"What's that, baby girl?" I braced for a litany of Nana D's ridiculous comments.

"She said, '*Tell your father he owes Mr. Paddington an apology. And as punishment for making unsuptions, there won't be any dessert again for two weeks.*' What did you do now, Daddy? How come you always get yourself into trouble when I leave the room?" Emma led me outside and to the parking lot, so I could drive home and forget the whole evening. "I'm tired, and I have school tomorrow. You really shouldn't keep me out so late next time, Daddy."

"Oh, and it's *assumptions*, baby." After buckling Emma in the back seat, I shut the door and opened my own. A large, menacing man stood nearby, looking in my direction. "You Kellan Ayrwick."

I nodded.

"I've got a message for you." He reached into his pocket.

I gulped and backed up against Emma's door. "From whom?"

"She says you should never hang up on her again. Nor should you turn off your cell phone. The line should be kept open for whenever the boss wants to speak with you."

My mother-in-law had tracked me down at the diner. Within an hour. She had contacts nearby who were willing to do her dirty work. "I'll take that under advisement." I felt my legs weaken but was confident Cecilia would do nothing to hurt Emma. Like killing me in front of my daughter.

"I know the boss pretty well, Mr. Ayrwick. She only warns someone once. I believe you've exhausted that count a few times. I suggest you do more than *take it under advisement.*" Although he disappeared into the darkness, I could hear his heavy shoes pounding the pavement and a bubble bursting in his mouth from the gum he'd taken out of his pocket.

CHAPTER 17

"I barely slept last night, Nana D. It's a good thing I don't have to teach any classes today. Maybe I'll swing by Danby Landing after tracking down Timothy. I need to know what he and his mother talked about just before she died." Nightmares about my mother-in-law's henchman had haunted me every hour while I'd laid in bed trying to forget our encounter in the parking lot. My restless body twitched every time a tree branch scratched the roof, or the wind whistled through the eaves. Sleeping in the attic bedroom had both its benefits and its downsides. Last night was definitely a downside.

"Good boy, that's the priority for today. I'll ask Eustacia to come by for tea at three o'clock. It'll do her some good to get out of that mansion. It's sucking her dry worse than an evening listening to your father talk about himself. And that old bat needs to quiz me for the debate on Friday." Nana D was familiarizing herself with what type of jobs people held in Wharton County and what policies had changed over the last decade under Mayor Grosvalet and Councilman Stanton.

After agreeing to meet them for tea, I dropped off Emma at school and drove to campus to experience my weekly harassment with Myriam. I was able to convince her to let Arthur remain working until the end of the King Lear run, then we'd reevaluate his position at the end of the semester. She ended the meeting quickly, citing the need to complete some research. Her more hospitable attitude pleasantly surprised me, but it only reminded me she was likely sugaring me up to execute a sneak attack as all hairy spiders did.

With my work activities on track, it meant I had time for a run. There were a few hidden trails scattered throughout the western section of Wellington Park, which also happened to be close to the Second Chance Reflections rehabilitation facility where Timothy was recuperating. I'd never been there before, but a few people I'd gone to college with had sought their help after turning to drugs and alcohol. It had been built in the 1970s after an excessive amount of addictions cropped up in Wharton County. We'd been a dry county for most of our existence, then granted licenses to a few establishments shortly after World War II ended. Unfortunately, as the years passed, the county government lost control of the situation and citizens turned to dangerous substances as distractions once the fiscal crisis hit.

Timothy had voluntarily checked himself in, but it was still up to him whether he accepted visitors. I stopped at the front desk in the reception area before beginning my run. "I'd like to request a brief visit with Timothy Paddington. He's not expecting me, but his family asked that I talk to him for a few minutes today," I said to an older gentleman named Buddy who'd dressed in a comfortable-looking cardigan, beige t-shirt, and brown corduroys.

"Has he put you on the approved list of visitors?" Buddy had a gentleness about him that made me think I stood a chance of getting inside.

"Probably not, but it's important. His mother passed away recently, and his family is worried Timothy's taking her death very hard. His aunt and uncle aren't doing well themselves. They're in their seventies and having some health problems." I appealed to Buddy's humanity and the need to protect the patients. Perhaps it would win him over.

"Timothy's a good lad, but he's struggling. I knew the boy back in high school. I was the school doctor and checked him out a few times. Now I'm here trying to make ends meet. Not easy. This town is all messed up when it comes to protecting its senior citizens." Buddy veered off into an entirely different topic.

I needed to get him focused before I lost my chance to get inside. "I wasn't aware you knew Timothy. He's had a rough life from what I understand."

"He played on the football team. Quarterback in his senior year," Buddy said with a nostalgic gleam in his eye. He told me more about Timothy's days back at Braxton High School, explained how tough it was to grow up in the Paddington family, and offered his sincere hopes that Timothy could wrestle with his current demons. Buddy agreed to check if Timothy would grant me a few minutes, even though it was against the facility's rules for random guests who weren't on the list to be admitted.

"I'm grateful, Buddy. I know his family would be, too." As he walked away, I remembered seeing him in my first year of high school. I didn't play any sports, but I also thought he had retired that year. He'd probably completed his years of service to the high school, collected his pension, and found a new part-time career to earn some additional income. Like most other places across the country, teachers and school administrators weren't paid properly and had tough times surviving after retiring from their positions.

While Buddy disappeared behind a locked entrance to the principal part of the facility, I perused a pamphlet about Second Chance Reflections. I found some information noting how they were funded both from government assistance and private contributions. I also stumbled upon a few metrics I thought might be helpful for Nana D to use in her campaign plans that would benefit her and the patients at Second Chance Reflections. I slipped the pamphlet into my back pocket as Buddy returned to the reception area.

"You're in luck. Timothy needs your help. Follow me, and I'll get you set up in one of our visitation rooms. The South Room has the best view of the gardens. They're not maintained well, but at least you're not staring at the back of the bus station or the parking lot." Buddy verified my identification, entered me into the system, and navigated us through a narrow hallway. Although the facility was clean and organized, the décor hadn't changed since the 1980s. I suspected the funding they received from the government didn't cover the look-and-feel, given it wasn't a sizeable amount of money to begin with. I was certain Nana D could convince the garden club to donate a few hours of time each week to spruce up what looked like it was once a grand landscape.

When I arrived at the South Room, Buddy opened the door for me and returned to the reception area. Timothy greeted me while standing near two wooden chairs and a small lime-green Formica-covered table with a few chips in the surface. The room was no more than forty square feet and looked remarkably similar to the county prison's visitor rooms, minus the bars and glass partition. Its walls were a dimly painted white and littered with scratch marks. Several water marks stained the ceiling. I wouldn't exactly call it a dump but give it another year or two with no tender loving care, and that's where it would end up.

Timothy looked about the same as when I'd briefly noticed him at Paddington's Play House on the day Gwendolyn was murdered. His face was pale and withdrawn, he was at least a month overdue for a haircut, and his clothes were a size larger than his body required. He'd apparently lost weight, likely from his drug addiction, and couldn't afford a high-end rehabilitation clinic since he'd also suffered with a gambling and debt problem. I'd seen a picture of him as president of Paddington Enterprises a few years ago when Lara Bouvier had done a special report for the local news network. It was like a whole different man occupied the room with me. Unfortunately, not in a good way.

"Kellan, I was surprised to hear you came to visit me," Timothy said, shaking my hand and directing me to take a seat. "I know your parents, but I haven't seen you since you were a toddler."

"I appreciate you agreeing to meet with me. I told Buddy that your family asked me to visit, which is true, but not the whole reason." I folded my hands on the table and smiled at him. This would not be an easy conversation.

"Buddy's been taking care of me. I didn't want the royal treatment. I screwed up in the last year, and part of my recovery includes living like a regular guy. I can't expect people to go out of their way because I'm a Paddington." Timothy's legs must have been shaking underneath the table because I could feel the heavy piece of furniture vibrating. "Before sharing why you came, how's my family?"

I wasn't sure which members he cared about, so I told him about the funeral and my interactions with Millard and Eustacia. "I know they both are worried about you."

"Aunt Eustacia is one in a million. She's a tough cookie, but that woman has been there for me more times than I care to remember," Timothy noted, clutching the end of the table with both hands hard enough to turn his knuckles a blotchy mix of white and red.

I wasn't sure if I should jump in with my questions or let him talk for a few minutes. He was nervous, and his eyes darted around the room a lot. Was he going cold turkey or gradually decreasing the amount of drug usage to wean him off everything? "Do you want to tell me about how you ended up here? I'm not family, but I can listen if there's anything you need to get off your chest." I didn't know him all that well, yet he clearly was suffering from everything swirling around him.

"That'd be great. You're a good guy. Few people would visit me here. I chose Second Chance Reflections for two reasons. One, I'm broke, and they were the cheapest place available. Two, no one in my family would show up. It's not like I never want to see them again, but... well, I realize part of the reason I'm so messed up is because of my family."

Timothy explained that he'd been placed under a microscope ever since he was a child. His parents expected him to be a perfect child, perfect business-man, and a perfect family man. He'd spent so much time focused on meeting Charles and Gwendolyn's expectations that he'd forgotten his own needs until he couldn't handle the pressure anymore. It sounded a lot like Millard's story, and that's when I realized how lucky I had it in my own family. Despite feeling pressure from time to time, I'd never felt as if I'd been scrutinized so closely I needed some sort of medication or drugs to escape. I might've run all the way across the country to disappear from them, but that was different. At least that's what I told myself to get by each day.

"The year my father retired, I was on top of the world. But it soon went downhill. Every minute became consumed by the family business. I worked sixteen-hour days and traveled all over the world, never knowing what time zone I was in. I had no one by my side to have a better work-life balance. I began sneaking out for thrills just to feel something shocking and different." Timothy stood, walked to the window, and stared into the desolate garden. "It started out as making wagers on silly things. Even when I lost, I still felt alive. That's when I fell in with the wrong crowd and started using too many drugs that I eventually lost track of night and day. My father convinced the Board of Directors to put me on temporary leave, insisting I couldn't come back to work until I finished therapy."

"Is that what led you to finally check into Second Chance Reflections last week?" I asked, knowing it wasn't the full picture since it'd had been almost a year between the two events.

"No, I escaped for a while. Spent all my money," he said, turning back to look at me. I could see him visibly shaking. "Ever since I stopped the drugs last week, my body is always freezing cold. Raw."

"You're doing the right thing, Timothy. You've got to get sober and find a better path in life. There's a lot of time left in your future to make things right again," I added, thinking he might have a son to get to know.

"Exactly. I promised my mother the day she died that I'd fix things." Timothy wrestled with his conscience while rocking in his seat. I could feel the pain and fear emanating off him.

Although I wanted to help him, my purpose for the visit was to determine if he could be Brad's father or whether he might've killed his mother. "What did you talk about at the theater?"

Timothy clenched his fist. "It was the night before when everything changed. I only stopped by the theater to say goodbye. I had already contacted Second Chance Reflections to check myself in."

Timothy explained what had happened the weekend before Gwendolyn passed away. He'd gone to Philadelphia and gotten outrageously wrecked. When he was walking back to his hotel after drinking in a bar, he stepped off the curb and was nearly hit by a car. Someone tried to help him, but he pushed the Good Samaritan away and berated her for no reason other than he was plastered. He woke up the next morning, sleeping half on the sidewalk and half in the street covered in mud, littered with garbage, and lying next to a drugged-out teenager. His wallet and shoes were missing, and he had a large open wound on his forearm. "I'd hit rock bottom. I went home that Saturday to tend to my injury, sober up, and apologize to my mother. I told her I was planning to get help."

"What time was this?" I asked, trying to organize the chronology of events.

"Late. She'd just gotten home from a friend's place. It might have been your grandmother's. I was still out of it, but I remember most of the conversation. I cried in my mother's arms for the first time since I was a kid. I didn't even cry at my father's funeral. I was high on cocaine and pot the day he was buried." Timothy shielded his face with his hands to hide the shame of the past. He explained how grateful he was to have that last chance to make things right between them before she died.

I realized by the way he spoke, Timothy was under the impression his mother had a heart attack and died from natural causes. I didn't want to be the one to tell him she was murdered. I would confirm with Sheriff Montague to be sure she'd never told him about the results of the autopsy. Timothy had seen no one else, and the sheriff smartly kept the news out of the papers until she could find the killer.

"What did your mother think about you getting treatment?" I wanted him to focus on something positive, but I also needed to know how they'd left things.

"She was supportive. We had such a friendly conversation that night. Mother even told me she would put me in her will again once I proved I could get back on the right track. I didn't care about the money, I wanted to fix things with her. She's my mother, and I screwed up too many times."

I nodded at Timothy. He knew he wasn't in the old will, which meant he had no financial reason to kill her. "I'm sure that night meant a lot to her. Do you... I'm sorry to have to ask you this, but do you know if she ever got around to putting you in a new will?"

Timothy shook his head. "I don't know. I left her house shortly afterward and went home to pack my stuff, so I could come here the next day. We didn't speak again until the following afternoon."

"She was at the Play House watching the show with me," I explained.

"Right. I'd gone to the estate to say goodbye but had missed her."

"Did you see anyone else at the house?" I needed to know if he'd admit to seeing Brad in the kitchen. If he lied, I thought that could mean he'd been up to something bad like swapping the pills.

"I came in the front door and went directly to my mother's room. I knocked, but she didn't answer. I thought I heard her moving around in there, but I didn't want to just walk in. She was a private woman. So, I went downstairs to see if Brad or Mrs. Crawford were around."

"Were they?" I asked, feeling as if I might be about to learn vital information.

"Mrs. Crawford was in the kitchen talking to the cook about meals for the upcoming week. Brad came in a few minutes later to say he had to go up to the Play House to bring my mother's medicine."

"Could Brad have been whom you heard in her room?" I asked, wondering if Timothy had still been drugged out of his mind that morning. When he shook his head, I asked, "When did you leave for the theater?"

Timothy rubbed his temples. "I offered to drop off the pills for my mother, but Brad said he was in a rush. About an hour later, I guess. Is there a reason for all these questions? Did Brad do something wrong?"

"No, sorry. I didn't mean to alarm you. I was trying to understand the timing."

Timothy nodded. "I was supposed to check in here at four o'clock. I went to the Play House to catch my mother during the intermission to thank her and to say goodbye. I originally wasn't going to see visitors for a month once I arrived at Second Chance Reflections. I needed to focus on my recovery and to think about my future. But something else happened, and now you showed up today."

"You looked upset while you were talking to your mother at the theater. What happened?" I asked, trying to understand the full picture. I'd ask what he meant about *something else happening* next.

"She didn't want me to leave until after the show. She wanted to go with me, but I insisted I had to do this on my own. We argued about it, but I told her I'd see her soon. That's when she touched my arm, and I felt the pain from my wound. I pushed her wrist away and told her she had to trust me."

"And then you came here?" If he and his mother hadn't been on bad terms, there was little chance he'd killed her. It would make no sense, and he didn't appear to be lying to me. There was genuine pain and heartache in his demeanor, and if he was truly coming off years of drugs, his body and mind weren't strong enough to create some elaborate ruse for me to believe.

Timothy noted he was getting tired and needed to be alone. "Before you go, there was a reason I agreed to see you. I need your help based on what happened."

"Sure, what can I do?" I also wanted to find out if he'd ever been romantically involved with Hannah, but I'd let him ask his favor first.

"Can you give this to Aunt Eustacia? I'm not allowed to send or receive mail from here while I'm going through this early recovery stage. It's a thank-you letter. She recently paid my gambling debt for me, so I can start fresh when I finish the program." He handed me a small envelope from his pocket.

"Of course. She loves you and wants to see you get better," I said, feeling nothing but respect for the cantankerous woman who loved to berate me. She might be difficult at times, but Eustacia was truly an admirable woman. "Before I leave, one more question. Do you recall a young maid that worked at your family's mansion about twenty-five years ago?"

Timothy smiled. "Sure, Hannah. She was only around for less than a year. Why do you ask?"

"I ran into a family member of hers, and he was looking to learn more about Hannah. She died a year ago." I didn't want to say too much. It'd be better to let Timothy tell me what he knew.

"She was the newest maid right after I started working at Paddington Enterprises. The former one had retired, and my parents accepted the first girl who applied. I still lived at home with them and my grandparents at the time. I didn't know her all that well, to be honest. I probably couldn't help whoever was asking about her."

"I thought maybe you and Hannah were closer... ummm... since you were about the same age at the time, you know..." I hesitated to say anything that might upset Timothy, but I needed to know if he could be Brad's father.

"You thought Hannah and I were together?" Timothy laughed for the first time since I'd arrived at Second Chance Reflections. It softened him and showed me he had a possibility for a better future. "No, definitely not. I was too caught up in being the perfect kid. If Father or Grandfather thought I was messing around with one of the family servants, they'd have punished me for years. I guess that ended up happening anyway, huh?"

If Brad's father wasn't Millard or Timothy, that left Charles or someone else I didn't know about. "I appreciate it. I'll let Hannah's family know. Do you remember whom she might have been close with?"

"Not off the top of my head. If I think of anyone, I'll let you know," Timothy said before shaking my hand and leaving the room.

Although I'd learned a vast amount of information by meeting with him, it only eliminated suspects from my list. I left the rehabilitation facility and went for an hour-long run. After I finished showering and changing, it was lunchtime. I grabbed some food at Braxton's cafeteria and stopped at my office in Diamond Hall to meet with a few students who had questions on an upcoming paper. In between their visits, Maggie and I caught up.

Me: *How's the library today?*

Maggie: *Good. I'm putting the finishing touches on the invitations for the masquerade ball.*

Me: *For the new building? When is the ball?*

Maggie: *In May, right after graduation. It'll be the first of a series of events to raise money.*

Me: *Great! Reservations Friday at eight at the new French restaurant on the Finnulia waterfront.*

Maggie: *I'm looking forward to it. We have lots to talk about. Got a meeting. See you soon.*

I rested my head on the desk to nap. Luckily, Emma would be at a play date after school, so I could rest my eyes for a few minutes before going to Nana D's for tea. I had only a few more days to let Francesca know if I was going to come back to Los Angeles. Could I tell Maggie what was going on? Would she be able to help me with no personal feelings getting in the way? With no answers to any of my questions, I forced myself to drive to Danby Landing. I needed the distraction, and Nana D would provide the best way to make me feel better —dessert!

CHAPTER 18

When I arrived, Eustacia and Nana D were setting the table for tea. Nana D had baked a chocolate cheesecake with peanut butter frosting. It looked and smelled so delicious, I could barely stop myself from picking crumbs off the top and sides. Nana D smacked my hand a few times. "Leave it. Wait until the tea is done steeping. Let's talk about Gwennie."

"Yeah, what have you learned, Kellan? You're not as good of an investigator as your grandmother made you out to be. Why don't I have answers yet?" Eustacia chided me.

After telling them all about my visit with Timothy, Eustacia gave me points for making some progress and confirmed she'd paid his debt. "I can't see my brother, Charles, cheating on Gwennie, but I guess anything's possible," Eustacia said while slicing into the cheesecake.

"I want to talk about your great nephews and nieces. I haven't been able to get a solid reading on them. As far as we know, they could've been included in the new will. Let's pretend for a minute Gwendolyn left one or more of them the Paddington family fortune."

"Good idea. What might the little rascal's motives be?" Nana D added while pouring tea into three cups.

"Dana told me Sam was fighting with Gwendolyn about something in the days before she was killed. Anyone know why?" I asked.

"Sam's always been a good boy. Gwennie thought he'd look after her if she ever got too sick. I'm not sure what they could've been fighting about," Eustacia explained, struggling to drink her tea without spilling a few drops on the table. The lack of answers was wearing her down.

"Whom is Sam closest to? Someone needs to ask him, but I don't see it being me. The kid runs away whenever I try to talk to him," I noted while handing Eustacia a napkin.

"I'll do it," Nana D said. "I'm good at talking to young guys. They seem to confide in me."

Nana D had a good point. I spilled my secrets to her in the past. Failing to tell her about Francesca being alive was the only thing I'd ever kept from her, and it was nearly killing me. "Tread lightly. He might be dangerous, we still don't know enough."

"Gwennie used to complain about Lilly all the time. She got herself into trouble years ago when a friend of hers died in a skiing accident. It was right before her grandfather passed away, but he thought Lilly was capable of pushing her friend down that mountain. Gwennie always thought Charles' grasp on reality was fading near the end. She believed Lilly was difficult, but not pathological. I'm inclined to agree with her on this one."

"I've seen Lilly be nasty, and she was quite rude to me at the funeral. From what I understand, Lilly believes she's found the money to get her new business started." I scooped up my first piece of cheesecake. "This is amazing, Nana D."

"Of course, it is. Nothing I do is ever short of perfect. Now, about Lilly... I saw her and Brad talking several times in the past few weeks. She seems to like him, but I don't know what they've been talking about," Nana D said. "It didn't look romantic, but I couldn't say for certain."

"Lilly and her mother never got along. She blamed her for Richard's frequent disappearances. She's been much better now that Ophelia and her father are back together."

"Could Richard have loaned her the money? Someone told me he's going to be the new president at Paddington Enterprises," I asked, contemplating how to locate him.

"With Timothy out of the picture in rehab, Richard's the only one left in the family who knows enough about the business. The Board approved him as the new president for a one-year term. He might invest in Lilly's business. And if that's the case, then she had no reason to kill her grandmother to get the money," Eustacia said, slamming her fist on the table. "Then there's Dana."

"Yes, she's a handful, too. I've heard a few people talk about the way she chases after guys. There was an incident in the library once, and I suspect that Dana was involved with Arthur in the..." I stopped when I realized my audience. I was telling two seventy-something year old women about the risqué actions of a young girl they knew.

"Well?" Nana D shouted. "Don't leave us hanging. What did she do?"

"Kellan, my grandniece is a bit of a trollop. I'm aware of her behavior. If you have something to say, out with it," Eustacia commented before handing me her cup to pour more tea.

"I'm sorry. I wasn't sure how to say it. She's been excessively flirtatious, but my understanding is Arthur initially rejected her advances. Something doesn't add up," I explained, thinking about how Dana was also the one who'd found and ordered the placebos.

"Arthur was outraged with Gwennie. Maybe Dana convinced Gwennie to leave the fortune to her, and she helped Arthur get revenge."

"Did she realistically have access to swap the pills with cocaine the morning Gwennie died?" Nana D asked, tapping her fingers on the table.

"Dana was with us at the theater, not at a brunch at the mansion. She lives on campus, right?" I said. "Could she have come home to the estate on Sunday morning to steal her grandmother's medicine, swap it with cocaine, and return to the theater with no one knowing?"

"Probably not, but that's where Arthur could've helped," Eustacia said.

"I'll ask Myriam. I'm certain Arthur couldn't have left Paddington's Play House before or during the dress rehearsal. He was running the place and had way too much to do," I explained.

"I'll ask Bertha if Dana was around at all over the weekend. You find out from Myriam," Nana D instructed. She began cleaning up the plates while we were talking. "You know what you have to do, Kellan."

Me? What was she talking about? "Ummm, what did you have in mind?"

In unison, Eustacia and Nana D shouted, "The sheriff, Kellan. Go see the sheriff."

Although April Montague had softened the last time we'd chatted, I didn't think she'd share any important news about the case with me. I did need to update her on my discussion with Millard about his non-intimate relationship with Hannah. Was that going to help any? "Fine, I'll take one for the team again. But I'm not gonna like it."

"That's life, Kellan. At least until you reach our age," Eustacia scoffed.

"And then you can make everyone else do the actual work!" Nana D added with a high-five in Eustacia's direction.

After Nana D's, I picked Emma up from her play date. On the ride home, we told each other about our days. I left out the part about the murder investigation, although part of me wondered if she might have an interesting take on the possible culprit. Children often weeded out the extraneous information and pointed out the one thing you'd missed all along. Should I try?

I was considering it when my father's name appeared on my cell phone as we pulled onto their street. "Hey, Dad. What's going on?"

"You have a visitor. I thought you might want to return home as soon as you could," he said in the same way he used to nudge me to come home for dinner more often to see my mother while I was in college. I pulled up in front of the house.

Given the motorcycle parked in the Royal Chic-Shack's driveway and my dumb luck, it was probably the sheriff. For a really long moment where even Emma had to remind me I was still on the phone, I considered passing the house as if I'd never been there. That's when I heard the knock on the passenger's side window and hung up the phone.

"Daddy, some lady cop is here to see you. And she looks angry. Or like she swallowed a bunch of nasty lima beans. Ewwww!!!" Emma squealed in a high-pitched voice.

"Just don't look into her eyes, baby girl. She's not a real cop. She's a mean demon, and you don't want to get on her nasty side, okay? Pretend you don't see her and back slowly into the house. She'll ignore you." I muttered while smiling at the sheriff through the closed window. Before getting out of my own seat, I reached around to unlock Emma's seatbelt and told her to rush inside to see Grandpa. After shutting the door, Emma decided not to follow my instructions and instead marched toward the sheriff. "Can I see your badge? My dad said you're a fake cop, but I don't believe him. You look like a real one. Just a mean one. Did you eat something bad just now? Cause your face looks like it. Are you trying to hide your monster fangs? I'm confused, but I'll sort this out."

April looked from Emma to me. I guessed what was on her mind by the subsequent twitches in the corners of her lips. She was awful at hiding her feelings. "Kids. They say the strangest things, huh?" I offered, shrugging and pointing toward the house. "Inside Emma."

"But Dad, if she's truly a monster, I'll wave a magic spell on her and send her far away. And she didn't answer my question. That's rude!" Emma threw her hands to her hips and stared at the sheriff. "My friend Shalini at school says boys pick on you when they want you to be their girlfriend. Are you mean to my daddy because you want to be his girlfriend?"

April's eyes opened so wide she looked like she'd stuck her finger in an electric socket. "Is she for real, Little Ayrwick? Did you rent a smaller version of yourself for the day?"

I had no choice but to introduce Emma to April. "She's six and sometimes doesn't know when to keep her mouth closed. I'm not really sure what my daughter's saying half the time."

"I can see the resemblance," April said to me, then turned to Emma. "It's a pleasure to meet you, Emma. I'm not a monster, but I am a real cop. I might've looked a little angry because your daddy was supposed to call me earlier to tell me something important. He was also not supposed to talk to anyone else about it. For some reason, he seems to have forgotten what we discussed recently. I'm a stickler for rules, and I expect others to follow them."

"I like rules, too. Daddy's forgetful sometimes. I think it's because he does too much. I guess you wouldn't want to be his girlfriend. He'd probably forget your birthday. Although, he's never forgot mine. I wonder if he needs a girlfriend to help keep him in line. That's what Nana D told me the other day," Emma announced walking toward the house to see my father.

"I think you've got your hands full with that one, Kellan," the sheriff advised.

"Kellan? I think that's the only time you've called me by my first name." I made a mental note to read my nana the riot act for saying something about getting a girlfriend in front of Emma.

"Yeah, well... based on what you're dealing with between your nana and your daughter, I might take it easy on you from time to time. I certainly don't want to be the one to cause your complete and utter breakdown," the sheriff said while pulling out her notepad. "As for the revealing comments you shared about me in front of your daughter, at least I know where we stand. And to think I was going to be a little more forthcoming with you in the future."

"Perhaps there might have been a wee bit of exaggeration. Can you honestly tell me you haven't said something equally controversial about me? Surely, Connor's been a good sounding board in the past. I've seen the way you look—" I said with enough sarcasm to prove my point but was stopped mid-sentence.

"Let's move on. Neither one of us wants to have that discussion. So, what did you find out from Timothy? I feel the need to remind you that you were only supposed to discuss Hannah with Millard. I'm not at all sure how you thought you had approval to hunt down Timothy. I was only joking when I told you where he was and that you could check for yourself." Sheriff Montague ambled toward the garage to avoid the chilled wind whipping by us.

We agreed to disagree on my approach, then I updated her on everything Timothy had told me at Second Chance Reflections. "He doesn't know his mother was murdered, I take it?"

"Nope. I was trying to keep that as quiet as possible, but Eustacia told several members of the family. She's a piece of work, ain't she?" Sheriff made a note on her pad, then continued after I nodded in agreement at her remarks. "We were able to confirm that the cocaine given to Gwendolyn was nowhere else in the house, nor in any of her other medication. We did find some in Timothy's apartment, but I'm uncertain we'll be able to prove that's the source where it came from. Dr. Betscha isn't an expert in recreational drugs, but he's doing his best."

"As for Brad's father, I'm at a loss. Could we attempt a DNA test?" I said.

"I couldn't get a warrant for it at this point. We can't prove Brad's done anything wrong," the sheriff explained. "However, I did learn something interesting when I was poking around Brad's background."

My curiosity piqued. "Can you share it?"

"If you promise to follow all of my instructions going forward, yes, I can," she said narrowing her eyes. "This is against my better judgment, but if you step out of line, apparently all I need to do is talk with your daughter to put you back on the straight and narrow."

"Scout's honor," I replied with one hand showing the proper gesture, and the other behind my back crossing my fingers. She also didn't need to know I was never a scout.

"Brad Shope doesn't have a nursing license. He's completed most of the coursework, but he never received his formal certification. Apparently, he failed one of the exams, and then he was released from a prior position after there was a mix-up with several patients' medications." When the sheriff's phone rang, she stepped away to take the call.

It was unexpected news. What was he hiding? Maybe Eustacia could talk to Dr. Betscha about a DNA test. Whether Brad was guilty of killing Gwendolyn or not, if he was a legitimate member of the family, everyone would have to know. Or should know. They probably didn't want to know.

"It seems there are several large withdrawals the Paddington's accountants knew nothing about. I'm on my way to find out more," Sheriff Montague said upon returning. "Don't speak with Brad about any of this. I will let you know when I have any additional information about his background."

"Can I suggest a DNA test to Eustacia?" I asked.

"Yes, but that's all. By the way, your daughter is adorable. I can see you're a great father. Maybe I will reconsider letting you call me April instead of Sheriff Montague," she said before jumping on her motorcycle and tearing off down the driveway.

I stepped inside with a smile. Maybe Emma did know exactly the right things to say! We spent the rest of the evening together with my parents eating dinner, baking cookies, and watching an episode of Emma's favorite television show. Normally she wasn't allowed to watch it during the week, but she deserved a reward. Then we read a bedtime story and discussed getting a puppy. She was winning.

* * *

On Wednesday after teaching classes, Fern had a working lunch to prepare our first major presentation on the structure of the new communications department at Braxton University. Once finished, she asked, "Have you talked to Myriam yet about letting Arthur stay on?" Fern looked like she needed to hear good news. Her head hung a little low and her eyes looked weary.

"Temporarily through the end of the show. I'm going to check again with her this afternoon. She asked for a few days to consider my input. I'll let you know what I find out." I unwrapped the plastic from the double fudge brownie I'd bought in the cafeteria and offered half to Fern.

"I needed it, thanks," she said, accepting the dessert. "Arthur's gotten himself into some sort of trouble again. He called last night to tell me things had gotten complicated, but he wouldn't say why. I'm hoping it's not something with the Play House or the show. He needs to stay focused on his career."

"You're a wonderful mother, Fern. Arthur's a little too dramatic sometimes. Maybe he's exaggerating about how complex things are." I'd already seen his outbursts occasionally since I'd been back home. I was also certain his news had something to do with Dana. There was more going on there than I could put my finger on. "Is he dating anyone?"

"Not that I'm aware of. He was seeing someone in New York before he came home, but that ended. I knew nothing about the person either," she said, careful not to say the gender of his former significant other. "He's generally secretive about whom he's dating."

Living in LA had exposed me to a much larger community, unlike our small town, where people were still fairly quiet about revealing their sexuality. I wasn't sure if Arthur dated men or women, but his reaction to Dana and his secrecy led me to believe that his preference had something to do with why he stayed clear of her. It wasn't something I felt comfortable bringing up to Fern, especially if his mother wasn't aware.

"Has Arthur said anything about Gwendolyn's death? I know they weren't always angry with one another, but how has he been reacting lately?" I asked with a tentative approach.

"Kellan, we've known each other for years. I'm also aware you investigated the two deaths on campus last month. Are you asking because you think Arthur had something to do with Gwendolyn's death? I thought it was a heart attack," Fern said with concern rising on her face.

"I won't lie. We need to work together and trust one another. I've heard rumors there was foul play with her medication and that her family might be involved. I know Arthur is friendly with one of her granddaughters, Dana. A thought or two has crossed my mind if he might have been coerced into doing something... and now that you mentioned he is in trouble, well..." My stomach cramped up knowing I was turning our meeting into something uncomfortable.

"I doubt it. Arthur can be difficult, but he's not a killer. He also stands up for himself, and if someone in that family tried to push him into doing something illegal, Arthur wouldn't have allowed it," Fern said with a hint of doubt lingering in her voice.

"Are you sure? I don't think he did either, but I can't rule it out. I've heard he's been... how shall I say... intimately involved with someone recently."

"I know my son. He's never been able to lie to me before," Fern said while collecting our trays. "And don't think I am upset with you for asking. I understand why you're doing it. You've always been a stand-up guy, even back when you used to fight for your fraternity when you were a student here. I admired your courage and strength then, and I admire it now."

"Thank you, it means a lot to hear you say it." After Fern left, I noticed a missed voicemail from an unknown caller. Why couldn't people leave me alone to focus on my priorities?

CHAPTER 19

I listened to the voicemail only to learn I'd forgotten to reschedule my annual exam with Dr. Betscha. I had to cancel it when I'd gotten Francesca's letter and couldn't push myself to do anything for a few hours other than sulking and reminiscing. Knowing I also needed to talk to him about Gwendolyn, I called the office and picked a new date and time. "Is there any chance he's available to speak?"

"Sure, he's got a light afternoon. He was supposed to be offsite at a conference, but the schedule changed last-minute," she said before putting me on hold.

A few seconds later, he picked up. After we caught up on the important things going on in our lives, he said, "So, what can I do for you today, Kellan?"

I told him about the possibility of the Paddington's maid giving birth to a child that might have been fathered by someone in their household. He was unusually quiet before finally responding.

"I'm sorry, I needed to give the question proper thought. Someone in the Paddington family recently asked me the same question," Dr. Betscha said. "I suppose now that she's gone, I'm not breaking Gwendolyn's confidence, especially if you're helping the family figure out who killed her."

His news surprised me. "Did Gwendolyn ask you for a DNA test on Brad Shope?"

"Yes. She'd come to find out the same thing you've learned about Brad. I got her in contact with a friend of mine who runs a DNA testing laboratory over in Woodland. I don't think she had time to get the final results, but she did have two different tests run if I understood correctly. It was only a couple of weeks ago," Dr. Betscha said.

"Did she say whom she suspected of being his father?"

"No, but she wanted to know if he was or wasn't a Paddington. I believe she was fond of the lad." Dr. Betscha put me on hold to speak with another patient who demanded the doctor make himself available. "Sorry about that, Kellan. I'm not sure how you deal with those Paddingtons all day long. That was one of them begging for a minute of my time this afternoon," he replied. Dr. Betscha was a good doctor, and he made as much time for his patients as possible. Sometimes he didn't know how or when to say *no*. Which Paddington was calling him? I didn't think I could ask him to reveal that, too.

"I won't keep you much longer. Can you send me the same info you sent Gwendolyn? It's a last resort to understanding who might have wanted her dead. If a relative thought she was going to add a new beneficiary or take someone else's name off the list, I'm worried that person might have killed her."

"It's a theory. There were lots of people in that family who disliked Gwendolyn. Even her daughter, Jennifer, threatened to kill her, and she was often the most level-headed of the bunch. At least she was before the incident, that is." Dr. Betscha coughed, then said his goodbye.

I wasn't sure what incident he was referring to. "Wait, is that something you can share?"

"I probably shouldn't, but it wasn't said to me in confidence. I learned about it through conversation with Jennifer one day afterward. Apparently, the reason she suffered the last miscarriage which ultimately ended her engagement was a fight with her mother. Gwendolyn accidentally pushed Jennifer down a flight of stairs during an argument at the mansion."

"Really? I knew about the miscarriages, but not the rest. Did she tell many people?"

"No, it wasn't like that. At first, she told the emergency room it was an accident. When she came to see me a few hours later, I had a consultation with her ob/gyn. We told Jennifer she might have difficulty conceiving a child again, and she became quite upset. That's when she started ranting and raving about her mother pushing her down the stairs."

"Do you think that's how it happened?" I asked, suddenly seeing a stronger reason why Jennifer might want to hurt her mother.

"Jennifer was angry and upset at the thought of not having a child. We never said she couldn't, just that it would be more difficult from some of the damage. You might want to talk to her about it. It's been four or five years, and I don't know how she felt about the situation anymore." Dr. Betscha hung up to deal with his other patient.

The Paddington family was full of so much drama, hatred, and long-held grudges. Any of them truly could have snapped in the last few months and concocted a plan to murder Gwendolyn. I would not be able to solve it unless we could find the missing will or force someone to confess out of guilt. Maybe the best next step would be to call a family meeting and put all the cards on the table. Could we trigger the murderer to say something that would reveal his or her identity?

After unsuccessfully trying to reach Nana D and Eustacia following my conversation with Dr. Betscha, I went to the library to do some research on how to have someone redeclared alive after they'd been previously declared dead. Surprisingly, there was quite a list of articles and a few books on the extraordinary topic. Most of what I'd learned focused on the financial and legal side of being declared dead when there wasn't an actual body to prove it. That wasn't my problem. There was definitely a body; it was just alive. And I was dealing with a crazy mob family who bribed cops and a coroner to issue a death certificate. Who was going to believe me?

Three hours later, after banging my head on the desk several times, causing a small red bump to materialize, I took some aspirin and drove home. My mother had picked Emma up after school and gone to a friend's daughter's birthday party, which meant I was on my own for dinner. No one else was around. I either needed to get myself some additional friends or take advantage of an early night given I felt like my body was fighting off a cold. I texted my mother that I was going to sleep, and she was responsible for getting Emma to bed. I also told her that I owed her big time. She agreed and sent me the number of a florist with a hint that she could use a little something for her office. I ordered two gigantic bouquets of Easter lilies and conked out listening to an episode of the Great British Baking show.

* * *

On Thursday morning, I awoke with a congested head and frustrating cough. The clock on the bedside table read nine o'clock. A note next to it from my father said he'd taken Emma to school that morning. When I hadn't woken up, even when Emma tried to nudge me, they knew I was in no condition to get through the day on my own. I sent my parents each a text message thanking them for being the best parents in the world. My father replied, saying he'd kept track of the favors I'd needed since returning home and that I should expect a bill at the end of the month. Was he being facetious? Why could I never tell with that man? My mother replied, saying the flowers were delivered at precisely eight thirty and smelled so fragrant, everyone in the admissions building stopped by to check them out.

After foregoing my run and workout, I showered and ate a leisurely breakfast. Nana D called to tell me I was off the hook if I needed to skip the mayoral debate. She'd heard from my mother, who said I was on my deathbed. I'm not sure how it went from a cold to almost dying, but the game of telephone between my mother and her mother often went off the rails easily. I let Nana D know I'd be at the debate as soon as I dropped off my dry cleaning, made a few phone calls, and picked up some decongestion medicine. Thirty minutes later, I sat at a tall table in The Big Beanery with a cup of tea to alleviate my throat, which was getting scratchier.

I connected with the DNA testing facility and left a message that I was inquiring on behalf of Gwendolyn Paddington, who'd recently passed away. I wanted to see if they could provide the results to me or to her lawyer, whichever they felt comfortable doing. I knew it would go to the lawyer, but I had to try.

Finnigan would undoubtedly share them with Eustacia, so I'd ultimately see them. As I sulked over feeling like a truck had hit me, and wishing I could crawl back in bed, I heard a familiar voice. I turned around and saw Sam Taft sitting at the booth to my left. I listened to his conversation.

Sam said, "I never expected this to happen, but ever since I met you, everything seems so much better in my life. You're amazing. I can't wait to see you again."

His voice was so full of glee and bliss, I could feel it a dozen feet away. Was Sam seeing someone new? If so, I was happy for him, but whom?

Sam continued, "I understand why you don't want anyone to know right now. It's complex, I get it. I'm not asking you to share the news until you're ready. Sure... yeah, I can do that."

Was his girlfriend trying to keep it under wraps? I felt bad listening in, but it was an opportunity to learn more about him. The kid had been secretive and standoffish whenever I was near him.

Sam laughed, then said, "I'm falling in love with you. I don't care what anyone thinks. My family might not be okay with it, but who needs them? Grandmother was the only one who listened to me. I still can't believe she and I fought over telling the others about you. Then she died without closure."

Interesting. I'd learned two things from Sam's phone conversation. One, why would he kill his grandmother if she were the only person who seemed to care about him? Two, he had a secret lover. Did Dana not approve of whom he was dating and that's why she told me about the fight?

Sam said, "I think Kellan knows. He's shown up a couple of times when I didn't expect to see him. I know we need to keep this a secret right now. But what do we do if he figures out what's going on? I'm already freaking out that my grandmother died because of it."

What did that mean? As I considered everything I learned, I wondered if Sam didn't have a girlfriend. Could he have a boyfriend and be scared to come out of the closet? And if the guy he was talking to also wasn't ready to tell anyone, could it be someone Sam's family knew? I gasped when another thought crossed my mind. Was it Arthur or Brad? I hardly knew anything about Brad's personal life, but that would be incestuous if Brad turned out to be a Paddington. My mind was so busy racing all over the place and processing all the information that I never heard Sam approach me.

"Kellan, I didn't see you there. Did you overhear me?" Sam inquired intently, biting his lower lip.

Should I say yes, or pretend I didn't? "Ummm... I... noticed you, yes, but... I didn't want to interrupt when I saw you on the phone."

"It's not what you think. I didn't want to keep it hidden." Sam's eyes narrowed to the floor.

"I didn't hear much. Is there something you want to tell me?"

He shook his head. "I was talking to a friend, that's all."

I threw out a little bait to see if he'd bite. "Ah, that wouldn't be Brad, by any chance, would it? I need to speak with him and couldn't find him this morning."

Sam looked at me with a puzzled expression. "Brad who?"

"Your grandmother's nurse," I replied.

"Oh, no. It wasn't Brad. I barely know him. I thought he was done working at the mansion already," Sam noted haphazardly gathering up his school bag.

"Brad's helping your great Aunt Eustacia with several things. I believe he's staying on a few more days," I explained, searching Sam's face for any sign or clue.

"Well, I gotta run. Can't help you on Brad. By the way, I know you said you overheard nothing, but if by any chance you did, please don't tell anyone. I'm not ready to share the news. I'm still dealing with it myself, and well, it's only half my news to share. There is someone else involved, too. I'm sure you understand why it's important to wait until we're all ready to sit down and discuss it, right?"

I nodded, only half understanding what he meant. Was he concerned I would reveal that he was gay? Or that he had something to do with Gwendolyn's death? "Sure, it's not my place to say anything. I want everyone involved to be happy."

"Thanks. I figured you of all people might understand, Kellan. Maybe I'll see you around again." Sam tossed on his coat and left The Big Beanery looking partially relieved.

I needed time to process the entire conversation, but I was fairly certain Sam's attitude toward me had suddenly changed. Maybe he'd seen I wasn't bothered by his news and didn't need to worry about hiding the truth from another person. Or maybe he was cleverly keeping me confused, so I wouldn't discover what'd really happened to his grandmother. I stood from my seat, realizing I had to get to the debate. Nana D had forced Marcus to stick to the original date and location despite his every effort to change both.

Twenty minutes later, they both took to the stage alongside Lara Bouvier in Wellington Park. We sat in an outdoor amphitheater protected from the cool weather by dozens of heat lamps. Lara asked both candidates to share a personal message to the constituents. Marcus talked about how his family had been in Wharton County for over two hundred years, highlighting all the donations they'd given to build the hospital, promote the concert hall, and redevelop the Finnulia waterfront. Nana D countered with all the benefits her ancestors, the Danbys and Betschas, had given to everyone, including creating jobs at the Betscha mines, developing the farmland, and organizing all the volunteer programs. She even cited the new opportunities she would commit to, plus the suggestions I'd made to help clean up the Second Chance Reflections facility.

For almost the entire debate, they were neck and neck. Until it came time for the audience to ask questions. The first speaker asked Marcus how he would handle addressing growing concerns about the environment. Crilly Lake was shrinking due to limited water from mountain run-off properly draining off into its basin, and several of the older chemical companies in the area had been dumping toxic waste into the Finnulia River. A few had been caught, but the latest readings on the cleanliness of the water showed a major focus was soon needed. The councilman had already been researching the impacts on the environment in the county and announced several plans he would put in place to stop the current offenders and increase the fines on future ones.

When it came time for Nana D's speaker to ask her question, she focused on Wharton County inhabitants who were worried that as the county grew more populous and offered opportunities for bigger businesses, how would it impact the percentage of funding we'd receive from the state in the future. Unfortunately, Nana D's full grasp on the political structure within the town of Braxton, Wharton County, and the state of Pennsylvania was still limited. While she was aware of what the county's citizens needed in terms of more jobs and less red tape, she hadn't learned enough about the risks of increased profits and revenue impacting the balance of what the state contributed to the county. She misspoke a few times about what she thought we should do, and Marcus called her out on it in his rebuttal. In the end, Nana D's supporters still rallied for her, but she took a painful step backward in the eyes of big business and corporate groups who had yet to reveal which candidate they planned to back.

As the debate ended, I listened to a few conversations, and the news didn't bode well for Nana D. As much as the county's inhabitants wanted change, they were afraid of money being taken away from them as well as supporting a candidate whose experience wasn't as strong as they needed. I comforted Nana D, who barely spoke on the walk back to the SUV. When we reached the parking lot, we saw a woman standing near a car and trying to keep herself from falling over. As we got closer, I realized it was Jennifer Paddington. I grabbed her hand and steadied her against my body. "Are you okay?"

"Kellan, yes, thank you," she mumbled. After regaining her composure, she handed me the keys to her car. "Can you grab the bottle of water from the bag on the passenger seat, please?"

I gave the keys to Nana D, who opened the door and reached for the bottle. When she got back to Jennifer and me, Nana D reached into her purse. "You look like you could use something to eat, too. Here, have an apple," she said after taking a Macintosh from her purse.

"What happened, Jennifer?" I asked when she leaned against the side of the car.

"I was feeling a little faint. It must be the morning sickness," Jennifer said, looking green.

"Ummm, are you pregnant?" Nana D asked.

Jennifer nodded. "Yes, I only found out a couple of days ago. It was a complete surprise."

"But I thought you were going to the fertility clinic, Jennifer?" I said, feeling dumbstruck by her last statement and our discussion at the toy store.

"I'd been going for the last year, but I ran out of money after the last one. I was shocked when I took the home test earlier this week and it said I was pregnant. I went to Dr. Betscha, who confirmed it. I'm six weeks pregnant," Jennifer said with the beginning of a smile forming on her lips.

"Congratulations! I guess the procedure must have taken after all," Nana D added.

"No, that's not what happened. I know for sure the last one didn't work out. I got pregnant the old-fashioned way this time. I'm sorry to be so blunt," she said, wiping her cheek. "I'm still shocked!"

"You must be thrilled," I added, wondering what it all meant.

"Yes, definitely. Don't get me wrong. My body's been through a lot. It's trying to adjust to different drugs, getting pregnant, and my mother's death. I need to go home and rest, I think," she said while climbing into her car.

"You shouldn't be driving right now, Jennifer," Nana D demanded as she looked at me. "Kellan can take you home. I'll follow him and we'll come back for his afterward."

"No, really. I can't trouble you both. I'll be okay," Jennifer replied.

"If you think you can drive, that's fine. I'll follow you until you get home to be sure everything's okay. Is that acceptable?" I asked. Jennifer nodded, and Nana D left for her car. As I got into mine, she texted.

Nana D: *What was that all about? You're not the father, are you?*
Me: *What is wrong with you? Of course, I'm not.*
Nana D: *I'm just sayin'. I wouldn't blame you if you needed to address that side of your life.*
Me: *What side's that? Having children with a strange woman who might have killed her mother?*
Nana D: *Don't be a fool! If it's not you, then who's the father?*
Me: *I haven't a clue! I'm not even sure what this means regarding Gwendolyn's death. Or will.*
Nana D: *By the way... are you seeing anyone? I think it's time you moved on. Emma might like a baby brother or sister one day. She'll stop asking about that puppy.*
Me: *This is none of your business. Especially right now. Go do some research for your campaign.*
Nana D: *Sometimes you can be a bad grandson. I've got a nerve to leave you outta my will now!*
Me: *Not funny! Maybe I ought to get you a glass of iced tea?*
Nana D: *Do you need another margarita lesson?*

That shut me up quickly. When I got back to the house, I spent the rest of the afternoon and early evening updating my 'Who killed Gwendolyn?' chart. I had more questions than answers, but at least everything was written down. As I prepared to pick up Emma from gymnastics class, my phone rang. It would likely be the rotten cherry on the pinnacle of my bad day. "Hello, Myriam."

"Good evening, Kellan. I just received the mail for the department," she said in a perfectly normal voice. There wasn't a hint of sarcasm coming from her. Was she preparing for a sneak attack?

343

"Is there a reason you called to tell me this?" I asked as pleasantly as possible.

"Correct. There's a package addressed to someone who doesn't work here, but I believe you are the best person to handle it," Myriam replied. Still no rage or peculiar Shakespeare quotes.

What could she be talking about? "Okay, I'll come by to pick it up in the morning. Who's it addressed to?"

"Gwendolyn Paddington. It's also from Gwendolyn Paddington. She sent herself something at Paddington's Play House," Myriam noted.

There was only one thing I thought it could be—we finally found her revised will!

CHAPTER 20

Another night passed with hardly any sleep since my cold had turned into something much worse. While living in LA for a decade, I'd avoided every possible germ and illness there was to catch. A month back in Braxton's harsh winters, and my body was ready to abandon me. I suppose that wasn't the only reason I couldn't sleep.

Once Myriam notified me about the package Gwendolyn received at Paddington's Play House, I immediately thought about rushing off to collect it. Then I realized it was a violation of federal law to open someone else's mail, even if the person was no longer alive. Actually, it was Myriam who brought up that last part. When I'd told her I'd stop by to get it last night, she discreetly tried to explain why she couldn't give it to me without proper approval. When I asked whom she expected to provide said consent, I listened to a litany of ways to legally transfer the document. I wanted to suggest holding a séance where Eleanor could contact Gwendolyn's ghost and ask her to haunt Myriam until she caved in, but I was certain that would send my vindictive boss to Second Chance Reflections for therapy. Even I knew that wouldn't be very nice of me.

Myriam had been too busy with the *King Lear* performance to discuss next steps, but she agreed to give me the document this morning if I had approval from both Gwendolyn's attorney and her estate's executor. Finnigan and Eustacia were kind enough to send me an approval via email while I'd been sleeping. All I needed to do was show them to Myriam when I went to teach my courses at Braxton. Except I felt so awful, I moved as slow as a snail with a hangover and broken shell. But my hangover wasn't from drinking alcohol, it was from a combination of cough medicine and various over-the-counter drugs I'd bought in a mad dash raid at the Nutberry Pharmacy the day before. Not only did they run one of the funeral parlors, but the Nutberry family also kept us well-medicated in life. I was still trying to avoid one of Nana D's infamous cures. She probably wanted me to drink some worm root and ground-up euca-lyptus leaves. I was only hazarding a guess as to her holistic cures, as the last time I had a four-day leg cramp from running, she made me drink the most awful concoction ever. I still had freakish hallucinations and swore to myself I'd never again accept her brand of medicine.

I replanned my lecture on the drive to campus, settling on showing a thirty-minute film and organizing the class into groups for discussions. I could walk around and comment as they were discussing it, then request a one-page paper summarizing their thoughts. It was not the way I preferred to teach, but there was little chance I could make it through the entire day when my body needed more sleep.

I called the sheriff to let her know about the package at Paddington's Play House. She asked me to meet her at Finnigan's office that afternoon to open it while she was present. I printed the emails—including signatures—after I finished teaching both classes and stopped in Myriam's office. "Good afternoon. How's your day going?" I said, followed by a loud sneeze and several unattrac-tive sniffles.

"Better than yours, Kellan. You look worse than usual. Out partying too much? I'd hoped you would take this job much more seriously and stay in good health. The students depend on us to educate them using our full potential," she said while opening her desk drawer. She pulled out a small package of disinfectant towelettes and began wiping her desk as though I'd sneezed on her belongings.

"I'm not in any shape to engage in our usual combat fighting. And your wife asked us to play nice," I said while handing her the printed approvals. "Signed by both Finnigan Masters, esteemed attorney for the recently deceased Gwen-dolyn Paddington, and Eustacia Paddington as the executor. I assume this will be sufficient for you to give me the package you received yesterday?"

"Leave them there on the desk. When I have a pair of gloves, I will sanitize them and put them in my files. *It seems there is a plague upon both your houses.*" Myriam's lips frowned as she stood and walked to the other side of her desk to read them.

Both my houses? Either she'd become more obtuse than usual, or my various symptoms were playing games with my hearing. "Come again?"

"Not only are you riddled with some sort of disease you've brought on campus, you're caught up in another one at the Paddington estate with drugs and murder. I spoke with the sheriff this morning. She told me Gwendolyn didn't just die of a heart attack. There's murder most foul in the air." Myriam used a pencil to move the top copy away from the bottom print-out, so she could finish reading the approvals.

"I guess you felt the need to double-check my work. Shouldn't there be a stronger sense of trust between us?" I asked, followed by another sneeze. I was certain I covered my mouth, but Myriam jumped so far away from me, I couldn't tell.

"I trust no one. Your papers appear to be in order. If you don't mind, please take your virus-ridden presence elsewhere. The package is over there," she demanded and pointed to the corner chair.

"Well, you're a haven of comfort in a sick man's time of need. A regular Mother Teresa and Florence Nightingale all wrapped up into one generous human being," I snarled before grabbing the package and leaving her office. As I turned the corner, I caught her nose wrinkle in anger and shock. There was no visible guilt or sorrow in her expression, only a satisfied repugnance I wanted to slash with a cleaver.

Although I had several administrative tasks to complete, I left knowing I couldn't focus on anything to save my life. As I drove by North Campus, Maggie texted to tell me she was looking forward to our date. My stomach sank when I realized I might not be well enough to socialize with her. I decided to first meet with Finnigan, Eustacia, and the sheriff, then go home to take a nap. If I felt horrible once I woke up, I'd reschedule the dinner with Maggie.

As I was leaving, the DNA testing facility called me back to indicate they weren't authorized to tell me anything, but they would be in contact the following week with the person Gwendolyn had named as the individual to receive the results. They couldn't give me any additional information, which made sense given the need for privacy and security in the current day and age.

Thirty minutes later, I entered Finnigan's law offices at the base of the Wharton Mountains. He'd inherited the practice from his father, who didn't want to be in the middle of all the action in downtown Braxton. He'd chosen a charming, converted log cabin as his law offices, so they could bask in a gorgeous landscape every day. When we all assembled in Finnigan's conference room, I handed him the package. Finnigan explained that he would need to authenticate the document by verifying signatures and ensuring it was the exact text copy he'd sent to Gwendolyn. He reminded us that all she was supposed to do was fill in a few names next to each of the bequeathals, sign the document in a few places, and obtain signatures from two non-interested witnesses.

Eustacia stared at him hard. "Just open it, will you? We've been waiting centuries for this dang document to show up." She banged her cane on the wooden floor. As it reverberated against the walls, Finnigan tore open the package with fervor.

"I will need a copy of that," Sheriff Montague said, pulling her chair closer to the table. "It might not have any bearing on the case, but I always keep my records clean and up to date." She turned to me as if I needed to be reminded of her keen attention to detail.

"Excellent point," I said, followed by another sneeze.

Eustacia handed me her handkerchief to stop the drip threatening to explode from my nose. "You should talk to your nana. She's always got those miracle cures. Just last week, she fixed this rash I had on my leg. I don't know where it came from, but Lord Almighty, it wouldn't go away. I kept scratching for weeks until she saw it all red and puffy like a rampant fungus. Seraphina fixed me up in less than forty-eight hours."

I choked on a small amount of bile that had propelled up my throat. "I'll do that." When Eustacia looked toward Finnigan, I rolled my eyes, wincing from the exerted pressure on my face.

The sheriff stifled a laugh as she leaned over in my direction. "You really do fit right in with your nana's friends, don't ya, Little Ayrwick?"

Finnigan cleared his throat. "I'll skip the normal approach when I read a last will and testament. Shall I focus on just the particulars?" he said, looking around the room. We all nodded in agreement.

"Get on with it, Masters. I could die before you spit everything out. I'm not paying you by the hour on this one," Eustacia snarled. Two more bangs of her cane on the floor.

Finnigan smiled and clapped his hands together. "Certainly. Let's see... okay, Gwendolyn Paddington split her fortune in half. Fifty percent was left to various charities and Paddington's Play House at Braxton. The remaining fifty percent of her estate was split equally among three people."

Interesting. She'd included someone new since the prior version. Eustacia coughed. "Go on."

"Millard Paddington, her brother-in-law. Timothy Paddington, her son. And Sam Taft, her grandson. She mentions leaving behind another letter that's meant to be read aloud at the final will reading. She explains why she made these decisions," Finnigan clarified. His gaze swept across the room, starting with the sheriff, then me, and ending with Eustacia. "Apparently, she left it with you, Eustacia. This note says it's safely hidden in something you depend on greatly to keep you living each day."

The sheriff stood. "I think we need to read it, Ms. Paddington. That letter might let us know who would be angry enough about her decision and want to kill her. Hand it over."

Eustacia withdrew. "I don't have any letter. I'm not sure what she's talking about!"

Sheriff Montague replied, "Well, give it some thought while we read through the rest of the will. This is important."

"What do you depend on, Eustacia?" I asked while walking toward her in confusion.

"Maybe it's somewhere back at my place in Willow Trees. I'll check tonight," Eustacia noted while squinting her eyes and tapping her cane against the floor. "Confounded woman."

"Who were the witnesses?" I asked, thinking that might help us move forward in the meantime.

"Brad Shope and Bertha Crawford," Finnigan replied. "The will appears to be in excellent condition. My legal secretary will match it word-for-word, but this is what we can use to probate the estate."

"Bertha signed it with no vested interest. She's just an employee who did Gwendolyn a favor that night by helping her get the new will finished. I'm more concerned about Brad being the other witness," the sheriff noted while twisting her fingers together.

I wasn't sure where the idea came from, but I suddenly thought of a way to lure the killer out of hiding. "What if we inform the whole Paddington family that the new will has been found. We tell them that Gwendolyn mailed it to herself and it's in Paddington's Play House, but we are waiting for the proper approvals to open it."

"Go ahead, I think I understand where you're going with this, Little Ayrwick." The sheriff had the early formation of a smile.

"If the killer wants to keep this new will from being found, he or she might sneak in to steal or destroy it. The murderer probably thinks it was lost or thrown away, but if the will were to show up, the killer would need to protect their interests." I felt my face flush, uncertain if it was the medication kicking in or the excitement over discovering a potential way to solve the case.

"Set a trap is what you're saying," Eustacia noted. She attempted to stand up but couldn't push the chair away from the table. "That's a smart idea. I can get the family together tomorrow to tell them we are reading the will. Then we can tell them about the new one!"

Finnigan rose to help Eustacia. "I'll play along if the sheriff thinks this will potentially help."

Sheriff Montague consented. "It's a strong possibility. Let me think through how I want to handle it. But go ahead, let's schedule it for ten o'clock tomorrow morning at the Paddington estate."

After we agreed on the basics, everyone left Finnigan's office. The sheriff pulled me aside in the parking lot. "I discussed everything with the Paddington accountants. It seems Ophelia was responsible for those unexplained withdrawals from Gwendolyn's accounts. She had access for years but had never used it until recently. I'm assuming Gwendolyn never realized her daughter could withdraw money when Charles died last year. Ophelia might be the person we're after."

"She's been cagey about the entire situation throughout the last week. Now that her husband is back, and he's head of the company, it looks like everything's coming together for her," I remarked. "If she was removed as a beneficiary with the new will, killing her mother before the new will turned up is definitely the opportunity and motive we need. Maybe we'll catch her tomorrow."

The sheriff was surprised at how quickly I had thought of the idea to bait the killer. "This approach is the best chance we have to getting close to solving the case. We don't have a weapon to trace, nor any alibis to confirm or deny. This kind of murder is always difficult to pin down."

"I'm glad I thought of it. We might solve the investigation together," I noted with a smile despite a desperate need to crash in my bed for a few hours. I decided to push my luck. "You're welcome, *April*." Sheriff Montague nodded at me as she got on her motorcycle and left the law office parking lot.

On the drive home, I called my parents to thank them for bringing Emma to Philadelphia. Emma had convinced them to take her to the zoo for the afternoon, and since her school was closed for a teacher conference that day, my parents offered to watch her. I pulled into the driveway at the Royal Chic-Shack dragging myself upstairs to take a nap. When I got to the top landing, my bedroom door was open, and a light shined through the crack. I knew I'd left the door closed and no one else was home.

I turned the corner while calling out, "Hellooo..." In retrospect, knowing the Castigliano family had sent a goon to scare me in the Pick-Me-Up Diner's parking lot earlier that week, I shouldn't have walked in the room so nonchalantly. Maybe it was the medication I had taken or the illness zapping any remaining common sense I had left. When the door swung fully open, I saw someone sitting on the edge of my bed. She looked back at me with a cunning yet comforting grin and said, "Surprise."

"What are you doing here? Someone could've caught you!" I stood almost paralyzed.

"Your parents are gone for the day. I knew I could hide out here until you got home," Francesca said, walking over to hug me.

"But how did you know? When did you get here?" I said, feeling lightheaded.

"My mother bugged the house the last time she was here. She's been listening to all your conversations to see if you'd said anything about me being alive. I overheard you and her talking the other day, and I caught a flight out here the next morning." Francesca explained that she'd stayed at a hotel the previous day, waiting for the right moment to reveal herself. I was glad to see her, and we needed to talk despite me not feeling well enough to focus. "But don't worry, I disconnected the listening devices in your room when I got here."

My body weakened. Just as I realized I'd never eaten breakfast or lunch, and that I'd probably overdosed on too much medicine trying to knock the original cold-turned-whatever-virus out of my system, I fell to the floor. The last thing I remember before passing out was Francesca leaning over me saying, "It's okay... you get some sleep. Let your wife take care of you."

* * *

As I rolled over onto my back, a stream of light hit my face. I was in my bedroom, but I had no idea what day or time it was. I felt around the night table for my glasses, then stared at a clock that read seven thirty. Something didn't feel right. I lifted the covers and felt a sudden chill. When I looked down, I had nothing on but a pair of boxer briefs. I didn't remember getting undressed. Then I realized if it was seven thirty in March, the sun had already set. Why was light coming through the window? I sat up in the bed and wrapped myself in an extra blanket lying nearby. That's when I remembered Francesca was in my bedroom. I was about to jump from the bed when the door creaked open.

"Good morning, sunshine. How are you feeling?" Francesca asked with a huge grin. "I'm so glad you slept through the night. I was worried when I took your temperature, and you had a high fever." She set a breakfast tray on the desk across from my bed and brought me a cup of coffee.

"What happened? How did you... where's Emma?" Then I recalled that my parents had taken her to the zoo in Philadelphia and were staying overnight.

But I also remembered I was supposed to meet Maggie for dinner. If it was morning, I'd missed the whole evening.

"Calm down. Don't get yourself even sicker. You were in terrible shape last night and passed out. I had to drag you into the bed and get you comfortable," Francesca said, sitting on the edge of the mattress and feeling my forehead. "No more fever."

I pulled the covers away and verified I really did have underwear on. "Did you take off my clothes, too?"

"You're acting like this is unusual. I am your wife, right?" Francesca patted my lap and kissed my cheek. "You're looking pretty amazing, hon. I missed snuggling up with you at night."

"Did we... do anything..." I asked, urging my brain to recall what'd happened the previous night. "Where did you sleep?" I wasn't sure that it mattered since she was my wife.

"You were way too sick to do anything like that, Kellan. I got you all tucked in by late afternoon. You've been asleep for almost sixteen hours. Not that I didn't want to, of course, but I prefer you to be awake enough to remember our first time together again," she cooed. "I slept next to you for most of the night to be sure you were okay."

"Where's my phone?" I asked hesitantly and feeling a weird grogginess in my head. When Francesca handed it to me, I unlocked the security code and checked what I'd missed. I had over twenty missed calls and multiple voice-mails from the sheriff, Nana D, Eleanor, Maggie, and my mother.

"Your phone kept ringing, so I turned it off while you slept. I tried to access it, but you must be using a different code now. I couldn't unlock the infernal device," Francesca noted. She grabbed a slice of toast from the tray and handed it to me. "Eat something, hon. You need your strength."

I suddenly felt a pit in my stomach growing so large I couldn't swallow a bite of toast. "Does anyone know you're here?"

Francesca explained her mother was horrified and incensed that she'd run off, but Cecilia ultimately backed down as long as Francesca would return that evening. "I called Eleanor, too. I let her know you were with me and not feeling well. I asked her to let Nana D know were fine. Your grandmother kept calling before I turned the phone off. I didn't want her to worry."

"Thanks," I mumbled while scrolling through all my text messages. I could respond to everything later except for the sheriff and Maggie. But I couldn't call Maggie with Francesca in the room. "Could you get me some ice water? I need something cold for my throat."

Once Francesca left, I dialed Maggie's number to apologize to her. She didn't pick up. Her voicemail and text message didn't sound like she was angry I'd bailed on our dinner, but I wasn't certain. I left her a voicemail apologizing for not calling. I told her I'd been so sick, I intended to wake up to call her but slept through the night. I'd fix it the next time I talked to her. Then I rang the sheriff.

"Where have you been? We need to discuss the plan for the meeting with the Paddington family. I thought I could trust you based on our last conversation," she yelled through the phone.

"I'm so sorry. I will be there soon. I'll explain everything later. Is it still ten o'clock? I'll arrive a little beforehand to talk with you." I squeaked out a quick apology before sneezing again.

"Fine. But you've taken quite a step down in my eyes, Little Ayrwick. I'll be watching the security camera at the Paddington estate to get a reading on everyone's facial expressions and comments," Sheriff Montague growled. She was beyond angry with me.

When I hung up, Francesca ambled into the room and handed me a glass of water and more medicine. "Take these. It's the same pills you took last night. The directions said every eight hours, but you missed a dose while you were sleeping. I didn't want to wake you."

For a moment, I debated whether to swallow them. Someone had been messing with Gwendolyn's medication, and it killed her. Francesca surely wouldn't do that to me, but I wasn't feeling like myself given everything that had happened in the last day. "Thanks. I need to be somewhere important in two hours, but we should chat."

"That's why I'm here, Kellan. Let's talk." Francesca climbed onto the bed and snuggled against my chest. "It's like before the accident. We're wrapped up in each other's arms discussing our future."

I swallowed the pills with a big gulp of water, told myself I'd thoroughly considered all my options, and prepared to have a tough conversation with my wife.

CHAPTER 21

"You know how much I love you, right? It absolutely breaks my heart to think about where we ended up after everything we've been through together," I said to Francesca as we held hands sitting on my bed. I was slightly more certain of my decision than I had been the prior day. Despite how well she took care of me, and the moments of happiness I felt being so close with her, Francesca's reappearance in my bedroom helped confirm the correct next steps.

"We're soulmates, Kellan. From that first day we met at the pier in Santa Monica, I knew you were the one. I can't wait to bring Emma back home, so I can see her all the time." Francesca kissed my cheek and squeezed my hand.

"I've thought about us a lot lately. Ever since I found out you were alive, I dreamt about cooking Sunday morning breakfasts together, teaching Emma how to read with you, and walking on the beach holding hands as we look for buried treasure." And it was the truth. For a little while, I was caught up in all the amazing things we could do as a family once Emma was a little older and we were back in Los Angeles. Then I realized how scared and nervous I was with Francesca in my parents' house.

"Let's go home today. My flight leaves in a few hours. I'll go ahead now, and you can meet me there with Emma later. I'm sure there will be two seats available for you both." Francesca shined as beautiful as always. The hope and desire in her expressions were as contagious as they had ever been.

I changed positions on the bed, so I could look directly at my wife. "But I've also felt scared and angry the last couple of weeks. Maybe even angrier than I was the first year after I thought you had died. When I wanted to kill that drunk driver and had almost no will left to live without you. The only thing that kept me focused was knowing I had to protect our baby girl. Emma needed me no matter what I was feeling." I found my strength and prepared to tell Francesca what I'd decided.

Every nerve in my body was on high alert. What if someone walked in on us? Could the Vargas family suspect something was going on if Emma and I returned? Were we being watched already? I couldn't live like that. As dreadful as it sounded and felt, letting my daughter think her mother was dead, even if the smallest chance existed to make this bizarre situation work, was the best solution. How could anyone be expected to know the right answer?

"I know it hurt you, but I'll make it up to you. We'll figure it out as long as you're back in LA. I promise this won't be forever," Francesca said with tears rolling down her cheeks. When she reached forward to hug me, I felt a few descend from my broken eyes as well.

"I'm so sorry," I whispered in her ear. "But I can't do it. I will not move back to LA and take any risks with Emma's future. I know it means you won't get a chance to see her, but that's my final decision. I'm so sorry, Francesca."

At first, she was quiet. I could feel her body tense up then quiver as if she'd been going through shock. I mumbled more words to explain how I felt, probably still trying to convince myself that I knew what I was doing.

Francesca eventually reached the point of anger and lashed out at me. "You can't, I won't let you. She's my daughter!" Francesca screamed, pushing me away from her. We continued to search for a solution, but one didn't exist. At least none that would work for the both of us. For a few seconds, Nana D's advice remained steady in my head. *'If you love something, let it go. If it's yours, it will come back to you.'* I didn't dare say those words to Francesca because I didn't know in this situation who was truly letting whom go.

When my phone rang and Francesca saw it was my mother, she went to grab it thinking it was Emma calling from Philadelphia to say good morning. She was about to hit the accept button, then stared back at me. "Answer it."

"I'll put it on speakerphone, so you can hear her voice, too." Francesca and I sat together, listening to our daughter excitedly tell us about her trip with her grandparents. When we hung up, I grabbed Francesca's hand. "Maybe one day things will change. And we'll figure out a way for you to see her. I'll come back on trips to LA and stay with your family, so you know what's going on with Emma."

"It won't be enough," Francesca cried. "I want my life back. I deserve it. You deserve it." Her warm, quivering lips kissed me with years of longing, reminding me why I'd fallen in love with her. As she rushed from the room and down the stairs, I felt each of her steps bouncing in my chest, breaking my heart into tiny little pieces. I had caused this pain by deciding not to put our family back together. I'd have to live with the consequences of lying to our daughter. If we ever found a way for Francesca to come back to life again, would Emma forgive me for what I'd done? I could hardly forgive myself.

* * *

An hour later, after a prolonged cry and an even lengthier shower, I made it to the Paddington estate with a cloudy head. Although I should've stayed in bed,

I'd grown accustomed to putting myself in uncomfortable situations and needed to draw out Gwendolyn's killer. In a weird and cathartic way, the potential to close the door on Gwendolyn's pain might ease my own.

Eustacia and I chatted with the sheriff on the drive over to establish a protocol for the family meeting. April and I would listen in from a nearby electrical closet. At first, I was not pleased about being locked together in a small space with the sheriff for an hour. Then I learned that an electrical closet in the Paddington estate was larger than my entire bedroom at the Royal Chic-Shack. April and I would have the comforts of plush recliners and soundproof padding, so no one could hear us talking, and a large video screen to monitor the Paddington family's every move and word.

Twenty minutes later, Bertha snuck us through a servant's entrance and led us to the electrical closet. When she closed the door, April turned to me and said, "Certainly not my idea of a fun way to spend a Saturday morning. Just keep quiet and do your part when the time comes. Don't veer from our script. I'm still not sure I can trust you after your disappearance last night."

My energy was so non-existent, I didn't even try to continue the repartee I'd come to enjoy the last few weeks. "Okay, I'll be ready. You don't have to worry. I'm truly sorry."

"Wait, who are you?" April replied with a confused glance. "Did Martians kidnap the real Kellan Ayrwick and replace him with the automaton I'm stuck in here with?" For added emphasis, April walked across the room toward me like a robot, swinging her arms in exaggerated slow motion up and down.

"I knew you could be witty and sarcastic, but I never expected regular, old-fashioned jokes," I said, trying to rouse a tease out of myself. I wasn't ready to laugh. "Sorry. It's been a rough morning."

"Well, I much prefer the old Kellan, even if he's a pain in my tuchus. The kind where it's so aggravating, I feel it radiating in every single limb to the point I want to throttle you with my bare hands. But of course, as the sheriff of this fine county, I would never do such a thing." She tilted her head and smiled at me.

I felt myself emit a tiny giggle. Was she trying to make me laugh, to help me feel better? "I didn't realize you were Jewish. Or did you borrow one of their words to make an eloquent point?"

"Born and bred. My mother would tan my hide if she knew I was working today. It's the sabbath, you know."

"I assume criminals don't stop doing terrible things because it's a Saturday, huh?"

"They're worse on weekends. If I got paid for the number of times I took a call between Friday evening and Sunday morning, I'd be a rich lady," April replied with a smirk. "Hopefully, whatever's got you down will dissipate soon enough. We've got a murder to solve today. And as much as I like to berate you, I don't enjoy seeing this side of you, Little Ayrwick. It's like kicking a puppy. And if I ever saw someone do that, I'm take 'em down with old Betsy here," she said, tapping the gun in her hip holster.

April raised the volume on the television monitor and indicated Eustacia was talking to her family. We both took seats in the recliners and observed them. I had my cell phone in my hand, ready to call at the appropriate time.

Eustacia sat at the head of the table, looking calm and collected. Millard, who had no idea that we were hiding nearby, or that this was part of a set-up, sat to her right pruning a small plant on his lap. He either had little interest in the will or was trying to distract himself. With each clip, there was a delicate touch and a clear sense of dedication to his craft.

Further down that side of the table were Jennifer and Sam engaged in a quiet conversation. I couldn't hear their words, but based on Jennifer's caress of her belly, I assumed she'd told her nephew about the pregnancy. When Sam smiled, her eyes opened wide, and she whispered, "Shhh" to keep him from saying anything. It seemed she didn't want to make it a major announcement at the family meeting.

"What's going on over there?" demanded an irritated Ophelia. From experience, she let no one keep her from knowing what was going on, nor did she like when her children had gotten too close to other people. She sat across the table from Jennifer to the left of her husband, Richard.

It was the first time I'd seen him, other than the moment at the funeral parlor when I was focused on other things. He scrolled through something on his cell phone, looking up every ten seconds to see what was going on around him. He neither smiled nor frowned. He looked more disconnected and bored, if anything.

"That Taft fellow is certainly interesting, don't ya think?" April said as Eustacia asked everyone to settle down. "I've been doing some research on him. He makes frequent trips out to Los Angeles to support the family business. Have you ever met him?"

I shook my head. "No. Contrary to popular belief, us Braxtonites don't all know each other!" I managed a smile, so she knew I was feeling a little better.

"Yeah, well, I never trust those west coasters... a little too... well, let's just say it's different from a place like Wharton County where we're rooted in old-fashioned values and beliefs," she said.

"Like murderers?" I knew April hadn't meant it as a dig about LA, so I let it go. She was just used to our comfortable mid-west surroundings. "Never been there, I take it?"

"Nope. But I might have to head out there soon enough. I stumbled upon a connection between Paddington Enterprises and an import/export business out in California called Castigliano International. Ever heard of it?" April casually shared while changing the position of the recliner, so she could relax.

I refused to look at her. Was she trying to hint about my connection to them? Did she know about Francesca turning up? "I've heard of it. How does it connect to the Paddingtons?" I asked, feeling my heart race.

"I'm not sure. I received an anonymous tip last week about a business transaction between the two companies from a year ago while Timothy was in charge. The informant apparently thought there was something illegal going on and wanted me to investigate it."

We both stopped talking as Eustacia addressed the family. April's message had unnerved me. What did my in-laws have to do with Paddington Enterprises? If it'd happened a year ago, that's roughly when Charles died, and Timothy was about to be removed from the company by the Board of Directors.

Lilly was the first to speak after Eustacia told everyone they were there to discuss Gwendolyn's will. She sat next to her sister, Dana, on the other side of their father, Richard. "What's this all about, Aunt Eustacia? I don't understand why you called us last-minute and demanded we show up today. This better not be a waste of my time."

Ophelia leaned over Richard to pat her daughter's arm. "Let's wait to see what she wants, hon."

Dana asked, "And where's Uncle Timothy? How come he gets to avoid this meeting?" I thought it was a good question, despite the arrogance oozing from the girl.

"Your grandmother died, young lady. The least you can do is keep your mouth quiet while we discuss her final words before she got called back to Heaven. Honestly, Ophelia... your daughters are both as spoiled as you were as a child. My parents are rolling over in the graves at what you've let them become." Eustacia banged her cane on the floor and shouted again, "Enough! I don't want to hear from any of you until I've shared some important news."

Eustacia informed everyone that a second, newer will had been located. As she told them about Gwendolyn's last-minute changes the day before she died, April and I searched everyone's faces and mannerisms to see if we could learn anything they might try to hide.

Ophelia reached for Richard's hand and leaned forward with a semi-shocked expression. He gently pulled her back and patted her wrist. It might have been a normal reaction to learning unexpected news. Millard's ears perked up, and he stopped pruning the leaves on the plant. He opened his mouth to speak, but then thought better of it. Jennifer looked disinterested. Sam, Dana, and Lilly all sat back in their chairs with alarmed expressions.

"Unfortunately, there will be a delay in getting to read the new will," Finnigan added. He was sitting opposite Eustacia at the other end of the table with his back to the camera. "Gwendolyn mailed the will to someone else, but I assure you it is valid. I reviewed it with her the day before she died. She wanted to make one last change that night, which she did. I asked her to drop it off the next day, but she was worried about being able to meet me on Sunday since she was attending the opening of *King Lear* that afternoon. Instead, she mailed it to a friend for safekeeping. I'm not exactly sure why she didn't mail it to me, but we must get the final version from him." It was a long-shot explanation, but we had to try it.

"That's outrageous," Lilly stood and yelled. "Why would she do such a stupid thing?"

Richard reached for his daughter's hand. "Your grandmother was a bit of an eccentric. Let the lawyer talk, so we can find out what happens next."

"Eccentric? She was a certified nutcase. You should've had her committed years ago," Dana added while crossing her arms and huffing as she slid down the chair into a sulk.

"Don't say such repulsive things, Dana!" Ophelia chastised. "No one in this family belongs in a psychiatric ward!"

It was my queue to call. Eustacia placed the office phone on speaker, so everyone could hear. "Hello, is that you, Kellan?"

"Yes, I'm here. Is this still the right time?" I replied.

Eustacia confirmed and explained to everyone that the package was locked in Paddington's Play House office but had been addressed to me. Jennifer laughed when she heard the news, then turned to Sam to shrug and clear her throat. Richard and Ophelia whispered something I couldn't hear.

"I received the package last night when I stopped at Paddington's Play House. When I realized it was Gwendolyn's will, I called Finnigan to let him know what I'd found. Unfortunately, I left it locked in the office and had to head out of town for today. I'll be back tomorrow and can drop it off with him."

Finnigan added, "Correct. I will validate the will and we can reconvene again on Monday to go through it once I've had a chance to understand the last updates Gwendolyn made."

"Can't Kellan tell us what it says? That makes more sense," Sam added. He sounded genuine, but I hadn't been able to get a solid read on him since we'd met the previous week. "It's already hard enough thinking about Grandmother being gone, but to delay this any further seems a little excessive."

"I agree. I don't understand what he has to do with our family, anyway. I'm the one in the theater. Why couldn't Grandmother make me the representative? Why's Kellan in our business so much these days? Is he trying to steal the family money?" Dana growled.

"Exactly! This is ridiculous. Do something, Daddy," Lilly exclaimed. "I'm done here. I don't want to hear anything else until the situation is under control. Mom's the oldest, she should be in charge."

Millard rushed over to stop Lilly from leaving, sticking his finger in her face. "Listen, young lady. I've been through this many times before. I know how hard it is, but your behavior is inappropriate. I suggest you sit down and wait until we have further instructions." He turned to Finnigan and said, "Can't someone else get the document right now, so we can close this out today? It seems urgent."

"Unfortunately, that won't work. Gwendolyn's will was enclosed in another envelope specifically addressed to Finnigan Masters. I didn't open that one." I glanced back at the sheriff and nodded. "I asked Finnigan the same question, but since the initial envelope was addressed to me, I need to hand it off to Gwendolyn's attorney or executor, so there isn't any question about the authenticity of the will or that anything was altered since my receipt. I will be back tomorrow to hand deliver it to Finnigan."

I hung up the phone after listening to everyone disagree and express their frustrations. They were all planning to attend the *King Lear* performance that afternoon, since they'd never gotten to see it in its entirety the first time when Gwendolyn died during the second half. The sheriff remained behind to finish listening to the conversation, and I rushed off to Paddington's Play House. I was meeting Officer Flatman to hide out in the office in case anyone tried to break in to steal the will.

On the drive, I called Nana D to let her know what had happened. "I'm proud of you, brilliant one. You put yourself in the middle of this debacle and trapped the killer," Nana D said.

"Let's hope. I couldn't get a feel from the room. Everyone was upset, but it could've been that we wasted their time, or they didn't care about the money," I replied, pulling into the parking lot.

"What about Brad Shope? Have you talked to him yet?"

"I'm going to call him after I hang up with you and ask him to meet me at the theater. He knows nothing about the will, but if Brad's working with someone in the family, he or she probably notified him already." If Brad were conspiring with someone, he might be concerned that I wasn't out of town, but I'd dance around that issue if he brought it up. It would tell me someone went running to him as soon as the meeting had finished.

"Do you think Brad will try to steal the will or ask questions about it while he's with you at Paddington's Play House?" Nana D asked.

"The sheriff couldn't produce a way to tip off Brad about the new will, so she told me to invite him over afterward. It covers all our bases, but it might not amount to much in the end."

Nana D repeatedly made an excited gurgle. "I almost forgot to tell you. I talked to Sam. He's definitely hiding someone. He had a date and couldn't chat, but he wanted to talk about something. He said his grandmother told him to trust me if he ever needed help."

"I wonder what that's about. Do you think he accidentally did something to Gwendolyn and might confess to you?" I asked, not wanting to believe he had crossed such a horrific line.

"I don't think so, but he had something important he wanted to share. Let's see what happens because of this trap you've set. Besides, if you don't solve it today, we'll come up with another plan. I'm liking solving crimes with you, Kellan," Nana D teased.

"It is exciting, huh? Although, the sheriff knows something she's not telling me. I have a feeling she already guessed the killer's identity. She mentioned something about the Paddington family doing business with the Castigliano family." I still couldn't figure out the connection, but I knew it was important. Part of me wanted to call my in-laws, but I worried it could cause a bigger issue. I also assumed Francesca had already told them I wouldn't be returning to LA. Incurring their wrath was not something I looked forward to.

"It's a good thing you moved back to Braxton. It's a better thing you're getting away from those people. I never cared for them much. They'll bring you down, and no one hurts my grandson except me!" Nana D laughed once she finished speaking. I desperately wanted to tell her about Francesca being alive. She would tell me I did the right thing by staying in Braxton.

"I gotta go, Nana D. The sheriff is calling," I said, hanging up to accept April's call. "Everything okay?"

The sheriff said, "Yep. You did well. Richard and Ophelia left together. Sam's outside talking to Eustacia. Jennifer and Millard went to that room with the flowers. I saw them as I sneaked outside."

"You mean the Great Hall. What about Lilly and Dana? Did you hear their nasty remarks?"

"I've got a name for people like them," April taunted. "But as a lady, I refuse to say any more."

I kept my mouth shut. Not that I didn't think April was a lady. I was still having a tough time figuring out that fine line between annoying her and staying on her good side. "I'll let you know what happens at the theater, April. I'm looking forward to my time with Officer Flatman."

CHAPTER 22

When I entered the lobby of Paddington's Play House, I saw Arthur walking into the Box Office. I checked my watch and confirmed it was almost time for the theater to open for ticket sales. There was only a matinee performance today since they were still in pre-show for another two days. "Wait up, Arthur. I'll follow you inside," I yelled, jogging toward the door.

"Kellan, what are you doing here? I sent you a bunch of tickets for opening night next Monday." Arthur held the door as I approached. He wore a dark suit and tie highlighting Braxton's colors, burgundy and blue. There was a relaxed sense about him since I'd convinced Myriam to let him keep his job, at least through the end of this show. Based on how the entire run turned out, we could extend an offer for him to manage the next production or let him leave on a high note. Unless he turned out to be the killer, which was still a minor concern floating around the cobwebs inside my head.

"I'll be there, thank you very much. I'm bringing Emma, my parents, and my sister with me. They're all looking forward to it, but that's not why I'm here today." I was curious about his indiscretion in one of the dressing rooms and how it fit into the entire overall puzzle. I closed the door behind me, noticing it no longer got stuck. "I guess they fixed that door?"

Arthur nodded while he flipped on the lights in the Box Office. "Earlier this week. Remember the electrician that helped your sister out? Same crew, they're jacks-of-all-trades."

We chatted about the performance before I realized I needed to contact Brad. "I'm gonna hang around in the Paddington office while the show is on stage. Just wanted to verify you didn't mind," I said, searching his expression for any concerns.

"You've got carte blanche. My mother told me you spoke with Myriam to save my job. I still can't believe how vindictive that woman can be. Thank you."

He looked calm and grateful, no trace of fear about me being in the office. It didn't appear as if he knew about the will. I had the package with me, but I had to slip inside soon. I wasn't sure how quickly someone might dash over here from the Paddington estate. "It's unlocked. I was in there to drop off some mail. I need to go back and lock up, but I wanted to grab a few ads I'd left in here first. Maybe you can take them with you?"

"Sure," I said, taking the envelope. "Can you tell me what Myriam was so angry about?"

"Ummm, well... I had brought a friend with me that afternoon to the theater... and we ducked into a space I thought was private, but... well, Myriam overheard us sorta... well... you get the picture," Arthur said as his face reddened. "It was unplanned. Myriam made a tremendous deal out of it. And the next thing I know... she's blasting me with some silly quote from *A Midsummer Night's Dream*. That woman is so thickheaded, she's worse than dealing with the DMV!"

"You gotta be more careful with Dana," I said, despite knowing Myriam thought it was someone else. I needed to see if he'd tell me his partner's name. I was certain it had to be Sam.

"Dana? No, I told you last time. I'm staying clear of that tart. She's straight up crazy! I'm more interested in a quieter, calmer... well, never mind. The point is, I owned up to my mistake, and I won't do it again," Arthur explained before telling me he needed to verify there was enough cash in the Box Office windows for the ticket sellers.

I followed him out and walked down the hall toward the Paddington Office. Along the way, I called Brad, who said he would drop by shortly to talk with me. He didn't seem to know I was supposed to be out of town. I also ordered a pizza since I hadn't eaten lunch. I verified the will was in my briefcase, tossed the strap over my shoulder, and walked into the far corner. When I approached the office, I saw Officer Flatman and waved in his direction. I was going to call out to him, but my phone rang. It was Maggie, and I couldn't let it go to voice-mail. I had a massive apology to convey.

I picked up the phone and said, "You have absolutely every reason to be angry with me, but I truly have a valid excuse." I felt my forehead to verify the fever was still gone. My head was loopy from the medicine, and my eyes were sore from crying over Francesca, but my health was improving. I explained what'd happened with the medicine causing me to crash.

"I understand. You're worrying too much, Kellan." Her voice was gentle and caring, but I knew Maggie well enough to guess my no-show had disappointed her. "Connor filled in. I figured there was no reason to waste the table, so he popped over. I've thought about us a lot this morning."

I felt a twinge of jealousy when she indicated Connor had taken my place. I wanted to tell her the truth, but I also knew I'd had an exhausting and emotional day already and needed to be careful in what I shared. "Me, too. I was excited to have some time alone with you. I've only been back a few weeks, but it feels like we hardly connected."

"I feel the same way. I realized this morning that we've tried to have dinner several times, yet something always gets in the way. Maybe it's Eleanor rubbing off on me, but could the universe be trying to tell us something?" Maggie laughed just enough to reveal her discomfort. I could picture her playing with her earlobes, guessing how nervous the conversation made her.

My heart was feeling stabs of pain as she spoke, and I prepared my response. I knew what I had to do. "I'm inclined to agree. You're still figuring out how you feel about Connor. You only just moved back to Braxton, too."

"Same for you. And Francesca's death is much fresher than my husband's death. I know what you're going through. Reaching out in the middle of the night just to feel if the other side of the bed is warm. Buying things she used to love, then not having the strength to return them. It gets easier, Kellan." Maggie always put other people first. She was trying to comfort me, although I'd been the one to cancel on her.

"You're an amazing woman. I've loved you for so long, but maybe we're both not ready to jump into anything," I said, burying my face into my free hand and hoping it could stop the inevitable.

"And you're a terrific guy. You need time to figure out how to raise your daughter in a new town. Even though you've been back a few times, Braxton's different from a decade ago." Maggie sniffled through the phone. I imagined her dabbing her cheeks with a tissue but smiling as though we were next to each other.

She was right. I was still married in the eyes of the church and in my heart. The law might think Francesca was dead and allow me to move on, but it was only a fantasy or a facade the Castiglianos had created for the world to believe. "Let's agree to focus on rebuilding our friendship, Maggie. And maybe in a few months or a year, we'll be ready to talk about something else."

"I think that's perfect, Kellan." As she hung up, I reminded myself of Nana D's advice about things coming back once they'd been set free. I still wasn't certain whether it applied to Francesca or Maggie. I also had little time to indulge myself in anymore grief or loss in my personal life.

Officer Flatman arrived with the pizza. "I believe you ordered this. The guy said it was paid for, but I gave him a couple bucks tip."

"We needed something to eat. We could have a long afternoon ahead of us," I replied. He declined reimbursement for tipping the delivery guy. We walked to the Paddington office and scarfed down a few slices. While we ate, we talked about the case.

"Sheriff Montague met with the Paddington accountants again. That's where she learned the details about the transactions with the Castigliano family. Someone at Paddington Enterprises was using their services to import goods into the country. She's trying to find out exactly who was involved and what exactly it was," he explained. "Apparently, it has something to do with hiding drugs."

I was about to respond when Brad's number appeared on my cell phone. I picked up, and he told me he was in the main lobby. Officer Flatman shut off the lights and hid in the closet in the room's corner. I placed the will on the desk, then went to find Brad.

As I led him back to the room, I said, "I appreciate you coming by. I had a few things to discuss with you, but I needed to stick around the theater this afternoon as the family's representative while the show is in production."

"I understand, and it's kinda funny. Something came up that I should talk to you about, too," Brad replied as we entered the Paddington office. I saw him look at the desk and assumed he'd noticed the will.

"Listen, I need to get rid of this pizza box and bring something to the Box Office," I said to Brad as I walked back toward the hall. "Can you hang around for a few minutes? I'll be right back." Officer Flatman watched through a small crack in the closet door. If Brad tried to leave with it, he'd stop him.

I left and tossed the pizza box in the garbage. I wandered the main reception area, watching a few guests head into the theater as the show started. After five minutes passed, I walked back to the Paddington Office. "Sorry about that. All clear, we've got some time to talk alone." The will hadn't been moved. He'd either looked through it and put it back in the same place I'd left it, or he hadn't even bothered to touch it.

"No sweat. So, you first?" Brad said.

"Sure, I wanted to ask you a couple of things. I'm not gonna beat around the bush, so pardon if I'm being a bit blunt," I explained, hoping to catch a reaction from him.

"That's the best way to be. My mother taught me never to keep secrets nor to waste people's time. Money was precious to her, she worked hard to support me and had little freedoms." Brad leaned against the desk with his hands buried in his pockets.

"Great. So... first, it's come to my attention that you were the second witness when Gwendolyn changed her will the day before she died. I'm not sure why you didn't share that piece of information with me at any point."

"Oh, well, I—" Brad began, but I held my hand up.

"Let me talk first, then you'll have a chance, Brad." When he nodded, I continued. "Then, I learned you don't have your official nursing license or certification. You were denied after something happened at a previous hospital or nursing home with a mix-up on several patients' medications. Ironic given that's exactly what led to Gwendolyn's death." I watched him carefully, but he only opened his mouth to interrupt again.

"That's not how it happened. If you'd let me—"

"Please let me finish, this will be a lot easier," I said, knowing I came across like a tyrant. Desperate times called for desperate measures. "I know also that your mother, Hannah Shope, used to work at the Paddington mansion twenty-five years ago. In fact, she probably conceived you while she was employed there as a maid. Gwendolyn had run a DNA test to determine if you were related to her family."

Brad turned white, but he didn't speak. He tapped his foot and swallowed with heavy force.

"When I add all these things together, you must realize, it makes you look guilty of something. Whether it's murder or conspiracy to commit murder with someone else, I don't know. But I don't get that vibe from you. You're hiding something, that's for sure." I stepped toward him to grab the will in case he tried to do anything hasty. "Before I update the sheriff with all this news, is there anything you want to share with me?"

Brad nodded, then pulled his hand out of his pocket. He unfolded a piece of paper and handed it to me. "That's the DNA test. Gwendolyn helped me find someone to conduct it. If you'll give me a minute, I'll tell you everything I know. But right up front, I assure you, I had nothing to do with her death. There was no reason for me to hurt the woman."

I looked at the DNA results but couldn't understand any of the medical jargon. I didn't know which sample belonged to which person. "Okay, go ahead." I knew Officer Flatman was listening to the entire conversation, so I didn't worry about missing anything important related to the murder. I wanted to figure out how Brad fit into the Paddington family.

"I previously worked for someone who kept pressuring me to go on a date with her. After I said no and threatened to report her to the hospital and the medical board, she finally backed away. I was weeks away from obtaining my nursing degree when one of my patients got sick. A few days later, another patient passed away. Something didn't feel right, but I didn't want to jeopardize my chances of finally reaching my dreams to become a nurse. I knew the woman wanted to get revenge against me, but I couldn't prove anything. She essentially caused my license to be detained." Brad shook his head with contempt and frustration. He shared that the other girl had been the one playing games, not him.

"That's awful you were taken advantage of like that. I'm sorry. How did you end up in Braxton?" I said.

"When my mom was near the end, she talked a lot about growing up in Braxton. With no job or family left, I moved here and got a new job as a nurse. I just need to get my formal certification."

"Okay, but that doesn't explain how you met Gwendolyn."

"I'd been working at the rehabilitation facility where she was recuperating. I didn't work in her wing, but she was friendly with one of my patients. I'd told my patient that my mom had worked at the Paddington household years ago. Next thing I know, Gwendolyn called and asked if I would be interested in becoming her private nurse. My former patient had told the story to Gwendolyn. I was upset at first, but it turned out to be a tremendous help."

If Gwendolyn had been aware of the baby, she might have realized Brad could be related to her. That's probably why she hired him, so she had access to get a sample of his DNA and find out more for herself. "Did you tell Gwendolyn about your mother?"

"I didn't have to. A few weeks after I began working for her, she brought it up. I wasn't interested in finding out my father's identity, but she kept pressuring me. She told me that a mistake had been made years ago, and if she was correct about my father, I would want to know the truth." Brad looked deeply upset. His face shrank and wrinkled as though he had little control over his feelings in that moment.

"Did she take this DNA test with your consent? Or behind your back?"

"I eventually agreed to. I was never interested in the money, just knowing more about my father and his family. Gwendolyn and I became friends over the last few weeks. She didn't need a nurse anymore. Just someone to talk to. Someone to keep her from being lonely and bored in the house. You've seen how awful that family is."

By the way he said *that family*, I believed he wasn't one of them. "I've seen them behave like animals. What do these results prove?"

"I'm not a Paddington. She thought Millard was my father, but he can't be. I don't share any DNA with Millard or Ophelia. Gwendolyn wasn't a Paddington by blood, so they couldn't try to match hers."

I was shocked at the response. He didn't appear to be lying. "Did she figure out his identity?"

Brad shook his head. "If she did, Gwendolyn didn't tell me. We got the results from that first DNA test the day before she died. She told me she had ordered a second one based on a hunch, but then she died the next day."

"How did you come to be the witness to sign her new will?"

"After she got home from your grandmother's house, she called Bertha and me into her room and asked us to sign the will. She filled in the new names, but I didn't see who would inherit everything. And then I left."

"So, you have no idea about your father's identity?" If it wasn't a Paddington, who else had been in the house that might have been Hannah's lover twenty-five years ago?

"Nope. For a while, I tried to get to know everyone in the family. I hoped maybe I would be related to them, not because I liked them but because I have no other family. Ever since my mother died, I've been on my own. My mother had no siblings, and her parents passed away before I was born."

Brad had no reason to kill Gwendolyn. "Thanks for sharing the DNA results with me. Is that what you meant when you said you had something to talk to me about?"

"Yes, I've been keeping it a secret from everyone because I didn't want the family to think I was trying to insert myself once Gwendolyn had passed away. Then Eustacia hired me to be her part-time nurse, and I started feeling guilty. I thought I'd talk to you first to help decide what to tell them."

I informed Brad that the DNA facility had told me they would be in contact with him soon with the results of the second test. I knew Brad's parentage wouldn't matter to the Paddingtons, but it was more important to figure out what this meant in relation to Gwendolyn being murdered over the change in her will. When he left, Brad pulled the door closed, and it automatically locked. I checked with Officer Flatman, who confirmed that Brad never touched the will while he was alone in the office.

We sat, pondering the entire situation, but failed to solve the puzzle. After an hour, we both heard someone trying to open the door handle. Officer Flatman studied me with large, excited eyes, and whispered, "Maybe that's the killer trying to get the will?"

I agreed and gently tossed the will back on the desk. I quickly shut out the lights, then quietly rushed into the closet and pulled the door shut. As we hovered in the darkness, I worried the person trying to enter the room was just an employee but remembered this was a private office the Paddingtons kept locked at all times. Besides the cleaning crew, Myriam, and Arthur, no one else had a key.

A few seconds later, we heard the door unlock. Someone turned on the lights and walked toward the desk. I couldn't determine their identity because he or she had been quick to get to the desk before there was enough light in the room. When the person turned around, I let out a quiet gasp. Everything made complete sense once I saw who'd shown up to steal the will. How could I have been such a fool not to guess who'd killed Gwendolyn?

CHAPTER 23

Richard Taft went directly to the desk and inspected the envelope. He didn't know that it was a fake copy I'd made that morning before leaving my parents' house. I didn't want to risk the real will being stolen, so I'd opened the envelope addressed to Finnigan and replaced the contents with a letter that read *'Surprise, this isn't the will you've been searching for!'*

As Richard opened the envelope and read the note, he muttered out loud, "What kinda trick is that Ayrwick dimwit up to?" He rifled through the rest of the papers on the desk but found nothing else. The real will idled in Finnigan's hands, as I'd lent it to the sheriff before I left the Paddington estate. She'd promised to give it back to Finnigan on her way out. Richard paced through the office, grumbling and slamming his fist on the desk. "That woman tried to chase me out of town for the last twenty-five years, but I got rid of her first. I'll find that will if it's the last thing I do!"

And that was my cue. I hadn't expected him to confess to the crime, and maybe it wouldn't hold up in court, but Officer Flatman and I both heard him say he'd done something to Gwendolyn. Flatman told me to step out of the closet first, and he'd stay behind to keep listening from his hidden vantage point. I heard a round of thunderous applause coming from inside the main theater, which meant the intermission was just beginning. I had a few minutes left to get a full confession out of Richard.

I stepped into the office while his back was to me, then closed the door almost all the way. "Did you find what you were looking for, Richard?"

He turned around with a snarl on his face and practically spat at me. "What's going on here? Where's the will? This isn't any of your business."

"Isn't that the will in your hands? Surely, it's what you came here looking for," I said calmly. "I must admit, you weren't on my radar for the last week. You've done a fantastic job coming and going so often that you were pretty much background noise. Until now." I stared him down like I was preparing for a kill shot.

"You don't have any clue what you're talking about. I just thought I'd help since I was at the show. What kind of games are you playing, telling us you left the will in the office and went out of town? You're right here, and this is a stupid note from an even stupider woman!" He stepped toward me with a panicked yet dangerous fury spreading across his face.

"I'd say Gwendolyn was pretty smart to change her will when she did. Look in the mirror before you throw stones, Richard. Did you kill her, so Ophelia would inherit all the money? Is your wife in on this with you?" I sized him up as I stood there, realizing he was several pounds heavier than me. I didn't see any sort of weapon, but I couldn't be certain.

"I guess I can tell you the complete story. It's not like you'll be around to share it with anyone else," he replied in a menacing tone while his gaze narrowed. "How much do you know already?"

As long as I stayed adjacent to the closet door, Officer Flatman could jump out at any moment to stop Richard from hurting me. I dug deep to play a role and get the answers in case he got away from us. I vaguely recalled Eustacia telling me Ophelia had just gotten married and she and Richard were living in the Paddington estate when the new maid started working there. I'd forgotten previously. "Were you friendly with a woman named Hannah Shope right around the time you got married? Perhaps twenty-five or twenty-six years ago sounds familiar?"

"It seems you've found out a lot of personal information in the last few days. Too bad it's not gonna help save you." He clenched his hands into giant fists.

"Let me see if I understand what happened," I implored, hoping to gain the upper hand before he attacked me. "You and Hannah were having an affair, even though you'd just married Ophelia. When Hannah told Gwendolyn she was pregnant, Gwendolyn thought it was Millard's baby. But it wasn't. It was yours. Only you didn't know until recently."

"I had no clue Hannah was pregnant. The Paddingtons sent her away, telling no one. I came home one night, and she was gone. Gwendolyn said Hannah had quit and left no forwarding contact information. I tried to find her those first few weeks, but I couldn't. That's when I realized I was stuck with Ophelia."

Although I could empathize with his pain, I'd never commit murder because of it. "Here's where I'm a little confused about what happened. You stayed married to Ophelia and had several kids but kept taking assignments out of town because you couldn't stand to be around her. Why did you suddenly feel the need to kill Gwendolyn now?" I knew it had something to do with the DNA test and Brad mysteriously showing up, but I couldn't pinpoint exactly what had changed.

"For years, Charles doted on his wayward son. Timothy got the family business. Timothy was set to inherit the family estate when Gwendolyn died. But behind the scenes, I was doing all the work. I secured new lines of business. I kept the operations running at Paddington Enterprises. I accepted my role until one day when Timothy and I were out at a club, and he started using recreational drugs. If he was going to hurt himself, maybe it wasn't so bad if I made it a little easier for that to happen. I decided to push him into trying different drugs until he became addicted. Cocaine was his downfall."

"And then he started gambling and screwing up several deals at the office because he was high or at various casinos betting too much?"

"Exactly. When Charles had the Board remove Timothy, I thought it would finally be my chance, but no, it never happened. Charles put Timothy out on a one-year leave of absence while he turned the company over to a silly leadership team who knew nothing about the organization. I was ignored just as they'd ignored Ophelia all those years. That pompous fool's a drug addict and almost lost the company!"

"And you wanted revenge?" I could see Richard unraveling in pieces.

"Charles died, Timothy was out. Gwendolyn had been depressed, broken her hip, and checked into the hospital. I should've been given the keys to Paddington Enterprises. Then Gwendolyn confronted me about the affair with Hannah from years ago. She'd found out about it and threatened to tell Ophelia. I thought it was buried."

"When the first DNA test failed to prove Brad was a Paddington, Gwendolyn realized it was you. That's when she had the second DNA test to be certain before telling anyone." I asked, assembling the whole sordid picture together.

"And my pre-nuptial agreement with Ophelia stated I got nothing if I had an affair." A wicked grin smiled back to me. Richard Taft was a cunning man. "I couldn't acknowledge Brad as my son."

"So, you switched Gwendolyn's medicine with placebos. Is Dana in on this deceit with you?" I worried he wasn't the only person in the family who'd tried to kill Gwendolyn.

"No, my daughter had no idea I stole them from her. It was a coincidence when she told me she'd located them for the next show at the theater. The sun was shining on me that day. I could slowly kill Gwendolyn and watch her suffer the way she made me suffer all these years. It just took too long."

"That's when you concocted a plan to overdose her with the cocaine?"

"I told her I couldn't go to the show. I went to LA for a quick deal and returned early Sunday morning on a private plane. I made it look like I'd taken a flight back after I heard the news Gwendolyn had passed away." Richard had little shame or remorse over his actions. He assumed no one would request an autopsy, and if they did, it'd incriminate to Timothy.

"How did you get the cocaine?"

"Hah! That's easy. One line of business I started with Paddington Enterprises is a front for smuggling drugs in and out of the country. I took some from the shipment and gave it to Timothy, so he'd have a long supply to keep destroying his life. I kept enough to put in Gwendolyn's medication that morning."

"When did you make the swap?" I asked.

"I snuck into the house Sunday morning after my plane landed and when everyone was still sleeping. I hid downstairs while everyone ate brunch." Richard stepped closer to me, scanning the room for a weapon.

"That's when you saw the bottle sitting on the table in the hallway. You knew Gwendolyn would take them at the show, so you dropped the replacement ones laced with cocaine into the bottle," I added, realizing he'd had an advantage sneaking around and knowing all the hiding spots.

"Unfortunately, that interfering grandmother of yours was coming back down the hall, and in the rush, I knocked the pill bottle to the floor."

"Clever... to think you almost got away with it." I blurted, recalling the company he was working with was Castigliano International. That meant my in-laws were involved in smuggling drugs. Did Francesca know anything about this dastardly side of the family business?

"I will get away with it. Just as soon as you tell me where the new will is. As it stands, Ophelia inherits a quarter of her mother's estate with the old will," he said with the smile of a devil growing wider with each moment that passed. "Now hand it over, and I'll be very gentle when I kill you."

Officer Flatman stepped out of the closet with his gun pointed directly at Richard at exactly that moment. "I don't think so. Put your hands up."

Richard grabbed hold of a bookcase on the wall to his right and pushed it toward us, providing him enough time to rush down the hall. While Officer Flatman and I shoved the books and the shelves out of our way, Richard opened the door and ran into the hall, not realizing guests were leaving the performance. As he tried to dash toward exit, Eustacia stuck out her cane, causing him to fall to the ground. The sheriff rushed across the lobby, pushing a few guests out of her way, and aimed old Betsy at Richard. Officer Flatman and I soon followed and surrounded them, so there could be no available escape route.

Eustacia guffawed. "That's the fool responsible for Gwennie's death?"

"Yes, ma'am," I said, leaning against the side wall. In the scuffle, I'd lost my breath and felt sick from over-exertion. It was wearing me down to the point I was almost going to pass out again.

Ophelia and her children dashed over to see why Richard was being put in handcuffs. Officer Flatman said, "He confessed to killing Gwendolyn while we were in the office. Not only that, but he also admitted to having an affair with Hannah Shope twenty-five years ago."

"And Brad is Richard's secret son," I added, watching Ophelia's eyes glare like a laser.

Lilly looked at her father and shrieked. "He's my half-brother? How could you do that to Mom?"

Dana turned to Jennifer, who stood nearby. "I don't understand it. How could he never tell us?"

When I caught my breath, I saw Nana D, Lindsey, and Millard comforting Eustacia. Ophelia rebuked Richard as Sheriff Montague handed him off to Officer Flatman to read him his Miranda rights. Sam looked shocked and devastated. He wasn't sure whom to turn to and kept shaking his head. When I walked toward him to ask if he was okay, he took off and never looked back.

Sheriff Montague approached me. "Excellent job, Little Ayrwick. Flatman informs me you convinced Richard to keep talking, so he could tell you exactly how everything happened."

"For some reason, I wasn't surprised to see him show up in the office when he did. It took putting him in the right environment for me to realize he'd been behind everything the whole time." I watched Eustacia turn to Lindsey, then I noticed Nana D's response. She still cared for Lindsey, even though she'd been backing away to let Eustacia have a chance with him. It was rare to see Nana D look disheartened, but I knew it wasn't the first time.

"Don't feel bad. He wasn't on my radar at first either. Then I got a tip about the Paddington and Castigliano business connections. That's what led me to seeing who signed the deal between the two companies. It was Richard," the sheriff noted as she idly ran a hand through her bristly hair. "If those drug deals happened in Wharton County, I'm going to make it a big focus in the coming weeks to nail those dirty traffickers. I read up on that Castigliano mob. They are one vicious family, but I'm not afraid of them. I'll take them down one by one if I have to." April's determined stare shot right through me.

All I knew is I needed to get some sleep. "I'm sure if anyone could take down the Castiglianos, it'd be you, April."

"Yep. Maybe I'll have to call on you for help. I don't like to admit when I'm wrong, but this is twice in a row you've stuck out your neck to protect our town. I'm not saying I misjudged you, so don't let that pretty boy head of yours swell up any larger than it already has. I'll call you next week to discuss my plans a little further." As the sheriff left Paddington's Play House, I wobbled my head in disbelief. I kept telling myself I wanted to prove to that woman I was better than her. But she wanted to talk with me about working together. What was wrong with me? It's like I wanted to repeatedly punish myself. Wasn't there a support group for those kinds of people?

"Kellan! What took you so long to figure this one out? I could've told you Richard Taft was a no-good loser," Nana D chided as she stepped away from her fellow septuagenarians and sidled up next to me to share her diatribe. "You look like death. Here, take this bottle of juice. I just opened it."

"Thanks, Nana D." I was tempted to ask her if she put cocaine it, but it was too soon to crack such a joke. "Just juice, right?"

"Would I poison you? Seriously, drink it. You really need to listen more closely. I told you that family was trying to kill poor Gwennie from the first day it came up at Danby Landing. But no... you wouldn't take it seriously until she keeled over in your lap. What kind of sleuth are you?"

I understood why I was constantly subjected to relationships like the ones I had with April and Myriam. I was surrounded by sassy women who liked to torture me. If I loved Nana D, did that mean one day I'd grow to love April and Myriam, too? My stomach ground and churned. I feared if I didn't do something soon, we'd have a situation in the lobby of Paddington's Play House. I was about to drop to the ground to take a well-deserved nap when an unexpected commotion brewed nearby.

"Jennifer, I heard what happened. I was stuck backstage. I'm so sorry. Are you okay?" Arthur rattled off before reaching us and hugging her. "Please tell me nothing happened to you or our baby!"

"Baby? Arthur is your baby daddy? You're cheating on me with my aunt? She's like ancient and close to my mom's age. I can't believe it," Dana shouted and beat Arthur's chest.

"I'm going to be a grandmother," Fern said, covering her mouth in shock as she joined the group.

Arthur grabbed Dana's wrists and stopped her from attacking him. "Enough, Dana. I've told you from the first day you tried to seduce me, I'm not interested. You're a little girl who throws temper tantrums when she doesn't get what she wants. You've heaved yourself at every guy within a five-foot radius. You'll never be anything like your aunt and need to stay away from us and our baby."

"You're a monster. I can't believe I ever liked you," Dana snarled while looking around, but her mother had already left with Officer Flatman when he'd escorted Richard Taft to the precinct. "I'll get even with you, Aunt Jennifer! This isn't the end. I'm a Paddington, too!"

As Dana stomped off, Lilly grabbed her sister's wrist. "Dad was just arrested for killing Grandmother. We have a new half-brother named Brad. Sam's taken off, and we don't know where he is. I think our family has enough to deal with, little sister. Grow up and stop being such a child!"

While Lilly's words were highly appropriate, she hadn't been the best role model in the past. As Lilly and Dana departed the lobby, I nodded at Fern, hoping she interpreted my mixed show of congratulations and sympathy for her. Fern and Arthur would be forever tied to the Paddington family.

I said goodbye to Nana D and drove home to finally get some sleep. I checked with my parents, who confirmed they were staying over in Philadelphia one more night and would bring Emma back the following evening, so she'd get plenty of rest before school on Monday. I verified Francesca's flight had taken off, which meant she was mid-air back to Los Angeles. I had no calls from the Castiglianos threatening me. Francesca likely hadn't told them my decision yet. Perhaps I would wake up with a brand-new focus and outlook on my life.

As I pulled into the driveway at the Royal Chic-Shack, Ursula Power stepped out of her car and waved me down. What was my boss doing at my house on a Saturday evening? After stepping to my car window, Ursula said, "Something urgent has come up, and I need your advice. Don't tell anyone, especially Myriam. She can't know how much trouble I'm in. You're my only hope."

I wasn't sure how to respond, but I needed downtime before I could take anything else on. "Sure, can we meet tomorrow? I'm about to pass out."

Ursula hesitated before leaving. "Yes, but this is important. My past has come back to haunt me, and I don't know how long before it explodes again."

"I promise. We can meet for dinner tomorrow if you'd like."

Ursula nodded and got back into her car. Before shutting the door, she turned toward me and said, "If I may speak freely, Kellan... you need a haircut. That mop on your head is ridiculous. I've been waiting weeks to see if you'd fix it, but I need to step in before it gets any worse. You're looking like a punk rock star and not in a good way." Ursula pulled out her phone and typed something. "Check your text messages. I've sent you the name and number of my stylist. He'll be able to save you from further embarrassment."

CHAPTER 24

I woke up on Sunday morning to a flurry of messages and what felt like an entirely new body. All the over-the-counter drugs I'd taken must have finally kicked my cold symptoms to the curb. I was glad I didn't develop a full-on flu, as I had no time to rest with everything suddenly heating up in Braxton. Even though I'd solved the latest murder, I couldn't help but worry the hits were going to keep on coming. Something in the air told me I was only given a temporary reprieve and that I should prepare for a bigger battle. Eleanor would tell me the stars were warning me to stay in bed all day. I went through my missed messages, then got in touch with everyone to organize my day before seeing Ursula for dinner. Nana D was the first person I followed up with.

Me: *I'm a whole new man this morning. Life is good.*
Nana D: *I knew you just needed one of my special cures to fix you.*
Me: *What are you talking about?*
Nana D: *You didn't think that was just juice yesterday? I added a few things.*
Me: *You drugged me? I knew you were up to something. Wait, why didn't it taste bad?*
Nana D: *Surely you don't expect me to give away all my secrets?*
Me: *You should be locked away somewhere. There's something wrong with you.*
Nana D: *Eh, I'm not gonna argue with you based on what I did last night.*

I replied and called a few times, but Nana D didn't explain her last line. I assumed I'd see her soon at the Paddington thank you brunch being held in my honor. I showered, dressed, and headed to the Paddingtons, fearing whatever first disaster awaited me. Bertha greeted and led me to the Great Hall. "Is my nana here, too?"

Bertha shook her head. "No, Kellan. Eustacia and Seraphina had a minor disagreement last night. She won't be attending brunch today."

I suspected it had to do with Eustacia turning to Lindsey at the theater. "Are you able to share what caused this minor disagreement?"

"Well, I'm not exactly certain how it began this time. They were fine yesterday when Seraphina came by for dinner. Until Councilman Stanton showed up. Things got a little ugly," Bertha said as she buried her hands in her face. "It took me three hours to get those stains off the wallpaper in the dining room last night."

"Ummm... are you saying they had a food fight?" I pictured Nana D throwing a handful of asparagus or broccoli at the councilman. She didn't know when to stop and would get herself locked up again if she didn't learn to control her distaste for that man.

"If only it were that simple. It all started out calmly, but then Lindsey said he agreed with one of Councilman Stanton's new political plans. He was donating to the campaign, it seems. Seraphina wasn't too happy about that."

"I don't blame her. I thought the Septuagenarian Club was supporting my nana!" What could've gone wrong to cause such a change?

"That's when Seraphina grabbed the entire pot of meatballs and sauce I'd put on the table. It was buffet style last night since we weren't originally expecting company, but then they all showed up. Seraphina is stronger than she looks!" Bertha wiped her hands with the bottom of her apron.

"What exactly happened?" I asked, alarmed over how the night had ended up.

"I'm not sure how to tell you this, Kellan. Seraphina started racing around the room, throwing meatballs at everyone like it was a war zone. One by one, she picked them out of the saucepan and tossed them like little water balloons. When she was all out of meatballs, she dumped the entire pot of sauce over someone's head."

"Over Lindsey's head? Or the councilman's? Either way, that's horrible!"

"No, Kellan. Over Eustacia's head. Seraphina told her it was payback for inviting the devil into their little party and being a ruthless jezebel trying to steal Lindsey again. I don't know what she was talking about, but your nana was a possessed woman." Bertha and I reached the Great Hall. She stopped before I stepped toward the fountain and pool. I couldn't help but think about the water wheel plant and its need to keep eating meat.

"I guess Eustacia wasn't too happy with my nana, huh?" I felt the need to stifle my laughter. The devil was likely Marcus Stanton, which made sense, but to call Eustacia a jezebel in front of everyone was not productive nor a truly kind comment.

"Nope. Apparently, Eustacia set the whole thing up as a trick to convince the councilman that he had the Paddington support, then they would rip it away from him at the next big debate. Eustacia just forgot to tell Seraphina in advance," Bertha said before she walked toward the kitchen. "Silly women!"

And Nana D had started her rivalry back up again with Eustacia. This was going to be quite a mess for me to solve. "Why do you do this to me?" I said out loud, looking up through the glass dome at the sky. I didn't expect anyone to respond, but when a voice did, I startled.

"You're the only one who can control her, Kellan." Millard had been standing in the Great Hall not too far away and had heard the whole conversation. "There's not much time left. We need to get Seraphina and Eustacia talking again if there's any hope for your grandmother to win the mayoral race."

"I believe you're right, Mr. Paddington. I'll talk to Nana D this afternoon. You convince Eustacia to give her another chance. We'll get them together tomorrow to figure it out," I said, shaking his hand.

"I'm glad to see you today. I wanted to thank you for helping my family. I think we're in for some rough times soon, but ultimately, it's the best thing to happen to us in years. With Richard out of our lives, and Timothy finally getting help, this family might reclaim the power and respect we once had." Millard and I took a seat near some fruit trees to his right. The scent of lemons and limes was overwhelming, yet comforting in a way I desperately needed.

"What's gonna happen at Paddington Enterprises now?"

"I will step in and help for a few months. Just until Timothy finishes his recovery at Second Chance Reflections. Once he gets back, we'll talk about getting Ophelia's son and daughters involved in the family business. They're still young, but I think we can get them focused." Millard ruffled his moustache when he finished speaking.

"Sounds like a good plan. What about Brad? How does he fit into all of this? He's not a Paddington, but he's tied into the family now," I asked, feeling bad for the nurse. He finally learned whom his father was only to discover the man had murdered someone to keep the news quiet.

"Brad's staying on to help Eustacia. She's gonna sell her place at Willow Trees and run the Paddington estate for a while. At least until she decides if Ophelia or Jennifer will step up to the plate for this family."

"Speaking of Ophelia, I had a question about something I saw the other day. You handed her an envelope that looked like it was from a bank." I felt awkward asking Millard about a private affair, but leaving it unaddressed would bother me forever.

"Yes, that... I believe Gwennie's final letter should explain everything. Eustacia found it last night after everyone left. It was inside her cane, that's what she meant by Eustacia *needing it to live* each day. When she dropped her cane last night, the bottom part fell off and out rolled the letter. My sister-in-law always knew how to motivate the rest of this family. I suppose Gwennie lost confidence in herself after Charles died, but this shows she would've gotten us aligned again. As much as it hurts, Gwennie's death served a purpose," Millard noted, handing me the letter she'd mentioned in the will.

To my family...

Ever since I lost Charles, my life hasn't been the same. His death impacted me in ways I never expected. We did the best we could to raise our three children and lead by example for our grandchildren. On some levels, we were successful. On others, we were not. I'm not sure how much time I have left on this planet... but should anything happen to me before I've fixed things, I leave behind these final thoughts.

Millard, you've been a wonderful brother-in-law to me and uncle to my children. You had a soft spot for my girls ever since they were rebellious teenagers and hoped one day to teach them how to be better people. While I didn't enjoy finding out you'd been giving money to Ophelia, so she could support herself and that fool of a husband, I know it was done with good intentions. It needs to stop until she learns how to help herself. I also need to correct your father's wrong when he left you out of his will. I've left behind a portion of the estate for you to administer on behalf of my daughters and to use at your own discretion. When they grow up and fix their immaturity, you can share some of the inheritance with them. Do something nice for yourself, too. Thank you for always being there for us.

Timothy, I'm glad you got help. You screwed up in the past, but of all my kids, you're the one finally getting better. I'm thrilled you've checked yourself into the rehabilitation facility and can't wait to see your progress. It was a mistake to remove you from the will years ago, so you're back in. Take care of your sisters. Find yourself a wife and have some kids. You're not getting any younger, but I think this is just the start of your new life.

Jennifer, I'm truly sorry we fought so much in the past, but you need to stop blaming me for your mistakes. I will always regret slapping you that day on the stairs, especially since it led to you falling and losing your precious child. Now is the time to get your life in order. If you want to be a better person, get a job and stop chasing after no-good men. Find someone worthy of you. Once you've proven to Millard that you can stop being a whiny and petulant girl, he'll share the inheritance, so you can have another chance at becoming a mother through that ridiculous fertilization clinic. It makes little sense why you can't do this the old-fashioned way, but good luck to you.

Ophelia, your husband is a louse. Someone's been stealing money from our accounts, and while I don't know if it's you or him, it needs to stop. I've ordered a DNA test to prove he cheated on you years ago. The results will be sent to the gentleman I believe is his son, but in case anything happens to me, I wanted you to know what he'd done in the past. You need to grow up and set a better example for your children. I'm teaching you a lesson here, and you better pay attention. Leave Richard. Be a better mother. Work at the family company. Millard will get you a position, so you can turn your life around, and maybe then he'll give you some of my inheritance. I believe in you.

Lilly and Dana, there's not much to say right now. You're both spiteful and spoiled. So was I at your age. Grow up. Stop relying on men to make you happy. Make something out of yourselves and your lives will amount to something better. If Lilly's business has that much potential, prove it to Millard. Work together on it, and he'll guide you through all the necessary steps.

Sam, of everyone in the family, you've always been the most precious to me. Not a day went by when you didn't sit with me at the hospital or at the estate during my recovery. You're the future of this family. You need to make those sisters of yours see reality. You need to find a way to love your mother more, even if she's been difficult with you. I know you're struggling with a big decision, and I'm sorry we fought about it before I died. This family's not exactly open-minded, but in time, they'll be okay with what you tell them. And based on what you'll eventually tell them, I suspect things are gonna get a lot more complicated. I'm leaving you part of my estate because I believe you'll be the one to steer this family back to greatness. Don't disappoint me, or I'll haunt you from beyond.

Eustacia, you've been my best friend in the family for most of our lives. It's your job to keep this family on the right track. That's why I left this note in your beloved cane. Your lifeblood. Everyone should have the right to live at the family estate, and I want you to oversee the place. You decide what happens to it on your own time. Perhaps someone in this family will step up and show us they're worthy.

Gwendolyn must have known she was getting sicker, or she truly believed someone was going to kill her. She died without confirmation that Richard was Brad's father, which meant she probably never knew it was Richard who'd been trying to kill her all along. After I handed the letter back to Millard and we said our goodbyes, Brad walked into the Great Hall. We exchanged a quick greeting, then he thanked me for helping him find his father. Eustacia had called him after the arrest at the theater to reveal the secret. "You've been a good friend. I need some of those if I'm going to stick around this town and live with the knowledge Richard Taft is my father."

"You've got two half-sisters and a half-brother to get to know. I think maybe you'll be a beneficial influence on them. At least Lilly and Dana. They've been left to their own devices for far too long. Sam's a good kid. I just can't figure him out," I said, hoping Brad might take his younger brother under his wing.

"Sam's a cool guy. He confided in me this morning that he's met someone and previously told Gwendolyn all about it. She was accepting of his life choices, which was a good thing to see. Not all families are supportive when someone comes out of the closet." Brad would be an exemplary role model for his younger siblings with that attitude. "I'm meeting with the DNA facility tomorrow. They will have the second test completed, but it looks like I already know the answer. Huh, Richard Taft, a murderer!"

"I'm so sorry it turned out this way. I wish you luck getting your nursing license. If I can help, my late wife used to be a nurse. I know a bit about what it takes to get that completed," I explained before saying goodbye. Brad and I made plans to grab drinks the following week to discuss everything. I needed to make some new friends, and since he was cleared of any suspicion, he'd be a great guy to hang out with.

Since the brunch was cancelled because of last night's catfight and meatball extravaganza, I headed to my favorite eatery. I pulled into Pick-Me-Up Diner's parking lot at the same time as Maggie. We walked inside together, doing our best to abide by the conversation we'd had the prior day.

"So, we're friends, right?" she said with a giant grin.

"I think so. I'm ready to reconnect and do things together like other friends do," I said.

"Friends hug one another, right?" Maggie said.

"They certainly do," I replied and stepped closer toward her. When we embraced, I knew there would always be something between us, but I also knew it wasn't the right time to explore it again. "Come on, let's go inside and see how your new diner's doing since opening last week."

Maggie talked to the chef while I tracked down Eleanor. "Hey sis, tell me all about your day. I think it's time we stopped talking about me and started talking about you."

"Wow! I lead a dull life. I don't have a back-from-the-dead wife, killers trying to do away with me, or mayoral campaigns blowing up in my face. I'd say you're the one with the stuff to talk about," Eleanor teased with a mouth full of sarcasm and a piece of apple pie.

"Really? You don't call visiting a fertility clinic *something to talk about*? It might be none of my business, but I've been telling you everything about my life. So, spill it. What's going on?" I pushed her into the office and shut the door.

"You can't tell anyone," she demanded, barely able to contain her glee. "I've decided to have a baby. I know it's a crazy idea, but I want a child. And I'm not getting any younger. I'm only thirty, but this feels like the right time. I could wait until I find the right guy and do everything the old-fashioned way, but the stars have been pointing me in this direction for months. I finally listened."

"And what exactly did they say?" I wasn't sure how I felt about her decision, but she was my sister and I'd support her in any way she needed.

"They said I should stop waiting for things to happen and go after what I want. I'm gonna do it. I've just got to figure out who's gonna be the father!" Eleanor tossed her hands in the air and did her version of a happy dance that looked more like a drunken macarena to me. "What do you think?"

I wanted to tell her she was doing too much at once between assuming ownership of the diner, going after Connor, and trying to become a single mother. But if I could do it, so could she, I ended up deciding. "I think it's fantastic. I don't want to know any of the details on how you get pregnant."

"You really need to grow up. Didn't I already tell you this recently? Nana D is right, you can be a giant baby sometimes," Eleanor chided, then asked me to go with her to the clinic the following week to discuss her options. She needed to pick out a sperm donor and wanted my input. The things I did for my family were getting way too weird.

As I stepped into the parking lot, I cleared my head of everything except heading home to spend the afternoon with my parents and Emma once they arrived. I walked to the last parking row and was about to unlock the SUV with my remote when I noticed Sam talking to someone near the sidewalk.

At first, I looked the other way, not wanting to intrude and knowing how uncomfortable he'd been around me. I had no idea why I made him so nervous, but if he didn't want to talk with me, I had no choice but to respect his wishes. Then I had to step into the space between my SUV and the car next to it, so I could leave. As I turned, I found myself close enough to witness Sam lean in to kiss whomever he'd been speaking to. It was the kind of kiss you only see in movies when two people who love each other finally give in to their passions and don't care what the world has to say about it.

Given I could be as nosy as Nana D, I might have stared longer than I should've, hoping to glimpse the guy he was making out with on the pathway. If it wasn't Arthur or Brad, I was clueless. When Sam pulled away, I got the shock of my life.

Sam Taft was kissing someone I knew—my brother. Not only was Gabriel back in Braxton and hadn't told any of us, but it also seemed he'd been keeping another big secret, too. I stood paralyzed for a few seconds. Should I interrupt them? Was I supposed to hide, so they didn't see me? Maybe that's why Sam had been so nervous around me. He knew I was Gabriel's brother. Before I could decide what to do, my cell phone rang.

I knew they'd heard it too, so I dropped to my knees and hid on the side of the SUV. I glanced at the phone's screen only to curse when I saw it was Cecilia Castigliano. I grudgingly pressed accept and whispered, "Hi. I can't talk right now. I'll call you back in a few minutes. I'm guessing Francesca told you what I decided."

"No, Kellan. She didn't tell me anything because she never got on the flight back home. Francesca is missing, and I blame this entirely on you. What did you do to my daughter?"

FLOWER POWER TRIP

BRAXTON CAMPUS MYSTERIES BOOK 3

ACKNOWLEDGMENTS

Writing a book is not an achievement an individual person can accomplish on his or her own. There are always people who contribute in a multitude of ways, sometimes unwittingly, throughout the journey from discovering the idea to drafting the last word. *Flower Power Trip: A Braxton Campus Mystery* has had many supporters since its inception in December 2018, but before the concept even sparked in my mind, my passion for writing was nurtured by others.

First thanks go to my parents, Jim and Pat, for always believing in me as a writer as well as teaching me how to become the person I am today. Their unconditional love and support have been the primary reason I'm accomplishing my goals. Through the guidance of my extended family and friends, who consistently encouraged me to pursue my passion, I found the confidence to take chances in life. With Winston and Baxter by my side, I was granted the opportunity to make my dreams of publishing this novel come true. I'm grateful to everyone for pushing me each day to complete this third book.

Flower Power Trip was cultivated through the interaction, feedback, and input of several talented beta readers. I'd like to thank Shalini G, Laura Albert, Anne Foster, Mary Deal, Misty Swafford, Anne Jacobs, Nina D. Silva, Candace Robinson, Lisa M. Berman, Carla @ CarlaLovesToRead, and Valerie for supplying insight and perspective during the development of the story, setting, and character arcs. I am indebted to them for finding all the proofreading misses, grammar mistakes, and awkward phrases.

- A special call-out goes to Shalini for countless conversations helping me to fine-tune every aspect of the setting, characters, and plot. She read every version and offered a tremendous amount of her time to advise me on this book over several weeks. I am beyond grateful for her help. Any mistakes are my own from misunderstanding our discussions.
- A big welcome to Carla, Anne, and Mary for joining the beta reading and proofing team with this book and providing helpful comments on things that needed to be fixed or updated to sound better. Thank you!
- Many thanks to QueNtiN who determined the options for the 1993 Chicago lab explosion. Without this guidance, I wouldn't

have known what to do with fertilizer, a Bunsen burner, or various powders and mixtures. I appreciate their patience and help finding the perfect solution.

- Many thanks to Timothy J. R. Rains for turning my simple hand drawn map into an awesome software-generated map I could include in the book.

Much gratitude to all my friends and mentors at Moravian College. Although no murders have ever taken place there, the setting of this series is loosely based on my former multi-campus school set in Pennsylvania. Most of the locations are completely fabricated, but Millionaire's Mile exists. I only made up the name and cable car system.

Thank you to Creativia / Next Chapter for publishing *Flower Power Trip* and paving the road for more books to come. I look forward to our continued partnership.

WHO'S WHO IN THE BRAXTON CAMPUS MYSTERIES?

AYRWICK FAMILY

- Kellan: Main Character, Braxton professor, amateur sleuth
- Wesley: Kellan's father, Braxton's retired president
- Violet: Kellan's mother, Braxton's admissions director
- Emma: Kellan's daughter with Francesca
- Eleanor: Kellan's younger sister, owns Pick-Me-Up Diner
- Gabriel: Kellan's younger brother, returns to town
- Nana D: Kellan's grandmother, also known as Seraphina Danby
- Deirdre Danby: Kellan's aunt, Nana D's daughter
- Alexander Betscha: Nana D's cousin, doctor
- Francesca Castigliano: Kellan's supposedly deceased wife
- Vincenzo & Cecilia Castigliano: Francesca's parents, run the mob

BRAXTON CAMPUS

- Ursula Power: President of Braxton, Myriam's wife
- Myriam Castle: Chair of Communications Dept., Ursula's wife
- Fern Terry: Dean of Student Affairs
- Ed Mulligan: Dean of Academics
- Anita Singh: Chair of Science Dept.
- Connor Hawkins: Director of Security, Kellan's best friend
- Maggie Roarke: Head Librarian, Kellan's ex-girlfriend
- Yuri Sato: Student, Works at Roarke & Daughters Inn
- Sam Taft: Recent graduate, Millard's great-nephew
- Jordan Ballantine: Recent graduate, Fern's nephew

- Carla Grey: Recent graduate, Judge Grey's granddaughter
- George Braun: Visiting professor

WHARTON COUNTY RESIDENTS

- Helena Roarke: Maggie's sister
- Doug Stoddard: Karen's husband, chef
- Karen Stoddard: Doug's wife, event manager
- Cheney Stoddard: Doug and Karen's son
- Sierra Stoddard: Doug and Karen's daughter
- Lissette Nutberry: Owns multiple pharmacies and funeral parlors
- Millard Paddington: Sponsor for Mendel Flower Show
- Dot: Owns the costume shop
- Brad Shope: Nurse

WHARTON COUNTY ADMINISTRATION

- April Montague: Wharton County Sheriff
- Marcus Stanton: Braxton Town Councilman
- Detective Gilkrist: Retiring Detective
- Officer Flatman: Police Officer
- Bartleby Grosvalet: Current Mayor
- Judge Grey: Wharton County Magistrate
- Lara Bouvier: Reporter
- Finnigan Masters: Attorney

CHAPTER 1

A postcard with an image of lush sprawling foliage and a rust-covered antique carriage taunted me from the cushy passenger seat of my SUV. I almost veered off the road twice on the drive to campus because I couldn't peel my eyes away from its persistent glare and blatant reminder of Mendoza. It had to be from Francesca. No one else knew about the remote South American vineyard we'd visited on our honeymoon many years earlier. I shook my clenched fist at the spooky vision of her vanishing in the rearview window. Was she following me everywhere now?

It was Francesca's seventh message since leaving town and failing to inform anyone she wasn't returning to Los Angeles. A torturous weekly mystery high-lighting her whereabouts but leaving no way to contact her. At first, I thought she'd accepted my decision to remain in Pennsylvania and would wait until her parents, the heads of the Castigliano mob family, discovered a way to bring her back from the dead. Let me clarify—she wasn't truly dead, but everyone thought she was. Upon getting caught in a vicious war with Las Vargas, a rival crime family, Francesca's parents had faked her death as the only way to keep her safe. No one else besides Francesca's parents and my sister knew Francesca was alive.

My wife just needed space to adjust to the changes. For two-and-a-half years, she'd been sequestered in a Los Angeles mansion watching from a distance as I raised our seven-year-old daughter on my own. Emma stayed with her nonni a couple of nights a week which made Francesca feel like her daughter was never too far away, but she couldn't actually talk to Emma. Once I moved back home, Francesca lost her ability to see Emma and materialized from seclusion hoping to reconcile. Based on the postcards, she was visiting all the places we'd once traveled to together. Perhaps she needed to feel close to me since I'd refused to participate in whatever game her family was embroiled in with Las Vargas. Unfortunately, now that the Castiglianos blamed me for Francesca's inexplicable disappearance, I anticipated their goons lurking around the corner and following me all the time. Dramatic stuff, huh?

I drove along Braxton's main street cutting through the center of our charming, remote town and parked in the South Campus cable car station's lot near Cambridge Lawn, a large open field filled with colorful flowerbeds, bright green blades of thick grass, and moss-covered stone walkways. It was Saturday, which meant graduation day at Braxton College—also my first one as a professor at the renowned institution. Although I'd only been back for a few months, it felt like I'd never left given my mother, Violet Ayrwick, was still its director of admissions and my father, Wesley Ayrwick, had just retired from its presidency. He would co-lead the ceremony with the new president to complete his responsibilities, thus allowing him to concentrate on converting the college into a university.

Although I'd been apprehensive in accepting my professorship, I grew excited about the opportunity to reconnect with family and friends whom I'd hardly seen since originally leaving town a decade ago. When my cell phone vibrated, I clicked a steering wheel button to display the text message on the SUV's dashboard screen. The previous owner, a family friend who'd been murdered earlier that year, had added all the bells and whistles making it easy to remain hands-free. Was I the only one slightly unnerved by driving a dead woman's car?

Nana D: *Are you still coming by after the graduation? I've got sticky buns and a broccoli and Gouda quiche for a late brunch... and I'm getting nervous about the race.*

My grandmother, known as Seraphina Danby to everyone else, had finished the third and final debate in her surprise quest to become the next mayor of Wharton County, the larger geographical area encompassing Braxton and three other villages in north-central Pennsylvania. She was neck and neck with Councilman Marcus Stanton, her dreaded enemy for reasons she refused to share with anyone. I secretly suspected she was angry with him because of a bad date or his failure to flirt with her once Grandpop had left us for the great big afterlife in the sky.

Me: *You'll be the new mayor. I'm confident. Focus on the numbers. Emma doing okay?*
Nana D: *Yep. She's in the stable talking to the horse groomer about finding her a puppy.*
Me: *Never committed to it! You told her she could have one if we moved into Danby Landing. Not me.*

I'd been living with my parents in the Royal Chic-Shack, a huge modernized log cabin they'd built before I was born thirty-two years ago. When it became clear I needed my own space, Nana D thoughtfully suggested a move to her farm's guesthouse to provide Emma and me some privacy. We'd agreed to give it a chance for the summer, but if it didn't pan out, I'd look for our own place posthaste.

Nana D: *Emma loves it here. She keeps me out of trouble. You and your mother should be grateful.*

She was right. Without a chaperone or extensive supervision, Nana D often found herself skirting too close to disaster. I parked the car and told my seventy-four-year-old cross to bear—I mean that as lovingly as possible—to expect a two o'clock arrival. The graduation ceremony would last longer, but I was only making a brief presentation to declare this year's cable car redesign winner.

Between North and South Campus ran a one-mile electrical track transporting students and faculty back and forth to dorms, academic halls, administrative offices, and other student buildings. The old-fashioned cable car was the only one of its kind in the area and often brought in visitors—and much-needed surplus income—from all over the country. Braxton's graduating class voted each year to redesign the interior as its outgoing gift to the college. There was a surprise victor this year which would make my friend and colleague, Dean Fern Terry, quite relieved. At one point, she worried an apocalyptic dystopian world of aliens would litter the inside of the two-car transportation system she used daily. It was not happening under my watch. I checked the time, stole one last glance at the ominous postcard, and walked across Cambridge Lawn.

As I approached the last stone pathway, I heard my name being called in the distance. I turned to see Ed Mulligan talking with an unknown bald man in his mid-to-late forties. Dean Mulligan, the head of all academics at Braxton, wore an impeccably tailored three-piece suit—his normal highbrow approach to dressing—and scuttled toward me as if he were in a desperate rush to the finish line.

"Kellan, I'd like you to meet George Braun, a visiting professor who arrived in town a few weeks ago to teach a summer course," Dean Mulligan said. When the sunlight landed on George's face, it highlighted the rippled, leathery texture of his skin. Perhaps he suffered from the effects of a recent sunburn or battled a case of rosacea.

"It's a pleasure to meet you, Kellan. Dean Mulligan tells me you recently joined Braxton and might lend a new guy some pointers about how to survive on this exquisite campus," George replied with an unusual accent. Although I was adept at picking up common enunciations, his was a mixture of too many unbalanced inflections to be certain of its origin. There were hints of a gruff Midwest tone with drawn-out vowels, yet I sensed a cultured European style as he finished each of his words.

When Dean Mulligan nodded to confirm George's statement, his jowls jiggled like Santa's belly. "I can think of no one else more qualified," he added with an exaggerated wink.

"Certainly, happy to play tour guide. I'm late at the moment, or I'd stay and chat. I have ceremonial duties for this morning's graduation." Upon shaking George's hand, I noticed he wore a pair of thin leather gloves despite the warm temperatures making it unnecessary. Germaphobe?

I wanted to ask what area he'd be working on given my boss, the indomitable Dr. Myriam Castle, head of the communications department, had brought in a new professor for curriculum redesign and expansion. It was supposed to be a chunk of my role at the college, but she'd quickly made a play for additional money to hire someone other than me to prepare the future vision. Now that my father was no longer the president, but Myriam's wife Ursula Power was in that role, things were changing.

"Perhaps we could have breakfast on Monday morning? I'm due on campus at ten o'clock to meet with Dr. Anita Singh about the courses," George explained. A dark gray sportscoat covered broad shoulders and attempted to slim his stocky figure. Given he was noticeably several inches taller and wider than me, it didn't appear to help.

"That sounds like a plan. Let's meet at eight thirty at the Pick-Me-Up Diner?" I proposed, knowing it'd lend me an excuse to judge the eatery's latest renovations.

Dean Mulligan haughtily teased," Ah, George, you'll soon come to learn the Ayrwick family has a long-standing establishment in and around Braxton. Eleanor, Kellan's sister, owns the diner, a favored restaurant by most employed at or attending our fine institution."

As Dean Mulligan provided directions to George, I caught a puzzled expression on the visiting professor's face. He muttered something unintelligible before his gaze narrowed and highlighted two ultra-thin blond eyebrows. "Pardon?" I inquired.

"Ayrwick, you said?" he added, cocking his head to the left and focusing on the pastoral landscape behind me. He wouldn't look me in the face without glancing away. Was he sensitive about his skin condition or his funny way of speaking? I hoped I hadn't offended the man with my transitory stare and state of confusion.

"Yes, Dean Mulligan's correct. My family's been in Wharton County for close to three centuries. I look forward to speaking with you on Monday," I replied, excusing myself and dashing toward the backstage area to locate Dean Fern Terry. Since she oversaw the graduation as head of student affairs, Fern could tell me when I was needed for the ceremony.

George Braun not only seemed familiar with the name Ayrwick, but I was certain that was concern or alarm etched on his face. After a quick catch-up with Fern, I found a spot on the east side of the stage as the ceremony began. I could stand there until it was time to declare the winner of the contest. Although I knew a few students in the graduating class, I hadn't been at the institution long enough to serve as an announcer of graduate names nor to deliver any inspirational departing speeches.

Fern initiated the ceremony by reminiscing about the school's history and highlighting the graduating class's accomplishments. She introduced Ursula who took the stage to congratulate the outgoing students, then turned it over to my father for his last opportunity to say goodbye to the future alumni. As he spoke, Ursula navigated the stage's steps like they were a catwalk and headed toward the back of the seating area.

Once my father finished boorishly riffing about something in Latin, Fern commandeered the stage and announced my name. I walked to the center and stood behind the lectern looking out at a mostly unfamiliar sea of people. With over two hundred graduates, the audience teetered around a thousand guests including their families and nearly all the college's administrative and academic staff. I talked about the process to nominate and vote for different cable car designs, then explained how it was an awfully close race. Only two people had been told the final winner. Ursula and I agreed to surprise Fern with the results given how disappointed she'd be if the apocalypse had won. She'd tried to bribe me with a homemade coconut cream cake at Easter, but I stood firm. Where desserts were my weakness, keeping secrets was my strength.

"It gives me immense pleasure to reveal today's winner," I said, pointing and clicking the button on a tiny remote toward the digital screen. "I've been a huge fan of these two larger-than-life characters since I was a small boy, and I often find myself involved in solving a few mysteries of my own." A series of conversations between Agatha Christie's famed detectives, Miss Marple and Hercule Poirot, materialized on the large screen behind me. Various quotes and images from the books, movies, and PBS shows would appear inside the cable car to share different interpretations of the characters.

"It's because you're our inspiration for solving those two murder investigations," Jordan Ballantine shouted followed by a bunch of cheers. "We wanted to honor your service to the campus!" Jordan was one of the graduates who'd be leaving Braxton to attend an MBA program in New Orleans.

In my three months at Braxton, I'd solved a couple of murders and been deemed a campus hero. I looked at Fern, Jordan's aunt, and smiled with humility. We'd come a long way from her disciplining me when I'd been the president of my fraternity pleading forgiveness after various mischievous activities. Fern beamed back at me and lifted her hands in the air as if to say 'holla' like the bellowing students. Somehow the image of a sixtyish woman built like a quarterback in a gray pixie-style haircut performing such a move was frightening beyond any comfort.

As I thanked everyone for their votes, I noticed one of the graduates, Sam Taft, speaking with my brother, Gabriel. I'd caught the two of them in a cozy embrace last March shortly after someone had killed Gwendolyn Paddington to ensure an inheritance of the family fortune. I'd been shocked to see my brother after eight years but even more astonished to learn he might be gay. If you'd seen that kiss, there wouldn't have been any question of *might be*, but until I spoke with him, I didn't want to assume. Neither one had realized I'd seen them that day, and for the last seven weeks, I'd kept the information to myself. I didn't know whether to ask Sam about it or hire a private investigator to track Gabriel.

Once I finished my speech, I sprinted down the steps to interrogate or to hug my brother—still hadn't decided which one. I tried to reach him, but Gabriel winked and escaped in the opposite direction. Before I could rush off to beg Sam for help, Ursula stepped in the way. "Kellan, I'm glad we ran into one another. I was curious if you found out anything new?" she said with a gleam of hope.

By now, Sam had lined up on stage to receive his diploma, and Gabriel was long gone. I breathed a gulp of warm air and felt my body begin to wane. For the third week of May, the heat had come from nowhere and grown inordinately stagnant. All the comforting breezes were blocked by tall fir trees surrounding one side of Cambridge Lawn and the massive church holding firm on its southern border. I liked the hot weather, but this was intense.

Ursula had recently pleaded for help with a problem involving the past finally catching up to her. I'd learned a lot about my new boss during our conversations, some of which explained the reason she was taciturn about her history and some of which shocked me to the core. Not even Myriam knew about her wife's tragedy or the years she'd been running and hiding from the truth about her real identity. While I felt the palpitating fear emanate off Ursula's normally serene exterior, I tried not to judge her for the damage her prior actions had caused.

"Not a whole lot, I'm sorry to say. Whoever is blackmailing you has gone to great lengths to keep their identity a secret. Are you sure this isn't an angry student playing a prank on you?" I asked, knowing the chances were slim. The person stalking Ursula had detailed knowledge about the complex science experiments her family had conducted in Chicago over two decades earlier.

"I don't see how anyone would know. Hans and my parents died because of what I did. Unless someone other than their assistant was loitering in the laboratory that day, no one else could still be around. That nuisance of an employee already tried to ruin me before I was forced to change my name and disappear!" Ursula cleared her throat and leaned her head in the direction of the graduation ceremony. Based on my father's latest announcement, graduate names were being called.

"I've got one more angle to try, but I don't think it'll turn up anything else. We might have to wait until he or she delivers another message to you. It could provide a clue to the identity of your stalker," I said with fading confidence. I'd been unable to track who was pursuing Ursula nor establish any leads thus far, but I felt certain no one would keep threatening her without demanding something in return. "What could they possibly want from you?"

"To die. Just like those victims who suffered when I destroyed all the possible cures for... never mind!" Ursula sat on a wrought iron bench scrunching her fists in the hope she wouldn't lose her cool. The twitch in her right eye barely held back a flood of emotions. "I appreciate your help, Kellan."

A chilling, nasal voice cut through the air inciting me to roll my eyes with vigor. Myriam had found us and was likely on her way armed with another acerbic Shakespearean barb. "Just what are you doing to my wife, Mr.

Ayrwick?" Myriam blasted while furiously stomping the remaining few feet before approaching our bench. "*Come not within the measure of my wrath.*" She resembled a dark and gloomy ghost with a pointy cardboard hat floating through Cambridge Lawn in search of someone to haunt to death. I'm certain the cap's sole purpose was to hold her *Jamie Lee Curtis* spiky gray wig in place. No other professor wore the full academic regalia. I reminded myself that Myriam, in all her expressive and ruthless glory, was a special breed of querulous pomp and circumstance.

"Don't start with me, Myriam. I'm holding a private conversation with Ursula that has nothing to do with you. I thought we agreed to stop causing scenes by arguing all the time?" I said with half a grin. We'd had several run-ins over the last few months but ultimately found a way to co-exist with each other during the final weeks of the *King Lear* performance at Paddington's Play House.

"Kellan hasn't done anything wrong, M. He's helping solve an important problem at Braxton," Ursula responded with a tentative stare in my direction. I took it as a reminder not to tell her wife anything. "Is everything okay? You look rather annoyed right now."

"Annoyed? Well, yes, my love, I am *more* than annoyed. I finished directing students off the stage and followed them down the aisle once my group's degrees were delivered. As I reached the end, an unruly, frightening man jumped out of the last row and grabbed my arm." She brushed imaginary dirt or unwelcome fingerprints off her flowing black graduation gown.

"Do you know who it was?" I asked. Would it be wrong to send a thank you gift to them?

"Of course not. Do you think I associate with such vulgarity, Mr. Ayrwick? He interrupted our graduation!" Myriam scowled. Why did she always say *mister*? Professor Ayrwick, Kellan, Prince of Awesomeness—anything else would be acceptable. *Mister* always conjured images of my father, and that's not something I relished even on a good day.

"I only meant—was it someone we could identify? Perhaps we'd recognize this supposed *monster* you encountered. Where is he now?" I wanted to strangle her with the honor society cords meticulously draped across her shoulders despite knowing it wouldn't help. Myriam tried to describe the man, but he sounded like a regular delivery guy who'd been hired to drop off the note, not an actual hoodlum. My boss tended to exaggerate any and all situations as well as choose the most peculiar words. "It was probably just a messaging service employee."

"You two have been sneaking around and conspiring about something. I want to know what's going on and how it connects to this letter," she said, thrusting her hand toward Ursula. Clasped between her fingers, besides a four-carat diamond ring, shook a piece of cardboard folded lengthwise in half. "Open it. The *delivery* hooligan pointed at you and said I should give it to *Flower Child.*"

Ursula's normally pale skin blanched to an alarming shade of white.

Worried she might pass out, I reached to steady her. When Myriam batted my arm away, I stepped on the pathway to see if I could find out whether the delivery guy was anywhere in sight.

Ursula opened the note, swallowed deeply, and closed it in a balled-up fist. "Myriam, could you get me a bottle of water? I'm a little parched." When Myriam appeared to balk, Ursula whispered something causing the woman to step away. "Thank you, M."

"You certainly seem to be the only one who controls her. No offense intended, *Madame President*," I said, trying to minimize the sudden cold front in the atmosphere. "Is it from the stalker?"

Ursula nodded, then handed me the note.

You thought you could run and hide, but life doesn't work that way. I tracked you down and plan to reveal myself at the upcoming costume party. Revenge is a long time coming, Flower Child. You'll never see the explosion this time! Nor will you make it out alive unless you follow my instructions very carefully. Remember, don't tell anyone else.

My eyes opened wide with an equal amount of shock and fear. All the previous notes were menacing and accusatory, but none had directly threatened Ursula's life. "We have to talk to Sheriff Montague at this point. I don't like where this game is going anymore."

CHAPTER 2

"You were almost too late for brunch, Kellan," Nana D teased while standing in her cozy farmhouse kitchen pouring mimosas by the bucketful. "I was outvoted by your sister and your daughter." She'd selected giant, frosted-green goblets as the holder of the traditional beverage we'd been sharing at our weekend brunches. Ninety percent champagne, ten percent orange juice. I'd be tipsy after the first two since the bubbles always went straight to my head. Give me several cans of beer or a few cocktails, I'd be as sober as a Baptist minister in Utah.

"I thought I saw Eleanor's car out front. Isn't she working at the Pick-Me-Up Diner?" I grew antsy, something fishy was going on. There were only four place settings which meant I wouldn't be surprised by another Nana D-engineered blind date. A setup was guaranteed any day now.

Emma raced into the kitchen, hugged me tightly, and jumped into the open banquette seat near the window. "Auntie Eleanor hired a new manager. He's easy on the eyes." When I'd left that morning, Emma had been wearing her pajamas and suffering from major bedhead. Now, she rocked a fresh blowout, an empire-cut blue dress, and a cashmere sweater with a butterfly pin clasped to the collar. Eleanor must have dressed her in anticipation of what future motherhood might be like. If Nana D had her druthers, Emma would wear overalls and pigtails.

"Easy on the eyes?" I said, squinting at my grandmother. "Where'd she learn that expression?"

"Your sister's words, not mine, brilliant one." Nana D sat and guzzled a third of her mimosa. "I offered to let Emma taste mine, but she said it smelled funky. Like your cologne. Is that acid-reflux?"

"I suppose I should focus on the fact she declined the drink rather than harbor any concern you suggested it to begin with?" I loved my Nana D, but she rarely listened to any of the rules I'd laid down when moving back. I trusted her with my life, yet after the margarita incident a few months earlier, I wouldn't drink anything she didn't also drink from. In equal parts. In front of me. Between that revenge tactic and her homemade cold and flu medications, it's no wonder I wasn't already six feet under.

"Of course," Eleanor chimed in as she sashayed into the room. "Didn't Nana D rub whiskey on our gums when we cut new teeth?"

"It kept me sane. Your mother would've killed me if she knew how many times I'd used that trick. New parents in the last thirty years think they invented all the rules. It's the old ways that always work." Nana D sliced large wedges of quiche for everyone and directed us to dig in. We sat in silence devouring our food until I couldn't take it anymore.

"So... care to explain who's easy on the eyes, little sister?" Last time I checked, she'd been practically ogling Connor Hawkins. At the same time, she rotated through several picture books to select a possible sperm donor for the baby she wanted to have. On her own, as in, sans anyone to co-parent with. Was she trying to mimic my life? She'd always repeated everything I did in the exact same manner as me when we were children.

"The renovation brought in loads of new customers, I couldn't keep up. I hired a part-time manager to cover Saturdays. Now, I have a full day off. I thought I told you," Eleanor mumbled while swallowing and moaning over the quiche. "I'm moving in if you keep serving this brunch, Nana D."

"The more the merrier," our grandmother replied, clinking her mimosa goblet against Emma's, which I prayed was only full of orange juice. "Maybe Gabriel will come home soon and need a place to crash. It'll be a family reunion."

I stopped midway from shoveling a sticky bun between my lips and peered up at Nana D. Had Gabriel been in contact with her? "What makes you say that, Nana D?"

She wiggled her shoulders and fiddled with her bright red, three-foot braid. I didn't think she'd cut her hair in over a decade given it was long enough to touch the floor when she sat down. Nana D ignored me and said, "This might be my best brunch ever. Whatta ya think, Emma, dear?"

Eleanor and I glanced at one another and simultaneously downed the remaining contents of our goblets. I poured us both more while she responded. "I'm not interested in my new manager. I'm quite sure he doesn't play for my team, if you get my drift," she whispered while nodding in Emma's direction.

"Ah. Well, that would make it difficult. Probably wouldn't stop Nana D from setting you up with him," I quipped, remembering the bevy of inappropriate women our grandmother had thrown in my direction in the past. Was Eleanor trying to hint at knowing about Gabriel's secret, too? Something was going on between my sister and Nana D, but I couldn't clear away the cobwebs to find the prize.

"Since you two aren't making any sense, let's change the topic. The graduation ceremony went well. I ran into a few people I hadn't seen in a while," I noted, mostly thinking about Ursula. When I left, she was planning to tell Myriam the note was about an issue with one of the college's alumni donors who called her *Flower Child*. I couldn't imagine explaining that name to my other boss.

From what Ursula had previously shared, *Flower Child* was a nickname given to her by her brother, Hans. She'd spent most of her childhood collecting flowers and researching their potential uses in medicines and herbal remedies. Their parents had been scientists who were close to finding a cure for a horrific disease. They'd only been close to discovering the answers until the explosion in the lab eliminated any records or verifiable, repeatable results.

"Did you see Maggie on campus?" Nana D asked, balancing a few plates on one arm and the tray of quiche on the other. Emma stood to clear the table. I'd taught my daughter proper manners despite what anyone else dared tell me.

While Eleanor knew Francesca was still alive, Nana D did not. Eleanor understood my reluctance to pursue a relationship with my former college girl-friend despite Nana D always trying to match me up. "No, Maggie wasn't involved in the graduation ceremony. She's busy planning tomorrow night's costume extravaganza. I'm dropping by later to help with the final details."

When Maggie had assumed the role of head librarian of Braxton's Memorial Library, she'd quickly realized the structure and its contents were outdated. She pitched an idea to the Board of Trustees who unanimously supported her request to raise money for a complete remodel and modernization. Although they'd received large contributions, they were several hundred thousand dollars short. Maggie had proposed a grand event to show everyone what the building looked like now and could become in the future. She invited a hundred of Braxton's wealthiest families hoping they would donate the missing funds needed to start renovations. The costume extravaganza was called *Heroes & Villains*. Guests were encouraged to dress as their favorites from any historical period.

Emma helped Nana D dry the dishes while Eleanor and I moseyed outside to catch up on Francesca's latest postcard. "I'm certain my wayward wife will come home as soon as she realizes I made the right decision," I explained.

"Cecilia didn't sound happy last time," Eleanor reminded me. Cecilia Castigliano was Francesca's mother, and the brains behind the family business. Francesca's father, Vincenzo, handled the mob's daily operations ensuring his wife didn't get her hands dirty.

"Not at all. She's threatened me on a throng of occasions. I've been given two more weeks to locate Francesca. The best I can do is to list any of the remaining places we'd visited in the past. Maybe Vincenzo's thugs can check them out and find her before she's discovered by Las Vargas."

"You certainly lead an interesting life," Eleanor said as she unlocked her car door claiming she had errands to run. The inside of her car looked like a bomb had exploded and needed a massive decluttering. "Can you come with me next week to meet the doctor at the clinic? I think I've nailed down the top three options for a donor."

I consented and suggested she text me the date, time, and location. I'd given up trying to talk her out of the plan to have a baby and figured it would settle itself. Sometimes keeping one's mouth firmly closed delivered the desired results.

Nana D took Emma with her to the orchard to check on Danby Landing's latest saplings. I hopped in the car to meet Maggie at her family's bed and breakfast, Roarke & Daughters Inn. Maggie's parents, former hippies in their younger days, and her four sisters ran the ten-room Victorian stunner. Maggie was the only daughter who opted not to get involved, instead choosing to enter into business with Eleanor as a fifty-percent silent partner in the Pick-Me-Up Diner. Ben and Lucy Roarke were supportive of their eldest child, but it was obvious they preferred she join them at some future point.

Roarke & Daughters Inn was located near Crilly Lake in the northern part of the county. Formed by melting glaciers during the shaping of the Wharton Mountains, the lake was a popular haven for swimming, fishing, and boating during summers. During the spring and fall, it offered striking views of the landscape where exercise and nature lovers spent countless hours surrounded by unmatched inspiration and dreamt of the future. When I pulled up to the front of the historic bed and breakfast and parked in the circle driveway, Maggie and one of her sisters, Helena, stepped into the enclosed wrap-around porch. From the twenty-foot distance, I could see they were having a disagreement about something. Maggie's finger waggled at Helena who crossed her arms on her chest and groaned loudly enough for me to hear in the distance.

I hadn't seen Helena in close to a decade, back when Maggie and I'd been about to graduate from Braxton. Helena was once the proverbial unruly teenager who'd failed her driver's license exam at least twice yet still demanded a brand-new car. She'd also gone to school with my brother, Gabriel, for a few years. Where Maggie had porcelain skin and soft, girlish features, Helena resembled the rest of their sisters—tall, incredibly thin, voluptuous, blessed with thick luxuriant hair, and immortalized with tons of makeup. Basically, the complete opposite of Maggie who was often mistaken for a ceramic statue or a timid doll. Helena recently celebrated her birthday by doing a pub crawl across all four villages in Wharton County. Eight hours, eight bars, eight different drinks. I wouldn't have survived that level of commitment.

Ivy crawled up and around each of the ornate shutters on the building's front windows offering a sharp contrast to the recently repointed beige brick and iron-colored mortar. Roarke & Daughters Inn had once been the home of a former mayor who'd passed away with no immediate descendants at the end of the nineteenth century. The three-story Victorian home passed to a distant cousin, one of Maggie's ancestors, and was used for most of the last century as their family home. Once their hippie days were over and their kids had grown up, the Roarkes converted it into an income-generating property. "Afternoon, ladies," I said, crossing the threshold into the enclosed porch.

"Kellan Ayrwick, I heard you returned to town. Not that my darling sister ever mentioned you would dare show your face around these parts again," Helena hollered as I walked across the porch. She scooped a handful of platinum-blonde hair into her palm and tossed it across her shoulder, revealing the thin spaghetti-straps of a hunter-green silk camisole that dipped incredibly low across her ample chest. "Dang, you look finer than I remember, hot stuff!"

I blushed when she pulled me into a tight hug and I inhaled her perfume, a cross between a bouquet of overly sweet flowers and freshly-baked cinnamon rolls. She'd matured into a fully grown-up knock-out with more curves than I'd remembered. Gorgeous. Dynamite. But not really my type, if I'm being honest. I preferred a woman with both a shy and a bit of a wild side, not someone like Helena who flirted with any man between eighteen and sixty-two and pushed her best assets out for everyone to admire on every possible occasion. "Maggie and I have put the past to rest, Helena. I hope you'll be able to, as well," I noted, withdrawing from the temporarily enticing embrace.

Had it really been over two years since I'd let myself *lose control* with a woman? One drunken night a month after Francesca died—or supposedly died —forcing me to realize I'd made a grave error trying to torpedo myself forward through the pain. A man can only be celibate for so long, and judging by the way I'd felt lately, my stint as a self-anointed priest was way past its prime.

Helena began speaking in a seductive tone but was abruptly stopped. "Does that mean you're up for grabs? I could see myself grabbing a piece of your—"

"Stand back, kiddo. Kellan's not interested, are you, Kellan?" Maggie firmly responded as she swatted at her sister's arm, then looked directly at me. A second set of chills cascaded down my back before I nudged myself out of fantasyland. "Besides, aren't you enamored with a new guy in town?"

"Yeah, a girl can never have too many friends," Helena teased as she pursed and licked her full lips. "Cheney's definitely at the top of my list, but I could permit another gentleman caller if he's able to handle all of me."

How two sisters could be so dissimilar was beyond me. When I considered the personality differences between Maggie and all four of her sisters, I truly had respect for Ben and Lucy Roarke. "Are you helping with the costume extravaganza, Helena?" I changed the subject to keep the greeting, or me, from overheating.

"You bet. Maggie needs someone to spice up her initial designs. Wait until you see my costume," Helena added before opening the front door and inviting me inside the house. A narrow staircase led guests upstairs to the second and third floors where all the bedrooms were located. In the front of the main floor were two parlors, one for afternoon cocktails and social occasions, another functioning as a reading or movie room depending on the night. "I'm not supposed to dress provocatively since I'll be serving appetizers and drinks, but I've got a few tricks up my sleeve."

From where I stood, she had no sleeves. And her skirt barely covered essential parts. Not that I was complaining all that much. Months ago, I'd been judging one of my students for dressing in skimpy couture. Today, I was fine with it. I suppose that's what happened when I went long enough without any physical connection. I either had the strongest willpower known to man or I was about to make a big mistake again—potentially with someone I shouldn't. "Looking forward to it," I said before turning to Maggie. "Have you decided on your costume?"

Maggie wasn't bringing a date given she would spend most of the night catering to all the wealthy donors. Connor Hawkins, my former best friend, and possibly new best friend again, had asked Maggie to go with him, but she indicated she'd rather go out the following day on a real date. Despite Eleanor's attraction to Connor, I stood by my promises and let the comment go. Maggie and I had agreed to focus on our friendship. Besides, I still had to figure out what was going on with Francesca. Can you divorce a dead person? I know you can't marry two women at once in Pennsylvania—not that I wanted to—but according to the government, Francesca was dead. According to the truth, she was alive and kicking. Furiously. Yeah, I'm a little frustrated these days.

"It's a surprise, but I did tell Connor. I expect him to wear something similar. I'm a heroine, but whether he chooses my mortal enemy or goes with someone she loves will be very telling!" Maggie sat across from the fireplace in a tall wingback chair that had been covered in a Scottish tartan pattern.

"Cheney and I are gonna coordinate our duds," Helena said. "He's perfect for his costume, or at least his lack of costume, I should say. Do you think he'll be too chilly in a loincloth, Maggie?"

Maggie's eyes burst open wider than one of Nana D's duck eggs. "We talked about this! You're serving food and drink, you need to dress like you would at Mom and Dad's inn. Respectable. I don't care if you spruce it up a little with something sexy, but there should be more body parts clothed than not clothed. Got it?"

Helena appeared to acquiesce, then poured herself a tumbler of brown-colored liquor from a crystal decanter idling on the bar cart. I checked my watch—only four o'clock. "I take it your shift is over, Helena?" I didn't want to get her in trouble, but Maggie needed my support to rein in the boundaries.

"It is not over. She only started an hour ago. Put the whiskey down, Helena. Isn't it time for an update on tomorrow's waitstaff? I got you that job with the catering service, you better not make me sorry I went to bat for you." Maggie had hired a catering event manager who recently opened a new company, Simply Stoddard. She always tried to support local businesses, especially start-ups trying to build up clientele. Cheney was the owner's son, and once Helena had met him, she begged Maggie to recommend her for a part-time position at Simply Stoddard. "Karen Stoddard and I are meeting tonight to finalize everything for the event. Are we ready?"

Helena confirmed, then excused herself claiming she had rooms to clean and beds to turn down before the guests retired for the night. I raised my eyelids when she disappeared to the second floor. "As brazen as ever, I see."

"I adore her, but she's driving me crazy. At twenty-eight, I'd gotten my second degree, had a full-time librarian job, and set up a genealogy research service as a side gig to earn extra money. Helena's always caught up with some guy these days, I can't keep track," Maggie said with a dash of exhaustion. "I'm sure she'll be an asset tomorrow. Hospitality is *supposed* to be her strong suit."

"I'm looking forward to the costume extravaganza. Do you think you'll get the rest of your donations to begin the renovations soon?" I asked. Maggie shared the names of a few folks on the guest list—the usual Stantons, Paddingtons, Greys, and Nutberrys but also some of the upper-middle class families who were interested in contributing to the cause.

After helping with the final details for the signage, giveaway bags, and surprise lottery drawing, I hugged Maggie goodbye and returned to campus. I had a priority task from a demanding barracuda to finish in my office—posting my syllabus and required class reading for the summer session before my last drop of patience with Myriam had evaporated.

Once work was completed, I walked to my SUV and noticed Millard Paddington exiting the cable car platform. I hadn't seen Nana D's septuagenarian friend since the last mayoral debate but welcomed a chance to speak with the brilliant businessman-turned-landscaper. After a recent disaster at his family's company, Millard had stepped back in to run the multi-layered conglomerate until things stabilized, but his heart belonged to the vast gardens he'd built on his family's estate.

"It's late for you to be on campus on a Saturday night, Kellan. Burning the near-midnight oil?"

"I could say the same for you, Millard. Not out with Nana D this evening? I thought you were going to help her and Emma with last-minute votes for the mayoral race." I shook his hand and leaned against the wooden railing. The pale color of his skin and the stoop to his normally erect posture made him look tired and worn down.

"I had to cancel. Needed to mediate the ridiculous disagreements between Anita Singh and George Braun about the plans for the upcoming Mendel flower show. George is serving as our master of ceremony next week when we cut the ribbon and open the doors to a special new exhibit. It'll be quite spectacular." Millard noticed my uncertain haze and brought me up to speed on the event's history.

Gregor Mendel, an Austrian monk who'd discovered and studied principles of hereditary, genetics, and botany in the mid-1800s, was the inspiration for an annual flower show held in Europe over many decades. It'd crossed the Atlantic Ocean five years earlier and stopped in a handful of major US cities. Scientists, botanists, and doctors would present their research from the prior year and share new knowledge with one another. Each brought extensive samples of the flowers they studied to make the exhibits more interactive for the general public. The team also spread key news about how communities could save the bumble bee population or use herbal medicines rather than non-homeopathic manufactured solutions.

It sounded fascinating to me, but I wasn't sure why it ended up in a small town like Braxton. "Why were they fighting?"

"Dr. Singh runs the entire science program at Braxton. I believe she's threatened by George's presence and fought with Dean Mulligan about allowing him to teach a class this summer."

I was about to ask him for more details when I noticed a few drops of sweat rolling down his cheek. "I appreciate the overview. Are you feeling okay?"

Millard dabbed his neck and forehead with a kerchief from his coat pocket. His bushy caterpillar eyebrows knitted together as he sighed. "Long days, Kellan. My nephew is at Second Chance Reflections focusing on his rehabilitation for another month. I can't keep running the company for Timothy much longer, all the while maintaining the Paddington estate gardens in tip-top shape and coordinating the whole flower show by myself."

I'd been wondering how much longer before Timothy would be released to the helm of the family company. After a nasty substance and gambling addiction, he'd finally sought help in the form of a three-month recovery program. "I assume George Braun can take a larger load of the work?"

"Yes, but it requires a tremendous amount of effort to add in this unplanned location. We're incredibly lucky to get someone of his caliber at Braxton. George is working with an event management company to organize the guest attendee portions of the show, and he's hiring an assistant to work in the labs for his summer class." As Millard shuffled toward his car, I followed him to hear the rest of his response but also ensure he didn't collapse from exhaustion.

"That should free up a few hours each day for George to oversee the Mendel flower show and its upcoming exhibits. To give you a break, right?" I gently guided his arm along our path down the steps.

"He's also presenting the personal research he's been working on for most of his life. George is an expert in botany, blood carcinogens, and the medicinal uses of plants and flowers. Maybe I should ask him for an herbal supplement to keep me going," Millard quipped.

Interesting. George Braun worked in the same field as Ursula's parents. Was he familiar with them or their past research? Did he have something to do with the notes from Ursula's stalker? I couldn't think of a reasonable approach to discuss it at the moment, but I'd give it thought before meeting the professor the following Monday for breakfast. "Don't push yourself. I'm sure it's been a difficult spring after losing your sister-in-law and controlling the tumult within your family."

"After George and his assistant get settled next week, I'll take a step back. Good seeing you, Kellan. Please tell Seraphina I'll reschedule with her in a few days," Millard uttered as he slid into his shiny white Cadillac and drove off.

The man looked quite peaked. I made a note on my phone to ask Eustacia, his sister, to check on him the following day. I worried Millard was doing too much and might be unintentionally harming himself. I also entered a reminder on my calendar to research George Braun before meeting him at the diner. I couldn't reveal Ursula's true identity, but maybe the professor knew someone who might have a grudge against her family or whether the assistant from twenty-five years ago was still causing problems about the loss of all the research. Or was he the assistant?

CHAPTER 3

After a relaxing Sunday together, I hugged my daughter goodbye and left for the costume extravaganza at Braxton's Memorial Library. Nana D was babysitting Emma, who claimed her throat was scratchy and didn't want to visit her friend for a play date. My daughter secretly preferred Nana D as her caretaker for the evening. I also suspected it was collusion to give my nana a night off from the campaign trail. Nana D didn't agree with me that the event would offer a perfect photo opportunity to show her raising money for a great cause. She worried people would think she was goofing off.

I dressed as Sherlock Holmes since I wouldn't be taking a date to the party and those around me would expect an ironic yet fitting costume. Sherlock was hardly ever seen with a woman on his arm but frequently noted as resembling a handsome devil. I thought of myself in the same manner, at least years ago before I became a mature and dedicated parent. Now, my free time was spent hunting down a wife who baffled me at every turn the last two months.

I wore a charcoal-colored, A-line tweed suit with a well-fitted black dress shirt that accentuated the impressive results of my last few workouts at Grey Sports Complex. I needed to amaze my colleagues, and the muffler, leather gloves, and classic waterproof, long gray coat only made the outfit more authentic. I liked to dress well, but when it involved locating clothing from one-and-a-half centuries ago, I had to do extensive research. I chose a few key accessories to hit home exactly what kind of hero I would be for this campus. Nana D swooned and whistled before I left Danby Landing.

When I walked through the front entrance of the library, I was astounded at the rapidly deteriorating building's marvelous transformation. The drab, outdated walls were covered in a silk fabric that had been draped from the vaulted ceilings to the sunken floors and tied back with gilded curtain rods. At the end of each was a picture of a famous hero or villain affixed to a crystal

405

plate. Each had a small, glowing reading light that looked like an old-fashioned candlestick. Velvet ropes and a long, narrow red carpet guided guests through the foyer into the main reading hall. All the research tables had been moved to the outer edges of the room creating space for everyone to mingle and socialize.

I scanned the room making a list of everyone I knew, which was more difficult than expected given the number of people whose costumes either masked their identity or distorted their appearance. I assumed that Ursula's stalker would be unfamiliar to me. There was a minute chance it could be someone we knew attempting revenge, but I couldn't worry about it until I found the culprit. He or she said they'd be attending the costume extravaganza. I'd promised Ursula I'd do everything I could to scour the room for a list of potential candidates. She'd begged me not to tell Sheriff Montague anything about the notes until we had some idea of who it might be. I'd given into the pressure knowing it was the wrong decision but also recognizing it was Ursula who'd originally asked me to investigate her past.

Two cocktail bars had been fashioned from elegant French credenzas the Paddington family had donated to the costume extravaganza. A parchment scroll advertised various champagne drinks available to guests, and several waiters and waitresses navigated the room carrying silver trays with canapes and hors d'oeuvres. I'd seen the menu beforehand and couldn't wait to sample the fig and prosciutto crostini the Stoddards had included as a complimentary thank you for choosing their catering service. I hadn't encountered Helena, but based on the description of her costume, she'd stand out from the others.

A four-piece string orchestra that was flanked by two bars played a Vivaldi classic. Dressed as King Henry VIII, Judge Grey led his granddaughter, recent Braxton graduate Carla Grey, to the dance floor. Carla dressed as Anne Boleyn, one of Henry's dead wives, and had included an unsavory gash across her neck with what appeared to be fake blood. Beheaded for witchcraft, Anne was seen as a villain by some, a heroine by others. The magistrate's choice in costumes was befitting given all I'd known about him and his many wives over the years. As I passed by, Carla said, "You always were the artful detective, Professor Ayrwick." Carla would be staying in Braxton and had obtained a junior dealer job at an art gallery. I continued walking toward the bar where I hoped I could count on a group of faculty to provide cover from the daunting Grey family. If not, a potent drink would be a good fallback.

"Kellan, you look dashing," Lara Bouvier noted as I stopped behind her in the short line. Lara was a local news reporter whom Maggie had invited to cover the event. I expected to see her boyfriend when the gentleman next to her turned around, but to my surprise, it was Finnigan Masters. I'd been close friends with his brother, a famous hockey player, and had run into Finnigan a few months earlier when he'd probated Gwendolyn Paddington's last will and testament.

Lara wore an ultra-classic, elegant brown skirt with a small slit up the side of one leg, a pink beret, and a cinnamon-colored top molded to her shapely figure. Finnigan's dark gray pinstripe suit, cotton-candy tie, and slicked back hair with accompanying chocolate-brown bolero hat reminded me of the famed 1930s killers, Bonnie and Clyde. "We're from different countries and time periods, but perhaps I ought to run you two criminals in," I teased, wagging my finger in their direction.

Finnigan shook my hand and offered me a bubbly drink served in a rippled copper flute from the bar. "Champagne Moscow Mule. My second of the night, and we've only just begun." After I sipped it, he said, "Maggie's done a wonderful job here. I'm sure the Board of Trustees will be impressed."

"Absolutely, she worked day and night the last few weeks to accomplish this. By the looks of the official sign showing how much money she's raised, the cup will overfloweth quite soon!" I clinked his flute and turned toward the right. Upon seeing Maggie in the opposite corner, I excused myself and meandered in her direction. I had an energetic crowd to circumvent before I could reach her.

Bartleby Grosvalet, our current seventy-something recluse mayor whom everyone couldn't wait to see retire, spoke with Fern Terry. He wore a rotund black and white tuxedo which reminded me of Danny DeVito's *Penguin* character from the second *Batman* movie starring Michael Keaton. For me, Keaton would always be the original even though several actors had played the famed superhero many times before my life had begun.

As Fern turned, I saw a true heroine's costume—Marie Curie, the first woman to win a Nobel Prize and conduct pioneering research on radioactivity. I waved to her, noticing the uncomfortable smile as she tried to escape from the mayor's clutches. I shrugged my shoulders and whispered that I'd be there soon, so she knew I'd try to save her. Unfortunately, someone else tapped me on the shoulder. Fern would have to wait.

When I circled around, three faces came into view—Frankenstein's Monster, the Bride of Frankenstein, and what I assumed was Professor McGonagall from the amazing Harry Potter children's books. Hiding under a magical witch's hat and black turtleneck dress, complete with billowing robes and an emerald green cape, was the belle of the ball. Maggie's porcelain skin shined through the makeup she'd slathered on to age herself appropriately for the role. Quite the heroine! Just what would Connor be wearing? "Kellan Ayrwick, let me introduce you to Doug and Karen Stoddard, the owners of a new restaurant downtown by the Finnulia River waterfront and the Simply Stoddard event management company helping make tonight's gala such a splash."

After we exchanged quick greetings, I learned they'd moved to Braxton several months earlier to launch their own business and an upscale American fine dining establishment. Doug had worked as a chef at several mid-level restaurants in the Midwest but had dreamed of owning his own place. Karen had a couple of jobs in her early career and had begun running events for corporations throughout the last decade. "Cheney is your son, if I understand correctly," I noted, remembering what Helena had said about him the day before. I still hadn't found her at the event. Perhaps Maggie had mandated strict instructions for her sister to stay out of the limelight.

"Yes, have you met him?" Karen asked with an inquisitive expression. In her Bride of Frankenstein getup, it was difficult to picture what she normally looked like. An oval-shaped head, large forehead, and snub nose were evident but had been covered in excessive character makeup. She was a few inches shorter than me, had a slender body, and boasted extremely attractive legs. A tasteful, knee-length ivory dress and bouffant dark hair with a streak of white completed her outfit.

"I believe my sister is to blame for that. She talked Cheney up yesterday to Kellan," Maggie explained, re-sorting the hat as it tipped forward too far. "Helena seems smitten with your son."

Doug laughed. His face was painted a bright green, and the two fake bolts on the sides of his neck jiggled. "Cheney's mentioned Helena a few times. She was over for dinner last week. A lovely girl," he added with a glance toward his wife.

Karen pursed her lips and cocked her head to the side. "Certainly, she's very pretty and... what's the word I'm looking for, dear... popular, yes? Cheney's diligently focused on his career right now. He's not looking to get involved with anyone seriously. I'm sure he's told her already." There was an obnoxious pattern to her speech as if she thought she was better than everyone else.

Maggie nodded and scratched at the costume jewelry dangling off her forearm. She always fiddled with something when she was nervous or uncomfortable. Karen quelled any burgeoning love affair between her son and Helena. I wondered whether there was a larger story brewing. "Young kids, what can you do? As for this event, you've all done a spectacular job," I chimed in, hoping to change the topic. Luckily, it worked.

"You should see our restaurant. We've only been open a few weeks, but it's getting super busy," Doug said with an excess of pride in his voice as he reached for Karen's hand.

"That sounds like a good plan. I'll bring my daughter and grandmother with me. They're quite the food enthusiasts," I replied, knowing Emma was getting more finicky by the day, and Nana D, well, she wasn't a fan of eating out all that much. She preferred more homey and comforting meals without too much grandeur.

Maggie raised her eyebrows before excusing herself to introduce the Stoddards to several other guests. I refilled my drink at the bar, devoured two of the fig and prosciutto appetizers, and glanced around the room. Marcus Stanton, Nana D's opponent in the mayoral race, spoke with a woman I recognized but couldn't remember why. I wiped my greasy fingers on a thin paper napkin, tossed it on a tray as a waiter scooted by me, then popped over to greet them.

"It's a pleasure to see you here, Councilman," I said while extending my hand in his direction. By the looks of his near-orange skin pallor and the wispy blond hair half glued to and half flying about his scalp, I could only hazard one guess at his costume. "Using my powers of keen deduction, you're aspiring to be a certain outspoken leader of our fine country?"

He laughed loudly and patted his growing stomach. "Oh, Kellan, you are the clever one. I'm only staying within the guidelines for costumes. *Heroes and Villains*, right?" Which was he? I'm sure we'd know in time, at least once the country found its footing again. I had tried to avoid politics most of my life, but Nana D's mayoral hopes dictated otherwise.

The woman standing next to Marcus, a late-forties brunette with a heart-shaped face and a trim body, dressed as Clara Barton, the founder of the American Red Cross. She wore a checkered blue polyester dress with a white apron hung around her neck and cinched at her waist. Bright red crosses were patched on her arms and chest, and a standard white nurse's cap adorned her head. The woman looked entirely too familiar, but I was afraid of introducing myself if we'd already met and I'd forgotten her name.

Marcus, leaning in too close for the woman's comfort judging by the frown on her lips, solved that issue for me. "You must know Lissette Nutberry, I presume. Her family runs a few funeral homes and the local pharmacy down on Main Street," he noted with a boisterous laugh.

Ah, yes! I'd not spoken to her in a long time, but she looked like her mother who'd played bridge with Nana D. I couldn't remember hearing much about Lissette recently other than she'd been covering at the family businesses for her sister, Judy, who'd left town a year or two earlier. "Yes, I know the Nutberry family quite well. I saw Tiffany last month. She helped track down my friend, Brad, who was interviewing at the hospital."

Brad Shope had been the late Gwendolyn Paddington's nurse for a few months before she died of a cocaine-induced heart attack at a performance of *King Lear* earlier that year. We'd met for dinner and drinks a few times in the last month and were quickly building a friendship. I needed some guys to lean on since I'd returned to town and had few friends left in the area.

"Oh, yes, Tiffany is my niece. She's doing well at Braxton General, just got a promotion, I hear," Lissette said as she stepped away from Marcus with a shiver.

"Where in Europe is Judy these days?" I asked.

"Oh, I wish I knew. I've been having some trouble tracking down the old girl lately. Judy wasn't feeling very well and had been confined to bed rest after an intensive attack of angina. She has a bad heart, you see, and often pushes herself to do too much at once," Lissette melancholically whined as the words rolled off her tongue. Someone had a flair for the dramatic.

"Don't fret now, my little Lissy, I'm sure she'll return your call soon," Marcus comforted and patted her back. Were those two dating or simply having a friendly conversation?

"If I don't hear from her by Tuesday, I'll take a trip to hunt her down. Deirdre offered to do some searching for me, so I didn't have to rush across the pond too hastily," Lissette said, her mood suddenly brightening.

"You know my aunt, Deirdre Danby?" I asked, curious if they'd gone to school together. Aunt Deirdre was my mother's youngest sister and a well-known author who'd penned several historical fiction books and a couple of romance novels. Aunt Deirdre had lived in London for the last two decades and rarely returned home for anything other than funerals and weddings, of which we'd had none in the immediate family for several years.

"We were sorority sisters back in college. We chatted on the *Facebook*, and your aunt thinks my life story might be a plot for one of her new books," Lissette laughed haughtily while a slightly amusing smile commandeered her face. Although she was thin and gaunt, her lips contained enough collagen for an entire tribe of *real housewives*. "Judy was in Deirdre's graduating class, so she offered to have her London detective inspector friend investigate my sister's recent silence. At least that's the story she's selling beneath those expensive bedsheets of hers, if you catch my drift." She eyed me up and down, then moistened her lips. "We should have lunch, darling boy."

Councilman Stanton said to Lisette, "Maybe Kellan could help you find Judy. From what I hear, he'd be the perfect man for this job!"

Time to pull the ripcord, baby. I needed to hatch an immediate escape plan. What was it about me attracting middle-aged women who thought I wanted to know everyone's personal details or become their boy wonder? Sure, I might've developed a minuscule reputation for investigating mysteries, but I didn't need to know what my aunt was doing in the bedroom nor entertain the notion of flirting with the crazy, rich women from her inner social circle. "I'm sure Aunt Deirdre will help you find Judy. If you run into any trouble, we can revisit the topic. Unfortunately, I need to find Dean Mulligan to discuss something about my classes. I saw him earlier talking with Dr. Singh from the science department, but they've disappeared. Have you seen either?"

Both shook their heads enabling me to wish them an enjoyable evening and make a speedy exit. I waited in line for several minutes before grabbing another drink at the bar, then listened to Maggie's speech about donations for Memorial Library's renovations. When it ended, I scanned the room to determine whom I hadn't yet spoken to. Dean Mulligan, wearing a Zeus costume consisting of a white tunic and multiple layers of ill-fitting robes and lighting bolt-shaped trails of garland, suddenly appeared in the far corner.

I stepped to the outer perimeter of the room hoping I could reach them quickly but was distracted when Anita Singh rushed by me in a tizzy. "Wait, I need to speak with you."

Without stopping, she yelled back, "I'm sorry. I'll talk to you another time, I need to locate Maggie Roarke. I left my cell phone in my lab coat pocket, but someone seems to have picked up the wrong one. It's gone, and I have an urgent call soon." She clutched a bunch of folders against her chest as she dashed through the crowd and away from me. For what was supposed to be a fun and exciting evening, she certainly seemed distracted and busier than necessary. Her costume choice was also poorly planned and executed. Although she'd attempted an Albert Einstein persona, all she'd done was add a bushy mustache and teased her naturally white hair, so it looked like she'd been shocked by electricity.

I made a one-eighty-degree turn to determine where she'd been running off to and stopped dead in my tracks when someone more familiar walked toward the east set of double doors to access the private employee spaces. Just beyond them was a narrow hallway leading to a few offices, a pair of restrooms, and a courtyard between the two wings of the library. It was usually off-limits to patrons and only left unlocked for employees during business hours. Was that Francesca or a lookalike? I thought I'd seen her holding a feathered mask in front of her eyes, but I hadn't gotten an unobstructed view. Since I suddenly had an urge to use the restroom from drinking all the Champagne Moscow Mules, I decided to investigate what was happening on the other side of the wall.

I dashed through the center of the room unable to chat with my cousin, Dr. Alex Betscha, who looked dapper in his Superman costume. I wasn't sure if he'd brought a Lois Lane, but his dancing partner was quite attractive in a white nurse's outfit with a patch over one eye. I mumbled an apology and gave them two thumbs up to their costumes.

By the time I reached the double doors close to ten minutes later—the dance crowd wouldn't stop to let me through—I felt a hand grab my wrist and quickly yank me to the side behind one of the flowing silk drapes. I stared at Frida Kahlo, the famed Mexican artist my grandmother loved to celebrate. It took me a minute to separate what her costume was—a bright magenta floral skirt, a royal-blue traditional Tehuana-style embroidered blouse and silver shawl, and a headpiece with dozens of colorful flowers—and the woman I'd come to know the last few months.

"Kellan, I think the stalker is here. Look," Ursula demanded while passing me a handwritten note on a cocktail napkin. "I put down my drink for five seconds to fix the strap on my shoe. When I went to get it, I saw this message." Ursula's tribute to the Mexican culture offered the opposite of her normal Scandinavian genetics—long flowing blonde hair, almond-shaped green eyes, and shy composure. Today, her eclectic jewelry and colorful ensemble echoed a more cultural and rich divinity.

I glanced away from the doors feeling torn between tracking down Francesca and protecting Ursula. "But I need to..." I growled until a prevailing temptation to read the note won out.

You loved riddles as a child, Sofia. Here's one for you... What's tall and clever, wearing a white costume, and planning to capture you when the clock strikes nine? I'll make it easy for you. It's me, and if you have any sense left at all, you will keep this to yourself. I've got a deal to make with you. Look for me in the donations line. – A Blast from the Past

I pulled out my cell phone and glanced at the time. It was eight fifty. We had ten minutes before Ursula finally figured out who'd been harassing her for weeks. "Okay, whoever this is wouldn't show up in the corner by the donations table until exactly nine. They'll be watching you to verify it's not a trap. Let me wander around to inventory anyone in a white costume."

"Thanks, Kellan. They used my real identity. No one knows my name is

Sofia. I'm not normally frightened so easily, but this is getting out of control. I'll meet you back here in five minutes," Ursula whispered. As she left, I saw a spot of red on her shawl. I'd have to remind her about it later, she hated any sense of imperfection. I assumed that was why Myriam loved the woman.

I watched her walk past the first bar and wondered how she'd kept the secret from her wife this whole time. From what Ursula had told me, Myriam would be dressed as Eleanor Roosevelt. While I was certain Frida Kahlo and Eleanor Roosevelt had never met, could my two bosses be hinting at a secret affair with their costumes? Doubtful, but intriguing. I found it ironic that I adored the former U.S. president's wife, but I couldn't stand our college president's. Luckily, I hadn't yet seen Myriam, but I knew my other boss hid somewhere in the room planning her next sneak attack on me.

I strolled casually along the far wall looking for anyone in a white costume. I saw a couple of additional people who fit the bill, but they all seemed deep in conversation with someone else and unconcerned about Ursula's presence. Only a few minutes left to check if it'd been Francesca sneaking through the double doors moments ago. I gently turned the handle, pushed open the left door, and backed through the narrow space. The restroom would have to wait.

When I turned around and got my bearings straight, I activated the flashlight on my phone. On the left were the offices and restrooms. On the right, about twenty feet away, was a large glass door leading into the courtyard. It looked like someone was standing in the outdoor space, but I couldn't be sure if the shadow I'd seen from my angle was a person or a garden statue. I quietly snuck down the hallway past all the closed doors and reached for the courtyard's door handle assuming it wouldn't be open. The courtyard was for employees only, and Maggie didn't want patrons lurking in restricted areas.

A slight shock escaped my lips when the door budged. I leaned in and peered around the corner to where I'd seen the shadow. The silhouette of a woman hovered near a table, but it was too dark to make out her costume. Was that who'd just left the main room? I checked my watch. Only four minutes before Ursula's stalker revealed himself or herself. I should've gone back to see who wore a white costume at the donations table but needed to verify if Francesca had snuck back here.

I carefully stepped on the slate tiles ensuring my footsteps were as inaudible as possible. As I approached, I could hear the woman crying and whispering something incomprehensible. When she leaned to the side, a dim light from an outdoor sconce landed on her. Something metallic moved near her hands. Helena, Maggie's sister, had dressed as a French maid in a short black and white lacy uniform. While she'd obeyed her sister's instructions to cover up most of her body, fishnet stockings and a see-through netted top were not what Maggie had imagined a server wearing at an upscale party.

When I stepped backward, I slipped on a slate tile and my new Cole Haan dress shoes made a loud scraping noise. I hoped I hadn't scuffed them too much. Helena turned toward me. "Who's there?"

"It's Kellan. I'm sorry, but I've got to find someone. I'll come back to check on you." I'd turned to walk away, but when Helena jolted upright, I could see she wasn't alone. Behind her, someone possibly unconscious was sprawled on the ground. Near Helena's feet was the sharp object that had been glistening from the light shining from the wall sconce. "Wait, what's going on?" I asked hesitantly before startling when a distant clock began to chime loudly. Was it already nine o'clock?

"You've got to help, I think he's dead. I can't find a pulse," Helena cried. When she moved to the side, I realized the shiny object was a knife. Covered in what looked to be a red, sticky substance.

I rushed over and gasped once the entire picture came into view. Whoever was lying on the ground had been stabbed and bled all over the slate tiles. "Who is it?" I whispered while comforting Helena, but she didn't respond. Instead, she fell into my arms and sobbed with a great force. I looked more closely at the victim and realized it was a guest who'd dressed as Dr. Evil from the Austin Powers flicks. Based on the amount of blood on his abdomen, I needed to call 9-1-1. Sheriff Montague wasn't going to be pleased that I'd found another dead body.

CHAPTER 4

I studied my immediate surroundings in search of the best path to avoid further disturbance to the crime scene. Judging by the amount of blood and the knife lying near my feet, this was not an accidental death. I nudged Helena to the side of the courtyard nearest the wall sconce, where a raised garden bed offered a place for her to temporarily relax. "Just sit tight, Helena. Everything will be okay," I murmured almost incoherently.

Several thoughts clouded my judgment at that frightening moment. Did Helena stab the man? Was she drunk or on drugs? Was this the man in white who'd been stalking Ursula? Although Dr. Evil's traditional garb was more of a light gray, it could pass for white in a dim light. I knew I needed to call the paramedics, but I didn't want to turn the entire party into massive chaos. As I carefully walked toward the body, I heard the door to the courtyard click. It was then I realized if Helena didn't stab Dr. Evil, could the assailant be hiding in the darkness somewhere nearby? If so, was the perp coming or going?

"Kellan, I can see a shadow approaching you!" Helena shrieked.

I turned to my left as someone grabbed my arm. I immediately jerked my elbow directly at what I guessed was a man's shoulder. If I could knock him over, I might get the advantage to pin him down.

"Kellan, what the heck are you doing? It's Connor," a deep voice with a Caribbean accent shouted. He swiftly wrenched my arm behind my back and yanked me several steps toward the door. "Stand down, dude." His choice of Dumbledore was fitting for the costume extravaganza, and I particularly enjoyed seeing what Connor might look like in forty years. A long, gray mane and beard flowed seamlessly together and landed on what I could only describe as a woman's caftan. While Connor was exceptionally well-built, his blue and white starred garment was a loose mess. The wand sticking out of his pocket was a humorous touch, but it'd do us no good right now.

"Connor," I said, tensing as he set me free from his impossibly firm grip. "Someone's been hurt."

"I followed you. Too many people were coming in and out of those double doors. What's going on?" His concern made sense because one of his responsibilities as Braxton's director of security was to check out anything suspicious.

After I explained what I'd stumbled upon, Connor instructed me to keep an eye on Helena while he contacted Sheriff Montague. I walked the outer perimeter of the courtyard, a forty-by-forty-foot space enclosed on all sides with only the one entry point. My phone provided enough light to ensure I didn't trip over anything, but I couldn't be sure someone wasn't crawling beneath a bush or under a table. As I reached Helena, Connor scanned the courtyard for any secluded place where someone could be hiding. Once he hung up with the sheriff, Connor checked the victim to locate a pulse or sense any sign of breathing.

"Connor is getting help, Helena. Are you able to tell me what happened?" I asked, pushing away a trace of guilt for not waiting until the cops showed up to lead the investigation. I held her hand and listened to her practice a yoga technique to control her breathing and relax her body.

"I found him like that. I... I'd come outside for a second, and when I saw him lying on the ground, I bent down to see if he'd fallen," Helena cried. She wiped away a tear as it rolled down her cheek and pulled me into a hug. "I didn't know who it was, but I saw him earlier fighting with—"

Connor interrupted Helena's response. "Sheriff Montague is on her way. She's locating Maggie in the main room and will venture back here as soon as she's posted police officers at all the exits. We don't want anyone leaving the library until we know what's going on."

"Did you see who came back here?" I couldn't be sure if Helena had anything to do with the victim's demise. Had the knife been in her hands or just near them? I hadn't told Connor that part yet.

"It was just too dark to tell from where I stood in the main room. No one's supposed to have access to these private offices, but the door was open when I arrived," Connor said.

When Sheriff Montague swooped in moments later, Maggie was at her side. The sheriff said, "Good thing I was already near the campus checking on a robbery. Talk to me, Connor. Who's the victim, and what do we know about the woman standing over the body?"

As the sheriff glanced at me, Maggie rushed over to Helena. "What's happened, sis?"

I realized Connor hadn't told the sheriff I'd found the body nor that it was Helena who'd been out here. Was he protecting us or providing enough cover at the time to get the police on site and cordon off the area? The poor guy lying dead on the ground behind me was covered in blood. I'd walked in seconds after it'd potentially happened. Was the killer hiding in one of the offices or restrooms? A shiver ran through my body despite the warm May weather.

"What are you doing here, Little Ayrwick?" the sheriff snarled. We'd, for the briefest of moments, begun calling each other by our first names, but I'd gotten the distinct impression she didn't want me to address her right now as *April*. "There have been four homicides in the last three months, and you are at the center of them all. Care to explain? Are you a magnet for seedy criminals skulking about in our normally respectable town? Have you unleashed your incendiary ties to the Castigliano mob family upon Wharton County?"

That answered another of my questions. April Montague knew all about my in-laws' shady business transactions. "No comment. All I did was step outside and stumble on a body. Again. I don't want this to keep happening. Never again. Really."

One of the sheriff's detectives I'd met in the past trudged into the courtyard and began surveying the scene. April introduced him to us and said this was likely to be his last case before he retired to Florida, but he was the best she had. "Too bad you picked tonight to work, Gilkrist," she teased. While he made notes on the surroundings, April asked Helena to share what she knew.

Maggie wrapped her arm around her sister's shoulder and urged her to speak. "Go ahead, Helena. Tell them everything. You can trust Connor and Sheriff Montague."

Helena explained that she'd gone to the courtyard to sneak a quick smoke break. While she was walking toward the picnic table, she tripped over something. As she bent down to see what it was, she noticed a person or what looked like a person. Helena shook the man, assuming it was someone who'd been drinking too much, fallen, or suffered a heart attack. When she touched the body in search of a wrist or throat, she'd felt something sticky. That's when she realized the person had no pulse. She was about to attempt CPR before I'd walked in. In the confusion, she might have touched the knife when I entered the courtyard.

"Why would you pick up a knife, Miss Roarke?" the sheriff asked with a suspicious glare. The detective approached and indicated the victim was indeed deceased. He'd already called the coroner, who'd be onsite within twenty minutes.

"I... I don't know," Helena said, her hands shaking with an intense tremor. She'd never looked that scared before. "It was just there. I was trying to find a pulse, and I didn't realize what it was until it was in my hands."

A few splashes of blood on her palm and fingers were now noticeable. I also saw some on the front of her blouse and skirt. Had the blood been transferred when she was leaning over the body or while she'd been stabbing him? I couldn't believe Helena was capable of murder, even as fiery as I'd seen her get in the past. I looked down and saw a few blotches had also rubbed onto my coat.

Over the next twenty minutes, the sheriff separated Helena and me to unleash her ruthless interrogation techniques. The detective questioned Helena with Maggie present. Connor and Sheriff Montague took me to a nearby office to explain what I'd seen. "I only came back here to use the restroom. It was closer than the public ones on the other side of the main room."

As I shared the rest of what I could recall, I realized the buzzing in my pocket had been my cell phone. I took a quick peek once Connor and the sheriff scampered away in a private conversation. Ursula had texted and called a few times. Nine o'clock had come and gone, but no one approached her at the donations table. 'Where are you?' she kept asking, then finally telling me she saw Sheriff Montague onsite. 'Did something happen?' was the latest text.

"Ursula Power is demanding to be told what's going on, Sheriff. I think we need to let her back here," I added as April walked toward me. If the person under the Dr. Evil mask was indeed Ursula's stalker, she couldn't keep her secret any longer.

"Really? And tell me, Little Ayrwick, do you think I should let every member of the general public, like yourself, just wander back here in the middle of a murder investigation? Perhaps we could have a coffee klatch while we play a game of *Clue* to decide who did it. Let's see... we know it was the knife in the courtyard, but I'm sure not smart enough to figure out whether it was the cook or the butler this time!" April's voice increased with each insult to the point her face reddened to a worrisome shade. Given that I was familiar with her normally prickly personality, I knew, despite appearances, she wouldn't explode on contact.

"Well, no... but... there might be a—" I started to say when Ursula hurried into the office pushing a very frustrated Officer Flatman aside.

"Back off unless you want me to sue you for harassment," Ursula yelled coming to an abrupt stop at seeing the situation in the office and out in the courtyard. Despite being cloaked in partial darkness, the courtyard was visible from the hallway. "What is the meaning of—"

"I attempted to prevent her from entering, Sheriff. She elbowed me in the chest, and then her wife grabbed my arm and pretended to trip. I tried to stop the woman from falling, and that's when Miss Power busted through the double doors. They're quite a pair of—" Officer Flatman said, upon finally reaching the rest of us.

"Just stand inside the main room and don't let anyone else in, Flatman. You're certainly not showing me any reasons why I'd consider you as the new detective when Gilkrist retires next month," Sheriff Montague advised in a slightly calmer manner. She narrowed her gaze at Ursula. "You're lucky I don't arrest you for assaulting an officer."

"That *officer* knocked over my wife with excessive force when I *accidentally* bumped into him on the way to chat with Mayor Grosvalet. You're lucky I don't inform the mayor I plan to sue you for police brutality. Let's get to the point here rather than decide which woman in this room has more power, Sheriff," Ursula countered with her head cocked to the side and her chin jutted out.

In a battle between Ursula and April, I couldn't be certain who'd win. While Ursula's past clearly revealed she was capable of standing her ground, April's knowledge of martial arts and wrestling—not to mention the stun gun and Old Betsy, her actual gun full of bullets currently attached to her hip— could clearly stop my boss in her tracks. "I attempted to warn you Ursula was determined to get back here, Sheriff Montague." I tried as hard as I could to keep the growing sneer off my lips, but I was powerless for the moment. She undoubtedly saw through my inability to keep a straight face.

The sheriff cleared her throat. "Enough. Since you're the president of this college, I'd need to share this news with you anyway. We're investigating a possible homicide. Keep that to yourself for the time being. A man wearing a Dr. Evil mask in a light gray or off-white suit appears to have been stabbed with a knife. A young lady working the event was caught standing over him. She's being questioned right now. Kellan Ayrwick, one of your..." she said tilting her gaze in my direction, "*esteemed professors...* happened to be the individual who observed the young lady stepping away from the victim with the probable murder weapon."

"Who is it?" Ursula asked, then turned to me. "Kellan?"

I lifted my shoulders. "I'm not entirely sure, but I find the *white costume* certainly strange. I suppose we need to wait for the cops to remove the mask." I emphasized the color of the Dr. Evil suit hoping Ursula would connect it to her stalker's latest messages. Judging by her partial nod, she did.

"I am sorry such a tragedy has happened. Braxton will certainly cooperate with the Wharton County Sheriff's Office. I will ask, Sheriff, how do you want to handle the ongoing party in the main room? We're about to wrap up soon, but I assume you'll need to speak with everyone at some point," Ursula noted in an authoritative yet understanding tone.

"My team has been monitoring the doors. We will need a list of every attendee or employee working at the event. I'll need to schedule interviews with everyone, but more importantly, I need to secure this crime scene," April instructed.

As the sheriff's team commandeered the courtyard and private office space, Maggie was released to announce that there'd been an unexpected death in the library. She was told not to say anything about it being a murder nor what the victim was wearing until the sheriff's office could contact the next of kin. While Connor stayed with Helena in one office, the sheriff spoke with the coroner and Detective Gilkrist in the courtyard.

"You have to tell them about the notes, Ursula. I have no idea if Helena saw anyone else. She mentioned whoever's wearing the Dr. Evil costume had fought with someone earlier tonight, but we were interrupted, and I was escorted out of the room shortly afterward." I didn't want to tell my boss what to do, but there was no other way to ensure we weren't accused of hiding anything.

"I need to see who's under that mask. If it's someone I know, I'll explain about the notes. If it's not, maybe the victim has nothing to do with me," Ursula demanded with renewed vigor and determination. It was clear her mind couldn't be changed.

"Fine. I'll ask if they'll let us see the victim's face," I noted while walking toward the sheriff and the coroner.

"Do not come any closer," April indicated with a tinge of annoyance in her voice. "We're about to remove the mask now that we have enough pictures and preliminary notes on how the body was found. The mask isn't connected to anything else. Lifting it won't interfere with the crime scene."

I tried not to stare, but I wanted to learn as much as I could about the victim in case it might help Ursula discover his identity. Although the man wore a full suit, his hands were hidden by dull white gloves likely added to match Dr. Evil's pale skin tone. The victim's face was fully covered in a mask, and he was lying on his back. One foot was slanted to the side, and a pool of blood had formed near his waist. It looked like he'd been stabbed in his stomach at least once. I had to look away, so I wouldn't get sick from what I'd observed thus far.

"Perhaps Ursula and I might be able to help identify the victim?" I asked, swallowing deeply to prevent the fig and prosciutto appetizer from projecting out of my throat.

"At this point, we need all the help we can get," April said as she began to record a video from her cell phone. As she stood near the body, she carefully positioned the camera to monitor the coroner's actions as he cut the elastic band near the victim's ears. Once loosened, he lifted the mask off with one hand while ensuring the man's head didn't shift from the movement.

As the coroner stepped away, I did a double take. I couldn't be certain if the man was Ursula's stalker, but I knew who he was. "I recognize him," I said in a faint voice.

"Care to share that information with the rest of us?" April said with a smirk.

"I think it's George Braun. I met him yesterday for the first time. The only time. He's teaching a class in the science department and working with Millard Paddington on the upcoming Mendel flower show." I drew in a deep breath and felt a bit lightheaded.

"Are you certain?"

I nodded. "Although... I only spoke with him for five minutes. We're supposed to have breakfast tomorrow before he starts working at Braxton." I looked at Ursula who clutched her upper chest and throat. After her loud and unexpected cough, I was certain she recognized the man.

The sheriff glanced at Ursula. "I assume you'd know one of your employees. Is Mr. Ayrwick correct in his identification of the victim?"

Ursula looked at me, then the sheriff. For five seconds, she entered a trance where I thought she might pass out. "No. I wouldn't know all of the professors. I've just been here a few months at this point," she replied in a distracted tone.

My boss was clearly lying. She didn't know this man was teaching at Braxton, but she definitely recognized his face. "Okay, well, that's all you need from us, right? I know the routine by now. Be prepared to review and sign a statement. You'll have more questions. Keep quiet. Right?"

The sheriff nodded, then told the coroner to continue preparing the body. She extended her hand in the opposite direction, so Ursula and I would follow her to the courtyard door. "Detective Gilkrist will arrange interviews for everyone in the main room. The coroner needs to conduct his investigation. I will meet with Helena Roarke myself. It's not every day you find the potential culprit standing over the body with the murder weapon."

The shock of her statement flustered me for a moment. "You can't think Helena did this. She told us she found the body and accidentally touched the knife." How did Helena know the professor? Or had she just seen him arguing with someone but not recognized him? I looked to Ursula who remained silent. What else was she hiding? I remembered the red stain I'd seen on her shawl.

"Leave the investigation to my team, Little Ayrwick. I've had enough of your interference in the past. If the Wharton County Sheriff's Office needs your assistance, we will ask for it. As of now, consider yourself dismissed. Both of you. Neither of you should leave town, nor discuss this with a soul. Not your nosy grandmother," she directed at me. "Not your difficult wife," she said, squinting at Ursula. "Not each other nor Helena or Maggie Roarke. No one. Got it?"

We both confirmed our understanding of the sheriff's vitriol. Did she think we were children? As Ursula and I walked down the hall toward the main room of Memorial Library, she stopped me. "Kellan, I know you saw the shock on my face when the coroner removed the mask."

"How do you know George Braun if you didn't recognize him as one of your new professors? And don't lie to me, Ursula. I'm on your side." I wondered if he was one of the investigators or the assistant from the explosion twenty-five years ago who'd recognized her and had come to town to blackmail her. By now, Ursula was trembling. I hadn't realized while we were walking that the intensity of her grip bored holes into my forearm.

"I don't know exactly how to say this. It's a coincidence, but..." she paused.

"What is it, Ursula? You're scaring me." I waited for her to look back up at me.

"That's my brother, Hans. I thought he'd died in the explosion, but could he have survived?" Ursula said as devastation and alarm flooded her eyes.

"Using a different name. Like you?" I shook my head in confusion.

"Yes. If he survived the explosion, he might've needed extensive plastic surgery. I saw my brother's eyes when I looked at that dead man. At George Braun. Do you think it's possible that—"

"Your own brother has been hiding all these years and finally found you?" I exclaimed, feeling stunned and uncertain. I recalled seeing him wearing gloves the day before. Was he hiding burns on his hands and fingers? "I guess that's the first place we need to look. Then maybe we'll know who killed him. Since it wasn't Helena. I can't see her doing something like that." When I finished speaking, Ursula turned away from me and opened the double doors. After she stepped through the open space into the main room of the library, she rushed directly into Myriam's waiting arms.

I couldn't help but wonder if Ursula had known who was stalking her and had taken the opportunity to get rid of him once and for all. It would explain the red stain. Could the surprise on her face at discovering his identity be as real as it seemed? Or had Myriam taught her wife how to act the part of an innocent, stunned, and perplexed bystander?

CHAPTER 5

When I returned to Danby Landing after the costume extravaganza, Emma was already asleep. Nana D thought she'd recovered quickly from her symptoms and would be fine after a solid night's rest. Before I went to bed, I remembered failing to discover whether Francesca was actually on campus that night. If it had been Francesca heading toward the courtyard, where had she gone and why had no one else seen her? Had I imagined it?

Although I'd tried to reach Maggie several times after the horrendous incident, she was either focused on helping Helena get through the interrogation with Sheriff Montague or they'd needed healing time to process what'd happened. I couldn't imagine either of the women had encountered a dead body in the past. The nightmares had been almost traumatic the first few times I'd found one. Suddenly, my phone vibrated with an incoming text message:

Maggie: *Stop by the library at lunchtime tomorrow. Helena needs your help to find the real killer.*

I confirmed I'd be there, then put my head on the pillow to let the comforting darkness lead me into slumber. It turned out to be filled with laughing masks and epic battles between heroes and villains.

* * *

On Monday morning before I dropped Emma at school, we had breakfast together. She only had a month left before school let out for the summer but was excited to present her show-and-tell project to the class. She'd been working on drawings of the landscape of Nana D's farm. I once thought Emma wanted to become a veterinarian when she grew up, but in the last few weeks, she'd become obsessed with sketching buildings and rearranging rooms in her dollhouse. I'd introduced her to a new custom version of the game *Clue* with a zoo animal theme, which led to her learning about the various parts of Danby Landing. Rather than animals as killers, this version of *Clue* focused on which animal had stolen the key to the food supply cabinet and guessing what they'd dropped outside the door in the rush to get away.

I drove to Braxton and parked on South Campus since I had my summer class to teach that morning—Screenwriting in a Digital World. It was an intense eight-week course where students met for two hours each day from Monday through Friday to learn about technique, develop their own scripts for a pilot episode, and understand how to present it to a production company. I entered Diamond Hall and ascended the stairs to the second floor where my humble office resided. As I passed through the hallway, I noticed my boss sitting at her desk.

"Good morning, Myriam. How was the rest of your evening?" I inquired pleasantly, wondering if Ursula had shared anything about discovering the victim resembled her dead brother, Hans.

Myriam slid tortoise-shell glasses to the bridge of her nose, huffed slightly, and glanced back at her laptop screen. "*Constant you are, but yet a woman and for secrecy, no lady closer for I well believe thou wilt not utter what thou dost not know.*"

I couldn't recall which of Shakespeare's plays that barb with ulterior motives had come from. "Let me guess, you're still angry with me?" I stepped one foot into her office waiting for something heavy to be flung in my direction. When she ignored my comment, I took another step inside, so that I was technically in her office but able to duck behind her coat rack if necessary. I'd learned that lesson the hard way the first time around. "Give me a hint. Is it from a tragedy or comedy?"

"Of course, you wouldn't know it's from Henry IV. What do you want, Mr. Ayrwick? I've got plenty of problems to attend to without you dropping more nonsense in my lap," Myriam grumbled as she turned to the credenza behind her to retrieve a document from the printer. "Hurry up, please. Some of us work around here."

"True, some of us do. I thought I'd see how Ursula was doing this morning. She was quite distraught over the death in the library last night," I said, taking a seat across from her. "I'm well aware Henry IV is one of the Bard's historical plays, neither a tragedy nor a comedy."

"Redemption will not erase the truth. I know you and Ursula have been keeping something from me. She was distressed last night and immediately went to sleep. I'm sure she'll have an expedient recovery today given she's meeting with the Board of Trustees." Myriam signed the document she'd pulled off the printer and handed it to me. "Your syllabus for the fall is approved. Is that all for today?"

I considered my next approach to determine what Myriam knew. "I know so little about your wife. Given that we all work together, I'd think Ursula could be a little more open and friendlier. Where did she grow up?"

Myriam stared past me at the whiteboard on the wall opposite her. "Now that the *King Lear* production is finished and we're beginning to cast our summer production, we need to agree on a few protocols for the remainder of the year I'm... *blessed*... to be working with you at Braxton."

I assumed she wasn't going to discuss Ursula's past. It would be all business. When I'd been offered an assistant professor role at Braxton, it had come with two clauses. First, it was only a one-year contract to provide time for the new executive administration to decide my fate. Second, given a few too many public disagreements Myriam and I'd shared in the past, Ursula mandated we work together at the college's theatre, Paddington's Play House, to conquer our glacial differences.

"I'm certainly glad you saw the light and extended the permanent stage director role to Arthur Terry. He and Jennifer will need the money now that they're having a baby together," I noted while turning around to see what Myriam had been reading on the whiteboard.

"Perhaps I'm learning the art of compromise, Mr. Ayrwick. I'll schedule our first meeting with him for later this week. Be sure to pick up a copy of the script. Time is of the essence here. I expect you will keep yourself from entanglement with anything else." Myriam pursed her lips, then smiled like a jackal about to consume its prey. "I'm sure Ursula would appreciate you keeping your distance from what's happened with Professor Braun's recent appearance and death."

The way Myriam spoke, she knew something I didn't. She paused and ever-so-gently cleared her throat when she said his name. "Of course, I will do whatever *Madame President* asks me to do. Just as I do whatever you, my immediate supervisor, asks me to do. I think we understand one another." I wished her a splendiferous day and walked down the hall to my office to prepare for the first set of courses.

A few hours later, encouraged about the excitement in the classroom, I stopped by The Big Beanery to buy lunch for Maggie. The cozy café on South Campus was a virtual hotspot for anyone to hang out with friends, study for an exam, or cruise the student population for a next date. Not an ideal path for me, but a sizable percentage of the college's near-one-thousand enrollees often spent hours socializing and hobnobbing with one another. With tons of comfy alcoves, free Wi-Fi and charging stations, and the best coffee in all of Wharton County, it was the place to be.

I wasn't sure if Helena would be visiting Maggie at the library, but we could all share a few sandwiches, chips, and a bowl of fruit. Maybe a couple of chocolate chip croissants for dessert, a necessary part of any meal. I took the next cable car to North Campus wondering when they'd start the summer redesign. It meant two weeks of walking back and forth between campuses—helpful for staying in shape but a dreadful experience in the sweltering heat.

After I left the station, I stepped on the central cobblestone pathway and ventured to the mailroom in the student union building to check for new deliveries. Besides a catalog advertising the latest genuine leather satchels—I might have an addiction—and office supplies, Braxton's alumni magazine with my father on the cover appeared. Although it was his highly candid outgoing interview, I'd read it another time. I also had a new postcard that'd been postmarked three days earlier in Vancouver. It read:

You were never one for air travel except for that one trip to Mendoza; you always wanted to Vacation by train given your fear of flying. I know a precious six-year old girl who'd love to visit this area with you one day. Maybe we'll all meet again at the VanDusen Botanical Garden where we can take center stage for a second wedding.

It had to be from Francesca. She and I had embarked on a two-week train excursion from Los Angeles to Northern Canada. At the botanical garden, we got mixed up with a celebrity couple who decided at the last minute to get married that afternoon. We served as their best man and matron of honor since none of their friends were in Vancouver. If Francesca had been in Canada three days ago, surely that was enough time to show up in Braxton last night. I snapped a photo of the message and sent it off to Cecilia and Vincenzo Castigliano. Maybe it would help them figure out where my wife was hiding.

I was feeling stalked like Ursula. What was it about people who couldn't be truthful nor accept things happened outside of our control? Ursula had only been trying to stop her brother, Hans, from stealing the cure when she accidentally caused the explosion killing their parents, and maybe him, too. Francesca was the one who got sucked into her family's shenanigans with Las Vargas. Couldn't she put Emma first and stop this hide-and-seek game? We couldn't magically become a family again nor pretend she was suddenly alive. Emma deserved a life without unnecessary fear. Until Vincenzo solved the Vargas family vendetta, this was how it had to be. Why couldn't Francesca understand that approach?

I turned at the end of the pathway and made a left up the steps leading into Memorial Library. Connor approached from the opposite direction. "Hey, Kellan. Maggie tells me she's expecting you for lunch."

"On my way now. Is Helena doing okay?"

"She spent most of the night at the Wharton County Sheriff's Office. They let her go early this morning, but she's acting highly suspicious. Sheriff Montague thinks Helena is hiding something important. Until April can produce a realistic motive, there's no reason to hold her." Connor shook my free hand before putting his own back in his pocket.

"I'm not sure there's anything I can do if Helena won't talk. I'm not inserting myself into the investigation again, so don't give your bestie any ideas that I'm going to interfere with—"

Connor interrupted. "Listen, April is not my bestie. I've given you a hard time in the past about putting your nose in other people's business. I think this is different. Helena is Maggie's little sister. She was standing over George Braun's dead body. We gotta look out for the Roarke family."

I hadn't expected Connor to support my involvement. "Did you learn anything else after I left?"

Connor indicated the autopsy was scheduled for today. The coroner had done preliminary work last night, and they had a positive identification from Millard Paddington. He was called to the morgue and confirmed it was George Braun. Millard had provided George's local address in Braxton. The guy had bought a cabin outside the Saddlebrooke National Forest on the other side of the Finnulia River. Millard knew nothing about the man's family, but suggested the sheriff follow up with Dean Mulligan and the college's human resources department. They could provide any paperwork George Braun had submitted that might identify his next of kin.

If he was truly Ursula's brother, Hans Mück, I knew the name of his next of kin. I needed to speak with Ursula as soon as possible. "I wish I knew where he'd come from before moving to Braxton."

Connor shrugged his shoulders. "You know the sheriff only tells me the minimum. She needs my cooperation as the director of security at Braxton, but there's a wall she puts up when it broaches revealing too much. Millard might know a little more than he's said. You're close to him. Perhaps you could find out if he remembers something else."

"I'll give him a call later today. Hey, not sure if this is important, but Anita Singh lost her lab coat last night. It was part of her Einstein costume. I wonder if that has anything to do with the murder," I said recalling she was in quite a hurry when I'd run into her.

"Do you think she's the killer?" Connor said with a distorted face.

I hadn't thought about that angle, although Dr. Singh had fought with George according to Millard. "Or the killer used her lab coat as a disguise to escape?" When Connor said he'd look into its disappearance, I replied, "Okay. Any chance Helena said anything else about knowing George Braun, other than meeting him at Memorial Library's costume extravaganza?"

"Nope. I haven't talked to Helena myself and only know what Maggie's shared with me. I gotta run, there's an administrative meeting with my staff in a few minutes. I have a lengthy list of security changes to drop on them." Connor suggested a time to meet at the gym the next day and took off for his office. Didn't he know my body was still complaining from his last inhumane workout regimen?

As I entered the library, I read a text message response from my in-laws. Vincenzo dispatched someone to Vancouver to learn anything new. He'd be in touch again soon. I hadn't told them about seeing their daughter at the party. I still couldn't be sure if I was hallucinating or whether Francesca had something to do with George Braun's death. My wife would never be able to kill someone, but it didn't mean someone else in her family wasn't somehow involved.

Maggie's office was in a different area of the library, which meant I didn't need to enter the private employee offices nor approach the courtyard. I wanted to check it out during the daylight, but she should escort me in case there was a police officer ensuring it'd remained locked down. When I found her in the office just past the history section, Maggie's head rested on the desk and her fingers massaged her temples in small concentric circles. The space wasn't large, but she'd added a personal touch to the room—a diffuser sputtered lavender-scented steam, a sound machine released a gentle rainstorm, and photos of all the great historical libraries adorned the walls.

"Is it really that bad?" I lifted my hand to show her the lunch I'd brought. "Salt and vinegar potato chips included. Free of charge, as always." I couldn't resist, knowing they were her favorite.

"Based on what I'm about to ask you, I'm the one who should be paying this time." Maggie lifted her head and motioned for me to come in.

Puffy red eyes indicated she'd been crying recently. "I'm so sorry this happened to you. Before we talk about your sister, did you raise everything you needed for the renovation fund?"

"That's the only positive thing about last night. I checked the figures my staff recorded from everyone who visited the donations table. We're ahead by five percent. We might be able to afford a brand-new, state of the art security system, which is apparently necessary at Braxton these days."

"That's probably a grand idea." I thought I saw a small upward curl on Maggie's lips. Was she coming out of her daze? I hugged her, then sat across the desk and opened the sandwiches and chips. "Eat up, it'll help you feel better. As for security around Braxton, I'm not sure what's going on, but something is out of order. I'm sure Connor is on top of it all."

"Thank you for coming today. Helena is at home. Mom and Dad want to keep her safe for now. Lara Bouvier from the WCLN news station followed us home last night and tried to interview her about the murder." Maggie ate a chip and opened a bottle of seltzer. I could see a bit of her color coming back.

"How is Helena doing?" I wondered whether she'd told Maggie anything else important.

"Insists on returning to work this morning. She's cleaning rooms and working a normal schedule," Maggie noted, then revealed George Braun had been a guest at the Roarke & Daughters Inn.

I guess that meant Helena knew him before the library event had kicked off the previous night. "Were there any issues between them? Did she tell the sheriff about it?"

"Yes, once Mom and Dad showed up at the sheriff's office last night, everything came out. George Braun rented a room three weeks ago claiming he'd bought a cabin but was having repairs done on it before he could officially move in. He was due to check out of the bed and breakfast next week."

"Meaning she mingled with him while cleaning his room and attending to normal guest needs?"

"Yes. And this morning, one of the other chambermaids told the detective that George and Helena were recently engaged in a heated discussion. Yuri didn't know the details, but apparently George slammed the door shut and told

Helena to stay out of his room for the rest of the weekend." Maggie brushed a few crumbs off the desk into a wastepaper basket as a student worker knocked on the door. "Yes, what do you need?"

"Ummm... some lady detective or cop stopped at the front desk and asked me to locate you. She said it was important," the student worker nervously advised. "And I gotta go. Dr. Singh's science lab starts in ten minutes."

Maggie told him he could leave but to let the sheriff know she'd be there in five minutes. "Helena won't listen to my parents or to me. I called Finnigan Masters this morning to ask for his help in case the police arrest her for George Braun's murder. The inn is swarming with police officers. The library's private employee offices are sealed off, so I had to let some of the staff stay home today. I've got to keep this place running, but I also need to meet with the chief of staff and Ursula today to discuss the situation."

"Should I visit your sister? I can try to persuade her to let Finnigan help or find out what she's hiding. Maybe she'll be more comfortable talking to someone outside her family." I needed to clarify if George and Hans were the same person. I also had to find out why Anita Singh and George didn't get along. Maybe Helena knew or saw something in his room at the Roarke & Daughters Inn.

"Yes, please, but first come with me to see the sheriff. There's one more fact Helena neglected to tell the detective about. I'm worried," Maggie noted as she shut and locked her office door.

"What?" I walked up the steps to the main floor. "Does it make her situation look worse?"

Maggie shook her head. "I'm not sure. She told me who she saw arguing with George Braun shortly before she found his body."

I worried it was Ursula. I had been with Ursula around that time, but I wasn't with her the whole night. "Anyone we know?"

"Cheney Stoddard. He's the son of the couple who recently moved to town to open the restaurant and event management company. Remember, they catered last night's party for me." Maggie stopped when we reached the front entrance. The sheriff stood a few feet away at the desk. "Don't say anything until you talk to Helena about it."

"Isn't she dating him?" I asked Maggie as Sheriff Montague walked toward us. What did the Stoddard family have to do with George Braun? Was it a coincidence, or had they known the professor prior to moving to Braxton? I remember Maggie saying the Stoddards came from the Midwest. Could it have been Chicago where Ursula had caused a lab explosion all those years ago?

CHAPTER 6

Sheriff Montague frowned when she saw me, then asked Maggie for a minute alone. Maggie said, "You can speak in front of Kellan, Sheriff. He's my eyes and ears while I'm protecting Helena."

I was about to provide assault and battery coverage for myself when my phone buzzed with a text message. "Excuse me a moment," I noted, leaving Maggie and the sheriff to chat.

Ursula: *We must talk today. Can you come by around five o'clock?*
Me: *Sure, but I'll have Emma with me. Need to get her from after-school activities.*
Ursula: *I can meet you at the Pick-Me-Up Diner for an early dinner. Myriam's teaching class tonight.*
Me: *See you then. I'm doing some research today and might have news.*

When I finished texting and looked toward the front desk, Maggie was gone. I thought it was time to leave until a grumpy voice startled me.

"I asked her to review her statement with Detective Gilkrist. She'll be back in a little while. What are you doing here?" a charged-up Sheriff Montague grumbled from a short distance away. Her standard blazer and dark blue jeans were crisply pressed. Her brassy blonde hair was well-styled for a change. Usually her motorcycle helmet squashed portions down like permanent bedhead.

"At the risk of sounding rude, this is the college's library and I am a professor in the communications department. I'm often in the building doing research and checking out these awesome paper, ink, and glue things called books." I rolled my eyes, adjusted my glasses, and lifted a *Brian L. Porter* novel from my new leather satchel, as if to make an indisputable point about why I was there.

"You don't say! And here I thought you were just another pretty face around campus. Thanks for clarifying your prestigious occupation for the umpteenth time, Little Ayrwick." April leaned against a desk covered in magazines and searched in her leather folder for something. "Since you just happened to be here, and I just happened to have your statement with me, maybe you could do us both a favor and help me cross one more item off my very lengthy list of to-dos."

"Don't you have someone to take care of those pesky things for you?" I asked, intending to acknowledge her own importance. I'd think the sheriff had more urgent things to do than carry around witness statements to be signed. "What I'm trying to say is I understand how busy you must be with last night's unexpected murder."

"Murder is always unexpected, at least in my world. I suppose in the mafia world, it's anticipated, eh? If I knew someone was going to be murdered, don't you think I'd try to stop it?" Sheriff Montague uncapped her pen and gently pushed it across the periodicals desk in my direction.

I wasn't helping the situation. "We keep getting off on the wrong foot, April. I'm sorry. Maggie asked me to stop by to cover a few things. I am not trying to get in your way." I looked at the written report and made a few notes of facts that weren't one-hundred percent accurate. "May I ask a question about the murder weapon?"

"Is it pertinent to your statement, Mr. Ayrwick, or are you exhibiting eccentric curiosities again?" She ran her fingers through her hair and straightened out her bangs. April had been growing her do much longer during the last few months. It made her look a bit softer in a positive way.

"Possibly. I should clarify that when I encountered Helena in the courtyard, I was aware of the knife before she stood up. I vividly remember the blade glistening when the light hit it. I thought I noticed some sort of design or scroll on the handle before it fell to the ground. If that's the case, she couldn't have been holding it, right?" I knew it had some sort of writing on it, but it was too dark and far away to read the exact wording.

"What you're saying is you didn't see her stab the victim, nor pull the knife out of his body. But you did see her drop it when you were walking toward her. Fair?" April typed a few notes on her mobile tablet as she spoke.

"It looked as if the knife just fell away from her body. I'm not exactly sure she'd been aware it was even there at first. Do you understand what I mean?" It had all happened so fast, but it didn't look like Helena was trying to hide anything.

"That's helpful. I'm not sure what it means, but after we run all the fingerprint tests and determine who owns the knife, I'll be in touch with additional questions. Thank you."

The sheriff indicated she'd have a revised statement available the following day.

While she exited into the private employee office area, I gathered my belongings and prepared to leave. The clerk at the main desk wanted to reconfirm one of the books I'd requested, which took a few minutes. Unfortunately, she was only using it as a chance to flirt with me. I informed her I had a no dating policy when it came to students. Just as the student was done sulking, Maggie returned to the floor.

"Oh, I'm glad you're still here. I didn't get to thank you for keeping quiet about Cheney. Once you find out from Helena what she knows, I'll understand if you need to tell the sheriff. I wanted to ask that you get all the details before saying anything. I'm sorry to put you in a difficult spot." As Maggie hugged me, it felt like she was reaching ten years into the past to a time when we first became friends.

"I'm here for you. There's only a handful of people who could get me to risk my sanity and freedom being hauled off to jail by our *unkind*-hearted sheriff for obstruction of justice."

"She'd never do that. April Montague is all bark and no bite when it comes to you. Trust me, a woman knows these things. By the way, she showed me a picture of the murder weapon and asked if I recognized it. They're trying to find out if it belonged to the victim, killer, or came from the library." Maggie shared that she saw German writing on the handle. It was partially discolored and diffi-cult to read, but she noticed a family crest with a lion fighting a bear. It looked like it had a ü, an umlaut symbol. "It definitely didn't come from the library, and I highly doubt Helena would even carry a knife. She's been afraid of them since our sisters forced her to watch slasher movies when we were kids."

Maggie had to return to work, and I had to pick up my daughter. As I left Memorial Library, I couldn't help but wonder if the knife belonged to someone else in my life. Might it be a letter in Ursula's former last name, Mück? If it was, did it belong to George Braun, formerly known as Hans Mück, or to Ursula, formerly known as Sofia Mück?

* * *

By five o'clock, the Pick-Me-Up Diner would be crowded with rowdy teenagers who were overly excited about finishing their last weeks in high school before summer break. I'd forgotten it would also be packed with half the population of the Willow Trees Retirement Complex and Braxton's infinite social circle of economically-savvy senior citizens. I hadn't expected to run into my favorite blue-haired rabble rouser, but in the far corner booth Eustacia Paddington slurped the daily blue-plate special, a bowl of lentil soup, with her brother, Millard. Since Ursula hadn't arrived, Emma and I strolled over for a visit.

"Is it supposed to be that icky mud color?" Emma asked while climbing onto the dark gray leather seat next to Eustacia. My daughter's nose wrinkled as she shook her head. "I like vegetables but that looks awful. Ewww… who cooked that mess?"

"It tastes delicious, but your manners need a slight improvement," chastised Eustacia as she adjusted the collar on her fuchsia-colored silk blouse. "Your nana would not tolerate such disobedience. Come, little critic, let's take a walk to see if your Aunt Eleanor and her chef have a bowl for you to taste."

As Emma waited for Eustacia to gain her balance from stepping off the platform, she giggled and said, "Daddy, her cane almost crushed my toes!" Emma's eyes bugged out as she followed Eustacia toward the kitchen. From Eustacia's exaggerated wink that looked more like the beginning of a seizure, I could tell she was giving Millard and me a moment alone.

"Your daughter might teach my sister a thing or two, Kellan," Millard quipped and motioned a hand to the seat across from him.

"They grow up way too fast. We just celebrated Emma's seventh birthday a few weeks ago." I pushed Eustacia's nearly empty soup bowl to the side and sat. "How're you holding up? I was planning to check on you today. George Braun's unfortunate death must mean you're busier than you'd hoped."

"Ah, Eustacia's surprise invitation to dinner tonight. I suppose that was your doing, eh?" Millard said as he wiped a dollop of soup from his lower lip. "I appreciate your concern. It was a shock. I'd only begun chatting with him a few months ago, but the world has lost a brilliant researcher and scientist."

"Indeed. How well did you know him?" I asked. Millard had only shared a brief history with me when I'd run into him on campus over the weekend. What else would he be able to tell me now?

"We'd corresponded a few times over the years but hadn't met in person until I'd caught one of his speaking engagements at a conference in January. I asked him to visit Braxton, but he declined indicating his busy schedule wouldn't allow for it." Millard explained that George contacted him a few weeks later feverishly excited to offer a chance to bring the Mendel flower show to Braxton if Millard would contact the college about his availability to teach a summer course.

"Did he say what changed his mind?"

"No, but I contacted Ed Mulligan and Anita Singh to suggest they consider him for a summer course. Anita was vehemently opposed to it. The dean was excited about the prospect of someone with George's credentials temporarily teaching at Braxton." After Millard explained their history, I wondered if during his research George had come across a news report highlighting Ursula's acceptance of the school's presidency. Could he have recognized her from the photo and finally found a way to track down his long-lost sister?

"Was there a formal interview process or anything odd about why he was hired?" I hoped to learn more of substance about George's relationship with anyone he'd met in his brief time at Braxton.

Millard noted George had interviewed with Dean Mulligan, Dr. Singh, the school's chief-of-staff, and someone in the human resources group. "Standard approach for a visiting professor teaching one class," he added, as Ursula walked into the diner and toward our booth. "Based on my limited experience working with her, Anita Singh is an overly complicated woman. Dean Mulligan ultimately reassigned responsibilities as the co-chair of the Mendel flower show from Anita to George. There were some ruffles over presenting George's personal research between the three of them."

"What was his research focused on?" It felt promising to add two possible suspects to my list.

"George claimed to have made a huge discovery about a certain flower having a powerful impact on a well-known disease. I'm hoping the details are still in his files or belongings. Either he kept nothing at Braxton's Cambridge Hall of Science, or someone stole his work."

I waved to Ursula and pointed at a table a few seats away. As she sat, I turned back to Millard. "I appreciate your help. Maggie's worried about Helena finding his body at the library. I'm trying to learn a little about George to see if there is any other connection that could help April Montague."

Millard nodded. "Sure, Kellan. I had nothing but respect for the man's work. As a person, he was arrogant and ruthless. While I'm confident the sheriff will determine who killed George, having you investigate the matter seems like an advantage she's not yet realized. At least as far as past experience tells us. Right, my friend?" His embellished smile was enough to indicate he knew I loved a good mystery. "By the way, George hired that new assistant. He or she was supposedly staying at the cabin George bought to assist with the renovations. Maybe that might provide some additional information to point you in the right direction."

"Don't tell me, Kellan's pushing you to gossip all about that dead professor," Eustacia chortled as she approached the table, flicking her fingers at me. "I assume you've gotten what you needed from my brother. I'll take my seat now. I imagine you've got some investigating to do."

I thanked Eustacia for her generosity and inquired into the whereabouts of my daughter. Emma was having chicken fingers and celery stalks in the kitchen with Chef Manny. Eleanor also agreed to watch her while I had dinner with Ursula. Before I stepped away, Eustacia reminded me, "You took a little too long finding my sister-in-law's killer, Kellan. Please try to wrap this one up sooner. Your reputation is on the line, you know."

I shook my head and walked away without responding. I knew better than to ask her what she meant or to challenge any of her opinions. I didn't need to be reprimanded in the middle of the Pick-Me-Up Diner. Upon sitting across from Ursula, I said, "I think we've got a lot to discuss."

"I've been researching George Braun during the last few hours. There're no formal records for the man before 1995. His bio says he grew up in and around the Chicago area, attended a post-graduate program in Washington D.C., and began his career at a Swiss institute. I've got a friend checking at Georgetown University to confirm his attendance." Ursula looked exhausted despite her attempt to conceal a heavy pair of dark under-eye bags.

"You said the explosion happened in 1993, right? Two years for him to recover from his burns and injuries, then maybe he changed his identity from Hans Mück to George Braun and created a new life. It's possible, but why?" My fingers idly tapped on the table while a waitress approached and took our orders. I wanted a glass of wine or a cocktail, but it was not an option since I was driving with Emma. Even though I now knew Francesca hadn't been killed in a drunk driving accident, I still couldn't bring myself to imbibe a drop of alcohol whenever my daughter would be in the car with me.

"Yes, twenty-six years ago later this summer. I won't ever forget it," Ursula said with an almost unwatchable sense of pain cascading across her face like a powerful ocean wave. "It's possible that he is Hans, of course, depending on the extent of the injuries. He'd just turned twenty-one, but I was still a minor and couldn't change my name for a few more years."

"Walk me through it one more time. Maybe something new will come to mind," I said, sipping my water while picturing Ursula's parents, Mila and Josef Mück. From what I could recall, they were both famous botanists who'd emigrated from Germany to Chicago in the late 1960s before having two children, Hans and Sofia. Given how focused they were on their research to cure unknown and rapidly developing diseases, they weren't attentive parents. They'd spent every waking moment studying the effects of various plants species on the human immune system.

While the waitress dropped off two Greek salads, Ursula explained her past to me once again. "Hans and I raised ourselves. We were inseparable even though he was five years older than me. Once we were mature enough, our parents forced us to work in the lab with them after school, sometimes until extremely late in the night. It made us both astonishingly dedicated and focused, but that much pressure can also have its negative impacts."

"You once mentioned Hans developed a god-like complex, almost as if he felt compelled to discover the cure by himself," I said, contemplating the line between working too much and working just enough. Parents should never push their children too far beyond their limits, or it can hurt them eventually. I tried to find the right balance with Emma, but I always worried if I'd done the right thing.

"A few weeks before the explosion happened, Hans challenged my parents more frequently. He would alter their test plans, hide results from them, and mislead them with metrics and details. He didn't know I was paying close attention. He was an obsessive megalomaniac on a power trip trying to ensure it appeared like he was leading the search for a cure. Then he discovered that I had possibly stumbled upon the right formulas to help my parents achieve their goals," Ursula continued as she pulled a photograph from her purse. "This was a picture of him and me in the lab shortly before everything went up in flames."

I studied the photograph, comparing it to what I could remember of George Braun from my limited discussion with the man. While there were some similarities, it was hard to say with any certainty if they were the same person. "We need to find out why he stayed hidden for all those years and suddenly tried to contact you. Could he be after the formulas that were destroyed? Do you even remember them?" I explained what Millard had told me about George's wavering reactions to Braxton, suggesting he could've recognized his own sister.

"No. After the accident, I was traumatized. I've intentionally distanced myself from anything with science or botany since those days. When Hans last saw me, I was only sixteen. I've changed a lot, but you can still see a resemblance," Ursula said grazing the picture with her thumb. "If he saw my photo in the college newspaper or some online article, he might've come here to verify for himself. The timing lines up with when I started receiving the notes mentioning my past."

Ursula recounted the remainder of her story. One evening after her parents had retired to their offices to prepare an application for a grant for new funding, Ursula overheard her brother talking with one of the lab assistants about a big breakthrough in the earlier test results. Hans had indicated he was planning to alter the research so it looked like his parents' tests had failed, but he would keep the actual results and build a case to present them himself to the institution's executive board members. "I still don't understand what happened. After the lab assistant left, Hans confronted me to steal the formulas. I begged him to talk with our parents together, but he said he was tired of them neglecting us and forcing us to work all the time with absolutely no credit or future of our own."

"You mentioned he attacked you that day, right?" I recalled Anita Singh having concerns about working with Hans. Was something going on between the two of them? Could she have once been his assistant? Anita was at least ten years older than him, so she might've been working for the Mücks. Surely, Ursula would've recognized the woman from the past. Had they ever met?

Ursula nodded. "I'd been in there all afternoon tabulating results on one of their experiments. Everyone else had gone home. Our parents were in the office on the other side of the floor. I thought if I could get them to listen to us, it would all be okay in the end. Before I could get away, Hans pinned me against the metal table where he was preparing a mixture for an experiment."

"It's understandable you needed to distract him. He sounds like a monster."

"I reached backward as he held my body against the cold surface demanding I share the formulas with him. I noticed a few powders he'd planned to use sitting in a nearby glass bowl. I tried to grab the bowl to hit his head but knocked it over and out of my reach. Hans had taken out an excessive amount of potassium nitrate which can be dangerous." Ursula paused and trembled over what looked like a series of erratic post-traumatic stress syndrome reactions.

I felt awful watching my friend relive a painful memory. "What's potassium nitrate?"

"A fertilizer. My parents had been using it to expedite growth in the flowers as part of their research. When you combine it with something else like sugar or honey over an open flame, it creates a small explosion or boom. Enough to startle someone, so they'd stop what they were doing at the time."

Ursula explained there were several Bunsen burners connected to a large supply of natural gas. She turned on the gas and twisted the top of the burner, so the flame reached out to ignite the potassium nitrate and sugar mixture, instantaneously causing a reaction similar to firecrackers launching and popping. Hans had been caught off-guard, which enabled Ursula to kick him in the shins and run out of the lab to find her parents.

Unfortunately, while Ursula's plan created a distraction in the lab, it unexpectedly caused a second, more explosive reaction. She'd been unaware that in one of the supply closets, Hans had foolishly kept an excessive amount of glycerine, a liquid fertilizer, for a future experiment. As she ran out of the room and across the hall, a full-scale fire broke out from the Bunsen burner continually shooting flames over the potassium nitrate mixture and across all the lab equipment. She tried to get back into the lab, but the fire spread too quickly. Ursula raced toward the other office to alert her parents but passed out from inhaling too much smoke. The building's smoke alarms signaled the fire department who arrived to find Ursula unconscious on the curb across the street from the flame-covered building. When the flames in the lab had reached the large tank of glycerine, the building detonated in a huge explosion despite the firefighters' attempts to contain it. With all the chemicals in the lab, it was an uncontrollable combustion that left only one known survivor —Sofia.

"Given the extent of the damage, we assumed whoever dragged me out must have gone back inside to save the rest of my family. We thought it was my brother and that he'd been knocked unconscious while trying to find our parents. Everything had been incinerated after the explosion. While they found some human remains, DNA testing was only in its infancy," Ursula explained. She was eventually forced to confess to the investigators that she'd inadvertently caused the explosion, and it was ruled an accident by the forensics unit covering the fire. Her parents and brother had been listed as the only three victims from the incident, which also destroyed any research or test results they'd documented on their experiments.

The lab assistant eventually revealed to the investigators that the Mücks had discovered a cure for a rapidly developing disease. She leaked the information to the press, which led to a public humiliation and attack on Sofia as the only survivor who'd set the entire situation in motion. With no relatives or anyone to take care of her, Sofia stole whatever money her parents had left, sold some of their belongings, and ran away. She lived on the streets for three months, then took up residence at a boarding house, and eventually obtained her GED. Once she turned eighteen, Sofia had changed her name to eliminate anyone connecting her with the explosion and began a new life as Ursula Power. Power had been chosen so she'd never forget what had happened and would remember not to get caught up in her own power trip in the future. Ursula had been chosen because she felt as ugly on the inside as the sea witch from 'The Little Mermaid.'

"It sounds like your brother may have been the one to save you that day. He must have gotten caught in the explosion but somehow survived, escaped, and needed reconstructive surgery," I added. If George was the supposedly deceased Hans Mück, had someone else helped him leave the building and recover? "Do you remember anything about the assistant? Is it possible that one of Braxton's professors, Anita Singh, worked with your family years ago?" I pulled up the college website and showed Ursula a photo of the woman.

"I haven't been at Braxton long enough to meet the entire staff," Ursula replied studying the photo. "Anita Singh doesn't look too familiar."

"It's been over twenty-five years. People can change their appearance."

"I didn't know the assistant all that well. I think Hans called her Lambertson. It was probably her last name, but I only saw her one time after the explosion when she told me I was to blame for taking her precious Hans away from her. I hadn't even known they were dating," Ursula explained as the waitress took away our salad bowls and dropped off our entrees.

"We could probably research who worked at the lab with the last name Lambertson. Do you have any other contacts who might remember?" I asked, then made a mental note of how I could track down the former assistant's identity. Could it be the same person Millard mentioned was now working for George Braun? Maybe they'd gotten in contact again to retaliate together against Ursula. I needed to find the cabin George had bought and take a gander at his belongings. Assuming he was Ursula's brother, it would probably be legal. If he wasn't, I'd have to deal with the aftermath later.

"No, I left that life behind," Ursula said, stabbing at her pasta Bolognese with disinterest. "I'm not sure I can eat anymore right now. I feel sick. We have to confirm George Braun was my brother, Hans. If he is, I'm worried I could be the next victim. Someone might be after us."

"If you haven't gotten any new notes, the likelihood of your stalker being someone other than him is pretty slim. If he had a partner, I can see why you'd worry for your own safety, but you need to focus on something else far worse," I added, remembering the red stain on her Frida Kahlo shawl.

Ursula looked like a frightened doe. "What could *that* possibly be?"

"If it's your brother who was murdered, the police might think you killed him. You told me yourself, you snuck off for a few minutes when you got that note at the costume extravaganza. Did anyone notice you in the thirty minutes before I found the body, or were you hiding the whole time?

A look of desperate fear shot across Ursula's face. "I was alone after the note showed up and before I found you. I don't think anyone saw me in that time frame. I was purposely staying hidden."

"I couldn't help but notice the red stain on your costume, right near your—"

"It wasn't blood. Somebody dropped sauce on it while I was walking through the crowd," Ursula said before I could finish speaking. Her eyes were glued to the table. "It was my mother's shawl, one of the only things I managed to keep from my old life. You believe me, right?"

We finished our meal in silence. I promised to dig into George's stay at the Roarke & Daughters Inn. I needed to talk to Helena about George's fight with Cheney in the courtyard, but maybe something in his room would identify the next best step. It might also reveal which cabin he'd purchased, so I could search for his new assistant. If it was the same one from the past, and I got a picture of her, Ursula might recognize the woman. Anita Singh's arguments with George were equally as important to investigate, and I'd have to talk to Dean Mulligan. Although my theories made sense, was I missing something from this puzzle? It couldn't be as simple as Hans and his assistant, Lambertson, had a fight that led to her killing him in some weird power struggle or as revenge for something he'd done.

Ursula picked up the tab, which included a generous twenty percent discount from my sister. I accompanied my boss to the parking lot and waited until she drove off. She shouldn't be alone until we confirmed who was stalking her. After she pulled away, I started my walk to the diner. I heard footsteps behind me and worried about who'd been following us so closely. Was it Ursula's stalker? The person who killed George Braun? Or would I turn around and come face-to-face with another vision of Francesca?

CHAPTER 7

I stopped short and broke into defense mode. With my legs firmly planted on the ground, I swung my body around and unexpectedly collided into Sam Taft. He was startled when he saw me and tensed up. "Kellan, I'm sorry. Didn't notice you there."

Sam wasn't aware I'd witnessed him and my brother kissing weeks ago, but Gabriel knew I'd seen them together at the graduation. Had Gabriel told Sam he'd noticed me? I wasn't in the mood to play any games, so I blurted out what was on my mind. "Where is he, Sam? I know my brother is back in town. Why hasn't he told his family?"

Sam took a step backward. "Who? I think you've got me confused with someone else. I don't know your brother."

"Don't lie to me. I'm sure Gabriel asked you to cover for him and not to tell me anything. I know I was the reason someone in your family was put in jail for killing your grandmother, but I was on your side during the whole situation." I hadn't spent any time with Sam since I'd discovered who had been playing games behind the scenes, but I didn't think he would hold a grudge against me.

Sam appeared conflicted. "You did, and as much as it hurt to learn the truth, I don't blame you."

"But you still won't help me with my brother, will you?" I grabbed his shoulder as he stepped toward the diner's entrance. "Please, Sam. He's been gone for eight years. I want to talk with him. To tell him I love him and that..." I worried that Gabriel was in hiding because he didn't want to reveal his life choices to his family. "I want to tell him that there's nothing he can say that'll make me upset with him. I want him to come home. I'll be on his side no matter what."

Sam relaxed but still pulled away from me. "It sounds like you care about your brother. Did something happen between you two? Not that I know him or can help you. Just curious." He shrugged his shoulders and looked away as if it were a casual conversation about someone he didn't know.

I could tell Sam was lying, but I also realized he didn't want to be doing it. "I do care about him. I've been gone for a long time, but I'm back. If he were home right now, I'd make him understand. No matter what's changed or what he's doing with his life." I needed to convey that I supported Gabriel, but I didn't want to scare Sam. If Sam was still hiding the truth about his sexuality, revealing what I'd seen might cause him to refuse to help me on any level.

"If I could help, I would. I see what it's like to have a brother. Brad and I have been talking recently, and we have a lot in common," Sam noted before turning away to leave. "Good luck with finding Gabriel."

I had the distinct impression Sam winked at me when he walked into the diner. Maybe he would tell Gabriel what I'd said. If I didn't hear from my brother in the next three days, I'd try again. But for now, I had more urgent business. Before heading back into the diner to collect Emma, I texted Helena.

Me: *It's Kellan. I need to see you about something important. Can we meet?*
Helena: *I'm busy with Cheney. It might be my last day of freedom if the cops arrest me for a murder I didn't commit. A girl needs to have some fun before she goes up the river.*
Me: *I believe you. I want to help. But I also need something from you. A favor. Just between us.*
Helena: *Sounds kinda fun. Are you hitting on me? Come by the inn tomorrow. I'm on the breakfast shift.*

I knew she'd bite if I told her I needed her help. While I wasn't above flirting to get answers, maybe if we worked together, I could prove her innocence and figure out who was stalking Ursula. Then life could return to normal again allowing me to focus on finding Francesca. Wait, what had my days come to when it was normal to have a wife who'd been resurrected from the dead?

* * *

After dropping Emma at her elementary school the following morning, I hopped on the highway heading north toward the base of the Wharton Mountains to reach the Roarke & Daughters Inn. There were two hours before my first class began, and I'd already prepared my lecture the prior night upon returning home from the diner. Nana D had left early to meet with her campaign manager about last-minute events at the upcoming town council meeting. Voting day was one week away and depending on which side of the county you spoke with, either Marcus Stanton or Nana D could be in the lead.

When I entered Maggie's family's bed and breakfast, I waved to her mother who was busily checking out a guest currently throwing a tantrum about the bill. Maggie's father was in the kitchen preparing breakfast dishes. They usually served a scrumptious spread of pastries, cereals, yogurts, fruits, and a full oatmeal bar. I nabbed a to-go cup of coffee and a vanilla scone as Helena bounded around the corner and ascended the ornate multi-level staircase.

With my mouth full of succulent, moist crumbs, I managed to mumble, "Wait up, you promised me you'd talk." Except it came out muffled like a dog who'd drunk too much beer, not that I advocated giving alcohol to a dog.

"I thought English was supposed to be your primary language. How can you eat all that sugary stuff and still look like you belong on the cover of Men's Fitness?" Helena teased in her usual histrionic tone. She stopped at the base of the staircase, curled one of her fingers, and motioned for me to follow her. "I need you in the bedroom right now."

With bulging eyes, I slanted my head and said, "I'll have you know, I run several times a week to offset everything I eat. I also speak three other languages and can tell you to 'pop a cork in it' in twelve different international tongues. Don't mess with me before I've had enough coffee, soon-to-be-prisoner twelve-oh-four-six-ninety-one."

Helena stopped on the second floor, turned completely around, and growled. "You're hot when you act all cocky. Is that how they're going to refer to me in jail? Hopefully, I don't get stuck wearing stripes. They don't look good on a girl with my curves."

If I was about to be arrested—whether or not I'd actually done the crime—I wouldn't be this flippant. "You aren't taking this seriously, are you?"

"Look, Kellan. I've got nothing to hide. I was in the wrong place at the wrong time. That sheriff knows I'm innocent, but she's got to follow all the rules." When we reached the third floor, Helena unlocked room three-oh-five with what appeared to be a master skeleton key.

"Do you have access to every room?" I asked, thinking about finding a way into George Braun's recent residence. As she walked into the room, I peered down the hall at a door with a yellow sign that read 'Keep out. No access without permission from Mgmt.' in bold black print.

"We're cleaning a room for a guest who just checked out. The one you're looking at across the hall belonged to the guy who bit the dust," Helena said in a very matter-of-fact tone. "This key opens everything. What else do you need to know, Nancy Drew?"

"Oh, you mean the dead guy whose body you were caught kneeling over?" I said with a hint of sarcasm as I walked into room three-oh-five and stood across the bed from Helena. I surmised the police had insisted no one access the other room while they were still investigating George's murder. "Have you been inside since it happened?"

"Ewww... that's creepy. I don't have a lot of time to chat, even if the thought has crossed my mind how sexy you look in that body-hugging dress shirt and how much fun it'd be to take it off you. Maggie should never have given you up the second chance around," she said while ripping sheets off the bed. "This would go a lot faster if you helped. I might even tell you what you want to know."

While we stripped sheets and I learned how hard maids work, Helena explained what she knew about George Braun. He was generally quiet and kept to himself, but he asked a lot of questions about the college, its executive administrative staff, and the costume extravaganza.

"How'd he know about the event?" I asked as she emptied all the trash bins in the room. I wasn't sure why he'd attended given he'd just arrived in town and wasn't a wealthy donor.

"Karen Stoddard invited him. She was here meeting with Maggie to plan the event. He'd been sitting downstairs in the lobby reading a book and having a glass of wine. We put out a small spread late afternoon and encourage our guests to mingle, you know."

That was the second possible connection I'd made between the Stoddards and George Braun. It could've been a coincidence he was from Chicago and they had moved from the Midwest, but this was beginning to set off alarm bells. "Didn't Maggie find it odd he was invited?"

"Yeah, but Karen talked about his friendship with Millard Paddington and how George could cross-promote at the upcoming flower show to encourage additional contributions. Maggie bought into the idea." Helena sashayed into the bathroom and turned on the faucet in the tub. "Care to join me?"

When stepping into the simple yet elegant white-tiled room, I was reminded of a woodsy spa retreat. "I'm not cleaning the bathroom. I have limits when it comes to my research."

"Who said anything about cleaning? I thought we might get a little dirty before—"

"Enough, Helena. I know you're joking around, but murder is serious. I'm also not going to flirt with my former girlfriend's little sister who, from what I understand, is already dating at least one other man named Cheney." It was a good segue, as I needed to learn more about the guy before I visited his parents' restaurant that afternoon to inquire about their past.

Helena marched to within inches of me and kissed my cheek. "Such an innocent. You need to have more fun in your life, Kellan. It must be boring and painful to act so straight-laced all the time."

I wasn't granting her the satisfaction of knowing her words rang truer than I could imagine. Except for the whole dead wife and mafia thing and finding a few dead bodies, I was kinda boring compared to my former life in Los Angeles. "Talk to me about Cheney."

Helena explained he'd moved with his parents to Braxton a few months ago. He was super excited to see his younger sister, Sierra, who'd just come home from her first year abroad at law school. Helena and Cheney had gone on a few dates, and she liked him a lot, but he could be possessive at times. "He doesn't like that I am a free spirit. Wants me to stop seeing anyone else, but I told him that's not gonna happen anytime soon. I just go with the flow. Peace is the way."

"Has he been too aggressive about it?" I asked, growing concerned for her safety.

Helena sighed, then began scrubbing the pedestal sink. "Not really, I mean, like he hasn't gotten physical in a negative way with me, but..."

When she hesitated, I leaned in closer to put a hand on her shoulder. "But what?"

"Remember when I said I saw someone arguing with George Braun at the library?"

"Yes, I know it was Cheney." I became concerned about her potential next statement.

"Cheney had grabbed George by the collar of his suit and was shouting at him. I stood in the hallway while they were in the courtyard." Helena's cautious speech pattern showed her nervousness.

"Did they know each other?" I asked, trying to deduce how they could be connected.

"I don't think so," she hesitated and tapped her foot against the tub. "But Cheney saw George and me arguing in his room the other day. He was flustered over the way George yelled at me. I had to stop Cheney from knocking on George's door that afternoon. Made him promise to let it go. Guests sometimes get difficult over how we leave their room or if we move things around."

Helena was giving me helpful information and potential suspects. "I have to ask you two things. Both of which you probably won't like."

"Besides my possible freedom, what do I get in return?" Helena pouted, but when she saw I wasn't biting, she continued. "Fine, what are they?"

"Did you have anything to do with George's death?" I asked as our eyes connected in the mirror.

Helena started dusting the furniture but stopped to look at me while she responded. "No, I swear. I've talked to the guy a few times at the inn. We had an animated discussion about his room, and I told him I'd leave it alone. He was completely nice again by the following morning, the day of the costume extravaganza. Then I saw him and Cheney arguing in the courtyard. When Cheney stepped away and appeared to calm down, I dashed off to the main party room to refill a few food trays."

"And how did you wind up back in the courtyard again? How many minutes had passed?" I asked, mapping the timeline in my head.

"Twenty minutes, no more than that. I refilled two trays, dropped off the party favors in the main room, decided I needed a smoke break, and thought I'd verify whatever scuffle Cheney and George had gotten into was truly over. When I went back there, no one else was around. I lit my cigarette, and that's when I stepped on something. I told you the rest," Helena said in a frustrated and whiny tone. "And before you ask, I talked to Cheney. He promised he left George alone in the courtyard and went back to tend bar. He'd been on a break and had to return before he'd get into trouble with his parents. You can confirm with them he was there."

It would be something I looked into, but I wondered how much of this the sheriff already knew. Helena said that once Cheney confirmed he had nothing to do with George's death, she conveniently neglected to tell the detective she'd even seen them fighting. "What does your lawyer say?"

"I didn't tell him about Cheney. Finnigan is meeting with the sheriff right now to find out what evidence they have, or if anything came back from the tests they've run. I wore gloves, so my fingerprints won't be on the knife. Can they arrest me just for being near the body?" Helena, for the first time, looked worried about the whole ordeal of going to prison. "I guess this could be bad for me, but I've always believed if you didn't do anything wrong and you had nothing to hide, it'd turn out okay. You know, ignore the cops."

The girl was a dreamer and almost too naïve to realize that wasn't how things worked out. "You need to be careful. And you need to tell Finnigan about this, or I will. He must know everything to help you get out of this debacle. Maggie's worried about you."

"I'll think about it. I don't want to get Cheney into trouble. So... what's the second thing?"

I gripped my hands together and seesawed back and forth on the balls of my feet. "Can you get me into George Braun's room?"

Ten minutes later, I'd vacuumed room three-oh-five, cleaned its toilet with a nasty scrub brush, and replenished all the towels and toiletries. Helena casually sat on a chair blowing cigarette smoke out the window, then agreed to let me into the dead man's room.

As I shut the door behind us, Helena laughed. "I feel his spirit in here. Almost like he's angry about something. I guess I'd be angry too if I was murdered."

"You need to spend more time with my sister, Eleanor. She's into all that stuff," I moaned while scanning the room. The bed was turned down, there was a chocolate on the pillow, and everything seemed to be in tidy shape. "So, from the looks of it, George went to the library for the party after his room had been cleaned for the evening, but he never came back. Who attended to his room? You were at the party which means this isn't your handiwork."

"Yuri Sato. She's a student at Braxton but has a part-time job with us when we need extra help," Helena noted as she opened dresser drawers. "The police have been through here with a fine-tooth comb already. Something about it being rather funny how I was found with the murder weapon in my hands and the victim was staying at my family's inn."

"Yep, certainly more than a coincidence," I said, rolling my eyes. I remembered meeting Yuri a few months earlier at Paddington's Play House during the *King Lear* rehearsals. I could ask her if she saw anything odd in George's room on the day of the party. "Did George meet with anyone while he was staying here?"

Helena sighed. "A couple of people, I guess. Millard Paddington was here once. Some other woman came in all dressed up to the nines. He was chatting with her in the front parlor. Something concerning the upcoming flower show, I think."

I assumed that could also be the person George worked with to stalk Ursula. When I asked Helena to describe the female visitor, she couldn't remember anything about her. "How about paperwork? Did you see anything lying around? Names? Dates? Something that might tie him to his killer?"

"That detective asked me the same questions. You know, you're kinda good at this investigation stuff." Helena ran a finger across the night table and laughed. "Oops, Yuri missed a spot."

"That's unfortunate," I said with indifference. "How about you answer the question?"

"Nope. George was very neat, never kept anything out for me to find, but he did ask me about the wall safe," Helena gleefully shared.

"Wait, did he put something in there?" I thought I was about to catch a break, but I knew we needed to get out of the room quickly before someone realized we'd entered it illegally. I also needed to get back on campus to teach today's class about honesty in writing publications and reporting news. Isn't irony grand?

"Nah, George thought it was too risky, which is why I showed him the secret hiding spot under the mattress." Helena lifted the bedspread and pointed to a floorboard near the top side where the pillows laid. "And before you ask, no, I don't know if he actually kept anything in there. I also didn't tell the detective about it."

"But why?" I scowled. "This could be something to help the sheriff look at other suspects!"

"The detective didn't ask, nor did I think of it at the time." Helena dropped to the floor, rolled onto her back, lifted a loose piece of floor board, and reached her hand into the dark space. When she popped out from under the bed and angled her head to me, she was smiling.

"I didn't ask about it either, but you told me it was there. Wait, did you find something?" I asked with exasperation. Helena was truly the opposite of Maggie in every way possible.

"Feels like a folder full of newspaper clippings and other assorted papers," she said as she withdrew her hand from under the bed and tossed her discovery on the throw rug near my feet. "I told you because I like you."

As it slid across the floor, a picture of Ursula landed on my shoe. I briefly flipped through the folder and saw many photos of her and others, as well as a copy of the news article about the explosion in 1993. The last document was a handwritten note with an inventory of things to do. The first item on the list read 'Find my sister.' The second read, 'Get revenge.' Jackpot, it might not be scientific proof, but it certainly seemed like George Braun was really Hans Mück who'd stumbled upon his long-lost sister after many years.

Just as Helena was about to grab one of the documents from my hand, we heard footsteps in the hallway. I couldn't see anyone through the peephole, but we didn't want to get caught in the room. We gave it a few more minutes, and when we verified the squeaking of the staircase, we snuck out of George Braun's room, rushed to room three-oh-five, and closed the door. "I would love to look through this entire file, but I should probably turn it over to the police, right?" I asked.

Helena walked over to me and looked directly in my eyes. While she spoke, she unfastened all the buttons on my dress shirt and lifted its tails from underneath my belt and pants. Then she spread the shirt open. "I knew you had at least a six-pack hidden under there."

I shivered as her fingers touched my abdomen and chest. "Ummm... what are you doing?" The words barely escaped my hesitant lips as I tried not to let my mind wander.

"Don't you trust me?" Helena traced a finger across the small dip between my pecs, ran her long red-stained nail down my stomach across a few patches of dirty blond hair, and stuffed the bottom of the folder into my waistband stopping short before we were about to enter a danger zone. It had been the first time in two years I'd taken off my shirt in front of a woman. Helena patted the folder, so it laid flat against my chest, then pulled my shirt closed and refastened the buttons until I was fully clothed again. "See? That's the best way to sneak out of the inn with this file, so you can check it for any evidence that might help my case. If my parents knew you had this folder, they'd insist we turn it over to the Wharton County Sheriff's Office and to Finnigan Masters right away. They follow the law, unlike us."

"Um, that's illegal, and I always follow the law," I said in a weird staccato pattern of speech. I think I was still flustered that she'd placed her hands on my shirtless torso seconds before. Did I enjoy it, or was that temporary shock? "I can't take this off property. It doesn't belong to me." I grunted at myself for being a good guy and not caving to my instincts.

"Too late. Your fingerprints are probably on it. I've watched enough crime shows to know how this is done, Kellan. Take it home to read."

"Besides crossing a few too many lines, how does that help us with the cops?" I shook my head at her and closed my eyes.

"When you're done, wipe it clean and bring it back. I'll put it in the space between the two floors again, tell the detective I remembered my conversation with George Braun, and suggest that he check under the bed. Voila!" Helena looked like she'd done this before. She also proved she was a lot smarter than I'd given her credit for in the past.

Once Helena kicked me out of the room, I finally succumbed to the risky plan and cursed myself for knowing how wrong it was. I decided to take the folder with me, but before I dug any further into the details, I needed to consider the options. There were lines I was willing to cross, but I didn't want to interfere with an ongoing investigation. On the other hand, this could help me prove Helena's innocence and solve Ursula's stalker problem.

When I sat in the car, I transferred the newly found evidence to my briefcase, drove to campus, and taught my two-hour class. I felt both dirty and electrified over what I'd done. It had been a while since that kind of thrill had tempted me. I had no idea what to do about the sudden change in my attitude and actions. Was Helena going to be bad news for me? Did Maggie know her sister could be so devilish? And if she could steal and lie, how much further away was murder?

CHAPTER 8

Three hours later, I finished teaching my class and made a call to Dean Mulligan's office. His secretary quickly transferred me when I said it was urgent. "Thanks for taking my call," I began.

"What's the problem? I have a meeting with Ursula momentarily." Dean Mulligan's voice was gruff and distant. "I don't have time to deal with everyone's complaints today."

Someone was grumpy. How could I get him to reveal what he knew about George Braun or the disagreements between him and Anita Singh? An idea began to formulate in my head. "Do you know who will be helping with the Mendel flower show now that George Braun passed away?"

"I never should've agreed to it. That man has done nothing but given me grief since the day he showed up! Are you asking to take his place? What do you know about botany and science, Kellan?"

Nothing, and that wasn't my intention. "No, no. I meant Millard Paddington has a lot on his plate right now, and I'm worried about his health. Just trying to look out for him. Was anyone working closely with George Braun? Maybe I could ask them to take a bigger load off Millard's plate."

"In my opinion, George Braun was only concerned about getting funding for his lab experiments. When I approved the money for his salary for the summer class, I never expected he'd ask for so much more. I don't want to get involved. Talk to Anita. She's the only other person close enough."

"I would, but I heard they didn't get along very well. It sounds like George wasn't well liked," I replied, feeling weird about the conversation but encouraged to learn George might have enemies.

"Ursula's all over me about this flower show... asking questions about how I hired such a pompous man to represent Braxton. I'm glad he's no longer with us, if you ask me. Death was more than that man deserved!" Dean Mulligan shouted before hanging up the phone.

Was this how Dean Mulligan normally behaved? Could there be a chance he had something to do with George's death? I hardly knew anything about the man, but immediately recalled Myriam's frequent digs about her boss's unprofessional style and superiority complex. She was one to talk! Feeling more confused than ever, I got back in the SUV and drove to Wharton County's central downtown quarter to finish my research on the Stoddards before I focused on Anita Singh's and Ed Mulligan's gripes with George.

Set in the middle of all four local villages, the amiable and well-frequented hotspot contained the county's main government branches and agencies as well a cute shopping and restaurant district along the Finnulia River. I parked in the public lot nestled south of all the civic buildings, paid the meter, and walked five blocks until I found and entered the Stoddards' restaurant.

Their new space occupied what was once a waterfront warehouse for storing grains before they'd been shipped by boat along the river. High-ceilings with exposed mechanical and plumbing ducts, cabling and wiring, and wood beams made the place feel industrial yet modern. To my right was a heavy metal door with a frosted glass window and the words 'Simply Stoddard,' the catering and event management arm of the family business, etched in fancy scroll font. To my left was the bar and dining room of Karen and Doug's new restaurant.

"Can I help ya?" a young guy in a royal blue polo, tight-fitting khakis, and dirty tennis shoes asked as I approached the front counter in the small vestibule. On the wall behind him was a glass-covered board filled with antique daggers and corresponding scrolls. Despite one being missing in the right corner, it was clear someone boasted an avid enthusiasm for dangerous and elaborate weapons.

"My name is Kellan Ayrwick. I thought I'd drop by for a bite to eat and to chat with the owners." I paused to read one of the scrolls that indicated the corresponding and missing knife had been German.

The guy turned to see what I was looking at. "My dad's fascinated by knives and has collected them from all around the world for years. Loves to hunt and keep his skills current."

"I met him last weekend with my friend, Maggie." I nodded, feeling lucky to have run into Cheney without inventing a need to track him down. I also considered what he'd just told me about his father's obsession with sharp weaponry.

"Surely. I know Maggie, she's Helena's sister. I'm Cheney, and you're looking for my parents." Cheney's smile displayed nearly perfect teeth as he grabbed a menu from the shelf behind him and walked toward the dining room. "You probably want something by the back window, right?"

"Yes, please. Helena's told me a little bit about you." He was at least six-feet tall, carried wide shoulders across his muscular frame, and had gotten an early bronze tan for the summer. A chiseled structure to his face and a small indentation in his chin stood out as his best features. Classically handsome, but he walked with a slouch and slow gait. For a moment, images of Neanderthal men popped into my head as I waited for Cheney to end his quandary over which table he'd seat me at.

"Yup, quite a chick. Been seeing her for a few weeks now. She might be the one, if ya know what I mean," he said, dropping the menu on the table with a thump. His hospitality skills needed some work.

"Oh, I think I understand what you're saying, but she's still young. Might want to keep an open mind, right? You've only been here for a couple of months, if I recall." I pulled out my own chair and sat facing the gorgeous view of a small waterfall and windmill near the riverbank.

Cheney turned to me with a dark, brooding gaze. "She didn't say something to you, did she? About not wanting to see me anymore?" When I shook my head slightly, he calmed down. "Sorry, man, I just really dig her. I guess I'll get your server."

As Cheney walked away, I called out his name and waited for him to turn around. "Maybe you could bring me a glass of water and tell me more about yourself." I wasn't particularly highbrow, but it was clear he hadn't adapted well to the service industry. "Are you in school or is this your only job?"

Cheney shrugged his shoulders. "I'm in construction, but there aren't any jobs available right now. So, I'm working here with my folks till something comes through. Kinda sucks, but what are ya gonna do, right?"

Maggie's sister sure knew how to pick them. "I think I saw you the other night at the costume party in Braxton's Memorial Library. You were working the event with Helena." I'd have to ask simple, specific questions to get anything out of this one.

"Yup. My parents needed the help, and it was good money. The costume stuff was kinda fun. I went as Robin Hood. Did you see that awesome bow and arrow slung across my shoulders?" Cheney fiddled with the back of a chair, tossing it left and right, so that it dangled only on two of its four feet.

I shook my head not truly remembering him in the costume. At least he didn't go with the loincloth as Maggie's sister had originally intended. "Helena's certainly got herself stuck in a tricky situation. I can't imagine what it was like for her to find, well, you know... that professor in the courtyard."

Cheney's eyes grew wide and alert, then his hand missed the chair on its return sway back toward him leading it to fall to the floor with a loud crash. "She had nothing to do with it, so don't be giving her a hard time!" He leaned down to pick up the chair but continued to stare at me. There were a few other diners at several tables in the center of the room who looked over at us.

"Whoa, I'm trying to help clear her. I'm a friend of the Roarke family, Cheney," I whispered, hoping to calm the guy. Helena mentioned he had a bit of a temper, but the panicked look in his eyes read as pure anger and innate fear.

"Yeah, sorry, man. I worry about Helena. That guy made her feel all sorts of skived out." Cheney motioned to a busboy walking nearby, so he'd stop at my table to fill the water glass. "I gave him a piece of my mind in the library that night right before someone axed the loser."

"What happened when you grilled him?" I asked as Doug and Karen entered the main dining room. They'd probably heard the crash and came running to see what'd happened.

"The guy claimed he was asking for more towels, but I knew better. He'd already broken his promise to me a couple of days earlier. I didn't trust him anymore," Cheney said, softening a little. Maybe he needed to vent his frustrations to someone.

"Had you met George Braun before his run-in with Helena?" I wasn't sure I understood the specific timing of the past events. Cheney clearly had something to share, but we were interrupted.

"Is everything okay here, son?" Doug said curtly as he reached the table with Karen hovering at his side. "Oh, we met the other night. You're Kevin, was it?"

I smiled. When a guy had a unique name, he's used to hearing the wrong one called out. "It's Kellan, Kellan Ayrwick. We met at the costume extravaganza. You invited me to stop by for lunch at the new restaurant. It's a stunning space."

Karen put her arm around Cheney's waist. "There's something wrong with the computer in my office, honey. Can you take a look at it? Sierra usually fixes that stuff, but she's been busy since she got home this week."

As Cheney stepped away without saying goodbye, I realized his mother was trying to keep him from speaking to me. Had she overheard what he'd started to tell me or was she being an overprotective mom? "Technology can be difficult." I glanced back toward Doug. "No issues, we just bumped into one another, and the chair fell over."

Doug didn't look like he believed me, but he wasn't about to question me in front of the rest of the patrons. "Sorry to hear, but I'm glad all is well. I'm pleased you came by. Lunch is on us."

Karen pushed the chair further against the table, then said, "Of course it is. Were you and Cheney getting to know one another? He's a good kid. Both my kids are great. Sierra's in law school at Queen Mary University in London."

"He's attentive and helpful," I lied. No need to anger his parents any further. "Cheney mentioned you moved here recently but didn't say from where. What led you to our secluded town?"

Doug began to speak, but Karen put her hand on his forearm. "We lived in a few places. Cincinnati, St. Louis, and Chicago most recently. One of our daughter's friends attended college across the river over at Woodland. She raved about it so much, we took a trip and fell in love with the surrounding villages."

"There's something about starting fresh in a small town that makes you feel part of the community," Doug added while removing the extra place settings and looking strangely at his wife. "Can I recommend anything for you? I am the executive chef, you can trust me. The salmon was caught fresh this morning."

"Sounds perfect," I noted while handing him the menu. "Tell me all about your experience moving here. I grew up in Braxton but took off to the West Coast for a few years. I only returned again this year, hence why I'm curious what others think about the place."

While Doug seemed interested in talking, Karen was distracted and wanted to get away. "Oh, it's quite lovely. We both worked for other people for so many years, we got to that point where it was time to take our chances and start our own business. The Roarke family has been generous with introducing us to some of the more influential folks in the county."

Doug added, "If I had to get sweaty in the kitchen and stick it out until well after midnight, it might as well be for my own restaurant, right? And Karen was tired of the late nights constantly checking on her results at the—"

"Office. I had a lot of projects that often kept me working around the clock," Karen interrupted gently tugging on her husband's arm. "We should sort through the upcoming events, Doug. Let's give Kellan a chance to look around and eat his lunch."

I thanked the Stoddards for their hospitality and assured them I'd share how my meal turned out. I couldn't push Karen or Doug any further without causing a scene, but I'd learned enough to let them scurry away. It would be more helpful to corner each of them by themselves in the future. One of three would share something that might confirm a stronger connection to the late George Braun. For now, I could follow up on the leads I'd gotten thus far. What promise had George broken to Cheney? What kind of work did Karen do that caused her to check on results late at night? Who or what really led them to Wharton County? They hadn't been completely truthful, I was certain. I'd share what I learned with Ursula, and maybe she could decipher what was going on.

While devouring my lunch, I checked with the Wharton County Sheriff's Office on the updated statement I needed to review and sign. Officer Flatman confirmed I could stop by that afternoon to take care of it. I couldn't help but notice the new confidence and maturity in his tone. He was gunning for the detective spot on the force that would be open once Gilkrist retired.

The salmon was brushed with a delectable horseradish-flavored glaze and broiled until a perfect char coated the crispy skin. For a side, they roasted Brussel sprouts with pancetta, shallots, garlic, and red chili flakes. The combination of sweet and spicy was mouth-watering and comforting, I'd definitely recommend the Stoddards' restaurant to friends and family. And it had nothing to do with the hazelnut crème brûlée dessert that magically appeared on my table after I complimented the entire experience. When finished, I left a twenty-dollar tip for the server because the check was on the house.

Given that the sheriff's office was only a few blocks away, I walked along the riverfront and breathed in the faint scent of honeysuckle and the blossoming rose bushes lining the path. When I reached the Wharton County administrative building that contained the courthouses, jail, and town offices, I felt a flood of renewed energy consume my body. I was prepared to navigate the muddy waters of my tepid relationship with Sheriff April Montague. I needed to encourage her to divulge anything useful about George Braun's untimely death.

Flatman escorted me to the sheriff's office noting Detective Gilkrist was offsite on an interview. He declined to answer my question of who the detective was interviewing. "Can't discuss open cases, Mr. Ayrwick," he rattled off like a squeaky robot needing more oil or to be fed better canned lines.

Sheriff Montague looked up from a mound of paperwork on her desk and told me to take a seat. "I needed to talk with you anyway. That's why I'm doing this instead of my team." The blazer and jeans were gone today, replaced by a pair of jade-green dress pants and a cream-colored V-neck light cashmere sweater. She'd applied product to her hair, parted it on the right, and neatly combed the rest across the top of her head. There was a gentle wave in the classic cut making April look more styled than usual. She wore a silver locket around her neck and had a small amount of cleavage showing. It was the first I'd ever seen her look so feminine.

After sitting, I looked around the sparse room and grumbled. "This might be the blandest and most impersonal office I've ever seen, April."

"Not that I need to explain myself to you, Little Ayrwick, but I prefer a pristine working environment. No distractions. It's important that I focus on the cases hitting my desk and nothing else," she said in a cordial tone while handing me the revised statement. "Let's get business out of the way, then I'll talk to you about something else that crossed my path recently."

After reading the statement, I signed it and placed it on the desk just out of her reach. "You made every correction I asked for. How come?" I wasn't surprised she'd included the proper updates as much as I was that she didn't purposely leave in something incorrect to frustrate me.

"I'm good at my job. There's no need to waste this county's time or money. Believe it or not, you're beginning to grow on me like harmless barnacles to an undocked ship." She sat back in her chair until she found the most comfortable position. "Don't let that go to your head."

Was she comparing me to a parasitic sea creature that latched itself on a boat and traveled the world in search of greener pastures? "I appreciate it. So, before we jump into this other topic you mentioned, can I ask a few questions?"

"As long as it's not about a current case, certainly," she said while cracking her neck to the left in quick motion.

I tried my best but squirmed a tiny amount when her neck made an incredibly loud popping sound. "It is, but I'm not interfering this time. I promise."

"Go on."

"Hypothetically speaking, of course, if someone were to find... let's say... a folder of papers in a room... let's say... at the Roarke & Daughters Inn. And still hypothetically speaking, of course, the said papers belonged to someone who'd recently been murdered... how should they handle it?" I asked while staring directly at the sheriff's perplexed face.

To her credit, not a single muscle or nerve twanged on her face. "Hypothetically speaking, of course, an intelligent and reputable detective would have

451

clearly marked such a room as off-limits to the general public. I'd also assume the said papers must have been found by the inn's staff who'd been given permission to enter only because the detective supposedly completed a thorough search of the said room and no longer needed anything within it."

"One would think, yes."

"In that case, hypothetically speaking, of course, the employee who found the said papers should be the one to notify the sheriff's office. If it was to happen under my jurisdiction and someone else had taken the said papers from the said room, I'd feel compelled to arrest the said person who wasn't an employee of the inn for as many crimes as I could sway a judge to render a guilty verdict on," April said, still with the only movement a faint rising of her chest as she exhaled a breath of air.

"I think we're on the same page. I appreciate your candid and detailed advice on such a complex matter. I'm confident if this particular situation were to happen, the inn's owners would notify the sheriff before the day was over. But, since this is only hypothetical," I continued, pausing as April's jaw set a little tighter, "we should move on to my next question."

"Go on."

"Maggie Roarke, a very good friend of mine for many years, asked me to talk with her sister about the experience of finding a dead body. As you know, I've had the unlucky occasion to stumble upon a handful of them myself in the last few months." I was trying to tread as carefully as I could before her jaw unhinged and she injected venom from two of her fangs into my neck. I'd either die from her poison or a nasty bleed-out from the wound itself.

"You've certainly been much closer to any murder investigation than I'd like." April leaned forward and took the signed statement from me despite my fingers pressing it tightly to the surface of the desk. "Please get to your point more quickly. I'm growing age spots listening to you ramble."

"Okay. I'll be blunt and ask you about the knife. Maggie told me it had some writing on it. She mentioned seeing some unusual letters. I happen to be a bit of an expert in different languages and believe it's from the German alphabet. Perhaps I might be able to lend a hand?"

"In exchange for?" April said while snapping my photo and scanning the statement into her computer files. Who knew the Wharton County Sheriff's Office had current technology at their disposal!

"Finding out if the victim's name was really George Braun or if that was a fake identity he'd been using." I tapped my fingers on her desk, patiently waiting for her to respond.

April stood and shut the door to her office. "Obviously, you know a lot more about this case than you're letting on. I'm going to forget you are a private citizen and that it annoys me to no end that you have firmly planted your feet in my shoes ever since you showed back up in Braxton. So, spill it now, and if I like what you tell me, I'll consider being more open with you."

I knew it was my only chance at helping Helena and Ursula but also at building a better relationship with the sheriff. I shared as much as I could without revealing anything confidential. I told April that Cheney had seen Helena fighting with George at the inn and that it seemed to revolve around something in his room. I explained what'd happened at the Stoddard restaurant and how I knew beyond any doubt they were hiding something. I also mentioned Millard's news about George renting a cabin and hiring an assistant, as well as the notion George could be someone who'd had facial reconstruction. I left out what his real name might be, to see what the sheriff would actually reveal to me.

"The autopsy's not complete, but I can confirm George Braun had extensive plastic surgery done to his face and various parts of his body. The coroner suspects he'd been marred in a fire or an explosion at some point in the past. The skin-grafting work was intricate and probably handled by an experienced specialist, but it's at least twenty years old based on some of the scarring."

"Do you know what his real name might be?"

The sheriff shook her head. "Not yet. We found no evidence in his room at the inn or office-space on campus that points to anything other than George Braun. If he's changed his name, it was done a very long time ago. He has records dating back to at least the mid-1990s, but we've sent out an alert to check a wider area and period." She opened a file on her computer and turned the monitor around, so I could see the screen. "This is a close-up picture of the knife. What can you tell me about it?"

I cleaned a smudge on my glasses with a tissue from the box on the corner of her desk, then leaned in to study the photo. It was a touchscreen monitor, but when I attempted to double tap with my finger to magnify the results, it didn't work.

April extended her hand near mine and enlarged the image with two fingers. "You have to use both with this software program, not one finger." When I turned my head in her direction, our faces were inches apart. Her breath smelled like a tempting peppermint candy covered in dark chocolate and magical dreams. My finger slipped, brushing against hers, causing us to both flinch from the encounter.

"I'm sorry." I might have blushed at the sudden intimacy between us. It was weird and soothing at the same time.

April took a deep breath, glanced away for a few seconds, then said, "Well, anything?"

"Oh, right," I mumbled trying to push a very unexpected and alarming thought from my head. Did I feel something or was my brain playing tricks on me? "It says Mück. I'm sure that's someone's last name, perhaps a family crest. It's German." Guilt began to consume me for leading April directly to Ursula, but it needed to be done.

"That's helpful, I appreciate it." April turned the screen back around to only face her.

"I was just at the new Stoddard restaurant. Doug Stoddard collects knives. You might want to check out the display on the wall when you first walk in."

"I get the feeling you know more than you're saying."

Had one of the Stoddards stolen the Mück knife? Was it just a coincidence? "I'd like to speak with someone before I reveal anything else. It might not be important or even have anything to do with this case. I promise I'll share whatever I know. Can you give me a day?"

"No." There was a hint of yes somewhere in her voice.

"A few hours?"

"No," she said emphatically. Maybe I was wrong about the hint. It could've been a hiccup.

"One hour?"

"Fine," April consented, pushing her chair backward in a grand flourish.

"I should get going. Either I'll contact you again, or someone else will call to share what he or she knows. Is that fair?" I stood and backed up a few steps like a teenager awkwardly entering puberty.

"You have one hour, but if I don't hear from either of you, I'll have Officer Flatman arrest you for obstruction of justice. Am I clear, Kellan?"

"You called me Kellan." I ignored the electric shock racing inside my body. What was going on?

"It's a segue into the other topic I need to discuss with you," April added with noticeable discomfort. "It's of a more personal nature."

I wasn't sure where the conversation might go next because I was still keenly focused on whatever peculiar moment had happened when we were both touching the monitor. "I'm all ears." I silently kicked myself for taking the bait. What was she about to scream over now?

CHAPTER 9

"You probably realized I mentioned in the library the other day that you were connected with the Castigliano family. More specifically to Vincenzo and Cecilia's dastardly branch of criminals."

I gulped. Was she about to say she'd located Francesca? "I was once married to their daughter."

"I knew your wife had died, but I didn't know about the circumstances." When the sheriff clasped her hands together on the back of the chair, her face showed a touch of empathy. "I know what it's like to lose someone you love unexpectedly, especially when the facts surrounding their death don't add up."

I couldn't tell what she might be trying to convey to me, but I wasn't about to interrupt her with more questions. "Thank you."

"What I'm trying to say, perhaps not as well as I could be, is that I hope I didn't offend you when I talked about connections to a mob family. I'm starting to understand why you behave the way you do."

"Meaning?" I asked apprehensively, staring at a water stain on the ceiling. My right hand couldn't stop squeezing my thigh. I was certain I'd bruised myself from the pressure, but at least my hand was hidden in my pants pocket so she couldn't see it flinching.

April went on to say she'd taken a step back after I helped her team solve the Gwendolyn Paddington murder investigation earlier that year. When part of their discovery revealed the culprit's connection to the Castigliano mob, April was determined to get to the bottom of the shenanigans. She wanted Wharton County to be free of any crime family's dominance and shady deals. "When I learned Francesca Castigliano was your wife and that she'd been killed in a car accident, I felt awful for you and for your daughter. Emma is such a sweet girl."

"She's my reason to keep on living," I said as my heart skipped a beat. Did the sheriff know Francesca was still alive?

"Did you ever wonder if the circumstances of your wife's death were a little suspicious? I'm not trying to open old wounds, but I read many of the reports. They never found the other driver, but the car smelled like liquor which is the only reason it was attributed to a case of drunk driving. A witness reported seeing another dark-colored car pull up and take something in a black bag away from the scene." She paused to see if I had any reactions.

I hadn't been aware of that detail. When I showed up at the accident scene, they wouldn't let me get close to Francesca's car. I also couldn't verify the body at the morgue and asked her father to do it. In retrospect, I couldn't imagine what Vincenzo Castigliano would've done if I'd wanted to see my wife one last time. I trembled at my increasing fear over how far her family would've gone to keep me in the dark. "I was a mess when she died. I crawled into a hole for several weeks and barely paid attention to anything on the news. My nana came out to Los Angeles to take care of Emma for me."

April reached a hand in my direction but paused before actually trying to physically comfort me. "As I said, I know what it's like to lose a loved one. There's a reason I'm mentioning this."

"I'd rather not talk about the past," I said, worrying Francesca had blown her cover.

"Listen to me, Kellan. Your wife died in a way that you had no control over. I understand the cause was listed as a drunk driver t-boning her car and pinning her against a tree. I'm worried that you're letting yourself get too close to the couple of murders we've had here in Braxton, as a way to help you move on. To accept Francesca's death. To eliminate any traces of guilt you might still feel."

"Huh?" It's all I could manage. Was she trying to tell me that I wanted to resolve what happened to my wife by helping the friends and family of victims discover who killed their loved ones? "I don't understand what you're insinuating."

"It's a coping mechanism. Rather than process everything you've been through, you're throwing yourself into complex and risky situations," she added.

"Are you not convinced Francesca's death was an accident?" I muttered.

"I'm slightly concerned at this point. I've read all the reports, as I said earlier. I've also learned what that family is capable of, and one of my former colleagues who's now in the FBI has hinted at something sinister going on in that family's LA mansion the last few years."

I needed to escape. It didn't matter whether I could or couldn't trust April with the reality of what went on. I had to put Emma first, and no matter what happened or what the sheriff discovered, I would always focus on my little girl's safety. "I don't know what you're talking about, but I also can't discuss this right now. Francesca's gone. I had to accept it. Maybe in time, I can think about the past again, but not today." I began walking away quickly with loud, determined steps past Officer Flatman.

April followed and grabbed my shoulder, unwilling to let me leave. "I'm not trying to pry. Nor am I intentionally looking to hurt you. But I need to investigate that family based on what happened with the Paddington Enterprises drug case. I thought you might be interested in helping me at some point. I hope I didn't upset you by bringing up what my instincts are telling me about Francesca's death."

"I should go. I have to pick up Emma soon," I explained and rushed out of the sheriff's office. I heard April apologize but also remind me of my promise to share what I knew about George Braun's death within one hour. When I reached the front lobby, I exited without looking back.

By the time I walked to my SUV, my entire body was fueled with rage and anxiety. As much as I was furious with April for bringing up the topic, I'd already detached my emotions about losing my wife. Francesca wasn't dead. April's message didn't evoke pain or loss. It made me realize how frustrated I was that my wife was hiding from us and had left a horrid mess for me to deal with. Again.

Organizing my priorities, I called Ursula and explained what I'd learned. She knew it was time to tell the truth and promised me she'd talk to April within the hour. Ursula also mentioned the knife sounded exactly like a family heirloom she'd brought with her to the office weeks ago. "I kept it in the drawer to protect myself from the stalker. I'll have to check if it's still there."

"Did anyone know it was in your office?" Like Doug?

Ursula took a few seconds to reflect. "Dean Mulligan walked into my office the day I brought it on campus. He saw me put it in the drawer, even made a joke about having weapons on campus."

After we hung up, I spoke with my mother who agreed to pick up Emma from school and watch her for the evening. I wanted to hold my daughter in my arms, but before I could see her, I needed to lose the tense aggression building up inside me. I was grateful I had my gym clothes in a bag on the backseat and quickly changed into them to go for a run before dinner that night with Nana D. It was our last opportunity to strategize how she could pull off winning the mayoral race. I desperately needed a distraction that evening where I focused on anything but death. Whether it was Francesca's or George Braun's, my mind required a night off from morbid thoughts.

* * *

"He's bringing a surprise guest... a date... what's that all about?" I finished setting the dining room table in Nana D's house as the concern escaped my lips. While the run had helped, I wasn't completely relaxed. Millard and my nana had dated for a brief period, but it was not meant to last. All she ever said was that he could be selfish and too old-fashioned.

"I don't believe it's a date. Millard only told me he had someone who could assist with the campaign. We need all the help we can get, especially after that unfortunate incident at the Paddington estate. Eustacia still hasn't forgiven me completely," Nana D said raising her voice from the other side of the kitchen.

She pulled open the oven door and tasted the beef brisket. "Twenty more minutes and this baby will melt in our mouths."

I loved how she casually mentioned the Paddington estate incident where she thought Eustacia and Millard had been cavorting with the enemy, Marcus Stanton. The Paddington family housekeeper, Bertha, had told me Nana D went berserk by dumping a pot of meatballs and sauce all over everyone. Nana D had not been in the loop on Eustacia's trick to force the councilman to reveal some of his campaign secrets. "I thought you'd resolved your differences again. I can't keep up. You two are worse than twin sisters out to hurt one another over the silliest of misunderstandings."

"What's that, brilliant one? Did you say you needed a margarita?" Nana D shut the oven and poked her head in the dining room to see if I'd laughed at her idle threat. "Water glass on the right, please. Just above the knife. You never did learn to set a proper table. As far as Eustacia, we're still close, but I'm waiting for that old bag to get her revenge."

It was going to be a long night. I offered to answer the door when the door-bell rang. I wondered if Millard was bringing Eustacia to smooth over the whole situation. I checked the table one last time and walked through the main hall to greet our guests.

"Good evening, Kellan. It's always a pleasure to see you. Let me introduce you to someone," Millard said while stepping to the side so I could meet the person hiding behind him.

It was Lissette Nutberry. She wore a stylish little black dress that covered her knees and shoulders, with a turquoise-colored silk wrap draped across her chest and matching high-heel pumps. The radiant hue brought out the blue specks in her hazel eyes. She looked much different than when I'd seen her at the costume extravaganza with Marcus Stanton. Wasn't she on the enemy's team?

"Kellan Ayrwick, twice in one week. Aren't I a lucky gal?" Lissette said leaning in to kiss my cheek. "I'm very excited to catch up with you. There simply wasn't enough time the other evening."

I gave Millard an inquisitive look and ushered them both inside. After taking her wrap and his coat, I complimented them both on how they were dressed and escorted them down the hall. Nana D wasn't one for formalities and preferred they hung around the kitchen while she finished cooking.

Lissette rushed right to my nana. "Oh, Seraphina, it's been ages. I've missed you so much."

I recalled our families had known one another, but those two seemed quite close. "May I get you a drink?" After pouring four glasses of a California pinot noir Millard had brought with him, I decided to be blunt. "Lissette, it's wonderful to see you again. I didn't realize you and Councilman Stanton were so close. He seemed smitten at the library."

Lissette guffawed. "That old horse's patootie? Don't be a fool! I certainly know him from the social scene, but I wouldn't be caught dead on his arms. In his dreams!" She gulped a third of her wine and then raised the glass upward to offer a toast. "To Seraphina Danby, the next mayor, and her darling grandson, Kellan, who's finally come back home."

After a rousing round of 'hear, hear,' Nana D noticed my discomfort. "Kellan, dear, Lissette has offered to talk to all the ladies in her auxiliary league about supporting me on election day."

"We're also going to put up some campaign signs around the family pharmacy and the funeral homes. I thought it might be a little tacky, but Seraphina astutely reminded me she was counting on the senior citizen's vote. Who spends more time at a pharmacy or a funeral home than this county's elder population? Am I right, or am I right?" Lissette clinked Nana D's glass, and they both swallowed another huge gulp.

"Lissette grew up with your mother and your Aunt Deirdre. I've known this one since she was a tiny girl begging me to help shear the sheep every year," Nana D noted while dropping a few pads of butter in the bowl of mashed potatoes. If she didn't kill me with pastries, my arteries would clog up before Emma reached her teenage years. Oh, did I dread those days!

"Watching you spin wool was magical. I have the fondest memories of this farm," Lissette added with a distant stare in her eyes. "I do wish Deirdre would come home from Europe. She's been gone for far too long. Like my sister, Judy." Lissette's voice grew soft and held a momentary pang of sadness.

Millard grabbed the bottle of wine and refilled her glass. "Lissette and I had tea yesterday. We got to talking about the upcoming flower exhibit and how I needed to find someone to help me get it organized now that we've lost George Braun. Awful business, eh, Kellan?"

"Truly. I can't make heads or tails of what happened to the man." I turned to Lissette. "Are you a gardener like Millard?"

Lissette reached out to grab his hand and brightened the room with a huge smile. "Millard's not a gardener. He's a brilliant landscape architect with an immense knowledge of the world of flowers. I could never attain the success he's achieved, but I have won Braxton's annual *Grand Garden* award a few years in the past."

"Don't be shy. You and Judy ran the *Grand Garden* committee for years. It's a shame she felt Braxton was too small for her, but I'm glad she found happiness somewhere else," Nana D said as she carried a giant orange, enamel-coated cast iron pot full of brisket, carrots, onions, and delicious gravy to the table.

"I wish I could be sure she found happiness, Seraphina. Judy and I kept in close touch the last two years, but she's been hard to reach ever since she got sick and moved again," Lissette huffed as she poured water in everyone's glass. "I'm so worried about her."

"What do you mean she got sick and moved away?" I asked.

Since Lissette was swallowing another mouthful of wine, Millard responded. "Judy wrote to Lissette a few months ago telling her she'd met a wonderful man on the train one day. She planned to come home this spring to introduce him to everyone, but he whisked her away to some secluded little town where she could recover from her heart condition. You must remember what new love is like."

"Your Aunt Deirdre is trying to locate them," Nana D offered as she took her seat.

"I've booked a flight to London tomorrow. Deirdre's letting me stay at her place before I fly to Judy's new home to surprise her, assuming the detective can locate her. It's her first love, you know, and at our age, it's quite difficult to catch a man," Lissette said sneaking a quick glance at Millard.

If Lissette and her sister were about Aunt Deirdre's age, she was also in her late forties or early fifties—odd that neither sister had married before. I also realized Lissette might be after Millard, despite his being old enough to be her father, because Judy's departure left her all alone. "I wish you much luck in finding Judy. I'm confident Aunt Deirdre will locate them. As queen of the romance novel, she's bound to unearth two lovers hiding from everyone while they begin a new life together." An odd thought crossed my brain that Judy and my aunt were secretly together, but I let it drift away quickly.

After everyone sat, Nana D said a quick *grace*. While we all dug into our rich, home-cooked meal, we began chatting about the mayoral campaign. Lissette assured us she was supporting Nana D and provided a few unknown pieces of gossip about Councilman Stanton. We might be able to use them to get Nana D the lead she needed in the home stretch.

After a scrumptious black cherry pie and our guests' departure, I squinted sideways at Nana D. "Was I imagining it, or was Lissette possibly flirting ever-so-faintly with Millard?"

Nana D spit out her mouthful of wine. "Oh, I hope so. I would love to see those two get into a little spat once Millard tries to smother her with his insistence she stay home and cook his meals. He's never lost that warped sense of a woman's responsibilities. A very antiquated man despite his worldly ways in most other matters. "I'm done with that farakte foray into the past."

"Is Aunt Deirdre coming home anytime soon?"

Nana D laughed. "Last time we spoke, my daughter promised she'd be back before summer. That's only a few weeks away. Maybe she'll find Judy and bring her and the new guy to town."

I hugged Nana D and walked to my guest house. My phone vibrated as I unlocked the door.

Ursula: *It's done. I told the sheriff what I knew and that George is most likely my brother, Hans.*

Me: *I know you were worried, but she needed to find out. What's she going to do now?*

Ursula: *She wants to see both of us in her office tomorrow morning. Apparently, you have a folder that she needs to retrieve?*

I opened my briefcase and confirmed it was still inside. I would leaf through it before bed to determine if it had anything important prior to handing it over to the police.

Me: *Yes. I just got hold of it a little while ago. What about the knife?*
Ursula: *I'll look after our meeting to see if it's the one I brought to my office.*

After going home, I checked on Emma who was thrilled to have a sleepover with my parents at the Royal Chic-Shack. While she loved spending time at Nana D's farmhouse and setting up our new home in the guest cottage, my parents had a huge game room and every movie channel. They'd watched a new Disney flick and stayed up much later than I would've liked. But my mother would be the one to rouse Emma when it was time to go to school, not me. Emma had inherited her intense dislike for the early morning from me.

* * *

By seven thirty, I left to meet Ursula at The Big Beanery on South Campus for a prep session. Since I'd spent most of the previous evening reviewing all the paperwork in the folder Helena had found, we wanted to catch up before our scheduled appointment with the sheriff in an hour. I needed to be back on campus to teach my morning class, and the sheriff had promised Ursula she'd be expedient. As I grabbed the open briefcase, I banged my elbow into the console. A few minutes later, once my funny bone stopped torturing me, I gathered everything that fell to the floor of the passenger seat and went inside. What was I in store for next? Something told me it was going to be a dreadful day.

"Anything valuable in the folder? If it's my brother's stuff, I might recognize something," Ursula suggested as I placed two coffees and bowls of whole wheat cereal with almond milk on the table. She insisted on buying breakfast but also demanded it didn't include anything sugary or full of carbs, citing my normal obsession with desserts. I compromised only because she was my boss and had mastered the look of someone ready to throttle you if you'd disagreed with her.

"Have a gander." I pushed the folder across the table. "I'll tell you the key things I noticed."

"I appreciate it."

"Besides a handful of photos and articles from the explosion, there are extensive clippings from multiple newspapers. He's tracked your entire career in the last few months. My guess is George, or Hans, whatever you want to call him..." I said, stopping to verify she was handling the news calmly.

"Go with George for now. We don't know he's definitely Hans." Ursula sipped her coffee.

"My guess is George didn't know anything about you until he found out about your appointment to Braxton's presidency earlier this year. Given the newspaper clippings are well preserved and smell fresh, he probably gathered all these articles recently. He's got copies of things such as your wedding announcement to Myriam, your graduation from Columbia, and pictures of

461

your current home." I sat back in the chair and paused to let her absorb the news.

"He's angry with me. I can tell by some of the notes he's made in the margins. I don't understand why he would hide all these years," Ursula said, pounding her fists against the table.

"Look, we need to give all this to Sheriff Montague. She'll have more access to his records than we do. I'm sure she's planning to get Interpol files of George's time in that Swiss institute. My research noted he was employed there, but I'd bet money that's where he had his reconstructive surgery."

"I think you're right." Ursula was about to say something else, but Myriam abruptly stopped at the side of our table and cleared her throat so loudly that Shakespeare himself could've heard it.

"I've been patient. I've been open-minded. I've even been quiet about the amount of time you two have been spending together. But tell me, 'How poor are they that have not patience! What wound did ever heal but by degrees?'

In the entire three months I'd known Myriam, not once had I ever seen a hair out of place, a tiny quake in her composure, or a twinge of jealousy in her voice. I'd now seen all three *and* confirmed she wasn't wearing a wig! "Morning, boss."

"What are you doing here? I thought you were meeting with Dean Mulligan this morning?" Ursula said, reaching for her wife's hand. I turned away at their moment of intimacy to be respectful of their privacy. "Kellan, would you mind giving Myriam and me a minute to—"

Although I stood, Myriam raised her gloved hand in my direction and with the gentle press of one finger pushed my shoulder down until I was sitting again. "The three of us are going to have an honest and highly diplomatic conversation about what's been going on. If we do not, Kellan will find himself with the worst possible class schedule this fall. I'll assign him to the freshman writing center, so he's forced to correct grammar all day long."

There were very few things I abhorred. Other than Myriam, of course. Freshmen were the bane of my existence. At least the ones forced to take a writing course in order to satisfy Braxton's general requirements for all graduates. "You wouldn't!"

"Absolutely, I would. If you think Desdemona was the downfall of Othello, think again. He couldn't take the simplicity of everyone around him and thus caused his own demise. That'll be you working with all the little brats who can't tell the difference between *me* and *I*. Myriam dragged a chair from a nearby empty table to ours and scowled. "Start talking!"

I looked to Ursula, but the defeat in her composure was already apparent. So, we conversed as peacefully as three frustrated and suspicious people could. Myriam explained she'd begun putting odd details together and learned Ursula's secret weeks ago. She hadn't revealed her discovery hoping her wife would choose to come clean of her own accord. Unfortunately, someone at the sheriff's office called their house that morning to remind Ursula not to be late to an important meeting. That's when Myriam decided to rip the curtain off the charade and step in to save the day.

"Obviously, you need proof this man is your brother before we do anything further," Myriam directed at her wife. "Let's forget how furious I am with you both for a moment. We must focus on how to prove you had nothing to do with his death." Myriam glared at me and took a spoonful of Ursula's leftover cereal. "As for you, since I've known you, Mr. Ayrwick," she said, pausing as a drop of milk splashed on my chin when she raised the spoon in my direction, "you are nothing but a nosy, interfering, non-stop questioning, painful wart on the tip of my pinky toe that has aggravated me beyond any reasonable expectation. You're also, I hesitate to acknowledge, the perfect solution to this problem."

Ursula and I turned to one another with puzzled expressions. "Come again?"

"Isn't it obvious? He works for you. He works for me. The man is compelled to investigate anything from an unplanned change in the wind's direction to the exact time a speck of dirt clung to his shoe with a desperate need to find something inaner than itself." She settled into her chair, crossed her legs, and made a noise like everything had been agreed to between us. "I expect a daily report. Make that twice a day. You have seventy-two hours to find the person responsible for this entire horrid affair and to keep the love of my life from getting arrested or being killed by this vulture. I don't need to ask if I am being clear because that's a fact."

Sometimes I can be a little reticent to acknowledge a warped version of a compromise. Other times I can be a little dense if I haven't had enough coffee. That was not the case right now. "Ummm... don't you think that's why Ursula and I have been meeting so much lately?" I said, darting my eyes to the floor. Before the snakes had appeared in lieu of Medusa's hair, people thought they could trust her. I didn't want to make the same mistake as the ancient Greeks by staring directly at Myriam.

"Now you've got me involved, so best be on your toes." Myriam stood and shot an obsequious smile in my direction. "I've got work. Don't be late for the sheriff. I expect a full report as soon as you both get back." Myriam bent down to peck her wife's forehead. "I'll deal with your lack of trust later tonight. Be home by five o'clock. I wouldn't suggest being any later. The bell currently tolls for thee." Then she turned to me. "Do this properly, and you'll have only the best course schedule this fall. Fail me or my wife, and let's just say... George Braun's death won't be the only suspicious loss of life in Braxton this week!"

CHAPTER 10

Once Myriam left and I regained my wits, I leaned over the table. "She wouldn't really do anything to me, would she?"

Ursula shook her head. "I wish I could be certain. I've never seen her behave this way. Usually when she's upset, she screams lines from Chaucer at me. At least you get Shakespeare as her muse. I don't think I've ever seen her be this nice to you. I'm a little petrified right now, if I'm being honest."

That was her being nice? We agreed to move on and flipped through George's folder marking the important items for the sheriff to follow up on. While we waited at the Wharton County Sheriff's Office, I prepared for my second dress-down of the day. I still hadn't fully interpreted what'd happened with April in her office the previous day when our fingers accidentally brushed against one another.

"Ah, if it isn't two examples of the most perfect, upstanding leaders of Braxton College. Tell me, are you proud of yourselves? Do you think this is how a college president and a supposedly well-liked professor and mentor to graduating students should behave?" April tore the folder from my hands, pointed at the two chairs across from her desk, and slammed the door shut.

After we listened to April's tirade about the need to protect evidence, the stupidity of trying to determine on our own who'd been stalking Ursula, and a litany of crimes that she was tempted to arrest us both for, she popped a glazed donut in her mouth. "Talk to me. What do you see as our next steps?"

I eyed the last donut knowing I shouldn't reach for it. April would probably shoot me, so instead, I offered to summarize what we'd learned to date. "George Braun is most likely Hans Mück. We need to find any proof that he changed his name after surviving the explosion. We don't know why he was trying to hurt Ursula, but if he hadn't done anything other than stalking her, it's probably because he still had a deal he wanted to make with his sister. Someone killed him, and we think he had a partner who was helping him with whatever sinister plan he'd concocted." Now I fully understood his choice to wear a Dr. Evil costume.

"We need to understand what he'd planned for his special exhibit in the Mendel flower show," Ursula suggested. If he'd been planning to expose her, there might be evidence we're missing. So far, it looked like he'd been focused on unveiling his latest research on how bees were the potential solution. He planned to stress the importance of saving them from rapidly declining numbers.

April said, "People don't realize how much of what they consume requires bees to thrive and transport pollen."

I glanced at her with a curious eye. "I didn't know you were so knowledgeable."

"I have several hives in my backyard. I'll invite you over to see them one afternoon," she replied.

Ursula cleared her throat. "I'm sure my brother was planning to hurt me. He held grudges when we were younger."

"Do you wear a full bee suit?" I asked unable to picture April in one.

"I do. I have a spare for when Myriam helps," April replied ignoring Ursula's presence. "You should check out the Indigo Acres Apiary website. Lots of cool stuff."

"As interesting as this bizarre connection is between you, and as much as this train wreck fascinates me, can we get back on topic?" Ursula said. After the sheriff and I complied, Ursula shared everything she could remember about the assistant who'd worked in the lab years ago. A couple of new suspects had risen to the top and warranted further investigation.

April confirmed they hadn't been able to find Anita Singh's missing lab coat, but she'd interview the chairman of the science department the next day to find out exactly when it disappeared. April was also going to interview Dean Mulligan at three o'clock that afternoon to clarify the crux of the disagreements with George about his research presentation at the Mendel flower show. "While these are all valid angles, my primary one right now is determining where the knife came from."

When she brought up its image on the screen, Ursula gasped. "That's definitely the Mück family crest. And it's my knife, or it was the knife my father kept in our house as a reminder of his ancestor's battles against French invaders in the seventeenth and eighteenth centuries. When I ran away after the explosion, I took it with me for protection."

"Are you telling me with certainty the murder weapon belonged to you, Ms. Power?" the sheriff said in an accusatory voice. It made Ursula look as guilty as Helena who'd been caught with the knife.

"I kept it in a drawer at the office but didn't know it was missing. I haven't looked for it in a long time," Ursula noted. Her eyes filled with worry and nostalgia over the death of her parents and her complicated past. "One of the

Stoddards must have broken in and taken it for display on the wall at the restaurant. It doesn't make any sense why or how Hans got hold of it."

"You don't know it was a Stoddard or Hans. All we know is that's what was used to kill your brother. Someone else might have found it and brought it to the costume extravaganza," I added.

April made a noise that sounded like she disagreed. "Based on the preliminary work-up of how George Braun, *possibly* Hans Mück, died, it was definitely from a knife wound to his abdomen. Actually, he was stabbed twice. The killer knew exactly where to cut George for maximum pain and almost immediate death. Oddly enough, only Braun's prints were found on the weapon. I might be going out on a limb, but I think he stole the knife from you because he planned to kill you with it that night. Perhaps he saw it as a fitting way to get revenge. It seems someone else got to him first."

The sheriff went on to indicate that because there were no other prints on the knife, it meant the killer either wore gloves or wiped it clean. Hans had likely tried to pull the knife out of his own abdomen but died in doing so, which explained why his bloody prints were found on it. I couldn't imagine how it felt to rip the blade from my own flesh and know I was about to bleed to death.

"If we're to believe Helena Roarke, she stumbled upon Hans moments after the killer escaped and Hans tried to remove the knife to save himself. Helena picked it up, but since she wore gloves as part of her costume, there wouldn't be any prints," the sheriff noted, flipping through a report on her computer screen. "Helena Roarke witnessed George Braun arguing with Cheney Stoddard in the courtyard at eight twenty-five. Multiple people will verify Cheney returned to the bar by eight thirty. Helena had already left to fill several food trays for the party and didn't return to the courtyard until eight forty-five. This suggests that George was killed between eight thirty and eight forty-five. Tell me again where the two of you were?"

Ursula said, "I found the note just before eight thirty. I was nervous and rushed behind the silk draperies near the doors to the private back office area in the library. I needed to decide what to do next and hid there for about fifteen minutes. That's when Kellan came rushing by me, and I grabbed his arm to show him the note."

"That's all true," I confirmed recalling the stain on her shawl. Should I believe her that it was only sauce? "I remember looking at my phone at eight fifty when I left Ursula to search for someone in a white costume."

"Perhaps Cheney is responsible. Cheney or his parents have some sort of a connection to George from what Kellan's told me," Ursula reminded us.

"Detective Gilkrist is meeting with Cheney and his sister, Sierra, today. She returned to town recently and has been hovering around her brother every time we visit him. She's a first-year law student and thinks she can protect him. I'll explore that avenue if it offers up any new leads. So, if we believe George is the one who left you the note just before eight thirty, it means he then snuck into the courtyard and argued with Cheney. Helena witnessed the disagreement but disappeared when she saw the two men stop fighting." April paused to let that information sink in. "If the killer isn't Cheney, then we have some mysterious person who managed to get into the courtyard between eight thirty and eight forty-five and found enough time to stab George and escape without being noticed by anyone. While it's possible, that's very tight timing."

"Helena admitted to leaving the door unlocked earlier in the night. Anyone could've snuck back there before Cheney did. There were several offices and restrooms to hide in," I said.

"True, but I can't ask over a hundred guests who might have had access. We're collecting statements from everyone and verifying any known absences from about eight until eight forty-five. I don't believe we've finished interviewing the Stoddards, but they are a priority for today. You must see this is currently pointing to three primary suspects," the sheriff noted.

"Helena. Cheney. And me," Ursula whispered.

"Unfortunately, I don't have enough evidence to arrest any of the three of you. I'll go through this file you found, and I plan to research your brother's likely stint as George Braun. At this point, I will be sending someone to your office with you right now to check for any fingerprints left behind during the supposed burglary. I'll need you to show us which desk drawer you kept the knife in." April stood and indicated it was time for us both to leave. "Do not speak to anyone else, and please stay out of this investigation, Kellan."

"I'll do my best, but Ursula has asked me to help figure out what happened to her brother," I reminded the sheriff. "And who might be trying to hurt her if it wasn't him."

"Stay out of my path while you do." April began closing the door after Ursula and I left her office. "I'll invite you over to see the bees when this investigation is done, Little Ayrwick."

"I'd like that. I'm fascinated by the whole concept." Did I really just say that? Was I feeling okay?

When we got back to campus, Ursula left with Flatman to check her office, and I taught my morning class. It went by quickly, but in the back of my head, something was bothering me about the timing of the entire situation and the connections of the people involved. I couldn't think clearly, but I was certain Cheney Stoddard hid something important. I had to find a way to talk to him again but needed a valid reason to show up and ask pertinent questions. Hopefully, Ed Mulligan or Anita Singh would confess something to help April find the killer, unless of course, it was one of them.

After class, I had a quick bite to eat and drove to the Pick-Me-Up Diner to collect Eleanor for her appointment with the fertility clinic. I'd almost forgotten we were going today, but I'd luckily carved out enough time.

After we were escorted past the nurse's station, Eleanor said, "You look different. Almost like when you were a teenager smitten with some new girl. Did you meet someone new today?"

"No! What are you talking about? I think it's all the hormone drugs you're taking. By the way," I replied as we sat in a private room waiting for the doctor to arrive, "have you told anyone else what you're doing here?" I hadn't seen anyone today, what was she talking about? I probably looked tired, it'd been a long day already.

"No, Mom and Dad can't know yet. Once I've got everything in order, I'll tell them it's already a done deal." She crossed her legs and squirmed with excitement and apprehension. "I still can't believe what they have to do to make this happen."

"I don't want to discuss it. I promised you I'd support you throughout the process, but I will not listen to a step-by-step itinerary of the procedures. I will help you select the donor. I will drive you to and from the doctor's office. I will be the first one to say congratulations when it's confirmed you're pregnant, but—"

Eleanor interrupted, "But if I bring up the words turkey baster, you'll throw me in the Finnulia River and claim a bear ate my body in the woods on a camping trip. I should've asked Nana D to come."

"Like she can keep a secret. She might be okay with you doing this, but you know Nana D would relish the thought of explaining the entire thing to Dad." I could imagine the props and pictures our grandmother would use to divulge the secret to our poor father. He'd die of a heart attack on the spot.

"While that might be true, please forget about that part for now. Look at these three profiles," Eleanor said while keying a few numbers into the computer. Everything was secure and advanced at this facility. She could look up only a certain amount of details at this point in the process, but she'd have a picture if the donor had included one to help make the ultimate decision.

Within seconds, the three images appeared on the monitor. I wasn't sure if Eleanor noticed my reaction, but I felt my own heart begin to race. "Ummm... Eleanor..."

"What? You don't think we'd be a good match? I see gorgeous babies!" she exclaimed.

Did she not realize it? "That's not the point. Do you see anything... about these photos... that might remind you of anyone?"

Eleanor leaned in further while I cleaned my glasses on the off chance the surprise I saw wasn't actually on the screen. "I guess the guys all look similar. Maybe I have a type," she quipped.

All three men had similar striking facial structure, light brown skin, and dark hair. One was from Barbados, another from South Africa, and the third from St. Kitt's. They had the exact same color eyes, a vibrant green that clearly stood out as a mesmerizing feature. As I read the bios, each worked in dangerous jobs ranging from airport security to personal bodyguard for a well-known celebrity. "Ummm... Eleanor, you have a type. And his name is Connor Hawkins."

To say I was shocked would be an understatement. Eleanor had gone on a few dates with my former best friend in the months before I'd returned to Braxton. She thought Connor was very interested in getting more serious, but he did a quick sidestep and dated Maggie Roarke. I'd eventually come to learn that Connor was attracted to my sister, but he'd also had a crush on Maggie ever since we'd broken up years ago. Instead of talking to me about the possibility of dating my sister, he shut the whole scenario down and almost broke Eleanor's heart. They'd been talking about giving it a chance again, but I did my best to stay as uninvolved as possible since I wasn't the most unbiased person to help Connor sort out his romantic dilemma.

Eleanor whacked my arm with an open hand. "That's not true. These guys are all... well, I mean... Connor has... oh no!" She crumpled against my chest and groaned loudly as the doctor walked in.

"Hello, Eleanor. I'm excited to review your choices. I see you've got someone here with you today. I'm Dr.—" he began until my sister stood and rushed out of the room leaving me behind to explain the situation.

"I'm her brother. We just got some urgent news from our parents. We need to help them with something. Eleanor will give you a call to reschedule, I'm sorry," I said backing out of the office. By the time I'd gotten to the reception area, Eleanor was already gone. I called her cell, but she didn't pick up. I felt awful for what'd happened, but she was hanging on to a hope that Connor would choose her, and she truly didn't realize what she was about to do until I'd pointed it out.

I waited a few minutes but couldn't find her. As I started the SUV's engine, my phone pinged. Eleanor said she needed some time to herself and would call me that night. She'd called an Uber to pick her up and would get back to the diner herself. Knowing my sister, a few hours of space and a focus on her job would help her feel better. I replied that I loved her and invited her to come by later that night for rocky road ice cream and *Reese's Pieces*, her favorite candy.

I drove back to campus and dashed to Paddington's Play House to retrieve a copy of the summer play. Myriam had indicated it was in the office behind the main stage. I needed to reread *Sunset Boulevard* before casting was finished. Upon arrival, I saw one of the students I'd worked with in the past. She was breaking down part of the *King Lear* set given its final performance had occurred last Saturday.

"Hey, Yuri. It's great to see you. I've been meaning to check in with you this week," I said, recalling she'd been working at the Roarke & Daughters Inn as a chambermaid in George's room the day he'd been killed.

"Professor Ayrwick. What's happening? I got confirmation I could attend your advanced filmmaking class in the fall. I can't wait," she gleefully replied. Just as last time, her hair was neon green, but it had been cut much shorter than before. She'd gained a few pounds and no longer looked waifish, but she'd added a new piercing to her left ear with a chain that ran to her nose ring. I was surprised the Roarkes allowed her to wear that at the inn. She must have caught me staring at it. "Cool, huh? I have to remove it at home or when I'm at work. Bummer, yeah?"

I wasn't sure how to respond to the last comment, so I didn't. "That's wonderful news. It'll be good to have a student of your caliber in the room next time," I noted. She had a lot of potential but preferred behind the scenes work, which was not my exact area of expertise. "Listen, I heard you work at the Roarke family's bed and breakfast."

"Yep, it's good money. I don't really dig having to clean up after some guests, but most are pretty solid about not making a huge mess." She wiped her hands on a towel and stopped fidgeting with the set. "What can I do for you?"

"I was curious if you happen to remember someone named George Braun. He was a guest there recently, and a friend of mine thought she—"

"The dude that died, right?" she said loudly with an excited expression. "I can't believe I saw him that afternoon and then poof! Life's too short. That's why I make every day count," she advised me.

"Definitely. Any chance you learned something about him? I'm looking out for Helena Roarke and her family. From what I understand, he could be rude to the staff." I tried to be tactful without setting off any alarms. Yuri was a nice girl, but I didn't know if she was the type to gossip about things with her friends.

"Oh, yeah. He was a pistol. I heard him yelling at Helena the day before the party. She picked up the phone when it rang in his room. He'd walked back in and gotten so upset about it," Yuri noted. She looked like she had more to say but didn't know where to begin.

"Really? Did Helena know who was on the phone?" I asked, assuming that was the incident where George kicked her out of his room and told her not to come back again.

"Nah, she was getting off work and her boyfriend, Cheney, was there. He looked real aggravated and said he wanted to teach that Braun dude a lesson." Yuri grabbed her keys from the table at the side. "I'm about to head out. Need anything else?"

I wasn't sure but wanted to find out what she might've overheard. "Did you see Cheney talk to George Braun?"

"No, Helena persuaded Cheney to leave. I had other rooms to clean, but I did see George Braun the next day when he asked me for extra towels. I dropped them off and overheard him talking to someone," she explained as we walked through the main lobby. "He'd been screaming at someone on the phone about not giving the money back and how sorry he was for the whole situation."

"Do you know who he was talking to?" I asked.

"I think he used the word marriage." Yuri pushed open the theater door to leave the building.

If George was married, then maybe the wife was his next of kin. Not Ursula. I needed to find out if he was married and to whom. "Did you hear any names? Locations?"

"Nah, he kept saying that he loved her, and it wasn't his fault. Then he hung up the phone and told me to get lost. Gave me five dollars and told me not to tell anyone about his call." Yuri shrugged her shoulders and waved goodbye. "Gotta jet."

"Hold up. Then why'd you tell me?" I said, puzzled over what had happened.

"If he'd given me twenty, I might have kept quiet. But five bucks doesn't even buy you a decent meal these days, professor. Plus, he was discourteous to us, so I figured he didn't deserve my silence." Yuri shrugged her shoulders as if she hadn't felt any guilt about what she'd done.

"Anything else you can remember? Other visitors?"

"Ummm... oh, yeah, I forgot. Dean Mulligan from campus came by after the phone call. I was cleaning another room and saw George's door open. I thought it was super odd, but then I heard George talk about the upcoming flower science exhibit thingy. The dean was yelling just like he always does, ya know? Something about if it was important enough to keep the secret buried, it was important enough to get hold of the money." Yuri indicated she hadn't heard anything else, then rushed off for an important dorm meeting.

When I got back to my car, my brain went into overdrive. I'd gotten lucky tonight in finding out several new important facts about George Braun. I would tell the sheriff what I'd stumbled upon, but that could wait until the morning. I wanted to analyze what Yuri's news meant. Could George's wife have snuck into the library and killed him for some unknown reason? Was Dean Mulligan involved in some sort of blackmail scheme with George Braun?

As I pulled out of the parking lot, the speed bump accidentally knocked my briefcase off the seat. When I leaned over to retrieve it, I saw an index card had fallen on the floor. I stopped the SUV on the side of the road, picked up the index card, and read the writing on the lined front side. It was an address I thought I'd recognized, so I checked my phone and realized it was one of the cabins near the Saddlebrooke National Forest. A bell went off in my head. I'd seen another index card just like it in the file Helena had found under George Braun's bed. This probably fell out of his folder when I pulled it out of my brief-case to deliver it to the sheriff.

It must be the cabin George had purchased, and if memory served, the assistant he'd hired was staying there to finish some of the renovations. I looked at the time but needed to pick Emma up from school and finish preparing lesson plans. I decided to stop by the cabin after tomorrow's classes when I had more time. Three major leads in a row. Today was certainly improving!

CHAPTER 11

After dinner, I reviewed Emma's homework and was happily surprised she'd received an award for the best show-and-tell experience in class that week. Everyone loved her drawings of Danby Landing and the photos of the different buildings and crop fields. Nana D only kept a few horses and chickens around, but she was still faithfully planting tons of fruits and vegetables to bring in supplemental income. Although my grandpop had left her with a small inheritance and she'd sold a chunk of the farm to cover her expenses once she became a widow, the extra money came in handy throughout the year.

"Can we read a bedtime story before Auntie Eleanor arrives?" Emma asked as I tucked her into bed. It was her turn to pick a book since I'd chosen *The Lion, the Witch and the Wardrobe* the previous week. There was a rule in my house—you can't watch the film or television show until you've read the book, if one existed. She'd begged to watch the most recent adaptation, but I wouldn't budge as I knew what a treat it'd had been as a child when Nana D had read them to us.

"You've got twenty minutes before she'll be here," I noted while my daughter perused the shelves in her bedroom. That was another rule I'd made when Emma was born—electronic books are fair game, but you must always have more physical books than e-books. I wanted Emma to experience a multitude of technology at her fingertips from an early age, but she also needed to respect and cherish all that our country had accomplished in the history of bookmaking and printing.

While Emma decided between an item on her classics shelf and a newly published fairy-tale retelling, I quickly surveyed the rest of our home to ensure it was ready for company. Nana D's guesthouse was a two-bedroom standalone ranch-style abode on the south corner of Danby Landing. The ten-minute walk to her cozy farmhouse just beyond the apple orchard gave us both the right amount of privacy and proximity. We'd fixed up the smaller bedroom for Emma with a fresh coat of paint and some unused furniture from the attic. All our stuff was back in Los Angeles in the house I'd left behind. I'd signed a one-year lease for a young couple who'd wanted to rent something furnished before buying their own place. It worked out well for me since I was technically bound to the LA television network who'd put my reality show, Dark Reality, on hiatus for one year while they revamped the entire program. I'd have to decide about returning early next year, pending my contract at Braxton.

Eleanor texted that she craved a movie night as her way to regroup from the visit at the fertility clinic. Emma found me in the kitchen as I took two bowls from the cabinet in preparation for my sister's arrival. "Let's go, Daddy. I want you to read two chapters in this one," my daughter said thrusting a copy of 'Charlotte's Web' in my hands.

"Works for me, then you can decorate your room to match the farm Wilbur lives on." I followed her into the bedroom where she climbed into her single platform bed, tossed bright purple covers over her body, and asked me to snuggle up next to her.

Shortly after I began reading chapter two, Eleanor arrived and let herself in. She stood in the doorway watching Emma's eyes flutter open and shut as I continued to read. Eleanor approached us, kissed Emma's forehead, and scuttled off to the kitchen to scoop ice cream into the bowls I'd taken out. "Goodnight, Auntie Eleanor," Emma said groggily as she turned on her side. After she fell asleep, I put the book on her nightstand and drew a picture of a piglet and a little girl named Emma on a piece of construction paper. I wrote 'Rise and shine, you're gonna have an oinky day!' She'd find it in the morning and start out the day with a laugh.

Once the lights were turned out, I joined Eleanor in the living room and waited for her to initiate the conversation. She looked more relaxed than she had earlier in the day, but I could tell my sister was still out of sorts. From the comfort of a plush recliner, she sighed. "I feel like such a fool for not realizing all those photos resembled Connor."

I'd been thinking about her situation all afternoon. Eleanor had always been the favorite child among the five Ayrwick siblings. She'd done everything the exact way our parents expected her to except for when it came to marriage. Eleanor went to college and later obtained a master's degree, ensuring she could support herself in the future. She traveled around the world for six months to get life experience, as our Dad referred to it. He'd offered to pay for each of us to take a trip upon graduation, but I didn't snatch that prize since I wasn't keen on airplanes. Those aluminum cans on steroids will kill you!

When she returned and searched for a job, Eleanor decided she wasn't ready to join the business world. She volunteered at various charities and not-for-profit organizations throughout Wharton County and built a vast network of contacts. One connection led to a job as the manager of a diner, and she accepted it because it meant she could interact with people daily and learn a new trade. Over time, she grew obsessed and turned it into a career culminating in her purchase of the diner from the previous long-time owners who'd moved out of town. Somehow along the path, finding a husband never happened. Unfortunately, our parents were known to frequently pressure her about it.

"Is this about something bigger, Eleanor? You've always been motivated by your job and inspired by your hobbies. Do you even want to get married? Is Connor the right guy or are you fixated on him because he flirted with you a few times?" I knew my best friend was a solid guy, but he couldn't make up his mind either. Maggie or Eleanor?

Eleanor slurped a huge spoonful of rocky road. "I know I'm attracted to him. I know I want to be a mother. Maybe I'm confusing the two things and trying to force something between us."

"I think you need to decide what you want out of life. You're thirty years old and have lots of time to get married and have kids. Don't push it if you aren't clear about your needs and desires right now. Maybe you and Connor will work out. Maybe he belongs with Maggie. Maybe you will have a baby and won't need someone to help. I can't answer those questions, but I can tell you how proud I am of you," I said while reaching for the candy hidden behind the pillow. "Here, I know these are your favorite."

"I guess I need to screw the lid on my juggernaut jar of jealousy over their budding relationship." Eleanor smiled and tore open the *Reese's Pieces* bag with her teeth like a ravenous animal. "You're the best brother I could ask for. Seriously, I'm so glad you came back home."

Eleanor was laughing by the end of our talk about our older siblings' current adventures. I didn't bring up our younger brother, Gabriel, because I didn't want to tell her what I'd seen him doing. It wasn't my secret to reveal. Instead, we downloaded a new horror movie and pretended not to be scared. By midnight, she left agreeing to think things over before making any permanent decisions, and I went to bed. I needed to teach my class and hunt down George Braun's cabin the following day.

* * *

After my normal routine dropping Emma off at school and educating the future of America for two solid hours, I popped in to update my truculent boss, Dr. Myriam Castle, per her orders. "I'm heading over to the cabin to see if George left anything behind. Ursula is aware I'm going, but she can't make it. She has a meeting with Maggie Roarke and the Board of Trustees about the library renovation."

'*Travelers never did lie, though fools at home condemn them.*' Since you don't seem to always recognize the quotes I generously share, I'll give you this one free of charge. The Tempest," Myriam replied while gathering her purse, a Coach bag that matched her trim brown and white Chanel suit.

"Yeah, thanks. I gotta go," I shook my head to detach her particular brand of crazy from nipping at my brain. There was only so much of the woman I could take without theorizing all the illegal ways to silence her.

"I'm coming too," she insisted. "We'll take my car, it's faster."

Five minutes later, after countless threats, she entered the address into her GPS while her black four-door BMW zoomed across the river. At one point, I thought we'd been airborne, but I had to close my eyes to prevent getting sick. "Are you not aware of the village speed limit?" I remembered she'd earned a reputation for an almost Indie-500-like erratic driving style.

"Pish. I'm the safest driver out there. Look, we're already here," she snapped as the car came to an abrupt halt in front of a cabin. "Must be that dilapidated-looking one over there."

We exited the car. She walked to the front door of a building that needed an overhaul. I rested a moment until my stomach found its proper location inside my body again. I was grateful I hadn't eaten lunch since I was sure my entire digestive system had made a complete loop from the crown of my head to the soles of my feet. "We should be a little careful, don't you think? Someone murdered the man."

Myriam didn't pay attention to my warning. By the time I'd reached the front of the cabin, she was already halfway around the side heading toward the back. "Don't dawdle, Kellan. I have to be back in an hour for a meeting." Her shuffle through the muddy terrain looked like one of Nana D's farm animals clumping through the dirt after a rainstorm.

As she approached the rear entrance, I noticed something useful. "There's a box that might be tall enough to climb into this open window." I moved the wooden crate closer and stepped on it.

Just as I was peering through the window, a shadow moved inside the cabin. It was followed by two hands unexpectedly appearing at the bottom of the sill and pushing the window upward. "I'm already here. Would you please try to keep up?" Myriam scolded in her usual haughty tone.

"How did you get inside?" I said, leaning into the window. Then I fell back and crashed through the wooden crate. At this point, I could heave myself into the cabin easily and didn't want to wander all the way through the mud around back.

As I fell to the floor and found myself covered in dust, Myriam made a tsk tsk sound. "You really are an oaf, aren't you? The door was unlocked. Not very safe, if you ask me."

I hadn't asked her but debating the topic any further wouldn't help the situation. We devised a plan to each search half of the cabin as quickly as possible. There were two bedrooms, a kitchen, living room, and a shared bathroom. It wasn't very large, but it had a quaint woodsy feel about it. One bedroom was fully renovated, and the other appeared to be half-finished. The bathroom had also been upgraded, but the kitchen and the main living area needed work. The inside had fared better than the exterior had over the years. It wasn't too far off from being habitable.

Thirty minutes later, we'd completed an exhaustive search of the premises. "There's not much here, is there?" Myriam said in a disappointed tone.

"At least we know this is definitely George's cabin. He has a few pieces of mail addressed to him," I noted before doing a final sweep of the bathroom, including checking inside the toilet tank in case something had been hidden there. No luck.

"And we know the assistant must be staying here based on the items in that finished room. The outfits in the closet did not belong to George Braun. Ursula's brother was a big guy, but those clothes fit someone thinner and shorter. Given today's gender non-specific approaches to wardrobe, I can't tell if those belong to a man or a woman." Myriam checked her phone and sighed. "I need to return to campus. Let's go. This was as useless as your non-existent knowledge of anything valuable."

I ignored her insult assuming it was meant in jest. She'd been toying with diverse ways of torturing me lately. "I'm not sure what I was hoping to find, but I feel like I'm missing something. Whoever the assistant is doesn't have anything personal here. Either he or she is incredibly careful, or we missed a spot." I followed Myriam out the back door, verifying we didn't leave anything out of place. We'd worn gloves so our fingerprints didn't show up, but I was still worried whoever killed George might appear at the cabin and kidnap us. Wait, maybe that's how I could escape from Myriam!

As we walked around the side of the house, a car pulled up. Myriam's BMW was in the front driveway, but we couldn't reach it without being seen by whomever had arrived. "Let's go, get behind this tree with me," I whispered. Myriam followed me across a side patch of grass, and we took cover behind a giant oak.

A blue Volkswagen SUV parked next to Myriam's car. We both watched with bated breath to see who stepped outside. Between the slight tinting on the windows and the shade from the foliage on the trees, I couldn't get a solid look at the person's face. The driver opened the door and walked to the front of the cabin calling out, "Hey, I'm back. You around?"

It was a younger guy's voice I thought I'd recognized. When he finally came into view, I gasped, inhaled a fly, and began choking. Myriam covered my mouth and said, "Keep your trap closed, he'll hear us, you ninny. It's a good thing I'm wearing gloves. I'm not thrilled about touching you!"

"No, it's okay. I know him. I haven't a clue what he's doing here, but I think we can approach him," I added, flicking her hand away. My mind was a sea of confusion trying to sort out what I was viewing. I stepped back onto the lawn and looked toward him. "Hey, it's Kellan."

Sam Taft jumped backward and glanced in our direction. He'd turned bright red when he saw us approaching him. "I... I... think I must be lost."

"Mr. Taft, ah, yes, I do recognize you now. Just what exactly are you doing here?" Myriam chastised the kid. He'd graduated five days earlier, but she still treated him like a student.

"I was visiting a friend. Guess I must have the wrong cabin," he said with eyes darting back and forth from the cabin to his car.

"Are you living here?" I asked, suddenly wondering if he was caught up with George Braun's plans for revenge on Ursula.

"Ugh. I guess I can't hide from the truth anymore," Sam said leaning against one of the poles supporting the roof of the front porch. "It's not what you think, Kellan."

Myriam tapped her foot on the ground. "I don't know what's going on here, but I need to get back to campus. Kellan, maybe you could stay to talk with Sam about this situation."

"That's a good idea. There are a number of things I need to discuss with Sam," I replied to Myriam, then turned to Sam. "Can you give me a lift back to campus when we're done chatting?"

Whether it was Myriam's presence or plain old guilt, Sam assented. "Sure, no problem."

I walked Myriam to her car and confirmed I'd call her as soon as I learned anything. Once she left, I narrowed my gaze on Sam. "Talk."

Sam sat on a chair under the covered porch. "As I said, this isn't what it looks like. I had nothing to do with George Braun."

"Perhaps you better tell me the full story," I urged him wondering if he had the skills to renovate a cabin. Although I'd only known him for a bit, he didn't seem particularly handy or experienced in home repair. He grew up in a family who hired servants to do everything except go to the bathroom for them.

"I really was visiting a friend. He's been staying here until he could get his own place," Sam explained while fiddling with his phone. "I'm guessing you're about to put two and two together now."

"Gabriel," I said feeling my heart begin to race. "Is that who's staying here?" Was my brother aware that George wasn't who he said he was?

Sam nodded. "He wants to talk to you, but I don't think he's ready to see your parents again."

I pushed Sam to explain everything. Sam had no clue about Ursula's connection to George Braun. I also couldn't figure out how much Sam knew about George's past. "Is Gabriel working for George Braun? Are you in cahoots with them?"

"Cahoots? Did we suddenly slip into a western movie? Let me get out my boots and spurs, cowboy. We're gonna have ourselves a good, old-fashioned duel with pistols." Based on his exaggerated slow speech, Sam had a funny side. "We're only ten years apart, Kellan, but you act much older sometimes."

Did I get sideswiped by a millennial? I thought I still was one at thirty-two. "Just tell me what you know, Sam."

"He was. At least until the man was killed," Sam said. Of all the people Sam and Gabriel could have found themselves connected to, George Braun was not someone who came to mind. "Gabriel had nothing to do with his death."

"You need to tell me everything. Start at the beginning." This couldn't be real. What happened to my shy, sweet, and innocent brother? How could Gabriel return to town to work for a man with a huge vendetta and a nasty past. Was the guy holding something over Gabriel? Had my kid brother gotten into trouble and needed help?

Sam nervously shared what he knew. "Gabriel came back to town about three months ago for his own reasons. I met him at a bar one night but didn't know he was your brother. We hung out a few times and felt a connection. I know you probably weren't aware of this part of his life, but he's an awesome guy, Kellan."

"I had no clue. I assure you I'm cool with it, but I wish Gabriel would've told me the truth." Things were beginning to fall into place. My brother was angry when our father took the job as president of Braxton College eight years ago. He must have been going through so many discoveries about himself at the time, he took off to learn how to deal with and accept it. "Why did he come back?"

"You'll have to ask him. It's not my place to say." When Sam looked at his phone, a panicked expression appeared.

"I'd ask him if I could find him. You haven't been willing to help me in the past." I knew I was getting closer to locating my brother, but I was suddenly afraid he might run again. "What exactly was he doing for George Braun?"

Sam was ignoring me and intently reading his phone. After scrolling through a few screens, he stomped his foot and looked toward the sky. "No, this is awful."

"What's awful, Sam? Who are you texting with?"

"I'm not sure what's going on, but Gabriel was brought to the Wharton County Sheriff's Office. He texted me twenty minutes ago and said he'd been hauled in for questioning regarding George Braun's death. I didn't see the messages while I was driving here." Sam's eyes were beginning to tear up. "You have to come with me to help him."

"Of course, he's my brother. Let's go," I said as we rushed to his SUV and drove downtown. What had my brother gotten himself into, and how would he react when I showed up with Sam?

CHAPTER 12

Sam and I sat in the Wharton County Sheriff's Office for over an hour while April Montague and Detective Gilkrist spoke with my brother. Sam wouldn't tell me anything else until he could visit with Gabriel. The sheriff left the interrogation room at one point to get Gabriel a cup of water. She popped into the main lobby where we nervously waited. "He knows you're both here. We're almost done questioning him, but he'd like to speak with Sam first."

"Are you arresting him?" I asked. It reminded me of when we played cops and robbers as children. Gabriel always wanted to be the criminal. He said it was more fun that way.

"Not today, so don't go lawyering up already, Little Ayrwick. He's a person of interest who knew the victim. I have no reason to believe Gabriel was at the library or had a motive to murder George Braun." The sheriff motioned to Sam to follow her down the hall. "You can chat with him for a few minutes after you and my detective have a conversation about that cabin."

While I paced the precinct's lobby floor, I considered whether I should call my parents, Eleanor, or Nana D to let them know about Gabriel's triumphant return. I ultimately decided it would be better to reveal his presence after I'd gotten the chance to speak with him. I sent Myriam a text message that I didn't yet know anything from Sam but would update her that evening. I also checked in with Helena to let her know that I'd turned over the folder we'd found in George's room to the sheriff.

April returned ten minutes later and escorted me to her office. "I spoke with Mulligan and Singh. Both agree George Braun was difficult to work with. Mulligan claims Braun was obsessed with his research and only out for himself. I can tell something more serious was going on between them, but I haven't gotten far yet."

"Maybe I can get him to talk. He hung up on me the other day when I asked questions, but I have an easy way to follow up about the flower show. What about Anita Singh's relationship with Braun? Was she the assistant from the past?"

"Anita Singh is an Indian-American who was born in Connecticut and grew up in New York City. I can't place her in Chicago during the 1993 lab explosion, but I'm not done with my research. She was married earlier this year, but she's very reticent to give any details about her husband. Detective Gilkrist is tracking down those records," April noted.

I updated her about Yuri Sato overhearing Mulligan and Braun arguing, as well as Braun having a wife somewhere. "Could he and Anita be married and working a scam together?"

The sheriff shook her head. "I appreciate you giving me Yuri's news, but I've told you enough so far. Now that we're alone, can you explain to me what your brother is doing by getting mixed up with this George Braun aka Hans Mück character?"

I shrugged my shoulders. "I found out an hour ago. I ran into Sam Taft who finally told me the truth." I left out the part about my trip to George's cabin. It didn't seem important enough to include in my response. "Wait, do you know for certain it's Hans Mück?"

"Yes, we have confirmation. Our European contacts were more than happy to cooperate once they knew George Braun was dead. They'd also documented reasons to locate him. I can't reveal any of those details at the moment." April handed me a cup of coffee from the sizzling pot behind her. "You look like you could use this. Now talk to me about Gabriel."

"Thanks, it's been an unusual day. Is my brother okay?" Had he shared anything with the sheriff about his past or why he left?

"Your brother is fine. He reminds me a lot of you. Not so much in attitude but in looks," April replied. She answered a brief call then asked Officer Flatman to escort Gabriel to her office in ten minutes once he was done meeting with the detective and Sam. "Kellan, from what I can tell, your brother was shocked to hear about George's death. He'd already known from the newspaper what had happened, but he claims he barely knew the guy."

"I wish I could help. I know nothing. I want to find out where he's been, what brought him back, and whether he's okay."

"You're a good brother. He's lucky to have someone like you in his corner right now. I'll tell you what I know," she said. For the first time, I noticed the vivacious lime green color of her eyes. "When we went through George's room, we found an employment contract he signed with your brother. I didn't know about it when we last spoke. I would've told you if I did, but this all happened overnight."

"Gabriel was George's assistant? I had no idea he knew anything about science or botany. Or even construction. He was an unusually sensitive and nervous kid the whole time we'd grown up. Always by himself reading *Business World* or the *Wall Street Journal*. Smart as they came, but I thought he'd get into stocks or banking." Sam had said Gabriel was working for George, but it just fully hit me.

"For whatever reason, he hasn't said, your brother returned to Braxton and overheard George Braun at a coffee shop talking about his search for an assistant. Gabriel applied and was one of the final candidates based on his prior experience. He'd also gotten the job because he was quite handy and could renovate Braun's cabin." April leaned against the padded seatback and waited for me to respond.

"I'll find out more when I can talk to him, thanks. You're definitely letting him go today, right?" When April nodded, I said, "If George has an angry wife, then maybe you have a new suspect."

April said, "I'm considering all leads right now. Are you okay with everything else we talked about yesterday? The Castiglianos, the drug case I need to investigate?"

Truthfully, I hadn't much time to think about it. I still didn't know where Francesca had escaped to next. I needed to check in with Vincenzo to see if he knew anything additional about his daughter's whereabouts. Since it seemed like April didn't realize Francesca was still alive, I told her I was fine. "I'm not sure I can help with the Paddington and Castigliano drug connection, and I don't spend a lot of time with my former in-laws. They're in my life only because they're Emma's grandparents."

"I understand. I don't need anything from you right now, but if the time comes, I was hoping I could count on you," April added as someone knocked on the door.

"Okay, we can chat in the future," I consented, knowing I was only able to focus on one shock at a time. "I would like some time alone with my brother."

April opened the door. Detective Gilkrist, Sam, and Gabriel were waiting in the hallway. "It's really you," I said.

April gave me the use of her office for as long as I needed it. She and her detective brought Sam back to finalize his statement confirming anything he knew regarding George Braun. Before he left, Sam hugged Gabriel. "Give him a chance, babe. I'll wait for you in the parking lot."

Once Sam left, Gabriel turned to me. While there was something different about him, many things hadn't changed. He was still five nine, the same height as me. He still had dirty blond hair like me. Where I'd cut mine short recently, he'd let his grow out, so it curled around his ears and at the back down his neck. He looked a little worse for the wear, but he had the same innocent smile and angelic hope in his eyes. "I've missed you, brother," I said with misty eyes as I hugged him tighter than I ever had before.

Gabriel hugged me back just as hard. "I'm sorry. I shouldn't have left the way I did. It had nothing to do with you."

After Gabriel assured me that he was fine, we talked about his relationship with George Braun. "It was pure luck. I'd only been in town for a couple of weeks. Sam and I had met the night before and enjoyed a couple of drinks. We stayed up to watch the sunrise over the Wharton Mountains and stopped at a coffee shop on the way back. After breakfast, Sam took off for class and I stuck around."

"And that's when you overheard George talking on the phone about needing an assistant?" I pieced together what April had shared and what my brother was starting to tell me. Gabriel had heard enough on the call about what George was looking for and located the ad posted on a local job site. He updated his resume, applied, and was called by the recruiting company right away. He'd matched his resume to exactly what George had said on the call, so he was a shoo-in.

"Smart thinking. I assume you actually knew how to do everything he required?" I'd never known my brother to lie. He was almost too truthful in the past.

"I'm not a kid anymore, Kellan. I've done a few things I'm not proud of. Sometimes you have to push the boundaries if you want to achieve a goal." Gabriel's face took on a darker tone, and in those few seconds, it became clear my brother was hiding something from me.

"Did you have anything to do with George's death?"

"Do you think I did?" As Gabriel stretched his back, his shirt sleeve rose a little higher on his arm. I noticed a colorful tattoo on his upper bicep. It was a circle broken into four separate pie-shaped quadrants, each dyed a different color. There was a word listed on the outer perimeter of each quarter—honor, knowledge, love, and respect. He'd spent more time at the gym since we'd last saw one another eight years ago. Gabriel had been scrawny in the past. Even though I wasn't as built as I am now, I could still pin him to the ground anytime we'd wrestled or played football with our friends.

I didn't want to believe my brother could commit murder, but a lot of time had passed since I'd last seen him. "When did you get the job?"

"I interviewed with him the next day. It was down to me and one other person. When he talked about his cabin, I clinched the deal by offering to fix it up in exchange for a place to sleep for a few months. I made it so he couldn't say no to me." There was a slightly wicked smile forming on his face.

"Do you know any reason why someone might have killed him?" I asked my brother, feeling my stomach tighten over his purposefully vague and shady answers.

He shook his head and told me the same thing he'd told the sheriff and Detective Gilkrist. "Nope, George was always kind to me. I spent a good chunk of my time running lab experiments for him in the first week, but then he asked me to focus on the flower show. I planned the whole thing for him."

"Have you met Millard Paddington? He's the guy sponsoring the event." I wondered if Millard had been keeping Gabriel's secret from me.

"Nah, I only worked behind the scenes. George gave me specific assignments to coordinate shipments, work with vendors, and sometimes interface with an event company who's doing the guest relations." Gabriel yawned, then apologized for being so tired. He'd been working too much lately and hadn't gotten a lot of sleep. "We done here?"

I felt bad for pushing him, but he was connected to all the bizarre events happening around me. As soon as he said there was an event company, I remembered I hadn't asked the sheriff if she'd found anything out from her interview with Cheney Stoddard. "What company was that?"

"Simply Stoddard. I worked with someone named Karen who was the account manager overseeing the flower show," Gabriel explained. "Is that important?"

Things were getting clearer for the first time. "Maybe. I'm not sure how it fits in, but it can't be a coincidence," I said, then explained what I'd known about each of the Stoddards.

"I only spoke to Karen on the phone. George spent most of the time with her, but occasionally I had to help. I don't know anyone named Doug, Sierra, or Cheney," my brother added.

Gabriel indicated he needed to use the men's room. We left the sheriff's office, and I waited for him in the lobby. April was heading out but stopped by my bench. "I'm off to meet with Cheney Stoddard. He was out of town with his sister yesterday and just got back to me this morning. Then I'll swing by Paddington's Play House to garner anything else I can from Yuri Sato. I appreciate the tip." As she left, she yelled back, "Good luck patching things up with your brother. Go easy on him. I'm sure you know what it's like when you first come back home."

For the first time since I'd known April Montague, it felt like she was warming up to me. Maybe we could find a way to be friends in the future. Perhaps that's why I had such an odd reaction in her office the other day when we were looking at the photo of the knife on her monitor.

The Stoddards, George Braun, and my brother had all come to town around the same time and been involved with an exhibition completely new to Braxton. Between Karen working on the flower show and Cheney's run-in with George, there had to be something I was missing. Sierra living in London and George previously working in Switzerland sounded like an angle to follow up on. Ursula's parents worked with flowers and had found a cure, but it had been lost forever when she accidentally caused the explosion. Could someone have figured out what the Mücks had discovered years ago and was now trying to recreate it? If they were, it'd be amazing to help people recover from an awful disease. Then it hit me—what if they were only trying to profit financially from the discovery?

Gabriel returned from the bathroom anxious to catch up with Sam. He promised to explain why he'd left town in the first place but begged to get some rest. "I'm not ready to see everyone else. Can you give me a couple of days?"

Although I didn't like the idea of hiding his return from our family, I was afraid if I said no, Gabriel would run away again. "Sure, but where are you going to stay? I doubt you can live at George Braun's cabin now that he's dead and the police know about the place. It'll be off-limits to everyone."

"You're right. I only have some clothes there. I keep everything else in my car. Sam's gonna take me back to it, and then I'm gonna crash at the boarding house over in Woodland where I stayed before I met George." Gabriel left the sheriff's office and walked to Sam's car in the parking lot. When he arrived, Sam kissed my brother like he had the first time I'd seen them together.

I gave them a moment alone before walking toward them. "How do I reach you, Gabriel?"

Sam looked at my brother. "You promised you'd make an effort to trust your family again, right?" When Gabriel nodded, Sam sent me a text message with Gabriel's number. I'd already had Sam's number from earlier in the year when I was helping his grandmother, Gwendolyn Paddington.

"Lunch tomorrow?" I asked Gabriel.

"I guess that'll work. I've got no job at this point. Why not push off my search for a couple of hours so we can catch up," he replied.

An idea began to formulate in my head. "Do you still want to work on the flower show?"

"Of course. I'd love to see it through." Gabriel perked up. "It's important I get a job quickly."

Sam and I looked at one another and smiled. Sam said, "I never thought of asking Uncle Millard to assist. I haven't told them anything about what's going on in my life. They still think I'm figuring out the next steps after graduating from Braxton. But Kellan could."

"I'll talk with Millard tonight. I'm sure he'll be willing to give my brother his job back once he knows Gabriel was doing a lot of the work for George before he died. Millard has a friend volunteering her time, but I think she's left town to visit with her sister." I didn't bother explaining to Gabriel that Lissette was going to be staying with our Aunt Deirdre who might also be home for a visit soon. I couldn't overwhelm my brother with the whole family at once.

"You'd do that for me?" Gabriel asked. When I confirmed, he hugged me again and promised to meet me for lunch the following day. I agreed to find a remote place since he didn't want anyone to know he was back. "You have no idea what I've been through the last few months. A man has limits."

After Sam, Gabriel, and I left the sheriff's office, they dropped me off on campus to pick up my car. I called Millard and told him all about Gabriel. I left out my brother's connection with Sam and begged Millard to keep quiet about Gabriel's return for now. He offered to meet for lunch the following day to work out the details. I couldn't shake my concern over the secrets my brother was keeping.

On my way to collect Emma after school, I called Vincenzo to get an update on my mysterious wife. Although talking to the man was a surefire way to sour my mood, it needed to be done. I pictured him sitting behind his beloved old banker's desk with a lit cigar in his fingers, the tip glowing like a firefly, and a Billy Joel classic kicking off his favorite Spotify playlist. "Any leads on Francesca?"

"Good of you to call. My daughter will be incredibly pleased to hear you are worried about her," he said. *We didn't start the fire* clearly played in the background. "How is my granddaughter? It's about time she came home, don't you think?" Although he'd grown up in the United States to American-born parents, he often spoke in a rugged, broken version of the English language I'd only seen in every stereotypical mafia movie. His voice somehow made it sound more frightening than the films.

"Emma's doing well. I am planning a trip to visit you this summer. You're always welcome to fly here, Vincenzo. I've never kept you from her." I parked the SUV outside Emma's elementary school and watched the buses form a line outside the entrance. A crossing guard was beginning to direct traffic.

"We see this three-thousand-mile distance a little differently. When I grew up, children respected their elders. Listened to them. Honored and obeyed them. It's a pity your parents didn't teach you those lessons, Kellan. I might have to do that." Vincenzo paused and mumbled something I couldn't understand. It probably wasn't meant for me but for one of his many hundred employees. "Eh, things change. I'm sure you realize that. Easily. One day you wake up in Pennsylvania. The next, maybe a lovely little ranch I know in Venezuela where there are more coyotes than human beings."

"You're a funny guy... you know I'm not a huge fan of travel. I appreciate the offer, but I think I'll stay where I am for now." Was he serious? He'd never been this obvious with death threats aimed directly at me before. "What about Francesca?"

"You tell me, Kellan. She was in your care last anyone saw her. We followed up on this lead you provided. My daughter is not in Canada anymore. Are you keeping her from me?" In a moment of near-silence, the only noise heard was the crisp pop as his cigar was relit. Vincenzo's manservant always stood a few feet away, ready to react to his boss's every whim.

"I've provided you everything I know at this point. The only two remaining places we visited together that she hasn't mailed a postcard from are Yellowstone Park and Savannah, Georgia. My guess is she's stopping there next." I'd convinced myself she wasn't appearing in Braxton the last few times I thought I'd seen her, in particular entering the private back-offices in Memorial Library. It had to be my imagination or someone who looked like her.

"Teams will be placed there. You will know if I hear anything. Should we not be able to locate my daughter within the next week, Kellan, I trust you understand what happens next." A loud buzzing indicated the conversation was over.

I didn't have time to deal with this situation. The Castiglianos had the resources and money to track Francesca down. Why weren't they doing more to help find her? I turned the car radio on to keep myself from thinking about anything until Emma exited the school. I flipped to the first station with a clear signal and listened to a country song about a girl who'd been kidnapped by her daddy.

Suddenly, I had an intense panic attack and a stunning revelation at the same time. It's amazing what a lack of oxygen will do to a desperate man. What if Vincenzo and Cecilia had known all along where their daughter was—in their house safe and sound. They'd faked her death once, could this be another scheme to frighten me enough that I'd be forced to move back to Los Angeles? Maybe Francesca was part of their plan to trick me and had fed them details about all the places we traveled to, so they could send someone to mail personalized postcards from each destination. They'd been sent to my office at Braxton which ensured none of my family saw them, keeping the whole thing a private affair. If they'd arrived at my house, someone else might realize the postcards came from my dead wife.

As I pondered how to prove my theory, the car door burst open and highlighted the sound of children's laughter. I'd been so distracted, I hadn't realized Emma was already finished with school and ready to leave. "How was your day?"

"Better than ever. I'm next to bring Rodney home on the weekend. Let's go to the store, Daddy," Emma screeched at the top of her lungs. "I got some research to do, so I'm ready to handle the responsibility."

It took me a solid thirty seconds to realize Rodney was the class pet, a rabbit who went home with a different student each weekend. "I got some research to do, so I'm ready to handle a few things, too, baby girl." Mine didn't exactly involve rabbits, but I'd need to move as quickly as one if I wanted to solve each of the puzzles controlling my life.

CHAPTER 13

Emma and I spent the rest of the afternoon at the pet store talking to a friendly salesman about how to care for a rabbit. Had I thought ahead, I would've called to see if the shop had any puppies available to adopt. As luck would have it, they did. Unfortunately, it was bad luck for me. Emma cooed over a ten-week-old black and tan shiba inu that'd arrived at the store the day before. Although it was adorable, the puppy bit and growled at the glass cage. Shibas were known for their severe dislike of restraint and the word *no*. Did I really want to subject myself to someone or something else who didn't listen to me?

I danced around the entire topic of why we needed to wait until the summer started to properly train a puppy, but it didn't work. I still left the pet store with a very sad little girl who cried the whole car ride home. Nana D was on-hand to cheer Emma up during dinner and even kept her distracted by planning for the rabbit's weekend stay.

While Emma visited with Nana D, I had time to strategize how to handle my situation with Francesca. I had a former colleague who was in Orlando for a film shoot. I asked him to send me a postcard from one of the Disney properties with a message about our time with Mickey and Minnie Mouse being the most fun ever. It didn't matter which resort because Francesca and I had never been to Orlando. If Vincenzo and Cecilia were faking her absence, this new postcard would certainly cause a reaction. If they acted as though it was just another one of Francesca's trips, maybe they really weren't behind her mysterious disappearance.

By the next morning, Emma was one-hundred percent focused on Rodney, so we didn't discuss the shiba inu puppy. For some reason, I had a dream where he'd come to live with us, and I'd named him Baxter. What a rambunctious little tyke he was, too!

While Emma was in school, I went to work and caught up with my boss. Myriam had learned nothing new from Ursula but steamrolled right over me with her normal disgruntled attitude and perseverance. "I don't know what all the fuss is about you, Mr. Ayrwick. Students seem to love you, but all I see is a lot of talk and no action. *What a terrible era in which idiots govern the blind.*'"

I ignored her as she clomped down the back stairs of Diamond Hall mumbling to herself about the ignorance and limited necessity of men. How did Ursula put up with that dragon-lady? Instead, I taught my class and looked forward to lunch with Gabriel. When my session with the students was finished, I checked my cell phone. Unfortunately, Gabriel canceled lunch without giving me any reason. He promised to be available the following day whether it was a meal or a quick beer at a remote pub in one of the nearby villages.

I strolled over to the student union building to grab a quick lunch. Situated in the center of campus, the building was one of the more modern structures on campus. It held the student cafeteria, a quick access to-go sandwich and salad outlet, the mailroom, two bookstores, an auditorium for holding assemblies, a lounge, and a few other student hotspots.

Dr. Singh and Fern were in line ordering lunch when I arrived. I waved and waited for Fern to finish paying for a large cup of oatmeal. "Dr. Betscha says my cholesterol was a little high and insisted I eat more oatmeal. Who does that in May?"

We reveled in hilarious banter about food choices in our thirties versus our fifties, catching a few puzzled expressions from students as they wandered by. I asked Fern how her son Arthur was doing with the big changes in his life, namely a new baby that would be due in about five months. "Do he and Jennifer have a wedding date set?"

"I keep asking, but Jennifer is adamant about keeping it simple. I was worried about my son marrying into the Paddington family after the whole sordid affair with that murder," she said shaking her head back and forth. "But she's been nothing but pleasant and down-to-earth lately."

"Speaking of weddings, I hear you were married recently," I said, turning to Dr. Singh.

She nodded. "My apologies, I must be going. Class starts in ten minutes."

"Congratulations. When was it?" I didn't want to let her escape without answering me.

"I'd rather not discuss it. It is a private affair, and I don't understand why everyone keeps asking me about it today," she replied and began to scamper away.

"Oh, okay. I'm sorry. By the way, did you ever find that missing lab coat?" The timing of her marriage shouldn't be something to make her nervous. Would questions about the night of the murder?

"No, someone must have accidentally taken it or thrown it out. I'm very late. Goodbye." She briskly jogged out the front entrance toward Cambridge Hall of Science.

"Anita's usually much more composed and friendlier," Fern said.

"Definitely surprising." Dr. Singh's behavior was suspicious, but I knew little about her to offer any reasoning behind the sudden chilly attitude. Suddenly remembering Fern had asked for my help with a recommendation for a caterer, I said, "How did your conversation go with Karen and Doug Stoddard to discuss the plans for the engagement party?"

Fern indicated she'd made the appointment with Karen, but when she went to meet her at the downtown office and restaurant, the woman never showed up. "It was odd. She called later to apologize and cited an urgent meeting with Dean Mulligan on the Mendel flower show."

"That's certainly not a stellar way to grow her business. I thought she was more dependable, I'm so sorry," I said feeling a bit guilty, then considering what kind of emergency could happen with a flower show. I theorized very little could justify her absence other than something peculiar and devious going on between anyone involved in the event. I clearly was missing relevant information.

"No, it's fine. Doug was there, and he and I spoke about the party. Since it's going to be a small affair, it was mostly about food and beverages. He was very helpful," Fern added. She explained they'd gotten along well and talked about their vastly different careers. "He mentioned how unsure he was of moving to such a remote town to open a restaurant on his own. But apparently, it's worked out. He'll never doubt Karen's suggestions when she picks a place to live based on a new job opportunity."

Fern's response confused me. When I'd spoken with Karen, she'd told me that their daughter's friend had shown her a picture of Crilly Lake. She and Doug booked a long weekend trip the following day. "Are you sure he said that Karen picked Braxton? I could have sworn it was more random."

"Yes, he said Karen came home one day all worked up about leaving the big city. Mentioned she had made a big-time connection and pushed them to move here to handle some major events." Fern nodded vigilantly as she pocketed some napkins from the counter. "Gotta go. Let's do dinner soon."

Something wasn't adding up with Karen and Doug Stoddard. Although Millard and Maggie had both hired them to manage or cater their events, and they both had good instincts, I needed to do my own verification on their background. I also wanted to find out how Sierra fit into the puzzle.

Since I wasn't too far from Memorial Library, I checked on Maggie. I was curious about her meeting with the Board of Trustees and Ursula regarding the incident in the courtyard and the future renovations for the building. I called to ask if she needed any lunch, but she'd already eaten. "Come on by, I have pictures from the event to show you," she excitedly rattled off.

I scarfed down a healthy chicken and avocado wrap as I walked to the library. The yellow tape had been removed from the double doors leading to the private employee offices. I crossed the entrance and made a right in the opposite direction to locate Maggie's office. As Maggie hung up the phone, I noted, "Looks like things are getting back to normal around here."

"Finally, it's taken the whole week for the detective to collect all his evidence," Maggie sighed. She flipped the monitor around on her screen and keyed in a few commands to bring up the pictures. "Helena tells me you've been helping her with a file she found in George Braun's room at the inn?"

Maggie and I caught up on everything we'd known about the professor's death and Helena's involvement in the case. With no prints other than George's on the knife, it wasn't looking good for her sister. The sheriff still hadn't made an arrest because Judge Grey wouldn't issue a warrant until they had more sufficient evidence. "I hope she's not trying to prove collusion between Cheney and Helena. He fought with George, but she claims it was about access to his room. That's not enough to kill someone."

"Detective Gilkrist and his team have been through the bed and breakfast. They aren't sharing much except they have other potential angles they are considering," Maggie sulked.

"The usual tactics. April Montague likes to let her suspects sweat it out for a few days. Then she comes at them like gangbusters once all her evidence is irrefutable." I smiled at Maggie and hoped she could feel my support and friendship shining through loud and clear. Although I wanted to explain Ursula's connection to George Braun, it wasn't fair to reveal someone else's secret. "They know whom the knife belongs to now. It might help them figure this out more quickly."

"That's good news. My parents are worried about the inn's reputation and Helena's future. They still can't rent out the room until the police are finished and they find the next of kin." Maggie's melancholic voice struggled to push past the fear and hold on to hope. "I thought if you looked through the photos with me, maybe you'd see something."

"Did you share these with the sheriff?" I asked, assuming April must have thought about whether there was any video recording or photo coverage in the library.

"Yes, she dropped by to get a copy this morning. She asked me not to share them with anyone," Maggie winked as she clicked open the first photo. "I am pretty certain she was referring to you, but to her credit, she only said, 'nosy non-pertinent people' and didn't mention any names."

"April definitely meant me. At least she's getting nicer about it," I replied. I confirmed with Maggie that there were no video recordings in the library, as it hadn't been upgraded like other parts of the campus were the previous semester.

"We talked about putting in some temporary cameras when I first took over, but with the renovation happening soon, it didn't make sense to spend the additional funding. Nothing bad has happened in the library since I started," Maggie quipped. "Until you came back to town."

"Just show me the pictures, funny girl," I said as I stuck my tongue at her. We flipped through several, focusing on anyone I saw dressed in a white costume or at anyone who stood near George Braun in his Dr. Evil costume.

Based on the time stamps from the digital camera the photographer had used, most of the photos were taken as people entered the library or during the brief presentation about the library's renovation donation fund.

Maggie saved a local copy of each photo that matched anything we were looking for. When we were finished going through them all, she opened all the images at the same time on her computer. "We should connect these to the projector in the movie room. If they're enlarged, we might catch something we don't see on this small screen."

"You're quite the detective yourself, Miss Roarke," I said as she downloaded the ten files to a thumb drive and left her office. We stopped at the front reception desk where she grabbed the key for the movie room in the basement of the library. "Did you ever find out how someone opened the door to the private office area the night of the costume extravaganza?"

Maggie groaned as she inserted the key in the lock. "Yes, the wonderful Helena Roarke strikes again. We have my sister to thank for the whole mess." Maggie had given the set of keys to Helena earlier in the night so she could unload some of the presentation materials and the bottles of champagne. The temperatures had dropped enough that the champagne could chill in the courtyard since there weren't enough refrigerators in the library for all they'd bought. Helena had conveniently forgotten to return the keys or lock the door, as it was the only place where she could sneak in a smoke break or spend a few minutes making out with Cheney when no one needed them.

"That girl is gonna be her own downfall one day, Maggie." I followed her into the movie room and thought about what the news meant as she loaded the files. A large rectangular space without windows, the place felt like a cave. There was a chill in the air since we were technically in the basement of the library, but the heat had also been turned off for the summer already. Stadium-style seating supported up to two hundred guests, and the place was used either for weekly movie nights for students and staff or for anyone majoring in film production who was sharing projects with the rest of the class. I'd used it once last semester for a project, but I hadn't yet attended any flicks myself.

If the door to the private employee entrance had been open all evening, anyone could have gotten to the courtyard at any point. The killer could have been in hiding and lured George to the courtyard. Or the killer could have seen George follow Helena or Cheney back there. "Wait, did Helena ever tell you why George was out there? I just remembered she saw him with Cheney earlier. Did Cheney ask George to meet him in the courtyard?"

"Cheney saw George follow Helena into the private office area. He then followed the guy, worried about what he was up to. George must have gotten lost and wound up in the courtyard where Cheney confronted him. Helena was in one of the offices getting a box of party favors I wanted to hand out to guests." Maggie flipped a switch on a nearby console, and our ten pictures were displayed on a large screen on the north wall.

"That's when Helena saw them fighting but walked away after they'd calmed down. So, if Cheney's not the murderer, someone else snuck in. He or she must have been watching George all night and saw him leave the main room." I met Maggie in the middle of the seating area so we could focus on the pictures together.

With a laser pointer, she aimed the red dot on the first picture. "There is George talking to Karen in the Bride of Frankenstein costume. They look like they're having an argument, don't they?"

"Yes," I huffed. "How much do you really know about the Stoddards?" I shared my concerns with Maggie that I knew George had lived in Chicago at one point. I didn't tell her it was when he was known as Hans Mück, but I wanted to gauge her trust with the owners of the newest event management company and restaurant in Braxton.

"Connor and I had dinner there one night earlier this year. I can't exactly remember, but somehow it came up that I worked at Braxton. Karen mentioned she was chatting with a few departments to cater some events."

"So, you don't know her well? Karen suggested her company to you, not the other way around," I clarified. Something told me Karen was trying to get herself involved in the costume extravaganza.

"You're right, now that we're talking about it. I didn't think I needed anyone, but she offered a discount and gave me some great ideas." Maggie pointed the laser at another picture. "You could be right. Here is another one of Karen and George standing near the door to the private offices."

I noticed Doug was also in the picture, and he had an angry look on his face. "Of the ten photos George shows up in, five also contain the Stoddards."

"Here's another one with George talking to Dr. Singh and Dean Mulligan. It looks like they walked into the event together. None of them look pleased with one another, huh?" Maggie enlarged the photos.

I agreed. "And in this one at eight fifty, Dean Mulligan's costume looks different. See where the lightning bolt was on the left side in the first photo. Now it's on the right and further down across his stomach." Could he have been trying to hide any blood evidence from attacking George?

"Check this photo of George with Ursula and Myriam. He looks a little perturbed there, too. Maybe he always has an angry face, Kellan. Some people don't smile very often." For added emphasis, Maggie chuckled and poked me in my side, hoping to tickle me.

"Stop it! You know I can't stand that," I practically screamed like a teenage girl and grabbed her wrist so she couldn't do it again. I pushed her back toward one of the seats and leaned in to tickle her, knowing she was just as weak as I was when it came to that form of torture. Not realizing how close we were to the seats, she lost her balance, began to fall and in the process, took me to the floor with her.

For a minute, we couldn't stop laughing. Neither of us had been hurt, but we also hadn't heard someone else enter the room. Just as Maggie reached a hand out to me so I could help her stand, Nana D sauntered over to us. "Is this how you spend your days at work? No wonder your father had to retire if his son was embarrassing himself by crawling on the floor in the basement of the library with the head librarian. Tsk tsk."

I would have been much more embarrassed if it had been Myriam, April, or Connor who'd caught us, but given it was my seventy-four-year-old grandmother who was also trying to push the two of us together, I didn't worry. "I dropped my glasses. Maggie was helping me look for them. You know how blind I am without them."

"Absolutely," Maggie added, handing me my glasses which had actually fallen to the floor. Nana D didn't need to know it was due to a tickle fight. "All good now, Kellan?"

I nodded while Nana D rolled her eyes in an exaggerated fashion and said, "Isn't that what you'd do if the situation were reversed? I might be a few years older than you, but my hearing's not going. I heard your laughter."

I did not want to think about a reverse situation where Nana D was rolling on the floor with a man. I also needed to stop her from further talking. "What are you doing here?"

"I came to campus to meet with Ed Mulligan but also drop off a book I borrowed from Maggie. Since I'm a woman with proper manners," Nana D said while holding out a *Mary Deal* paperback with her right hand, "I thought I would say hello before I left. That kid up at the circulation desk told me Maggie was down here." Wow! Everyone in my house was reading Mary Deal's books this month after the library recommended her as its author of the month.

"Why are you meeting with Dean Mulligan?" What was Nana D up to now? I couldn't shake the concern growing in my head over the dean's reaction on our phone call and his skewed costume.

"I'm not sure. He called the meeting, but I plan to convince him to vote for me next week, brilliant one."

Maggie added, "Thank you, Nana D. I am always happy to see you. Why don't we have a cup of tea before you meet with the dean? You've got fifteen minutes before he's expecting you. I've got a new vanilla caramel tea I want to try."

Before Maggie left with Nana D, she handed me the thumb drive and told me to figure out how it could help her sister. The only immediate way I knew how was to see the Stoddards again, hoping I could straighten out their reasons for moving to Braxton and learn whether they knew George Braun in Chicago. Since I planned to pick up Emma after I met the Stoddards, I drove rather than walked downtown.

All the storefronts on the side of the road opposite the river were mirror images of one another. The Wharton County Civic Center and Merchants Association wanted to maintain a small-town aesthetic and minimum standard with red brick facades, gold and white signs with black scrolled writing, and wrought iron window boxes filled with colorful flowers. On the riverside, each restaurant could design its own exterior, but it had to employ a similar color palette. At Christmastime, it was meticulously decorated with gorgeous fir trees, antique holiday lights, and real garland. It felt magical.

I arrived at two thirty which would be after the lunch rush. As soon as I was inside, I heard shouting. "You've been disappearing for hours ever since we moved to this town. And you never have an explanation! What is going on, Karen?" Doug yelled in an aggravated voice from behind the office door.

I was going to knock so they knew I was in the building, but I thought I might learn more by listening to their argument. I stepped toward the restaurant section and hid behind the reception desk wall where I wouldn't be seen. It appeared they'd been closed for lunch today.

"I'm with prospective clients trying to drum up more business for us. What's gotten into you lately? You've gotten so jealous ever since we moved," Karen responded in a high-pitched voice. She must have slammed a file cabinet drawer shut as I heard the metal vibration.

"I'd believe you except you vanished in the middle of the costume extravaganza for over thirty minutes last weekend. What was that all about? I've tried to ignore it, but you're up to something," Doug complained. He was incredibly angry but also asked rational questions. "Ever since that George Braun character hired us to oversee the Braxton stop for the Mendel flower show, you've been secretive and short-tempered with me. Are you having an affair?"

"What? No! I'm busy focusing on making a name for us, so we can stop worrying about the future. Don't we want to be successful here? We don't need more problems like we had in Chicago. Cheney's been through enough already," Karen said in a softer voice. It sounded like she was trying to calm her husband down. "I was talking with Maggie about the success of the library event. I spoke with a few people about new catering job opportunities. I never disappeared at the costume extravaganza."

Was Karen and Doug's marriage on the rocks? Had the sheriff known Karen disappeared for thirty minutes? If she was lying to someone about where she'd gone, could she be hiding something important? Listening to their conversation had also given me some key information about the problems they had with their son before moving. While I considered everything I'd just learned, the door opened.

"You suggested we move to this isolated place, Karen. I only agreed so we could give Cheney an opportunity to start fresh where no one knew about his past. I'm going to the store to get some last-minute supplies we need for this weekend's dinner events," Doug said as he stepped into the vestibule to grab his coat. "We need to fix this marriage, if you still care about me."

"I'll go. I need to meet with Fern Terry about her son's engagement party. Give me the list. I'll pick everything up on the way back," she said before clearing her throat loudly. "Maybe if you weren't focused on opening up your expensive restaurant, we'd be able to spend more quality time together."

Karen left without any additional conversation or even saying goodbye. If she was trying to fix whatever spat they'd been having, she would have kissed her husband or at least apologized. She was in a hurry and definitely had something to hide. Doug must have returned to the office as I heard chair wheels rolling across the floor. I was grateful he didn't walk into the restaurant and find me standing there listening to their conversation.

I quietly snuck into the main vestibule and opened and shut the door so he would hear someone entering the building. "Hello, is anyone around?" I called out preparing myself to play a new role.

CHAPTER 14

Doug stepped into the vestibule. "I'm sorry, we're closed for lunch today, but we'll be open for dinner in two hours. Oh, wait, I know you."

After I reintroduced myself, Doug offered to make me a cup of coffee as he was having one for himself. I followed him into the server's side station where he brewed a new pot. It was hidden behind a large movable screen that kept diners from seeing the prep area. "Thanks again for the great comments you left on Yelp about the place. We appreciate it. What brings you back again so soon, Kellan?"

I had to think on my feet. Now that I knew he suspected something occurring between his wife and George and that there was an issue with their son in the past, I had the ideal path. "You're welcome. I was looking for Cheney. I need to speak with him about something that happened recently." I glanced away to make it look like it was a difficult topic for me to bring up to Doug.

"Oh, no... has he done it again? Look, I'm so sorry. Cheney's basically a good guy, but he's got a bad temper and shoots his mouth off. What happened this time?" Doug grabbed two cups from the top shelf and sat them on the counter. "Milk, sugar?"

I nodded trying to keep my responses to a minimum so he would keep talking. "I didn't mean—"

"Did he cause any damage? We'll pay for it. We moved here so he could start over again. I'd appreciate your help in keeping it quiet," Doug said while he poured coffee into both cups.

"I think I've given you the wrong impression. I needed to talk with Cheney about his relationship with Helena, but now you've got me worried. Is there something I should know before anything gets too serious with those two? I'm very good friends with the Roarke family and don't want anything bad to happen to them." I sipped some coffee as we sat at a nearby table.

Doug hesitated at first, but then he ultimately gave in. "When my daughter Sierra left for college, Cheney fell in with the wrong crowd back in Chicago. She'd kept him in line even though she was younger. He was lost on his own and tried to prove himself with a troublesome group of guys. Last summer, he got picked up for breaking and entering into a couple of houses in an affluent part of town."

"Has he been in prison?" I asked, wondering if Helena knew anything about it.

"A couple of months. The judge gave him a light sentence as a first-time offender. We needed to get him away from the negative influences," Doug explained. Cheney had gotten kicked out of college after he failed two classes and had an incident on campus with aggravated assault. The college had agreed not to press charges if Cheney dealt with his anger management issues. Doug and Karen thought he'd matured until he started hanging out with a gang in Chicago, which is what ultimately led to his arrest.

"I'm sorry to hear it, but you made the best decision to get him out of there. Is that why you chose to move?" I'd overheard Doug and Karen say that was why, but I needed the rest of the details.

"Yes. We were looking at a few smaller cities on the West Coast. I thought the nicer weather in California might help Cheney relax more. Karen and I had always wanted to open our own restaurant, but we couldn't afford to at the time."

"It's great she wanted to support you. Why'd you end up choosing Braxton?" I asked.

"Karen met a scientist who was running the Mendel flower show and made the arrangements. She'd come up with a brilliant plan to open the event management arm of the business, so we could be a full-service company." Doug offered to refill our cups, but I'd already had too much for one day. My hands were getting jittery.

When his cell rang, Doug stepped away to answer it. I didn't want to push my luck when I'd already gotten a bunch of helpful information. I needed to know how Karen had really met George Braun but decided it might be better to talk to her separately. It seemed she was the one lying to people. If Doug didn't know much, and he told Karen I'd asked questions, she might clam up around me.

Doug returned to the table. "Sorry, it was Karen. She couldn't read something I'd written on a shopping list and wanted to verify it with me. I do need to get ready for tonight's dinner seating."

"Oh, right. Sure. Listen, I appreciate you sharing what you did about Cheney. I won't tell anyone, but if you see him, can you ask him to give me a call?" I wrote my number on a napkin. "I want to look out for Helena."

"I understand. I think they're growing closer, but he does need to take things slow. I want my son to get his life in order before he settles down with a girl," Doug added.

I guess he hadn't realized that Helena wasn't looking to be in a committed relationship right now. "We have a deal. I'll keep what you told me about Cheney quiet and try to convince Helena to take it slow for a while. Maybe you shouldn't tell Karen what you told me about the past."

"I think that's a good idea. Karen can be high-strung at times. She doesn't want anyone to know about Cheney's problems. She's afraid it could set him back again if people started talking," Doug said as he stood from the table to escort me to the front door.

"Oh, one more question," I said upon noticing the German knife that'd been missing from the display in the vestibule was suddenly back. "Didn't I see an empty space there the other day?"

Doug pursed his lips. "You're an observant fellow. Yes, you did."

"I didn't know you were such a fan of hunting weapons until Cheney mentioned it," I noted.

"I had to clean that particular knife. I noticed a smudge the other day and took it down. With everything going on, I finally got around to it." Doug couldn't usher me out the door quick enough.

I left the Stoddards' restaurant after amassing a great deal of new information, but how did it fit together? Doug's knife wasn't used to kill George, but the display clearly showed his advanced skills. April had mentioned whoever killed George knew exactly where to stab him for almost immediate death. I put a call into the sheriff's office on the drive to the elementary school to pick up Emma.

"Officer Flatman speaking, how may I assist you and keep crime down today?" the wannabe detective said with an overly cheery greeting and newly polished customer service skills.

"This is Mayor Grosvalet. I must urgently speak with Sheriff Montague about a cat stuck in a tree," I teased and lied to the junior cop hoping to unnerve him enough to cause a slip of his tongue about the case. "That Braun murder solved yet?"

"Oh, good afternnnnoonnn... Mayor, sir... I... ummm... she's not here. Sheriff Montague is out making an arrest right now. I can call and track her down immediately for you," Flatman anxiously spit out. "Ummm... what's wrong with that cat, sir?"

Upon hearing of the arrest, I'd forgotten about the lie I'd just made up. "No bother. I'll climb the tree myself." I hung up worried who'd been taken to jail. Where should I go first—to see Helena or Ursula? Which one had April planned to take into custody?

I parked the SUV in the guest lot across from the school. Since Emma would bring Rodney home today, I couldn't wait in the normal parental pick-up line. She couldn't carry his cage and supplies on her own, so I met her inside to collect the rabbit. I remembered Fern had an administrative meeting with Ursula beginning in a few minutes, so I texted her to see if the meeting was still on. If Ursula had been arrested, the meeting would've been canceled. As Emma and I left the elementary school, Fern replied that the meeting was about to start, and Ursula was standing in the doorway speaking to her assistant. I told Emma we needed to make an unplanned stop at the

Roarke & Daughters Inn and cut through a few side streets to avoid downtown traffic.

When I pulled up to the front part of the circle driveway, I looked for the sheriff's motorcycle or any police vehicles in the main lot, but there were none present. Since I was parked right outside the front door, I told Emma not to move from the car and asked her to wait five minutes for me. I could see her from the front parlor of the inn and only planned to run in for a moment to see if Helena was okay. I hopped up the stairs, entered the screened-in porch, and opened the front door. When I stepped inside, Helena and her mother were setting up for the daily afternoon cocktail hour. "Hey, sexy man. Finally decided you couldn't get enough of me?" Helena said as she planted a kiss on my lips. "Why are you all flushed? Do I make you nervous?"

Lucy Roarke gave her daughter a disapproving look. "Leave your sister's friend alone. Kellan is trying to help you, now stop being such an instigator, young lady."

I might have skipped a run or two, but the mad dash up the stairs knocked the wind out of me. "Mrs. Roarke, you look lovely as always," I said, then turned to her daughter. "Helena, you sound as silly as always. I'm here to save you from the sheriff." Both women looked at me like I had flies swarming around my head. "Has anyone tried to arrest you today?"

Helena laughed. "As if. I told you, she can't arrest me because I didn't do it."

"That's not how the law works. I'm sure Finnigan told you this already," I reminded her. Had Officer Flatman been mistaken when he said the sheriff was out making an arrest?

"My lawyer probably mentioned it, but I wasn't paying much attention to his words. That man is dreamy!" She shrugged her shoulders. "He might be almost a decade older, but that wouldn't stop this girl from saying yes to a date with him."

"I thought you were still dating Cheney," I began, but her mother interrupted.

"I can't listen to this nonsense, Helena. Finish setting up the tables and quit acting so juvenile. I need to get the cakes and pastries ready for our guests," Lucy ordered her daughter. "If I remember correctly, Kellan, you loved my shortbread cookies. I'll bring you a few extra, love."

When her mother left the room, Helena latched on to my arm. "I thought she'd never leave. I need to run to the store to get a birthday present for Cheney's party tomorrow night. He'll be twenty-five. I guess being three years older than him is okay, right? It's acceptable in modern times even though my mother thinks he's way too immature for me."

"I believe you have that backward, Helena. She probably thinks you're too immature for him," I scolded her. It was too much to accept the combination of Helena's flirtatious ways, her inability to stick to one guy, and her focus on Cheney who I'd come to learn had quite a past. "How much do you know about Cheney's life before the Stoddards moved to Braxton?"

"You're making way too big a deal, Kellan. I'm too young to settle down. I talk a big game, but I'm not all that crazy when you think about it," Helena sulked. As she laid out napkins and wine glasses, a loud siren began wailing on the street.

I felt my stomach begin to turn over. I needed to check on Emma, my five minutes were close to up. I'd suddenly made a connection with something Helena had said. "Wait, when does Cheney turn twenty-five?"

"His actual birthday is tomorrow. I'm having dinner with him, his sister, and his parents. That's how he wanted to celebrate." Helena stepped toward the front door, walked onto the porch, and turned as white as a ghost. "That siren is coming from a police car pulling into the parking lot."

Helena's second statement about the cop car hadn't registered. I was too busy calculating the math in my head. If Cheney turned twenty-five tomorrow, it meant he'd been born in Chicago roughly nine months after Hans and Ursula's family's lab had blown up. It couldn't be a coincidence that Cheney was conceived within days of the explosion. If Karen and George had known each other, was she the assistant who told the news outlets all about Ursula's involvement? I began to wonder if it meant George, formerly Hans, could be Cheney's father. If it were true, I might have found a reason why he'd been killed. I could see motives for several members of the Stoddard family lining up.

"It's the sheriff, Kellan, and she's walking toward Emma," Helena shouted.

I raced out to the parking lot to limit my daughter's exposure to the situation. She and April had chatted a couple of times before, but Emma did not need to see anyone being arrested. "April, what's going on? When I didn't see you at first, I wondered whom you were going to arrest. But now you're here. How did I get to the inn before you?"

"I've tried to give you the benefit of the doubt, Little Ayrwick, but you show up wherever there's a murder or an arrest happening. It's like you've got radar detection for whatever crime's about to occur in Wharton County," April growled at me. She nodded in Helena's direction and handed one of her cops an official looking piece of paper. Once he went to arrest Helena, April turned back to me. "How is it you guessed I'd be coming here?"

I knew as soon as it'd left my mouth, I'd said too much. "Just visiting, I needed to borrow a cup of sugar from Helena's family and—"

"You shouldn't lie in front of your daughter," April said with a stern and judgmental frown in my direction. "Now it makes sense."

I shook my head back and forth, then peeked my head into the passenger window to tell Emma to sit tight for a few more minutes. "I'm not sure what you're talking about."

"Since Emma's here, I'll be brief. Officer Flatman called me as I was leading my team here to arrest Miss Roarke for the murder of George Braun. Mayor Grosvalet supposedly called the sheriff's office to interrupt whatever it was I'd been doing. I found it odd because I'd only spoken to him and Councilman Stanton two hours earlier when both urged me to make an arrest in this case."

Why was Marcus pushing for an arrest? It had to be something he wanted to tout as a win for his mayoral campaign before next week's election. "But I don't understand what it has to do with me."

"Flatman is a very good beat cop. Do you think our heavyset, north of seventy-years-old, asthmatic mayor can climb a tree? Flatman needs to learn how and when to call bulls..." April said as she glanced at Emma. "To call baloney on a prank caller. Given you knew I was about to make an arrest and that ridiculous story about a cat, I'm quite certain you were the caller. As soon as you heard, you rushed your whiny little behind over here to be the knight in shining armor for Miss Roarke."

I whistled for ten seconds and avoided eye contact with the sheriff. It often felt like the *Looney Tunes* cartoon where she was the roadrunner and I was Wile E. Coyote. I needed to turn the tables on her, so I didn't constantly feel like an underdog who always lost the race. "Since we both know you have something more important to do right now, perhaps we can ignore Officer Flatman for the moment. It seems neither of us thinks he's got anything important to say."

"Agreed, but I will caution you not to disparage a Braxton police officer in the presence of others, Little Ayrwick," April said. The officer had begun reading Helena her Miranda rights.

"Kellan, please help. Contact Maggie for me. Call Finnigan Masters and let him know to meet us downtown," Lucy Roarke begged, indicating she was going with her daughter to the sheriff's office, so she wasn't alone. Ben was going to keep things running at the inn until one of their other daughters arrived to watch the place and take care of any guests.

As Detective Gilkrist went inside with a warrant to search the place, Helena was driven downtown by the arresting officer with Lucy following closely behind them. I turned to the sheriff. "We need to talk."

"Yes, I agree. It seems you have a few favors to do for the Roarkes. Why don't you make those calls? I'll keep your daughter company," April said as she gently tapped Emma's window.

"Wait, why are you being so nice right now?" I asked.

April told me to do as I was told and began talking to Emma about her rabbit, Rodney. I stepped back onto the porch and quickly updated Maggie. She was leaving the library and would meet her mother at the sheriff's office. Connor was with her to help keep things under control for the time being. I also contacted Helena's lawyer, but Finnigan's assistant informed me he was still at court for a deposition. She assured me it would end in the next thirty minutes, so he could be there for Helena.

As I descended the stairs back into the main driveway, the remaining cops carried a bag of evidence to a police van. I looked at my daughter, who was sitting on an outdoor bench with April, and listened to their conversation from a few feet away.

"Rodney likes you, Emma," April said while gently stroking the rabbit's ears. The rabbit seemed content in her arms as if he had no concerns in the world.

"He's a good boy. I hope he doesn't get scared at home. There are lots of other animals on the farm who are bigger than him," Emma said with a growing look of panic in her eyes.

"He might get worried, but that's where you come in. He's gonna depend on you to be his caretaker. You'll have to ensure he's loved, fed, and cared for. Don't let the other animals near him until they've calmed down. And maybe only the smaller ones. You're a big girl, I'm sure your Daddy will help you," April said before looking up at me as she handed the rabbit to Emma. "As I get to know him a little more, I can see how good of a parent he is. I'm sure that's rubbing off on you, so you can be a good parent to little Rodney."

Just when April did something foolish like arresting Helena Roarke for a murder she would never commit, the self-righteous sheriff paid me a compliment. Now, I had to be nice to her even though I wanted to lock her in a closet until... never mind... whoa, that was going somewhere I hadn't intended it to go. "Hey Emma, why don't you run inside and get a cookie from the parlor. I'll watch Rodney for you."

Emma put Rodney in the cage, then handed it to the sheriff. "You're not so bad even if Daddy complains about you all the time. He complains about everyone." She hugged April and started jogging toward the front steps. "Nana D says he's a tool. I'm not sure if he's a hammer or a screwdriver."

I closed my eyes and leaned against the SUV's passenger door. "Don't have children, April. They know how to make you love someone unconditionally and then rip out your heart and stomp on it!"

"At the risk of sounding sappy, I meant what I said. You're a damn fine father, Little Ayrwick," April said patting my shoulder twice. "You should also know I don't believe Helena Roarke had anything to do with George Braun's murder, but I've got a few pieces of evidence I can't deny at the moment. There is a lot of pressure from Mayor Grosvalet and Councilman Stanton to make this arrest."

"He's trying to make a point here, isn't he? The Roarke family is close to my family. This will be bad news for my nana, huh?"

April nodded. "Listen, I shouldn't be telling you this. I'm not sure why I am either, but you're starting to whittle me to the bone. I'm investigating a few other leads, but maybe the killer will let down his or her guard now that we've arrested Helena."

"Finnigan will get her out. She's not a flight risk," I added checking the time on my watch. "I'm guessing you have to hold her until Monday. No judge is gonna take her case at five o'clock on a Friday."

"I'm afraid you're right. I should drive downtown to process Helena and be sure she gets adequate accommodations for the extended stay. I'm sure she could use a visitor this weekend, that is, if you're around," April said, stepping away from me.

"Why Sheriff Montague, are you trying to help Helena, or do you want to see me again tomorrow?" I snickered. Laughter was sometimes the best way to handle an awkward situation. I didn't know how to behave around April if we weren't enemies anymore. We weren't quite friends, but that in-between, middle ground often caused more problems than necessary.

"For one thing, I'm not working tomorrow. You can spend all day in a jail cell talking to your former girlfriend's sister, buddy. For another, I do believe I've had my fill of Kellan Ayrwick for the month. I'm perfectly happy to wait until Braxton's next murder to deal with the likes of you," April taunted with an evil grin.

"Before you head out," I said, pulling my thoughts together. "I overheard a peculiar conversation between Doug and Karen Stoddard. Not only has their son, Cheney, been in some trouble in the past, but it occurred in Chicago. There also seems to be a different explanation between the two of them on how they ended up deciding to move to Braxton." I told the sheriff everything I'd learned from Doug about his wife's thirty-minute disappearance.

"I'll do some investigating about their arrival in Braxton. I already know about Cheney Stoddard's stint in prison. It makes him look guiltier, but Helena swears she saw Cheney back away from George in the courtyard. She's either covering for Cheney, or he left after his argument with the victim. Helena's case is growing stronger by the minute, even if my gut says she's not guilty." When the sky began to turn gray and mist, April blinked. Her vibrant green eyes glowed like an LED light.

"But you'll check into where Karen was during those thirty minutes?" I asked.

"Of course. Unfortunately, they backed one another up that neither had left each other's side most of the night, so I'll need to figure out how to introduce this topic. If I catch Doug and Karen separately, tripping one or both up should be relatively easy." The sheriff warned me not to talk to them again, as it could make her own investigation more difficult. I promised I'd do my best, but I knew if given the chance, I'd poke around. I couldn't help it. Two of my friends were in trouble, and the sheriff hadn't yet proved her dependability to me. I'd been essential to solving the earlier two murder cases, and if I hadn't kept my nose away from where it might not belong, a killer could've gone unpunished.

"Anything else you learned about the phone call Yuri overheard the day of George's murder?"

"I thought you agreed to stay out of it," April grunted. She crossed both arms and stood next to her motorcycle, glaring at me before putting on her helmet.

"Just following up on a lead I provided, that's all. Closing the item out, so I don't have to think about it ever again once I know you've got it under control," I said, hoping to appease her concerns.

"In that case, yes, Yuri's information was helpful. I followed up on what you were told, but let's just say... I'm not convinced she was being truthful. Yuri Sato is currently in trouble with Dean Mulligan over something she did at Braxton."

"Did the dean actually meet with George that afternoon, or did she make the whole thing up?"

"I can't comment on it right now. I need to finish my investigation. Don't push me on this." April clenched her jaw indicating she was nearing her boiling point over my persistence. "I will tell you that based on some of the documents left behind in his room at the inn, we confirmed George Braun was married. However, we do not yet know her full identity nor her location. She is a person of interest, and as soon as we can track her down, we'll have another possible suspect." April verified the bike was in neutral, pulled the clutch on the handlebar, started the engine, and roared out of the driveway.

I needed to find out why Anita Singh wouldn't talk about who she married. Now that Yuri was involved in a peculiar lie, I worried how she fit into the whole puzzle. If we couldn't produce another legitimate suspect, Helena might be in more trouble than I realized.

Emma bounded down the steps with two cookies in her hand. "She's so cool, Daddy. Here, have a gingersnap. Mr. Roarke said he was counting on you to help Helena."

"Thank you, baby. Let's head to dinner with Grandma, Grandpa, and Nana D. I promised them we'd stop by." Someone needed to stop Marcus Stanton for trying to push the sheriff around. Grosvalet would be out of a job soon enough, but I had to do everything to stop Stanton from becoming the next mayor.

CHAPTER 15

Emma and I got Rodney settled in for the night. Once we were sure he had enough food and water and fell asleep in his cage, we prepared to meet the rest of the family for dinner. Emma begged for a piggyback ride, so I pretended to be a farm animal and raced around Danby Landing snorting and squealing. I wasn't sure if making that awful noise or the actual running had worn me out first. Before driving to the Royal Chic-Shack, I called Ursula to let her know Helena had been arrested and that I suspected she might recognize who'd been recently consorting with George Braun. I explained who Karen and Doug Stoddard were without talking about their son's jail experience in Chicago. Ursula couldn't remember the assistant's first name and had still thought the person who worked in the lab was named Lambertson. It may or may not be the same person, I reminded myself.

"Myriam has a dinner this evening with all the other department chairs from neighboring colleges. Since I'm on my own, perhaps I should try the new Stoddard restaurant to see if I recognize Karen," Ursula suggested on the phone. "Care to participate in the fun?"

"I think it's a good idea. I'd join if I could, but I'm pulling up to my parents for some family time with Eleanor, Nana D, and Emma. Be careful, I don't exactly trust the Stoddard family right now," I cautioned as I parked the SUV and unbuckled my seatbelt. "Don't push her if she's combative or difficult. And be warned, Cheney's got a bit of a temper."

When we arrived, Emma placed a *My Little Pony* page holder in her book and waited for me to unlock the back door. My precocious daughter jumped into my arms saying, "What did we bring for dinner?" As I shut the door, I realized I hadn't asked my parents if they needed anything nor volunteered to bring part of the meal. I was a bad son.

"Well, honey, Daddy's had a busy day, and—"

Emma interrupted and said, "Auntie Eleanor just pulled up. She'll save the day." She jumped back down and ran to my sister's car once it parked behind us. When Eleanor stepped out of the driver side, she and Emma whispered like gossipy schoolgirls. I heard a second car door slam shut and watched Nana D exit the passenger side.

"Really? Your daddy forgot to bring something, how unusual," Eleanor teased.

"Oh, brilliant one, if the women in your life weren't on top of things, you'd be the worst sort of mess," Nana D reprimanded me as she walked between the two vehicles. "Take this," she said, handing me a fragrant bouquet of white daisies and yellow solidago. "Harness some flower power."

Since I'd been back in Braxton for three months, I could count on one hand the number of times we had dinner together as a family. When Eleanor, Nana D, and my parents congregated in a room, the zingers flew so fast they bounced off the walls and nipped you in the rear before you could get the next one out. As sarcastic as I could be, keeping up was not an option. I knew my place in that viper pit. Would it change now that Gabriel was back? I worried about keeping his secret from everyone tonight as I had only just found him again. Now I had to purposely not mention his name or risk a new world war.

"For me? You shouldn't have." I kissed Nana D on her cheek and took the bouquet and a cake plate she'd been carrying. "Far out. Were you ever a hippie, Nana D? Lay it on me." I thought I'd flavor up the evening with a little slang she might remember.

"You bet your sweet bippy I was, now don't bogart my stash! Does that answer your question?" Using her now-free hand, Nana D smacked me with a large canvas bag. "That's what I'm bringing. German chocolate cake made with the cocoa beans Deirdre sent me from her travels to Brazil. Supposedly doing research for her next romance novel, my bippy."

"What is in that tote, a thousand roles of quarters?" I said, switching the bouquet of flowers to my other hand so I could rub my shoulder. "Nana D's got her freak flag on and is repeating herself," I said in a drawn-out slur as if I were intoxicated. "She must be like way high on the grass!"

"Stop. No one finds you funny. Emma is probably ashamed to be your daughter," Nana D said.

"She's been carrying them around for a week and threatening to knock the councilman out if he keeps spreading rumors about her," Eleanor chimed in and grabbed Emma's hand to walk inside. In her other hand was a bag with at least four bottles of wine poking out the top. Good, one for each of us. My father drank scotch, but the rest of us would need a bottle to get through the night.

"That scoundrel told a group of downtown merchants that I wanted to knock over their stores to build a puppy mill. He's an arrogant son-of-a..." Nana D raised her voice until I leaned my head in Emma's direction. "Poop head! Anyway, you can give the flowers to your mother, so you don't look like a creep who forgot to bring something."

"Thank you, Nana D. I love you." I followed everyone inside and prepared for battle.

My father studied his formidable mother-in-law, searching for his best opening line. Then it arrived like a twister. "Mommie Dearest, it's wonderful to see you without your broom this evening. All out of gas? Or did you give the little monkeys the night off, I see?"

He reached for the cake, but she swatted his hand away. "Make yourself useful and disappear." Nana D pushed past him with a shoulder check and went looking for my mother in the kitchen.

Eleanor dropped off the wine on the dining room sidebar and immediately slid out the top drawer in search of a bottle opener. While Emma told my father all about her day at school, I approached my sister and whispered, "Should you be drinking if you're trying to get pregnant?"

"I'm not pregnant now. I'll stop if and when it happens, but until then I consider this special grape juice a necessary coat of armor for the evening," she replied and uncorked the first bottle of white. "A French Sancerre ought to get us started in the right mood."

Emma hopped to the kitchen making rabbit noises to help her grandmother and nana. My father opened the lower liquor cabinet, grabbed a shiny new bottle, and poured himself a scotch. "What's new in your life, son? Ever since you abandoned ship, I hardly ever see you anymore."

"I've been busy planning the next theatre show at Paddington's Play House. *Sunset Boulevard* should bring in extra folks while there are fewer students this summer," I replied, hoping to avoid a few topics he'd undoubtedly bring up. "Last year's Broadway revival caused quite the stir."

"Excellent choice. Ursula and Myriam are treating you well, I presume." He swirled the half a glass of liquor and breathed in its heavy, oaky scent. "How's that dirty old farm shed of Nana D's working out for you? Your mother definitely misses seeing you and Emma around the house. She's been sulking more than usual lately."

Nana D chose that moment to enter through the other side of the room. "That's because Violet's stuck spending all day with you, Wesley. There's only so many cantankerous, old academic scholarly bowel movements she can take at once." And just as quickly as she entered the room, she grabbed the freshly poured wine glass Eleanor had handed to me and strolled back into the kitchen. "Who picked this dry dud? We should only be buying American wine. And scotch, Wesley. Don't think I didn't notice your fancy schmancy liquor on the sidebar. Entire villages in Africa could eat for a month with what you spent on that bottle."

"Who invited that wet blanket?" my father asked as he refilled his tumbler. "Doesn't she have a campaign to lose?" Although they often traded ruthless barbs with one another, it was all in jest. They'd never genuinely liked each other, but our family supported their own when it counted in public.

"Actually, Dad, she's picked up a few points based on the latest news reports this morning. Nana D is currently ahead of Councilman Stanton," Eleanor added as she poured another glass for me.

"Speaking of Councilman Stanton, I ran into him today. He mentioned an arrest in the George Braun murder but wouldn't tell me who it was until it became official. Anyone I know?" my father said.

"Five more minutes until dinner," my mother cheerfully noted when she poked her head in the dining room. "Hello, my son. It's been so quiet without you here lately. I know you needed your privacy, but if you ever want to come back home, you are welcome." She stepped to the bar on the side of the room and poured herself a glass of wine, then cupped my cheek with her hand. "I love this face."

I knew the order of things around the Ayrwick household. "Of course, Mom. I appreciate it," I said and handed her the bouquet of flowers.

"These look just like the ones I saw at Nana D's house last week. You two must shop in the same florist," Mom teased before making a complete circle in the room and heading back to the kitchen to finalize our meal.

Eleanor shrugged her shoulders. "Kellan knows about the arrest, Dad. He was there when it happened."

How did she know? I hadn't had a moment of peace to tell anyone. I cocked my head at her and gave a confused look at her words. "Dish."

"Emma told me that you and April Montague wanted to be alone at the Roarke & Daughters Inn," Eleanor said, purposely and playfully throwing me under the bus with our father. "I'm not sure what she meant. What about it, Kellan? What's going on in your love life these days?"

I cleared my throat and cast a menacing look at my sister. "I think you've had too much to drink already. I heard you went to the doctor recently. What was that all about?" I turned to my father and let him know that while Helena had been arrested, it was not going to stick.

"Finnigan will clear the charges, since she's not guilty. Those Roarkes are too wonderful to do anything bad. It's a shame that things didn't work out with you and Maggie, huh, Kellan?" My father had finished most of his second scotch by then and was eyeing the bottle.

Eleanor knew we were swimming in rough waters. My father had made it clear in the past he didn't like Francesca. Given she was alive and only Eleanor and I knew, we needed to steer further away from the topic. My father would be smart enough not to say anything rude in front of Emma, but I still needed to put a pin in the conversation. Eleanor jumped in first. "You know, Dad, Maggie is definitely worried about her sister. Kellan has been helping to investigate. He's looking into the Stoddards and George Braun's history in Chicago. Do you know anything about them?"

I poured more wine into Eleanor's glass. She deserved it. "That's right, did you ever meet them on campus?"

My father took his seat at the head of the table. "Yes, I met Karen when Millard Paddington introduced us. She's also helping plan the Mendel flower show, I believe." He and my mother had skipped the library's costume extrava-

ganza, so Ursula could assume full leadership of Braxton without her predecessor still looming over the campus. "Never met the Braun fellow. It's
unfortunate he was murdered in the library. That won't make things any easier
for Maggie with the renovation plans."

My mother, Nana D, and Emma marched into the dining room like three
wooden soldiers carrying dinner. The housekeeper had prepared the meal
earlier in the day. All my mother had to do was heat it up when she got home
from work. Cooking was not one of her strengths. "We're having a divine lobster
risotto with homemade cheese biscuits and haricot vert."

"She means green beans with fish and rice," Nana D reminded everyone.
"Between you and Deirdre, half my kids think they're *Food Network* gour-
mands. I think not!" She exaggerated her words as though she were a high-class
snob with an ego the size of the eastern Wharton Mountain range.

"Yes, Mom. Thank you for clarifying our meal, so Emma knows what she's
eating," my mother said in an increasingly agitated voice. Although they got
along well under most conditions, they had little in common when it came to
domestic affairs. "Speaking of Deirdre, she's on her way home. I'm so excited."

"Really? I didn't know," I said. Her name had been popping up quite a bit
lately, but I never expected a visit. No one died or got married. That I was
aware of. Wait, I needed to check today's obituaries.

After my mother scooped portions of lobster risotto, Nana D added the
vegetable as each plate circled around the table. Emma dropped a biscuit on
everyone's dish and said 'order up' in a deep voice like Chef Manny. Was she
spending too much time at the diner? At least there were two biscuits dropped
on my plate. My daughter knew my fondness for bread came second only to
desserts.

Nana D sighed. "She's flying back with Lissette Nutberry. The poor
woman has been trying to track down her sister. From what I understand, she
learned some shocking news and asked Deirdre to accompany her."

"Lissette mentioned Judy was hard to reach lately. I wonder if she ever
found her." I helped Emma to cut her green beans in small chunks. She loved
vegetables but hadn't mastered using a knife.

"I don't know. Deirdre promised to call me when she arrived. She'll be
staying at the farmhouse for a couple of days." Nana D said *grace* prior to
eating, and at the end felt compelled to add, "And may the good lord bring
home all the other members of our family, such as Gabriel, who was forced to
leave Braxton when some of us couldn't be more open-minded about their jobs
and egos."

Dad was quiet for the rest of the meal until dessert arrived. By the final
course, they'd always broker a truce. He couldn't ignore her baking skills and
had finally thrown down that gauntlet years ago. "It was delicious. Thank you
both very much, but I have a call to return from Hampton. He's looking at real
estate in the area and wanted my advice. It's always wonderful to know my children still need me. Not everyone is smart enough to recognize that." Had he
scowled at me as he left the room?

My mother and Nana D retired to the den to watch a television show. Eleanor opened the third bottle of wine. We'd agreed to clear the table, wash the dishes, and clean up the kitchen. The cooks deserved a break, and we were happy to get a few moments alone. Emma emptied the dining room, but then I told her she could hang out in the game room. My parents kept tons of toys, puzzles, and surprises for all the grandchildren when they visited.

"Not too difficult tonight," Eleanor thoughtfully tossed out while we scraped the plates into the garbage disposal. "I only counted seventeen dirty hits. Lower than average."

"I thought I'd lose it when Dad brought up my break-up with Maggie," I responded while practicing my three-pointer shot with the tablecloth in the laundry basket. "Thank you for helping redirect that conversation."

"Anything new on the dead-not-so-dead-wife front?" she inquired. I shared my theory on Francesca's parents still hiding her away in their mansion to torture me and influence me to move back to LA. Eleanor didn't think they'd do something so underhanded. "Despite everything that's happened, they want the best for all of you. I think something else is going on."

"Speaking of something else going on... have you talked to Connor? I know he's been supporting Maggie through this whole ordeal with Helena." I checked my phone, wondering how Ursula's reconnaissance mission to the Stoddard restaurant was going. She hadn't updated me since we last chatted three hours ago.

"He and I scheduled a date for next week. He is seeing Maggie, but they're not serious right now. It's the modern way of doing things, Kellan. We millennials date a few people at once until something clicks. It's not the olden days when couples like Mom and Dad went steady," she said in a flourish while loading plates in the dishwasher.

Why did this millennial thing keep coming up around me? Was there that big of a generational difference to account for? "I suppose I could get behind that. What about the whole baby thing?" I asked hesitantly. She hadn't brought it up in a couple of days.

"I'm not sure. I told you that earlier. When I know, I'll spill. For now, zip it, big brother. You made your point loud and clear the other night." Eleanor wanted to seal the gap on that topic for now, which I happily understood and agreed to.

My phone vibrated. "It's *Madame President*. I need to take this. Can you check on Emma?" Eleanor agreed and ambled to the game room. I answered Ursula's call.

"You were right. Karen's the assistant."

"What happened?" I asked, hoping to learn something important to clear Helena. I didn't exactly dislike the Stoddards, but if one of them killed George Braun, they should be held responsible.

"It's a long story, but I'll give you the condensed version." Ursula explained that Karen was shocked when she showed up at the restaurant. The woman first acted confused, but once Ursula mentioned Hans and the explosion, the look on Karen's face gave away the truth. "It was almost like she relived the past right there in front of me."

"So, she's definitely the assistant who was around the day of the accident? I'm so sorry." I shook my head at the drama unfolding around everyone in my life.

"Karen claims she loved Hans and was devastated when he died. She blamed me for his death, and that's why she told the cops and the newspapers that I caused everything. She purposely wanted the media to spin all the coverage, so it looked like I was the bad guy."

"How does Doug fit into the picture?" I said.

"After Hans died, she married Doug. They'd been casually dating, but the fire brought them closer together. Karen moved on and never looked back once she got pregnant with Cheney."

The timing sounded awfully convenient. "I suppose that's a possibility. Do you think she's lying about which man is Cheney's father? Could Cheney be your nephew?" I asked trying to compare and contrast their facial features and mannerisms. I hadn't spent enough time with either Karen or Cheney to make a solid assessment.

"I need to see a picture of Cheney, I can't be certain." Ursula indicated she'd been worried Karen might reveal the truth to someone in the media again, but when she asked her about it, Karen was apologetic. "The woman told me the past is in the past. Hans was dead at this point. She wants to rebuild a life with her husband, son, and daughter in Braxton. She won't hurt me, she promised."

"Did she know George was Hans this whole time? Was she helping him?"

"I outright asked Karen if she'd been involved in delivering the notes. I told her George was stalking me and threatening to hurt me at one point." Ursula noted that Karen acted upset, almost as if it was all unfamiliar news.

"So, she denied being involved with George or Hans on any level?"

"Not exactly. Claims they ran into one another at the Mendel flower show. He asked for her help for old time's sake. She thought it'd be a great event to launch her and Doug's company in Braxton."

"Be careful. I don't think she's telling you the whole story." If Hans was Cheney's father, Karen might have killed him to keep the truth from coming out. On the flip side, if Doug learned he wasn't Cheney's father, or that Karen was having an affair, he might have murdered Hans in revenge.

Ursula asked for a day to think about everything that had happened. We agreed to reconnect once I had a chance to speak with Helena and Sheriff Montague. If the sheriff found anything new contradicting what Karen had told Ursula, we'd have a solid lead. As I hung up, I saw in the reflection of the window Emma and Eleanor skulking past the kitchen with foam Nerf guns. They were going to sneak attack my father in his office and my mother and Nana D from behind the couch. I was definitely on board for that type of distraction.

CHAPTER 16

Nana D agreed to watch Emma on Saturday while I organized a schedule around the various conversations I needed to hold. Gabriel agreed to meet after his lunch with Millard to discuss the upcoming flower exhibition. Since Maggie and her parents were visiting Helena at the prison in the afternoon, there'd be time in the morning to see me. Detective Gilkrist led me to a second-floor waiting room in the Wharton County administrative building which housed the county's entire court system and main prison. Petty criminals were kept overnight at the local jail in the nearby sheriff's office until they were seen by the judge for a decision on bail. If it was granted, the arrestee could leave the building until their hearing or trial began. If they were denied bail, they were moved to the main prison. Since Helena was being held on a murder charge until she could see Judge Grey on Monday, they'd transferred her to the main prison immediately.

Security buzzed me into the visiting area after I was allowed to speak with Helena. The space was painted an off-white color and had little room to move around. Detective Gilkrist told us he'd return in twenty minutes and that a guard was posted outside the door. Helena sat on the other side of a glass wall preventing us from any physical contact, and we spoke via two phones that connected underneath the thick barrier. She was in a dingy, light gray jumpsuit and wore no makeup but looked better than I'd expected.

"At least I'm not wearing those stripes yet," Helena teased after we'd sat down and picked up each phone receiver.

"You survived your first night. Only two more to go before Finnigan gets you out hopefully," I said. Helena told me he'd explain everything he'd learned about the case against her later that afternoon. They would prepare on Sunday and present the best possible scenario of why she should be released on her own recognizance at Monday's hearing with the judge.

"Finnigan doesn't think they'll deny bail. I'm not a flight risk. Their case isn't completely solid."

"I'm sure he's got your best interests in mind. There are a few questions I need answers on, if you expect me to help." I offered my best pseudo big brother worried look and hoped the glass window between us didn't distort my intentions.

"Ask away. I've got plenty of time apparently." She tapped her fingers on the counter in front of the glass. Helena handled her stint in prison better than I would if the roles had been reversed.

"I need to get hold of Cheney without his parents around. I think he's hiding something. If you won't tell me anything else, I'll have to ask him directly."

"I didn't hear any question there," Helena said, shrugging her shoulders and looking at me with a coy expression. "Should I assume you want me to tell you how to find him?"

"That would make my job a lot easier," I noted.

"Cheney didn't do anything. I trust him, but I wouldn't have blamed him if he did. His parents aren't very honest people. He found something out that upset him when he spoke with George. I don't know all the details. You'd have to ask him."

"Go on. I'm glad to see you're opening up and trying to protect yourself. What if the Stoddards are involved in George Braun's death?"

"Doubtful," she said scratching her nail on the counter. "I don't know them all that well, but they don't seem like killers to me."

"Someone murdered the man." I knew in my heart Ursula hadn't murdered the guy. Looking back, the shock on her face was one-hundred-percent authentic when she realized he was her brother. I wasn't certain at first, and the stain on her shawl had confused me, but she would've told me the truth if she'd done something stupid and accepted the consequences of her actions. "How can it hurt if I talk to Cheney? I won't tell him you sent me. I'll feel him out to see if he's comfortable talking about whatever he'd learned." I waited a minute before Helena finally responded with something helpful.

"You might find him at happy hour at Kirklands, a pub in Woodland." Helena indicated they had two-dollar beers starting at four o'clock every day. It was remote enough that I could also suggest the location to Gabriel for our catch up.

"What else do you want to know?" she asked. "I appreciate everything you're doing. I don't mean to be rude, but this place is boring. I want to get out as quickly as possible."

"Working on it. Are you sure there's nothing else you recall about George Braun that might lead me to another suspect? How about the name Hans Mück?"

"Don't recognize it. I told you he met with some woman about the flower show. Maybe it was his girlfriend or wife. He had one but rarely talked about her." Helena leaned forward on the counter and rested her head against the glass.

The guard banged on the door to startle Helena before poking his head in the room. "Don't forget I'm watching through this window." She turned halfway around making a quick gesture in his direction.

Since Helena's back was to me, I couldn't see what it was, but I had a feeling it was highly inappropriate. "Young, old? What'd she look like?"

"I only saw her for a second. She could've been anywhere from early twenties to late forties, maybe even fifty. She had a kerchief around her head, so I couldn't see her hair or any facial features."

It might've been Anita Singh. I also hadn't seen a picture of Sierra Stoddard. "Have you met Cheney's sister?"

"Nah, she just got back last week from Switzerland. She finished her first year at law school in London, then went skiing before coming back to the States for the summer. Cheney was gonna introduce me to her this weekend."

"Could the woman you saw with George have been Sierra?" I asked. Had they met in Switzerland at some point?

"I guess it's possible. I don't know the exact date Sierra arrived in Braxton, but I think it was before I saw this woman talking to George. Cheney would know for sure." Helena cradled the phone against her neck and fluffed up her hair. "I need shampoo. Maggie better bring the good stuff. I think they gave me generic body and hair soap to use this morning. How uncivilized!"

"You look fine. Focus on listening to Finnigan this afternoon. Do whatever he tells you, he's the best." I had no other questions for Helena, so we said our goodbyes. The guard escorted Helena back to her cell. Detective Gilkrist was tied up, but the sheriff wanted me to stop by if I had time.

On the walk next door, I considered everything Helena had revealed. If Sierra was in Europe at the same time as George, Sierra could've been the one helping him get revenge on Ursula. Maybe she had something to do with his death? I texted my brother to meet me at Kirklands in Woodland at two thirty. It'd allow us enough time to chat before Cheney showed up for his afternoon buzz.

I let the receptionist at the front desk know April Montague asked for me. I was brought to her office right away. "Little Ayrwick, I appreciate you stopping by. How'd your conversation go with Helena? Is she sticking with the same story?"

"Helena is one tough cookie. She gave me a few ideas to follow up on, but nothing concrete. I'll let you know if anything comes to fruition," I said.

April's office was as understated as it'd been earlier in the week, except she now had a picture on her desk with a man she'd had her arms wrapped around. I knew she wasn't married but didn't know anything else about her. Where had she moved here from? Did she have a special someone in her life?

In the brief silence, April caught me staring at the photo. "Darren was my fiancé. We'd been engaged for two months until someone gunned him down in a drive-by shooting six years ago."

That's what she meant the other day by *knowing what it was like to lose someone.* "I'm so sorry, April. I had no idea."

"I rarely talk about it. It wasn't a good period for me. The jerk who killed him had been released on bail after stealing a dozen cars and shooting a parking lot attendant back in Buffalo. I'd been the arresting officer. I could never prove it, but I think Darren was killed as a revenge message to me."

"That's awful. You keep things locked up pretty tight, don't you?" I asked.

She nodded. "As I said, it wasn't a good time for me. That's why I took this job when it came up. I needed to get away from cities with a lot of crime."

"And you thought Wharton County would be a calmer place to work?" I began understanding more about April Montague in the few minutes she let her wall down in front of me.

"I want to keep the citizens of my jurisdiction safe. I couldn't do that in Buffalo anymore. There wasn't a huge amount of crime, but there were murders and gang shootings. I thought it'd be different here," she said gently caressing the picture frame.

"And now we've had four murders in Braxton in the last three months." It was a statement, and I didn't expect a response, but April laughed.

"I told you earlier this week. I'm worried you're a magnet for disaster. It was quiet my first few years running this county. Now, you've got me a little flustered about things." April paused for a moment to collect her thoughts. "That's why I put this picture back up again. I needed a reminder of what I was fighting for. What I came to this beautiful place to do."

"Saving fine, upstanding citizens like myself from the bad guys?"

"The jury's still out on whether you're one of these fine, upstanding citizens, but you get the point. I'm not afraid of a challenge, and I won't let things get out of control around here. I'm supposed to keep the law and order. And that includes reminding you of appropriate boundaries."

"Duly noted. I consider myself protected and warned, but please remember, April... I'm only trying to help my friends."

"I know that. It's why I plan to go a little easier on you. I'm not about to share everything on this case, but I'm glad we're collaborating rather than antagonizing. In the interest of protecting Ursula Power and Helena Roarke, let's talk about some new things that've come up." April retrieved a bank statement from a folder on her desk and handed it to me.

After looking it over, I said, "If I'm reading this correctly, George Braun made many large transfers from another account into this one in the last four months. Who owns the other account?"

"Very good. You're asking the right questions. I'm not sure, but we're trying to pull those details. I suspect he was financing his lab experiments to find the cure he'd lost twenty-five years ago. I think someone was helping to back his research. None of the big medical companies would handle it this way. They'd publicize their work to keep getting more funding. He made efforts to hide it."

"You think this other account belongs to George's partner?"

"Maybe. I should know within the next twenty-four hours. I've also been able to locate his last known residence in Switzerland and confirm he'd been living there up until taking the Mendel flower show to the States. It was held in Chicago last January, then he made this special stop in Braxton."

"Can you share anything about George's relationship with Anita Singh or Ed Mulligan?"

April waffled but eventually conceded. "Mulligan admits he went to see George the day of the costume extravaganza. George wanted more money and claimed he had information that would embarrass the dean."

"Did he?" What had Dean Mulligan done? It'd explain the dean's anger on our phone call.

"Ed Mulligan has a temper, and he did something he shouldn't have done. It's certainly compromising for Braxton, but it only impacts a few people. That's all I can reveal right now." April pressed her fingers against the bridge of her nose to relieve pressure or tension.

"Okay. You mentioned Yuri was angry with Dean Mulligan and probably exaggerated what she told me that day?" When April appeared to agree, I said, "Ursula did mention Dean Mulligan saw where she'd kept the knife in her office."

"I'm aware and following this closely. The same goes for Anita Singh, even though you didn't ask me. The lab coat never turned up, but she has been keeping a secret about her marriage. I can't tell you anything additional at this time."

I knew it was best to back away, but it felt comforting to know she was pursuing all the leads I'd suggested to her. Before taking off, I updated April about Sierra Stoddard's skiing trip in Switzerland. She agreed to check it out with her international contacts to find out if Sierra and George were ever in the same place. I was glad to develop a newfound tentative partnership with the sheriff. After I left her office, I squeezed in a workout for the day, quickly downed a protein shake for lunch, and drove across the river to Kirklands to meet Gabriel.

He sat in a corner booth intently staring at something on his phone when I arrived. Despite the trim beard and leather jacket, my brother still looked naiver than his twenty-eight years. I wasn't sure how he'd explain the nose piercing and tattoo to our parents, but it did give him a certain edge. His dirty blond hair was still spiked and messy, making him look like a cross between a well-known British model and the lead singer of any popular rock band.

When Gabriel heard my footsteps approaching, he greeted me with a hesitant grin and removed his earbuds. "Just listening to some Callum Scott. His voice is off the charts. So, I ordered us both two of whatever was on tap."

"That works for me. I lifted for the last hour, so it'll burn off quickly. I might be drinking here for a while," I said, explaining my hope to run into Cheney at some point.

"Where do you want to start?" Gabriel asked.

I had a lot of topics. How long had he known he was gay? Had he been involved in any serious relationships? Did anyone else in the family know?

Why did he jump ship eight years ago? What had he done with his life? When did he decide to come back to Braxton? I didn't want to overwhelm him, so I suggested he tell me whatever he was comfortable with right now.

"Sure. Let's start with why I left Braxton," he began as two pints of lager were delivered to our table. "I think I always knew I was different, but I couldn't do anything about it. I met someone when I was a sophomore at Braxton. He changed my life." Gabriel finished his story, and when it ended, I was proud of my little brother.

After a few weeks of hanging out with the guy between classes or during meals, Gabriel knew his old life was about to end. The guy was transferring to Penn State and wanted Gabriel to come with him. Gabriel applied and was granted the transfer, which is when our father also accepted the role of president at Braxton. Unfortunately, my brother's fling ended weeks later when the other guy's parents found out and sent their son off to some psychiatric institute for evaluation. Gabriel had gotten one last email before he disappeared, and while it devastated him, my brother knew he couldn't transfer schools on his own. He returned to Braxton, but our father wouldn't budge about giving up his new position. Gabriel didn't want to get special treatment if his father ran the college. In a last-ditch effort to work it out with him, Gabriel confessed his secret to our father and begged for the same opportunity to finish school like all his older siblings without any influence. They fought about it, and our father wanted to talk to our mother, but Gabriel wasn't ready to tell everyone else.

"So, I took off. I made him promise to keep my secret, which he agreed to do since he didn't relinquish his new job. That's when I moved to San Francisco. It's where I thought I was supposed to go... until I got there. Let's just say it wasn't for me." Gabriel rolled his eyes.

April was right. We did have similar mannerisms. "Why stay away for eight years?"

"It's a difficult thing to go through, Kellan. At first, you think because you're different, there's something really wrong with you. Then you go through your own acceptance phase. Enough time went by that I was afraid to tell you guys. I liked my life. I grew up sheltered and quiet, almost as if I never had a chance to become me. It's no one's fault, but it happened."

Gabriel stuck it out for two years in San Francisco, earned his bachelor's degree in biology, then moved to Seattle and got a job in a pharmaceutical company. "I focused on my PhD, made good money doing construction work on the weekends, and held a nine-to-five lab role weekdays. Everything was working out great."

"But now you're home again. Why?" I asked, wishing we'd known we were both living in California for all those years.

"I don't want to talk about it. Something happened, I got angry. Can we just forget it for now?" Gabriel immediately changed topics noting he'd kept tabs on the family by reading local papers. "I'm sorry about Francesca, but I can't wait to meet Emma."

What was my brother hiding? I wanted to tell him the truth, but it wasn't the right time. "I think you'll be welcomed back with open arms. Seriously, everyone will be fine." I explained how Wharton County and Braxton had become more open-minded and tolerant in the last few years, citing Ursula Power as the school's president. I hadn't heard a negative thing about her, which showed our growth.

"That's what Sam tells me. He's a really honest, caring, and supportive guy. But we're taking it very slow," Gabriel said, signaling the bartender for two more beers.

By the time Gabriel and I finished talking about what'd happened to each of us since we'd last seen each other, it'd felt like old times. Part of me was concerned he still concealed something about his connection to George Braun, especially given how withdrawn Gabriel had become at several points in the conversation. We decided I would schedule a family dinner the following week where Gabriel would show up and attempt to reintegrate.

"Where are you planning to live?" I asked my brother.

"Not with Mom and Dad. I need my privacy. I was thinking about buying some land and building a house once I got a permanent job again," Gabriel said as he swallowed the last of his beer and checked if I wanted another round.

I looked across the bar as Cheney Stoddard hopped on a stool. "I do, but somehow I gotta get that guy to spill some secrets." After explaining to my brother what I needed to know from Cheney, he offered to handle it.

"Cheney can be a little rough and has been looking for a job. I think he's angry about the whole situation," I said as my brother walked away and sidled up to the bar. A few minutes later, he bumped into Cheney causing the beer to spill out of his mug. I worried if my brother was about to start a brawl in the bar. I monitored the situation for at least ten minutes while they drank a couple of beers together followed by at least two shots of a clear liquid. When the two of them turned around and began walking toward the table, they laughed like they were lifetime friends.

"Hey, Kellan, this is Cheney. Cheney, this here's my brother Kellan," Gabriel said introducing the two of us like we hadn't already met earlier that week. "You called it, bro, I'm always causing accidents. I totally sideswiped him ordering more beers. I offered to buy him another, and we started chatting. Turns out today's his birthday."

Cheney said, "Yes, and I'm celebrating all alone. Did you know your brother's in construction? He knows of a possible job to help me out... hey... wait, don't I know you?"

I adopted my brother's more relaxed, friendlier attitude, ignoring how much he'd probably already drunk. "Yeah, we do, this is too funny. I came to your restaurant for lunch this week. You're dating my friend, Helena. Such a small town!"

Cheney clunked his beer on the table, sat across from me, and smacked his hand against his forehead. "Helena Roarke. That beautiful vixen is gonna be my downfall. You won't believe what she's doing to protect me this time. I could use some cool dudes to talk to about how screwed up my life is right now."

And just like that, my brother returned to town and busted open the best lead I had on the murder investigation. Wow, it felt good to be home again with Gabriel.

CHAPTER 17

Cheney finished his beer, summoned a waitress to order three refills, and pounded his fists on the table. "Ugh, did you ever live your whole life knowing something wasn't right? Then you find out it's all one big lie!"

I emphatically agreed with him. "Not my whole life, but definitely a few of those years," I said thinking about the last couple when Francesca was supposedly dead. Gabriel chimed in with similar woes, and we all commiserated for at least ten cathartic minutes. I didn't want to push Cheney, but the more he drank, the more he might reveal.

After the waitress dropped off the newest round and took away the rest, Cheney's gaze widened and he whispered, "I can trust you guys, right?"

I noticed Gabriel's previous glass had still been full when the waitress took it away, and his new one now had a clear liquid that I guessed was vodka. I leaned over to smell it. There wasn't any liquor in that glass. What was he up to? "Sure, of course, you can, Cheney."

Gabriel bugged his eyes out at me, then turned to Cheney and took a swig from his glass. "Totally. You were saying something about Helena, right?"

"Yup." Cheney belched and shook his head. "She's covering for me because of a stupid argument I had with someone."

"Is this about what happened in the library?" Out of the corner of my eye, while Cheney focused on telling me his story, I watched Gabriel pour my drink into an empty glass at his side. He dropped a ten-dollar bill next to it, and a minute later, the waitress came by to collect both the glass and the money. He hadn't been drinking anything since he bumped into Cheney at the bar. Gabriel was keeping us sober, so we could convince our new friend to talk.

"Exactly. That dead guy... my mother knew him years ago. Twenty-five years today to be exact."

Oh, I knew what he was about to say next. My detective skills were becoming top-notch. "That's some weird stuff, man!"

"Get this. He's my real father. He and my mother had some fling going years ago before he disappeared. So, she married the guy I thought was my father and has been keeping it a secret this whole time." Cheney growled under his breath about all the disappointments in his life. "You think you can get me a job, so I can get outta this place?" he mumbled at Gabriel.

"Yeah, I'll definitely try. I've got lots of contacts," my brother replied as he took another swig from his water glass. He clinked Cheney's, encouraging him to finish his own. "Did the dead guy know he's your father?"

I didn't exactly approve of Gabriel's ingenious plan to get Cheney intoxicated, but he'd probably have drunk this much on his own if he was by himself on his birthday. We'd be sure to hire a cab to get him home safely.

"Not this whole time, but he found out last week." Cheney swallowed the remains of his beer and waved for another before finishing his story. He'd overheard his mother talking to George one afternoon about giving birth to his son but thinking he'd been gone forever. Cheney wasn't aware George was really Hans Mück who hadn't been killed in the explosion. Cheney's impression from overhearing the conversation was that his mother had simply lost touch with his biological father and moved on.

"I don't understand how Helena fits into this," I inquired, knowing there was some connection, but perhaps it wouldn't be logical. Cheney wasn't the brightest guy I'd ever met.

"Helena knows I confronted George in the courtyard. I'd found out the truth the day before the costume extravaganza and tried to talk to him, but he wouldn't cut me any slack. That man originally promised me a construction job. When he found out who I was, he took it away."

"George didn't want to acknowledge you were his son?" Gabriel asked while swapping his drink again. My brother just realized George had hired him instead of Cheney to work on the cabin.

"Nope. I told him we were both lied to and deserved a chance to get to know one another. We got into an argument when he told me to leave him alone and forget I ever found out the truth. I don't need another parent to tell me what to do. What a loser!"

"Sorry, that's some dysfunction," I said supporting the guy. "Did you tell all this to Helena? Is your real connection with George what she agreed not to share with the cops?"

"Yep. She only told them about her disagreement in his room. Turns out, someone else overheard me tell Helena I wanted to teach George Braun a lesson and confessed to the cops what'd happened at the inn." Cheney was getting too drunk to keep talking anymore. "I walked away!"

Yuri was the person who saw George hassling Helena at the inn and Cheney subsequently defending his girlfriend's honor. Was she playing games in the background to cast suspicion in a different path? "No disrespect meant, but did you have anything to do with the guy's death?" I didn't get the vibe that he had, but without asking the question, I might've missed something valuable.

Cheney stood up and flailed his arms around. "Hell no! I told that jerk he wasn't ever gonna be my father because I was too good for him. I grabbed him by that stupid costume to shut him up. That's when he showed me the knife he had in his pocket. I backed away. I wasn't stupid enough to take the risk he'd stab me. He was acting all sorts of crazy about the way I'd confronted him. I left the courtyard and went back to tend bar for the rest of the night."

Cheney leaned too far to the side, but Gabriel jumped up to catch him. Despite Cheney having at least forty pounds and five inches on my brother, Gabriel was able to hold him upright. "We need to get him in a cab," Gabriel said.

I nodded and was about to pull out my cell phone when a woman's voice scolded us. "Leave my brother alone. What's going on here?"

Sierra Stoddard had shown up finally. Layers of curly ebony hair cascaded down her back with a large bunch pulled together at the top and wrapped in a tight bun. High, prominent cheekbones and a beauty mark just above her lip made her look mysterious and contemplative. She wore a mid-thigh black skirt, knee-high leather boots, and a gold-colored silk blouse mostly hidden by a trim business coat. In a way, she reminded me of what Francesca had looked like before the massive makeover.

Cheney hugged his sister. "It's my birthday, sis, but I gotta use the little boy's room."

"Can't you wait, honey? I'll put you in the car and take you home," Sierra pleaded as she swung a tiny beaded purse across her shoulders. It collided with a chunky necklace and made a popping noise.

"Nope!" Cheney grimaced and took off toward the men's room.

Gabriel rushed after him. "I'll take care of him. We'll be back as soon as we can."

I turned to Sierra. "Hi, I'm Kellan Ayrwick. We were having drinks with—"

"I know exactly who you are. My mother told me all about you nosing around with questions about our family. What gives?" she said, dropping her purse on the table and pulling out a chair to sit.

I threw my hands up in the air and backed away. "Innocent. I was having drinks with my brother. Cheney showed up on his own, and then we all sat down to shoot the breeze."

"My brother's gonna be a while in the state you got him into," she said kicking the leg of another chair toward me. "Sit and shoot the breeze with me." The excessive confidence in Sierra's voice and her intense attitude was not winning her any points in my book. Was this a tactic she'd learned in law school or her natural cosmopolitan charm?

"I'm not sure why you're being defensive. Cheney's dating Helena who happens to be the sister of a good friend of mine. I've known her for over ten years. As for your parents, I've met them two or three times. Who said I was nosing around?" Doug wouldn't have shared our conversation with his daughter, he wanted to keep that situation quiet. Karen must be worried about something.

"I'm not defensive. I'm cautiously protective of my family. They're all I have, and I'd do anything to keep them safe." Sierra crossed her arms and relaxed into the seat. "I don't mean to be rude."

"Fine, I can understand looking out for those you love."

"My mother said you have a reputation for digging into people's personal lives. Ours is just fine, we don't need a mole inventing drama for the sake of drama," Sierra warned as she dabbed a napkin on a few sticky spots on the table. "If you need to know anything about us, funnel your questions through me in the future. Capiche?"

"Law school agrees with you. You'll make a fine ambulance chaser one day." I doubted I'd get very much out of the girl if I annoyed her, but maybe she'd echo her brother and say something in frustration or anger. I signaled to the waitress to bring me the tab. "I think we're done here."

"No, we're not," she said, pointing an index finger at me. "What did Cheney tell you?"

"Nothing for you to worry about. The guy's alone on his birthday, just needed some company. Tell me, why weren't you celebrating with him tonight if you're such a fantastic sister?" I stood and pulled out my wallet to collect a few twenty-dollar bills.

"I was helping my parents with legal documents for the business. We were supposed to have a family dinner tonight, but Cheney never showed. I know he likes to hang out here, so I came to get him."

"Then you admit your brother caused his own problem tonight. It wasn't me." I saw Gabriel and Cheney walking back from the restroom. Her brother appeared to have sobered up some.

Sierra snorted. "Consider this a formal warning or free advice, whatever you want. My parents are good people. My brother's trying to get his life in order. I'm fiercely loyal to them and will stop anyone from hurting a Stoddard. So back off!" She smiled and turned to the waitress to snatch the bill from her hands. After rummaging through her pocketbook, Sierra grabbed a handful of cash and handed it to the server.

"I was gonna buy, you know, it is his birthday," I said.

"No, thank you. You got Cheney into this mess, I'll get him out of it," she said almost indifferently. When Cheney reached the table, she grabbed his hand and pulled her brother closer. "Come on, let's get to dinner, babe. We've got a fun night planned."

Cheney followed his sister to the front door but leaned back and whispered to me with a wide grin, "I'm in trouble. Don't ever piss her off, she always wins in the end!"

Gabriel sighed. "That was fun. Is this what things are like for you all the time, brother?"

I didn't think they were, but he had a point. People always had extreme reactions around me, whether good or bad. Had Sierra been listening to our conversation and heard Cheney tell us about George being his biological father? Was she responsible for getting rid of the man, so he couldn't hurt their family anymore? I needed to find out when she flew to Switzerland and Braxton as well as if she'd been a guest at the costume extravaganza that night.

"It's unintentional, Gabriel. I don't know what happened here tonight, but the best thing about it was seeing you in action."

"You learn how to survive when you're on your own. I'm a people person. I know how to connect and get someone to talk. You should try me some time," Gabriel said. He verified we left nothing at the table. "Let's motor. I need to meet Sam."

"You promised you'd come for dinner next week with everyone," I reminded him as we walked to the parking lot. "I'm proud of you." He kept walking to his car without any response.

After Gabriel left Kirklands, I called the sheriff and let her know what I'd learned from talking with Cheney and Sierra. She was stunned to learn the truth about George being Cheney's father, but Sierra wasn't on her radar. April promised she'd check into Sierra's travel records and would consider how to move forward with Cheney.

"I want to haul him in for obstruction of justice, not to mention add those charges to Helena Roarke's rap sheet. Why do people lie about something this important?" April asked.

"I think you know the answer to that question. Either this secret has nothing to do with why George was killed, or they're all scared about something." I wasn't an expert in human psychology, but Cheney was emotionally devastated on many levels. His mother had been lying to him all his life, and George rejected his son without knowing much about him. Cheney had anger management issues, and they could've escalated to the point he grabbed the knife from George and stabbed his newly discovered father in a moment of delusion or extreme anger and pain.

"That is what I'm going to find out," April insisted. The woman needed a night off. Too many unresolved leads were ripping her apart. "I appreciate you sharing this news so quickly. I need to remind you not to discuss it with anyone else. Not even Maggie. Helena is in enough trouble for keeping this from me. I'm stopping all visitors the rest of this weekend, so she and Cheney can't communicate."

April hung up. I understood why she had to limit Helena's conversations with anyone else. If she'd shared what Cheney had told her sooner, Helena might not have been arrested. Cheney might have been, but it wouldn't have wasted the Wharton County Sheriff's Office's time for the last few days. They could have been investigating other angles instead of a disagreement about access to George's room at the Roarke & Daughters Inn. Although I didn't want Helena to get in more trouble, perhaps something a little stronger than a slap on her wrist when this was done might be a good thing.

Before heading to Nana D's to pick up Emma, I stopped on campus to get my mail and dashed into the faculty mailroom in the student union building. I punched my code into the keypad and collected my post. The Orlando post-card I'd asked my friend to send had arrived, but so did another from Yellow-stone Park. It read:

Emma loves Animals so much, I thought she'd never let us leave. Between the elk and the bison, she could barely contain herself. I wish we had the chance to return together as a family. So much has changed in the last few years. If only I could see her reaction as the snow fell on her face and made her laugh like she did when Old Faithful erupted.

Recalling our family trip to Yellowstone comforted me in a way I hadn't felt for a long time. As much as I wished we could have that life back, we couldn't right now. I needed to push back on the Castiglianos if they were playing games with me. I snapped a photo of both and sent them to Vincenzo. There were several days between the dates on the two postcards, so it didn't look suspicious when he read them. It looked like she'd left the West Coast and flew to the East Coast to finish her tour of the past. If things continued, the next and last one I'd get would be from Savannah. Would she go back to Los Angeles afterward, or visit Braxton to convince me to give us another chance?

When I arrived at Nana D's, I called out to them and dropped off my satchel on the couch. No one answered me. My stomach rumbled as I checked in the kitchen. A whole chicken was roasting in the oven, and gravy was on a slow simmer on the stove. Sage and rosemary tempted my nose enough to taste a spoonful. I peered out the back window and saw them feeding the horses in the barn. Nana D always followed the same rule—animals eat first, then humans can have their chow. When I waved to them, Emma jumped up and down and began running up to the house.

While I waited for their return, my phone rang. I picked up the call. "Did you get the photos?"

"I did. You never told me about Orlando. You said Savannah and the park. Is this a trick you are playing on me?" he asked in an eerily calm tone. *'Only the Good Die Young'* played in the background.

Bingo! Vincenzo took the bait. Now to figure out if he was upset because I didn't tell him about Orlando or because he was sending the postcards and didn't have a clue where this one came from. "I must have forgotten. Your daughter and I were married for six years before she disappeared, Vincenzo. We went to a lot of places."

"I will send people there tonight. I do not have anyone in Orlando, but they are close by in Miami. Maybe she's still at Disney." Vincenzo sounded like he believed she was there.

"Perhaps Francesca needed this time to decide her future. She'll come home again soon. It must have been difficult being cooped up in the house for so long." I was treading a thin line by annoying my father-in-law, and he was much better at games than me. Giving my plan a shot was necessary.

"No! My daughter would not ignore me for this long. She sends these postcards to you. I get nothing. Her parents have no messages. She is a good daughter. She does what I tell her to do." Vincenzo began losing his perfect composure.

Maybe he wasn't sending them. Maybe Francesca did this on her own. I'd soon find out, but in the meantime, Emma came running in the room and hugged me. "Hey baby," I said to my daughter. "Talk to Nonno." I told Vincenzo his granddaughter was getting on the line and that I'd let him know when the next postcard arrived. Emma took the phone and raced into the living room.

"Trouble with the Castiglianos?" Nana D asked while washing her hands. Although my parents never knew about the devious underworld my in-laws lurked in, Nana D had hinted a few times in the past that she was aware. "Need me to get involved? The Septuagenarian Club has always wanted to take a trip to Los Angeles. We could be a major distraction to keep them off your back!"

Just what I needed. Nana D stepping into some mafia war to protect me. While she was clever at getting revenge and verbally torturing people, the mob was not a world she needed to experience. "It'll be okay. They just miss Emma."

Nana D pinched my cheeks. "This new shorter do looks good on you. I'm glad to see you're taking care of yourself again. I can't imagine what it's like to lose your wife at such a young age and have to raise your daughter on your own. You are truly an inspiration, brilliant one."

No sarcasm? No backhanded compliment? Who was this woman and where was my Nana D? She's one to talk. Nana D and Grandpop were together for almost fifty years when she lost him to a heart attack. We were grateful it happened quickly and there was little if any pain, but she was the inspiration. "I love you, Nana D. I don't know what I'd do without you."

"You'd probably screw up a lot more often." Nana D took the chicken out of the oven and instructed me to pour iced tea for the three of us.

She was right. I probably would, but so would she. "How are your last couple of days as a free woman working out? Stanton concede yet?"

"Nah, that rascal won't give up until he counts every ballot himself. The team tells me I'm pulling ahead enough they aren't too worried. It's still a close race, so I can't—"

"Can't get your hopes up. Just keep on being your confident and humble self. You're what this county needs to fix the sins of the past," I said.

For too long, Wharton County had been led by wealthy families who took bribes, bought cops in their pocket, and let fear hold back any change. When the former sheriff retired and the people voted in an out-of-towner, the beginnings of a new future had emerged. April had no tolerance for bureaucratic ways and ruffled as many feathers as possible. It worried me when she arrested Helena due to pressure from Councilman Stanton and Mayor Grosvalet, but she had an ulterior motive to draw out the real criminal. She was smart enough not to let them win at their game.

"You bet I am," Nana D cheered. She handed me the knife to carve up the chicken. "Any news on that murder you're all hopped up about? You still helping out Maggie's sister?"

"I am. What did Dean Mulligan want from you?" The curiosity was almost killing me.

"To ask me to convince you to stop looking into George Braun's murder."

"What?" I hadn't expected her to say that.

"He overheard you and the sheriff talking about him being closely involved with the flower show, the disagreements with Anita Singh, et al. The dean didn't want to cause a problem for the college by confronting you himself, so he asked me to do it."

"That makes no sense. He's actually a suspect right now."

"Ed Mulligan and I go way back. He thought I could get you to leave him alone before he had to file a formal complaint about it," Nana D replied.

I felt like the man had stabbed me in the back. "What did you say?"

"Oh, brilliant one. He and I might be friends, but you and I are family. I told him to fight his own battles, and that if you were poking your nose in his business, there was a valid reason!"

"Did that shut him up?" I remembered the two pictures showing his rearranged costume. Had we found our killer?

"Yep. He assures me he had nothing to do with offing George Braun. But I'll leave that to you to prove." Nana D might believe him, but all killers said they weren't guilty. He knew something important.

"Thanks, Nana D. I'm working with April who's checking into him as we speak."

"*April?* Since when do you call that mooncalf sheriff by her first name?" Nana D banged the lid on the gravy pot.

"We're getting along better these days. I'm tired of fighting with her," I said, wondering who I was convincing—Nana D or myself. I enjoyed the banter, but was that the most effective approach to eliciting pertinent facts from a sheriff who was supposed to keep quiet about the details of crime? "Aren't you the one who taught me about catching more flies with honey?" As I finished slicing the chicken, Emma entered the kitchen and stuck the phone in my pocket.

"That woman is made of vinegar. She doesn't count," Nana D blasted.

There was no use pushing Nana D on that situation. Ever since the sheriff almost arrested my nana several years ago, she'd held the biggest grudge I'd ever encountered. "Dinner looks amazing, doesn't it?" I said, turning to Emma.

"Nonno said your time ran out. What does that mean, Daddy?" Emma tugged on my shirt as we walked to the table with the rest of the side dishes—mashed potatoes and carrots jubilee.

"We're playing a game and he's afraid to lose, that's all." Vincenzo knew better than to pass messages to me through Emma. I wasn't gonna let this proceed any further.

Nana D looked inquisitively at me as she poured gravy on her chicken. "He's gonna lose if I have anything to say about it." Did my grandmother know more than she was letting on?

"Can I play?" Emma asked.

"No, it's an adult game. We can play a different one tonight with Nana D."

"I like Uno. Can we play that?"

"Yes, baby."

While we finished dinner, we chatted about their day on the farm and how Rodney was adapting to his weekend home. Before we settled down with Uno, we played with the rabbit and fed him a carrot stick. As I watched my daughter comfort the little tyke, I remembered our jaunt to Yellowstone. She had only been three years old and still too young to appreciate the trip, yet she'd had the best time that summer despite the unbearable temperatures. We never should have gone hiking in that weather, but Francesca made sure we'd all had sunblock and taken plenty of water breaks.

Wait! We were in Yellowstone during the summer. Why did Francesca's postcard mention snow? There was definitely no snow on our trip. Had she been confused?

"Rodney's back in his cage, Daddy. Let's play Uno," Emma said.

I couldn't shake the feeling that something weird was going on, but what did it mean? Emma grabbed my hand, and we met Nana D in the den to play cards. After an hour, Emma won a few hands, but Nana D triumphed on the rest. I was in last place by way too many points to admit.

We left Nana D's and went back to our cottage. I tucked Emma in bed at her normal time without any issues. My daughter truly was the most perfect child. Every parent said it, but I was certain, unlike the rest. I got lucky and would never forget it.

I debated calling Ursula to let her know what I'd learned about George being Cheney's real father. She now had a nephew, but would she be able to acknowledge him? I sent a text to see if she was awake. It was still before ten on a Saturday, yet I didn't want to risk calling and have Myriam answer the phone. Who knew what quote she'd blast me with at this hour?

Ursula called me instead. "Hi. Myriam's making popcorn. We're about to watch a documentary on PBS. What's going on?"

I'd never thought Myriam would watch television. Actually, I never thought about what she did outside of torturing me and working at Braxton. Did she have a personal life where she did normal things? "I spent some time with Cheney this evening. Our suspicions were correct. He is your nephew."

There was a long moment of silence on the phone. "I have to talk with him. He's family."

"I wouldn't do that yet," I cautioned Ursula. "He's a troubled kid." Although he was twenty-five years old, he seemed a lot younger. Perhaps all the misfortune he'd gotten into and his immature attitude and actions made it feel that way. I relayed everything I'd learned about Cheney. "I don't think Doug is aware Cheney isn't his son. Sierra is a wild card. Karen might be lying to you about not wanting to kill George."

"Do you believe one of them killed my brother?" she asked.

"I think it's highly possible. Karen is the only person I haven't had a one-on-

one conversation with, but you have." I wasn't sure how to move forward next, but Karen definitely hid key information.

"She's wily and talks in circles. Let's think through it overnight. Then we can hatch a plan to confront her tomorrow," Ursula suggested.

"The Mendel flower show starts on Monday. Maybe we'll catch her off-guard while she's trying to get ready for it?" I said before hanging up the phone and preparing for bed. It had been a long day and too many miscellaneous facts had been dropped at my footsteps. I had a strong inclination the answer was buried somewhere in the details of what I'd already learned, but I couldn't connect the dots.

CHAPTER 18

On Sunday morning, Emma and I met my parents at church. My family grew up Catholic, attended weekly mass, and celebrated all the major holidays, but beyond that, we weren't particularly religious. I wasn't sure what I believed anymore, but Emma needed to learn as much about the world as possible. She could make her own decisions about where religion fit into her life once she was old enough.

I suggested a family dinner for Thursday evening since that was also the day of the mayoral election. We could spend the afternoon together and support Nana D once she won. She had to win, I'd convinced myself. Aunt Deirdre would want to see everyone, and I had the biggest surprise of all, assuming Gabriel showed up. I was half convinced he'd take off beforehand, but I had to keep focused.

Emma went home with my parents for a few hours. She wanted to select new perennials for their flower garden. Since I was planning to confront Karen Stoddard at some point that day, I was more than happy to let my daughter spend some quality time with her grandparents.

When I arrived at the Pick-Me-Up Diner, Eleanor was chatting with Connor. I was meeting Ursula and Myriam for brunch to discuss everything we'd learned the day before. I waved to them and took a seat across from my two bosses. "Morning, ladies. Are you as starving as I am? Chef Manny makes the best Belgian waffles covered in real maple syrup and—"

"A diabetic coma? How lovely for you, Mr. Ayrwick," Myriam blasted. "My wife has learned she has a long-lost nephew, her family's antique knife was used to kill her brother, and her entire sordid past is about to become a public relations nightmare. And the only thing you can bring up is food! Well, I've got news for you, you *poisonous bunch-backed toad*—"

"M, please don't overreact. Kellan was simply—" Ursula attempted to squelch the battle of puns about to be unleashed, but it was unsuccessful once another of Myriam's humorous tirades interrupted.

"*'He hath eaten me out of house and home, he hath put all my substance into that fat belly of his.'* The man is truly a selfish and useless waste of space on our campus, my darling. How do you continue to put up with him?" Myriam exploded with pent-up frustration.

"Oh, Myriam. That's the second quote this week from Henry IV. I thought you were more careful than that with your invectives," I replied, suppressing a desire to gloat with a song and dance.

"Stop antagonizing her, she only responds with more—" Ursula warned.

"At least I know what plays the lines come from, *thou elvish-mark'd, abortive, rooting hog! You boil, a plague sore on my—*" Myriam shouted.

"As opposed to saying something original? Are you incapable of insulting me with your own fresh barbs? Must you always use five-hundred-year-old phrases that make you sound just as antiquated?" Oops, I might have gone a little too far. She was my boss after all.

"Enough!" Ursula screamed at the top of her lungs. Complete silence suddenly overtook the diner. Every patron in the place turned to look at our table.

When I looked at Myriam, she nodded. "Sorry folks," I announced to the room. "We're rehearsing lines from this summer's upcoming theatre production at Paddington's Play House. We got carried away with our love of the script."

"Please come check it out, we're looking forward to seeing everyone there," Myriam added. Knives and forks scraped plates again, giving my table a chance to calm down.

"Are you two finished?" Ursula reprimanded us. "I ought to fire you both."

We both looked at Ursula, lowering our glasses to the tip of our noses. Myriam spoke first. "Doubtful, my darling. You love me too much."

Ten minutes later, we agreed Ed Mulligan hid something, Anita Singh behaved strangely, and that it was my turn to push Karen for answers. If Ursula approached the former assistant from her parents' laboratory about Cheney being Hans's son, it might prevent us from learning anything else.

"I'll talk to her about the flower show and transition into her relationship with your brother. If she doesn't tell me exactly how and when she reconnected with him again or what he was up to, then I'll spring the truth on her." I dug into my Belgian waffles. They were so delicious, I even offered a piece to Myriam. She declined with only a frown. I wanted to tell her that frowning caused wrinkles, but I promised Ursula I'd be on better behavior mode.

"Meaning?" Ursula asked for clarification.

"I'll tell her I'm aware Doug isn't Cheney's father and that I'll inform the police if she doesn't fess up about Hans's ultimate motives."

"But you already told the police," Ursula countered.

"Karen doesn't know that, dear," Myriam said. "Keep up with us now."

Ursula shot her wife a look that sent a chill through my body. Those two

531

were a formidable match, and I could only imagine what kind of power struggles happened in their house.

"April isn't going to talk to her until she has all her ducks in a row," I reminded Ursula and Myriam as they left the diner. "I'll update you afterward."

"I'll also call Anita Singh and Ed Mulligan into my office today to find out what's going on between them," Ursula replied.

Before leaving, I stopped by Eleanor's office to check on her and Connor. "Hey, kids. What's going on? Brunch was delicious."

"That was quite a scene you caused earlier," Connor jested as he stood and shook my hand. "You really ought to be acting in those productions on campus."

"Oscar-worthy, huh?"

He nodded. "Are we still meeting at the gym tomorrow before your classes?"

"Yes," I confirmed. I planned to attend the flower show in the afternoon, so we'd agreed to an eight o'clock morning workout. "Anything new from your bestie on the George Braun murder?"

Connor shook his head. "Nah, nothing April's shared recently." He attempted a smile in Eleanor's direction, but it was an awkward one given he didn't want to mention anything in front of my sister about Maggie or her family.

"I'm sure Helena will get bail tomorrow," Eleanor said. She opted to be the brave one and not hide behind the elephant in the room. "You can talk about Maggie, guys. We're all adults."

"Just being careful," I said looking at Connor's relaxed reaction.

"I've got something to discuss with you tomorrow at the gym, Kellan. It's important," Connor said as he stood. "But I need to do my rounds on campus right now. I'll see you all soon." He glanced at me, then at Eleanor deciding what to do. Eventually, he kissed my sister's cheek and left the diner.

"Phew, that was fun. He must be such a romantic, it goes directly over my head!" I said.

"You can be a nuisance sometimes!" Eleanor scolded me and left her office to check on the main dining room.

I drove downtown to the Simply Stoddard catering offices. Karen had been avoiding me all week. Sunday brunch was a memorable event in Braxton, she had to be onsite helping her husband run the new restaurant. When I walked into the main vestibule, a hostess greeted me and asked how many members in my party.

"None. What happened to Cheney?" I thought he was usually at the front desk. Maybe his hangover prevented him from working today.

"He just fills in during the week on occasion. I'm the hostess most nights and weekends. How can I help you?"

"Are Doug and Karen around?" I asked the young woman, noticing her solid hospitality skills.

She pointed to the door on my right. "Karen is working in the office over there. Doug is in the kitchen cooking. I think Sierra is helping her father today. Cheney was supposed to stop in, but he wasn't feeling well."

I smiled and thanked her. She greeted a couple who'd walked in behind me while I pushed open the door to Simply Stoddard's catering offices and called out for Karen.

"May I help you?" she said, standing from behind the desk. When I came into view, she looked upset. "Oh, Kellan. I know you left a few messages. It's been unexpectedly crazy around here lately."

"I've heard. I ran into your daughter, Sierra, yesterday."

"I'm actually quite busy right now. Maybe we could make an appointment for next week if you need to plan an event." She sat back down and moved the mouse. Her computer screen lit up, but I couldn't see what was on it from the other side of the desk.

"I had a few questions for you. Surely, you can spare a few minutes for me right now. Maggie and Millard have said nothing but wonderful things about working with you." I wasn't lying, both had praised the work Simply Stoddard had done for them.

"Look, I don't mean to be rude, but you got my son drunk yesterday. You've been asking questions about us all around town. People talk a lot about how you like to get involved in private situations you don't belong in. I don't have time for idle gossip or manufactured small-town drama." She waved her hand at the door, indicating I should leave.

"Now I see where Cheney gets his customer service skills." I wasn't going to debate my involvement in other people's situations, but I was always asked to do the investigation. "I'll consider leaving if you give me the name of one person who said anything negative about me."

"I'll give you two, then maybe I can also skip our second meeting." She didn't bother to look up as she typed away on the keyboard. "Ophelia Taft and Myriam Castle. Goodbye."

Ophelia, I could understand. I had words with the woman a few times while determining if she had something to do with her mother's death earlier that year. Myriam would disparage me on most occasions, but she wouldn't have done it while I helped her wife. "When and what did Myriam say?"

"Myriam contacted me to plan a cast party for a recent show. Probably a month ago, but she ultimately decided not to spend the money. She mentioned I should ignore anything you brought up, but you and I've never had the pleasure of meeting. Is that all?"

I knew it wasn't recent. Myriam must have been excluding me from the *King Lear* celebration at one point in time. I'd ultimately convinced her to hold the cast party at the Pick-Me-Up Diner, which is why she never went with Simply Stoddard. "Fine, we can play it this way. I'll take my questions about George Braun being Cheney's biological father to Sheriff Montague. Have a good day, Lambertson."

I turned and walked back into the vestibule, then tried to leave the building. Karen called out, but I ignored her. She finally rushed from the office, grabbed my arm as I stepped into the outdoor patio, and dragged me back to the desk. "On second thought, now might be a fine time for us to chat, Kellan. How did you know my maiden name was Lambertson?"

"A mutual friend told me. How kind of you to consider sticking around right now. I'll be sure to remember the best way to motivate you in the future, that is, assuming you don't end up in prison for killing Hans Mück." Karen responded to threats, which meant the more I could frighten her, the more she might consent to tell me everything she knew.

"What exactly do you know?" she asked. Most of her face blanched white, but her cheeks brightened like two shiny red delicious apples when I said the name Hans Mück.

"No, I'm in the driver's seat right now. If only you'd been more open-minded in the beginning, we could've had a quiet, civilized conversation about the past." I took a seat across from her, rested my right foot and leg on my left knee and put my hands behind my neck. "Tell me whatever you'd like. I'll give you a few hints. You already know I'm close with the Roarke family and that Helena didn't kill him. I work for Ursula Power, who's shared her past as Sofia Mück. She also didn't kill her brother."

"I didn't kill him either!" Karen snarled.

"Maybe someone in your family murdered him. The sheriff will figure it out eventually, but I'm giving you this opportunity to help me help you. If we can work with each other, everyone could come out of this disaster without getting further singed."

"Fine! The Mücks hired me to work in their lab right after I graduated from college. I was fascinated by their research and spent a lot of time with their son, Hans. I'd been helping them with a bunch of experiments, mostly documenting results each night and early morning."

"That explains Doug's slip last week about you working late nights."

She nodded. "Hans flirted with me. He was smart and worldly. I fell in love, but he was too focused on making a name for himself. I'd met Doug one night at a bar. He paid a lot of attention to me, and I threw myself at him. Next thing I know, Hans asked for my help to fudge test results at the lab. I didn't want to do it, but he told me once he got famous, he wanted to marry me and travel the world."

"Hans took advantage of you," I said. It had happened more often than people realized. "But you didn't know it at the time."

"Exactly. He would sneak breaks with me to hold my hand or make out with me in the closet. I thought he was serious. Then he asked me to switch some chemicals to invalidate his parents' experiments. He was running the same experiments but with excessive amounts of glycerine and other fertilizers. He had me buy and store substantial amounts of it in the lab. I'd no idea someone would purposely create a fire that day."

A pit began to deepen in my gut. Ursula thought she was only creating a small boom to stop Hans from hurting their parents. "You caused the explosion that killed him."

Karen threw her head against the desk and began crying. "Yes, it was my fault."

Ursula didn't know about this part. "You need to tell me everything right now.

Karen continued to explain what'd happened twenty-five years ago. She'd kept all the Mücks accurate results in a separate file cabinet. Hans didn't want them to leave the lab, but he also didn't want anyone to know about what he was doing.

"I thought Hans died in that explosion for the last twenty-five years. Once his sister told me what she had done, I realized I was to blame but couldn't tell the police. So, I leaked it to the press that she had caused the explosion and destroyed all the results. They were close to finding a cure for certain forms of cancer."

"What happened next?" I shook my head at the damage Hans Mück had caused over the years.

"A few weeks later, I found out I was pregnant. Once I knew the timing, I figured out Hans was probably my baby's father, but he was gone. I liked Doug well enough, so I told him he'd gotten me pregnant. It was only a few weeks difference, he didn't think to ask questions."

At that point, Karen left Sofia alone because she had to move on. Sofia ran away and became Ursula Power. Karen moved around the Midwest with Doug, had Sierra a few years later, and pretended the past never happened.

"I loved working with plants and flowers, running laboratories, and being part of something complex and challenging. I eventually got into planning medical conferences and fundraisers. When my daughter, Sierra, chose to attend law school in London, I visited her more often and even accepted a couple of event planning jobs over there. That's how I ran into Hans. He'd been running the Mendel flower show in Europe and planned to take it to the United States at some point." Karen explained that Hans had earned a name for himself as George Braun, a botanist who taught at various medical schools and colleges. He'd still been trying to recreate the experiments from years ago, but he never could find the right balance of all the formulas and inputs. He believed his sister would remember them.

"How did you end up getting to Braxton?" I asked, feeling unclear how it brought everyone to my hometown.

"I wanted to confess the truth, but he seemed so different. I decided not to tell Hans about Cheney until I got to know him a little better again. Hans, going by the name George at that time, pressured me to remember as much as I could about the experiments, but it wasn't enough. I went back home and would occasionally talk to him on the phone." At that point, Karen wasn't sure how it had happened, but George told her he'd found his sister again. She was living in Braxton, Pennsylvania, and he'd asked Karen to move to Braxton and help him rediscover the cure again.

"Now I understand how you got to Braxton, but what does Doug know?"

"Doug knows nothing about this. I convinced him we could start over here.

That's when we decided to open the restaurant for him to focus on, and I set up the event management company."

"Is it real, or a cover to help George?"

"Completely legitimate. My company helped George coordinate and transition the Mendel flower show to the United States. He was using all the plants in his experiments to find a cure."

"Why did you agree to help him after all these years?"

"At first, it was because Doug and I were having problems. Cheney had gotten into some legal troubles back in Chicago. Doug and I were thinking about splitting up. I thought I had a chance with Hans again. After we got situated in Braxton, Hans and I grew close. I told him I never stopped loving him and that..." she paused and stood behind the desk.

"What?"

Karen was panicking about something. "Is someone there?" She rushed past me and into the vestibule. When she came back in, she looked frightened.

"Was someone listening?"

Karen shook her head. "No one was out there, but I saw a shadow."

"Maybe it was the hostess or a patron walking in." I waited for Karen to sit again.

"I might be nervous. My family doesn't know about all of this." Karen continued to explain what'd happened after she updated Hans about Cheney being his son. "He told me he couldn't think about it until after he found a way to compel his sister to remember everything about the experiments.

"Did you help him stalk Ursula? Or Sofia... however he referred to her."

Karen nodded. "In the beginning, I collected information about her and dropped off a couple of notes. I thought if I could push his plan along, we'd be finished sooner. Then he and I could be together."

"What stopped it from happening?"

"He'd broken into his sister's office and realized she'd created a whole new life for herself and had forgotten about him. Hans was angry that his sister had disfigured him. He wanted revenge."

"Was he going to kill her?"

"I was afraid he might. That's when I stopped helping him and tried to ignore him. But he wouldn't let me. He blackmailed me."

"That he'd tell Doug and Cheney the truth?" I asked.

"Yes." We sat in silence for a few minutes while I debated my next move.

"Karen, did you kill him?"

"No, I told you I didn't. He kept forcing me to do things right up until the end.

"Like drop that final note off for Ursula at the costume extravaganza?" I asked.

"Exactly. I finally told him that was the last thing I'd do. He confirmed he wouldn't need my help after that night anymore."

"Why not?" I asked.

"He showed me a knife. He was going to kill his sister after he got the formulas out of her." Karen explained that Hans had followed Helena into the private employee offices to find a quiet place to bring Ursula once he confronted her at nine o'clock. Unfortunately, Cheney snuck back there delaying Hans from returning to the main room, ultimately giving the killer an opportunity to strike.

Everything had finally fallen into place. Except understanding who killed him. I realized at that moment Karen didn't know Cheney had learned the truth. "Your son confronted Hans that night."

"I know. He was upset about the way Helena had been treated at her family's inn."

"No," I said shaking my head. "Cheney overheard you and Hans talking about your past together. He knew the truth and tried to bond with his father." I updated Karen with everything Cheney had told me at the bar.

Karen was overwhelmed. "Cheney might have provoked him, but my son wouldn't kill him."

At that moment, Sierra poked her head in the office. "Mom, do you know where Dad is? The sous chef is holding the entire kitchen down, but he needs help." When she saw me sitting across from her mother, she froze. "What are you doing here? I told you not to bother my family anymore."

Karen looked back and forth between me and her daughter, deciding what to do or say. "Kellan, I need to put out a couple of fires. Can we finish this conversation later or tomorrow?"

Although I was concerned we might lose momentum if I let her go, she had a restaurant to run. I also needed to update April on what I'd just learned. "Sure, but you know this conversation needs to be held with someone else, right?"

"As soon as I locate my husband and talk to my son. That's my priority right now. Goodbye, Kellan." Karen pushed us out of the office and into the vestibule. She locked the door and told the hostess not to let anyone inside again. "Sierra, let's get the kitchen organized before I find your father."

When they disappeared, I walked to the parking lot. Had Doug overheard our conversation and left the restaurant? Based on what Karen told me, her entire family had good reason to murder Hans Mück. Which one actually did it? I put a call into the sheriff's office, but Officer Flatman informed me she was on an international line. He was not able to comment on whether she'd found out when Sierra Stoddard arrived in Braxton, but he'd tell Sheriff Montague I urgently needed to speak with her.

CHAPTER 19

On the drive to the farmhouse, I updated Maggie with my progress on the case. I couldn't tell her about Ursula's involvement, but I mentioned the Stoddards had a past connection with George Braun. "I'm not sure what it all means. It could depend on when Sierra Stoddard arrived in Braxton."

"I don't know exactly when she flew here, but she was back by the costume extravaganza. Karen asked me if her daughter could stop by that night. She even had time to rent a costume. I think she was some sort of nurse. I guess that's a hero, but there was a patch over her eye."

"Dancing with my cousin, Alex!" It suddenly smacked me upside the head why Sierra had seemed familiar. "You've been such a help, you can't even imagine."

"Do you think Sierra had something to do with George's death? She wasn't supposed to be at the party. It was a last-minute request, Kellan. I was shocked she got the costume from the shop. Dot told me she practically sold out after I recommended her place to all the guests to choose between a hero and a villain."

"I'm not sure, but she might know something she hasn't shared with anyone." I told Maggie I needed to hang up and make another call. I tried to reach Alex, but his phone went directly to voicemail. I sent him a text message and called his assistant. He was affiliated with the Wharton County General Hospital and often turned off his cell phone if he was in surgery.

While driving home, I tried to piece together what I knew about Sierra. She'd been skiing in Switzerland, she'd come home in time to attend the costume extravaganza, and she was fiercely protective of her family. Yuri had told us she overheard George fighting with a woman about something not being his fault. George was married, but the sheriff couldn't track down the name of his wife. Could it be Sierra Stoddard? Had George gotten mixed up with Sierra in Europe which was how he subsequently ran into Karen again?

I arrived at Danby Landing excited to see my daughter but desperate to learn anything my cousin, Alex, knew about Sierra. I knocked on Nana D's door and entered the living room expecting to see my grandmother and my daughter reading or working on a puzzle.

"We're in the kitchen cleaning up, brilliant one," Nana D called out. "Guess who's here!"

I wasn't in the mood for those kinds of games right now. "My parents?" I knew Eleanor was working at the diner. Who else could it be? I found out when I slithered into the kitchen.

"Kellan, you look amazing!" Aunt Deirdre shouted while looking up from the counter. She must've forgotten she was drying a sharp knife. Her hand slipped, and a pool of red welled up leaving a bloody trail down her sleeve. "Ouchhh!"

Emma screeched and covered her eyes. She didn't like the sight of blood and was known to faint upon seeing any. Nana D said, "Kellan, check on your aunt. I'll go to Emma."

"Raise your hand above your head." I rushed to Aunt Deirdre and covered her wound with the towel. I also wasn't thrilled to see blood but had to see how deep the cut was. "Let me take a peek."

As I glanced at the situation, Deirdre laughed. "I'm such a klutz. Bollocks! It's all over the brand-new blouse I bought with Lissette at the airport yesterday." While her finger looked tender and cut up, she didn't appear to need stitches.

"I think if we put a butterfly bandage on it and wrap the wound tightly, you'll be fine," I said.

Once Emma calmed down, Nana D took Aunt Deirdre to the bathroom to attend to her injury. I breathed a deep sigh of relief followed by one of the biggest *aha* moments I'd ever had.

April had shared with me that George was stabbed twice. If his killer pulled the knife out of his body to stab him again, blood had to have splashed on the killer. It was a costume extravaganza, everyone dressed up—even the servers rented costumes for the night. If there was blood on the killer's costume, the store might inadvertently know who murdered George Braun.

I called the costume shop, but they were closed for the evening. It was after eight o'clock on a Sunday, of course, they'd be closed when I needed them most. I left a message to call me back the next morning as soon as they could.

Once Aunt Deirdre was all patched up, we sampled an apple pie Emma and Nana D had baked earlier that day. Deirdre explained that Lissette had traveled all the way to her sister's place only to find out she'd passed away two days before. Since Judy was new in the small town where she stayed, no one knew who her family was, to inform them about her death. Lissette was heartbroken and begged Aunt Deirdre to meet her at a London airport, so she had someone to fly home with. They'd only arrived in Braxton that afternoon, but Aunt Deirdre would check on her friend again soon. As I said, it was always funerals and weddings that brought her home to Braxton. No one was getting married that she knew, so I counted this as a visit for a funeral. Lissette would be arranging services for her sister in the near future at their family funeral home.

I took Emma home and tucked her in bed since she had school the following day. When I went back to my bedroom, I checked my phone. Fern Terry sent me a text message that I'd dropped a piece of mail near her the other day when we met up in the student union building. I had a postcard from someone in Savannah, Georgia which she'd give to me on Monday. For now, she sent a screenshot of the front picture and back message:

You wanted to move here after a trip to the hostess city of the South. Imagine what that would have been like for Emma to grow up in the grand world of antebellum style. Too bad you broke your ankle and couldn't stay the whole week to experience the possibilities. Maybe another trip without so much pain is the answer.

Savannah was a gorgeous city, and I wanted to move there at one point. I preferred more humid climates and missed Los Angeles weather. But Francesca was mistaken again. I'd broken my ankle at the airport on the day we left Savannah. It didn't interrupt our trip at all. Maybe the flight home was worse than usual given I was doped up on painkillers the whole five hours. Had she confused another one of our trips? It didn't make sense, but other messages were more important at the moment.

Alex left me a voicemail stating he'd only met the girl at the costume extravaganza. Her name was Sierra, they'd spoken about her visiting her parents for a few days and that she lived in London. When I called him back, he was on rounds and had to keep it quick. "Nope, I danced with her twice. She talked to a few other people. Honestly, don't recall who."

"Did you ever see her enter the private office area?" I asked my cousin.

"I don't know. Right after you came running by us, she excused herself to go to the ladies' room. I never saw her again that night."

"What was her costume? A nurse?"

"Yes, she was Elle Driver from the movie, *Kill Bill*. Remember the evil nurse Daryl Hannah played?" Alex had to visit with a patient and hung up after mentioning a day to have dinner next week.

At least I'd learned from my cousin what Sierra's costume was and that she'd disappeared just before George had been stabbed. Could she have left the event because she had blood on her costume?

Sheriff Montague had also left me a message that she'd been following up on the leads for George Braun's wife and would connect with me in the morning to discuss whatever I'd learned that night from my discussion with Karen Stoddard.

Despite an early bedtime, I slept poorly given everything on my mind.

Visions of Francesca chasing me around Braxton plagued my dreams. Every time I'd try to catch her, she'd vanish into thin air. At another point during the night, I was tied to a pole while four women in masks chanted in a circle. One by one, each removed her mask. Myriam, April, Sierra, and Karen were casting spells to torture me. Shortly before I woke up, a mysterious shadowed figure kept plunging a knife in my gut. I'd come back to life each time, and just as I was about to open the door to see who killed Hans, I'd die again. Maybe Eleanor would be able to interpret it all because I certainly couldn't.

After dropping Emma at school the next morning, I met Connor at the gym for an hour of weights, then checked in with Maggie. Helena was Judge Grey's first case of the day. "Is she ready?"

Maggie sighed. "I couldn't talk with her yesterday. She was only allowed to meet with Finnigan. He said she's been cooperating with him."

"I wish I could be there, but I've got class. Then I'm heading over to the costume shop you told me about. If the killer got blood on his or her costume, we might be able to solve this more quickly." I knew we were getting closer, but it wasn't far enough for me to slow down and let the sheriff handle it on her own. My curiosities were aroused, and there was little chance of this dog letting go of his bone.

After Maggie and I hung up, I chatted with Ursula and Myriam. They were having coffee in Ursula's office before the day got too busy. Ursula said, "I met with Dean Mulligan. I expected better of the man, but it seems retirement should be looming for him next semester."

Ursula explained that Dean Mulligan had developed a crush on Dr. Anita Singh over the last year. Both had been single and weren't too far apart in age, but he knew, as her boss, nothing could happen between them. Anita begged him not to hire George. She'd known of the man's ruthless and underhanded schemes from various international science conferences. Mulligan had already signed the contract and had to play arbiter between them for weeks. George later discovered Mulligan's secret crush and tried to extort more money from him for the Mendel flower show and his own personal experiments. The dean refused at first, but to protect Anita from any backlash, he'd ultimately given in. He'd confronted George at the Roarke & Daughters Inn the afternoon of the costume extravaganza, which is what Yuri overheard and used to get favors from the dean. When it didn't work, she'd exaggerated the story to get even with Dean Mulligan.

"It's all very childish. It doesn't explain why the dean's costume was so disheveled later in the evening," I noted. What had the dean done to Anita?

Myriam hooted. "I can explain that. His Zeus getup consisted of a rather large Greek robe. Each time the man used the restroom, he needed to pull the whole thing off. It just never got put on the same way again. What a fool!"

While Myriam made sense, it clearly pointed out a silly mistake I should've realized myself. "That leaves us with figuring out what Anita Singh's hiding."

"Pish! I know Anita, and she's much too gentle to stab someone. I'm now

541

leaning toward Sierra Stoddard. She has a motive, and I think she had the opportunity," Myriam retorted.

"The timing is really tight, but she could've snuck into the courtyard right after I saw her on the dance floor and stayed in hiding until Cheney and Helena left," I said.

"I was too busy telling you all about the note I'd found. I didn't pay attention to anyone walking through the double doors to the private offices while we were behind the silk draperies," Ursula reasoned out. What came out of your discussion with Karen?"

"She hasn't gotten back to me. I suspect she and Doug are getting their stories straight, or she's avoiding me until I force the issue again," I explained. Ursula wanted to talk with Cheney, but I convinced her to wait until we found out who killed her brother. She could already be in a dangerous position because of him.

I left to teach my two-hour class for the morning, then grabbed a snack bar out of the vending machine. There was no time to waste on lunch. Maggie texted that Judge Grey was delayed, and Helena would see him at one thirty. Finnigan had gotten additional information from Detective Gilkrist about a new lead the sheriff was on top of. Maggie didn't know if it hurt or helped her sister's case. April still hadn't returned my second call from the night before. I wanted to text her, but we really weren't close enough that it felt appropriate to blur the lines between us.

I hightailed it to the costume shop on the town border in Woodland. The costume shop hadn't called, but an emergency to them and an emergency to me were probably two different things. I parked the SUV and climbed down a few steps to the garden-level floor of a brownstone building.

I walked through the door, noticing dozens of mannequins artfully arranged in scenes. Each held a sign describing the type of costumes and which floor and section to find them in. The building had five floors and was divided into four quadrants or rooms on each one. In the lower garden-level were steps going up to the second floor and another door leading to the cellar. They probably kept all the returned costumes in the basement either to be cleaned on premises or sent out to a separate facility.

There were two other patrons nearby. One was flipping through a book in the front parlor, another was talking to an older woman wearing a tie-dyed dress and light-colored wrap around her shoulders. She had a peace sign tattoo on her left wrist. When the guest left, I marched to the counter, introduced myself, and asked if she'd listened to my voicemail.

"I haven't been able to return any messages today. My new girl didn't show up, and Mondays are always rough. People need to chill like we did in the sixties," she mumbled and huffed.

"Does that mean you have an answer for me or no?" I said with a scrunched-up face.

"You asked about a Tarzan costume for a weekend getaway? Lay it on me, dude." The woman had a name tag pinned to her waist that caught my attention as she flowed from side to side in a daze.

Was she on the wacky stuff right now? "Ummm... no. I called about all the costumes that were returned from Braxton's Memorial Library extravaganza." I was, however, curious who called about the Tarzan costume. I would never show that much skin, but more power to someone who felt comfortable in their skivvies in front of the entire world. "Listen, Dot, this is really important. I need to know if a certain costume was returned."

"All my customers are important. What's your bag, man? This shop is my pride and joy. I take my job very seriously, and I make sure I do everything I can to help them out." She caught her ring on the wrap and spent thirty seconds trying to remove it. "Well, ain't this a gas!"

When desperate exasperation bubbled inside me, I reached over to help her. "Let me." After it came loose, we laughed about the chances of it happening again. I really didn't care, but I knew I needed to be as sweet as pie. Not only would Nana D whack me upside the head for treating one of my elders poorly, she passionately believed you got more answers by being kind. And with this hippie, I'd have to be extra patient. "Could you tell me if someone returned a costume with a stain? Something red all over the front."

"Like pasta sauce?"

"Not exactly." I shook my head. I felt a headache coming on.

"Red wine stains are the hardest to get out. My momma taught me a trick years ago. Hydrogen peroxide with..." she said with unbridled gusto before pausing to remember what she meant to say.

"No, but I appreciate the tip. Something a bit stickier. Trust me, you'd probably know the costume if I described the stain." Please don't make me tell you it's blood. No store owner wants to find out someone bled on one of their garments.

"We could try that approach, but I can't give names out. I respect my customer's privacy. The fuzz don't like it when I talk." She reached behind her to grab a clipboard. "The law clearly states—"

"Dot, I need you to work with me here. I understand you have privacy concerns. If we need to have the sheriff ask the questions, I'll get hold of her right now." I knew that probably wouldn't work, but I had to take a chance Dot wouldn't challenge me. I painfully curled my toes inside my shoes until I felt the seams begin to separate.

"Don't get your knickers in a twist, boy." She closed the book and sipped from her cup of herbal tea. "Tell me again. What did this costume look like?"

Okay, maybe we were getting somewhere finally. I explained what I could from memory. I flipped through the ten pictures Maggie had given me a copy of, but there were none of Sierra in the white nurse's uniform. I described the patch and the shape of the dress, but not until I said it was from the *Kill Bill* movie did Dot know which one I meant.

"Yeah! Elle Driver. She's a popular Halloween rental. I've seen that movie five times. Much prefer Uma Thurman's yellow leather and spandex costume, you know what I mean. No foam domes hiding in that chick's costume!" She clicked a button on the keyboard and searched for *The Bride* costume Uma Thurman had worn. "Here we go."

"No, that's not what I want."

"Are you sure? It's a great costume. Although, you might not fit in it with those broad shoulders. What size coat do you wear? Forty, Forty-two?" Dot was falling into that category of older women who flirted with me too much. We were also getting nowhere on this midday train to crazy.

"Let's try this again. White nurse costume. Eye patch. Was it returned with a red stain?" My face must have turned redder than the strawberry stickers on Dot's cheeks.

"Is that all you needed to know?" She clicked another button on her screen. "You really should've asked that the first time. You need to hang loose a little more, sir."

"I'm not a sir! I'm only thirty-two." I pulled my bottom lip into my mouth and crunched down hard. Dot was doing her best. I needed to have patience. "Did you find it?"

"Oh, I didn't need to look that one up. It was returned the next day. Cleaned it up quick and sent it back out two days later for another party. Lickety-split!"

"Did it have a stain?" I asked.

"I just told you I sent it right back out, sir. Do you think I'd give it to someone else with a stain on it? We're the top costume shop in all of Wharton County. That ain't no way to do business. Definitely no stains on that costume." She turned to a new customer who'd entered the store. "Be with ya in a jiffy, hon. Almost done teaching this young kid how we operate around here."

This was useless. Could the killer have worn the lab coat to protect their costume from getting blood on it? That would mean it was premeditated murder, but April thought this crime happened unexpectedly. No one would choose to murder somebody in a place with a huge crowd. I needed to have Sheriff Montague question Dot, maybe put a little fear into her so we'd get better answers. "I was kinda hoping you told me that costume had a stain on it. It would have made my life a lot easier."

"I'm not rightly sure why you want a stained nurse costume, but to each his own." She smacked her hand on the counter and laughed. "My ex-husband used to tell me people were fickle when—"

"Thank you for your help." Maybe Nana D would've gotten the answer instead of me. These two would have gotten along famously.

"You're welcome. That costume extravaganza made this month our best sales record in a while. Peace out!" She smiled at me and left the counter holding two fingers in a V-shape as we walked to the front door.

"I'm glad you're doing so well," I said, finally remembering my manners. I'd only been distracted by my desire to find a murderer. Definitely not important. I slapped my head and began to leave.

"Yesiree. And we only had one item that never got returned. That was quite a shame, too. Had to keep the deposit. It was a costume we'd just started selling on the one-hundredth anniversary of the person's death." Dot yelled back to the other patron that she'd be right with her.

"Why didn't the customer return it?" It was a long shot, but Dot might surprise me.

"The renter told me the costume just vanished. I don't know how a costume gets up and splits on its own, but at least I got my money to buy a new one." She pulled the door open and waved as I stepped through the threshold.

"Wait, Dot, can you tell me the customer's name?" Please let this be the lead I need.

"Didn't you hear me earlier? I got to keep customer data private. The fuzz man, the fuzz!"

"Right, you mentioned that," I growled.

"But I'm sure there's no harm in showing you a picture of the costume, right?" She winked and waved me back in. "I kinda like you. It'd be a shame to send away an unhappy handsome customer."

She brought me back inside the store and flipped through a few screens on her computer. When she stopped on the one she wanted to show me, she cheered. "Great Mother Earth! I found it."

I gaped at the screen in complete disbelief. I knew who'd worn that costume, but I couldn't make heads or tails of why the person would kill George Braun or Hans Mück. "Thank you, Dot. You've just made me a very curious man." Maybe it was a coincidence?

* * *

As soon as I got back in the SUV, I called my brother. Gabriel picked up on the second ring. "Hey, great news! Millard hired me to help him with the rest of the flower exhibit and wants me to come work for him on the landscaping over at the Paddington estate."

"That's awesome. I can't wait to hear all about it. I need to ask you an important question." I wasn't sure if he'd remember, but I had to give it a shot.

"Sure, go ahead. We can chat later about my new job."

I loaded up the ten photos Maggie had shared with me. "You told me you briefly met the other person who interviewed for the job with George Braun. I know Cheney was hoping to do the cabin renovation, but it was someone different who wanted to work on the flower exhibit, right?"

"Yeah. George said the other candidate was very annoying and had ulterior motives."

I texted Gabriel all the photos. "Are any of these the person who interviewed with George?"

Gabriel took a few seconds to respond. "It's hard to be certain with that costume, but I think it's that first photo. I only got a brief glimpse when I left the interview at who talked with George next."

"One more question. Did George ever say anything about having a wife?"

I'd never thought to ask Gabriel that question when he told me about his work with the man.

"He shared very little about his personal life, but he did mention being married at one point. Are you going somewhere with this, Kellan? I'm not sure I understand all the questions."

"I'll explain everything later. Did he say his wife's name or what happened to her?" Things were coming together, but I had a couple of pieces that didn't quite fit into the puzzle.

"You know, I'm sure he mentioned she passed away a little while ago. Never got her name."

I hung up with Gabriel after telling him I might need his help with something else. What a fool I'd been! The answer was right in front of me the whole time. I needed to find the proof. The culprit was extraordinarily clever and had built an elaborate ruse to provide the perfect alibi. There was only one other person who might be able to bang the final nail into the coffin. Time to make another phone call!

CHAPTER 20

"Hi, brilliant one. Did you need me to pick up Emma today? You were supposed to let me know earlier," Nana D said.

"Yes, that's exactly why I was calling. Well, that and another reason too."

"Sure, I'll get Emma when she's done with school. What else can I do to help?" Nana D was hands-down the best grandmother in the world. I could count on her at the last minute for almost anything. I asked Nana D to put my aunt on the phone.

When she picked up, she said, "Hello, Kellan. What's going on?"

"Aunt Deirdre, I have a weird question for you. But first, how's your finger?"

"Those are the best kind of questions, sweetheart," she said with a boisterous laugh. "It's healing, thanks to your quick thinking."

"Great! Now for the odd question. When did Lissette Nutberry find out her sister, Judy, died?" I knew something was off with the timing but needed to prove it.

"A couple of days before we flew home, I don't remember the exact time. Is it important?"

"Not the specific time. Are you sure Judy Nutberry only died a few days ago?"

"That's what Lissette told me. It's why I rushed back here with her. I wasn't planning to come for a visit until next month. It's changed all my plans and nearly ruined the surprise I have for all of you."

Surprise? I couldn't get distracted right now. "Where was she before she met you in London?"

"Switzerland, I'm sure about that. I waited with her at customs and immigration when we arrived in the States," Aunt Deirdre replied. "I also noticed her passport stamp."

"I knew it. There's a connection between her and George Braun." What was their relationship?

"It was odd. I didn't go up to the booth with her since we're not family. I thought I heard the man behind the counter ask Lissette if she often traveled to Switzerland for work. Apparently, she'd already been in and out of the country a few times this year."

Bingo! Lissette had claimed not to know where her sister was living. She lied. "Thank you. You're the best aunt in the world. Do me a favor, don't tell her about this conversation. It's important."

"Okay, but I'm heading over to the college campus to meet her for the opening of the Mendel flower show today. I hope I don't forget and accidentally say something, Kellan. You know me, I get caught up in my book ideas and next thing I know, I prattle on—"

"Please stay home today. I think something terrible has happened." I hung up the phone after extracting a promise from my aunt that she'd keep her lips zipped or fake a stroke if she couldn't stop herself from babbling.

I had to try reaching the sheriff again. After Officer Flatman transferred me, April picked up the phone. "You are pushing your luck, Little Ayrwick. I am trying to solve a murder case and couldn't call you back until this afternoon."

"I think I've unintentionally solved it for you, April." I covered everything I'd learned including my discussion with Dot at the costume shop, my conversations with Gabriel and Aunt Deirdre, and the photographs from the library's extravaganza.

"I've been busy myself. I have confirmation on the exact date George's wife passed away. According to the death certificate, Judy Nutberry Braun died of heart failure four weeks ago," April confirmed. "Given what you just told me, Lissette is lying about discovering her sister died only last week. Why would she do that?"

"I have my suspicions, but only Lissette will be able to tell us the truth. I have an idea how to force it out of her. How much do you trust me?"

* * *

Maggie and I had just hung up our call when I arrived at Braxton. Helena had been granted bail, and her parents were paying the necessary ten percent to get her released. After the paperwork was processed, Ben and Lucy Roarke would escort Helena home to shower and get some uninterrupted sleep. Maggie knew Helena would rush off to find Cheney but couldn't stop her sister from doing what her heart told her to do. Maggie wouldn't attend the flower show as she needed to get back to Memorial Library after being absent most of the morning waiting at the courthouse for answers.

The Mendel flower show was held in Cambridge Hall of Sciences on North Campus. Tomorrow was the official opening day of the show, but today there was an invitation-only preview for a select group of Wharton County citizens. Millard Paddington wanted to offer an opportunity to Braxton administration, faculty, and students to attend for free without a massive crowd standing in their way.

Simply Stoddard, Karen's event management company, had handled most of the coordination for the public and press while Millard worked behind the scenes with the botanists and scientists who would be sharing some of their recent research. Gabriel agreed to assist in the back offices even though he was concerned someone might discover his return to Braxton sooner than he preferred. I couldn't tell anyone about the plan to force a confession from Lissette Nutberry, but I required Gabriel's and Karen's help to be successful.

"Kellan, I don't understand why you need to present at today's opening ceremony. Why wasn't I told about this sooner?" Karen asked. We stood in a lecture hall on the second floor of the building preparing the opening address before it was time to allow folks into the show.

"Millard asked me to say a few words to everyone. I won't take too long." Millard had no idea what I wanted to say, but he trusted me and knew I wouldn't have asked him unless I had a solid reason.

After Millard's opening remarks at the ribbon-cutting ceremony, he'd introduce me to those who'd gathered in the main hall. He'd already confirmed with Lissette that she planned to attend given how much she loved flowers and had helped him with a few details before my brother was rehired. I prepared a succinct memorial, a eulogy of sorts, for the late George Braun. I had a few key messages to convey. If everything went according to plan, Lissette wouldn't be able to resist herself.

"That's fine, but you have five minutes. Seven, tops. Everything's been coordinated down to the smallest of details," Karen advised me as if I'd asked her to rearrange the whole schedule. "You might think I'm an awful person for lying about the explosion and the identity of Cheney's real father, but I'm determined to make this event a success."

I told Karen I found her previous actions difficult to accept and that she should apologize to Ursula for everything that had happened. "Cheney is her nephew. She lost her brother and has no family left. Maybe she won't want to reveal her true identity to the world, but I'm certain she won't ignore a blood relation."

Karen shuffled to the main hall to verify everything was ready. I instructed Gabriel on what I needed him to create for me. Then, I called April to verify her team was in place.

"I've got two undercover officers at the front entrance and a couple more stationed throughout the main floor. She has two possible exits, and we'll stop her whichever route she takes," April confirmed. She hadn't been comfortable with my proposal, but the evidence she'd collected to date wasn't enough to arrest Lissette. "We have a fifty-fifty chance of getting her to react today. Be careful you don't ruin any opportunity I have in the future of getting her full confession."

"I understand." As we hung up, I kept repeating the same lines to convince myself our plan would work. I didn't want to shock Ursula and Myriam at the opening ceremony, so I shared the gist of my strategy. They fully supported the approach and would watch for reactions from the room. I hadn't told them we suspected Lissette of killing Ursula's brother, but both knew I was focused on the mysterious wife whom Ursula's brother had left behind.

I found Millard in one of the nearby offices and walked with him to the main hall. Millard waved to Lissette who was chatting with Fern Terry. I wasn't comfortable with the idea of a good friend standing so close to a possible killer, but there was little to be done. About two hundred Braxton College employees and Wharton County citizens had gathered outside the doors brimming with excitement over seeing all the elegant flowers, lush foliage, and brilliant research conducted in the past year. Beyond those doors on the other side of the room was the first exhibit, George's personal unfinished research, on extracting vascular and epidermal tissue from certain flowers to cure diseases.

At the front of the room was a stage raised three feet off the floor. Lined up on either side of the podium was a bevy of pots of various shapes and sizes filled with robust colors and species of flowers. There were common ones most people were familiar with such as roses, tulips, daisies, and lilies, but there were also strange and rare species such as the Kadupul flower from Sri Lanka and candy cane sorrel from South Africa. The marvel of beauty in front of us was intimidating. Was George Braun on the precipice of a major discovery before he died? Would his death be in vain?

As Millard took to the podium, Karen sidled up next to me. "Gabriel says your slides are loaded. All you need to do is click the top button, and they will appear. Don't cause me any delays!"

If it had been someone kinder and more honest, I would've felt worse about causing a big scene at Karen's second major event for Braxton. She skirted by the first disaster with George Braun's death in the library, but if we arrested the killer at the second event her company had handled, Simply Stoddard might earn an unfortunate reputation. Or worse yet, bad reviews on Yelp!

Millard introduced himself to the crowd explaining how his love of flowers had blossomed at an early age. He spoke about what'd initiated his involvement in the Mendel flower show while traveling in Europe. He shared some highlights they could expect in this year's exhibitions and experimental findings, then introduced me by noting I had a special presentation before everyone entered the show.

April nodded at me. I caught a glimpse of Old Betsy, her black SIG P227 .45-caliber handgun, pushing the bottom of her plaid coat a few inches away from her hip. Too obvious in my opinion, but everyone knew she carried protection with her wherever she went. I shook hands with Millard, thanked him, and adjusted the microphone.

"Good afternoon, everyone," I began. Lissette was front and center, which made it both easy and difficult for me to concentrate. "As everyone is aware, we lost a much-honored and cherished colleague last week. George Braun had achieved remarkable success in his field over a long history of time. Today, we will see his recent work and take a moment to say goodbye to a pillar of the science community."

I caught a sneer forming on Lissette's lips. Her nose wrinkled and twitched as I spoke. A few folks applauded while I paused to click the button Karen had shown me earlier. Gabriel's efforts had worked. A photo of George Braun taken on his first day on campus was projected on the screen behind me.

"Before we show you George's special exhibit this afternoon, let's take a minute to get to know the man behind the flowers and the science." I clicked the button again and watched as a picture of George and Judy burst on the screen.

I felt a tad guilty goading Lissette in such a manner. She was a friend whom my aunt and Nana D had known for years. I assuaged my concerns knowing all I planned to do today was say enough to force Lissette to react. She had little way of knowing I'd discovered the truth. Once the sheriff showed me a picture of Judy Nutberry, I recalled seeing a similar one of her in the folder George had kept under his bed at Maggie's family's inn. We didn't realize who she was at the time given how she'd been sick and had deteriorated in the last year. I, unfortunately, had to besmirch Judy to push Lissette over the edge.

"We're privileged to have a photograph of George and his wife, Judy, from sometime earlier this year. We don't know a lot about his private life given the professor rarely spoke about himself, but judging by the look on their faces, George and Judy had a happy marriage. It's a shame Judy hasn't returned our calls to be here with us today. Perhaps she was jealous of the man or wasn't a very supporting wife."

Lissette gasped. Fern turned to her with a mixed sense of shock and apprehension. I glanced at Ursula who'd made a concerted effort to hold it together, but it was obvious this exercise was a painful experience. I'd come to know her well in the last few months and recognized when she was frightened, saddened, or worried. I had to keep pushing further.

"As we all gather today to launch the Mendel flower show, let us remember this bright and kind man for all he's accomplished over the years. Let us hope George Braun can rest in peace and that we can locate his indifferent wife to share some important news with her about his profound legacy."

Lissette took a step forward. Not a huge one, but enough that I could see a tear rolling beneath her eye. A thin line of mascara traced the contour of her cheek. It took all the remaining energy I had left, but I pushed myself to deliver the final blow.

"We're building and dedicating a memorial to the late George Braun, a scholar, a brilliant scientist, and an honorable humanitarian who deserved our gratitude." I clicked the button for the last slide to appear. A memorial plaque Gabriel had created using Photoshop earlier that afternoon—beautiful stone background, crisp and elegant black writing, and a flowerpot etched in all four corners.

George Braun, In Memoriam of a Beloved Professor, Friend, and Husband.

"No! This is nonsense. He wasn't any of those things. George Braun was a monster," Lissette shouted as she climbed to the stage and trembled uncontrollably. She dropped her purse and walked up to the podium.

"Lissette, are you okay?" I asked while reaching a hand toward her shoulder.

She shoved me away, grabbed the remote aiming it randomly all around the room, and pressed buttons until the picture with Judy reappeared on the screen. "That devil killed my sister." She rushed behind me and thrust her hands on the image as if she were trying to connect with Judy. "He abandoned her. He stole her money and left her to die all alone."

One of the sheriff's team members moved closer to the steps on the opposite side of where Lissette stood. I walked toward her and gently removed the remote from her hands. "Lissette, let's get you some water in the other room. I'm sure you're confused. George is the one who died. We need to honor him before we cut the ribbon for today's exhibit opening." I clicked the power button and let the image fade from the screen. I felt awful further torturing the woman, but she'd killed a man and needed to pay for her sins.

"No!" she screamed at me as she scanned the room for someone to believe her. "That man deserved to die. That man killed Judy. But I got revenge. I made him suffer for everything he did to her." Lissette morphed into a mad and raving animal who'd been trapped and cornered only five feet away from me. She seized one of the flowerpots on the table and rushed toward me with fury in her eyes.

I had only a moment to turn to the side and protect myself as she raised the pot and forcefully slammed it against my head. I fell to the floor while she ran across the stage to the other set of steps. The last thing I remembered seeing before my vision went pitch black was April whooshing toward us.

* * *

"He's come to," someone said. I recognized the voice, but my head was too groggy to properly connect it to a person.

Another one, definitely a woman's this time, said in a soothing tone, "Don't get up. Do you know where you are?"

I mumbled a yes or a no, I wasn't sure what sound came out of my mouth. Suddenly, the focus in my eyes began to clear. I seemed to be lying down. Fern sat next to me. Why did she have dirt on her hands? I tried to get up, but a strong grip held me back.

"Stay put. You might have a concussion," the first voice said again. Whoever he was cradled my head in his hands. He leaned over me and smiled. "Do you know who I am, Kellan?"

I did. "Brad Shope. You're a nurse. Did you give me the good drugs?"

Brad and Fern laughed. "No. You were hit on the head with a flowerpot, and it knocked you out," Brad replied.

"Apparently, your head isn't as strong as you think it is," Fern added.

I began to recall what'd taken place before I was rendered unconscious. "Did they catch her?"

Fern explained what'd happened. As soon as Lissette reached for the flowerpot, April leaped up the stairs to prevent her from throwing it at me. The sheriff had been too far away, and in the rush to escape, Lissette clunked me on the head. When I fell to the ground, Lissette tore across the stage finding herself caught between Officer Flatman and the sheriff. "It was quite a scene for two minutes. Lissette ran back and forth until they closed in on her, then she jumped off the stage to escape through the crowd," Brad noted.

"She got away?" I mumbled feeling my strength come back. How could that happen?

"No, someone tackled her," Brad said, rubbing something on my head. "This might sting a bit."

Footsteps approached from the other side. "How's he doing?"

"He's doing fine," I told April. "Was it you who tackled Lissette Nutberry?"

"Not exactly."

"I guess that would be me," Fern said with a hearty laugh. She was built like a quarterback, there'd be no getting past her.

"Thank you." I felt the pain in my head settle in for what would be a long night.

Brad cleaned out the wound with antiseptic and applied a bandage. "I think you'll be fine, but we should really get you to the hospital to see if there's any damage."

April laughed, "I'm not sure how they'll be able to tell. He must've been brain damaged already to come up with this hokey plan."

"You went along with it," I retorted. It hurt to laugh, though. "Did Lissette confess?"

April nodded. "We took her into a private office to let her calm down and vent. We got enough to arrest her, but she's asked for a lawyer before saying anything else."

While Brad helped me sit upright to see if I was able to walk on my own, Fern told me that Millard ushered everyone else into the first exhibit. He'd given them the choice of continuing or going home and coming back tomorrow for the full show. Most wanted to move forward to see George's special exhibit. April and her team interrogated Lissette. Brad and Fern attended to me while I laid stretched out on the stage. They'd put a pillow under my head and called Nana D, so someone knew what had happened.

Although I was able to get up, I needed more time before I could walk to a car. April grabbed a chair and helped me get situated. "Lissette told us she'd finally tracked her sister down to a small town in Switzerland over a month ago. She'd been sending Judy money to help with all the medical bills. Judy couldn't work on account of her heart condition. She left the United States last year because she thought her family made too big a deal of it and wanted her privacy. That's when she met George."

As April paused for me to process what she said, Connor walked over to us.

"Hey, man. I hear you lost a fight with a flowerpot. Definitely an uneven match. You never had a chance."

"Ha! We'll see about that when I kick your butt in the gym tomorrow," I jeered as my head throbbed. "Maybe the day after."

Brad laughed, "I've seen you both at the gym. Connor will destroy you in under a minute."

"Let's give it a few days before exercising again. I don't want to shame you two days in a row," Connor teased. "We'll do coffee tomorrow. I have to chat with you about something."

For friends, those two sure liked to gang up on me. Since I remembered that was the second time Connor had mentioned needing to talk to me, I knew I hadn't sustained too much damage from the whack to my head. He'd also failed to tell me his news at the gym earlier in the day. "Were you just meeting with Lissette?" I asked.

"Yes. It happened on college property, so I sat in with the sheriff and her team while they grilled the woman," Connor noted. His role as director of security at Braxton came in handy. "George had been stealing all the money Judy's family had been sending her for the medical bills. He used it to further his research, finance the special flower exhibit, and track his sister."

"Lissette went to visit Judy four weeks ago and found her near death. She was all alone in her bed without anyone to take care of her. Judy died that evening, and when Lissette searched the house, she discovered George Braun's deception and the missing family money. Lissette followed him to Braxton, even tried to get a job with him at the flower show. She used a fake name with a perfect resume, then showed up to meet him. She wanted revenge, but he never hired her." George hadn't recognized Lissette in their interview because his wife had looked much different due to her illness.

"He didn't hire her because George gave the job to Gabriel," I said.

Connor choked. "Your brother's back?"

"Let's chat about that another time," I whispered. At least I hoped I did. Either the acoustics in the room were off or my head was worse than I'd thought.

Brad said, "You ought to take a break right now. Your head needs rest to properly recover."

April supported Brad's insistence that I head to the hospital. "This is the second time you've put yourself in the line of fire to get a killer to confess to their crime. Do you have a death wish?"

I shook my head. Probably too quickly because everything was fuzzy for the next twenty seconds. Trails of blurry dots followed me wherever I focused. "I do not. I'm motivated to protect people I care about. Fears are meant to be conquered."

"Does that mean you want to hop on a flight with me to Antigua to visit my family this weekend?" Connor asked with a sly grin.

"Stop messing with me. I'm a sick man," I finally relented. There would be no flying in my future. Brad and Connor helped me stand. When I declined to go to the hospital to have any scans or tests run, we cut a deal. Brad would take me home to Nana D's and monitor me for a few hours. Fern agreed to follow Brad in my SUV, so it wasn't left on campus overnight.

As we prepared to leave, Officer Flatman escorted Lissette in handcuffs into the main room. She stopped him when they passed us. "Kellan, I'm sorry I hit you. I... I... was so upset at seeing Judy's picture with that arrogant bastard. How could you say all those wonderful things about him?"

"I'm sorry. I know he hurt your family." I felt bad, but I couldn't tell her I'd tricked her in case it caused any issues with her future trial. As far as everyone else was concerned, Lissette simply broke down and confessed when she heard me talking about her sister.

"I'm sure my lawyer will fix this. It was a misunderstanding. I confronted George at the costume extravaganza. He pulled a knife on me. I had to protect myself." When Lissette began to struggle, Officer Flatman yanked her away.

"Maybe that defense would work if she stabbed him once and rushed out to get help. But she stabbed the guy twice and lied about the timing of her sister's death. The rest of her family still thinks Judy only died a few days ago. Lissette's going away for quite a long time," April advised.

"Will the charges be dropped against Helena now?" I asked April.

"We're working on it. She did lie to us, and she helped someone we know remove evidence from George's room." April had her hands on her hips and cast a warning look in my direction.

"But if that didn't happen, we'd never have—"

"Take Little Ayrwick home, Brad. He's sounding a bit delusional." April followed Officer Flatman out of the building and waved her fingers goodbye in my direction. "Toodaloo."

That woman was truly going to drive me up a wall. I needed a vacation from her before I got myself put into jail for crossing lines I knew better than to cross. "I need some pain medication. Stat!"

CHAPTER 21

As we walked toward the parking lot, a woman's voice called out to us. "Hold up, can I have a minute with him?" Ursula said with Myriam closely in tow.

"Sure. Make it quick. He needs some downtime." Brad stepped to the side to talk with Fern as I leaned against his car.

"I don't know how to thank you, Kellan. My brother wasn't a good man, but he didn't deserve to die that way. It doesn't really matter now, I made peace years ago. It's time to move on," Ursula said.

Myriam swallowed something that must have been stuck in her throat. "I suppose you will be needing a day or two to recuperate, Mr. Ayrwick?"

Ursula swatted at her wife. "M, I'm sure we can find someone to cover his classes for a few days. We owe Kellan that much."

"*Let not sloth dim your horrors new-begot,*" Myriam replied in my direction with a gentle bow. Henry VI. I couldn't muster the nerve to fight back, but as she walked away, I caught her wicked little wink in my direction. Myriam had been grateful for my help, and her choice of apropos quotes made it obvious. Was this a turning point in our relationship?

Fern and Brad helped me get situated in the car. As we pulled out of the parking lot, I fought the urge to fall asleep. I hadn't gotten proper rest in a long time, but even now I wouldn't be allowed to sleep until Nana D knew I wasn't concussed. I'd finally come to realize that despite winning a battle here or there, I'd never win the war when it came to the women in my life.

The rest of Monday was a blur. Nana D informed me Brad and Fern stayed until I was beginning to function normally again. Of course, my grandmother told all her friends I'd drunk too much that evening. While I was in and out of brief naps—she'd wake me every hour to be sure I was okay—all her cronies called to check on me. A few had been at the flower show and wanted to know why Lissette Nutberry went crazy living up to her name in spectacular fashion.

Although usually one for gossip, Nana D had been close to the woman and wasn't ready to talk about what had gone wrong.

"Thank you, Nana D. Everything is coming together, but I still can't figure out why Anita Singh was so upset this week when we asked about her marriage. At one point, I thought she might have been George's wife." Lissette had confessed to taking Anita's lab coat to hide the blood stains on her costume. She eventually threw everything out, which is why nothing had been returned to the shop.

"Oh, I wish you'd asked me that," Nana D replied, heading to the front door. "Anita Singh got married earlier this year, but the folks at the immigration office are harassing her about it."

"I didn't realize she wasn't an American," I noted finally realizing why she was apprehensive to talk to us.

"No, you have it backward, Kellan. Anita was born here, but her husband wasn't. He's from Iran, and with all the focus on border patrol, travel restrictions, and the reticence to grant citizenship, they've been threatening to deport him. Her family also hasn't been supportive of her marrying outside her culture."

"Did she marry him for love or to keep him in the country?" I said.

"Don't be a fool! Anita is one of the most honest and caring people I know. Of course, it's legitimate. But she's been fighting with the government all year long. Unfortunately, Ed Mulligan is the one who reported Anita's husband to immigration. He thought he was protecting her."

"Meaning what... he might have had a chance with her?"

Nana D nodded. "If he couldn't have her, then no one else could. I told that man he was a stupid fool. I think he's learned a lesson this time. Once George found out what Ed had done, it was easy blackmail to elicit more money for his lab experiments."

* * *

While Nana D dropped Emma off at school on Tuesday morning, I had breakfast with Aunt Deirdre. Myriam had found someone to teach my class that day, which meant I could take some time off. I knew I'd be back to work on Wednesday, so I didn't worry too much about the impact.

"I'm devastated for her," Aunt Deirdre said, sulking in her Earl Grey tea and crumpets. She'd brought them from London knowing Nana D wouldn't have anything like them at Danby Landing.

"People do crazy stuff when someone they love is hurt." I comforted my aunt in words and with a great big bear hug before I sat at the table. "I'm not sure we'll ever know the full story of what went on between Judy and George."

"Oh, Kellan, I have to confess something to someone, or I'll go batty thinking I'm the cause of all this drama." Aunt Deirdre pulled up a seat next to me and slung her head on my shoulder. She still wore her satin nightgown and a silk robe. The garment covered the essentials, but it was like looking at a younger version of my mother parading around in very little. I would've imagined this was how the heroines in her novels dressed, but they were from at least a century earlier.

What could Aunt Deirdre possibly confess about the situation? "You didn't kill Judy or George. I'm sure whatever you're anxious about is a lot less worrisome than you think."

"I'm the one who sent Judy the article about Ursula Power becoming the new president at Braxton. It was that big newspaper article the Wharton County Gazette published earlier this year about the transition of the decade when your father announced his impending retirement." She moaned and wallowed in her own little world as if her actions were as horrific as the murder itself.

I didn't understand what she was trying to tell me. "How does this make you responsible?" I poured myself another cup of coffee on the off chance I wasn't awake enough to understand her incoherent explanation.

"Judy was reading that article on a train ride from France to Switzerland. She'd just come from visiting me in London and had taken the Chunnel to Paris. She was tired of her family watching every little thing she did back home. That's why she moved to Europe in the first place. I encouraged her to travel more as a way to meet new people." She tugged at her robe as if a spook had entered her body.

"Okay, so she was reading the article on the train and George saw it. It doesn't mean you pushed them together."

"But I did. Judy called me after she met him. George wined and dined her in those first few weeks. He convinced her to move to Switzerland to be with him. She'd no idea how to take care of herself and let him lead her on. When she asked me what to do, I told her to enjoy falling in love." Aunt Deirdre sighed and pulled out her cell phone. "I've begun falling in love myself, you see."

"Are you saying you knew Judy was living in Switzerland but didn't tell Lissette or the rest of the Nutberry family?" I ignored her statement about falling in love. She'd suggested something the previous day about having a surprise for us. I'm sure we'd hear soon enough. Some English lord or land baron, I surmised.

"I did, but I never knew who the man was. Judy referred to him as *her doctor friend*. I guess because he had a PhD and was fussing all over her at the beginning about her heart condition. I didn't know they'd gotten married." Aunt Deirdre's eyes were swollen and distant. "I wonder if I could have prevented her death."

"You couldn't have predicted the man was going to milk Judy for all her money and abandon her once he found a reason to..." I stopped realizing it wasn't appropriate to conjecture. We didn't know if he'd killed Judy or she'd died of her illness.

She perked up. "You're probably right. Besides, does anyone know why he chose to come to Braxton? It doesn't make sense, that's where Judy was from."

I knew the reason. His sister, Sofia, now living as Ursula Power, had moved here. But I couldn't tell my aunt or anyone else. That would be up to the sheriff and to my boss to decide. "I know it's hard to mourn the death of a friend and to accept that another one will be going to prison for murder. Take some time while you're visiting us and regroup. Nana D is so excited to have you here, Aunt Deirdre."

She stopped searching for something on her phone and chuckled. "I do have a secret to share. I was going to wait until the big family dinner Thursday night, but it wouldn't hurt if I told you before."

I braced myself for whatever shocker she was about to unleash on me. It couldn't compare to the one I'd bring to the table about Gabriel. "Sure, I'm curious to hear your surprise." I gulped the muddy coffee remnants at the bottom of my cup.

"I'm engaged. We're getting married next month. I think we'll do it here in Braxton," she cheered. Her mood had gone from sullen and distraught to frenzied and ecstatic. I thought I was on a roller coaster of the highest proportion when it came to her emotions. Maybe Brad had given me some sort of drug to keep me in a woozy state.

"Congratulations! I look forward to meeting him." What else could I say? It was the first I'd heard of it. "Where'd you meet one another?"

Aunt Deirdre handed me her phone. "That's his picture, isn't he gorgeous?" she said with a puzzling grin. "He wants to have a baby as soon as possible, and well, I don't see why we shouldn't when we're in love."

I wished I could have seen my jaw drop to the ground, but my eyes had exploded from their sockets and landed somewhere in Danby Landing's eastern apple orchard. I knew Aunt Deirdre was younger than my mother, but I didn't think she was that young. I couldn't think of the most tactful way to ask, and I had to stop myself from going into a choking fit. "Water, please."

She jumped up and filled my coffee mug from the kitchen tap. "Drink up, Kellan."

When I regained my composure, I did a double-take on the photo staring back at me from her mobile phone. "That's Timothy Paddington!"

"Yes, I've known him all my life, but we drifted apart. We found each other on the *Facebook* again this year. All us girls have been getting more into social media. He's such a generous and caring man." The smile on my aunt's now happy face was so bright I couldn't look at her. If there were ever a female counterpart to *Batman*'s Joker, she was it right now.

"But... you know he's... I mean, not that it means you can't, what I'm trying to say..." I couldn't get the words out of my mouth.

"He's in rehab for an alcohol and drug addiction. I'm aware, but he gets sprung from Second Chance Reflections in two weeks. I was planning on meeting him that day to start our new life together, then Lissette asked me to accompany her back home. It was fate!" she proclaimed before doing a little dance on the kitchen floor.

Another voice in the kitchen laughed raucously. "I thought I'd check on you, but I can see your aunt has you in stitches," Connor teased. He hugged my aunt who thanked me for cheering her up, then demanded I keep her secret. While she went to take a bath, I poured myself another cup of coffee and offered one to Connor.

"Don't ask. I'm not sure if I'm loopy or she's actually here. Am I seeing people? Are you real?" I grabbed a few crumpets from the bowl and threw them at him.

"Oh, I saw her dancing that broken Irish jig. That woman needs to take a few lessons on how to find some rhythm." Connor caught one, leaned against the counter, and slurped his coffee.

"No doubt about it. It's good to see you," I said.

"I couldn't keep the news to myself anymore. I had to share it with you before you found out from someone else." Connor was beaming, and it was unusual for him to wear his emotions on his sleeves. Ten years in security had made him rigid and hard to read.

Was he about to tell me he was getting married too? It couldn't be Eleanor. My sister wouldn't have been able to contain that news. Then I realized he wouldn't have proposed to Maggie with everything she's been doing to support Helena this week. "Out with it. You've got that devious look on your face like you're about to sideswipe me with something big," I replied.

"You're looking at the newest detective in the Wharton County Sheriff's Office. Or at least as soon as Gilkrist is finished at the end of this month." Connor rushed over to hug me, spilling coffee all down both our backs. He went on to explain that he and April had been talking a lot about their partnership to keep the town of Braxton and its college campus safer. "You know I quit the force in Philadelphia because I didn't want to be around all the gang fights, high murder rate, and urban crimes."

"You wanted something more laidback where you could make a real difference," I said. We'd previously spoken about it when I'd returned to Braxton.

"She suggested it. I talked to Gilkrist, and it's a great fit. I'll really miss working at the college, but Ursula understood." Connor had been interviewing all along and never told me. Neither did Ursula. I guess there was a distinct line between business and personal relationships.

"Does Maggie know?" I asked.

"We're meeting for an early lunch. I hinted about it but never told her I interviewed with April," Connor noted. He checked his watch and mentioned he had to leave to pick Maggie up on time.

After he left, I had a moment where I felt depressed. I was happy for my friend who found a great new job, but with him and April working so closely together, it might make any future homicide investigations harder on me. Then I realized something. Why was I predicting there would be another murder I wanted to solve? At the rate things had been going since my return to Braxton, maybe there was some truth to April's jokes about me being at the center of all the crime in our charming and secluded town.

When Aunt Deirdre finished bathing and dressing, I said goodbye and headed to the guesthouse to determine how to introduce Gabriel back into the fold. I needed to wake up, so I decided to get my own shower out of the way. Just as I stripped naked and turned on the water, my cell rang. It was Maggie. "Hey, you caught me at a bad time. Can I call you back in fifteen?"

"Connor is on his way to pick me up. I wanted to thank you for everything you did. Helena is home with all the charges officially withdrawn from her record. It's only because you stuck your neck out for us," Maggie said in a soft, gentle voice. "I'm grateful more than I can say."

"I only did what you would've done for me, if the situations were reversed. Let's get together soon."

"That sounds perfect. I need to run. Helena and Cheney set up this brunch for the four of us to get to know one another."

"Say hi for me."

"Maybe we could meet next weekend. I'd love to pick your brain about the renovations at Memorial Library. We start construction in twelve weeks," Maggie added with a passion in her voice.

"That's great news!" I told Maggie we'd catch up again soon and hung up. I checked the water temperature and hopped under the full blast. My shoulders were sore and needed the relief. I only stepped out again when I heard someone moving around in the hallway. I quickly dried off with a fresh towel and called out, "One minute. Just throwing on some clothes."

I grabbed the jeans and black tank top I'd hung on the back of the door and slipped into them. I located my glasses and wandered into the living room. No one was there. I poked my head into the kitchen, then my bedroom, but they were also empty. Emma's door had been shut and was still shut, so no one was in there. Maybe I'd started hearing things as well as seeing things.

I grabbed my satchel and flipped through all the postcards Francesca had sent. Now that we'd found George Braun's murderer and I'd received postcards from all the places my wife and I had visited, it was time to figure out what she was up to.

As I reread each one, I realized there were other mistakes besides the two I'd recognized on the postcards from Savannah and Yellowstone. Not only had Francesca incorrectly mentioned snow on one of them and my broken ankle on the other, but she'd referred to Emma as being six years old. Emma had turned seven years old several weeks before that postcard had arrived the previous month. I laid them all out on the table and tried to make sense of what was in front of me.

The front door opened and in ran Emma with Nana D following closely behind. "I'm back from school!" She had an early release today.

"Hey kiddo! Did you just get here, or were you in the house a few minutes ago?" I asked my daughter. Maybe I hadn't been hallucinating about the noises.

"Mmm, you saw us walk in, Daddy. Is your head still hurting?" Emma asked while tapping my nose. "Rodney is back at school. I miss him."

Nana D looked at the table in front of me, then at me, and finally at my daughter. "Why don't you make yourself a snack, Emma? I left some cut-up apples in the fridge earlier. Maybe some peanut butter with it, okay?"

Emma cheered and rushed off to the kitchen. Nana D sat next to me and picked up the Mendoza postcard. "What's going on, brilliant one?"

I wasn't ready to share with my grandmother that my wife was alive. I needed to find her first. "It's nothing, Nana D. I was looking at old messages from Francesca. Are you ready for election day?" I took the postcard from her hand and tucked it under the rest of the pile.

"I think so. I'm feeling good about it, but you never know what dirty tricks Marcus Stanton has up his sleeve." Nana D leaned forward to study one of the other postcards, but I confiscated it from her before she could. "Nothing good comes from focusing on the past. I'll put these away later."

"Never be afraid of history. Those who forget the lessons they've learned are condemned to repeat the same mistakes. It's like all those jewelry thefts that started up again," Nana D cautioned.

I hadn't been aware of any but recalled the sheriff mentioning something about a burglary she'd been investigating the night of the costume extravaganza. "What do you mean *again*?"

"You don't remember?" she asked inquisitively while leaning over the table to get a better glimpse of the only postcard still accessible. "Oh, that's right, it happened while you were in LA."

Was I going to have to beg for details? "And the award for the best dramatic reveal goes to—"

"Slow your roll, brilliant one. I'm getting there." Nana D knocked over a pillow as she stood from the couch, but I was aware of how tricky she could be. "Get that, will ya?" she said while swooping down to collect the postcard.

I shuffled the entire lot into a pile, gathered them into my left hand, and reached for the pillow with the other. "Go on. I'll put these away now."

"Oh, about eight years ago... right around the time Gabriel left Braxton... there were a bunch of robberies on campus. Started out small at first, but the thief worked his or her way up to expensive jewelry and a lot of money." Nana D thrust herself back into the couch with a long sigh, obviously disgruntled that I'd kept her from nosing into my business.

"His or her? Didn't they catch the person?"

"Nope. By the time it was all done, a fifty-thousand-dollar donation had been stolen from the alumni building. Some fool had dropped off cash. It was pinched before the night fell." Nana D shrugged her shoulders and tossed her hands in the air. "Never found the culprit or the money. It just happened again last week."

"As in more money was stolen?"

"Don't you read the newspapers? Get with it, you're losing touch with reality." She wagged her finger at me disapprovingly. "Same calling card was left, but a lot more was stolen this time. Your father thinks it was one of the professors. Maybe it's a case for you to get involved with?"

Emma interrupted us from continuing the conversation about the stolen money and jewelry. It was intriguing, but I needed some downtime to relax. "What's up, baby girl?"

"Can I go play on the iPad in my bedroom? I want to beat my high score on *Candy Crush Saga*." She giggled and put on her adorable pleading face.

"Your homework is done?" I asked. When she nodded, I let her have thirty minutes on the device. Then she'd have to help prepare dinner with Nana D and me.

Nana D cleared her throat after Emma rushed out of the room. "When were you gonna tell me Gabriel was back?" She narrowed judgmental eyes in my direction.

How did she know? "I... ummm... he asked me to keep his secret."

"I don't like when you lie to me, brilliant one." Nana D made a tsk tsk noise to shame me. Unfortunately, it was beginning to work.

Before I could reply, a scream came from Emma's room. We both jumped off the couch and rushed to check it out. I thought she'd fallen and hurt herself.

When I got to the room, Emma was bent over a wicker basket on her bed and crying tears of joy. "It's a puppy. It's the one we saw at the pet store, Daddy. You got him for me!"

I didn't get him for her. I looked at Nana D who vehemently shook her head. "Not me."

While Emma clutched the shiba inu puppy against her chest, Nana D sat on the bed and ruffled her hair. I looked in the basket and found another postcard. It read:

It seems Francesca has run out of places to visit, so she stopped back home. Emma loved her trip to the pet store the other day. She took such great care of the rabbit last week. Maybe this puppy will keep her happy until Mommy comes home. If you'd ever like to see her mommy alive again, you need to convince your in-laws to do exactly what I say. I'll be in touch soon. Don't try to locate me, or Francesca will truly be dead this time.
-Familia Las Vargas

I hurried into the living room to look at the nine postcards. I checked the first one thoroughly and found the letter 'L' written under the handwritten address. In the second, I found an 'A' hidden under the postage stamp. By the time I scanned them all, there were nine letters scattered on each of the nine cards. She'd capitalized some of the letters in her words to make a point. It wasn't random. They spelled out *LAS VARGAS*. But it spelled out way more than that. Francesca hadn't been visiting all the places we'd gone to together in our past. Her parents weren't keeping her safe in the Castigliano mansion. The Vargas family had kidnapped my wife and forced her to share details about our trips, so they could send those postcards. They didn't want us to find her!

Francesca must have been sending clues to reveal what was going on. I had no idea what to do next. Should I confess everything to Nana D? Was it best to contact Vincenzo and Cecilia for help? Did I need to get the FBI involved?

My phone rang shrilly, jerking me out of the unexpected stupor. The puppy barked in Emma's room while I panicked at the number on the screen. It was the sheriff. I suddenly knew exactly what to do at that moment. "April, I need your help. Something insane has happened, and you're the only person I can trust right now."

MISTAKEN IDENTITY CRISIS

BRAXTON CAMPUS MYSTERIES BOOK 4

ACKNOWLEDGMENTS

Writing a book is not an achievement an individual person can accomplish on his or her own. There are always people who contribute in a multitude of ways, sometimes unwittingly, throughout the journey from discovering the idea to drafting the last word. *Mistaken Identity Crisis: A Braxton Campus Mystery* has had many supporters since its inception in February 2019, but before the concept even sparked in my mind, my passion for writing was nurtured by others.

First thanks go to my parents, Jim and Pat, for always believing in me as a writer as well as teaching me how to become the person I am today. Their unconditional love and support have been the primary reason I'm accomplishing my goals. Through the guidance of my extended family and friends, who consistently encouraged me to pursue my passion, I found the confidence to take chances in life. With Winston and Baxter by my side, I was granted the opportunity to make my dreams of publishing this novel come true. I'm grateful to everyone for pushing me each day to complete this sixth book.

Mistaken Identity Crisis was cultivated through the interaction, feedback, and input of several talented beta readers. I'd like to thank Laura Albert, Mary Deal, Misty Swafford, Anne Jacobs, Nina D. Silva, Carla @ CarlaLovesTo-Read, Tyler Colins, Anne Foster, Lisa M. Berman, and Valerie for supplying insight and perspective during the development of the story, setting, and character arcs. I am indebted to them for finding all the proofreading misses, grammar mistakes, and awkward phrases. A major thanks to Tyler for encouraging me to be stronger in my word choice and providing several pages of suggestions to convert good language into fantastic language! A special call-out goes to Shalini for countless conversations helping me to fine-tune every aspect of the setting, characters, and plot. She read every version and offered a tremendous amount of her time to advise me on this book over several weeks. I am beyond grateful for her help. Any mistakes are my own from misunderstanding our discussions.

Much gratitude to all my friends and mentors at Moravian College. Although no murders have ever taken place there, the setting of this series is loosely based on my former multi-campus school set in Pennsylvania. Most of the locations are completely fabricated, but the concept of Millionaire's Mile exists. I only made up the name, grand estates, and cable car system.

Thank you to Creativia / Next Chapter for publishing *Mistaken Identity Crisis* and paving the road for more books to come. I look forward to our continued partnership.

WHO'S WHO IN THE BRAXTON CAMPUS MYSTERIES?

AYRWICK FAMILY

- *Kellan:* Main Character, Braxton professor, amateur sleuth
- *Wesley:* Kellan's father, Braxton's retired President
- *Violet:* Kellan's mother, Braxton's Admissions Director
- *Emma:* Kellan's daughter with Francesca
- *Eleanor:* Kellan's younger sister, owns Pick-Me-Up Diner
- *Gabriel:* Kellan's younger brother, dating Sam
- *Nana D:* Kellan's grandmother, also known as Seraphina Danby
- *Deirdre Danby:* Kellan's aunt, Nana D's daughter, Timothy's fiancée
- *Francesca Castigliano:* Kellan's estranged wife
- *Vincenzo & Cecilia Castigliano:* Francesca's parents, run the mob

BRAXTON CAMPUS

- *Ursula Power:* President, Myriam's wife
- *Myriam Castle:* Chair of Communications Dept., Ursula's wife
- *Fern Terry:* Dean of Student Affairs, Arthur's mom
- *Arthur Terry:* Engaged to Jennifer, Fern's son
- *Maggie Roarke:* Head Librarian, dating Connor, Helena's sister
- *Quint Crawford:* Electrician, Bertha's son
- *Raquel Salvado:* Current student
- *Imogene Grey:* Lara's daughter, Paul's fiancée, former college sorority girl
- *Siobhan Walsh:* Office Manager, current student

- *Krissy Stanton:* Marcus's daughter, former college sorority girl

WHARTON COUNTY RESIDENTS

- *Cristiano Vargas:* Runs the mob, kidnapped Francesca
- *Bertha Crawford:* Quint's mother, Silas's brother-in-law
- *Tiffany Nutberry:* Lydia's daughter, former college sorority girl
- *Lydia Nutberry:* Tiffany's mother, runs Whispering Pines Funeral Home
- *Helena Roarke:* Maggie's sister, former college sorority girl
- *Nicholas Endicott:* Construction company owner, former college student
- *Karen Stoddard:* Restaurant owner
- *Cheney Stoddard:* Karen's son, was dating Helena
- *Timothy Paddington:* Deirdre's fiancé, Jennifer's brother
- *Eustacia Paddington:* Head of Paddington family, aunt to Jennifer and Tim
- *Jennifer Paddington:* Engaged to Arthur, Timothy's sister
- *Sam Taft:* Dating Gabriel, nephew to Jennifer and Timothy
- *Chef Manny:* Cook at Eleanor's diner

WHARTON COUNTY ADMINISTRATION

- *Silas Crawford:* Former Sheriff, Bertha's brother-in-law
- *April Montague:* Current Sheriff
- *Connor Hawkins:* Detective, Kellan's best friend, dating Maggie
- *Paul Dodd:* New Braxton Town Councilman, Imogene's fiancé
- *Marcus Stanton:* Former Braxton Town Councilman, Krissy's father
- *Judge Grey:* Wharton County Magistrate, Imogene's grandfather
- *Lara Bouvier:* Reporter, Imogene's mother

CHAPTER 1

"The first time we met, I knew you'd cause me to gray prematurely," April griped while clawing at clumps of her brassy blonde hair and squeezing her golden badge until a star-shaped imprint marked her left palm. "But I honestly thought I'd have a better chance at predicting the Pennsylvania state lottery numbers before guessing you'd paint a bullseye on your own forehead for the Castigliano mob family. Seriously, Kellan, you've made a royal mess of this situation. Are they gonna take potshots at me next?"

We bantered steadfastly in her downtown office at the Wharton County administrative building with the door glued shut. Very few people knew what'd happened to my supposedly dead wife, Francesca. I shrugged and offered my best apology face, which unintentionally resembled a confused puppy in search of a warm place to sleep, rather than a truly sorrowful man who'd never intended to wreak such havoc. "We've covered this several times in the last three weeks. I should've immediately informed you that Francesca's family faked her death. I didn't know what to do until that last note from Cristiano Vargas confirmed they'd kidnapped her as a revenge tactic to punish the Castiglianos." I rested both hands and my chin on the heavily papered desk, grinned widely as if my jaw were about to unhinge, and blinked twice through stylish glasses to endear myself to the sheriff.

At least she'd stopped calling me *Little Ayrwick*. Of all the nicknames I'd heard during my thirty-two years, that was the most insulting. There was nothing *little* about me anymore. Upon graduating from Braxton a decade ago, I'd transformed from an awkward middle child in a complex, overachieving family into what many women eagerly deemed a devilishly handsome and well-built guy blessed with clever wit and a charming personality. Don't get me wrong, I'm not an egomaniac. I've merely settled into myself and accepted the positive and the negative. Lately, there were tons more negative than I cared to tolerate. At least Nana D still called me *brilliant one*, which melted my heart every time.

"That's your apology?" April vigorously shook her head and slammed a *Tweety Bird* coffee mug on the desk's smooth metal surface. Drops of cold, muddy brown liquid splashed across it and landed on my upper lip. "*I'm sorry*, I didn't mean to do that," she whined repentantly while handing me a napkin from a squeaky drawer. "Oh, and in case you forgot, that's how you ask for forgiveness."

Had it not been for the tiniest of curls at the sides of her sarcastic mouth, I wouldn't have known April was teasing me. We'd spent an inordinate amount of time joined at the hip, organizing everything that'd happened in the last two-and-a-half years since *the accident*. Okay, backstory time—Francesca and I had arrived separately at a Thanksgiving party because I'd been working out of town earlier in the week. Our daughter, Emma, begged to ride home with me— a monumental blessing in disguise—rather than her mother. Little did I know at the time, Francesca's parents, Vincenzo and Cecilia Castigliano, had orchestrated the entire façade. When I received the call that my wife had been struck and killed by a drunk driver, I did my best to rally with the help of Nana D, my five-foot-tall spitfire grandmother. Meanwhile, Francesca lived covertly in the Castigliano mansion until her parents could divine a way to resolve the turf war with Las Vargas, the rival mafia family controlling much of the West Coast. Two years had zipped by without a viable solution or anyone learning their secret.

A few months ago, Emma and I moved back home to Braxton, the small town in north-central Pennsylvania where I'd been raised and now worked as an assistant professor specializing in communications and film studies. Francesca chose that moment to materialize from hiding, jealous and angry about the sudden inability to watch her daughter grow up in LA. After I refused to *hibernate in captivity*, she took off, letting her parents and me think she was visiting all the places we'd once vacationed in—a blissful trip down memory lane. At some point, Cristiano Vargas had discovered Francesca was alive, captured my not-so-dead wife, and forced her to mail postcards from every location to dangle us in a state of confusion. Now, we pondered their next move.

"I'm sorry, April. I know you intended to leave this spectacle of intense drama when you relocated from Buffalo, but I'm confident we'll find a solution." I wiped the coffee from my lip and internally chuckled over her persnickety comments. "I should teach you to brew a better cup of joe. I guess it's true that cops will drink any sludge someone—"

"Don't continue with that stereotypical, inflammatory insult unless you want me to handcuff you to my desk and head out for the day!" April released a long pent-up sigh and shuffled through stained papers in a worn manila folder. "Let's focus on our next steps. The Castiglianos will soon arrive in Braxton, and they better have answers. I agreed not to *formally* include the FBI until we received an official ransom request. We also need proof Francesca is alive before they'll get further involved."

April and I hadn't been friends previously, especially because I'd unexpectedly solved four murders sooner than she had—not a helpful icebreaker for our relationship. She mostly viewed me as a prickly thorn that irritated every nerve in her body. We'd brokered a tepid alliance in the last three weeks, and I convinced myself that the intense display of awe-inducing fireworks in her office, when our fingers had accidentally brushed against one another, was only a freakish blip on the radar. Then, a visceral flash of lightning surged inside my body and a sensual, steamy dream left me quite flushed and bewildered. I was technically still married and shouldn't have welcomed those types of thoughts about other women, right?

Once the war ended between the two families, Francesca could reveal herself to the rest of the world, and we'd deal with the repercussions. I only cared about the impact on our seven-year-old daughter. Emma didn't deserve this level of pain and confusion. Neither did I, but in the few encounters I'd already had with Francesca upon her triumphant reincarnation, it'd grown clear we were both different people. As a good Catholic—my family attended church on Sundays—divorce was a tricky solution. I knew I loved Francesca, but I was no longer in love with her. After all the lies and deception, how could I forgive her? Yes, her life had been in danger from Las Vargas, but she could've told me the truth years ago. I'd only discovered the reality of her shady family business by accident after she 'died.'

"Cristiano's latest update said he'd contact me soon with next steps. Maybe he'll offer easily attainable ransom terms for the Castiglianos. Then, this whole mess will blow over." All remaining confidence drained from my body with each reticent word. "Ugh! Why am I in the middle of this quandary? Las Vargas should work directly with Francesca's parents for her safe release."

"Excellent point. Perhaps your uniquely innate charm just begs for more attention? Regardless, I'm collecting evidence on the Castigliano drug-trafficking exploits to put them away for good. Someone will go to prison over this entire ordeal. I won't be able to protect her, you know," April said convincingly with a pointed stare. "I get she's your wife, but the mafia princess committed several crimes. I'm glad you never collected any insurance payments upon her death."

"I was a fool not to ask more questions about her background when we'd met." Although my immediate family members were a fantastic crew, the Ayrwicks also liked to pry into each other's business much too often. When I'd moved to Los Angeles to escape their clutches, an all-encompassing, powerful first love had blinded me from recognizing the truth. Francesca and I married way too quickly, and before long, I'd obtained my PhD, gotten a job as an assistant director at a Hollywood television show, and become a father upon Emma's arrival in this world. We lived a good life, but I'd always known something important was missing between Francesca and me.

"We'll sort it out, Kellan. You're going through a lot, but you can't tell anyone else until we dismantle Las Vargas. Anyway, I have to follow up on another jewelry heist that happened last week."

"I've been meaning to ask Nana D about those pesky robberies. Anything you can share?"

April swallowed heavily. "Jewelry was stolen. Victims are unhappy. Is that what you need to know, oh holy meddlesome one? Don't even think about inserting yourself into another one of my—"

"Blah, blah, blah. I read the papers and have some clue, April. I'll just ask Nana D. She tends to dig up the latest facts. I vaguely recall something about an unusual calling card being left behind, right?"

"I'd rather not discuss it. The ineptitude of the former sheriff still infuriates me. My predecessor had a penchant for burying facts from his townspeople." April grunted and shook her head.

"Nana D claims he took bribes to hide petty crimes," I said, hoping to keep her talking about it. "Maybe you and I should compare notes about the case. I *have* been helpful in the past."

"And we're officially done here," April muttered as she advanced toward me with alarming concentration in her eyes. "Let's talk tomorrow about your wife's kidnapping." Moist, hot breath from her lips passed over mine, and her skin smelled like black peppercorns and coriander—spicy yet fresh.

Although tempting comfort swayed between us like a pendulum jam-packed with uncertainty over its destination, I retreated before April and I approached a line we weren't prepared to cross. Too many intimate moments had encircled us lately, and I couldn't fathom how to properly interpret them. "Sure, I'll update you as soon as I hear from Cristiano."

Leaving her office, I noticed my reflection in the shiny glass pane of the door. Several days of dirty-blond stubble peppered my cheeks and chin, and dark circles occupied the sunken spaces below my disconcerted blue eyes. At least I'd managed to comb my frequently untamable hair, so I didn't look horribly disheveled. Nana D would slap my bottom silly—her words, not mine —for drawing shame to her, especially now that she'd won the election to become the new mayor of Wharton County.

* * *

Later that Saturday afternoon, I drove to Wellington Park in Millner Place to celebrate Nana D's seventy-fifth birthday in style with the party of the century. Millner Place and Braxton made up two of the four towns in Wharton County —the others, Woodland in the northwest and Lakeview in the northeast. Ninety miles south of Buffalo, New York, our county was one of the earliest settlements in Pennsylvania and had been founded by my ancestors.

"Is today the double wedding, Daddy?" Emma asked as I steered the SUV into a narrow spot.

Aunt Deirdre, a famous novelist and one of my mother's siblings, had returned from England and coordinated Nana D's party while simultaneously planning her own upcoming nuptials to Timothy Paddington, an international business mogul.

"Nope, that's in two weeks on Independence Day," I reminded my precocious daughter. Timothy's sister was also engaged, prompting their family to suggest a double wedding to make it easy on all the guests. Both couples had only recently met one another, and it made more sense as a way to reunite the Paddington family who'd experienced several traumatic events earlier in the year. "Do you know what Independence Day is about, honey?"

When Emma nodded with enthusiasm, mahogany-brown pigtails bounced feverishly against her slightly chubby, olive-tinted cheeks. My mother had located a picture of seven-year-old Nana D and designed a matching outfit for my daughter since Emma looked so much like her at that age. "We talked about it on the last day of school. It's when we shoot firecrackers into the sky!"

"Yes, that's part of it, but it's also when we became our own country. Aunt Deirdre thought it would be amusing to shed her independence on the same day America officially separated from England two-and-a-half centuries ago," I explained. Having lived there for half her life, Aunt Deirdre deemed herself British for all intents and purposes. She also lived *inside her head* where she dreamed up Victorian romances all day. Ply my aunt with more than two glasses of wine and her American roots were more obvious than the henna rinse in Nana D's wild, three-foot-long braids.

"That sounds like an adult joke. I don't get it." Emma gave a thumbs-down symbol. "When will Nonna and Nonno be here?" My daughter referred to Francesca's parents by the Italian words for a grandparent. Her hazelnut-brown eyes were darkening this summer, highlighting how much she also resembled her mother before my wife had adopted various disguises. Emma was being kept far away from any conversation about her not-so-dead mother, something even the Castiglianos had easily agreed to with everything exploding around us.

"Monday evening." I grabbed her hand and rambled toward Wellington Park. Nana D had chosen the cherished location across the Finnulia River, touting it as a critical place to rebuild. She'd also promised *free ice cream every weekend* in her campaign speeches during the mayoral election. "Look, here's Uncle Gabriel," I added when my brother caught up with us at the tree-lined entranceway.

At a complicated and sentimental family dinner earlier in the month, Gabriel had announced his unexpected homecoming and the not-so-earth-shattering news that he was gay. Not surprisingly, the Ayrwicks openly welcomed him back into their fold with minimal concern. My mother cried the entire time at her youngest son returning to the roost. Our older siblings couldn't visit for that dinner or for Nana D's birthday party, but I hadn't expected them to travel. When both had mentioned they would come back for the birthday party *or* the double wedding, Nana D vehemently insisted on the wedding.

"Emma? It can't be! She's grown two feet in the last few days," Gabriel teased while picking up my best girl and swinging her from side to side. In observance of the warm late June weather, Gabriel donned a pair of dressy long shorts and a collared, black polo shirt. One of his many tattoos peeked out from the shirt's sleeve as his taut, muscular arms carried Emma in near-perfect circles.

"It's too fuzzy! Does it hurt?" Emma giggled as she touched his lip piercing and trim, dark-blond beard. He was four glorious years younger than me, as he always reminded me, but our semblance remained uncannily similar. Although he projected a mysterious and rugged appearance, I erred toward the clean-cut side—except for days like today when I hadn't shaved. I secretly clung to the worthy excuse of dealing with a back-from-the-dead wife. Also, Gabriel had been accepted by the family and was currently the favored, treasured sibling whom our parents and Nana D couldn't stop fawning over. Even our father, the resolute Wesley Ayrwick, seemed overjoyed at his prodigal son's return.

"Nope! But you can't get a tattoo either, I already asked your daddy. He's a party pooper," Gabriel responded, smiling as his boyfriend, Sam Taft, meandered to his side. After releasing Emma, who excitedly jumped to the ground, Gabriel shrugged and narrowed his eyes at me. "Isn't that so, brother?"

I shot a spectacular warning look at him. He earned only one of those before I'd tackle him for saying such nonsensical and controversial things to Emma. I'd already mandated she wasn't allowed to wear makeup or jewelry, go on a date, or talk to a boy—or a girl, if that's what she decided—until she turned eighteen. I wasn't overprotective. I was cautiously aware and attentive. At least that's how I justified my helicopter parenting. "Why don't you and Sam find Auntie Eleanor? I need to remind Uncle Gabriel about the many afternoons he spent sprawled on the dirty ground as a dumb teenager."

Sam, the essence of compassion, cocked his head and groaned. "Will you two ever grow up? I'm younger than you both yet more mature than the combination." To Emma, he said, "Let's go, bean sprout. Grow some legs and race me to the deejay. I bet I can do a better Chicken Dance than you!"

During my distraction while watching them take off, clucking and flapping their arms at their sides, Gabriel tackled me and jumped on my back and shoulders. "Like this, you mean?" he shouted before hooking his legs around my waist, pressuring me to fall, and torturing me with a noogie.

We tossed each other back and forth for fifteen seconds, each of us trying to gain and maintain the upper hand. We only stopped when Nana D intervened and chastised us.

"What is wrong with the two of you? Can't you act like civilized men instead of delinquents who don't know any better?" As we separated, she grabbed each of us by an ear with nimble hands, lowered our heads until they were closer to her own height, and held us side by side. For a moment, we expected a harangue over our behavior, even though we were completely goofing off and not at all fighting. Then, she released our ears and gave us both noogies. "Ha, got you both!"

"Not cool, Nana D," Gabriel shouted, rubbing his head after escaping her bizarrely strong grip.

"That's not very becoming of a new county mayor. You should be ashamed of yourself," I added.

"Pish! I'm glad to have two of my grandsons back home. You have no idea what it means to this middle-aged lady to spend quality time with you before I—"

"Move into the Willow Trees retirement complex?" Gabriel interrupted saucily.

The sly smile plastered across his face was more than I could handle. I burst out laughing, grateful he'd said something sarcastic instead of me. Middle-aged at seventy-five? Nana D had not only pushed the envelope, but she sent it reeling over the edge of a cliff to its ultimate death on arrival.

"Gabriel, if you want to keep on living at Danby Landing, you better shut your pie hole. I'll kick you out as quickly as I offered you a temporary place to crash," Nana D reprimanded, hugging him and kissing his cheek. "I've got big-time control now that I run this county."

After squashing Town Councilman Marcus Stanton in a landslide victory, Nana D wouldn't stop reminding everyone about the power she'd gained. Of course, she only planned to use it for good, but there was something unnerving and dubious about a woman with a Napoleon complex wielding control over us. "Everyone here already?" I inquired as we marched into the park like wooden soldiers.

"Yes, I'm sorry my other grandchildren couldn't attend. I also wish my two sons could make time for their mother, but I'm glad to have *some* of my family here to celebrate with," Nana D said, fighting back a small whimper. She wasn't sentimental very often, but on a grand occasion like a seventy-fifth birthday, the well-hidden side of my nana's personality snuck out for a brief respite.

For the remainder of the afternoon, we shared stories of Nana D's past and presented her with a custom-made drawing of our family tree dating back to the 1600s, the earliest records she'd been able to trace of her ancestors. A local artist specialized in transferring computer-generated genealogical family trees to a 3D-like graphical print format. Everyone had chipped in to make Nana D's birthday as extraordinary as she was to us. Even my father made a brief announcement about how, despite their fervent and frequent disagreements, she was a remarkable woman and a treasure to the family and the county. She frowned when he said *ancient* treasure, and I knew she'd engineer a way to implement revenge. There'd be a summons from the mayor's office in his mailbox when she officially took charge the following week. As I said, her Napoleon complex was going to have an infinite impact on our lives.

After a delicious picnic spread and tons of games, we watched brilliant colors cascade across the sky as the sun set. Sam exited to join a dinner party with his mother, and Gabriel indicated an urgency to check on something at the lab where he worked. His questionable timing prompted me to suspect he suffered from a hangover and needed to sleep it off. Emma requested a sleep-over at my parents' house, the Royal Chic-Shack, and departed with them. Although Aunt Deirdre had driven Nana D to Wellington Park, she'd wandered away an hour earlier with Timothy to discuss wedding preparations. I was graciously assigned responsibility for getting my nana home safely.

Other guests exited too, lamenting the few remaining hours before ushering in a new workweek. While many of my colleagues from Braxton College had attended the celebration, I hardly had time to socialize with them. Nana D had insisted Emma and I stick close to her side most of the afternoon. Did she want me nearby to prevent another small breakdown, or had she known I was distracted thinking about Francesca's disappearance?

"Penny for your thoughts, brilliant one?" she asked while we loaded her gifts in the trunk.

Nana D had been present when the final postcard and new puppy, a gift notifying me that Las Vargas had kidnapped my wife, had arrived. She supported me while I'd contacted April, in her official role as the sheriff of Wharton County, to ask for help. "It feels like this was my last moment with Emma before I rip off the Band-Aid. How do you tell a little girl her mother isn't dead, and that the woman *chose* to leave her?" I sighed with exasperation and leaned my head against the side of the SUV.

"You tell her the truth, Kellan. She's your daughter, which makes her brilliant, remember? Francesca caused this debacle, and you'll need to wait for her to resurface. When she does, I plan to give that little harpy a piece of my mind!" Nana D smiled at me and stepped into the SUV's passenger seat, unfazed by the entire kidnapping tribulation. "I have faith you'll determine the best approach—"

Nana D was interrupted when Connor Hawkins, a good friend who'd recently changed jobs from Braxton College's security director to a Wharton County Sheriff's Office detective, approached us. "Happy Birthday, Nana D! What are you now, a half-century?" he said with an infectious beam of excitement gushing on his chiseled face. While I was usually a pasty and pale-skinned kinda guy who couldn't ever find the proper length of time for a good suntan, Connor inherited the perfect balance of skin color from his South African father and Caribbean mother. It even *offset his brooding, stormy eyes*, as he selflessly and frequently pointed out. Called an Adonis by some, to me he was the mere mortal who managed my workouts so that someday, I might look more like him. Don't tell him I admitted that!

I stepped to the side to let him embrace my grandmother. They'd known each other for a long time since Connor and I had grown up together. While we'd lost touch when I moved to LA, we'd bonded again in the last few months. "I'm glad you stopped by. I worried we'd missed you."

"Sorry about that, Kellan. I'm still pulling double duty until the college finds my replacement. Just finished organizing the team for the upcoming week, and now I'm headed out on a call. There's been another jewelry heist," Connor explained as he elbowed the passenger door shut.

"That's awful. Who was it this time?" Nana D settled into her seat and pulled out her phone to make notes. Through the open window, she said, "I was alarmed before, but this is the third one, right?"

Connor replied, "Fourth, ma'am. I suppose I can fill you in on the little I know from today, especially since you're soon to be our new mayor. The Grey family was hit hard this time."

The Greys, a prominent and wealthy clan, controlled a sizable portion of the county. Judge Hiram Grey, a few years younger than Nana D, sat on the bench for over thirty years. I'd taught his granddaughter the previous semester before she'd graduated from Braxton. "What did the perp steal?"

"I'm not sure. A uniformed officer was called to the scene, but once he realized who it was and what'd really happened, the sergeant contacted me. I'm on my way now." Connor responded on one of his many technical communication devices that he'd be onsite in ten minutes.

"Was anyone hurt?" Nana D asked as I shook Connor's hand to say goodbye.

"Yes, Imogene Grey is being treated by the paramedics for a head injury. She caught the assailant trying to abscond with a piece of her jewelry and endeavored to stop him before he escaped. I'll let you know later tonight if I find out anything more, Your Honor."

Once Connor took off, I boarded the SUV and buckled my seatbelt. "It's getting out of control, huh? Imogene is one of the students in my summer session starting Monday."

"You don't know the half of it, Kellan. This seems inexplicably analogous to the last time we had those unruly jewelry thefts in Braxton. Imogene's mother, Lara, was here recording some video of the party for a news segment. She was one of the victims during the previous round," Nana D harrumphed.

"That's right, I forgot. You never did tell me what happened." Lara Bouvier, a reporter for the local news outlet, WCLN, had been married to one of Judge Grey's sons years ago. Their daughter, Imogene, had lived in France for a big part of her life. Imogene was the cousin of my former student, Carla, who'd just graduated and become an art dealer. "I don't think I've ever met Imogene."

"Sure, you did. She used to run around with Gabriel when they attended Braxton together. Come to think of it, that's the last time those jewelry heists occurred. They stopped right before Gabriel vanished during that nasty thunderstorm." Nana D cracked her knuckles, lost in a pensive reflection. "Oh, you weren't around then, my mistake. Let's head home, brilliant one. It's been a long day."

"Are you hinting at something with that comment?" Gabriel had been secretive since his return, and he'd grown darker and more evasive, but he was a good guy at heart. That I was positive about.

"I'm not really up for talking about it this weekend, Kellan. Why don't you drop me off and come for brunch on Monday when I'm more relaxed? My schedule is slammed with meetings all day tomorrow for the upcoming inauguration."

I had no choice but to grudgingly consent to Nana D's wishes. It was her birthday. She made it acutely clear she wasn't up for discussing it tonight, and I could only handle one melodrama at a time. As we left Wellington Park, a couple dashed across the street and into the park, neglecting to check for any oncoming traffic. I slammed on my horn to warn them, and they briefly looked up with shocked expressions before blocking their faces from my headlights. Given their rush and my focus on the larger surroundings, I hadn't gotten a solid glance at them.

"What's he doing with her?" Nana D mumbled, scrabbling the side of her head.

"Who?" I watched them disappear on a walkway heading south once they crossed the street.

"That was Paul Dodd, Imogene's fiancé. Shouldn't he be home attending to her after the robbery? Not running around with some other woman!" Nana D reproved before reminding me Paul had been elected the new town councilman of Braxton, assuming the role from Marcus Stanton.

"Maybe he was rushing to get home to Imogene?"

"Heading *into* the park? Nah... and he's supposed to be a stand-up guy. I can't be certain, but the woman he left with looked like Krissy Stanton, Marcus's troublesome daughter."

Krissy was another student in my upcoming class, which made their sneaky behavior sound as suspicious as that persistent *deer* invading Nana D's orchard and stealing heaps of ripening fruit. Marcus had threatened to cause a rumpus and wouldn't acknowledge Nana D had officially won the race. He lived next door to us, hence why I also suspected him of being that *deer*! "Want to follow them?"

"No, I've got ways to elicit the truth from Paul Dodd, Braxton's supposedly perfect politician and model citizen. Leave it to me." Nana D tapped the dashboard and directed me which way to drive home. "Something's fishy in the state of Pennsylvania. And it ain't your father's feet this time, Kellan."

CHAPTER 2

I spent the following morning preparing for my new class, speeding through the lesson plans and syllabus to ensure maximum quality time with my daughter when I visited my parents. Gabriel and Eleanor played various board games with us that afternoon. Even my folks joined in for several rounds of cards and dominoes. Knowing I still had a few hours of work to complete before classes began the next day, I accepted my mother's offer to watch Emma for another night. My daughter reveled in glory, which was all that mattered to me in the insufferable situation with the Castiglianos and Las Vargas.

The evening and my work passed by expeditiously, enabling me to suggest meeting for a beer to Connor. I secretly wanted to find out what'd happened at the Grey estate, but he was too wrapped up in the case to take a break. All I'd learned was that Imogene hadn't been able to identify the jewel thief, despite being at home when the crook had broken in. Connor proposed a new time for our workout later that week, and I fell asleep early in preparation for the start of a new class schedule.

After a fierce battle deciding what to wear on Monday morning, I dressed in my finest professorial duds. The summer term had made its illustrious debut, and I wanted to appear mature enough to command respect yet modern and casual in a way that befitted the television and film industry. The end result: slim cut, well-tailored trousers in traditional checks and stripes; a heather-gray, open-collared dress shirt; a thin cashmere, V-neck sweater the saleslady called the color of eggplant; and sophisticated dark loafers sans socks. Despite Nana D's effusive insistence, I wasn't morphing into a popinjay!

I hurried to The Big Beanery, a student gathering house providing some of the richest and most flavorful coffee and the craziest and most unfortunate hookups in the entire county. Thankfully, I avoided the latter, except when Nana D had set me up on a blind date those few times. I ordered a couple of coffees and apple tarts sprinkled with powdered sugar and cinnamon glaze to go. I needed something to tide me over until brunch at Nana D's. My body craved desserts just as much as it felt energized by my daily workout, which had been fulfilled by a six-mile run earlier that morning. I assumed the two ends of the spectrum balanced each other out and refused to question the greater authority of a god who permitted me to have free will.

Braxton College was comprised of two campuses, North and South, separated by a one-mile tree-lined esplanade of cozy storefronts, student housing, and charming historical points of interest. One campus perched atop a semi-steep incline of the Wharton Mountains, the other sat near the base of a lower hill leading directly into the downtown district. Traditional Victorian and Queen Anne homes, painted in vivid colors and adorned with massive stone turrets and white scalloped shingles, reminded visitors of a smaller and quieter version of San Francisco. Without the Pacific Ocean nearby, Crilly Lake and the Finnulia River generously provided our daily water supply, a source of relaxation, and stunning views. Locals referred to the large estates set atop the hill as Millionaire's Mile, and that's where you'd find folks like the Greys, the Paddingtons, and the Stantons.

North Campus was the college's main site, but I worked on South Campus which catered to scholars in the humanities, communications, and music departments. An electric cable car system, currently under maintenance, transported students back and forth between the two academic spaces. For two weeks each summer, usually when the weather reached a scorching one-hundred-degree temperature, a local company would repair the mechanics and reconfigure the inside panels based on whatever the most recent graduating class had gifted the college. This year, as a dedication to the valiant efforts of a few folks—primarily me, who'd played amateur sleuth to locate a couple of murderers—the theme was a Hercule Poirot and Miss Marple, 1930s-style mystery car. Construction had begun ten days ago, and the final ribbon-cutting ceremony would occur at the end of this week.

I climbed the steps to the sturdy but chaotic platform and scanned the sweeping uptown view of mesmerizing foliage-covered hills. My latest routine included a visit to the cable car each morning to inspect its progress with the local contractor leading the effort. Quint Crawford was in his late twenties, had shaggy blond hair, and proudly boasted a full beard. Years of working construction sites had tanned his skin a golden color and transformed his lithe body into a solid machine capable of frequent hard labor. When I called out his name, the suave and shrewd craftsman poked his head out the car doors and saluted. While I dressed up for my first day of summer classes, Quint had chosen a white fitted t-shirt and a well-worn pair of jeans slung low on his hips from all the tools weighing down the thinning denim. Although he only stood an inch below me, a slight slouch made him appear shorter.

When I'd first encountered Quint two weeks earlier, the enigmatic electrician puzzled me. Quint fancied himself quite the ladies' man, evident by his wandering eye whenever an attractive girl would meander near the cable car station. Quint was a tad too full of himself, easily enchanting the women around him by posturing a rakish allure and approach to life. But he'd privately mentioned recent heartbreak over lost love and a desire to convince the ex to proffer him a second chance. Unfortunately, Quint hadn't shared specific details on what had gone wrong the first time between him and his beloved. Nonetheless, I'd been impressed by his mercurial attitude and ability to quickly dust himself off and get in the ring again, despite his painfully obvious attempt to conceal several wounds stemming from the end of the relationship.

Once he'd formally introduced himself, I'd realized his mother and I had met a few times earlier in the year. Knowing Bertha Crawford was such a kind and gentle soul, I settled on believing Quint was a sophisticated yet opportunistic version of his mother who didn't like to hear the word *no*. "Morning, Quint. How're things looking for your mother this weekend?" I asked, passing a steaming cup of coffee and a warm pastry to him.

"I appreciate you dropping by with breakfast again. You're a good man, Kellan." His eyes darted to the panel he'd been installing and instantly looked apprehensive about my arrival. "Momma's doing better ever since she retired from the Paddington estate. Being on her feet all day as their housekeeper, slaving away at their every outlandish whim, has taken its toll on her over the years."

"Does that mean the radiation treatments are going well?" She'd discovered a lump in her breast shortly after I'd met her months ago, then learned she had an advanced form of cancer. The Paddington family also confirmed she'd quit to focus on her deteriorating health. That's when Quint had made it a priority to take extra care of his mother, a widow for the last two decades. His father had perished years ago in an explosion at the Betscha mines.

"So far, the doctors aren't positive," he mumbled, unscrewing an interior panel near the door.

"That's not good to hear." From what I could see, the winning design was close to being installed. I noticed a few wires creeping out at the bottom and wondered how the repair portion of the work was going. "The new panels look fantastic. Is the electrical upgrade on schedule?"

"Got two cables to replace, but I'll be done tomorrow afternoon. Then we can run some tests to see how the old girl's working. Should be right smooth!" Quint tapped his knuckles on the side of his head as a sign of luck. As he bent downward, he gingerly flinched and moaned before rubbing his back.

"Did you hurt yourself on the job?" I asked, uncertain what company had been awarded the contract for the redesign project. Hopefully, he'd reported any injuries to the school's administration.

"Nothing to grumble about. A man in my line of work deals with rough spots." He gently kneeled to the floor and turned away to finish removing the lower panel. "How's that daughter of yours?"

I'd brought Emma to campus with me the previous time because she had reduced hours during her last week of school. Since she'd stayed at my parents' place last night, tagging along today wasn't an option. I'd also scheduled summer camp for her to attend while I'd be teaching my classes over the subsequent seven weeks. Orientation was scheduled for tomorrow. "Emma will visit again soon. I'll be sure to bring her by, so you can say hello. She had fun watching you work last time."

"That'd be cool of you, Kellan. Don't mean to rush you off, but I've got to finish this today. Fern Terry plans to stop by to check out my progress," Quint advised with an equal mix of hesitancy and substantial irritation, then winked. "Not that she's too knowledgeable about men's work."

Fern was the dean of student affairs as well as a good friend of mine. I needed to schedule lunch with her to catch up on the wedding plans. Her son was marrying Timothy Paddington's sister, hence the double wedding on Independence Day. I ignored Quint's shallow and ludicrous comments about Fern, keenly aware we'd already discussed his opinions in the past. He regarded women more as beautiful objects or conquests rather than equals, yet he easily disguised such views when he needed to appear polished enough to charm one into offering her affections.

"I understand. Do you own the company that won the project bid?" I paused and waited for a response, but an unusually long time went by without his trademark riposte. "Quint, did you hear me?"

"Sure did. My apologies, I was thinking about the best answer," he replied, unlatching a tool from the hook on his belt. "I'm working for someone else who promised me a cheap buy-in. I'll earn a stake in the company once this project is complete. Not to be rude, buddy, but I did mention I was busy. Gotta finish tinkering with this beauty until she's sparkling like a diamond again. Chat another time?"

Quint powered up a drill on full throttle. I waved goodbye to his back—he'd already moved on to his next priority without another word—and walked toward my office in Diamond Hall. My curious nature wanted to ask more questions about whom he worked for, but Fern could supply the answer just as easily. It'd also require less impudence than dealing with my edgy new acquaintance, Quint.

Diamond Hall had previously been a grand colonial home, a mansion by modern-day standards, before its transformation into the communications department's offices. The architecturally stunning building stood three stories high and was covered with a limestone façade mined from quarries owned by the Betscha side of my family. On the top floor were a large open working area and departmental library, and on the second resided offices for academic staff. The ground floor held four classrooms, and for the next seven weeks, I'd occupy the northwest one overlooking Stanton Hall.

As I stepped through the front door, my boss glared at me with a sour expression. It wouldn't be a typical day unless I experienced at least ten minutes of Dr. Myriam Castle's uncalled-for-but-amusing wrath. Even after I'd investigated her wife's stalker the previous month, Myriam still brushed me off with a chilly disposition and delivered ruthless Shakespearean quotes that made little to no sense.

"There's a man here to see you," she stated curtly, her hands locked on her hips. Adorned in her traditional exquisite couture, her trim frame sported a cream-colored suit and slate-gray blouse assuredly flown in from some European designer's latest collection. It was the spiky, more-gray-than-black, short, no-fuss, no-muss hairstyle that initially captured a person's attention. "He doesn't have a visitor pass, and I don't recognize him. You should tell your ne'er-do-well associates to follow the rules, and if I might remind you, we should be working, not socializing."

Well, this was a perfect start to a day at the office. "I don't have any scheduled meetings. Perhaps he's a student in my summer course." I tried to dart past her, but she swiftly grabbed my arm.

"See to it this doesn't happen again. I run a clean and tight ship, and strangers are usually up to no good. I don't like his swarthy looks." She paused as if she had more to say but thought better of it.

"I'll address it right now." Swarthy? I didn't know anyone fitting that description.

"Have you considered my recommendation from last week's meeting? *'God has given you one face, and you make yourself another.'* I'm thinking only of you." Myriam frowned as if she'd bit into an acidulous piece of candy, then dug her heels into the floor like a cat in heat.

She'd been harping about instructing students to refer to me as *Dr. Ayrwick*, not *Professor* or *Kellan*, beginning with this summer's courses. I wasn't excessively opposed to it, but my Ph.D. was in film studies. I didn't feel like a bona fide medical professional, and I was still considered a temporary assistant professor. "I'm not the type to be caught up over labels. I understand your opinion that we as doctorates have earned the respect and title, but if it's all the same to you, I'd—"

"It's not my decision, this is college policy. Your father was instrumental in choosing that outcome. Take it up with him if you care to debate it. As an employee in my department, you will follow the guidelines. Are we clear?" She nodded at the puzzled expression on my face and exited the building.

Lacking any and all desire to speak with my father, the result of our discussion was a done deal. He'd been the president up until he retired the previous semester. Lucky for me, the new president was Myriam's wife, Ursula. *Fate* and *Irony* were two of my least favorite divas! "Dr. Ayrwick it will be," I shouted as I mounted the steps, wondering who skulked outside my door.

When I reached the second floor and peered down the hallway, it looked empty. The door to my office was unlocked and ajar, and the light from my desk lamp was on—not the way I'd left it the previous Friday. I cautiously stepped inside to find the *swarthy* male sitting at my desk, except I wouldn't have considered him swarthy. Knowing Myriam often chose odd ways to describe people, I ignored her comment and focused on why this man sat in my chair.

He looked familiar from the side angle, but I couldn't easily place him. "May I help you?"

Once he stood, a six-foot-three solid frame coated with a bronzed skin tone proclaimed his stature as larger-than-life. Piercing golden-brown eyes stared directly at me, and floppy espresso-colored hair cascaded down his forehead in multiple layers, reminding me of genetically engineered male supermodels gracing the covers of fashion magazines. In an instant, I knew it was Cristiano Vargas. He'd finally decided to bestow his unblemished presence upon me.

"I'm confident there's no need for proper introductions, but if you feel that's necessary, I'm happy to oblige." He exuded confidence and spoke in a smooth, distinguished voice with a cultured accent containing slight hints of his Latino heritage. From everything I'd read about the man, he functioned like a finely tuned, expensive automobile, charmed all the women he'd met, and inspired fear in all the men he'd chucked down. A Harvard pedigree also made him a wizard in the business world, no doubt ensuring his success as *numero dos* in the Las Vargas syndicate.

"Not necessary. Just a brief explanation of what you need from me, then we can both proceed with our priorities." Wishing April could be present for the conversation, I discreetly reached for the phone in my pocket, trying to recall where I'd previously placed her on speed dial. After surmising he could've taken me out at any point in the last few weeks, I considered how fearful I should be of Cristiano Vargas.

"There's no need to call the authorities or make any sudden movements. I've no intention to kill you *today*, but if necessary, I will disarm you." He lifted a panel of his suit jacket to reveal a Beretta 92.

I wasn't sure of the specific caliber, but it was a lethal one. I'd been researching handguns with the aim of procuring one to protect Emma from anyone involved in this unfortunate and over-the-top situation, yet I hadn't executed the purchase. I abhorred the thought of brandishing a weapon in the house around a child or anywhere near Nana D, who'd undoubtedly want to target shoot with me. I fought the urge to chuckle upon remembering when Rose shot Blanche's favorite vase in the apropos *Golden Girls* sitcom. Nana D had forced me to stay up late watching it with her every night when I lived in Danby Landing's main farmhouse. "Fair enough. I can put a little trust on the table, Cristiano."

"Shut the door. Sit tight. Spend a minute with me." Cristiano effortlessly walked to the guest chair on the other side of my undersized desk and pointed to his original seat. "I'm not the enemy. As a show of good faith, I'll authorize you taking the more powerful position for this conversation, yes?"

Authorize? Why did I get the impression I already hated this man? I stepped cautiously inside, scanned for any makeshift weapons, and assumed the use of my regular chair. "I'm not sure I agree with that statement. You broke into my office and scared the bejesus out of my boss."

Cristiano laughed, boasting two winning dimples balanced below his perfectly structured cheekbones. "Women are never scared of me. They want to be with me. It can be a curse, but such is my lot in life. We all have, how do you say, an albatross around our necks?" When Cristiano crossed his legs, his sleek, burgundy Ferragamo shoes tapped the corner of my desk. "Based on my research, Myriam Castle does not frighten easily. Please do not start our cozy little meeting with a preposterous lie."

"You might have researched Myriam, but suffering through her brand of crazy is an utterly inimitable experience." She was certainly an albatross. I'd give him credit for that snarky comment. I sat with my hands folded on the top of the desk, willing my confidence not to falter in the slightest.

He snickered menacingly again. "Francesca said you were an amusing guy."

"So, you're the one holding her captive. Is there a reason you're not dealing directly with the Castigliano family? I have no power in this convoluted predicament." I'd watched enough mob movies and read countless crime novels. I needed to relax and approach the meeting as if we were negotiating a common business deal. I couldn't reveal my desperate fear or complete inexperience in this lifestyle.

"Francesca also said you were very smart and would cut to the chase. I think I'm going to like working with you." Cristiano matched my position, our foreheads barely six inches apart.

I squished my knee against the side of the narrow desk to stop my leg from quivering. "I'm hopeful we only need this one meeting to discuss resolving the dispute between our two families."

As I attempted to back away, Cristiano's hand pressed down on my right shoulder. "Don't move until I permit you to do so. I want to be certain you understand what I'm about to tell you. Is this clear?"

Why was no one else in the building at this hour? I'd even accept Myriam as my bodyguard for this brief moment. In his silence, I heard the clock ticking in the hallway and the air conditioner vent blowing from the corner of the room. What had Francesca gotten me into? "Yes, like a cloudless sky."

Cristiano's other hand landed on my left shoulder, applying enough pressure to be uncomfortably intimate and dangerous. It resembled a powwow or a huddle before a championship game, except in reality, this was a duel where one of us had a broken and bullet-less pistol. "It is excruciatingly important you fear what I am capable of doing. My wrath is boundless. Las Vargas doesn't play games we cannot win... one way or another. Nothing is as it appears. Your wife is a fascinating, resourceful woman who understands the art of a mutually beneficial deal." Cristiano gripped the back of my head with his hands, then thumped the top of my scalp repeatedly with both index fingers.

Being this close, I had an in-depth look at the immaculate skin adorning his face. Cristiano had no pores—it was as if he'd been blessed with a flawless complexion. Perfection frightened me because it meant someone would fight until death to retain every aspect of it. If he hadn't told me he wouldn't kill me today, I would've expected the next move to be a swift twist of my neck until it hung limply at the side of my lifeless body. "Leave me out of this mess. Just deal with Vincenzo and Cecilia who are used to this craziness. It'll be a lot simpler that way."

Cristiano released me, walked casually around the desk, and whacked my cheek with the back of his hand—powerfully enough that my eyes saw stars and my mouth tasted blood. When I stood and attempted to punch his perturbed face, he effortlessly grabbed my forearm and twisted it around my back. I couldn't move without intense pain shooting into my shoulder blade. "Do not ever tell me what to do, Kellan. Such consequences have been known to kill stronger men than you."

I stood still, unwilling to accept but forced to listen to his words. "Why am I involved?"

"Surprisingly, Francesca offered to sacrifice her own life to end the war. Yet, as much as she cooperated with me and as anxious as she was to get out from under the watchful scorn of her devious parents, I didn't completely trust your wife. Although an eye for an eye would make up for a lot, it wouldn't have made my family content." Cristiano released me and stepped backward, crossing his arms and casting a look that made it clear I shouldn't attack him again. "My family wants more than equivalent payback. Reparations for the Castiglianos' past indiscretions have become necessary."

"You didn't answer my question. Why are you looping me into this negotiation?"

"Patience, I'm telling you a story. I thought hard and long about why Francesca was willing to die. I wanted to locate any hidden motives that might harm the Vargas family. I tried a few different methods to break her, but after I threatened to hurt Emma, Francesca finally cringed, begged for mercy, and revealed all the plans her parents had made to destroy us. Don't try anything funny. I'd hate for anything bad to happen to that precious little girl," Cristiano said, a sinister shadow cast across his face from the glow of the desk lamp. "Once locating the right incentive, with Francesca on board, forcing the Castiglianos to agree to whatever I asked became simple. Using you as a middleman, Francesca and her parents are unable to talk to one another or pass any clues to play tricks on me. People are willing to cooperate when they're unable to hear or see what's happening to someone they love. Now, I'll have everyone's full collaboration and obedience. Fear can be a highly encouraging factor."

"The Castiglianos won't share anything with me. They've hated me for years," I explained, unclear how that would gain him any leverage or control over my in-laws. I only understood how Francesca would listen, knowing she wanted to be with Emma again—that was obvious.

"The Castiglianos don't want to sacrifice their daughter, but they're also frightened I'll harm Emma. No one wants to lose their entire family, do they?" The sneer on his face manifested all too easily when he handed me a phone from his jacket pocket. "Your monstrous in-laws have zero choice but to trust you if they want to see their daughter and granddaughter survive this ordeal."

"I get it now. Emma and I are your leverage. You want me to broker the deal between you and the Castiglianos because it motivates everyone to behave. If I don't or if any of the Castiglianos try to escape or retaliate, Emma, Francesca, and I end up dead. Then, everyone loses."

"You catch on quickly, Kellan. That phone is how we'll communicate in the future. Do not use it for anything else but our conversations. I will be in touch in forty-eight hours with instructions. My diligent staff is organizing stimulating bedtime reading that Francesca has generously shared with us."

"Do we have the same goal in mind? Are we expecting an outcome we'll both be happy about?"

"That depends. If you imagine moving forward with your life minus any future worries, we have similar desires. If you anticipate the Castiglianos retaining control of their business investments and interests, we do not." Cristiano removed a handkerchief from his pocket and rubbed a spot on his shoe.

"Will Francesca be safe until then?"

"This has never been about her. It was about revenge against her parents and accepting the consequences of their past actions. When I met Francesca two months ago, something fortuitous happened. She's not the woman I thought she would be. Based on her cooperation thus far, no harm should fall her way. If anything feels suspicious, harm will fall your and Emma's way. Agreed?"

"Not until I speak with Francesca." I ignored the bitter metallic taste overwhelming my mouth.

"In time. Do not contact me. I'll call you when I have the details you need." He stepped a few feet closer and faced me directly. "Emma certainly loves her new puppy. Baxter is the perfect name."

"How did you know we named him—"

Cristiano looked at me as if I'd spoken a foreign language or said the most ridiculous series of childish words, then furiously smacked my abdominals with the palm of his hand. His unexpected physical aggression was taking its toll on me, but I wouldn't let him see me retreat in pain. "I know everything, Kellan. Even how you skipped the last half-mile on your morning run near Crilly Lake. Imagine how much better shape you'd be in, if you challenged yourself and stopped devouring those insidious apple tarts. I'd be more worried those desserts are what'll kill you one day, *Little Ayrwick*."

Five seconds later, Cristiano was gone, and I rushed to the men's room. Either the coffee had cycled through me more quickly than usual or I was more scared than I thought. Once I felt normal again, I swiped my mobile's screen and began to dial April before realizing Cristiano might've tapped my phone line. I wasn't sure if one could tap a mobile phone or if the scheming mastermind had hidden a voice-activated recording device in the office to listen to my every move. I wanted to check with Connor, but April had warned me not to reveal anything to him unnecessarily.

I briefly searched the office but found nothing obvious. I abandoned the mission and instead downloaded student profiles for my summer course. I walked to Paddington's Play House, the campus theater next door, and commandeered their office phone. April and I made plans to discuss our next steps the following day, and she promised to locate someone to scour my office for any recording devices while I taught *Documentary Filmmaking* that afternoon. Shortly before noon, I left the Play House and called Nana D from my cell phone to let her know I was driving to Danby Landing for brunch and to solicit background on the jewelry burglaries. Knowing I only had a couple of hours before class started, she'd promised earlier that our meal would be ready when I walked through the door.

"On your way home yet, brilliant one? You better hurry up," she said in a muffled voice.

"Yes, I'll be on time. Why are you acting like I'm already late?" Punctuality was at the high end of Nana D's expectations, and I was certain to avoid punishment for something easily obtainable.

"You've got some early visitors. We're having a cocktail in your guest cottage —*Whiskey Sour* for me, *Death in the Afternoon* for them. It seemed appropriate for your in-laws. I hope you don't mind, but I saw the Castiglianos pull up and didn't want to leave them unattended," Nana D explained.

I slammed on the brakes and jolted forward. The last time Nana D had seen my in-laws was when she'd visited LA after Francesca had supposedly died. For the last two-and-a-half years, they'd managed to avoid one another like the plague. "Please behave, I've had enough drama for today!"

"Gotta run, don't want to leave them sitting by themselves. I need to find Grandpop's shotgun. Better to be armed than defenseless, eh? Toodle-oo, Kellan." Nana D hung up, snickering wickedly.

I drove twice the speed limit to get home before one of the three flamboyant caricatures in my life committed murder. If I were a betting man, Nana D would garner the best odds, but what was her aim like these days?

CHAPTER 3

Ten minutes later, I opened my front door to the sound of three distinct laughs. Nana D's garrulous and all-encompassing guffaw, Cecilia's pompous and high-pitched chortle, and Vincenzo's single grunt resembling a snorting pig searching for food in his empty trough. "You're extremely early," I said, tossing my keys on a nearby table. "What's so funny?"

Vincenzo's shiny bald head seemed to grow exponentially as he aged, and the salt-and-pepper goatee that insisted upon clinging to his chin in despair left me embarrassed for him. Nonetheless, his eerily calm tone and menacing, stocky body shape frightened most people to no end, including me. "I've missed this face. Hopefully, we can keep it this way. You need to visit more often, especially once everything is back to normal." He immediately greeted me with a big hug, then kissed both my cheeks.

Hmmm... had I entered *The Twilight Zone*? When he pulled away, I felt his fingerprints still etched into my back and shoulders. "I trust you had a safe flight." I directed my gaze at him, then turned to Cecilia. She stared at me coldly and offered no embrace, which was a relief after Vincenzo's salutation. Cecilia, willowy and gaunt, though pretty in the right light with her striking blonde coiffure, matched her husband in height. Neither had ever needed a stepstool to change a lightbulb in a ceiling fixture, not that they'd deign to do that kind of chore themselves.

She unclenched her teeth. "Let's skate past the small stuff, Kellan. We're not here to partake in afternoon tea. If Seraphina hadn't won her recent mayoral election, I would've suspected she poisoned our cocktails. Alas, she can't afford a scandal right now. I trust you are following our orders?"

Orders! Everyone wanted me to follow their orders. I was fed up with it all and felt like a puppet whose strings were mismanaged frantically by maniacs. Cecilia and Vincenzo instructed me not to speak with the police or the Vargas family, encouraging me to leave the negotiations in their capable hands. What kind of convoluted scheme were they kicking off this time? I couldn't tell them that Cristiano had visited me earlier that day. I also wouldn't reveal April's involvement in a secret investigation. "I'm aware of your directives. I intend to follow them to the best of my ability. Please cut me some slack; the world of ominous crime families is new to me."

Nana D cleared her throat. "For your information, *Don Castigliano*, or whatever you ridiculous mafia types call yourselves... I wouldn't poison you. I'd arrange for my sons to take you on a little trip into the Saddlebrooke National Forest to monitor our famous grizzly bears coming out of hibernation. Though I'm not sure they'd relish the taste of rancid meat." She downed the remainder of her cocktail.

Cecilia pranced forward until she stood face to face with Nana D, albeit an entire foot taller. "I thought we were getting along so well before Kellan arrived home. I suggest you be careful with the words you choose, Seraphina. You wouldn't want to get caught in the crossfire, right?"

"That's enough threats from the lot of you. Why are you here?" I asked my pugnacious in-laws.

Vincenzo explained that he and Cecilia had been spying on the Vargas family, looking for information they could use to prevent them from keeping Francesca. "I uncovered a few possibilities last weekend, but I need to set something in motion that will force Las Vargas to return my daughter safely. I cannot go into the details, but it seems Cristiano might not be as clean as he claims to be."

I grabbed the bottle of whiskey from the coffee table and poured myself a shot. I swallowed it immediately. Then I poured another and stared at the smooth golden liquid like it were the elixir of life. I downed it just like Nana D had. I debated pouring a third, but two were enough for the afternoon. There was a class to teach. "For years, you've caused nothing but grief for me and my family. Emma knows little about this, and I intend to keep it that way. Push me too much, I will shove back. Do what you want to rescue Francesca, but don't play games with me. Like you, my daughter will always come first."

"I assure you; we are just as much victims in this catastrophe as you are, Kellan," Cecilia tactfully tried to reason with me. "If you'd stayed in Los Angeles, this wouldn't have become a problem."

"If he'd stayed in Los Angeles, he might've been fish food," Nana D whined in a mocking voice, looking as if she was gearing up for a sucker-punch. "What a bunch of stupid—"

I moved near Nana D to assert control over her actions, which were problematic based on prior experience. "Look, you two plan whatever scheme it takes to find a solution," I directed at Cecilia and Vincenzo, "and I'll keep Emma sheltered from the truth. She's all I care about right now."

Cecilia blasted, "When offered a choice between saving you or my daughter, you'll always lose."

"And if there's a choice between saving Francesca or Emma, as I said earlier, I'll choose my daughter every time." How dare my psycho mother-in-law go down that path!

"Don't you love Francesca anymore? Don't you want her to return safely?" Vincenzo pleaded with me in a way I knew was meant to frighten and warn me.

"Yes, of course, but it's been a long time, and I have no idea how this will turn out. Francesca and I need to make that decision together when it's appropriate to do so." I'd already decided I couldn't recommit to my wife after everything that'd happened, but this wasn't the time or place to discuss it.

"You haven't heard from Las Vargas since the kidnapping, right?" Cecilia barked conspiratorially.

I shook my head. I didn't want to lie, but my best course of action was to trust neither side and to bide my time until April found something useful. "How long will you be in Braxton?"

"A few days," Vincenzo replied, grabbing Cecilia's arm and shepherding her out the door. "We will call you tomorrow for an update. Our agenda is quite full this afternoon with... other discussions."

After they left, Nana D said, "I'm proud you stood your ground. You're doing the right thing."

I prayed that she was correct, or that she had a direct line to someone who could protect us all. My mind and body were a wreck. The lies and fear were taking their toll on me, and the thought of what would still play out once Emma learned her mother was alive reminded me of someone who waited for a derailed train to pummel them. "I love you, Nana D. You're my rock throughout this entire fiasco."

"Of course, I am. Now, do you want to hear about those jewelry thefts from eight years ago, or did you already forget the purpose of brunch?" Nana D shuffled out of the cottage toward her house to prepare our meal, sighing the entire way about how long it took me to follow her.

"You're gonna drive me to an early grave. I don't believe anyone can keep up with you." When we reached her kitchen, she slowed down, enabling me to regain her attention. "What are we having?"

"Chicken salad with walnuts and cranberries. I know you love them." Nana D ripped the plastic cover off an oversized bowl. "Whole grain bread, avocado mash, and a small slice of lemon meringue pie on the side. Can't have your sugar dip too low in front of the students, but you need to watch what you eat at your age," she added, reaching over the table and poking the top of my already tender stomach.

Was she coordinating today's insults with Cristiano? "My metabolism hasn't stopped. Don't jinx me." I poured us each a glass of sun tea and selected the two largest sandwiches as my own crude way of fighting back. We sat side by side at the banquette in her farmhouse kitchen staring at the corner of the orchard, where many of the trees dangled and released blossoming fruit. We were experiencing the June Drop, a natural process where trees self-pruned and shed some of their gifts. "Have you heard anything further about the jewelry theft at the Grey estate? Or caught up with Paul about his park dalliances? Imogene is supposed to attend this afternoon's class. I wonder if she'll show up."

"I'm meeting Paul on Wednesday. All I know is that the crime happened at Imogene's mother's place, not the family estate. Marcus Stanton is monopolizing all the sheriff's time. He has a few days before leaving office, but he's trying his best to keep information from me." Nana D made an odd gesture with two curled fingers cursing the vitriolic man. Eleanor must have taught her —not that the women in my family believed in witchcraft, but several claimed to have psychic abilities and receive well-intentioned premonitions. Eleanor had once fastidiously learned to read Tarot Cards and tea leaves.

"So, that weird gnarly finger move means it's a *no*?" I asked, gobbling the avocado mash. I'd wanted to interrogate Connor at our workout, but he'd canceled again due to his caseload. Although the jewelry thefts had zilch to do with me, the curious devil inside me wouldn't let it go. Nana D crossed her arms as if my insurgence had insulted her—the epitome of a sullen child when it suited her needs.

"You really are the best cook in town," I patronized, hoping to appease her sudden disdain. Nana D shot me a staggering warning glance. "I mean county." Her added ruffled gaze gave me the willies. "Definitely the whole state. Indubitably." When she leaned closer, I finished expediently, saying, "Okay, maybe I'll just stuff my mouth full of pie."

"You've finally said something that makes sense!" she grumbled and handed her plate to me, indicating she wanted a large slice. Nana D shared what she knew of the jewelry thefts from eight years ago. Between May and June, five homes had been burglarized. The first item was an *en tremblant* brooch, an iridescent French floral spray with a striking trembling effect, owned by Gwendolyn Paddington. She'd been attending a theater performance at the Paddington Play House on campus when it had been purportedly lost. Her family couldn't remember seeing it clipped to her gown, but several witnesses had recalled noticing its glow from the candlelight of the wall sconces at the theater. "The following day, when it didn't turn up in the lost and found or at the Paddington estate, Gwennie contacted the sheriff who sent an officer to check both places. It was a useless exercise."

"No leads on who stole it?" I pondered the confusion about where it'd been lost and wondered whether it'd anything to do with the bribes April once mentioned in association with the former sheriff.

"No, Gwennie insisted the investigation be kept quiet. She was embarrassed at the uncertainty of when and where it had been stolen. Nine days later, Agnes Nutberry lost a choker while listening to her granddaughter, Tiffany's, concert in Stanton Hall." Tiffany was the daughter of Agnes's son, a pharmacist, and his wife, Lydia, the director of their family mortuary. I'd known the Nutberrys for years and had unfortunately stumbled upon one of their clan's roles in a murder the prior month.

"Did they publicize the loss?" Something didn't make sense if it had also been silenced.

"Yes, but no one connected the two crimes initially. Sheriff Crawford wouldn't broadcast the investigation's core facts until much later when he couldn't unearth the criminal." The former sheriff being Quint Crawford's uncle, who'd passed away a few years ago shortly after his retirement.

"Okay, what about the rest?" I wanted to ask if there were any suspects, but she was on a roll.

"In the third robbery, a pair of ruby earrings were pilfered while on display at an historical society event on campus. Lucy Roarke had donated them to the exhibition because they'd been one of the earliest documented gems in Braxton's history."

After Nana D noted that the third robbery occurred exactly nine days after the second one, I asked the obvious, "What's the significance of nine days?"

Nana D had no insight but thought it peculiar. She revealed that the fourth stolen item had also gone missing nine days later—a pearl necklace Lara Bouvier had been gifted at her wedding to one of the Grey boys. They'd married on her eighteenth birthday after she'd graduated from high school, but it wasn't for love. Lara had gotten pregnant while still in school, and Judge Hiram Grey forced his son to marry her to prevent Imogene from being born out of wedlock. Even though this had only happened twenty-eight years ago, his family had gone through enough scandals, and he'd been up for his first reelection to the bench that year. After the divorce, Lara had retained the necklace as part of her generous settlement. "When the Grey family offered to pay Imogene's college expenses, Lara was thrilled; however, they demanded the necklace be returned as part of the arrangement. To get even with them, Lara decided to sell the necklace at an auction, but it was stolen the night before she could present it for bidding."

"If Lara couldn't figure out what happened, the thief must've been highly intelligent and savvy," I suggested while sampling the smoothest and tangiest lemon curd filling I'd ever tasted. Nothing about the nine-day gap between each heist made sense, unless the timing was only a coincidence.

Nana D explained that fifty-thousand dollars had been pinched from the Stanton family in the fifth robbery, but she couldn't remember the entire episode's details. "A massive thunderstorm caused a power outage for twenty-fours during some big shi-shi party with hobnobbers clippity-clopping about all night. Marcus caused such a ruckus, everyone panicked, and no one knew what was going on."

While Nana D cleared the table, I perused the local newspaper but found nothing about the recent burglary at Lara's place. "And no one was ever caught eight years ago?"

"Nah, all those wealthy families were hesitant to go public and look foolish for being tricked. Silas Crawford, my friend's brother-in-law, was the former sheriff. Bertha knew of a few shady things going on back then but tried to dissociate herself once the rumors about him taking bribes increased." Nana D handed me a Tupperware dish with another slice of pie. "The thefts stopped after the fifth one, and then the whole affair quieted down. That's also when Gabriel disappeared."

"When did it all start up again?" I visualized a calendar to piece together the timing. "Just the basics, I've got to get back to campus for class soon."

"Last week of May, right before we had our big family dinner to welcome Gabriel home." Nana D pursed her lips and closed her eyes. "Talk to your brother to find out if he's concealing useful information from the police. I can't start my term as mayor with a black cloud hanging over this family."

"I understand." After a goodbye hug, I chatted with Emma to verify her visit with my father was going well. They'd just finished lunch at the country club and were delivering coffee to my mother, who was working in Admissions Hall for the afternoon. Emma begged to crash at the Royal Chic-Shack again, and once my father blessed the idea, I agreed to it. She needed to be far away from the Castiglianos.

On the drive to Braxton, I called Gabriel to propose meeting up for a beer, where I could also find out what he knew about the burglaries. He didn't answer, and his voicemail was full. I couldn't leave a message. What had he gotten himself into this time, and how did his former friendship with the latest victim, Imogene Grey, fit into the puzzle? Nana D had said they'd been close before he left town.

Documentary Filmmaking was my seven-week summer class meeting Mondays, Wednesdays, and Fridays for two-and-a-half hours in the afternoon. It was an elective course for any students majoring in communications, but it was also open that summer to any Braxton citizens interested in the film industry. As a result, much of the crowd were locals in their late twenties or early thirties who didn't work full-time. After taking attendance, reviewing the syllabus, and answering questions, I divided the class into three groups consisting of four students each. They were tasked with selecting and agreeing on topics for future group and individual documentaries. I spent the final hour walking around to provide clarification and input, then met with each team, who shared their proposed projects for my approval. The first two presentations went effortlessly, and I encouraged them to utilize their remaining time to get better acquainted.

I dragged a student desk across the linoleum floor and joined the third and final group, who'd gathered in a circle near the open bay window. Initially, all four women were silent. Disgruntled expressions occupied most faces. I recognized one of them, Siobhan Walsh, as she'd held the role of office manager in our department last semester. She'd gone on maternity leave two months before I'd begun working on campus. Upon her return, she'd quickly transferred to another department, something which had displeased my boss, Myriam.

I'd never met the other three women in the circle, but during a preliminary review of the course roster, I'd recognized two of their names. Imogene Grey showed up for class in spite of the prior weekend's burglary, and Krissy Stanton was the daughter of our outgoing, monosyllabic town councilman, Marcus Stanton. I worried about the possibility of tension in the classroom resulting from my nana defeating her father in the mayoral election but hoped we could handle the situation as mature adults. I wasn't certain Krissy was the same girl I'd seen running in the park with Paul Dodd, despite their similar body type. The fourth woman, Raquel Salvado, was unfamiliar to me and new to Braxton.

"How's this group working out so far?" I asked, eager to encourage their discussion.

Siobhan smiled and attempted to speak first. Her garish makeup and bright-red hair made her seem like an over-the-top exaggeration of herself, but she was actually a sweet, down-to-earth mother caring for newborn twins. The only concern I remembered from our interactions, besides thinking she might've killed a friend of mine, was that she could be impetuous and confrontational if you crossed her the wrong way. "We haven't made a lot of progress. Imogene and Krissy are unable to agree on a group topic. Raquel and I are flexible, and we're happy to—"

"All I said was that her proposal wouldn't capture an audience's attention," Krissy interjected while tossing her hand in Imogene's direction. "She's just too sensitive sometimes."

I'd forgotten how thick Siobhan's Irish accent was, despite her relocation from Dublin to the United States over five years ago. I looked at Raquel, who nodded in agreement with Siobhan, and smiled confidently. "Perhaps I can help. Have we had proper introductions from every member in the group? We should understand the reason each of you has enrolled in this course."

"I'll go first. My father taught me how to be a leader," Krissy said, then hesitated to continue as she realized to whom she was talking. Krissy, in her late twenties, looked overly pouty for this early in the summer session and had pulled her wavy dirty-blonde hair into a ponytail. She wore chic dark-colored jeans, four-inch crimson-red heels, and a flowery silk blouse that covered a few extra pounds she didn't want anyone to know about. I only knew because my sister, Eleanor, had shared her own tricks with me. "Anyway, my name is Krissy Stanton. I'm thinking of moving to California, and I've always loved the movies. I thought... why not take a class... maybe when I get to Hollywood, I'll be ahead of the curve. With this experience and my family's name and fame, I'm a shoo-in for a big-time director role."

"Great to meet you, Krissy," I began, pondering how to best temper her excitement and confusion over the way things worked in the film industry. "Not to alarm you, but sometimes it can be difficult to break into the business without any formal experience. I'll do my best to educate everyone on the different paths filmmakers might take, especially in terms of documentary-style movies."

"Thanks, Dr. Ayrwick." Krissy scrolled on her cell phone and grinned scornfully at Imogene.

"Excellent. How about you, Imogene? Please share a little about yourself." I turned my focus to a woman in her late twenties with expressive eyes and short, curly dark-brown hair. She appeared timid, but I couldn't be certain if it was the aftereffect of her encounter with the thief, her discord with Krissy, or simply her normal personality having been raised in the Grey family.

"It's a pleasure to meet everyone. I'm Imogene Grey, and you might know my mother, Lara Bouvier. She's a reporter at WCLN and covers all the major exclusives in Wharton County. I'm excited to be here," she said with a brief giggle, prompting her to cover her mouth and glance downward. "I grew up in Braxton before attending boarding school in Paris. I graduated from Braxton College six years ago and moved back to Paris to get an advanced degree, but I recently returned home to be with my fiancé. When I wanted to learn more about my mother's work, she suggested I take a course in communications."

Imogene spoke with traces of a French accent, and her wardrobe must've been inspired by her experiences in Paris. She wore a lace-trimmed designer black dress and a playful red beret, reminding me of the actress who starred in the movie *Amelie*. I noticed Imogene's strong resemblance to Lara as well as how lucky she'd been to avoid inheriting the protuberant jaw of the Grey family.

"I've met your mother a few times. She's a gifted newscaster. I won't be able to offer you every detail on the life of an investigative reporter in this particular class, but many of the skills required to create a documentary, such as in-depth interview techniques and summarizing events of the past, will be covered," I replied, finding no obvious sign of injury to her upper body. Knowing news of her attack had been semi-public, I questioned it. "I understand you found a spot of trouble this weekend. Are you well enough to attend class today? I'd love for you to stay engaged if you're feeling up to it."

When Krissy snorted in the background, Raquel shot her a disapproving look. Imogene and Krissy must've known one another previously from their la-dee-da social circles. If something were going on between Paul and Krissy, maybe Imogene had become aware of it. I could see resentment in the women's eyes. Raquel and Siobhan would hopefully function as the calming forces in the group.

"Oh, I'm much better today. The creep didn't hit me too hard, and as soon as I realized what was going on, I shoved him away and ran from the room. I'm lucky he didn't follow me," Imogene responded as she clasped her hands in her lap and rubbed her fingers together. "I am still shaken up but don't want to miss anything you're planning to teach us."

In a tone bubbling with excitement and energy, Siobhan said, "Good for you. I've had a few encounters with less-than-stellar jerks too. I always hit back. Did you get a chance to knock him out?"

Imogene looked downward. "I think... maybe... I cut his arm with my fingernail."

"How unlike you! I guess Paul, Mommy, and Daddy weren't there to help, huh?" Krissy scolded.

"I'm glad you're well enough to be here," I interrupted, "but I don't want to keep everyone too late. Siobhan, tell the group about your background and why you're taking this class."

"I previously worked in this building but needed to earn more money. Single mothers have it so hard. I accepted an offer in the admissions office last month. I've always been interested in documentaries, and this was the best way I could stay connected to all my former colleagues. I miss working with them." She beamed widely and sat back in her chair, waiting for me to respond.

"We miss you too, but to ensure everyone is clear, I plan to treat you equally in this classroom. It doesn't matter if you know someone in my family," I said, looking at Imogene and recalling she and Gabriel had once been well acquainted. I couldn't bring myself to look at Krissy. "Or if we've worked together in the past. So, let's hear from our final team member before discussing the presentations."

An exotically attractive brunette in her mid-twenties cleared her throat and introduced herself. "I'm Raquel Salvado, and this is my first class at Braxton. I recently moved to Wharton County, and I haven't been able to find a job. My husband told me about these summer classes. I thought it might be a productive way to meet new people and learn something fun." Her voice was soft but strong, and she spoke eloquently as if she'd attended elite schools and came from a well-to-do family.

"We're thrilled to have you here," I replied while analyzing the dynamics in the group. Krissy and Siobhan would be the two to vie for control. Imogene and Krissy's pasts might result in disagreements. Should I consider changing groups now before the projects began? I decided not to make any switches. If they couldn't act mature and find a way to partner together, I'd reassign their team at the end of the week. I owed it to the entire class to allow the situation a chance to work itself out. "Now that we know each other better, who wants to explain the two options you've come up with for the project?"

After back-and-forth negotiations, we settled on a new theme for their group effort, and all four women appeared content with the solution. I reminded them what to do for Wednesday's class, ushered them out of Diamond Hall, and drove home to finish my day sans all the crazy people in my life. Nana D was meeting friends for dinner, and Gabriel was probably working again. I wouldn't be interrupted by anyone and could get to sleep early. Once I returned a few emails and ate dinner, I called my mother to check on Emma. After a quick catch up, she passed the phone to my daughter.

"Daddy! I'm super excited to visit the summer camp tomorrow. What time do we go?" Emma's voice was so incredibly sweet and enthusiastic, it almost turned my evening around.

"We attend orientation at noon. Grandpa and Grandma will take you some-where special for an early lunch. I'll be at work for a few hours, but I'll use my magic lamp to find you." Being a single parent was not easy, Siobhan was right. At least I had the benefit of a partially flexible teaching schedule to ensure I could be there for all the notable events in Emma's life. Without my parents, Nana D, and Eleanor, I would be a royal mess, to quote the sheriff as she once described our current situation. Still, it was better than the alternative in LA where the Castiglianos had frequently cared for Emma.

"I love surprises. I bet it's the science lab. Last time, I got to eat lunch next to a giant tarantula!" She chuckled and continued dazzling me with the story I heard every single time she'd visit campus.

"I love you more than desserts, ice cream, and anyone else," I said, feeling my heartstrings twang over the disastrous war between Las Vargas and the Castiglianos. "Baxter misses you very much, but it's your bedtime, honey. We'll see each other tomorrow."

After hanging up and walking her new puppy, I began to feel better, or at least strong enough to get through another day. Pets and kids; they always made life brighter!

* * *

Tuesday morning came so fast, it was as if I blinked and the night had passed. In reality, I'd spent every waking moment staring at the ceiling and attempting to concoct a non-existent solution for my dilemma with Cristiano Vargas. After yielding to the lack of clarity on our next steps, I drove to The Big Beanery to buy morning pastries and coffee for Quint, choosing a French-vanilla blend on this occasion. Thinking about something other than the mafia or jewelry thefts had ensured my good mood. On the five-minute walk to the cable car station, chirping birds soared through the trees and someone's heavy footsteps jogged on a nearby pathway. When a pungent sandalwood scent wafted by, I gazed around and saw through the branches as the jogger picked up a pair of gloves from the path and took off in the opposite direction. Mornings on campus, especially in the summer, were often incredibly quiet. I ascended the steps to the platform and tossed out Quint's name, wondering whether he might recall anything his uncle, the former sheriff, had said about the past jewelry thefts. "Chocolate-glazed donuts, buddy. How's progress?" I rounded the corner and stepped through the entrance into the cable car.

Unfortunately, it was not the scene I expected to encounter or one I needed to encounter. Quint was there, but the sounds of his tools humming along as they finished the repairs and redesign weren't present. Quint quietly lay on the floor without a care in the world, except I knew it wasn't a brief morning nap between tasks. I'd seen the look of an extinguished life many times before. Quint was permanently sleeping, as in deceased for all eternity.

CHAPTER 4

After verifying Quint was unquestionably dead, I debated whether to call the sheriff or Connor. Grateful that my relationship with April had swung to the positive side, I notified Connor, hopeful it might unfold less painfully with him. While he rushed over, I surveyed the scene to determine what had transpired.

Quint laid supine on the floor of the cable car with his eyes wide open, staring at various pictures of Agatha Christie on the finished ceiling. He wore his usual jeans, white t-shirt, and construction boots, and his hands were slightly clenched. On closer inspection, I noticed red and dark brownish-black spots on his fingers as though he'd recently been burned by something. Two exposed wires from the panel across the cramped space carelessly drooped to the floor but produced no sparks. It was the only remaining panel disconnected from the body of the cable car. Had he accidentally electrocuted himself while doing repairs? My heart went out to the man who'd lost his life too early.

It appeared Quint had touched the exposed wires. I would be safe, assuming I avoided those. I'd need to advise Connor to confirm whether the main electrical power supply to the cable car was currently switched on or off. While searching the remainder of the car, a bouquet of black calla lilies resting beside Quint's immobile body seemed out of place. Had someone discovered the accident and put a remembrance token near him? Or was it a revenge message, a call of death? It raised curiosity about what'd occurred in the darkest hours of the night inside Braxton's beloved transportation system.

When a car pulled into the lot, I checked my watch and noticed it was barely eight in the morning. Connor exited his unmarked vehicle and trudged up the steps. "Kellan, are you inside?"

I called back to him and waited for him to reach me. "He's definitely gone. I'm not sure if he electrocuted himself or something else happened. Look," I said, pointing to the calla lilies once he arrived. "That's unusual, don't you think?"

Connor climbed under the platform and confirmed the power was off at the external supply box, which made little sense based on the burns on Quint's hands. Had he still been alive after the first jolt, enabling him to turn off the power, and died from a secondary issue? While Connor notified the sheriff and coroner, I continued looking around the cable car. Quint's open toolbox sat on a blanket on a newly cushioned seat. At least he took caution not to scratch or tear anything in the car while working. I inspected the floor and saw a shiny red object underneath the bench nearest Quint's feet.

I bent down to catch a better view without disturbing any potential evidence, in case this was a crime scene. My mind was inclined to enter over-drive, but I wouldn't let myself get too concerned this early in the game about Quint's death being unnatural. I pointed to the shiny red object as Connor walked back in the car. "Is that a piece of jewelry?"

To my chagrin, Connor asked me to step outside while he inspected it. "Wait on the platform, please."

I thought back to my conversation with Quint the prior morning. He'd been quick to dismiss me, noting he had work to do. Could Quint have discovered the thief coming back from another heist last night? Then again, Nana D told me they'd happened every nine days. The last one had occurred only three days ago. I gulped a large mouthful of coffee with a hope it'd alleviate my confusion. It didn't.

Connor stepped back on the platform and accepted the coffee I'd intended to give Quint. "I believe it's a ruby, but I don't want to touch anything until the forensics team arrives onsite. Did you notice anyone hanging around the cable car when you showed up? And what time was that exactly?"

I paused to mentally walk myself through every step I'd made after setting foot on campus, then grabbed The Big Beanery receipt from my pocket. "I paid for coffee at seven twenty-five. Takes less than five minutes to walk here, so I guess about seven thirty. Now that you mention it, I briefly noticed someone. At the time, I assumed it was a jogger out for a morning run. I never saw the person's face, just the silhouette of someone picking up a pair of gloves and continuing on his or her way."

"Okay. His body is cool to the touch. Rigor has set in. The coroner will confirm, but he's been dead maybe six or eight hours." Connor scratched his chin and shook his head. Something about the situation perturbed him too. "I took multiple photos of the crime scene before the team arrives."

"What do you think happened?" Based on Connor's math, Quint had died around midnight.

Connor peered at Quint's body with speculation, focusing closely at the collar of his shirt. "I assumed he was electrocuted, but there are red marks on his neck which look suspicious."

"I suppose they couldn't have been from the power of the voltage," I said, hearing the sheriff's voice calling Connor's name from the platform steps. "Could he have been strangled?"

"Possibly; they do resemble distinct finger impressions. To be honest, the calla lilies and the ruby suggest this wasn't an accidental electrocution." Connor nodded at April, who dipped her head before walking by us to enter the car.

"Gentlemen, not the best circumstances to be meeting one another this morning," April began, raising her voice from inside the center section. "Kellan, I hoped we wouldn't have to do this again. Do you go on walkabout quests searching for dead bodies as one of your cherished hobbies? If you're that bored, maybe you could consider needlepoint or ballroom dancing."

From the quick glance I'd stolen as she glided by, I'd originally surmised a calmer and more open-minded sheriff would be making an appearance today. I was wrong. "Your sarcasm knows no bounds. I purposely contacted Connor this time, hoping to avoid exactly this conversation—"

As she stepped out of the car, April covered my mouth with a gloved hand and guided me toward the end of the platform. "You finally did the right thing. It's bugged me for months why you insisted on contacting me instead of the detective I'd assigned to a case," April interrupted and glanced down at her car.

Someone sat in the passenger seat, but I couldn't sneak a fully unobstructed look at him. Other than recognizing he was on the younger and taller side, I was perplexed. She didn't wear a wedding ring, yet I'd never seen her on a date before. Had April Montague been on a clandestine overnight jaunt with a boyfriend?

"Perhaps I just enjoy your company," I said, shrugging and mentally slapping myself. Why did my mouth utter things I had no control over whenever April was around? "Or, I guess, I didn't know any of your other detectives before Connor joined the force."

"Now that you know one, I think it's best if you consider him your primary contact in the future. We're already working together enough on your personal situation. Let's keep it that way." April caught me gawking at the man in her car, but she didn't acknowledge him or offer any explanation.

"Sure, I'm hopeful I can walk away from this one after giving a formal statement." I hardly knew Quint. Why would I need to stay involved in this investigation?

"Good. I assume that means you unintentionally found the body this morning and don't know who it is. I'll verify Connor has this under control, then I need to take my...." April looked back at her car. "Then, I have an errand to run. Try not to get into any more trouble this week, okay?"

Hmmm... I didn't want to lie to her. "You should know that I've been chatting with the victim almost every morning for the last ten days. I purposely stopped by to see him today."

April's right hand slowly clenched. "I see. I'm confident Connor will take that into consideration. You're unfamiliar with his family or next of kin, right? Nothing to keep you here longer?"

"Oh, well... about that...."

"Little Ayrwick!" April's eyes burst open like a spring flower witnessing an unexpected flurry of snow and curling its frustrated petals.

"Hey, you said you'd stop calling me that!" I threw my hands in the air in pseudo-shock. "You also know someone in his family." I mentioned that Quint was the son of Bertha Crawford, a witness she'd interviewed in the Paddington murder case. I also noted the woman's current bout with cancer.

"That poor soul. First, she gets sick. Then, her son is murdered." April's lime-green eyes revealed a genuine sadness for Bertha. "That also makes the victim the nephew of the former sheriff."

"Definitely murdered." My ears tingled with curiosity about the calla lilies. What did they mean?

"Yes, I trust you'll keep that quiet. I'll wait for the coroner's report, but he was obviously strangled and electrocuted. Someone desperately wanted Quint Crawford out of the picture."

The sheriff exchanged a few words with Connor and the team who'd begun cordoning off the area. After she left saying she'd call about our other case soon, Connor escorted me down the steps. "Other than Quint's mother, do you know whom we should notify of his death?"

"No, I hardly learned much about him. I hadn't even known Bertha was his mother until he told me a few days after construction started." I'd volunteered to talk to the bid winner with Fern to flesh out the redesign timeline and details. We'd quickly learned that Quint was the type of guy who responded better to a male boss, despite Fern's stern warning and direct instructions. Rather than make a huge issue out of it, she asked me to monitor his progress. I found the whole redesign process fascinating and enjoyed my daily touch-base with Quint. "I don't know what company he's working for. Fern handled that part and just told me Quint was the primary point of contact."

"Endicott Construction," Connor replied, scrabbling his chin again. "I've seen the truck around, and there was a jacket with the name and company logo at the other end of the cable car."

I must've missed that on my initial scope of the space. "I could talk to Lindsey Endicott to find out if he owns the company." Lindsey, a retired attorney who'd opened a brewery in the downtown district, was one of Nana D's closest friends. I assumed he had family in the area but wasn't certain.

"You wouldn't be trying to take over my job, buddy, would ya?" Connor cautioned and walked me to the bottom of the steps. "I'll handle it from here. Come by the sheriff's office tomorrow to review a formal statement with me. You might've seen someone else talking to him recently."

Connor returned to the cable car, and I headed to my office to complete as much work as I could before picking up Emma for orientation at day camp. I updated Nana D, knowing she'd want to check on her friend, Bertha. My grandmother had taken the woman to chemotherapy in the early part of her diagnosis before Quint had gotten involved. Nana D planned to call on her friend later that afternoon, once she was certain someone had informed the woman of her son's death. I also called Gabriel, but he didn't pick up again, and his voicemail was still full. Something didn't feel right about his isolation.

* * *

"As much as I'll miss Nana D while I'm at camp, she's way too famous to worry about being a babysitter, right?" Emma asked as we entered the Woodland Warriors summer program for noon orientation.

I would've preferred to enroll her in Braxton's camp facility, but they were renovating the building this summer. Woodland College had an early childhood center for their students majoring in education, and during summers, they offered a local student teaching program for children from kindergarten through third grade. Emma had only just finished second grade and was eligible for this final year. It also helped that the bus would pick her up every morning at eight and drop her off every evening at five or seven on the Braxton College campus.

"You could say that. As mayor, she'll be busy babysitting an entire staff of county workers hoping to improve citizens' lives. You'll still see her at night." I dropped Emma's hand to let her buzz the entrance bell, which suggested the facility had dependable security. The structure was a typical two-story, red-brick school building with blue-tinted windows and an enclosed playground area containing a basketball court, resurfaced blacktop, and grassy field. Old and slightly chipped ceramic tiles covered the floor, and children's art projects and posters festooned the off-white-beige walls. It was in decent shape but in need of a makeover. Luckily, the technology, talent, and curriculum were top notch.

"I want to be like Nana D when I grow up," Emma declared while we walked to the main reception office. "She's more awesome than Wonder Woman!"

Francesca had forced Emma to watch all sorts of superhero shows with positive female role models. I supported the decision but sometimes thought it'd gone a little too far. My daughter had even higher expectations for herself than I'd developed at her age, and that scared me. Managing through the disappointment a harsh reality could deliver was never easy, but she'd taken it in stride thus far.

When we entered the head office, Helena Roarke, drenched in an overly sweet perfume, greeted us. Helena was the younger sister of Maggie Roarke, my former college girlfriend, and had gotten herself into some trouble the previous month when she was found standing over a dead body and holding a knife. What was she doing at Woodland Warriors?

"It's going to be a fantastic summer," Helena exclaimed, stretching her agile yet voluptuous body on the walk toward us. Blessed with huge thick hair, she often teased it to the point she couldn't fit through narrow doorways without brushing against the molding. Nonetheless, her feminine facial features and sultry disposition always made her the girl people wanted to know and converse with. "I'm one of two assistant teachers in Emma's classroom."

I rolled my eyes hoping they'd shoot lasers for once. Don't get me wrong; she was a fun girl and smarter than most people had acknowledged, but she was also inconsistent and flighty. Helena explained that she'd studied early childhood education during her years at Braxton but hadn't finished her student teaching. She was taking a final class this summer and would obtain her degree in the fall.

"How are you going to handle classes, teaching students, cleaning rooms in your parents' bed and breakfast, and working at the catering facility?" I asked, recalling she'd been all over the place trying to get her life in order the last time we chatted.

"Ugh! The Stoddards fired me when I broke up with their son, Cheney. He wanted to get serious, and I wasn't ready for that. Gosh, I'm only twenty-eight. I have ten years before I want to get married." Helena grabbed Emma's hand and mine, then led us to the classroom. "Walk with me. I'll introduce you to the head teacher."

After we arrived, I covered the basics with Emma's instructor, Jane O'Malley, granddaughter of the previous Braxton librarian whom Maggie had succeeded. Miss O'Malley wanted to chat with Emma for a few minutes to get to know one another. Helena and I sat at an art table in the corner of the room while Emma explained all about Danby Landing to her new favorite person. At least my daughter was open-minded and friendly when trying new things. She didn't inherit that from me.

"I take it Cheney wasn't happy. Did he push his parents to fire you?" I asked. Helena and Cheney weren't a proper fit, especially since he had a less-than-perfect background and spent time in prison.

"They never liked me. I doubt Cheney asked. He still sends flirty messages and pictures of his—"

I cut her off not wanting to know where that lurid statement was going. Knowing Helena, it was going exactly where I expected it to go. "That's great. It's nice to remain special friends with someone when you break up. So, they axed you, and you needed a new job?"

"Pretty much." She shamelessly grabbed my wrist. "After that whole ordeal of discovering the body and spending a weekend in jail, I kinda had a wake-up call. I decided to focus on getting my teaching degree and educating the kids in Wharton County."

Why hadn't Maggie told me her sister was working at Woodland Warriors? We'd just shared lunch the previous week and talked about Emma spending her summer here. Maggie must not have known; she and her sister weren't the closest—although, their relationship had seemed to improve lately. "Congratulations. It's wonderful to hear some positive news about the future. It's been a rough morning." I disentangled my hand from her unrelenting clasp and sat on it to prevent another attempt.

"Poor Quint. I can't believe he electrocuted himself to death." Helena fluffed her blonde hair and stretched her neck from side to side. "I'm gonna miss him."

How did they know each other? "Who told you he was dead? I just found him this morning."

"Seriously? This is Wharton County. Jane O'Malley, Emma's teacher, heard it from Calliope Nickels. Calliope works as a waitress at the Pick-Me-Up Diner for your sister. She overheard two cops mention it as they were gobbling down Chef Manny's fresh apple-cinnamon waffles at breakfast. They call you *The Unlikely Death Locator.*" Helena's hands gestured like two gossipy sock puppets divulging secrets about small town citizens.

That was *not* a name to be known by! I'd have to inform Connor his colleagues were talking too freely in the diner. Just as Helena ceased chatting, my mobile phone vibrated. It was my sister.

Eleanor: *Did you really find Quint Crawford's body this morning? Calliope Nickels said he was naked.*

Me: *No. You've got your information messed up as usual.*

Eleanor: *Umm, so he is alive? But his body was painted like the American flag for the 4th of July?*

How did shocking news travel and change so quickly? This was worse than a child's game of telephone. The whole town had forgotten how to be respect-ful. A man had died, and while we didn't know the cause, freak accident or murder, this wasn't the time to start fabricating rumors.

Me: *Ugh! I'll call you later. He IS dead. He was NOT naked. There was NO body paint. You ARE ridiculous.*

Eleanor: *Apparently, you're a divining rod for locating dead bodies. Makes sense, I'm psychic.*

Me: *Crazy does run in our family. Did you coin my new nickname as* The Unlikely Death Locator?

Eleanor: *Don't shoot the messenger. At least you got to see April, right? Hugs and kisses, Romeo.*

Me: *Mind your own business. Search your broken crystal ball for answers next time. Goodbye.*

And that was lucky reason number thirteen why I never should've come back home to *Hooterville.* I hid my phone away and focused on Helena. "Did you know Quint well?"

"Yep, we went to school together. There was a core group of eight of us who used to hang out all the time. He was the athlete in our group, always showing off how agile he was." Helena fastened a button that had popped open on her blouse as she shifted in her seat. She'd soon realize her wardrobe wasn't suited to working in a summer camp. "Quint and I were going to grab a drink this week, but we never picked a time." Helena's smile faded as she accepted her friend was truly gone forever.

"I'm sorry for your loss. I met Quint about seven or eight times in the last ten days. He was working on the cable car redesign." I patted her hand, hoping she didn't take it the wrong way.

"Oh, right. I forgot Nicky had hired him on that project."

"Nicky?" My eyebrows arched like a pyramid, highlighting my confusion.

"Nicholas Endicott. Lindsey's son, you know, the kid he had kinda late in life." Helena explained that Nicky was one of the four guys in their core group. When Nicky had graduated from college, his father had just turned seventy and retired from his law practice. Lindsey had sold it to Finnigan Masters and gone into the brewery business. "Nicky helped him choose the beers, but he always wanted to run his own company separate from his dad. That's when he opened Endicott Construction."

Quint had mentioned he hoped to get a piece of ownership in the construction business, but based on what Helena had said, Nicky wanted to run his own company. "Were they still friends?"

Helena wasn't sure, offering little explanation whether Quint and Nicky had communicated recently. "A lot of people from our little group have been coming and going lately. Like your brother."

I'd hoped she wouldn't reveal Gabriel was part of the illustrious octet. I knew he and Helena had attended Braxton together during their freshman and sophomore years, but while Gabriel had left town, Helena had remained here to torture me upon my triumphant return. Knowing Connor wasn't going to publicize any news indicating Quint might've been murdered, I'd have to be careful when posing any questions to determine potential or viable suspects. Perhaps I was jumping the gun and declaring it a murder too soon, but it wouldn't hurt to ask a few innocent ones. "Who else was involved in the—"

As two shadows approached us, Helena said, "Looks like Emma is done with Miss O'Malley."

Emma had a productive meeting with her new teacher and was excited to hang around for the remainder of the afternoon. I spent a few minutes digesting the various activities and subjects Miss O'Malley would be teaching, then headed back to Braxton to get some work done. Learning Helena would be with Emma was both a comfort and a worry, but I trusted her to take care of my daughter. Without a way to find out what else Helena knew about Quint, I gave up and left Woodland Warriors. I'd call Helena later to ascertain more details about their group of college friends, once I engineered an opportunity to pressure Connor into throwing me a few scraps of information about Quint's death.

While I didn't believe Gabriel had anything to do with the jewelry thefts, something suspicious had been encapsulating his recent return. Between the repeating robberies aligning with his absences from Braxton, the strange calla lilies and ruby on the floor of the car, and Quint's likely murder, the intertwining mysteries had become exceedingly fascinating and yanked me into their clutches. Truthfully, I wasn't yet certain the ruby in the cable car had a connection to the jewelry thefts. It might've just loosened from a ring Quint had been wearing when he fell to the floor.

Remembering how victims often knew their murderers, I considered whether the jogger wearing the sandalwood cologne who'd retrieved the gloves was associated with Quint's death. It would depend upon confirming the presence of fingerprints. If Quint had been dead for six hours, the jogger was more likely a random passerby. Just who was in the group of eight, and why did I have a tough time avoiding trouble? I couldn't help myself lately. I'd found the dead bodies and was inclined to punish the ruthless monster who'd cut someone's life too short. Some naysayers around me called it a sickness. I preferred to categorize it as generously doing my civic duty.

After arriving back at my office on the Braxton campus, I attempted to reach Gabriel who'd been ignoring me for two days now. I still couldn't leave a voicemail and had to assume he was up to no good. I decided to text one more time, knowing if he didn't respond, I'd sic Nana D on him.

Me: *Are you dead? Have you left town again? Talk to me, or I'll break out the big guns.*
Gabriel: *Get a life. I've just been busy working. I'll check in over the weekend. Promise.*
Me: *Need to talk to you about several things, including Quint Crawford. Don't play games with me.*
Gabriel: *I'm not, seriously. I heard about his death. Life is too short. Maybe I'll see you on campus.*

Several messages later, Gabriel still refused to respond. If he wanted to be evasive, I'd confront him when he wasn't expecting it. He'd be working at Cambridge Hall of Science for tomorrow's next public flower show. I could surprise him before my afternoon class. Get ready, brother. I'm on the trail, and you are being hunted down by an ultra-determined, intelligent wolf in sheep's clothing.

The rest of the afternoon focused on planning my upcoming classes and reading as many news articles as I could on previous and current jewelry thefts. I'd learned several interesting facts to review with Nana D, Connor, and April, but I wasn't certain they'd be able to answer my open questions. If they couldn't, or wouldn't, I'd consider going directly to the main sources. Lara Bouvier had been intimately involved in tracing the commonalities between all the robberies, but even she'd never postulated on potential suspects in her public news segments. Perhaps I'd convince her to share her private theories with me. At first, I just wanted to prove Gabriel wasn't involved, but now, with Quint's murder conceivably linked to them, I worried for a variety of additional reasons.

After Emma arrived at the bus stop, I carted her to gymnastics practice where she impressed me with her agility and strength. I demonstrated my excessive dose of pride to the other parents of less athletically inclined children, then we met Eleanor at the Pick-Me-Up Diner for dinner. While we shared a luscious dessert—Emma wasn't a huge fan of sweets, so I suppose I should confess to having eaten a majority of it—an unlikely pair discretely snuck into the eatery and hunkered down in a corner booth.

I racked my brain to conjure a legitimate reason for interrupting their meal, but nothing came to mind. I also didn't relish the idea of dealing with the wrath of a man who'd lost the election to Nana D. Marcus Stanton and Imogene Grey might not benefit from my wickedly delightful presence this evening, but I'd certainly ask Nana D what she thought of that duo when I visited her the following morning. As far as I understood, Krissy and Imogene disliked one another, and Imogene's fiancé, Paul, was taking over the role of town councilman from Marcus. There was something nefarious going on, and if it had anything to do with the jewelry thefts or Quint Crawford's death, April needed to know post haste.

CHAPTER 5

When I woke up the next morning, my body demanded exercise. I'd consumed too many desserts the previous week, and it always came back to haunt me. Once Emma was safely on the bus to camp, I changed into my running clothes and swung by Nana D's for a brief catch up. A few days remained before her official start as the new mayor of Wharton County. We'd been working on her speech whenever we found free time, but it wasn't complete. Nana D wanted to lay out a three-month plan on what citizens could expect, and she insisted on providing target metrics and deliverables that would be impossible even for an experienced politician. My gentle warning hadn't dissuaded her, suggesting I'd need to try harder. It wasn't that I didn't believe in her ability to get the job done, but without having a deeper background in county government, she might set herself up for a tumble way too soon.

Nana D was sitting at the dining table when I popped by and opened the front door. She waved me in and pointed to a chair. "Have you heard from Gabriel? That nincompoop won't return my calls."

"At least I'm not the only one he's ghosting." I took a seat across from her at Grandpop's custom-made table, tracing my fingers along the burnt scalloped edges he'd spent hours perfecting. I missed him more than I'd realized the last few years.

"What kinda cockamamie word is *ghosting*?" Nana D suspiciously looked up from whatever she'd been scribbling on a notepad.

"It usually refers to when someone stops returning messages after giving you some sort of indication that they were interested in—" I began to say, but Nana D twirled her finger in the air a few times to let me know I was taking too long to explain its meaning. "Basically, ignoring you."

"Why say something in thirty words when you can say it in two, brilliant one? Wasn't that part of your bachelor's degree? Master's? Doctorate? You've been in school so long, you must know everything by now." Nana D pushed a steno pad across the table. "Please weigh in. I think I've nailed it."

I knew better than to defend myself or take her bait. Yes, brevity was important, but sometimes an elaborate way of saying something provided context and tone. *Some people* struggled to understand that approach and preferred to be exceedingly direct in their feedback. "Sure, give me a minute." When I finished, I gave her a high-five. "Perfect. Looks like you came around to my way of thinking with—"

"Can it. We're done. You don't need to analyze who contributed which parts. Now, what about Gabriel?" she said, pouring herself another cup of tea.

"Well, he finally responded to me last night. I told him I needed to talk about Quint Crawford, but he ignored me and said he'd see me on campus. I might show up at his lab this afternoon." Gabriel had only been back for a couple of months, but he must've known by now that no one in our family walked away without paying the price. When an escapee finally returned to the zoo, the inmate was subjected to scrutiny until every last precious metal bar was soldered back onto the cage.

"Poor Bertha, she's beside herself with grief over her boy's death. She asked me to stick around after the funeral service to talk. She specifically requested you to be there too." Nana D sipped her tea and placed her speech in a folder on the table. She was all jazzed up in a navy-blue pantsuit with a white silk blouse that had a fluffy bow tied across her chest. Her hair was braided and wrapped around the top of her head, and she sported a pair of old-fashioned spectacles strategically placed on the bridge of her nose. She rarely donned them in public, but her eyesight had gotten worse lately, and even she couldn't deny it. Oh, the anguish that would be thrust upon me if I mentioned anything about the cheaters.

"I hardly knew Quint. We only met ten days ago on campus." What did she need from me? I was still trying to understand why Quint had never told me he'd been friends with my brother years ago.

"I guess we'll find out. My bones have been aching whenever I think about that ruby you saw in the cable car near Quint's body. I fear there's a connection between his death and the missing jewelry. Maybe he discovered the thief's identity and confronted him in the cable car. Or perhaps—"

"Or perhaps it's just arthritis?" After she flicked my ear, I conceded to her way of thinking and told her about the dinner between Imogene and Marcus. "I agree with you. Helena and Gabriel should be able to tell us whom Quint had been closest to. They might shed some light on his activities throughout the last few weeks. That's where I'll dig for clues about the contractor's untimely death."

"Maybe Marcus was supposed to meet both Paul and Imogene. Could Paul have shown up after you left, to discuss the transition of the town councilman role?"

"I suppose. Add that to your list when you talk to Paul later," I jokingly directed.

"Yes, master. Did you find out from Imogene if the bandit left another calla lily again this time?"

I considered Nana D's old-fashioned expression carefully, but nothing sparked other than reminding her no one had said the word *bandit* post last century. Then, I remembered the black calla lilies in the cable car next to Quint. "Wanna explain what you meant about the flower being at Imogene's place? Is the calla lily some sort of ironic calling card among thieves that I'm unaware of?"

"How would I know? All I'm saying is that in each place where he'd absconded with the goods, the perp left a single black calla lily. Didn't I tell you that the other day?"

"No, you conveniently left out that part in our rush to discuss all the jewelry thefts before my class began. I didn't know flowers came in black." I should've paid more attention at the flower show's debut last month but catching a murderer was ultimately the proper priority back then. Wait! Given there were calla lilies next to the body along with the ruby, it generated two definitive links between the jewelry thefts and Quint's shocking murder. I needed confirmation on whom the gem belonged to.

"It's a heavily debated topic in the botany world. Millard and I have often discussed it. What most people think of as black petals are dark purple," Nana D clarified as she tapped several bony fingers against the table in quick fashion.

"Do they spray-paint them for certain holidays, like Halloween or Valentine's Day?"

"Wash your mouth with soap, Kellan. That's just nonsense. I never agreed with altering nature's beauty in an artificial manner. Splicing various species is one thing, but spraying a flower with paint seems excessive." Nana D was adamant about organic farming and not messing with Mother Earth.

"Got it, black calla lilies are deep purple. I'll ingrain it in my memory next time. Are they rare?"

"Used to be. Nowadays, you can get anything off the Internet. It's rare to actually see a black one but not difficult to cultivate and grow them." Nana D fetched a gardening catalog from the shelf and flipped to an article on the flower. "While you peruse the magazine, I've got a few calls to make. If you don't talk to your brother today, let me know. I'll order him to the mayor's office to find out what he knows about the jewelry thefts."

"It says calla lilies represent elegance and mystery and are used at funerals. How creepy!"

"Grow up." Nana D crossed into the kitchen to retrieve her old-fashioned, daffodil-yellow wall phone and dialed a number. "Skedaddle. I've got to be downtown in two hours to find out why Paul Dodd was sneaking around with Krissy Stanton, and why his fiancée was sneaking around with Krissy's father. I feel like we've been tossed in the middle of one of your mother's kitschy soap operas. You still gonna drop me off after your little exercise routine to lose the flab you've been packing on?"

"Oh, right, I almost forgot. Wait... what did you say?" She was already talking to someone, so I checked my watch, set an alarm, and took off for my run. Normally I'd drive to Braxton, race the indoor track, and shower at the campus gym, then head to my office in Diamond Hall. With Nana D's new job and hesitancy to drive on her own, she'd become reliant on me until her chauffeur started the following week. A driver was part of the many perks she'd garnered by winning the election, but the current mayor wouldn't give up the town jockey until his final day.

I jogged across the orchard to where I could pick up a narrow trail running toward the eastern range of the Wharton Mountains. It was a four-mile distance to reach them and guaranteed me one uninterrupted hour of exercise. Along the path, I blocked out everything weighing me down and focused on keeping my adrenaline high and my running form solid. I reached the midpoint and took a brief water break to admire the cloudless sky and colorful trees and bushes. It was still early enough that the sun's heat hadn't peaked, and the air near the mountains was always a little cooler. My moment of complete relaxation was intruded upon by a ringing cell phone, except it was an unfamiliar tone. I'd also remembered turning mine off, ensuring only calls from Emma's camp would make any noise. I needed to escape from any distraction but couldn't be unreachable for my daughter.

When I retrieved the phone from my pocket, I gulped. Instead of taking my personal cell phone earlier, I'd mistakenly grabbed the one Cristiano Vargas had bestowed upon me as his personal lackey. I pressed accept and uttered a weak "hello," knowing the purpose of my run was now forever ruined.

"Good morning, Kellan. Four miles in thirty minutes, not too shabby," a cheery yet alarming voice greeted.

"You're certainly a man of your word, Cristiano. It's been exactly two days." Another reason to dislike the man, his impeccable timing and incredible accuracy. Of course, he was watching me right now. I looked around for a professional goon hiding around the edges of the mountainous terrain, but there was too much territory to cover in this brief amount of time.

"It brings me immense pleasure to know I can deliver on any promise I make. Perhaps under different circumstances, you and I would be good friends. Let's table that thought for now. I need your assistance." Cristiano was listening to the Hamilton soundtrack. I recognized one of the songs. Francesca and I had attended an early preview of the show several months before she'd faked her death. Her father had gifted us the tickets, which had shocked me at the time—it had been impossible to buy them! Now, I knew why he'd been so successful; running a mob family had its advantages.

"Are you finally ready to deliver Francesca to us?" I was feeling more direct than usual.

"Not exactly. I'm enjoying her company. She's introducing me to music and culture I know little about. The favor I need won't be too complicated." Cristiano cleared his throat to let me know he was finished speaking.

"Hit me with it," I replied. What could he possibly ask me to do that I'd be willing to entertain?

"You need to tell *Signor e Signora* Castigliano that I've learned what they're up to, and it will not fly. Be exponentially clear with them. If they do not retreat, I will be forced to punish those insolent fools." Cristiano informed me that his team was aware Cecilia and Vincenzo had recently sent a spy into the Vargas camp. "Tell them the friendly face who showed up to offer me a deal isn't looking particularly friendly anymore. I'm sure his battle wounds will heal in time. War can be brutal on someone who is as delicate as a soufflé. Remember that if you ever try to cross me, Kellan."

I'd never understood the idiom *felt my blood boil* until now. How was I stuck in the middle of this sick, twisted vendetta? "What did you do? For that matter, what did the bickering caterwaulers do?"

"Your only role is to be the messenger. It's better when you don't know any details. If the Castiglianos follow my orders, Francesca will be returned to you within the week. I must go now."

"Wait, I don't know what they did—"

"Goodbye, Kellan. We shall speak no further until I get a sign from them that they understand." Cristiano hung up on me. How would they give him a sign? Shoot up a Harry Potter *Dark Mark* in the sky? I had to be missing information that would clarify what was combusting into flames around me.

My energy level soared after the phone call, and I ran back to Danby Landing more quickly than it'd taken me to get to the mountains. Arriving home, I showered and changed, dropped Nana D off at the administrative building in downtown Wharton County, and zoomed to Braxton where I spent three hours preparing for my afternoon class.

I also suffered through a departmental staff meeting where Myriam notified everyone of changes in the fall schedule. An adjunct professor had backed out of a job because she'd been awarded an assistant professorship role at Woodland College. "I need a volunteer to interview a potential new candidate next week."

I had no time to take on anything additional, prompting me to keep my head down reading the remainder of the bullet points on her tedious agenda. I'd gotten distracted when the meeting ended and hadn't realized everyone else except Myriam exited.

"Thank you, Kellan. I appreciate your generosity," she said, thrusting a resume at me.

"Wait, what did I do?"

"You volunteered to help me with the interview process. Did you not stick around after the meeting as I informed everyone to do if they were interested?" Myriam adjusted her glasses and pursed her irksome lips while waiting for my response.

She had me there. If I confessed my failure to pay attention, it would hurt me eventually. No one else had stuck around. If I didn't accept the task, she'd just assign it to me anyway. "Happy to help save the day," I contritely replied and began to leave the room.

"*Let none presume to wear an undeserved dignity.*" Myriam cited a well-known line from *Merchant of Venice,* then waited for me to redirect my attention to her. "One more item. A student in your class visited me yesterday." A puzzling grimace danced eagerly on my boss's face.

"Another satisfied customer?" I pushed my glasses higher, above the small bump on my nose.

"That would make you quite pleased, wouldn't it? Unfortunately, no, that is not the case. While she didn't request any changes, the student wanted me to know that she was unhappy about the group she'd been assigned to work with." Myriam recited her personal opinion on how to handle the issue, then asked me what I planned to do about it.

"Will you at least tell me who it was?" I wouldn't confront the student, but I'd know to tread carefully in the future. I was convinced it had to be Imogene or Krissy. Both were frustrated when class had ended on Monday, even though they'd claimed to be okay with the compromise for the group's topic selection.

"It's best that I do not. If she returns, we'll have a deeper discussion about the problem. For now, please be certain you are more attentive to student issues and preferences. We can't always kowtow to their every single need, but we also shouldn't alienate them," Myriam warned as she collected her belongings. "You must be careful about this situation. It could become a problem for your future at Braxton. I'll be putting a note in your file with Human Resources."

Once *Barracuda Boss* left, I bought lunch in the cafeteria and chatted with a colleague about his summer lectures. I finished early enough to swing by Cambridge Hall to surprise Gabriel before my class. On the walk across campus, I noticed him entering the building's front doors. I picked up enough speed to almost catch up, but before I could arrive, the elevator door closed. Inside, he held an animated conversation with one of my students, Krissy Stanton.

Gabriel worked on the second floor in the science labs. Rather than wait for the elevator, I ascended the stairs at the end of the hallway. Upon arriving, I realized I didn't know exactly in which lab he'd spend his afternoon. I'd been in the building a handful of times but never to meet him. I asked a distracted lab assistant if she knew where Gabriel's office resided. With her hands flapping and bobbing about, she whined, "He doesn't have his own place, kinda hangs out in different labs and keeps things in order. He got off the elevator, but like, I don't know where he went. I'm not his keeper!"

"Got it, thanks." Was everyone nuts today? I walked around the entire floor but couldn't locate him anywhere. Ten minutes later, I exited the building and headed to class. Where had he disappeared?

I stopped at my office to collect my lecture notes, then strode to the classroom on the first floor. A few students were already assembled in their seats. Siobhan approached me at the desk. I didn't think she was the student who'd complained to Myriam, but I'd poke around to discover whether she knew anything. "How're the twins doing?"

"They're flying it... doing well, I mean. I sometimes forget you're not Irish. I'm knackered, I'll tell ya," Siobhan responded, collapsing into a chair across from my desk. "With Mrs. Crawford needing some time off this week, my schedule has been quite hectic."

"Come again?" I didn't understand her news. "Was Bertha Crawford working for you?"

"Aye. After she left the Paddington estate on account of the cancer, she needed more income. Mrs. Crawford watched the twins while I attended work or class. It's easy pay for a few hours when I couldn't bring them to daycare." Siobhan covered her mouth as she yawned. "After what happened to her son, Quint, she couldn't handle it anymore. I don't blame her. Just left me a bit stuck, ya know? I had to find a new sitter. Today is the new girl's first time watching my babies."

I hadn't realized Siobhan knew the Crawfords. "It's an awful shock for Bertha. How's she doing?"

"Haven't seen her since it happened. When the police contacted her, she was watching the twins. I left work and went to get them. Your mother was very understanding about me needing to take the afternoon off after I was already late that...." Siobhan paused as a few more students walked into the room, including her groupmate, Raquel.

"I guess you must've known Quint?" It wasn't my business, but I didn't want to jump directly into my question about any potential complaints with the groups.

"Oh, he was a clever bloke. I... uh... didn't know him all that well. I'm sorry that he died, but... well... I don't have much to say about that topic. Anyway, I'm a little worried what it's gonna be like in this group with those other two," she said hesitantly, then breathed deeply and waved to Raquel. "Not her, Raquel's a doll. I mean Krissy and Imogene. Krissy gave me quite an earful after our last class."

"Really? About concerns with the course? Were you happy with the last session?" I asked, finding my opening but also curious about the relationship between the other two women. Also, had I imagined it or did Siobhan clam up when I asked whether she'd known Quint well?

"This class? Aye, it'll be fun. I might just have to keep the others under control. Krissy and Imogene used to be best friends, but after—" Siobhan stopped speaking when someone rushed into the classroom, creating an uproar worthy of a bad referee call on a football field.

"Sorry. I'm late. Got held up talking. I'm here now. Class can start." A frowzy and somber Krissy squirmed through the desks, knocking over books and a chair, then plopped down in a frenzy.

While several students sighed profusely and picked up their belongings, I checked my watch. We were one minute shy of the lecture's start time. I really wanted to know what Siobhan had almost revealed, but I'd have to confront her afterward. I also sought an explanation for why Krissy and Gabriel had been together. "It's okay, we're just about to begin." I looked around the room, confirming all but one person was in attendance. "Let's give Imogene another minute before we dive in."

"She's not gonna be here today, you can proceed." Krissy huffed, grabbed a pen, and fixed her hair as she settled into the seat. "Everyone else has finally quieted down."

I wasn't fond of Krissy's overly direct and bossy way of speaking to others, but if she'd been the student who'd complained, it wouldn't help to provoke her in front of everyone. "Sure, I'll call Imogene tonight to let her know what she missed. Let's talk about Grierson's *Nanook of the North*, the first original American documentary produced in...."

I taught for ninety minutes, then took a ten-minute break. I motioned to Siobhan, but she frantically rushed out of the room, one ear glued to her cell phone. I assumed she wanted to check on her kids and didn't interrupt. Instead, I approached Raquel and Krissy, who were engaged in a lively discussion. "Pardon me, I thought I'd take an impromptu poll to see how you both felt about the class so far. We're still early enough if you had anything to share, I could make some adjustments."

Raquel was quiet, but Krissy speedily responded. "You're a great lecturer. I was very connected with today's lesson. I knew you'd be a good professor, just as a friend of mine told me," she said with a quick but obvious wink. I assumed she'd meant my brother, Gabriel.

Raquel nodded, "I agree. I'm really excited about the next chapter, but we only have a few minutes remaining, and I need to use the restroom."

When Raquel left, I refocused my gaze on Krissy. "May I ask how you knew Imogene wouldn't be attending this afternoon? I am only curious because I need to make a note of her absence. I'm allowing two for this summer's course without any grade penalizations."

"Did you hear about that guy who died working on the cable car, Quint Crawford?"

"Yes, I did. I was the one who—"

"Quint was Imogene's ex-boyfriend. They used to date back in college before she dumped him for Paul Dodd, the new councilman. Now, she's engaged and hardly ever sees her friends anymore," Krissy said with a defiant and palpable aggravation. "Except suddenly she's all broken up about Quint's death and couldn't bring herself to attend today. Ugh, I'm upset about it too, but...." Krissy paused and began to sob in front of me. A few students in the room looked over awkwardly.

"Are you okay? Did you know him well?" I asked, unsure whether to pat Krissy's shoulder or give her a moment of privacy. The relationship between her and Imogene was beyond odd. I handed a tissue from my pocket to her, wondering why she'd been with Paul the night of Nana D's birthday party.

"We were all friends years ago. I cared about Quint too, but I forced myself to show up today." Krissy hurriedly cleared her tears and fixed her makeup.

"When you say *all*, does it include my brother, Gabriel?" I figured it was the most apt time to confirm the names in their convoluted octet—my *innocent* questions re his death required answers.

"Yep, there was a whole bunch of us who hung out during our freshman and sophomore years. Then, the group sorta broke up, and everyone went their separate ways. I tried to reunite the rest of them, but not everyone stuck around Braxton. I guess you knew that already, huh?"

"Yes, I did. I just saw you with Gabriel, didn't I?" I lifted my eyes to match hers and held my ground. I wanted to see how she'd respond to my question before inquiring who else had left town.

"Oh, yeah, he saw you as we went up the elevator. I ran into him on the way to class. We were catching up, but he was in a rush to check on an experiment," she explained, as the door opened with a flurry of students rushing in. Raquel and Siobhan were included in the group who sat closest to Krissy.

"Looks like we need to get started. Maybe we could finish our discussion after class?"

After Krissy cautiously confirmed, I returned to the front of the classroom and finished the lecture. By the time it ended, she was packed and ready to leave. I had little chance to stop her before she exited Diamond Hall and tore off for the parking lot.

Raquel, tossing her long dark locks to the side, approached me. "She's a little scatterbrained. I wouldn't take it personally." She deftly applied pink gloss on her plump lips and smacked them together with a snappy pop. The color added a fresh glow to match her naturally smooth and silky skin.

"She's just lost a friend she'd known for a long time. I understand what that's like. What can I do for you?" I said, shutting off a display screen and laptop.

"I wonder if I could talk to you about the courses you'll be teaching next fall. I want to enroll in something else, but I'm not sure which would be best for me," she added, rearranging her books and pulling out her phone. "I'm free tomorrow morning. Could we get coffee at The Big Beanery? Isn't that where all the students and teachers hang out?"

"It is," I said guardedly. Her tone was more suggestive than I expected. I might have misread the situation, but it never hurt to be too careful, especially if she was the girl who'd complained. "I'll have office hours on Friday. How about we block thirty minutes at five o'clock after class ends?"

"Oh, sure. I guess I can wait until then. It will give me enough time to read up on a few things." Raquel batted her suspiciously thick eyelashes while entering the details of our appointment into her phone, thanked me, and withdrew from the room.

Siobhan was also out of pocket, so we couldn't finish our conversation. I headed directly to North Campus where Emma's bus would arrive momentarily. While walking, I considered everything I'd learned that afternoon. It unearthed more questions than answers, and I still didn't know which student had expressed concerns about my last class. Could Myriam have exaggerated what'd been said, to make me feel nervous or uncomfortable? Or had one of the students lied to me tonight about how she felt?

Emma and I spent the evening cooking dinner together and training Baxter how to sit and let us know when he needed to go potty. At sixteen weeks old, he was learning basic tricks, which made Emma as excited as a proud parent. After we read a short story, she nodded off to sleep. As I poured myself a glass of wine, the phone rang. When the caller ID indicated it was the Castiglianos, I chugged every remaining drop of liquid courage, poured myself another to guarantee an enjoyable time, and pressed accept. "What will it take to be rid of your constant barrage of complaints and intrusions?"

CHAPTER 6

After I explained Cristiano's instructions, Cecilia blasted me. "I warned Vincenzo his plan wouldn't work. Now, I must assume control. Do not be alarmed, Kellan, I have the solution."

I tried to elicit basic details or an explanation from my mother-in-law, but she told me there wasn't any room for children in the games she currently played. "I still don't understand why Las Vargas is involving you, but apparently they think it will make things more successful. If only they knew weak men like you weren't cut out for this life. I always told Francesca you'd be her downfall. Now, my proclamation has come to fruition."

"I don't like being the mediator either, but since Cristiano threatened Emma's life and informed me that I'd be his primary point of contact, we're stuck. Aren't we, *Mommie Dearest*?" My anger and frustration had reached its limit. I was being played on both sides, and there was little way I could ever assume control or gain the upper hand in this war. I had to sit back and wait for two devious players to move their pawns on an unstable board until someone dared to attempt the final gnashing kill.

After we disconnected, I needed a distraction from everything that was slowly eroding my sanity. I caught a couple of minutes of my favorite television series and watched a rerun of the episode of *Dark Reality* that I'd directed in Los Angeles the previous year. I'd been anxiously awaiting the executive producer's decision on whether he'd consider letting me direct my own true crime show, rather than the reality series I'd been stuck working on before my boss had been fired. I wasn't due to find out until the beginning of next year, which timed out well with the end of my one-year teaching contract in Braxton's communications department. I wasn't sure what I'd do if neither place offered me a permanent role, but that wouldn't occur for at least another six months.

Just as I changed into a pair of comfy shorts and a t-shirt, my cell phone rang again. I put the ringer on mute in case I forgot to do so after talking to Nana D. I was desperate for no further interruptions and a full night's sleep. "Hi. What's going on?"

In the background, a television blasted Lara Bouvier's local news segment covering the upcoming inauguration ceremony.

"Paul Dodd claims Krissy Stanton was harassing him at the park. He'd been at home working on his campaign speech and decided to go for a walk. She found him there and followed him around until he got a call from Imogene about the break-in at Lara's place."

"Do you believe him?" I heard voices talking on top of the news report. "Wait, where are you?"

"Kirklands. I'm having a drink with Eustacia. She heard it's a happening place. We came to check out my constituency. Let me guess, you're in bed already?" Nana D teased.

"Whether I'm in bed or not isn't the point. It's been a long day. You didn't answer my quest—"

"Can it, brilliant one. I don't want to keep you from your precious beauty sleep. I believe Paul, but he also said something interesting." I waited for her to continue speaking, but all I could hear was Eustacia debating what drink to order with their waitress. "Earth to the eccentric woman bugging me?"

"You're getting belligerent like your cranky old father, Kellan. Come meet us for a drink?"

"Emma is sleeping, and it won't help my social life to be seen hanging out at local bars with my grandmother, the mayor," I explained, hoping it would keep her from delaying the conversation any further. "What did Paul say?"

"I'll pretend I didn't hear that part about your social life. And you can pretend I didn't say your social life is equivalent to the existence of the Loch Ness monster," Nana D replied with a chortle and a burp. Then, Eustacia cackled and screamed through the phone at me, "Meaning you ain't got one, boy."

"I'm hanging up."

"Ugh, fine, you wet blanket. Paul told me Krissy tried to convince him that Imogene was cheating on him. He claimed he didn't believe her, but I saw the anger flare up in those dreamy eyes of his. He was mad as a hatter, especially when I told him Imogene was hanging out at the Pick-Me-Up Diner with Marcus. He offered no explanation, mind you."

Nana D and Eustacia continued to share their opinions on how attractive Paul was, then shifted to how crass Marcus Stanton and his daughter, Krissy, were. I could barely understand them once they began shouting over one another and the screechy television.

"Thanks for finding out. How is it you persuade everyone to talk to you, Nana D?"

"A girl's gotta have some secrets, brilliant one. Go drink your hot cocoa and tuck yourself into beddy-bye. Let the Sandman bring the baby a dream! Can't have you getting ill-tempered because I kept you up past the witching hour. To think, the sun just finished setting and you're conking out already."

"Who's the designated driver tonight?" I really couldn't take her anymore tonight.

"Uber, unless you want to be a good grandson and come get us?"

I hung up. I'd hit my limit of dealing with semi-inebriated grandmothers and their ridiculous frenemies. Sufficiently placated with a third glass of wine and Baxter curled up in the crook of my knees, I opened the latest mystery from my favorite author and began to read. Then, my phone buzzed again, leading me to mumble a few not-so-nice words. I'd turned the ringer off but accidentally left on the vibration mode. This time it was a text message from April, and as usual, I had no idea what to make of it. It wasn't a question or a suggestion. It was another order and the final nail in my coffin this evening.

April: *My office at nine tomorrow morning. Need to discuss your 'role' in* Quint's murder inquiry.

* * *

"Listen, I know I said to work directly with Connor on the cable car incident, but he's been pulled into another angle on this investigation and has gone out of town." If April's furrowed brows weren't enough warning, her harried countenance indicated it'd already been a rough Thursday morning.

"I had to chat with you anyway. A few things came up regarding Las Vargas yesterday," I confessed, checking what else I had to accomplish on this bright and sunny morning. I craved more coffee but wouldn't dare endure the nasty torture of the discarded remnants in April's office pot.

"By the way, your office is clear. We found no bugs," April casually notified me before asking what had happened the day before with my missing wife drama.

It felt good to be able to speak freely inside my office without worrying about who snooped on my conversations. I let April know what Cristiano had told me and how Cecilia had reacted to his threats. "I'm not sure how much more I can take of this disruptive seesaw."

"It's not easy, I understand. For what it's worth, you've handled this lunacy well. I've always admired how adept you are at keeping your cool and holding your own. Not many men could stand up to the mob, worm their way into a police investigation where they're almost killed, and push back on an amazing sheriff who threatens to arrest him for obstruction of justice nearly every day. You're a brave man, Kellan." April laughed at her attempt to assuage my concerns and boost my ego.

"Those might be the nicest and strangest words you've ever said to me. I don't feel very brave but thank you for that compliment."

April briefly dipped her head in my direction. "We've released Quint's body to the funeral home, and I'm under the impression it will be a quick service tomorrow evening."

"Although Quint's mother has been sick, she'll be present. A group of us from the college will attend to pay our respects," I declared. I'd never been fond of attending wakes, but they'd been prevalent in my life the last few months. Nana D and I had recently commiserated over watching some of her friends pass away. The sudden and wasted loss of life was both depressing and alarming, especially surrounding the current situation with Francesca's kidnapping. "Any leads on Quint's killer?"

"I'm the one asking the questions here, buddy. Tell me everything you remember about the time you spent with Quint Crawford," she countered with an obsequious grin.

I updated April with every tidbit I could remember from my previous conversations with Quint between the moment I'd initially met him and when I'd found him dead in the cable car. "He was often aloof, and while he hadn't kicked me out every time I visited him, I'd never felt fully welcomed. He seemed to have a knack for reading people and situations easily. At first, I'd only intended to verify his progress, but there were flashes when he got rather chatty. Or should I say, he asked a lot of questions."

"About you or the college? Was he particularly angry toward anyone?" April asked, hoping I had more information than I knew I had.

"Not really. I didn't know much about him. He asked about my teaching schedule and my daughter. When he told me how sick his mother was, I mentioned how difficult it had been to lose my grandpop. Quint brought up Francesca's death once, but I couldn't say much about it."

"Why did he ask about that?" April leaned in closer to focus on my response, a peculiar expression commandeering her face.

"Just said he'd heard about it from his mother, and he wanted to tell me how sorry he was that I'd lost a wife so young." I barely recalled the specifics of the conversation that day as it had been shortly after I'd pieced together Francesca's kidnapping and could barely keep my own thoughts straight. "What have you learned about the ruby I found in the cable car? Is it from the jewelry thefts?"

"I'm not sure why that's anything you and I should be discussing, Kellan. I'm grateful you noticed it, and Connor is investigating that angle in San Francisco right now. I asked you here in case you knew anything else important enough to share with me about Quint. Not the other way around." April was hesitant in her response, suggesting she'd learned something she didn't want to tell me.

"I'm only trying to help. I know some of the people involved. Maybe I'll discover a valuable connection, April." Gabriel had lived in San Francisco when he'd left town eight years ago after the first set of burglaries had occurred; that was certainly a connection. "What's Connor in California for?"

"Fine, I'll share a bit. One of the originally stolen jewels was recovered there years ago. It'd been sold at a pawn shop on Mission Street. Of all the lost items, the Roarke ruby earrings were the only ones returned or found. Connor is seeking a better description of the person who sold them to the pawn shop." April shifted in her seat and looked uncomfortable with our conversation's focal point.

"If they'd been recouped, wouldn't that information already be in the Wharton County police reports?" I knew I was pushing too deeply for answers, but I'd been willingly drawn into the enigma.

"It should have been, but my predecessor's files leave a lot to be desired," April groused with obvious contempt for the man. "The former sheriff never put out an alert on the missing jewelry beyond Wharton County. All he'd documented about the recovered ruby was that a *random* caller had notified the pawn shop in San Francisco of the owner's identity." After the pawn shop subsequently called Sheriff Crawford, he requested a picture and showed it to the Roarke family. Eventually, Lucy had been able to retrieve her family's precious gems. No other details had been included in the records.

"What happened to the rest of the jewelry and the money from eight years ago?"

"Why do you want to know?" April asked, narrowing her gaze as she stood to remove her blazer. *Old Betsy*, her prized threatening revolver, was strapped to her hip.

I didn't want to implicate my brother, but I couldn't lie to April any longer. I explained what I knew about Gabriel's disappearance and how there might be a link between him and the jewelry thefts. "Can you tell me anything about the past robberies and how they line up with the current ones?" I was focused on the missing jewelry because I now believed for certain the string of break-ins had something to do with Quint's death. There was little chance a bouquet of black calla lilies and a stolen ruby next to Quint's dead body were unrelated to the reason he'd been brutally murdered.

April considered my request, and by the pensive look in her eyes and the frequent crack of her knuckles, she wanted to alleviate my concerns yet also protect herself from revealing too much. "Most of this is public knowledge. I'll share the basics of what the newspapers had printed at the time. If I say something is confidential, please keep it that way."

Once I agreed, April filled in the blanks Nana D hadn't remembered or been aware of. "In the first robbery, only four students confirmed seeing the stolen brooch at the Paddington Play House. There was a black calla lily left in Gwendolyn Paddington's bedroom, similar to the ones found by Quint's body and all the other robberies. The brooch has never been recovered, and Sheriff Crawford's details were erratic at best."

"Bertha Crawford worked for the Paddingtons. Was she interviewed afterward?" There had to be an association if one of the filched gems was found near Quint and other jewelry had been stolen from the family who'd employed his mother.

"Not according to the files. Gwendolyn insisted she lost it at the estate and not the Play House. The report containing her input affirmed she'd personally interrogated her entire staff, but no one knew anything." April resumed explaining the previous occurrences, eyeing me dubiously the whole time. While I doubted the ability to learn anything new from the previous jewelry thefts, some obscure minutiae might surprise us.

"What did the Nutberry family do after their diamond choker was stolen?"

"Agnes died a few weeks afterward, and the whole affair was relegated to the backstage. Everyone in her family had rock-solid alibis, thus proving they weren't responsible for stealing the jewelry." The sheriff flipped to the next report in the file.

"I'm most familiar with the third victim, Lucy Roarke." I planned to visit Maggie and Helena's mother to find out all I could in the next few days. I didn't want April to know I was separately investigating on the side, so I navigated the conversation along a different angle. "How did the thief get access to all the houses and jewelry without getting caught?"

"Unfortunately, in three of those cases, there was little security protecting the jewelry. I see how it could've been stolen without the thief being trapped on camera. Back then, people were more trusting. Even Braxton's administrative department admitted they were too lax. The key for the exhibit room where the Roarke rubies were on display had been sitting in a tray on the secretary's desk. Anyone could've walked in and taken it," April complained. We agreed that the thief had to be clever enough to ensure never getting captured, but that he or she must've been someone whose presence people wouldn't have questioned for hanging out in all those places.

"You mentioned there was other jewelry on display, but only the Roarke rubies were stolen, right?" In the nine days between the burglaries and the specific targets who'd been chosen, there must've been a pattern we failed to distinguish—one that could lead to identifying Quint's killer.

April confirmed her agreement on my theory. "None of it makes sense. Could Gabriel have stolen the rubies, then tried to innocently return them to the Roarkes after a change of heart?"

"I suppose it's possible, but we'll have to ask him. San Francisco was one of the first places he'd visited and ultimately lived for two years." I remembered Nana D wanted to know if I'd gotten my brother to talk, but I never updated her that he and I hadn't connected the previous day. While April rooted around for the next police report, I texted Nana D to fulfill my commitment.

"After the original fourth robbery, Lara Bouvier searched for the thief herself, which is what ultimately led her to convince WCLN to hire her as an investigative reporter for their news segments. She wasn't able to find the responsible party, and the rift between her and the Grey family widened immensely," April explained, citing she'd already questioned Lara to obtain all the historical details.

"I met Imogene recently. She's spent a lot of time outside the country in France over the years. I can't imagine she had anything to do with it. Could the Greys have stolen back the jewelry and taken other things to avoid suspicion?" I worried that my brother had also known Imogene quite well back in the day. Had he been trying to help her get money for tuition since the Grey family wouldn't support her unless Lara returned the family necklace? Perhaps he was simply a modern-day 'Robin Hood.'

"The Greys have been out of town for weeks on business trips, so it's unlikely. Connor will interview everyone involved eight years ago to compile a list of suspects. Your brother will need to provide an alibi for each instance where jewelry was stolen, and possibly Quint's murder should it come to that," April declared before mentioning we needed to tread carefully in that part of the investigation.

"What about the fifth and final burglary from eight years ago?"

"Wendy Stanton, Marcus's late wife. Same timing except it was a bag of cash instead of jewelry. Her story is an interesting one. She'd been married to Marcus for five years, but there was a rumor she'd been looking for a divorce. During his reelection campaign, she suspected he'd skimmed money from alumni donors," April revealed. His opponent had been a no-name from the rural parts of town who'd little chance of winning, which meant Marcus didn't need to use the donations for marketing and advertising. Wendy confirmed Marcus had kept fifty-thousand dollars in cash from a recent fundraiser in the Braxton alumni office that weekend.

"I read that newspaper article. Marcus indicated he planned to bring the money to the bank the following Monday, but then it disappeared when the power went out during the thunderstorm. Wendy claimed her husband had stolen the cash and ratted him out to the erstwhile sheriff," I replied.

"Of course, that deadbeat didn't do anything to investigate if Marcus had been skimming money from the alumni event for personal gain. Our soon-to-be-former town councilman must've paid off the sheriff to focus only on finding the money." April closed the report and slammed her fist on the desk.

Wendy and Marcus reconciled after his subsequent reelection win eight years ago. Wendy also revealed that Marcus had found a calla lily when he went to retrieve the money. I asked, "Does anyone know if she was covering up her husband's dirty laundry or whether there really was a calla lily?"

April grunted. "Surprisingly, the one thing Sheriff Crawford did correctly was not immediately divulge to the public that a calla lily had been left at every theft. Wendy and Marcus had no way of knowing there was one present at the other crimes unless they'd spoken to those victims. Nobody publicly acknowledged that they'd been robbed at first." Silas Crawford had been smart enough to keep that calling card close to the vest until the burglaries ceased. He wanted to find the responsible thief, but when it looked to be an impossible feat, he slipped details to the public to trigger the memory of anyone who might've seen someone walking around with calla lilies.

"No one offered up anything?"

"Not according to the original reports. Based on the new interviews we've conducted thus far, either everyone's memory is a bit hazy or they throw out so many names that we'd have to haul in the entire town for questioning." While shaking her head in disgust, April indicated she'd only focus on the current round of thefts, hoping those would be more effective in determining the identity of the thief and Quint's murderer. "There's nothing worse than solving a crime someone covered up years ago."

"I agree, it's probably the same thief. You should be able to crack the current robberies and discover how they tie to Quint's murder. We're probably missing something simple and obvious," I said, worrying that it only made things look worse for my brother if his exit and reentry into Braxton coincided with the time frames of all the missing jewelry.

"It's possible. So far, there have been four thefts with nine days between each one." April opened a cabinet on her wall to reveal a whiteboard listing the dates, locations, and items stolen during the last month.

"Any theories on why nine days?"

"Not yet. It gets weirder with the way these crimes have now been repeated," April said before explaining the basic facts associated with the current robberies. "Could be an accomplice or a copycat."

The first victim had been Jennifer Paddington, who indicated a watch made of crystal and diamonds was stolen from the family estate the weekend of the costume extravaganza. Nine days later, Lydia Nutberry lost a pair of sapphire earrings while attending her sister-in-law's funeral. Eight-thousand dollars in the mortuary safe was also pilfered that evening. Another nine days passed before the matching ruby necklace and the same original pair of ruby earrings were stolen from Maggie Roarke's home. After they'd been returned to Lucy, she'd gifted them to her eldest daughter rather than leave them locked away in a safe, never to be used by anyone. Then, just a few days ago, Imogene Grey was attacked when she caught the thief robbing her mother's home. While she'd been sleeping, a diamond tiara, a present from her grandfather that'd been handed down from an ancestor who'd married into royalty, went missing.

"Let me guess. In all four instances, a black calla lily was left behind?" I knew the truth already but wanted indisputable confirmation.

April replied, "Yes. If the pattern continues, the Stanton household will be the next one hit in four days. Therefore, I need to speak with your brother to find out what he knows."

"It doesn't explain why one of the Roarke rubies was found in the cable car near Quint Crawford's dead body with a bouquet of spray-painted black calla lilies."

"I shouldn't tell you, but perhaps you'll have an explanation. The bouquet of calla lilies left near Quint's body wasn't spray-painted. Those were actual black calla lilies. Only the individual flowers left at the locations where jewelry was stolen were white ones that had been spray-painted."

"That's unusual," I remarked, not sure what the distinction meant. "Hopefully, Connor will find a lead while he's in San Francisco. Maybe he'll get a description or name from the pawn shop owner, indicating who'd sold them the ruby and who'd told them that it belonged to the Roarke family. Perhaps something will explain the calla lily connections. Can you tell me anything about those red marks around Quint's neck?"

April closed the whiteboard and glanced back at me. "That's one of those confidential things, Kellan. I've said enough for today, especially if your brother is somehow mixed up in this situation. He has a knack for getting close to criminals."

"I know my brother. He's acting strange, and I admit, he might've had something to do with the jewelry thefts. But he's not a murderer. He wouldn't hurt anyone, April. You have to believe me."

"That's why it's best for you to work with Connor on anything related to this case. You guys are close, and he knows your brother. I'm already involved deeply in your wife's kidnapping."

"My family must look pretty messed up, huh?" I wasn't being cavalier in sharing my thoughts, but a dark cloud shrouded the Ayrwicks, and I needed all the help I could obtain to disperse it.

"For the sake of our developing friendship, I won't respond to that question." April looked past me as the coroner arrived at her office. She waved him in and indicated it was time for me to leave.

I walked a few steps down the hall but kept my ears attuned to their conversation. The coroner said, "Based on the autopsy, I can confirm Quint Crawford's cause of death as strangulation. My analysis showed major damage. Bruising to his larynx and windpipe with a shattered hyoid bone, and petechiae, also known as blood spots, in his eyes. No DNA obtained from the killer, as far as I can tell right now. I have a few more tests to run later today."

April grunted. "Can you tell me anything about his killer to help the case?"

"Given the size of the individual marks on the victim's neck, the killer had medium-sized hands. Not too small, not too big. Based on past experience and research, males most often choose strangulation as a murder method. You should look for a man with average-sized hands."

I heard footsteps shuffling in April's office before she said, "You're being presumptuous about the gender. We've had our fair share of unusual female killers around here lately. Any fingerprints?"

I recently had a conversation with Connor about forensics being able to trace the killer's identity by picking up impressions on the victim's skin. Oils left behind had allowed for the unique qualities of a person's fingerprints to be more easily obtained. Had we gotten lucky this time?

"No fingerprints. My guess is the killer wore gloves or some sort of protection on his hands. However, let me tell you about the order of events the night Quint Crawford was murdered. A few things might surprise you. At roughly midnight, he was—" the coroner said as the door slammed shut.

CHAPTER 7

Later that Thursday morning, after working out at the Grey Sports Complex and drafting an article for a mystery journal about Alfred Hitchcock's early career, I texted Connor to find out when he'd return from San Francisco. I assumed he was still in the Pacific Time Zone, but his lack of a response meant he was either in flight or busily attending to the case. I desperately wanted to find out what else the coroner had shared with April, and I was certain Connor might be slightly more open to telling me. My brother and I had similar-sized hands, and they were unquestionably larger than average. If what the coroner had told the sheriff was accurate, Gabriel couldn't have been responsible for strangling Quint Crawford.

I strolled across North Campus and headed toward Memorial Library, hoping Maggie might know Connor's current location. During summer sessions, Braxton always held a mini four-week May-June term where students spent a majority of their day focused on one specialized class. From late June through early August, each department also offered two regular classes for those students continuing their studies in between terms who would work twice as hard in half the normal amount of time. It provided an option for transfer students, or those who might've failed a previous course, to catch up before the beginning of the next semester. Locals often used the summers to squeeze in extra classes to graduate sooner than the normal four years.

As I approached the last meandering walkway, I ran into Fern Terry, the dean of student affairs, exiting the main administrative building. Most of the college's non-academic departments had offices in the large colonial-style structure built in the early twentieth century, each with an identical single window peering across campus. Several chimneys poked out of the medium-pitched, dark-colored roof, and a giant circular clock in its center upper peak served to report the official campus time.

"We're overdue for lunch," I said, stopping at a nearby pink dogwood tree where the two paths crossed. "I'm probably free any day next week. How about you?"

"I've got an out-of-town conference, then I'll be in panic mode trying to get ahead of the curve. Any chance you have time this weekend? I'd love to pick your brain about this upcoming family wedding." Fern towered over me. Her wide frame often reminded students of a football player fully dressed in all his gear and padding. She'd been trying to lose a few pounds lately and had hired a trainer to focus on the problem areas, a suggestion Dr. Betscha posed while reminding Fern she wasn't getting any younger. I believe she body-checked my poor cousin when he'd cavalierly delivered that news.

Although Fern's son and my aunt marrying into the Paddington family wouldn't make us related, we enjoyed thinking somehow it meant we were suddenly some sort of step-cousins eighteen times removed from one another. "Let's do dinner on Saturday. Emma has a sleepover with a friend, and I'll have the evening to myself." One of her schoolmates would be celebrating a birthday and had invited her four best pals to spend an afternoon at the local gymnastics facility followed by dinner at a Chuck E. Cheese's restaurant and an animated cartoon movie night.

"Perfect. Want to check out Simply Stoddard?" Fern explained that they'd be catering the wedding, and she wanted to sample a few of their dishes again before making the final decision on what would be served. The Paddingtons were paying for everything else at the wedding but had agreed to let Fern fund the food. I'd met the owners of the new downtown restaurant the month prior and recently tried to repair the remnants of our awkward relationship, especially after previously pushing them hard for answers during a murder investigation about their relocation to Braxton.

We agreed on a time, and Fern offered to make the reservation. "What's the status of the cable car redesign project?" I knew the area had been released by the police, but I wasn't sure if Fern had found a replacement crew.

"Endicott Construction is sending over a new guy to finish the last few items. I met with Nicholas myself, and he hired Cheney Stoddard to finish it," Fern added, complaining that Nicholas had gotten black paint all over her new blouse that day. While she excused herself to attend a meeting on time, I wondered whether the same black paint had been used to change the color of a few calla lilies. What motive could Nicky be hiding for stealing jewelry or murdering Quint? There seemed to be some confusion or discrepancies over future ownership of the company. I added it to my mental follow-up list.

I was glad to hear Cheney had found a job after losing out on the last opportunity when my brother had been hired to fix several cabins near the Saddlebrook National Forest. I rambled down the rest of the walkway and navigated my way toward the library to visit Maggie. On display in the lobby were the plans for the renovation they'd undertake in the fall semester. I was extremely excited to see the boring old structure being razed in favor of a newer, more modern facility.

Once I reached her office, Maggie said, "What brings you by, Kellan?" Maggie had immaculate alabaster skin, and her luscious brown hair had recently been cut shoulder length. She easily charmed others with her girl-next-door personality, a pleasant change of pace from her former ultra-reserved self.

"A few things. I heard the new library plans were released and wanted to see what the place would look like. That's gonna be one fantastic building when it's finished," I said, noticing her sister, Helena, standing in the corner. Wasn't she supposed to be at Woodland Warriors with my daughter?

"Hey, gorgeous. Looking sexy as always," Helena teased, following with a serenade of 'Super Bass' by Nicki Minaj, complete with a brief booty dance that caused her sister to scowl.

"Helena, that's enough, we're in the library!" Maggie's face flushed bright red.

Helena repented by crossing her hands against her chest and bowing. "*Miss Innocent* over there says it's only going to take one year to pull off the whole remodel. Fancy that!"

"We'll be able to use part of the existing building while the new structure is built, but in the spring semester, we'll have a temporary library setup elsewhere. I'm still working through the final details," Maggie explained, before offering me a bottle of water and ignoring Helena. "What else can I do for you? Sorry, but I have a staff meeting to lead in a couple of minutes."

"I won't keep you. Have you heard from Connor? I need to talk to him about something."

"He should be landing at the Philadelphia airport around this time tomorrow, then he's driving back to Wharton County. Everything okay?" Maggie asked with a slight squint.

"Yes, just wanted to find out about his trip. I left him a message. He'll probably reply when he has time." I didn't want to say too much in front of Helena, but I also wasn't sure how close Connor and Maggie were these days. He'd been dating both Maggie and my sister, Eleanor, which wasn't something I could ever be comfortable with. I've always been a one-woman kind of guy, but if he was able to keep the peace until deciding which girl was better for him, I could easily keep my mouth shut about the situation. I was currently under the impression Eleanor's feelings for him had begun waning over time.

"I'll escort you. I need to get to work," Helena said, as Maggie led us back to the lobby of the library. While Maggie kept walking down the hall to her meeting, Helena locked onto my arm as we exited the building. "So, what's shaking, studly?"

"I heard Cheney is finishing the cable car repairs. A good move for him," I said while rolling my eyes, even though she'd previously told me things weren't going well since their break-up.

"He mentioned it this morning. Cheney's excited, but I'm not letting him get the wrong idea. I don't want to be in a relationship," Helena explained once we reached the main campus entrance.

"Are you attending the funeral for Quint tomorrow?" I asked when we stopped near the gate.

Helena repeated that she needed to get to Woodland Warriors for her afternoon shift. She and the assistant teacher split the day, guaranteeing there was someone onsite for early morning drop-offs as well as someone for late evening pick-ups. "Yes, but I'll be there late. I won't be done at the camp until seven o'clock. It's sad, but I'm looking forward to seeing the rest of the Alpha Iota Omega sisters," Helena replied while digging in her pocketbook for her car keys.

"I didn't know you'd been part of a sorority," I exclaimed. Helena, like Gabriel, was four years younger than Maggie and me, which meant we'd never attended high school or college at the same time. "Is that the group of friends you mentioned the other day?"

Helena nodded. "Imogene Grey, Krissy Stanton, Tiffany Nutberry, and I pledged together in the spring of our sophomore year. We had such an amazing time back then, but I was a lot pluckier femme fatale when I was younger, I guess."

From everything I knew and what Maggie had told me, Helena was still a wild child. "You were all in a pledge class together? Was Gabriel a part of this group of friends?"

"Sure was. Quint Crawford, Paul Dodd, and Nicky Endicott were the other guys we hung out with. The eight of us spent our free time together before eventually parting ways," she explained.

"Did Gabriel talk to you about why he left town that summer?"

"Nah. He and I weren't all that close. It was a little awkward because we knew you and Maggie had once dated... we kinda kept a little distance between us." Helena declared again that she had to leave to ensure on-time arrival at Woodland Warriors.

I hadn't realized Helena knew everyone involved. Could she have unexpected information about who might've stolen the jewelry or killed Quint? I planned to tread carefully. Most people believed Quint had died of natural causes, despite my inclination that electrocution didn't qualify as *natural*. I'd have to navigate the conversation gently from the jewelry burglaries toward motives for wanting Quint dead. "A couple of questions. It shouldn't take too long. Your family had some jewelry stolen lately, right?" I knew the rubies belonged to her mother and her sister, but what did she know about them?

"Yeah, it was kinda creepy. Maggie freaked out when she realized someone had stolen them while she was at work, but that calla lily was the strangest thing. I overheard Connor tell Maggie there was a flower left at all the places where something had been stolen. You can't tell anyone else, though." Helena looked at her watch and motioned for me to hurry up. "Sorry, can't lose this job, babe. Plus, Emma prefers me to the other assistant teacher."

I'm sure Emma did. She'd raved about Miss Roarke's lessons the prior evening. "It's a little strange that four of the girls in your sorority's pledge class had something stolen last time, and it appears to be happening again to the same crew of families. Anything you might know about that?"

Helena's face flushed, and she averted her gaze. "I really need to go, Kellan."

"Wait. This is important. If you know something, please tell me so I can... never mind why." I gently grabbed her arm to prevent her from walking away. "I don't mean this how it sounds, but I helped find George Braun's real killer last time, so you weren't stuck in jail. It's payback time." Helena owed me for everything I'd done to protect her when she'd been accused of knifing the professor.

"Ugh, okay. You can't tell anyone else." Helena made me swear on Francesca's grave, which made no sense, but she didn't know the reason. "It's about something we did to join the sisterhood."

My fraternity had done some questionable things back in the day, but there were lines we'd never crossed. It seemed like that wasn't the case for other Greek societies, but not everyone operated the same. Generally, each new semester, sororities and fraternities would hold social functions to search for new members during the *rush period*. It allowed everyone to decide which organization best matched their interests before officially moving forward with a decision. Some Greek societies requested formal applications for a board review; others accepted any new members. At Braxton, it had been more of an exclusive membership. The sorority or fraternity employed clandestine notification procedures when notifying potential members about entering their probationary period. During the subsequent weeks, the candidates became official pledges and would have to learn detailed facts about each official member. They'd also perform semi-shady actions before being inducted as a full sister or brother, hence the appropriate fear of hazing and bullying practices. As part of the pledging process to become a member of the Alpha Iota Omega sorority, each new pledge class had been burdened with a trifecta: something complex, dangerous, and unethical. It was considered a test to see how far each girl would go to become a full-fledged sister, but it'd also been designed to create a bond and a secret between the girls, ensuring they'd protect one another no matter what the cost.

"What exactly were the four of you tasked with doing when you pledged?" I pushed, worried about what she might reveal and how it connected to suspects responsible for Quint's strangulation.

"Look, it was foolish, but we only stole that first piece of jewelry. We were going to give it back, except then...." Helena revealed the entire sordid story.

The Alpha Iota Omega sorority had been founded by a group of women from five major families who'd lived in Braxton in the early 1900s—Paddington, Nutberry, Grey, Roarke, and Stanton. The year Helena pledged had been the one-hundredth anniversary, and the sorority's leadership had requested something preposterously massive to prove to all the alumni that they were the strongest members. The assignment dropped on the newest pledge class—steal a piece of jewelry from one of the original founding families, then present it on the night they'd be formally inducted into the sisterhood. There were only four members in Helena's class representing the Nutberry, Grey, Roarke, and Stanton families. None of the Paddington girls had been in college at the time, enabling the four of them to easily agree to steal the jewelry from the Paddington family.

"We were attending a performance at the Paddington Play House when Krissy saw the brooch on the floor. We decided to take it that night and agreed to keep our actions secret. The plan was to give it back to the Paddingtons at the induction ceremony, but then something went off-track," Helena added with noticeable discomfort over revealing her sisterhood's reprehensible secrets. "Krissy gave the brooch to the president of the sorority after the show. We all saw her put it in the safe, but when we went to retrieve it for the induction ceremony the following week with the alumni, it was missing."

Helena explained that they'd been too scared to go to the police, especially when more thefts kept happening over the next month. Once the burglaries had stopped, the girls vowed never to speak about them again. Helena and her pledge sisters had become full members of the sorority, the police never learned it'd been meant as a joke, and the girls had moved on with their lives. I assumed that one of the girls in the sorority must've removed the brooch from the safe, which meant she was potentially the same person who'd committed the crimes years ago. It didn't explain how Quint's death aligned with the burglaries unless one of the girls had started stealing again and had lost the ruby while killing him in the cable car for some other reason. Had Quint caught the thief and been punished? It also didn't explain Gabriel's involvement, but the timing of his departure from Braxton could've been an abject coincidence. It was imperative I found out what records the pawn shop had kept eight years ago.

* * *

I spent the rest of the evening researching a work project, training Baxter, and watching a few cartoons before tucking Emma in bed and nodding off on the couch. When I woke up on Friday, Connor still hadn't returned my text message which worried me that he'd unearthed troubling news about my brother. I dropped off Emma at the bus stop, watched her leave for camp, and spent the morning dealing with some administrative responsibilities at Braxton. Since I would attend the wake for Quint Crawford at the Whispering Pines funeral parlor after class, my mother agreed to meet Emma when the bus dropped her off after camp. I planned to pick up my daughter from the Royal Chic-Shack once my evening finished.

In need of a break, I escaped to run a few errands and order a sandwich at a local deli for lunch. By the time I ate and returned a few phone calls in my office, my afternoon lecture was ready to begin. I used the back staircase to access the first floor and walked toward the classroom. As I approached it, I heard two women chatting. I recognized the voices as Imogene and Krissy and remained in the hallway to snoop on their conversation. I usually wouldn't eavesdrop on someone else's private discussion, but if they knew something about the current burglaries or Quint's death, it would be beneficial for me to listen in and share any news with April and Connor. I just hoped it wasn't a conversation about shoes!

"Seriously, you've always wanted him. You tried to steal Quint from me years ago too," Imogene said to Krissy in a demure voice.

Krissy shouted, "I would've had him except you kept stringing him along with promises. You broke his heart when you chose Paul. And you probably broke his heart again this time, you fool."

"That's just silly. You've got it backward. Quint was acting strangely while we were together, and that's when I decided to get serious with Paul," Imogene countered with a curt, supercilious tone. "None of it matters anymore. He's gone, and I'm engaged to Paul. And I know things about *you*."

"You've been dating Paul for almost eight years now. I doubt our new town councilman will actually marry you. He'll want a wife he can be proud of, not a disingenuous French tart," Krissy yelled.

I heard the sound of a harsh slap and assumed Imogene must have attacked Krissy. The door opened down the hall and Siobhan called out to me. "Hi, Dr. Ayrwick. How're you today?"

Imogene responded, "You're jealous because none of the guys in our group desired you."

"That's not true. You don't know anything about—"

I interrupted by walking into the room. I couldn't stand there playing the role of slobbering spectator while Siobhan watched me, so I waved her over and attempted to calm the other girls. "Whatever is going on between the two of you needs to stop right now. Students are beginning to arrive, and it's obvious you're both terribly upset. Let's take a quick break." I asked Siobhan to accompany Krissy to the restroom while she splashed cool water on her face since she'd just been smacked.

Imogene stepped outside with me, and I said, "Do you want to talk about what just happened?"

"That's not necessary. Krissy is, and has always been, a bully. We were best friends a long time ago, but she's grown far worse over the years. We'll work it out. I promise it won't interfere with class," Imogene said, looking nervously at the ground and rubbing the hand she'd used to whack Krissy's cheek.

Something about Imogene's reaction felt insincere or forced. Given the sudden violent outburst I'd witnessed, her newly calm exterior wouldn't have been my initial expectation. If she were capable of such a quick transition, what else might she be hiding? Could Imogene have been the one to steal the Paddington brooch from the sorority's safe eight years ago, then gone on a rampage thieving all the rest of the jewelry? If that were true, she would've had to fake the robbery at her mother's place the prior weekend.

Then, I remembered that Quint had been distraught over a break-up. Krissy had mentioned Quint and Imogene had been in love years ago, and she'd ended it for some reason. The only motivation I could understand for Imogene killing Quint would be if he'd discovered the truth about the robberies and confronted her. Was Imogene truly capable of murdering someone she'd once been seriously involved with? Sometimes people surprised you with the secrets they kept. It was a long shot, but I needed to consider all theories and suspects while collecting more information about Quint's life and current relationships. "I'm glad your issues with Krissy won't cause further incidents in class. You're overwhelmed by your friend's death. Emotions run high during painful times."

"Quint and I were friends long ago, but we lost touch. I'd overlooked how much I missed him until recently," Imogene said as she perched modestly on a nearby bench.

A few students walked by, including Raquel. I'd forgotten she wanted to talk after class today. As Imogene's head hung low, Raquel checked if everything was okay. I nodded and told her we'd be inside momentarily. "Imogene, maybe the funeral will help provide a way to say a proper goodbye."

"You're right, thank you. I appreciate your kindness, but we should get back to class." Imogene jumped up and walked toward Diamond Hall with determined steps.

After she trotted away, I struggled to understand the exchange that had occurred between her and Krissy. It was clear Krissy had been jealous of Imogene, but what was Krissy's relationship with Quint before he had been killed? Neither girl seemed capable of strangling Quint under normal conditions, yet during an intense argument, it might be possible, especially if Quint had threatened to call the cops. Both women had average-sized hands, though Krissy's were slightly larger than Imogene's. What I struggled to understand was *why someone would electrocute Quint after they'd already strangled him.* It was unfortunate I couldn't listen to the coroner's explanation about the order of the events when Quint had been murdered. Was the electrocution simply to cover up evidence, or had it occurred first? Still, someone had turned off the power source before I'd arrived, making things even murkier. Could the jogger I'd witnessed have been the killer coming back to retrieve the gloves and turn off the power? Sandalwood was a strong scent, and I might stumble upon someone wearing it again. I wanted to ask more direct questions, but people believed Quint had died of an accidental electrocution. I couldn't even hint about murder, not without the repercussions of idle gossip. Ugh, so frustrating!

The remainder of my lecture completed smoothly. I made a last-minute change to limit the amount of time students would work in groups, theorizing it'd be best to keep the two girls from interacting with one another immediately after they'd had a fight. After everyone left, Raquel and I spent thirty minutes reviewing her background and discussing her interest in the film industry. "What was your undergraduate degree in?"

"Political science and economics, but I went to graduate school and earned an MBA with a focus on management and leadership. I worked for a few years before getting married. I'm still figuring out what's next," she responded and crossed her legs. Only a few inches of skin could be seen below the hem of her skirt and the top of her knee-high leather boots.

"Do you see yourself working in the entertainment business, or is this class just something to keep from being bored until you find the right job?" I asked, curious whether she planned to remain in Braxton or move elsewhere. There would be little opportunity to make movies or films in this part of the country, at least not as a full-time job. While a few production companies and studios had opened in New York City and the southern part of the country, I wasn't familiar with anything major in Pennsylvania that would attract her attention.

"Mostly to keep busy while my husband focuses on his career. We might move to the West Coast if his current job doesn't pan out. What's Los Angeles like?" Raquel flashed her colorful eyes at me and leaned in closer. "Did you work with any celebrities or important people? Were you on camera?"

"A few stars crossed my path. My expertise is in investigative reporting, historical crimes, and behind-the-scenes coordination. I'm not interested in acting or dealing with fans. I like my privacy." In the past, several colleagues had pushed me to audition for roles on the popular crime shows, but I didn't want to worry about always looking perfect, interacting with followers, and playing distinct roles. My skills were in getting things done, not projecting an image I couldn't possibly maintain twenty-four-seven.

"You're a handsome man. You've built a following, even if you don't want to admit it. I did some research when I saw you'd be teaching this class. How come you're back in Pennsylvania? Based on what you want to do, you'd be better off in LA." Raquel licked her lips and tilted her head to the side.

For a hot second, I wondered if she were flirting with me. While she was attractive, we were both married even if I intended to terminate my relationship as soon as Las Vargas released Francesca. "I'm not comfortable having that conversation. Let's focus on you and what I can do to help."

"Just trying to comprehend how you made your decisions. I thought it might help me understand if I'd be better off moving to Hollywood." She leaned back again, reining in her lingering glances and coquettish smile. "I've heard the rumors about you solving a lot of murders around here. You must be fantastic at your job. You should've gone into the FBI instead of directing and teaching."

"I considered it when I was younger. I've always had a knack for solving puzzles and figuring out people's secrets. It's easy to see through the walls people put up when you listen to the words they use, especially if I feel like someone's not being truthful with me." Once I'd moved to the West Coast and been granted a few lucky breaks, I'd grown too enamored with Hollywood and decided not to leave it until recently. But I was happier with my life these days, especially being closer to my family again.

"As long as you're careful. I overheard Krissy and Imogene talking about the jewelry thefts during break. It sounds dangerous. Hopefully, you're not getting involved in solving that crime!" Raquel handed me a print-out of next semester's courses. "This is what I hope to take. What do you think?"

"First off, I think the sheriff is capable of solving the burglaries. Second, my plate is full these days. Now, let's peruse your proposal." I glanced at her suggestions and agreed with her enrollment plans. Perhaps she was simply bored and nosy and wanted to get to know me better. I shared some background on how she could study the film industry outside of Braxton. After Raquel left, my phone vibrated with a text that accentuated the already disastrous aura surrounding the upcoming evening.

Connor: *Just landed. We need to talk about your brother. It's important.*

Me: *What did Gabriel do now? We can meet at the wake tonight.*

Connor: *Okay. For starters, it seems like he's involved in some or all the jewelry thefts.*

Me: *Perhaps it just looks that way? Give me some hope here, man.*

Connor: *Gabriel has also quickly risen on my list of suspects potentially connected with Quint's murder.*

Me: *That's not helping me! He's NOT a murderer.*

Connor: *I wish I had better news, but I might be forced to get a warrant issued for his arrest tomorrow.*

CHAPTER 8

Post Connor's last text message, my body yearned for positive distraction. When I checked on Emma, my mother had just arrived home and was heating dinner for all of them. The housekeeper had stored a meal in the refrigerator when she'd finished cooking earlier that day; my mother was not the most domestic person I knew. After our chat, I stopped at the Pick-Me-Up Diner for a quick bite to eat with Eleanor. With one before Quint's service, it would be beneficial to hold a sibling catch up.

"Look what the cat dragged in," she teased as I walked inside the recently renovated eatery a few blocks from campus. A turquoise and slate-gray sundress adorned my sister's solid and compact body, features she'd struggled to accept until realizing their value during her field hockey days. Wide hips and thick, muscular arms came from the Danby side of the family, and they weren't something she could change. Eleanor handed a receipt to a customer who dashed past me and into the parking lot.

"Good evening to you too. Do you greet all your best customers that way?" I asked as she kissed my cheek and handed two menus to a waitress who was seating someone ahead of me.

"Only the ones I love. Follow me to the office. I need to call back a supplier. You can stop in the kitchen to pick up our meals from Chef Manny. He should be done by now," Eleanor said while walking to the far corner of the diner. When she said Manny's name, I could swear her eyes brightened.

While she made a right toward her office, I stopped in front of the kitchen and gently pushed open the swinging door. Before I could lean my head inside to let Manny know we were ready, his voice echoed in the hall. It would either be an insurance issue or a health code violation for me to wander into the kitchen. I didn't work there and had no training; therefore, I wouldn't step all the way inside.

"Nah, she doesn't know. I'm afraid to tell her. What if it doesn't come through?" Manny said with an excess of hesitation in his voice. I couldn't see him because he stood behind the door cooking on the grill. He must not have been talking to me, given I hadn't a clue what he'd meant.

Another muffled voice responded, "She's the boss. You gotta tell her today if you're gonna leave town. It's an amazing opportunity. Does Eleanor know you got married on that Vegas trip?"

Manny replied, "Nope. I couldn't bring myself to disappoint her. We've worked together for years and gotten very close. I'd feel like a jerk to up and leave just when she took over the joint."

As far as I could tell, Manny was happy working at the diner. I'd always suspected he had the whisper of an attraction to Eleanor, but nothing had ever come of it. He'd gone on vacation after she'd bought the place that spring, but once he'd returned, Eleanor thought he'd begun acting strangely. She assumed he was solicitous because they used to be peers, yet as the owner, she was officially his boss instead of just the serving staff manager. It hadn't been an easy road for my sister, especially when the contractor she'd hired for the repairs absconded with some of her money and she later failed the initial electrical inspection. It would be a disaster if her chef resigned in the first few months.

Manny must have noticed the door was slightly ajar. "Who's there?"

I poked my head inside and smiled. "*Hola, amigo.* Eleanor says she's ready for our dinner."

"Hey, Kellan, I'll bring it to her office in a minute. Is Emma here?" Manny loved visiting with my daughter. She would suggest ideas for meals whenever Eleanor watched Emma for me.

"Not today. She's with my parents, but we'll be back again soon, I'm sure. How's everything with you?" I asked, wondering if he'd say anything to me about the news I'd just overheard.

"*Bueno.* Tell her I said hi," he replied without looking up from the grill.

As a waitress picked up a hot dish, I scooted out of her way and headed toward Eleanor's office. When I arrived, my sister hung up the phone and said, "All good?"

"That depends. Have you figured out why Manny was acting weird the last two months?" I didn't want to be the one to tell Eleanor but also wasn't sure I knew the whole story. What amazing opportunity had the other kitchen worker been talking about?

"We chatted a few weeks ago. I got the impression he was doing okay, but I know he's holding back. I'm not sure if he's upset that I bought the diner and he wanted to try to swing it himself, or if there's something else going on." Eleanor absentmindedly cleared her desk, so we had a place to eat. "I didn't think he wanted to buy his own place. He likes operating behind the scenes, kind of like you."

I told Eleanor what I'd overheard and offered a minor concession to make her feel better. "Maybe I misunderstood the conversation. I can be easily confused."

"Him quitting would be awful news. I'm gonna confront Manny." She marched past me in a fury.

I grabbed her arm. "Hold up, Attila. Maybe now isn't the best time. Wait until things slow down when you can talk to him alone."

Eleanor couldn't respond when Manny walked in with two plates and set them on the desk. "It's today's special. Chicken cordon bleu with scalloped potatoes."

"It smells amazing. You're the best chef around. I'm really glad we're working together. I should probably give you a raise, huh?" Eleanor said, patting him on the back. She was laying it on a little thick, in my humble opinion, but at least she didn't confront him.

Manny blushed and waved his hands at her as he stepped backward out of the office. "No, no. Everything is good. I need to get back to the kitchen." He glanced back at her longer than I'd expected.

Eleanor scowled at me. "He's got that same look on his face that you get whenever you feel guilty about something. Is it a man thing? Why can't you just tell us the truth?" She sliced into her chicken with a little too much energy and precision and grunted at me like an angry troll.

"Don't take your frustrations out on me, little sister. I do not keep things from people."

"One word," she said, looking at me with a devious smirk.

"Awesome?"

"Francesca."

She had a point. I was keeping my wife's reincarnation from our parents. "That's different."

"I know." Eleanor's entire demeanor had changed since I'd shown up fifteen minutes earlier. "I just wanted to bring up her name, so you could tell me the latest."

I updated Eleanor on my partnership with April, the calls from Cristiano, and the meeting with the Castiglianos. I expected something new to happen over the weekend but feared the outcome of it would be another unwelcome surprise. She helped me stay as calm as possible under the circumstances. "I should head to the funeral home for Quint's service soon."

"Poor guy. He used to flirt with me all the time when he'd come in for lunch or a late dinner. I liked him a lot, and he could be awfully persuasive and assertive, but Quint just wasn't my type. Although, I almost yielded to his seduction once. He knew how to make you feel special, but he'd also pined away for Imogene way too long and couldn't commit to another girl," Eleanor explained with a rueful sigh.

"I've heard that about him. Do you think he'd ever hurt a woman?" I'd experienced mixed responses from different people in Quint's life regarding his behavior. He'd worshipped all the ladies he'd dated but struggled to view others, like Fern, as an authority figure. I could only conclude that he was a bit of a chameleon, depending on the situation and balance of power in the relationship. I theorized someone had resented his quicksilver ability to dazzle a woman and then disappoint her when he snatched back his charms. Or had someone like Paul begrudged Quint's past with Imogene? It wouldn't be the first time a jealous man killed to protect the woman he loved.

"Nah, I think Quint pushed too hard, but he would stop when a woman said *no*. He always did with me. He was very smart, despite having an ego even bigger than yours." Eleanor mindlessly massaged the scar on her elbow she'd gotten from a grease fire years ago.

"Touché, Attila." I didn't want to gossip about Gabriel's potential role in the jewelry thefts until he and I talked through it, even though she was our sister. When we finished eating and I noticed it was time for Quint's service, I warned Eleanor to go easy on Manny and suggested he was only *thinking* about moving to Las Vegas with his new wife. Sometimes people mulled over their options before making a final decision—she shouldn't jump to conclusions. As the words spilled from my lips, I realized I should take my own banal advice. I'd already deemed Gabriel guilty of a string of crimes, regardless of discovering adequate proof or having a discussion with him about what'd happened in the past.

* * *

I stepped through the front door of Whispering Pines, shivering at the thought of having to attend another wake. The funeral home smelled like lilacs even when they weren't in season. It was the Nutberry's attempt to disguise the smell of embalming fluids and force people to forget what happened to dead bodies before they were put on display for grieving relatives and friends.

Lydia Nutberry chatted with Nana D and Bertha Crawford in the far corner. Unwilling to interrupt, I circulated the room to verify who else had attended. I stopped at the casket to pay my respects and say goodbye to Quint Crawford. I'd only known him for less than two weeks, but I'd never seen him dressed in anything other than jeans and a t-shirt. Today, he wore a dark-brown suit, off-white dress shirt, and a muted beige tie. He looked like a completely different man, one who was uncomfortable in his current attire.

"I told you I'd be here, Kellan. You didn't need to sic Nana D on me. She was all over me earlier, like a lion on a fresh carcass," Gabriel blasted once I stood from kneeling at the coffin.

I turned and stared at my brother. He wore a dark-colored suit and light-blue dress shirt and matching tie, looking just as uncomfortable as Quint and me. "I didn't force her to do or say anything. You know Nana D. She grabs the bull by its horns with her own hands."

Gabriel led me by the jacket sleeve to the side of the room. "Let's not do this tonight. I got all your messages. I know you have questions, but this isn't the appropriate place. Are you available tomorrow? We could grab a drink at Kirklands like last time, where I spilled my secrets."

"Sure, tomorrow's fine, but come by in the morning for breakfast. Emma would love to see you," I replied as Connor ambled nearby and jerked his head to the side to indicate where we should meet. "What I know doesn't make much sense, and you're foolishly hiding something from everyone."

"Tomorrow at nine. I'll be there," Gabriel said before walking away. I followed to remind him I was on his side, but he joined two guys sitting a few rows away near the front window. One of them was the new town councilman and Imogene's fiancé, Paul Dodd. Based on the resemblance, I assumed the other was Nicholas Endicott, the son Lindsey had procreated with a former girlfriend he'd met at his forty-ninth birthday party. It'd had been quite a shock to his friends and family when he'd become a father again at such a late time in life.

In another row just beyond, Imogene, Krissy, Tiffany, and Helena were deep in conversation. All eight members of the former close-knit group were present, except one would soon be buried six feet underground. What did each know about Quint's death and the jewelry thefts? As I strolled away, that familiar sandalwood scent I'd smelled near the cable car filled the air. I couldn't exactly walk up to each of them and sniff their necks like a pig searching for truffles; that would look bizarre. Which one had been the jogger I'd seen collecting the gloves the day Quint had died? It could've been a coincidence, but I no longer believed in them when it came to the murder investigations I'd become embroiled in.

"I'm glad you waited for Gabriel to step away before we talked," Connor began as soon as I reached the corner. "April told me she informed you why I was in San Francisco."

"I'm not going to like your news very much, am I?" Briefly abandoning my quest for the person wearing the cologne, I planned to sniff out the trail after Connor and I conversed.

"It's not all bad. I managed to track down the employee who was working the night the Roarke rubies had been pawned," Connor said, demonstrating why he'd been the perfect addition to the Wharton County Sheriff's Office. "Two people had initially come into the shop, but they both left after an argument in the main entranceway. Only one person returned afterward to fill out the forms to sell the rubies. The store still had the record."

"Why didn't they offer it to Sheriff Crawford? April indicated the information wasn't in her files."

"The shop owner swears he faxed over the record when the former sheriff requested it. What happened after that, I have no clue. I have my suspicions but can't be certain." Connor might do his best to protect my brother, but he wouldn't skirt the law. "This wasn't the shadiest shop I've seen. I think they tried to do the right thing, and they were cooperative with me. I'm quite sure they broke a few rules last time." Connor put his hand on my back and squeezed my shoulder. "The name on the record is Gabriel Ayrwick. Sorry, buddy."

A minute passed as the news digested. I looked at my baby brother as sadness crept inside my body like I hadn't experienced in a long time. "Does that mean he's the thief you're looking for?"

Connor explained that there was no record of the other person's name, nor were there any video recordings from eight years ago. "The worker handed the money to your brother. Do you know how pawn shops function?" After I shook my head, as I hadn't been one-hundred percent familiar, Connor shared the store's policy for loaning cash to a customer who pawned an item. If the hawker brought back the cash within one month, plus any additional amount for store fees, the item would be returned. If nobody showed up within one month, the item could be sold to someone else for any price. "There is an interesting fact about how this one turned out."

"Gabriel went back to try to retrieve the item, right?" I wanted to believe my brother was innocent, but the details Connor had learned on his trip were incontrovertible.

"He couldn't have. Just before the one month was up, an anonymous caller notified the shop that the rubies belonged to someone in Braxton. The shop eventually contacted Sheriff Crawford who requested photos. Formal paperwork was filed, and the rubies were returned to the Roarke family." The pawn shop dealt with their insurance agency, and the sheriff followed up on the report of who'd pawned them. But we don't know what Crawford did because the report wasn't included in his files. Something happened to stop him from searching for Gabriel.

"Do you have any idea whom Gabriel was with at the pawn shop?"

"The worker at the pawn shop couldn't remember if it was a woman or a man who'd initially walked in with your brother. Gabriel's tattoos and piercings had made too big of an impression on him that day," Connor replied, shaking his head and smirking. "I'll ask Lucy Roarke what Sheriff Crawford said when he returned the stolen rubies. He might have been covering for your brother."

"Do you think the Roarkes opted not to file charges because Gabriel was involved, and they didn't want to hurt my family?"

Connor nodded. "I'm afraid that might have transpired. It doesn't explain why no one tried to locate all the other stolen items, nor why similar thefts are happening all over again."

When we looked up to see what Gabriel was doing, my brother had already left the funeral parlor. So had Nicholas Endicott, Paul Dodd, and most of the girls from the sorority. I considered telling Connor what Helena had revealed about the hazing ritual to steal the original brooch from the Paddingtons, but I wanted to speak with Gabriel first. If he and Quint had gotten into a volatile argument together, could Gabriel have taken it too far? A man can go through a lot in eight years to change his personality; however, the size of my brother's hands and fingers couldn't have matched the marks around Quint's neck. Was there an accomplice, an unknown person who could be responsible?

Nana D interrupted me before I could ask Connor about his next steps. "Bertha would like to speak with you. Do you have a minute?"

Connor excused himself, indicating he'd follow up with me over the weekend. I didn't know whether he was going to arrest my brother or wait until he had more information. As far as I was concerned, Gabriel's role in the current round of robberies was circumstantial. It was likely Gabriel would only be a person of interest until they found something to tie him to the new crimes. Could they arrest him for the ones eight years ago? I assumed there wasn't any statute of limitations on robbery if you eventually found the guilty party. I followed Nana D to the small sitting area in the other corner where a worn-down Bertha Crawford leaned against the arm of the chair. The sandalwood smell had already been replaced by lilacs. I'd lost my chance to locate the potential culprit or accomplice.

"Thank you, Kellan. I'm glad you could spare some time." Bertha's shaky hand reached toward me, and her Georgian accent was still strong, despite the cancer's persistent grip on her life. The once plump and matronly woman, blessed with a head of thick gray curls, had deteriorated into a bony and sallow-skinned shell. She'd done her best to hide the painful changes in her body, but nothing concealed the effects of the rampant disease on her face and hair. A black scarf was elegantly wrapped around the top of her head, yet it was obvious she had little desire or strength to combat the truth.

"I'm truly sorry for your loss, Bertha," I said, remembering she'd yelled whenever I'd called her Mrs. Crawford in the past. "Quint and I had a few laughs the last couple of weeks while he was working on the cable car redesign project. I know how proud you were of him."

"I can't believe he's gone. I should've been the one to die first. I don't understand how an old lady like me can linger around with cancer, but a strong young man like him can be murdered by a crazy person." Her face was stoic, and she refused to cry in public.

"What do you mean murdered by a crazy person?" Had April or Connor told her more than me?

"That new sheriff promised me she's going to find his killer, but I saw how you tracked down what happened to Gwendolyn Paddington. I need your help, Kellan. I'm begging you to investigate who killed my boy." Bertha closed her eyes and buried her forehead in her hands.

I looked at Nana D with confusion and hesitancy over Gabriel's potential involvement in the situation. "I'm not sure that's the best idea. What did the sheriff indicate was the cause of death?"

Bertha mumbled a mostly incoherent response. All I could understand was that Quint had been electrocuted, but someone had also choked him to death with their hands. There were no fingerprints found on his body or inside the cable car. "I can't speak too much about Quinton's life outside of the little he'd told me. For the last month, all he'd done was work for Nicky Endicott and take care of me."

I'd investigate Nicky as a priority, but if I had any chance of finding Quint's killer, I needed to know everything he'd been up to and whom he'd socialized with recently. Bertha confirmed there were no other family members in the area, and they'd mostly kept to themselves since her diagnosis. "Was Quint dating anyone? He told me he'd fallen in love, but it'd ended poorly."

Bertha considered my question, then shook her head. "Not that he shared.

He dated a few women in Braxton, but he'd never gotten over Imogene. Isn't she engaged to another man, though?"

Paul Dodd was on my list, but I knew little about him. Had he been wearing the cologne? When I pushed Bertha for more information, she lost most of her energy. I squeezed her hand and told her I'd do my best to look into it. "Imogene told me they were once friends. I'll see what she knows. She might be our only other real lead right now."

"Is there anyone Quint fought with who might have tried to hurt him?" Nana D asked.

"I can't imagine who would've been that angry. The only person he had an argument with was that Irish girl, and she was just upset because my boy changed his mind about her." Bertha closed her eyes and rested her head against a pillow Nana D had placed on the back of the chair.

Irish girl? Who was she talking about? It took me a minute to piece together everything she'd said. "Do you mean Siobhan Walsh? The young woman whose twins you'd been babysitting?"

"Yes, that's her. Quinton and Siobhan went on a few dates, but it didn't work out. She was irate with him when it ended." Bertha's pleading eyes were cast in my direction. "Please find out who did this to Quinton. I must know soon... it's doubtful... I'll recuperate from this invasive disease."

Nana D suggested I search Quint's bedroom at Bertha's house to locate any potential clues. It was a solid idea, and I agreed to visit as soon as possible. We agreed that someone needed to chat with Siobhan to understand what'd taken place between her and Quint, even if it had nothing to do with his death. On the flip side, if Siobhan had a motive for hurting him, and they had a fight in the cable car, maybe she was somehow involved in his murder. She also mentioned not earning enough money before taking the new job with my mother in the admission's office. I vividly recalled Siobhan's response to Imogene on the first day of class about how she had to take care of a man who'd once hurt her. Had she been referring to Quint? It couldn't be, I convinced myself. This was merely another case of circumstantial evidence.

Bertha asked Nana D if she could accompany her to the casket for a last goodbye before the graveside service the following morning. As they shuffled away, I felt someone fiercely jab at my shoulder. Upon turning around, an awkward-looking Lydia Nutberry thrust one hand on her hip and waggled an index finger with the other. The last time I'd spoken with Lydia occurred before I'd provoked her sister-in-law into confessing to murder the prior month. What was I about to get myself into?

CHAPTER 9

"I'm very angry with you," Lydia scowled. Unfortunately blessed with an austere countenance, she also kept her dark-gray hair shellacked tightly in a bun on the crown of her head. Lydia wore an oversized suit jacket that hung on her body like last threads gripping a broken hanger in fear of eternal loss. Delicately balanced tiny glasses connected to a stringy beaded chain and chunky black orthopedic sneakers completed the peculiar outfit. Her pointy nose and chin, not all that different from a stereotypical cartoon witch, usually warned people not to mess with her.

Convinced she wouldn't make a scene in the middle of a funeral service, I let her quietly vent rather than defend my actions. "I'm terribly sorry for how everything exploded at the Mendel flower show opening. I had no intention of harming your family when my speech compelled your sister-in-law to admit what she'd done to Judy's husband." While it wasn't exactly a true statement, the Wharton County Sheriff's Office preferred that my involvement appeared unintentional to the general public. They feared Lissette's lawyer would claim she'd been coerced into a false confession, but the proof of her crime was irrefutable.

"At least you know well enough to begin with an apology." Lydia led me down the hall to her office. Our feet trod softly on a plush, emerald-green carpet as we passed endless walls covered on the top half with a floral print and the bottom half with burgundy wainscoting. "But you've got it all wrong. I'm not angry with you for discovering what my sister-in-law did."

Had I heard her correctly? "What do you mean? I thought you'd never speak with me again."

"Just like my husband thinks. The whole lot of you needs to be reeducated," Lydia pointed out as she took a seat behind her desk. "I'm ticked off because you didn't visit me after that incident happened. How long have our families known one another, Kellan?"

"Well, it's at least... oh, I'd say close to... um—" I began tracing our history and had just remembered attending camp with one of her sons when she interrupted me.

"Decades. That's long enough to expect a better reaction." Lydia explained that while she was saddened one sister-in-law had passed away and another had gone to the psychiatric ward for evaluation prior to a prison term, she passionately believed that people should be punished for their crimes and should seek mental help to recover whenever possible. Lydia was disgruntled with me for not checking on her or showing solidarity and support for her after all the bad publicity and rumors circulating around town about the Nutberry family.

"I should've known better. It's been a rough year for you." I recalled some of the reactions from the community. Sales had been down for her family's mortuary when customers went to neighboring villages to purchase funeral services. Nana D had also mentioned that the pharmacy was a ghost town since people worried about the unstable Nutberry family filling prescription drugs for patrons. After we repaired our relationship, Lydia flabbergasted me with her next topic.

"My daughter, Tiffany, is distraught over losing her friend at such an early age. You really ought to visit her this weekend; she could use some cheering up. But truthfully, there's another reason I wanted to talk to you." Lydia handed me a cup of tea from the Keurig machine on the credenza behind her. "With you being such a clever detective, I expect you are putting those skills to use and trying to find out what happened to Quint. Bertha is counting on you to solve this before she passes away. Quint didn't die from electrocution. He was murdered!"

I hadn't realized Bertha and Lydia were friends, but it made sense if their children had known one another. "Bertha asked me to help, but what if I discover something neither of you would want people to know?" Someone in that group of eight had stolen the jewelry, and my guess was that one of them had either killed Quint as revenge for something yet to be discovered or to cover up a role in the robberies. Quint couldn't have strangled himself, and I swore my brother wasn't capable of murder. It left six other options, despite nothing obvious connecting Tiffany, Lydia's daughter, to the crimes.

"The truth always has a funny way of clawing its way to the surface. I trust you will handle it with proper caution and respect," she counseled. Lydia was a strong woman who'd married into the Nutberry family and struggled to find her own place among a very stubborn crowd. She was direct but fair when listening to what other people had to tell her. "How can I help?"

"Since you've asked, perhaps you could tell me what you know about the jewelry thefts. Your family lost two things, right?" When she nodded in slight confusion, I added, "Not that Quint's death is necessarily connected to them, but it's important for me to understand everything. There was a stolen ruby found near Quint's body. Tell me what happened to your mother-in-law's choker eight years ago."

"I'm not sure what that has to do with the price of beans, but I'll share anything I can remember." Lydia removed her bifocals and pinched the bridge of her nose. "Agnes had taken it out of the safe that morning because she planned to wear it to Tiffany's concert. I know everyone thinks she bribed the director, but Tiffany was a wonderful musician. Maybe she wasn't the best flutist that season, but she was in the top three. What no one else ever admits is the girl who was the best had been suspected of a little powdered candy," she said, tapping the side of her nose and smiling ruefully at me.

Lydia finished sharing her story. Agnes had changed her outfit at the last minute and decided not to wear the choker. They were running late, prompting her not to take the time to lock it in the safe before leaving for the concert. When they'd returned home, it was missing. Agnes called the police, and the former sheriff personally visited the family the next morning. It had been the second theft at that point, but no one had made any connection to the first one until much later because of the confusion with where the Paddington brooch had been stolen and the revelation about the calla lilies consistently appearing at all the locations. Eventually, Agnes reported it to her insurance company and had been compensated for the loss. The choker was still missing to this day.

"How did Tiffany feel about the whole event? Quint was her friend, and his uncle couldn't help much," I said, wondering what Lydia might have surmised.

"Tiffany was barely twenty years old. She was acting a little strange, but all kids do at that age."

"Was she living in the Braxton dorms?"

"Yes, but she'd come home that weekend for a family party. I think she had friends over the day of the concert and was wrapped up in her social life. Come to think of it, Agnes showed everyone the choker that night while they were having dinner." Lydia confirmed all eight kids from the group, including Quint and my brother, had been at that meal before they'd left for the concert. All of Tiffany's friends had attended the concert, but they'd returned to the dorms once it finished. Lydia and Agnes had gone out for drinks. When they'd arrived home, the house was empty, and Agnes had discovered the choker was stolen. Tiffany confirmed she hadn't gone back to the house after the concert, so she wasn't sure either. She couldn't remember anyone disappearing, but it could've been possible.

"What about your earrings? Weren't they stolen a few weeks ago while you were at your sister-in-law's memorial service at the church?"

"Yes, Tiffany had worn them to an engagement party the night before, and she dropped them off at Whispering Pines. I also had eight-thousand dollars in cash in our safe that day." Lydia explained that she'd kept enough money in her office for incidentals and payments to vendors who offered discounts if she'd paid cash for certain services. She'd been the last one in the funeral parlor that evening and had thought she'd locked the safe but couldn't be certain. She was going directly to the church, so she left the earrings at the funeral parlor overnight. When she arrived the next morning, the safe had been emptied and a black calla lily left behind. She'd never needed cameras at the facility before, especially in her office, and there were no resultant fingerprints other than those of regular employees. "We've installed a new surveillance system already."

"Do you have any idea who might be responsible?" I asked, wondering if Tiffany had inadvertently revealed to anyone that she'd dropped the earrings off at the funeral home.

"Sheriff Montague mentioned there'd been a string of burglaries happening again. I just assumed it was random, but then she asked me this morning if I'd seen your brother lately. Surely, she doesn't think he's involved somehow, does she?" Lydia pulled back and gasped a little as if she'd just remembered something important.

"Are you okay?"

"Gabriel was driving Tiffany the day she dropped off the earrings. I forgot about it until just now. It was very quick, but she said he was waiting in the car as he had to make a call before they went to lunch." Lydia didn't know of other potential suspects who might've killed Quint, so I decided to hold off on any further questions. I needed to speak with Tiffany to find out what she was hiding from everyone.

Once Lydia and I finished chatting, we returned to the main room. I said goodbye to Nana D and Bertha, promising to call her soon with some questions and any updates on what'd happened to Quint. The room was mostly empty, and there was no one else I could follow up with about the situation. I'd had a long enough day and needed to pick up Emma from my parents. We were overdue to take the puppy out for his evening walk and read a bedtime story before Emma went to sleep.

* * *

Once Gabriel texted he was on his way over on Saturday morning, Emma and I prepared breakfast. It was less than a ten-minute walk from Nana D's place to the guest cottage, so I scrambled a half-dozen eggs and popped several slices of whole wheat bread in the toaster. I didn't have time for a full spread like Nana D would've, but mine would suffice for this morning.

Gabriel knocked twice and opened the front door. The bags under his eyes were heavy and as dark as mud. "Nana D sends her regards. She has an early meeting with Paul Dodd to prepare for their first year working together and sent over a coffee cake she made yesterday morning."

Emma and Gabriel set the table while I finished cooking. When everything was ready, we ate breakfast together, keeping the conversation civil and focused on lighthearted topics. Once we were done, Emma took Baxter outside to practice his tricks. I watched them through the window as they played in the small fenced-in area just outside the back door. I could hear Emma sternly warning the puppy that he wouldn't get any treats if he didn't properly listen to her. She was gonna turn into another Nana D if I wasn't careful!

"We have a lot to discuss, and you better be truthful," I firmly warned Gabriel, realizing my daughter was more like me than I'd previously acknowledged.

"Yeah, your non-stop messages and cruddy attitude has made that clear." He poured himself a glass of orange juice, kicked off his shoes as he sat across from me, and plunked his feet on the couch next to me. "There are two sides to every story. All I ask is that you don't judge me until I'm finished."

Gabriel and I had always been close as young kids, even though we were four years apart. I'd never shared that kind of relationship with our older brother, Hampton, who'd tortured me and treated me like his servant. By the time Hampton had moved out, I was tired of being the middle child in our family and went off to college to build a new life. I blamed myself for abandoning Gabriel when he'd needed me most. Accepting the truth about his homosexuality must have been difficult if he'd felt he had no one to talk to about his emotions and his fears.

"I promise. It might be a little too late, but I'll do whatever I can to help fix what you've done," I said, playfully slapping his thigh as a show of support. "Talk to me."

"That's just the thing. I already tried to fix it years ago and look what's happened." Gabriel grunted, jumped up from the couch, and walked toward the front door. "I didn't steal the jewelry eight years ago. I know people suspect me, but I'm innocent."

"I'm glad to hear it. Why do you think they suspect you?"

"Because I know who did. And that person forced me to get more involved than I needed to be." Brow furrowed and eyes focused, he paced the living-room floor.

"I know what happened in San Francisco at the pawn shop." I should have waited for my brother to share when he was ready, but I wanted answers.

"What? You've got to be kidding me. No one was supposed to know about that. He promised me he'd keep it hidden." Gabriel punched the front door to let out his frustrations.

"Who promised you that? Connor?" My head felt too cloudy to interpret his explanation.

"Connor? What does he have to do with the pawn shop? I'm talking about Dad. He took care of everything. That's part of why I left town." Gabriel had thrown out a curveball with that reveal as he leaned against the opposite wall and groaned loudly enough for Emma to check on us.

I ushered her back out the door and assured her everything was fine. "You've completely lost me, Gabriel. Connor and I found one of the Roarke rubies near Quint's body in the cable car. He realized it was from the original pieces of jewelry someone had stolen and that had eventually been hocked at a pawn shop in California." I shook my head, trying to make sense of the situation. "Connor thinks whoever killed Quint is the person stealing all the jewelry and lost control—"

"Are you saying the police suspect me of killing Quint? That's absurd; he was my friend. Quint might've done some stupid things and tried to take advantage of me, but I'd never physically hurt him." Gabriel looked as wounded as he was shocked by the thought of someone accusing him of murder again. "I gotta get out of here. It was foolish of me to return to Braxton. Nothing's changed."

"Wait! You said something about Dad. What does he have to do with this mess?"

"Ask him yourself. I need to talk to someone else before this gets out of hand again," Gabriel shouted and raced out the front door toward the main house.

Who was he going to speak with? I couldn't follow him since Emma was outside with Baxter and too young to be on her own. My discussion with Gabriel only confused the matter further. I called my mother and verified we were still on for lunch at Nana D's the following day once church finished. My father would try to avoid the conversation, but I intended to drag out of him whatever secret he and Gabriel had been keeping.

* * *

After Tiffany agreed to meet me for a drink at Kirklands, the rest of the early afternoon revolved around Emma. We straightened up her room, packed her overnight bag, and drove to the gymnastics facility near the Betscha mines. I watched her twist her body on the parallel bars and hang upside down on the rings. At one point, I had been fairly adept at it myself, but the thought of hanging upside down only made me nauseous these days. Emma hugged me goodbye and went back to her friends, worrying me that I only had a few more years left with her as my baby girl.

Tiffany was sitting, and slightly swaying, at the bar when I arrived. Considered a dive by most, the usual patrons at Kirklands were more than satisfied with two-dollar beers and five-dollar cocktails during happy hour. Its most appealing feature, besides the dark and gloomy corners where drinkers could easily hide, was a flair for playing eclectic music and showcasing local talent on weekends.

"Mom reveled over the chat you two had last night. I kind of expected you'd call soon." Tiffany partially hugged me and slid over a pint of beer. The light hit her in just the right way to highlight her mousy-brown hair, freckles, and petite waist. Her hands were not at all petite, which meant she might be the person who'd killed Quint. When she spoke, a trail of Cosmo breath fluttered by.

"First, let me say how sorry I am about Quint. I understand you two were very close." I offered to pay for the beer, but she waved my arm away and sprayed a flowery perfume on her wrists.

"What a pretty scent," I said, lifting her hand to my nose. "I've been smelling sandalwood cologne lately but can't figure out the name."

"You should ask Nicky Endicott. He's a cologne fanatic. I'm quite sure the woodsy ones are his latest obsession too. Everything is woodsy right down to his boxers, and don't ask me how I know that! That lumberjack of a hottie even prefers to jog through the wood-chipped trails at Braxton all the time." After sipping a mouthful from the mug and turning a little green, she seemed disinterested in her beer. "What can I do for you? It sounded urgent on the phone. I only showed up because I happened to be in need of an excuse to escape a brunch that wasn't going well."

That was a tip I hadn't expected to get today. Could Nicky have been the person I'd seen at the cable car the morning I'd found Quint's body? I'd have to track him down soon to find out as well as relay the news that Tiffany had a secret crush on him. "I've learned something I'd rather not share straightaway, but it's connected to the jewelry thefts that started up again. Can you share anything you know about them?" Was she drunk enough to tell me the truth, or would she be evasive on the topic?

"What do they have to do with me?" She pulled her bottom lip into her mouth and gently bit it.

"I'm hoping you'll reveal everything you know, starting with the sorority prank eight years ago and ending with what you and Gabriel talked about the day you returned the earrings to your mother at Whispering Pines." I picked up my pint, clinked hers, and said, "Drink up. We've got a lot to cover."

Tiffany was not thrilled to learn I knew about the sorority's hazing practices. "It was supposed to be confidential. I don't know who told you, but she's definitely going to be in big trouble for it."

"Forget how I know. Just help me connect the dots. Do you know who stole the jewelry?"

"It was just a harmless prank we played on Gwendolyn Paddington, but then the brooch really disappeared. When a second item was stolen, this time from my family, I wondered if it was a coincidence or connected in a warped way."

"Why didn't anyone say something to the cops? Or you could've told your parents. It might've stopped the thief from stealing more jewelry and cash from the Roarkes, Greys, and Stantons."

"We were scared. I couldn't tell my parents we'd stolen the original brooch. No one wanted to be accused of all the other burglaries or go to prison." Tiffany began slurring more frequently.

"Okay, I can buy that. Did you suspect one another of being the real thief?"

"Not really. I mean, I thought only the four of us girls in the pledge class knew about the prank. One of them must have told someone else," she snarled.

"Don't get snippy with me. I'm just asking questions." I wasn't the enemy, but it wouldn't help to push back. "Did you leave a calla lily at the Paddington estate after you stole the brooch?"

"No, are you kidding me? We took the brooch from the Play House, locked it in the safe at the sorority house, and moved on. Someone must have decided to keep stealing items and tried to make it look like it was connected to Alpha Iota Omega, but the culprit was never caught."

"How do Quint, Paul, Nicholas, and Gabriel fit in? Did they know about the sorority prank?

"I already answered that. No one was supposed to know what we did, but I can't tell you what anyone else was privy to." She slapped a ten-dollar bill on the bar and waved to the bartender.

"We're not done. Is there anything else you can tell me? I'm worried Quint confronted someone about the jewelry thefts in the cable car." I paused to let the news sink in. "If you know something, you might be able to determine what really happened to the poor guy the day he died."

"I'm devastated my friend passed away, but it wasn't anything more than an accident. I don't see how his death has anything to do with the jewelry robberies." Frustrated, Tiffany exhaled loudly.

"Where were you the night Quint died? I'm just curious how and when you found out," I said nonchalantly.

"Um, I don't remember. Didn't he electrocute himself in the middle of the night? I guess I was sleeping probably. My mother told me the next morning. Ugh, I need to get out of here." Tiffany jumped up from the barstool and faltered more than expected. She was partially drunk and couldn't look me in the face, yet she'd been reading something on her phone. It seemed like an act. Why?

"You're hiding something from me. If you're worried about Gabriel, you're in good company."

Tiffany closed her eyes and breathed deeply. "Gabriel is the one who disappeared after all that cash was stolen from the Stantons during the first round of robberies. I also saw him shove something shiny in a duffel bag when I stopped by his dorm room to surprise him the night he left town."

"Are you certain it was Gabriel?" I asked, wondering if it had been a case of mistaken identity.

"Unless I was confused about whom I saw through the crack in the door, your brother is involved. I guess I didn't see the guy's face, but it was your brother's room. I assumed based on a few coincidences and the timing that Gabriel might've been the thief, but I couldn't turn in a friend, so I kept quiet. Then, he mentioned leaving my concert early the night my mother's house had been robbed to—"

"Wait! Your mother said you didn't remember anyone disappearing that night. Which is the truth?" I wasn't thrilled to hear that change of news, as it made my brother look guiltier.

"I'd been too excited by the concert back then. When Gabriel told me recently that he'd left the concert to meet his secret boyfriend, it triggered my memory that he'd been missing."

"Do you believe he's guilty, or do you think he really met his boyfriend that night?"

"I'm not sure. No one else had enough knowledge and access to details about everyone's comings and goings both in the past and now. If Gabriel isn't the thief, then I don't understand who's robbing people again." Tiffany settled the bill with the bartender and stepped away from the bar.

"What about when you dropped off the earrings with your mother at the funeral home a few weeks ago? Did anyone else know you were doing that?"

"Gabriel and I had lunch with Quint, Krissy, and Nicky that day. I might've mentioned returning the earrings, I can't be sure." She dropped a few singles on the bar and hastily rushed out of Kirklands toward a taxi. Thankfully, she wasn't planning to drive.

I felt like my wheels were spinning—even my brother's friends thought he was guilty. I'd have to follow up on Krissy and Nicky's alibis at the time Lydia's earrings had been stolen. At this point, I could only hint about Quint's death being unusual, which meant asking people for alibis wouldn't be easy. Could I prove my brother's innocence that way? If not, perhaps when Fern and I had dinner, she'd have insight about the girls in the Alpha Iota Omega sorority. It was also time to check in with Connor to find out what he'd learned from the coroner about the exact circumstances surrounding Quint's death.

CHAPTER 10

"Connor is at an offsite meeting presently. Anything I may assist with?" April asked as I bumped into her in the lobby of the Wharton County Sheriff's Office. Her stereotypical tweed blazer and bootcut jeans were nowhere in sight this afternoon. In their place, she wore a pair of high-waisted gray dress pants, a canary-yellow blouse with a brown silk scarf draped across her left shoulder, and a pair of shiny pumps. She looked positively radiant and ready for an evening out on the town.

"It can wait. I don't want to interrupt anything," I said, watching her look past me as if she was waiting for someone to walk down the hall. "I had peculiar conversations with Gabriel and a few folks in the Nutberry family. Just wanted to compare notes."

"It's almost like you think you've got a sleuthing partner now that one of my detectives is your former best friend, huh?" She smirked and punched me lightly in the shoulder. "I'm only teasing, don't get too testy on me now. Did you need to talk about it?"

I did, but the timing didn't seem ideal upon running into her. "You're about to head out. I'll wait for Connor. Do you think he'll be back soon?" I checked my watch to confirm I had a couple of hours before meeting Fern for dinner.

"Doubtful. He's with the coroner reviewing the final report on Quint Crawford's death." April nodded at someone behind me, then waved at the person to join us. "I'm attending a sort of cocktail party this evening, but I can spare a few minutes for you."

Those were words I didn't expect to hear together—April and a cocktail party. Based on everything she'd ever shared with me in the past, she loathed that type of gathering. I turned my head to discover who approached us and instantly recalled having seen the guy in her car the other day. Was I about to meet the potential boyfriend she'd kept ensconced from everyone?

"I hope you two have a wonderful evening." I extended my hand toward the guy once he reached us, attempting to contain my shock at his babyface and wide-eyed, innocent expression. If her date were a day over eighteen, I'd cash in my 401K retirement plan and donate it to the least worthy cause I could find. "You will certainly get some looks wherever you're going tonight." Was April a secret cougar? Who could have guessed that she liked younger guys!

"August, this is Kellan Ayrwick, a..." April said while pointing at me and pausing momentarily, "friend of mine whom I'm working with on a case."

"Good to meet you, Mr. Ayrwick," he replied and stretched a confident hand toward me. His platinum blond hair was buzzed short on the sides but had several inches of length slicked straight back with gel on the top of his head. "Call me Augie. She refuses to listen to someone else's preferences, yet I'm in trouble when I don't do whatever she asks of me at home. Such a drag sometimes."

I liked him already. Anyone who gave April a tough time was golden in my book. "Have you two known each other long? You've got witty banter going on here." Wait! Did he say they lived together?

"You could say that," April replied, checking her watch.

Augie glanced at her, rolling his green eyes in grand fashion. "Way longer than I like to think about."

The guy jumped up another notch for performing my signature move. "You must know a few secrets about her." I slanted my eyes in April's direction. "In my experience, she can be a real handful."

"Dude, she's off the charts sometimes. It's like she was born to be a mother hen, ya know?" Augie wrapped a thin, long arm around April and kissed her cheek. "You ready to roll, Momma Dukes?"

That last comment felt like a sucker-punch. Was Augie her son? Who knew she had a kid? She'd never said anything before. Doing the math—we were roughly the same age—April must have been fourteen or fifteen when she'd given birth. I found it amusing they both had first names that matched months of the year beginning with the letter 'A.'

"Is that how you're gonna talk when you meet everyone on campus tonight?" April grabbed Augie by the back of his neck and squeezed hard. "How did I get stuck dealing with the likes of you?"

I feverishly needed to know what was going on more than I could stand. "For the clueless and those ready to vomit, is he your son or your date?"

Augie dropped to his knees and tugged on April's blouse. "Please, Mom, I mean, wifey, don't make me go tonight," he whined, then cackled so loudly, the police officer manning the front desk shushed him. "Can't you try to be a better sugar momma, love? I'll be a good boy at the party."

"Kellan... August is... not... my son." April turned and handed him her keys. "Get the car started, you tool. I'll be out in a few minutes."

"Thanks for the laughs, man. You made my night." Augie slapped my back, tossed two buds in his ears, and kicked off some music on his mobile phone before strolling out the front door. They shared identical high, prominent cheekbones that framed their well-structured faces, but he exited with a bit of awkwardness while April had a more confident and determined walk.

"He's my brother. August has been living with me the last five years since everything happened back in Buffalo." April sat on a nearby wooden bench and waited for me to join her. "My parents were older when August was born. It'd been a surprise, as my mother was in her late forties, and I had just started high school. She had a tough pregnancy but managed to live for another ten years. Unfortunately, when she passed away, my father wasn't capable of taking care of August by himself."

April shared that her father was an alcoholic who'd started abusing her brother that first year after his wife had lost her battle with a painful illness. He'd blamed August for his wife's death and taken it out on the poor kid who'd been too young to defend himself. April fought their father for two years before the courts finally awarded her custody on her twenty-seventh birthday.

"I'm so sorry. You never said anything," I replied. April had always been silent regarding her background until I'd learned about her fiancé's death in a drive-by shooting several years ago. "He seems like a strong kid. I like that he pushes back on you."

"He is a strong kid, but it took time to get him there. He'll be a senior this fall, and we're going to check out local colleges this summer." April sighed and showed me a picture of him and her from when she'd been granted guardianship. "Tonight is Braxton's meet and greet for prospective students. We're on our way there in a few minutes."

"You've got this entire life that I know nothing about, April. I feel like I've confessed everything about myself, yet I'm in the dark when it comes to you." I admired April's ability to protect her privacy. Learning about her relationship with Augie clarified a tremendous amount for me regarding who she was as a human being. "What you've done for him speaks volumes to me."

"Sometimes I forget I need to be a parent. He's always been smart for his age, especially having to grow up so quickly when our mother died. Our father took advantage of the situation." April put the picture away and grabbed one of my hands. "We're not all that different, you and me. It's hard to accept that as a fact, but when I saw you with Emma for the first time, I knew I'd been too rigid those early months."

The surrounding air seemed to contain a magic that desperately pined to pull us closer together. Part of me suppressed a desire to gently caress April's cheek and experience a physical connection like we had when our fingers brushed against one another last month. Could something be developing between us? April smiled when I cupped her slender fingers inside mine and looked directly at her. I was considering whether to lean in to kiss her, but a phone rang somewhere nearby.

"I think that's you." She separated from me and pointed to my leather satchel.

I jerked out of my temporary trance and reached for the device. It was the phone Cristiano had bestowed upon me earlier that week. "It's Las Vargas."

"Answer it. Hurry up, maybe we're closer to solving one of our dilemmas," April encouraged.

I clicked accept. "This is Kellan."

"It's Francesca. I'm glad to hear your voice."

My eyes opened wide and filled with excitement and fear. I was happy to know she was alive, but the reality of the situation had become fully apparent at that moment. "Are you okay?" I asked Francesca, before turning to April to whisper the name of who was on the phone.

"Yes, Cristiano has only permitted me a minute to talk to you. He's standing here too and wants you to know he's aware of your current location." Francesca's voice was calm and collected, as though she weren't afraid of what was happening to her. "Don't do anything foolish."

"Is he going to let you come home soon? What can you tell me?" I asked, looking from April to the floor when I couldn't settle on the most comfortable place to stare.

There was a moment of silence followed by a muted conversation before Cristiano hopped on the line. "I've fulfilled my promise to let you speak with Francesca. Now that you know she's alive, I must ask... have you fulfilled your promise to notify the Castiglianos with my instructions?"

"I told them, Cristiano. I can't force them to respond, but they understood your message." I switched seats so April could listen to the conversation with me. Our ears were pressed together in another unexpected intimate moment as we waited for his response.

"Excellent. Francesca convinced me that I could count on you. You shouldn't need to wait much longer. I'm arranging for a discussion early next week. The Castiglianos have something I want, and if they deliver it to you, we can put an end to this inconvenient situation."

April pulled out her phone and typed the word *where* on the screen.

"Will you be coming back to Braxton for this discussion? Do I need to meet you somewhere?" I asked, trying to ignore the pleasing tickle of April's fragrant hair against my cheek.

"For such a clever man, you certainly miss the obvious, Kellan. I never left Braxton after our last conversation in your office." He then whispered something I couldn't hear. "Francesca asked me to tell you that Emma looks happy at Chuck E. Cheese and that she misses seeing her daughter every day."

I closed my eyes and dropped my head to my lap. I knew Cristiano was spying on my every move, but did he bring Francesca with him to monitor me too? "Where are you? Why can't we just meet immediately and solve this?" A fire crept inside my body, threatening to incinerate everything around us. Why couldn't they just leave Emma alone? While April sent a text message on her phone to someone on her team to get to Chuck E. Cheese immediately, I felt her rubbing my upper back to calm me down. I turned my head and mumbled a thank you.

"A few more days, and this should all be over, Kellan. I'm sorry that kidnapping Francesca had to be my insurance policy, but if her parents do the right

thing, we will all get what we want. I'll be in touch." Cristiano abruptly disconnected the phone call.

"Wait!" I shouted, despite knowing he'd already hung up. "This is a nightmare. Every time I think we can get back to normal, that guy scares the crap out
of me by following Emma around."

"I've got an unmarked vehicle pulling into the restaurant parking lot. Have
faith, Kellan. Your daughter will be fine, and we'll catch the people responsible
for causing the war." April grabbed my shoulders and forced me to face her
directly. "Trust me. I've got your back."

We waited in silence for five minutes before one of her officers confirmed
he'd just missed two people walking out the side door of the restaurant. They'd
gotten into a limousine and pulled away in a hurry, but Emma had been
unharmed and completely unaware of their presence. April said, "Emma's
happily playing with her friends as if she had no cares in the world. Do you
want to visit her? I can drop you off on my way to Braxton."

I shook my head. Francesca would never let Cristiano harm Emma. "It's
okay. I'm just frustrated. I might swing by before dinner with a friend of mine.
You should go to Braxton and help Augie decide if it's where he wants to attend
college in another year."

April nodded. "I'll have my cell phone in case you need anything. Are you
sure you don't want to talk about your brother or what happened with the
Nutberry family?"

I briefly filled in April on my conversations with Lydia, Tiffany, and
Gabriel, excluding the part about my father knowing something important. I
needed to speak with him before revealing that piece of news. "Is Connor going
to arrest Gabriel for the jewelry thefts or Quint's murder?"

"Not yet. We don't have sufficient evidence, and I probably shouldn't be
telling you what I'm about to tell you, but you could use a bit of good news,"
April replied as she stood to leave. "We lifted a set of prints from the main
power source to the cable car. We don't know to whom they belong, but they
weren't a match to your brother's. We had his on file from the George Braun
case last month."

I breathed a small sigh of relief. "That's helpful. I'm sure the prints could
belong to any number of electricians, right?"

"Actually, there were only two sets—Quint's and the unknown person's.
We're strategizing how to check everyone involved. I can't tell you everything,
but a few of the folks in this group of friends aren't being totally honest." April
indicated she would check on me later that evening.

As she left the building, I reflected on the changes beginning to develop in
our relationship. When we'd first met, we were like two barnyard cats vying for
territory. During the last three months, I'd helped her solve several cases and
gotten on her bad side more times than I cared to remember. In the last few
weeks, ever since she'd begun assisting with Francesca's kidnapping, things had
been pleasant. I considered her a friend; someone I could trust to look out for
my welfare. After the moment we shared today, I knew something stronger was

percolating between us. I couldn't let myself process it until things calmed down. Wild gale-force storms tossed us about, and until this tornado dropped us on safe ground, it would be best to keep anything more serious from blossoming.

* * *

An hour later, after verifying for myself that Emma was okay, I drove back downtown to meet Fern at Simply Stoddard for dinner. The new eatery had a prime central location on *Restaurant Row* overlooking the Finnulia River, where a gorgeous octagonal cedar-shake windmill and cleverly arranged outdoor teak furniture welcomed guests in the summer and early fall.

I arrived before Fern and informed the hostess of the reservation. After learning our table wasn't ready, I sat at the cherrywood bar and ordered a Jack Daniels and ginger ale, minus the ice. It only diluted the drink, and I always quivered when ice banged my teeth. As the bartender handed me the cocktail, one of the owners, Karen Stoddard, approached from the opposite side of the room where a newly renovated, top-of-the-line kitchen with a traditional brick oven and delectable pastry counter teased customers. Karen's bright neon blouse and pencil skirt glimmered as she shimmied through the narrow spaces between two tables.

"It's nice to see you again, Kellan. I'm glad to see we can put our past differences aside and coexist in the same town," she quipped. Newly frosted tips accentuated her stylish shag hairstyle, an odd yet bold statement on a woman whose snub nose was all too prominent of a feature.

"I couldn't agree more. Your husband is a talented chef, and I always prefer to find common ground with someone rather than bicker over the petty things. How're Cheney and Sierra doing?"

"My kids are well. Sierra's back in London, and Cheney is happy to be finishing the cable car project. I'm hopeful he's capitulated on wooing Helena. She's a fine girl, but Cheney needs to focus on getting his life in order," Karen cautioned me, then told the bartender my drink was on the house.

"I appreciate it. I happen to agree. Helena should focus on herself. She's got a rambunctious side that needs to simmer down before she gets involved in a committed relationship," I consented.

"Exactly. She was in here earlier today with a few women. There was a shouting match and drinks being thrown across the table. I had to kick them all out," Karen explained, shaking her head and groaning. "For four women quickly approaching thirty, it was very immature."

"Really? Do you happen to know whom she was with?" I assumed it was her sorority class who'd been discussing the jewelry thefts and Quint's death. Tiffany had mentioned needing to escape a brunch that wasn't going too well.

"I knew two of the girls, Imogene Grey and Krissy Stanton. I overheard them arguing about calla lilies and who stole whose boyfriend over the years. Trivial stuff," Karen said, as if she couldn't understand what it was like to get catty with a girlfriend.

I described Tiffany Nutberry, and Karen confirmed she was the fourth girl. "I appreciate the update. It explains a lot." The girls had undoubtedly gotten together to compare information and agree on a story in case anyone else asked more questions. Tiffany had been extremely angry that one of them had fessed up about the sorority ritual.

As Karen left, Fern waved to me from the hostess desk. I dropped a few singles on the bar, met her at our table, and ordered another drink. We chatted about her day and the upcoming wedding. Her son Arthur was marrying my Aunt Deirdre's fiancé's sister, Jennifer Paddington. They'd begun dating earlier that year and when Jennifer had learned she was pregnant, Arthur proposed to her. It was an unusual match for their clan. Arthur was my age and a tad on the nerdy side while Jennifer was in her mid-forties and from a wealthy family. I needed to speak with Jennifer to find out the circumstances of the jewelry theft at the estate. She'd lost an expensive family watch in the current round of burglaries.

Once we covered all the major topics and finished our meal, I asked Fern about the Alpha Iota Omega sorority. Fern had worked at Braxton for over twenty years and advised all the Greek societies on campus. If there were any secrets to discover about the sorority's connection to the jewelry thefts, she'd know them. "What can you tell me about the current state of the Alpha Iota Omegas?"

Fern laughed. "Oh, that's easy. I shut down that sorority years ago. They were one of the infamous ones who liked to push my boundaries way too many times. I used to challenge you about some of your fraternity's initiation practices, but these girls were monsters."

"What do you mean? Did they do something illegal?"

"Hazing itself wasn't illegal then, but I've always believed it was highly unethical and hazardous. I was at the forefront of Pennsylvania's commitment to institute anti-bullying and hazing laws. Although I couldn't prove it all, there were rumors about excessive drinking, violence, and dangerous pranks with those girls." Fern asked the server for a cup of coffee when he passed by.

"How about jewelry theft? Did that ever come up?" I shared a little with Fern about what Helena had told me, knowing it wouldn't go any further, especially with the dismantling of the sorority.

Fern shook her head. "Not that I'm aware of. Most of my information came from witnesses who saw things happening on campus or girls who complained when they were treated unfairly. If you're referring to all those burglaries from years ago, no, I don't know anything."

"That's disappointing," I said, feeling disheartened that I hadn't learned anything new from my discussion with Fern. "I hoped you might offer some missing clue. Between those calla lilies showing up and the repetition of the original crimes happening this year, I'm baffled."

"Calla lilies? You know that's the official flower of the Alpha Iota Omega sorority, right? It's tradition for the house mother and big sister to present a white calla lily to each new inductee when she becomes a full member." Fern leaned in closer to me and whispered, "It was designed to mimic something special that the original founding families used to do when a daughter revealed which boy she was sweet on. A mother would send a white calla lily from her daughter to the boy for nine days in a row. It was a sign that he was welcome to ask her daughter on a date. If he was interested, he'd show up with a bouquet of white calla lilies on the tenth evening. If he was not, he'd send back a single black calla lily to the mother as his notice of rejection." Fern explained that in the *Book of Revelations*, Alpha and Omega meant the beginning and the end of life. Iota was also the ninth letter in the Greek alphabet, and it had a special meaning to the sisterhood in terms of the calla lily presentation.

"You've got to be joking me!" Fern had just filled in an important piece of the riddle. If the thief was leaving a black calla lily every nine days, was he or she trying to show his rejection for something? The puzzle was starting to fit together, but I needed more information. Unfortunately, Fern couldn't share anything else of value. Somebody in that sorority knew what was going on, or at the very least had shared the history of the calla lily being used to tell someone that you were or weren't interested in dating them. Now, I just needed to figure out exactly what the thief's symbols meant and whether we could prevent the next robbery from happening in a few days. It might also reveal Quint's probable killer.

CHAPTER 11

"Gabriel won't be here for lunch today. He took off late last night to do some soul-searching. He left a note indicating he'd gone camping with Sam up in the mountains," Nana D said as we fed the horses on Sunday morning while waiting for my parents to arrive from church. Although she was prepared to turn over the entire farm to her right-hand man, my nana wanted to cherish the last few days before getting bogged down with all the mayoral responsibilities she was about to absorb.

"He left because I confronted him yesterday. I didn't get a clear answer either." I never expected him to confess everything he'd done while he was away from Braxton, but his explanations left more open holes than Nana D's favorite pair of worn overalls—and that was saying a lot, not to mention scarier than all get-out! "Did he tell you anything else?"

Emma held the bucket while her favorite horse gobbled his morning oats. One of her friends' mothers had picked them up this morning from the sleep-over and dropped Emma off at Danby Landing for me. "Uncle Gabriel isn't gone for good, is he?"

"No, honey. He just needed to cool his jets," Nana D said, comforting my daughter and looking at me. "He's clearing his head before talking to some important people." Nana D grabbed Emma's hand and began walking back to the farmhouse.

By important people, Nana D had meant the sheriff's office. Although the police did not officially want Gabriel, he would need to discuss everything he'd known about the jewelry thefts now that Connor had found his name on the San Francisco pawn shop's reports. "Has Marcus finally conceded to you? Or is he just ignoring your inauguration?"

"He called yesterday to acknowledge I beat him. I also forced Marcus to explain why he'd been meeting with Imogene at the diner last week. Apparently, she requested the discussion to warn him that if his daughter continued to cause trouble for her fiancé as he was beginning his new role in Braxton, she'd sue Krissy for slander. Paul must've told her what Krissy had said in the park the night of my birthday party about Imogene cheating on him with Quint."

Nana D tickled Emma as we crossed through a flower garden, then chased her for several feet before finally throwing her arms in the air announcing defeat. The flowers reminded me of the news Fern had shared the previous night about the calla lily's role in the historical courting processes of the Alpha Iota Omega sorority. I still couldn't figure out the connection between the flowers and the jewelry thefts or with Quint's death. If Imogene had cheated on Paul with Quint, maybe Paul was angry about being cuckolded and killed Quint in retaliation. Had Paul left behind a bouquet of calla lilies to get even with his friend for backstabbing him? Nonetheless, I still wasn't certain Imogene had cheated on Paul.

Nana D explained that Marcus had only told her because he'd gotten drunk in order to find the wherewithal to admit defeat. "Marcus did blame the election loss on someone else, of course."

On the return path, Eleanor joined us. She was only able to visit for an hour before needing to attend to the lunch crowd at the Pick-Me-Up Diner, but she wanted to spend some time with the rest of the family. "Let me guess, he blamed Kellan?"

Go Eleanor! I assumed that man was going to cause trouble at some point. "Probably."

"Nope, Quint Crawford. Apparently, Quint had done some work on Marcus's house next door, and Marcus never paid him. I heard from a couple of folks that Quint was starting to tell people about it," Nana D indicated, then suggested I should find out if there was any truth to the rumor. As we meandered up the path by the orchard, Aunt Deirdre and Timothy Paddington pulled into the driveway.

A few minutes later, we sat in the living room and caught up on everything going on between them. Once Timothy had finished his three-month program at Second Chance Reflections, he'd moved back into the Paddington family estate. Aunt Deirdre had been staying with Nana D at Danby Landing, but she'd relocated to Timothy's after a separate room was prepared for her. An old-fashioned gal, she didn't want to share his bedroom until their wedding night, but she also acknowledged that it would be beneficial for them to spend as much time together as possible. Most of their relationship had developed via electronic communications while she'd lived in England and he'd been in recovery.

"*Facebook* brought us back together. We dated years ago, but a lot happened in the eighties that we both care to forget," Aunt Deirdre explained with a narrowed gaze at Timothy. My lovely aunt's shoulder-length, dark-blonde hair was tied back with a pink ribbon, highlighting the sleek curve of her neckline. It'd also been adorned with a silver and diamond necklace, courtesy of her wealthy fiancé.

"Exactly, pumpkin. Second Chance Reflections offered me a new lease on life, and now we need to take advantage of it." Timothy squeezed her hand and kissed her nose. His time in recovery had reversed many of the physical impacts of his addiction to alcohol, drugs, and gambling, but his hair continued to gray further at his temples and above his ears. He was a prime example of why people said men were *distinguished* as they aged. "I just adore this magnificent peach of a woman."

Nana D walked behind the couch, where only Emma and I could see her. She pretended to stick two fingers down her throat and expel whatever thoughts had gotten trapped inside her body. By the time she came into everyone else's view, she said, "Oh, aren't you two precious! Tell us about your *simply divine* post-wedding plans." It was such a blessing not to be on the receiving end of her sarcasm, yet I knew my time would come soon enough.

"Thank you, Mother," Aunt Deirdre said with a slight but noticeable twitch in a vein at the side of her neck. Evidence of her British accent slipping away as she drank, or grew frustrated and angry, was becoming clearer as she spoke. "Timothy is taking me to the Maldives for nine days, and then we're going to stop in England for a celebration with all my friends back home."

"Where are you planning to live after the wedding? Are you leaving Braxton that quickly?"

Timothy wrapped his arm around my aunt's shoulder. "We'll only be gone for a few weeks while I get up to speed on what's been happening at Paddington Enterprises. We'll return at the end of July when I can assume control and let Uncle Millard go back into retirement."

"Timothy and I plan to split where we reside. My London flat is large enough to accommodate a remote office for him as well as an extra bedroom or two for when we have little ones," Aunt Deirdre explained, resulting in an uncontrollable gasp from my grandmother. Seconds later, Nana D kicked the coffee table leg and casually blamed her outburst on an unexpected, painful leg cramp.

Out of the corner of my eye, I saw the strangest glare form when Eleanor realized Aunt Deirdre was hoping to get pregnant with Timothy's baby. My sister had been considering artificial insemination the last few months because she hadn't found her own husband. Aunt Deirdre was every bit of fifty, and while modern science had made gigantic advances, this was quite a leap for the family to accept.

"While we're here in Braxton, we'll run the Paddington estate. Aunt Eustacia is moving back to Willow Trees to resume her own life, but my sisters will remain in the mansion with us. There are plenty of wings to give us all the privacy we need," Timothy added.

"Do you really think you two need to have a child at your ages when—"

Nana D was interrupted when the front door opened, and my parents walked in carrying a box from a local bakery and a small gift for Emma. My mother spoiled my daughter, and there was little I could do to stop it.

As Aunt Deirdre sneered and whispered something to Timothy, Emma jumped up from her seat and ran toward my father. After we all exchanged greetings, I grabbed the box from my mother and walked with her into the kitchen. My father chatted with Emma about Baxter's latest trick. I'd find time to corner him later about his and Gabriel's dirty little secret.

"You look wonderful today, Mom. I miss seeing you all the time. We should arrange a weekly lunch. We both work on the same campus, right?" She'd been the director of admissions as long as I could remember, yet we rarely made the effort to meet around my teaching schedule.

"I'd love that, Kellan. At church this morning, Father O'Malley talked about the importance of family. I'm so grateful you and Gabriel are back in Braxton, and Hampton will be here at the end of the summer. Even my sister's come home again." She hugged me like I was a small child and gleefully flitted around the kitchen. "I convinced Nana D not to make dessert today. I wanted to bring those éclairs you love from that cute little bakery on Main Street. They are *simply divine!*"

"Thanks, Mom. I'll check my schedule and suggest a few days for lunch. Is Siobhan managing your calendar now that she's working in the admissions office?" I asked as she plated the éclairs.

"Your department's loss is my gain. Siobhan's very efficient, even when she's stuck at home with a sick baby. I adore my grandchildren, but I'm relieved those days are behind me." My mother might kvetch—a Jewish word April had taught me—about once being thirtyish and raising children, but her exceptionally youthful beauty and unparalleled attention to new products revealed her fear of aging.

"Are you two close? I know Siobhan had been relying on Bertha Crawford's help with babysitting, but after Bertha got sick and her son died last week, it hasn't been easy." I was curious whether my mother knew of any ill feelings between Quint and Siobhan, based on what Bertha had mentioned at the funeral parlor.

"That poor boy! I must admit, I never much cared for your brother's friend. Quint always seemed to find trouble, and I've seen him get too forward with women. He and Siobhan had a quarrel recently, and I didn't like the way he was behaving. Not very gentlemanly." My mother tut-tutted as we walked into the dining room and placed the tray on the table.

I asked my mother to give me an example, and she revealed what'd happened between Siobhan and Quint the previous month. When Siobhan had dropped the twins off at the Crawford house, Bertha asked her for a favor—to deliver Quint's lunch on the way back to campus. After Siobhan met Quint, chemistry sparked between the two of them. Quint must've convinced Siobhan to spend the night with him one evening while his mother watched the babies. "Siobhan thought he was genuinely interested in her. When she tried to get more serious with him, he backed away, claiming his heart belonged to another woman. She was terribly angry, and I don't blame her. I don't think Quint meant any harm, but it truly upset Siobhan. She wanted to teach him a lesson, but I kept telling her to let it go, that American boys can be foolish. That poor girl still gets bothered whenever I mention his name. Quint always thought he was God's gift to women, but unfortunately, he won't be able to redeem himself now that he's gone. It's positively disheartening when someone young dies from an accident like that." She fussed with a strand of auburn hair that wouldn't properly tuck behind her ear.

"Has he done things like that before? Or was it a one-time occurrence?" I asked, surprised at learning about this side of him. He could be persistent, but I thought he was a decent guy who knew how to treat a woman. Helena and Tiffany never mentioned anything negative that would lead me to believe otherwise. Imogene wouldn't have dated him if he'd been that callous. Could he have changed?

"I'm really not sure, but it'd gotten bad enough that Siobhan considered telling Bertha what her son had done. She didn't have the courage to break the woman's heart, especially during chemotherapy, with tales of her son's ill-mannered behavior. Instead, she searched for a new nanny."

"Do you think Siobhan tried to get revenge against Quint?" She was a strong woman and could strangle someone, especially if he'd been inebriated and unable to fight back. I needed Connor to confirm whether Quint had been drunk the day he died. I didn't recall smelling any alcohol in the cable car, yet Siobhan definitely had the right-sized hands based on the coroner's description.

"Siobhan has a temper, but she's a smart girl and wouldn't get into that kind of trouble." My mother shook her head and waggled her nose for emphasis on her point.

"Was she in the office the day Quint died?" I thought back to how Siobhan had acted in class the day before and the day after Quint's murder, but no alarms stood out.

"I'll have to check. I don't remember and will look at my calendar when I get to work tomorrow," my mother replied as Nana D entered the dining room.

"Let's get our meal out of the oven. Your dullard husband's getting crabby in the other room, Violet. I can't stand that man's voice sometimes," Nana D groused as she walked by us and then yelled back to the living room. "Get your butts in here, everyone. We've gotta eat before King Wesley bores us all to death with his oh-so-wonderful stories about himself."

"No need to shout, Your Honor, we all followed you into the dining room in case you accidentally tripped and fell over your ego. We wouldn't want you to break a hip, now would we?" my father announced while taking his seat at the head of the table. Even in Nana D's house, he assumed what he felt was his rightful place once Grandpop had passed away. Their battles for control had been epic over the years, and often I'd just sit back and listen to the wild accusations and hidden undertones flying by me.

Once the meal finished, Eleanor left for work. Timothy offered to wash dishes with Aunt Deirdre as part of their continued relationship growth exercises. "Those who clean together always shine together, right, Mom?" he said upon turning to Nana D. Calling her *that* wasn't going over well!

Nana D and I both turned away to make fake gagging sounds this round. Timothy's time in the recovery program had converted him into an overly sappy human being. I couldn't wait to see how things transpired once he returned to Paddington Enterprises, a corporation known for being as cutthroat as any of the major international companies it did business with. I grabbed two tumblers and the bottle of whiskey from Nana D's cupboard and nodded at my father to join me on the porch. Emma was playing fetch with Baxter while my mother discussed her sister's wedding plans with Nana D.

"Excellent idea, son. You know exactly how to turn the afternoon around," my father cheered while patting me on the back as we stepped outside. A gentle breeze carried the scent of fresh fruit from the orchard. I was tempted to take a walk but had urgent business with my father.

"Don't get too excited yet, Dad. I have an ulterior motive." I waited for him to sit on a wicker chair before pouring and handing him the whiskey. "We need to have a discussion about Gabriel."

"I see. Would you be buttering me up prior to dropping a bombshell on me? You definitely take after your mother more than me, son." He chugged half the tumbler and cleared his throat with a loud, raspy groan. "I'm ready. What are you two boys up to, and what do you need from me to get started?"

My father had once envisioned his three sons all going into business together to build a family empire. My oldest brother, Hampton, had joined a prestigious law firm years ago and would be relocating to Pennsylvania in the fall. When I'd left town to focus on the film and television industry, Dad's dream was crushed, but he often tried to redirect my interests. It hadn't worked until he'd convinced me earlier this year to help him build an advanced communications program at Braxton. We'd been playing well together in the sandbox, but that was mostly because there were multiple people involved in the project.

"Gabriel might be in trouble, and I think you know a lot about it. He mentioned that you took care of something when he left town eight years ago." I paused to let the silence linger, hoping it made my father uncomfortable enough to be honest with me.

"That business is all in the past. There's no reason to dig it up again. Besides, I don't know for sure what happened, and sometimes things are better left unsaid. Why don't we talk about something else?" My father stood and looked out on the horizon, jangling coins in his pocket.

I listened to him breathing until I found the right words. "Whatever you did years ago didn't work. Gabriel might be arrested for his role in the jewelry thefts, and honestly, Dad, he looks guilty to me. I want to protect him, but I don't have the information to do so." I stood next to my father and stared across the farm, trying to understand what he focused on. "I suspect you do. We could work together to solicit him some help, the way families do all the time when one of their own is in need."

A few birds chirped and a lawnmower idled in the distance while he considered my request. "You do your best as a parent to protect your children when they're young. And you hope they learn their lessons and don't repeat your mistakes." My father leaned against the corner post, slightly worn down and hesitant to continue. "Hampton's done well, but he almost didn't make it through his last year at law school. He quit one day because he wasn't the best student in the class, then took off for a couple of weeks. I didn't find out until the school called us to check if he'd gotten ill."

"I didn't know. He's always seemed quite levelheaded," I replied, feeling strangely saddened for my brother but glad to know he was actually human and had made mistakes.

My father told me how he tracked Hampton down and set him back on the right course to graduate on time. "Your sister, Penelope, pulled something similar, just as Eleanor and Gabriel made foolish mistakes at one point in the past. It seems to be part of this family's DNA."

I'd known about Penelope's elopement with her husband and how she'd confessed she'd done it just to spite my parents for trying to control her life. Eleanor had disappointed our parents when she didn't become a doctor and had taken a job as a waitress at the diner. Both my sisters had redeemed their actions years later, but it'd still been an awkward period for a while. "Maybe we get this rebellious strain from Nana D," I quipped, hoping to lighten the mood.

"Kellan, of all my children, you're the only one who's effectively stood up to me. You stop me from interfering in your decisions. You go out of your way to protect everyone in the family. I'm proud of you, son." My father leaned in to hug me, and for a moment, any proper response failed to rise to the surface. "I did something I shouldn't have eight years ago. Perhaps it's time you stepped in to fix it."

My father confessed a chilling secret that he and Gabriel had been hiding. After our father had accepted the offer to become Braxton's new president, Gabriel had decided not to transfer to Penn State. My brother's underground relationship had unexpectedly ended, and he knew he had to reveal the truth about his attraction to guys. Gabriel then moved to San Francisco to hide and buy himself time, but he'd stayed away longer than planned. We'd already discussed this piece the previous month when he'd returned to town; however, no one had known my father briefly decided to step down from his post as president to allow Gabriel the option of remaining at Braxton. Unfortunately, that's when Sheriff Crawford had approached our father with disturbing news that changed everything.

"The sheriff alleged that Gabriel was involved in at least one of the jewelry heists. He offered to cover it up, but he insisted both boys leave town to guarantee things would blow over for a while."

"What do you mean *both boys leave town*? Who else was involved?"

"Quint Crawford. Silas told me his nephew and Gabriel were involved together with the robberies. Didn't you just tell me you knew that already?" my father said with a cockeyed glance.

"No, I knew someone else had been involved, but I never had a name. When did Quint leave town?" No one had ever said that Quint lived outside of Braxton.

"About eight years ago around the same time as your brother. He only returned in April when he learned his mother was sick," my father replied, explaining that he'd initially refused to believe Gabriel was involved, but once he'd checked my brother's dorm room, he'd found pieces of the missing jewelry. My father then confronted Gabriel, who didn't deny the accusations nor admit to them. Instead, Gabriel focused on his struggle to accept he was gay and his frustration over our father's new job. My father made the decision to convince Gabriel to leave town not because he was ashamed of his son for being gay but because he wanted his son to have a better life and not be thrown in prison.

"I've felt awful all these years for being the reason he stayed away from everyone," my father said in a low and disheartened voice before explaining that Sheriff Crawford had later shared a copy of the pawn shop report with Gabriel's name on it. "I knew then your brother was guilty of something. Even if he didn't steal the jewelry himself, he'd stored it in his dorm room and hocked it in San Francisco. Maybe if I'd made Gabriel take responsibility for his actions, things would be different now."

I considered everything my father had just bared, including recognizing what his news confirmed: Tiffany had seen Gabriel with the jewels the day he'd skipped town. "Gabriel did this himself, Dad. Either he and Quint came back to Braxton to start stealing again, knowing that the sheriff had passed away last year, or Gabriel knows who's recreating the crimes now. Maybe there's an accomplice or a copycat."

We agreed to regroup the following day once Gabriel returned from the mountains. We assumed my brother hadn't disappeared again, but time would tell for sure. While my father went inside, I reflected on what I'd learned about his role and the story of the sorority's calla lilies. We were also missing records from eight years ago. The sheriff had been crooked. I wouldn't learn a lot from the past burglaries. I'd already spoken with Lydia and Tiffany Nutberry about the earrings that had been stolen from their place the previous month. Now, I needed to ascertain where Quint and Gabriel had been that night as well as the other three times more jewelry had been stolen.

Based on past occurrences, we had one day before the next theft would occur, if that nine-day pattern stayed consistent. If a theft happened, then Gabriel was probably responsible and needed help to turn himself in. If one didn't occur, maybe Quint had been the ringleader and Gabriel wasn't involved in the current round. I had to find out the truth to prevent my brother from making another mistake. More importantly, I had to accept that I'd failed to discover an important fact sooner—Quint had left town right after the original thefts too. While identifying the original accomplice and/or mastermind solved one problem for me, it created another more complicated one. If Quint and Gabriel had been the thieves, and they were back working together again, there was no longer a mystery accomplice to blame for Quint's death. I couldn't accept the killer was Gabriel, suggesting the only other logical solution was that Quint's death had nothing to do with the robberies. Now how would I solve his murder?

CHAPTER 12

After Aunt Deirdre told Emma about the newest flowers in the conservatory at the Paddington estate, my daughter begged to see them. Timothy offered to drive Emma back and forth, but I saw it as an opportunity to talk with Eustacia and Jennifer Paddington, his aunt and sister, to inquire what they knew about the robberies. We followed Aunt Deirdre and Timothy—I refused to call him Uncle Timothy this late in the game—to the estate. The three-story manor had been built in the early twentieth century and was approaching its one-hundredth anniversary. Timothy had mentioned throwing a soirée that summer for all their friends to celebrate his family's history and rise from the ashes of the year's tragedies. A small parking lot, a cedar-chipped path, and lush gardens with shrubbery and trees that'd been shaped into forest animals welcomed guests as they arrived at the mansion.

Bertha's replacement greeted us at the door. While Emma went with Aunt Deirdre and Timothy to check out the conservatory, I asked the new maid what she knew about the latest jewelry theft. Unfortunately, she'd started the week afterward, which meant she couldn't help me. "They didn't have anyone working the day of the burglary, sir. The Paddingtons were still interviewing for a replacement," she noted before leaving to locate Eustacia. When she did, the maid led me to a sitting room where Eustacia and Jennifer discussed wedding details.

"Kellan, what a surprise! What brings you by?" Eustacia sang from her baby-blue-tufted, chenille chaise longue. Her cane, topped with a brass lion's head, rested by the side of the long chair, enabling her feet to stretch out comfortably. I didn't want to make her get up, so I leaned in for a perfunctory greeting. I'd known my nana's frenemy for years, and I was grateful the two of them had been on good terms ever since the election had been decided. "We missed you at Kirklands the other night, sleepy."

"You're quite funny." I updated them on Emma's botanical interests, then brought up Bertha Crawford. "I saw her at the funeral on Friday evening. She didn't look well."

Eustacia shook her head and sighed. The normal blue color of her frenzied hair had been toned down, but she would never relinquish the comfort of her classic 1980's pink tracksuits. When at home, despite demanding that others dress more sophisticatedly, she chose comfort over fashion. "Life should never end so early. I can't imagine what it must've been like to be electrocuted, that unfortunate soul."

At least the sheriff had been able to keep the truth about Quint's death from reaching as few people as possible. "I imagine you knew him as a boy since Bertha worked here."

"Yes, he used to visit when he was a small child. Bertha had been with us for almost twenty-five years before she retired," Eustacia added while staring innocuously around the room.

"Was Bertha working here the day the Paddington jewelry was stolen?" I asked, introducing the topic in a hopefully inconspicuous manner.

"Which time?" Jennifer placed knitting needles on her lap. She'd been creating what looked like a blanket for her baby, due that fall. Sporting less makeup than usual and kinky chestnut hair that had been trimmed an inch, Jennifer looked pretty and relaxed. Impending motherhood and marriage had softened rough edges and tendencies to act spoiled.

"I suppose both," I said, feeling a tad guilty about leading them directly where I needed them to go. "Eight years ago, Gwendolyn misplaced a brooch, right?"

Eustacia chortled. "Misplaced? It was stolen, my dear. She swore up and down for days she did not lose it at the Play House, but no one believed her. I know for a fact that she was telling the truth."

Interesting news. Helena had told me they'd taken it from her while attending the performance at the theater, but everyone else said they'd never seen it there. "What do you mean?"

"The show took place on a Friday evening. I'd been unable to go because my arthritis was flaring up and I couldn't get hold of Dr. Betscha that afternoon. I can't speak to what happened at the Play House, but the next day," she said, looking quite pleased with herself, "the brooch was sitting on Gwennie's dresser just where she said she'd left it, as plain as the wrinkles on her face."

"Then, you believe the thief stole it from here, not from the theater?" I was puzzled by the two different stories but knew there had to be a justifiable explanation. Helena positively said that Krissy had picked it up off the floor in the main lobby at the Paddington Play House. When Eustacia nodded, I said, "How do you explain several witnesses claiming they'd seen it while at the show?"

"They must have been confused. It was just a bunch of sorority girls, they probably saw someone else's brooch and thought it was Gwennie's," she replied with determination, turning to Jennifer. "You were there. Did you see it?"

"I hadn't been paying close attention, Aunt Eustacia. Bertha is the one who suggested the police should ask everyone who'd attended the show. Her son, Quint, had been here that day for her birthday, and he'd mentioned his friends had been onsite and might remember seeing something." Jennifer nibbled on a dry biscuit before presenting a fancy plate layered with others in my direction, another sign that her manners were improving since watching her mother pass away earlier that year.

I declined her offer, only able to focus on Quint's presence popping up everywhere. Why had he decided to steal all the jewelry? Did he rope my brother into it? Krissy Stanton claimed to have seen the brooch on the theater floor. How did it end up back at the Paddington estate after someone put it in the safe at the sorority house? It increasingly looked like I needed to pay a visit to Krissy, who might remember more than she realized. "What about you, Jennifer? What did you lose recently?"

Jennifer explained that she'd developed an unusual reaction to wearing silver jewelry upon entering her second trimester. She'd stopped using an antique watch her father had gifted her on her eighteenth birthday. It had crystals and diamonds on the faceplate and was worth a lot of money. "I decided to have it cleaned, hoping that maybe I'd be able to wear it again without getting a rash. It had been sitting on my nightstand the day it was stolen. Arthur picked me up for lunch, and I thought I'd set the security alarm before leaving the house. I might've forgotten... you know, baby brain and all."

Jennifer explained that no one else had been home that morning or evening due to the costume extravaganza occurring at Memorial Library. Millard had been at the office, Eustacia was with friends, and Ophelia and her daughters were on vacation; the school year had ended and they needed a break from a hectic schedule. When Jennifer returned to her bedroom that evening, the watch had been missing and a black calla lily sat in its place. "The watch was the only thing we didn't have locked in the safe that day. Bertha's last day had been that week too. The place was truly empty," she said, then turned to Eustacia. "Which reminds me, Bertha mentioned Quint would drop off the keys that weekend, but I never saw him. I don't suppose we should ask her about it now, should we?"

After Eustacia looked at me, synchronizing our newfound clarity and noting that she'd handle it, I said, "Don't you have cameras hooked up throughout the house?"

Eustacia laughed like a small child. "We did, but after the tragedy of Gwennie's murder, we had to order a new system. Timothy wanted to handle it, but he wasn't home from the recovery program. The new system is installed now." She also indicated there had been no signs of a break-in, which was why Jennifer originally worried she'd accidentally left the front door unlocked.

"Did you tell the police everything you've just told me?"

Jennifer nodded. "Except about Bertha failing to give us the keys. I'd forgotten that part. You don't think Quint had something to do with this, do you?"

"I really couldn't say, but that would be a strange coincidence with the keys and no sign of forced entry. Maybe he accidentally lost them." I needed to let April and Connor know what I'd learned. "I hope the police find the watch, it sounds very special to you," I suggested, wondering whether I should also pay a visit to Bertha to deliver an update on what I'd discovered. If she'd coughed up the keys to Quint, we might have found our explanation for how Jennifer's watch had been stolen.

Emma and Timothy joined us in the sitting room. They'd had a fantastic time looking at all the flowers and the pond in the middle of the Great Hall. "There's a mean plant that bites the goldfish, Daddy." Emma shuddered, hiding something in her hand behind her back. "I don't want one of those, and we're never bringing Baxter here."

"Good idea. What have you got there?" I turned her around and gasped.

"Aunt Deirdre says it's a cow lily," she giggled and handed me one that she'd been holding behind her back. "Someone cut a bunch and left this one near the pond. Aren't they pretty?"

"It's called a calla lily, and yes, they are very pretty. Especially these black ones." It was beginning to wither and droop, which suggested it hadn't been cut recently.

Timothy replied, "I called Uncle Millard to let him know that there were several missing in the Great Hall. He hasn't been by to clean the pond or monitor the flower gardens in a week. The last time he checked was the day of Nana D's birthday party when all was fine."

"Do you have any cameras that would show who might've been near the pond?"

Eustacia said, "Maybe, but it was probably that new maid. Don't worry, we'll take care of it, Kellan. If I didn't know better, I'd suspect it was our jewelry thief, but it's probably just a coincidence."

"Why do you say that?"

"All the flowers that were left as calling cards after the robberies were white calla lilies that someone spray-painted black. The ones missing from our gardens are legitimate black calla lilies. We only started to grow those two weeks ago, after Jennifer's necklace was stolen."

While Eustacia had a point, she didn't have the privilege of knowing that the ones left near Quint's dead body were also legitimate black calla lilies. No spray paint had been used for that bouquet. "Can I see the video recordings? I can't tell you why, but there might be something important on it."

Timothy said, "Of course, I trust you have a valid reason, but unfortunately, there are no cameras pointing near the pond in the Great Hall. We only installed cameras to secure the entrances, exits, hallways, main rooms, and exterior of the house."

That wasn't going to help me. If I knew who was inside the Great Hall, I might confirm who cut a bunch of flowers to leave near Quint's body after killing him. "Can you put together a list of people who had access between the time Millard tended the flowers last Sunday and Tuesday morning? Visitors, employees, anyone in the family, please. It's important."

Jennifer looked to her aunt and brother, then shook her head. "Isn't that when you found Quint Crawford's body?"

I nodded.

"Sure, I'll talk to everyone in the house and come up with a list," Eustacia firmly announced, then leaned on her cane to prop herself off the chair. "Come, Jennifer, we have work to accomplish and a new criminal to catch."

* * *

On the drive home, I convinced myself to disclose to Connor the news of the calla lilies being cut down at the Paddington estate. By informing him, I risked him intervening with Eustacia and insisting she turn over the list to him and not me. I'd address that if and when it happened.

Emma and I spent the rest of the afternoon together. While she read a few chapters from her favorite author, I prepared for my upcoming classes. We would have our first pop quiz that week, and I needed to design the questions to cover a wide variety of topics. By dinnertime, Emma had a craving for Chinese food. Confident that delivery would take too long, I ordered a few different options and drove to the restaurant to pick it up. Our order wasn't ready when I arrived, and the hostess let us wait in a corner booth with a bucket of free fortune cookies. A gold-painted, ceramic kitty—a traditional Chinese sign of luck—continually waved to us from a nearby shelf. Emma connected her earbuds and played a game on one of her devices. I scrolled through my phone to catch up on any work emails I'd missed since Friday. I had just opened the summary of Myriam's staff meeting when my name was called.

It wasn't from the hostess about my food. "Fancy seeing you here, Dr. Ayrwick," Krissy Stanton said as she sidled up to the booth. "This must be your lovely daughter."

"Yes, that's Emma." I poked my daughter's elbow and introduced them. Emma told me she was about to enter the next level, so I let her keep playing. "Are you coming or going?" I asked Krissy.

"Coming. I'm having dinner with my father tonight. He hasn't yet arrived," she said, sitting across from me. "Do you mind?"

"Not at all. I wanted to talk to you anyway." Luck was on my side this evening. I'd have to thank the Chinese kitty before I left. I couldn't have planned this impromptu meeting any better if I tried. "How's Marcus doing in his last two days before his position as town councilman ends?"

"Don't gloat too much. My father doesn't accept defeat easily. He's probably planning some sort of coup, so you should tell your nana to be on the lookout," Krissy warned. Her tone was mostly friendly, so I didn't take it as a threat. "To be honest, I'm getting tired of Dad's games and planning to tell him at dinner tonight."

"Relationships with our parents are often quite painful, I hear you." Had I just found my way to bring up Quint's death to Krissy? "I'll be sure to caution Nana D. She spoke with him yesterday, at least he called her. By the way, I heard a strange rumor. I wonder if you'd know anything about it."

"What's that?" she asked, playing with a set of unwrapped chopsticks and tapping her foot against the side of the booth. When I asked her about the work Quint had done at her father's house, Krissy huffed. "It's not a rumor. Quint was my friend, and he did amazing work. I was home the entire time watching him rewire several rooms."

"Your dad's known to be a... piece of work. No offense intended to you, of course. Do you think he did anything to hurt him after Quint told people your father wouldn't pay up?"

Krissy's eyebrows arched high, and her mouth opened wide. "I... I... never thought about it. Dad's been angry ever since he lost the election. I haven't seen much of him. He can be vengeful, but Quint never mentioned anything." Her entire demeanor had changed in front of me once I suggested it.

"Well, I wouldn't worry too much then," I said, uncertain myself how far Marcus might go to stop someone from hurting his reputation. When the hostess told me that the food would be ready in five minutes, I leaned toward Krissy and quietly said, "Do you mind if I ask you another question that might be uncomfortable to answer?"

"Ummm... sure, is this about the incident with Imogene in class?" she asked, swallowing deeply.

"No, it's not." I clasped my hands together and cracked my knuckles. "I know what happened eight years ago when you were pledging the Alpha Iota Omega sorority. I was hoping you might fill in a few blanks for me."

Krissy recoiled quickly and looked in the lobby to see if her father had arrived. "I don't want to talk about that, and I should probably move to my own table."

"Krissy, wait," I said, holding up my hand. "I just want to know what occurred at the Paddington Play House the night Gwendolyn lost her brooch. The rest of her family swears she had it at the estate the following day, but you and the other girls had stolen it the previous night." I explained what I knew about the prank and how the brooch had disappeared from the safe, then suggested Quint might've been involved.

"If I tell you what I know, will you agree to drop it? This happened a long time ago, and I'd rather forget the whole thing," she begged. When I nodded, she continued. "I stole the brooch out of the safe at the sorority house and gave it to Quint to return to the Paddington estate. I felt guilty about what we'd done."

I'd suspected something like that had happened, but I wasn't sure which girl had been the Good Samaritan. "Does anyone else know?"

"No, just Quint. He helped me steal it in the first place. Quint spent a lot of time at the Paddington estate, and he'd seen the brooch a few times. He'd stopped by to visit his mother while she was working the day of the show and took it for me. I never told the other girls about that part."

"That's how you were able to tell everyone you saw it on the floor in the lobby of the theater?" Part of the story was beginning to make sense.

"Yes. Quint swiped it for me, so we could fulfill the sisterhood's request before we were permitted to become members of Alpha Iota Omega. He'd dropped it in Gwendolyn's purse right before she left for the show, then I grabbed it while no one was looking in the restroom and told the other girls I'd found it on the floor. Later that night, the sorority president put it in the safe. I saw the combination and retrieved it the next morning. I gave it to Quint, who snuck it back in when he went to visit his mother for her birthday. I'd felt too guilty about the whole thing and didn't want to go through with it."

"Do you know what happened afterward?"

"No, it really went missing because the Paddingtons reported it stolen afterward. I saw Quint put it back in her room. Eustacia Paddington wasn't lying. She must've noticed it the next morning after he'd returned it. I was there with him to say happy birthday to his mother."

If Quint and Krissy had returned it, then how did it disappear again? When I asked Krissy if she had any suggestions, she looked humiliated over her role in the past. "Are you sure no one else knew what you and Quint had done? Is there a chance my brother was aware?" I needed to discover whether Gabriel or Quint had acted alone or if someone else had been involved.

"I don't know. That was a really bad month for everyone. Imogene and Quint had been dating, then she abandoned him for Paul Dodd. Your brother started distancing himself from us, but now I know it was because he didn't know how to tell us about being gay," Krissy said, indicating her father was walking through the front door. "I recall Gabriel had been acting suspiciously the day he disappeared."

"Were you aware of the other jewelry thefts at the time?" I asked, unsure who had been told what back then, especially considering the sheriff was Quint's uncle and had hidden facts from people.

"Minor details until it hit the papers days after the last one, and by then, your brother and Quint had left town. The group fell apart." Krissy tapped Emma's arm and waved goodbye when my daughter looked up from her game. "I need to go. I'm sure you'd rather not run into my father."

Marcus scoffed at me as his daughter joined him in the lobby, and they strolled to their table on the other side of the room. When the hostess brought over my food, I paid the check and walked to the parking lot with Emma.

At least I now understood the confusion about the brooch appearing at the theater, but why had Quint double-crossed Krissy by only pretending to return it to the Paddington estate? I called Nana D and asked her to arrange a get-together with Bertha Crawford, curious whether she'd been hiding any information about the jewelry thefts. Could she know more than she'd confessed about her son?

After dinner and a game of checkers, Emma went to sleep. I contacted Connor to schedule our next workout. As I climbed into bed, he responded that we could meet Tuesday at the Grey Sports Complex before work. Then I saw several dots on the message appear and disappear. Connor had more to discuss but kept changing his mind.

Me: *Dude, you're gonna give me a seizure. Something else you need to say?*
Connor: *Was gonna call earlier but got wrapped up in something. Are you free tomorrow?*
Me: *I have a meeting, interview, and class, otherwise available. What's up?*
Connor: *Gabriel returned my call. I'm questioning him at four o'clock. April wants me to chat with you beforehand. She thinks you know more than you've said.*
Me: *Sure. The Big Beanery at 8:15, okay?*
Connor: *Deal. BTW, is something going on between you two? You once teased me...*

I began several replies only to erase each of them and try again. I gave up after six attempts, removed my glasses, and pulled the covers over my head. It was Connor's turn to see several dots on the message appear and disappear. I pretended not to recognize the irony of the situation, keenly aware he ultimately responded to me and I was abandoning him without an explanation.

There was always tomorrow when the promise of a better answer could arrive. I began to doze off, recognizing that if the thief had stuck to his or her pattern, tomorrow was nine days since the burglary at Lara's house when Imogene had been attacked. If a final robbery targeting the Stantons was going to occur, exactly where and when would it take place?

CHAPTER 13

Once Emma was safely on the bus the next morning, I drove to South Campus and met Connor at The Big Beanery. I checked my watch to confirm I'd made it on time, as punctuality had been instilled in me by Nana D ever since I was old enough to read a clock. She wouldn't let me use anything digital until I knew the difference between the big and little hands, just as I couldn't get Velcro shoes until I could properly tie my own laces. That woman never gave up until she got her way!

Other than a few people in line and my boss and her wife sitting in a corner booth, the place was empty. I waved at Myriam and Ursula, then got in the queue. Only one waved back, of course. By the time I was next to order, Connor joined me and added in his items. "Make that two more black coffees, skip the bear claws he idiotically ordered, and give us three fruit bowls, please."

I cast a disapproving look. "Desserts motivate me. If you want me to talk, then put them back on the list." I stared back and forth between the cashier and Connor, wondering who would win our standoff before the full weight of what he'd said hit me. In that temporary confusion, he inserted his credit card into the chip-and-pin device to pay for the order, minus the bear claws. "Why three?"

"For me," April said, as she idled over to the other side of the counter where the barista placed our breakfast. "I realized three heads are better than two when it comes to piecing together this doozy of a conundrum."

Once the fruit bowls were placed on a tray, April directed me to collect napkins and forks and located a table. I followed her and Connor, then slumped into the empty chair across from them. "I'm more jumbled than my mother trying to find her way around the kitchen. First, you tell me to stay out of your investigations. Then, you tell me to work with Connor but leave you alone.

Now, you're joining us before I've had enough coffee to process the tomfoolery happening around me."

"Is he always this chipper in the morning?" Yanking a fork and napkin from my hands, April ignored the frustration building on my face.

"You should see him try to lift his first set of weights. I stand pretty close by in case he falls and knocks himself unconscious," Connor replied as he handed out fruit bowls.

"Do I need to be here? I might have better luck not getting sideswiped if I stood in the middle of commuter traffic on the highway," I grunted as they sipped coffee.

"You are right, Kellan. I've been giving you mixed signals," April said, offering one of the rare concessions I'd usually witness only during full moons in a leap year once a millennium. "Connor and I had a lengthy conversation yesterday about your involvement in our jobs."

I briefly slid my gaze to Connor's stoic face, unable to read him. Was my name being called upon strictly for professional reasons or had a smattering of personal interests popped up? April began by explaining that it'd be better to share information, highlighting my familiarity with many of the people involved in the jewelry thefts and Quint's murder. She reiterated the inability for me to speak to anyone else about the case, stressing her reticence to reveal key details to a private citizen. "You're not an official deputy, and you haven't gained any special privileges, so don't let this go to your head."

"I promise I'll be worth it," I said in an unexpectedly confident and amorous voice, then winked at April. What was happening to my self-control around this woman? "I mean, you can completely trust me. Right, so...."

Connor must have noticed my startling tone because a crafty grin formed on his lips. "Did you want me to stick around, or would you rather talk to April alone, Kellan?"

"Let's just get on with our discussion," I replied and kicked him under the table. He and I would have an incredibly painful tête-à-tête the next time I was spotting *him* while *he* bench-pressed too much weight. "Shall we start with the jewelry heists or the electrocution-slash-strangulation death?"

"I assume they're connected, but let's start with the murder." Connor's revelation about Quint's death surprised me, especially when he clarified the order of the events. "The coroner worked with Dr. Betscha to confirm exactly what happened in the cable car. Quint was electrocuted before he was strangled to death." Based on the burn marks and the residual effects in Quint's system, he was electrocuted around midnight. He hadn't suffered a cardiac arrest, which meant the electric cables weren't what killed him. Quint must've grabbed a wire while installing a panel, thinking the power supply had been turned off, then passed out from his injuries. "It may or may not have been accidental. The autopsy showed little alcohol in his system."

April interjected, "What's odd is that the power was turned off when Connor checked it that morning. Someone, possibly the person who'd strangled him, tried to confuse us."

"Tell me what you know about the time of death." We'd seen the finger impressions on his neck. If Quint had been injured and weakened from the electrical surge, he wouldn't have been able to stop his attacker from choking him. Anyone involved could've killed him, pending the size of their hands.

"Between twelve thirty and one that morning, about seven hours before you found him," Connor replied, sharing the key details from his report. "There was major bruising on his larynx and windpipe, but it wouldn't have taken much force based on his condition from being electrocuted."

"Do you think the same person who tried to electrocute him stuck around and finished the job?" My stomach began to grind with disgust upon thinking about the cruelty Quint had suffered. What kind of person could do such a thing? Although he'd been a thief, his murder wasn't justified.

"It's definitely a possibility, but we can't be certain. We're checking alibis for everyone he'd been seen talking with the last few weeks," April said, finishing her coffee and signaling the waitress for a refill. "Which brings us to the jewelry thefts and the reason we want to speak with Gabriel."

"Before you say anything else, there's something I should've told you sooner. I only got confirmation this weekend, and it might change your approach." I hoped they weren't angry that I'd kept the details about the Alpha Iota Omega sorority's prank from them. I finished explaining everything I knew, including what my father had shared about the previous sheriff's blackmail and what Krissy had revealed about returning the brooch with Quint at the Paddington house.

Eyeing me intently, April snarled, "This changes everything!"

Connor said, "I'll contact Eustacia Paddington to directly submit to me the list of people with access to the flowers at the estate. I'll also have someone check for any fingerprints, but it's unlikely we'll find any at this point."

After we finished organizing the case, we devised a plan where Connor would interview all the girls who'd pledged the sorority, applying enough pressure to force someone to crack and share additional information. He'd also obtain their alibis covering the hours preceding and including Quint's death. April would follow up with Siobhan Walsh and Marcus Stanton to determine if either had been involved in the murder. I was tasked with convincing Gabriel to reveal everything he knew when they met later that afternoon. I let both Connor and April know that I planned to visit Bertha after my class, to see if she could remember anything else as well as inquire about the keys to the Paddington estate.

I tossed my glasses on the table to give my eyes a break from focusing on their livid expressions. "Look, I get that I screwed up by not contacting either of you immediately. I just talked to Krissy last night about that final part. I wanted to find out what Gabriel knew before I updated the Wharton County Sheriff's Office." I genuinely never intended to keep the information from them, but saving my brother was important to me. April grabbed the tray containing the remains of our breakfast from me when I attempted to pick it up. After a brief game of tug of war, I let it go, hoping something would accidentally fall onto her. Unfortunately, she was too careful and stepped away before anything spilled on her lap.

"I get it." Clearly frustrated and ready to wring someone's neck, April tossed out the garbage and hastily wiped the table with a napkin. "I'm not angry at you as much as I am at those who lied or hid information in the past. We could have prevented this second round of robberies and Quint's death."

Once they left The Big Beanery, I realized April had inadvertently thrown my glasses away with the trash. Unwilling to rifle through nasty garbage containers, I grabbed a spare pair from my satchel and made a mental note to read her the *Riot Act*. When I put them on, I noticed how crowded the café had become and scanned the room in search of my interviewee. Ten minutes later, a tall African American woman in her late forties, the candidate for the fall semester's assistant professor role, showed up. Dr. Lawson would be a strong addition to the department, but in the end, she disclosed a potentially complex connection to Wharton County, setting off a few glaring warning signs. I'd mention it to Myriam, who'd make the final decision whether to hire the esteemed historian.

Knowing I had a bit more time to kill, I verified with Bertha I would visit her at seven thirty that evening, then thanked Nana D for setting up the meeting. I also called my mother to see if she'd checked her calendar about the ideal day to hang out each week. I wanted to catch her before she got stuck in meetings. "Great, so we'll do lunch on Fridays at noon in the campus cafeteria."

"Perfect. While I have you on the phone, let me confirm that other thing you asked me," my mother added, clicking a few keys in the background from her office in Admissions Hall.

I'd forgotten she was going to verify if Siobhan had been working on Tuesday morning the day after Quint had been killed. "I appreciate it. I doubt she did anything, but at least we'll know for sure."

"I keep notes whenever my staff is late. I try to cut Siobhan a little slack because she has such tiny babies, but I want a record in case it ever gets out of hand." My mother was very observant, despite the disconnected glare and relaxed composure she'd outwardly display. "Ah, yes, she was late that day. Siobhan told me she had taken the twins to the downtown clinic for some emergency care the night before. Turned out they just had croup, I believe."

I thanked my mother for the information and considered how to prove Siobhan's alibi. With all the security around patient medical records, it wouldn't be easy. Then again, April was going to speak with Siobhan, so I should just let the sheriff do her job, right? As I stood to leave, I bumped into someone in my distracted state. "Pardon me," I apologized and stepped aside, so he could walk past.

"I was just looking for a table and thought you might be leaving," a familiar-looking man replied, glancing toward someone at the front counter. Then, the sandalwood scent filled the air around me.

"Nicholas Endicott?" I asked, noticing his father, Lindsey, was the person he'd been searching for in line. "I'm Kellan Ayrwick. I know your dad, and I think you might be friends with my brother, Gabriel."

"Oh, yes, I've heard your name in the past. It's great to finally meet you," he replied and thanked me when I offered him the table.

"No problem, I was just leaving. Listen, I'm sorry to hear about your friend, Quint."

"Thanks, man. He was definitely taken too quickly. Call me Nicky, everyone does." A firm handshake greeted me before he brushed a few crumbs from the table. They'd been in April's spot, not mine. Luckily, the interviewee had sat on the other side of me. April was such a hot mess! Nana D had always demanded that I clean up after myself. As he pulled away his hand, I saw a large scratch on his forearm and black paint on his chipped fingernails. Could he have gotten the scratch while attacking Imogene during the robbery? Were the black stains from spray-painting the calla lilies? Was Nicky the unknown accomplice? He noticed my stare and responded, "Construction work can be messy and painful. I was cutting and staining some beadboard at one of my sites."

I thanked fate for dropping this opportunity in my lap but wasn't sure whether to believe him about the cuts and black paint. "Quint once told me he was eager to buy into your company. It's great to hear friends can go into business together without any worries," I said, hoping to learn something of value during our exchange. I knew extraordinarily little about Nicky, but since he was Lindsey's son, I'd start with the benefit of the doubt by assuming he wasn't involved in any crimes.

"Yeah, that wasn't the exact plan. Quint wanted to be part of the company, and we were friends, but I didn't plan to share ownership with anyone else." Nicky waved at his father to come over.

"Oh, I must have misunderstood. Was everything okay between you two?"

Nicky nodded. "I prefer not to mix business and pleasure. Endicott Construction is my baby." He looked startled by my questions and finished speaking abruptly as his father reached the table.

"Nana D is preparing for tomorrow's inauguration. Thanks for your help all along," I greeted.

"Good to see you, Kellan. Such a small town, eh? How's Seraphina?" Lindsey replied.

"Swell." I decided to dive in. "I heard you're a runner, Nicky. Maybe we should hit the Braxton campus trails together one day. There are some great ones on the hills near the cable car station."

Nicky looked as if I'd suggested we become best friends forever and was suddenly unnerved by my presence. "I like to go each morning before I head to my job sites. Sure, maybe I'll see you around."

When the conversation hadn't led anywhere, nor could I come up with an approach to learn where he'd been the day Quint died, I said goodbye and drove to North Campus for a meeting with the team working on the college expansion plans to offer a graduate curriculum and convert Braxton into a university the following year. After an hour of reviewing the upcoming deliverables, we were released to finish the rest of our day. I had a few hours before class but needed to organize the pop quiz details. When I got back to my office on South Campus, I realized I'd left my satchel under the table at The Big Beanery. While walking past the cable car station to retrieve it, I visited Cheney who was applying the finishing touches. He indicated he planned to do a test run the following morning to verify the repairs had been completed and the car was ready for the grand reopening that week. He said that Nicky had also offered him a full-time job at the construction company, so things were finally looking positive.

I took the pathway to The Big Beanery and approached its front door, the handle fabricated to resemble the portafilter on a classic espresso machine. Through the glass, I saw the table was still empty, which would make it easy for me to dash inside to grab my satchel and hasten right back out. I collected my belongings, then heard my brother's voice booming through an open window. I left via the side door, walked around the corner of the coffee-bean shaped building, and peered into the parking lot. Standing in the outdoor seating area, Gabriel was chatting with Nicky. I stepped closer to listen to their conversation before interrupting them. Well there you go, call me an *eavesdropper,* after all!

"Listen, I owe you the money, take it," Gabriel pleaded while handing an envelope to Nicky.

"If I needed it that desperately, I would've tracked you down." Nicky pushed the envelope away.

"I'd feel a lot better if I repaid my debt. You did me a huge favor the night I left Braxton."

I couldn't lose my chance to confront my brother before they finished conversing.

"Gabriel, just let it go. Use the money to buy yourself something and move on," Nicky said as I approached them. When he saw me, his head retracted quickly, and he looked stunned. "Kellan?"

Gabriel said, "Are you following me? I was clear the other day. I don't want to talk to you."

"I know about your four o'clock meeting this afternoon. What I don't know is why you're handing an envelope of cash to someone in the middle of a parking lot. Care to explain, brother?"

Nicky backed away. "Sounds like a family dispute. I hope you guys work it out. I'll call you later."

My troublemaking sibling turned to me and shook his head. "You're a pain in my—"

"Just don't. I'm tired of the half-truths and partial stories about why you left town and what led you to return. Stop being an immature child, and do the right thing for a change," I chastised.

"Fine," he spit out and began walking away. "You wanna talk? We'll do it my way this time."

"Where are you going?" I beckoned while running after him.

When he stopped, Gabriel stood in front of his motorcycle and unlocked two helmets. "Hop on. I want to have this discussion where no one else can interrupt us." Gabriel fastened his helmet, knocked the kickstand up, and started the bike. Over its powerful roar, he yelled, "Let's do this."

CHAPTER 14

A warm, gusty wind parted my lips and flushed my cheeks as Gabriel's motorcycle instinctively navigated the highway heading northbound through the Wharton Mountain range. When we were teenagers, he used to ride his two-speed bicycle to Crilly Lake to escape the monotony of family life. He always preferred to be alone when he needed to think, and I speculated that he was taking me to the place where he'd once made all the major decisions in his life. I wrapped my left arm around his chest to keep myself steady and let the other loosely grip the side of his waist. Somehow, it felt wrong for me to depend on my brother for support. It was supposed to be the other way around right now.

At the last exit in Wharton County, he slowed to take Dead Man's Curve at a reasonable speed. A kid I'd gone to high school with hadn't been so lucky the week we'd graduated and lost the future he deserved by racing around that curve too swiftly. The new Gabriel could be reckless, but he would never endanger our lives. I'd only been on a bike once before when some buddies of mine in Los Angeles had taken me to a rally for a race they'd entered. The thrill of driving down the California coast with them one afternoon had left quite an impression on me. No wonder April and Gabriel had purchased bikes of their own, not that I'd ever let Emma chance a ride while I was alive. I had my limits, as hypocritical as it might make me, and being a doting and semi-controlling father was the priority.

Gabriel stopped about twenty feet before reaching the lake and waited for me to disembark. By the time I removed my helmet, felt my heart slow its excessive pumping, and wiped a dead bug from my glasses, he'd tossed off his shoes, rolled up his pants legs to his knees, and sat on the edge of the dock.

I plopped down next to him and said, "Remember when the head cheerleader, Misty Donovan, told everyone you tried to steal her panties in gym class... and the captain of the football team tracked you down while we were playing Frisbee at the park?"

Gabriel nodded.

"You weren't afraid of anyone back then, and you're not afraid of anyone right now. Are you?" I shoved his head a few inches to the side in a playful older brother manner.

He smirked and ran his fingers through his hair to fix the mess I'd made. "Clearly, everyone must know by now that I was never interested in Misty's lace panties."

"I guess, maybe, you desired the captain of the football team's lace panties?" I busted out laughing at my joke-slash-insult, cradling my head against my lap with my arms covering my neck to try to contain the potential damage. I never should've let my guard down because the next thing I knew, my brother shoved me off the dock, and I landed in the cool water fully clothed and highly embarrassed.

Gabriel crossed his arms. "Hey, you were right. I'm not afraid of anyone right now." He stretched an arm in my direction and helped me climb back on the dock.

"I've got class to teach in a few hours, you jerk," I said and handed him my glasses. "Dry those, if you don't mind."

"We can swing by Danby Landing to get you a change of clothes. You're such a prima donna, Kellan. And people think I'm the one they need to worry about causing a scene in public."

We sat in silence for ten minutes watching a couple of fish swim past. A large white bird soared close by and attempted to snatch one unsuccessfully. "If you're not more careful, Gabriel, someone's gonna swoop down and catch you when you least expect it. Why won't you let me help?"

"Because I screwed up and deserve to be punished." Gabriel confessed the entire story to me, and I knew he wasn't leaving anything out. At one point, tears were even shed over the loss of a complicated friendship when Quint Crawford had been murdered in the cable car the previous week.

Within the group, Nicky and Paul had been best friends, and Gabriel and Quint had been best friends. Nicky was always after his next girl, yet Paul and Quint both had a thing for Imogene Grey. Imogene and Quint had dated for a few months, until Lara Bouvier confronted Quint and told him that he wasn't good enough for her daughter. She'd threatened to launch an investigation into his uncle's shady behavior. Although there'd been persistent rumors about his uncle, Sheriff Crawford, being shifty and on the take, nothing had ever been proven. Quint didn't want any bad press to hurt his mother, so he agreed to leave Imogene alone. It'd destroyed him because he'd always felt like the weakling in the group—everyone's family had money but his. Quint then began instigating trouble on campus which caused the group to break up. At the time, Gabriel had been dating his secret boyfriend and was trying to stay under the radar. Except one day, Quint had stumbled upon the truth.

"At first, he acted like everything was okay, and that it didn't bother him.

But the more he pushed Imogene away to protect his mother, the more he became angry about anyone who'd fallen in love," Gabriel explained as fine worry lines formed along the sides of his mouth.

"That must have been tough on your friendship," I commiserated.

"Yep. It gradually got worse. One day, he told me he wanted to leave town, and he wanted me to go with him. I'd just broken up with that guy I told you about, and everything was falling apart for me. Dad wouldn't listen to me about not accepting the Braxton presidency, and I needed some space."

"What does this have to do with the jewelry thefts? I'm not sure I understand."

"Quint was the thief. He'd wanted to get back at everyone who'd angered him that semester. Krissy had asked him to steal something from the Paddington estate while he was visiting his mother. He helped her out, but then she ordered him to put it back. That was the last straw for him; he was tired of being treated like his mother—a maid or servant." Gabriel explained that Quint needed money to leave town and had attempted to blackmail a few folks, but when it hadn't worked, he'd turned to robbery.

"Quint would've been a good spy, based on what you're telling me."

Quint had originally thought if he stole a few pieces of jewelry, he could sell it in another state and start a new life. But then he was compelled to get even with the girls in the Alpha Iota Omega sorority. Imogene had told him the story about a girl's mother leaving a white calla lily on a boy's doorstep for nine days to reveal her daughter's crush, and how he would choose whether to return a black flower or a white bouquet, depending on his feelings. Since Quint wasn't interested in his friends anymore, he decided to punish them. When he couldn't find a black calla lily, he chose to spray-paint several white ones and left them at each robbery. "It was his attempt at a *screw you* to those who'd wronged him. Quint didn't know a black calla lily was a dark-purple one, and I didn't want to make him feel stupid," Gabriel replied with a contrite smile.

"I can see why it'd make the situation worse." I shook my head at what I'd just learned, realizing that the person who'd killed Quint must not have known he'd been spray-painting white calla lilies. The killer used real ones because he or she didn't know any better.

Quint had hoped it would lead his uncle to investigate the sorority and their families, throwing the cops off any trail leading back to him as well as getting revenge on people like Lara Bouvier. It'd almost worked, but his uncle had discovered the truth. "Sheriff Crawford overheard Quint and me recounting what his nephew had done. He misunderstood, thinking Quint and I were in on it together."

"But you never stole anything, you just knew what he'd been up to."

Gabriel nodded. "Everything got crazy that day. I told Dad the truth about the guy who dumped me and that I was gay. He wanted me to tell everyone in the family and work through it together. I begged him to withdraw from the Braxton presidency, and he asked for a day to think about it. A few hours later, he stopped by the dorm room while I was in class and convinced the cleaning staff to let him inside, so he could leave a note for me. That's when he found the missing jewelry in my room."

"How is that possible if you weren't involved?"

"Quint had my spare key and planted the jewels. He'd set me up, even dressed like me to make it look like I was up to no good," Gabriel said, the frustration and pain evident on his face. "He was afraid that I'd turn him and his uncle in, to the mayor. He wanted something to hold over my head. Quint had planned the whole thing to ensure he didn't get hung out to dry by himself. He wasn't just opportunistic. He was crafty and cunning about protecting himself."

I pieced the rest of the story together. Tiffany had seen Quint in Gabriel's dorm room, not Gabriel, and thought my brother was responsible for the robberies. What a mess! "That's why Sheriff Crawford told Dad that you were involved and to check your dorm room. The sheriff had offered to cover it up as long as Dad pushed you to leave town. He was protecting his nephew."

"Yes, only I'd already gone to Nicky Endicott and begged him to loan me enough money to leave Braxton. That's what you saw me doing just now, repaying the money I'd never returned to him." Gabriel stood and unrolled his pants. "When Dad found me later that night, it was storming pretty badly. Quint was busy stealing from Marcus Stanton's alumni event during the power outage. I was fighting with Dad, who told me he knew what I'd done. He tried to give me money to leave, but I told him I never wanted to speak to him again. Our father thought I was the thief, and he never believed I could be innocent after I'd hidden everything else from him. When Quint finished his last robbery, he blackmailed me to leave town together that night and hock all the jewelry." Quint had threatened to tell everyone Gabriel was the thief if he didn't let him come on the trip. Nicky's money was only half as helpful as Gabriel had originally planned. They went to the pawn shop with the Roarke earrings as a test run. "I had no money left, and I did a stupid thing. Quint forced me to put my name on the paperwork. Then, we waited a few days to verify nothing happened once we'd received the money for the earrings."

"But what about all the money Quint stole from Marcus Stanton's office?" I asked, bemused.

Gabriel groaned. "I didn't know about it until the night I went looking for something in his bag. He was out getting food, and I found the cash. We had a huge argument when he returned to the hostel. Quint hadn't wanted to spend that money until he was sure the bills weren't traceable, and he wanted my name on any formal records to ensure nothing could fall back on him. His uncle had warned him. That night, Quint packed up his stuff, the cash, and the jewelry, and he disappeared. I never heard from him again. I panicked and entered crisis mode. I knew I could never come home again for a long time."

I could've killed Quint myself for what he'd done to my brother. "Is that why you called the pawn shop to tell them where to find the owners of the rubies?"

"Yes, I disguised my voice and left a message from a random pay phone in another part of San Francisco. Then, I got a job, went back to school, and you know the rest, I guess." Gabriel indicated we should head back if I needed to get to class on time.

"I know the rest in terms of your time away from Braxton, but what happened when you came back this year. Did you confront Quint again?" I asked as we reached his motorcycle.

"I didn't see him the first few weeks, but we ran into each other at lunch one day. He told me how bad he felt about the whole situation and that he hoped I could get past it. He promised me he'd changed." Gabriel explained that he told Quint he'd give it some thought, but they never found a chance to talk again. My brother had no information about the current jewelry thefts, nor did he know who might've been angry enough with Quint to kill him. "Imogene and Paul never knew what Quint had done, and now they're happily engaged in their own world. Tiffany, Imogene, and Helena don't know that Krissy had asked Quint to steal the original brooch, so they'd never suspected him of being the thief. Tiffany thinks it's me because I was with her at the funeral parlor the day her mother had been robbed, and she saw Quint dressed like me in my dorm room with the stolen jewelry. Nicky only hired Quint because he didn't know what the guy had done to me until I told him a few weeks ago."

Gabriel confirmed he had no alibi for the night Quint had been killed. He was at home sleeping and couldn't prove that he wasn't anywhere near the cable car. Nana D was sleeping too. Gabriel knocked the kickstand away and drove to Danby Landing, so I could change clothes, then we headed back to campus. He went to work, promising to tell the whole truth to Connor later that afternoon.

As he left, I contacted Lucy Roarke to learn if she'd ever been told who'd stolen the rubies. She stated that Silas Crawford claimed he'd never discovered any names when the San Francisco police transferred the gems. He'd definitely been covering up his nephew's role and had chosen not to release any information he'd learned from the pawn shop to the Roarkes. I ended the conversation just as my father called to mention that he hadn't recollected anything else since our previous discussion. "But remember, bad blood runs through the Crawford men, so Quint's the true thief. I'm sure there won't be any more break-ins again, Kellan."

I wasn't so certain. Walking back to Diamond Hall, I contemplated everything I'd learned; new connections in the spiderweb of clues began to grow much clearer. Quint had been angry because he felt the girls in the sorority had taken advantage of him. Then, Lara forced her daughter, Imogene, to break up with him. Quint wanted revenge. He'd purposely chosen to steal from the families who'd founded Alpha Iota Omega, and he'd left the calla lily to implicate someone in the sorority for stealing all the jewelry. Except he'd gotten away with it and left town to cash in on his rewards.

When Quint returned to town, he'd begun repeating the crimes but in a slightly different manner. There was a more intricate pattern that no one else had figured out. In the first theft of each series, he stole from Gwendolyn Paddington and her daughter, Jennifer. In the second thefts, it was Agnes followed by her daughter-in-law, Lydia. In the third thefts, it was Lucy Roarke and her daughter, Maggie. In the fourth thefts, it was Lara and her daughter, Imogene Grey. When I considered the original fifth victim, Wendy Stanton, I found myself stumped. Wendy didn't have any daughters and her son was too young to be married. Then, I realized she had a stepdaughter, Krissy. If there was a new accomplice who'd killed Quint for an unknown reason, we might still have another burglary. Based on the pattern, it'd be happening very soon. Could we get ahead of the second thief and Quint's probable killer?

I needed to share my theory with Connor and April, but it would have to wait until after class. I made up an excuse, announcing that I needed to speak with Krissy and another student during the break about an issue with their transcripts. I wanted to ensure Krissy would be available to talk with me, in case she had any concerns about being targeted for a future jewelry heist. For ninety minutes, we discussed the pros and cons of changes in documentary-style reporting since the Internet had become available. While the first student came to see me during the break, Krissy did not. I told the first student that I was confused and had found what I needed for her files, so she could ignore everything. I searched the entire floor for Krissy, but she wasn't anywhere in sight.

Raquel saw me looking around. "Who are you looking for, Dr. Ayrwick?" After I told her, she said, "Krissy and Imogene went out the back door a few minutes ago."

I thanked Raquel and went to check for myself. Those exits were usually only for professors to get to our second-floor offices. The last time something unusual had sent me up that staircase, I'd found my first dead body. My stomach flipped at the thought of it happening all over again.

I ascended the first staircase, but they weren't there. Then, I heard a voice in the distance and realized someone had gone to the third-floor library space. I quietly climbed the steps, hoping not to make my presence known. When I reached the top of the platform, Krissy and Imogene were arguing. They couldn't see me through the small crack in the doorjamb, as far as I could tell.

"The police came by to see me today. They suggested Quint's death wasn't an accident. I know you were there." Imogene sounded nervous but determined to confront Krissy.

"I don't know what you're talking about. You really are a dumb little mouse. I don't understand what Paul sees in you," Krissy retorted with venomous anger in her tone, which I'd never heard before.

"Aren't you worried that I told them about you hanging around the cable car? I wonder if they're coming to interrogate you next, maybe arrest you for something, huh?" Imogene taunted, her normally calm demeanor holding firm.

What was Krissy doing in the cable car? Was Imogene referring to the day Quint was murdered?

"The cops called. I'm meeting them tomorrow. I have a lot to tell them about you too, you witch." Krissy took a few steps closer. "I was just visiting Quint that night. We were friends."

I reached for my phone to record the conversation, but I was afraid they'd hear me pressing buttons. I kept listening, curious as to what else they might say. My word would be good enough for the sheriff if anyone confessed that afternoon.

"At eleven o'clock the night Quint was electrocuted? I saw you before I went home to Paul's house that night." Imogene backed away and slipped behind a small chair.

I considered the layout of the room and wondered if there were any weapons around. Nothing came to mind, but I hadn't been up there in weeks. Even a book could hurt someone.

Krissy guffawed. "Yes, Quint and I had drinks that night. He mentioned needing to get something he'd left in the cable car earlier that day, so I went with him. That's all. You probably saw me leaving the parking lot while he remained behind working, before accidentally electrocuting himself."

"Odd time to be on campus, huh? Quint was very smart. I must agree with the police; I don't think he'd be foolish enough to leave the power on. I told them you'd been spending time there, that you tried to steal Quint from me back in college too. That detective was extremely interested in hearing what I had to say," Imogene replied.

I'd have to find a way to corroborate Imogene's story about going home to Paul that night. If Krissy had been there an hour before Quint died, did it mean she was guilty, or had she seen someone else skulking around the cable car? She'd known about the purpose of the calla lilies and asked Quint to steal the first item for her. Had I missed key clues when she revealed the story at the Chinese restaurant the other night? I tiptoed down a few steps, worried they might find me eavesdropping. I had to rethink my plan to talk to Krissy about the next potential robbery. Perhaps this girl was wound more tightly than I'd realized. Could she be Quint's accomplice, trying to cover her tracks?

* * *

After class finished, I wrote a few lesson plans and sent a text to Connor and April to inform them I had urgent information. When I checked the time, I realized they were still cross-examining Gabriel and I had to collect Emma from the bus stop. She'd taken the later bus home today. Once I did, we drove to Bertha Crawford's house to provide an update on what I'd discovered since Quint's funeral service.

Emma regaled me on the ride over by sharing stories about all her new friends at camp. I also learned that Miss Roarke, Helena to me, had gotten into an argument with someone who'd shown up that afternoon at the school. Emma recalled that the other woman kept saying, 'How could you not tell me he was a cheater?' She then asked me, "What's a cheater, Daddy? Is that like when Nonno hides cards in his jacket pocket?"

I hadn't realized Vincenzo was that obvious in front of Emma. "Oh, sorta, honey. That's why I always say it's best to be honest and learn how to be a good loser. You can't win them all." I'd have a word with my father-in-law the next time I saw him, to suggest he stop doing foolish things when Emma was nearby.

Would it be awful of me to wish he'd been kidnapped instead of Francesca? I still hadn't produced a reasonable plan on how I'd tell Emma that her mother was alive. Any day now, Francesca might be a free woman again. I should've been thrilled by the news, and perhaps six months ago, I might have been. Too much had happened this year, I supposed. Whom had Helena fought with at work?

Emma and I knocked on Bertha's door, and she yelled for us to come inside. She lived in a small three-bedroom home not too far from the Betscha mines where her husband used to work. Nana D had told me that her brother-in-law, Silas, the former sheriff, had moved in with her after his brother died, to help provide a male role model for his young nephew. Based on what I'd learned, he'd been successful. While the sheriff had been a corrupt law enforcer, Quint had grown up to be a thief.

"Have a seat. This must be Emma," she said. After quick introductions, Bertha told Emma she'd baked cupcakes that were cooling on the kitchen table. "You can put the icing on them if you'd like."

Once Emma raced to the kitchen, I said, "Thanks. I appreciate you giving me time this evening."

"Based on the darkness in those normally pretty blue eyes of yours and the hesitancy in your voice, I assume you've come bearing unwelcome news." Bertha removed the oxygen tube clipped to her nose and rested it on a nearby shaky table. "I needed to learn to breathe on my own again anyway."

"You're a smart woman, and I'm truly sorry to have to deliver this news." I sat on the couch next to her and rubbed her cold hand. Bertha had been putting up a good fight, but the chemo had taken a lot out of her. I worried she didn't have much longer to live.

"Out with it. My son did some foolish things, so don't worry about breaking an old woman's heart. I did the best I could to raise that boy, but when we lost his father, things never did improve. There were some bad influences hanging around." She sighed while glancing at a picture on a shelf across the room. It was a framed photo of her and her husband with Quint when he was a small boy.

"I know with certainty that Quint stole all the jewelry and cash from a few families eight years ago." I paused to let her take in the information. Unmoved, she continued to stare at me. "He roped someone else into hocking a few pieces, then he must've taken off and lived on the profits."

"It makes sense. I got a few expensive gifts in the mail from him shortly after he left last time. Did he continue to steal once he left Braxton?" Her chest heaved up and down with great force.

After Bertha recovered, I said, "I'm not certain, but I suspect he had something to do with the recent string of burglaries. I also know your brother-in-law covered up the original ones."

Bertha expressed sorrow for the son she'd lost when he was a young boy and the one she'd lost once he'd grown up and followed in his devious uncle's footsteps. "Your classic family tragedy. A mother always knows when her son is up to no good even if she can't admit it to anyone else until too late."

"The other person involved years ago is currently talking to Sheriff Montague."

"Do you think this person killed my Quinton?" Bertha's eyes teared.

I handed her a tissue. "No, ma'am. I believe with every fiber of my being he didn't harm your son. But my good friend is the lead detective on this case. I'm confident he will find the real criminal."

"You've been honest with me, Kellan. I appreciate that. You can search Quint's room if you want, though I don't know if you'll unearth anything. One of his friends came by wanting to be close to him one last time," Bertha said, drying her cheeks and reattaching the oxygen tube to her nose. "He hardly kept anything in there. Doubt you'll find much."

I was curious to hear a friend had rummaged through the room. "Do you recall who?"

Bertha closed her eyes and pressed her fingertips together. "She came in right after I finished baking. Mixing the cupcakes had knocked the wind out of me. I told her to just go ahead into his room. I didn't have my glasses with me, and I'd taken a painkiller. I was simply too out of it to remember much."

"Can you describe the girl?"

Bertha couldn't recall any specific features other than she had medium to dark hair. "About the same age as Quinton. I must've fallen asleep. Next thing I remember, you were knocking at the door."

It sounded like Imogene, but when I showed her a picture on my phone that I'd found online, it didn't help. Bertha was tired. It was time for us to leave. I checked Quint's room myself but only found a set of lock picks and other tools he'd used to break into various places. "Is there anything else you can tell me, before we head out?" I waved to Emma, who'd brought an iced cupcake to Bertha.

"Take a few home, sweetie. I don't have any grandchildren. It makes an old woman feel useful to bake them for someone who loves them so much." Bertha reached out and tousled Emma's hair, then turned to me. "Quinton did have some money the last couple of months. He kept paying all the expenses to keep the house up. The Paddingtons offered to pay my medical bills, but I wouldn't let them. My pride stood a little too firm, I suppose. I feel awful that my son stole from them years ago."

"If you remember anything about the woman, please give me a call." Before we left, Bertha confirmed she'd given the Paddington estate keys to her son to return and assumed he'd followed through on the task. We both agreed he must've used them to steal Jennifer's watch. The keys had either gone missing again or Quint tossed them, so they couldn't be traced back to him.

Emma and I left Bertha's place and spent the evening with Nana D. I lacked the energy to update Connor and April on what I'd learned from Bertha. When they contacted the distraught and sick woman, they'd find out. Gabriel confirmed he'd survived the discussion with Connor and promised to call soon to explain how it had gone. Knowing tomorrow was Nana D's first day as the new mayor, I climbed into bed to get some sleep. Then, I noticed a new message arrive on my phone.

Connor: *The Paddingtons sent me the list. This is confidential information. Lots of visitors but only four could've had access. Imogene and Paul brought an engagement present and were left waiting in the Great Hall for a few minutes. Krissy Stanton got lost using the restroom after stopping by to collect a donation for a charity she was sponsoring. Nicky Endicott dropped off a quote for some construction work on the ceiling in the Great Hall, and he was alone while the maid went to get him a glass of water.*

Four people with access, but just because one had dropped a bouquet of black calla lilies near Quint, it didn't mean they'd also killed him. I needed to produce a plan to interrogate everyone myself. Hopefully by morning, the best approach would reveal itself. As I nodded off, I realized tonight had been nine days since the jewelry theft at Lara's place, yet nothing else had happened. Based on the pattern, it should be in progress right now or within the next twelve hours. Would anything happen overnight?

CHAPTER 15

Nana D held her press conference promptly at nine the next morning outside the county administrative building. Mother Nature cooperated by delivering a glorious day with bright sunshine and a soothing seventy-five-degree temperature. It was an almost near-perfect moment, short of Town Councilman Marcus Stanton's rants at the back of the crowd. All four towns in Wharton County had elected a new councilman, which meant there were five new leaders joining the ranks at the half-year mark. What a welcome July had brought in!

I committed to letting Emma attend the inauguration ceremony but planned to drop her off at Woodland Warriors Day Camp later that morning. Lara Bouvier agreed to meet for lunch to discuss the jewelry thefts as long as I promised a quote for her television segment covering Nana D's first day in office. A little quid pro quo never hurt anyone if it focused on sharing information to solve a crime, at least I kept assuring myself that while worrying about what kinds of questions Lara might throw at me.

"Where is she? I can't see her," Emma said as she jumped up and down to get a better view of the coverage. We stood on the sidewalk at the front of the crowd listening to the first speaker, but no one would see Nana D until she stepped through the black curtain and up to the platform. Being five-foot-tall had both advantages and disadvantages, and she kept herself well-hidden until it was her turn to speak.

"Nana D's campaign manager is almost done," I explained, lifting Emma on my shoulders. "She's backstage rehearsing her speech and waiting for a memorable introduction."

Based on the final agenda for her first day in office, Nana D was on a mission to prove she was the best woman for the job. The morning would kick off with a press conference to highlight and thank previous town leaders for their service, followed by a thirty-minute inauguration ceremony where my grandmother would unveil her three-month vision. She'd coordinated an outdoor street fair and lunch where she'd meet and greet all the local business owners, visit the town's homeless shelter, and hold a question-and-answer session for the general population to suggest ideas her office should consider as priority tasks. In lieu of a formal cocktail party—Nana D wasn't a fan of fancy affairs—she invited the local choirs from religious organizations and schools to entertain the crowd over a picnic dinner in Wellington Park. Paddington Enterprises was funding both meals, ensuring no town resources were used to pay for her opening day. To close out the evening, Nana D scheduled her first official meeting with the new town board members for nine o'clock, assuring all citizens that her team wasn't afraid of working late hours to better help Wharton County.

When the outgoing mayor and Nana D's campaign manager finished speaking, and Nana D sauntered to the podium, Emma was the first to squeal and initiate a flurry of applauses. "She looks beautiful!" Emma shouted and bounced jovially on my shoulders. Nana D had dressed for the occasion in a vintage black pantsuit and open-collared strawberry-colored silk blouse. Her long red hair was elegantly braided and wrapped in a small cone shape on the top of her head, covered in black netting, and topped with a magenta-colored rose. She'd even worn her new pink horn-rimmed glasses, and her very presence reminded me of a younger version of a supreme court justice I greatly admired.

"Good morning, Wharton County," Nana D projected into a pumped audience who were thrilled about the potential changes new blood would bring to their cherished towns. "It is officially time to take my oath, and I can think of no one I'd rather see standing beside me than this beloved group of people."

After Judge Grey swore Nana D into office, she thanked her predecessor and offered to share the spotlight with him for the day. Former Mayor Grosvalet declined, citing a need to let the future begin today. Nana D began her speech, covering a few minutes of her background and credentials, a glance at what it took to get her voted into office, and what she promised to deliver in ninety days.

"I am not the type of leader you've had in the last decade. You chose me because you wanted change. And change is what you're going to get...." Nana D gracefully shined a spotlight on the corruption and laziness she'd watched happening all around the county but quickly introduced a focus on eliminating any form of bribery during her term in office. She reminded everyone there would be conflict, but unlike it'd been in the past, it'd now be resolved for the benefit of all citizens.

The horde around us was wild with hope and admiration at my grandmother's stories of the past, as was I until Nana D specifically called me out in the crowd when she talked about the future. "Kellan is the next generation of leadership this county needs, and I plan to work closely with him to ensure folks like him come back home to make Wharton County the top county in Pennsylvania."

I noticed my parents and Eleanor huddled at the back of the animated crowd. Why wasn't Gabriel with them? I wanted to know what'd happened when Gabriel spoke with Connor, but of course, he'd gone into hiding again. When the major activities ended, Emma and I headed to the parking lot, noticing Nana D approaching.

"Eleven o'clock tomorrow morning. My new office, please," she mandated while sidling up and hugging me.

"You were amazing today, but what's this meeting about?" I asked, trepidation in my voice.

"Sheriff Montague will provide a report to me about the Quint Crawford murder investigation. You need to be there." She kissed Emma's forehead and tightened the clip in her hair.

"I'm not sure that's a good idea. I have lots to do, and that won't make April happy to see—"

"You may not be on my staff," she interrupted with a wave of the hand, "but I pay you with enough desserts and a rent-free cottage. You don't have a way out of it unless you'd rather me not bake anymore... besides, you'll just casually show up to see how my second day is going, and *surprise*, the sheriff happens to be there." Nana D gave a severe and shifty glance that said she wasn't joking.

"Doesn't this contradict what you said about bribery an hour ago?"

"Emma, your daddy is a sour grape. I'm promoting you as my new assistant mayor. I expect you to convince him to show up tomorrow," Nana D directed at my daughter as she traipsed away. "Kellan, this wasn't a suggestion. Be a good grandson and do what the mayor tells you to do, brilliant one."

I fought the urge to kick the curb, especially when Emma turned to me and said with a finger pointing in my direction, "Yeah, brilliant one. Mayor Nana D gave you an order. I'd do what she says, or she'll put you in jail." I relinquished, dropped Emma at camp, and met Lara for lunch. It had to be an improvement to my day thus far.

Lara and I huddled up in a corner booth at the Pick-Me-Up Diner. Though somewhere in her mid to late forties, the buxom brunette, also one of the most intelligent people I'd ever met, could easily pass as her daughter's sister. Born to French parents, she'd grown up in the United States and had once been a fashion model before getting entangled with the Grey family.

"An historic day," Lara said, activating a recording device and opening a screen on her tablet to take notes. "Seraphina Danby, first female mayor. Paul Dodd, youngest town councilman. We should be proud of our families."

"Oh, that's right. I forgot, Paul is engaged to your daughter, Imogene. She must be busy planning their wedding and deciding what her position should be as Braxton's First Lady." I laughed at the thought of Braxton having someone in that role. Marcus Stanton had conveniently flaunted his single lifestyle after his wife had passed away several years ago.

"Yes to the wedding. Doubtful to being in the public eye. Imogene is very shy. She must have gotten that particular personality trait from my ex-husband." When Lara laughed, a wrinkle-free face lit up the diner. She was a beautiful and cultured woman, and I could see why she'd garnered

WCLN's lead investigative reporter and co-anchor position on the evening local news.

"I have enjoyed working with Imogene in class. She mentioned taking this course to better understand your job. It must feel great to have a daughter following in your footsteps."

Lara threw a hand up in the air. "Oh, I love her to pieces, but we are vastly different women and have very dissimilar taste in men. I'm just glad she finally accepted Paul's marriage proposal. Hopefully now that Quint Crawford is dead, she will kick the habit of trying to fix the men she dates."

I'd only met Lara a handful of times, but she was much more open than I'd expected. "I am aware Imogene and Quint dated years ago. Wasn't that over in college when he left town?"

"Yes, but she pined for him the whole time. She and Paul have been more off-and-on-again than a Hollywood power couple's rocky marriage. My daughter finally said yes to Paul this spring when she moved back home from France. A week later, she's having lunch with Quint and telling me how much she'd missed him." Lara waved over a waitress to order food.

I waited until the server walked away, then put forth, "Do you think something was going on between your daughter and Quint again?" I couldn't decide how it had fit in with what Emma had overheard at Woodland Warriors regarding someone yelling at Helena about a cheater.

"I'm not one to gossip, and that's not why we're here, is it? Let's stick to the key points today," Lara said, changing the topic to my grandmother. We spent the next thirty minutes discussing Nana D's plans over lunch.

When our plates were cleared and coffee ordered, I resumed the conversation. "You were going to tell me everything you knew about the jewelry thefts, right?"

She nodded. "Tell me why you care. I understand the journalistic need to find answers and seek the truth, but you left that life when you relocated from LA. I'm not entirely sure I understand why, but that's a story for a different day." Lara was direct but fair, an approach most people liked about her.

I took a moment to consider my answer. "Life is about balance. My daughter needed to be around her family, and I wasn't comfortable with some of the influences on the West Coast. In Braxton, I can teach her better values and provide a less stressful lifestyle."

"I assume you're referring to the Castiglianos?" she said, typing away on her tablet. "I'm not going to publicize any of this, so don't worry."

"Thanks. Yes, my in-laws are complex people. When I left the television show, I lost my analytical side. Teaching is fantastic and rewarding but cracking complex puzzles and holding people accountable for their actions is important to me." I'd been trying to find someone who understood my passion for solving crimes. Lara seemed to identify with this inner desire.

"You and I are a lot alike," she responded with a smile. "Maybe we should work together more often. Tell me what you know about the jewelry thefts. I'll fill in the blanks on anything I can clear up about Quint's death. I know they're related somehow."

Could I trust her? I provided a few quick points of interest without revealing anything the sheriff wouldn't want me to disclose nor mentioning Gabriel's role. "As near as I can tell, Quint had something to do with stealing the jewelry. His mother and I had a lengthy conversation about it. Someone visited her yesterday, but Bertha can't remember much about the girl."

"Imogene has always been fond of Bertha. I suppose she might have gone to see her. I'll see if I can find out, but I doubt she had anything to do with the jewelry thefts or Quint's death. The rumors circulating around the station are that Quint was murdered. That electrical issue wasn't an accident."

I shrugged. "I wouldn't know for sure. You'd have to ask the sheriff or Connor Hawkins, the lead detective on the case."

"And your best friend. I can see it on your face. The rumors are true. You wouldn't make a good criminal, Kellan. You can't lie to save your life, but I like that about you," Lara said, peeling the lid off a non-fat dairy creamer container and pouring it into her coffee. "I'll tell you what I've uncovered about the missing jewelry."

Lara explained everything that had happened at her house the previous week. Imogene admired a tiara her grandmother on the Grey side had given to her years ago. She wanted to incorporate it into her wedding ensemble and planned to bring it to the bridal salon for consideration. She'd been living at the Grey estate where she'd kept the family heirloom safely tucked away, but she'd planned to spend the night at Lara's place the night of Nana D's seventy-fifth birthday party. She'd also brought the tiara with her, so she could go directly to the wedding salon the next morning. Lara had been doing a news segment at Nana D's party, and Paul was at his house working on his plans as the new town councilman. A noise had woken Imogene while she was napping, and she thought it was her mother coming back home. When she got up to check, it was dusk, and she had trouble seeing from the glare of the setting sun. Someone knocked her over and tried to run out the door. She knew the layout of the room better than the thief, and when she was trying to escape, he tripped over her again. She struggled with him, scratched his arm, and he whacked her on the head with a bowl from a nearby table.

"Who do you think it is?"

Lara sat back and turned off the tape recorder, unwilling to say anything that might hurt her daughter while being recorded. "Imogene wouldn't inform the police, but she told me that very few people knew she'd kept the tiara that night. A couple of family members at the Grey estate, but they could've stolen it at any time in the past. She was afraid it was one of her friends."

"You think it was Quint, don't you?"

"She'd had lunch with him that day, and he'd asked her to give him another chance. He wanted her to break up with Paul, but Imogene needed time to think about it. Paul made her feel safe and offered her a future without worrying about money or what people would think."

"Quint must have been angry. Could he have stolen the tiara to make her feel afraid, perhaps to sell it for money to support them? Does she have her own money from the Grey family?" Whoever confronted Helena at the camp must've been talking about Imogene cheating on Paul, at least it seemed the best explanation so far. Maybe Emma had gotten it backward. Was Krissy upset about Imogene and Quint hanging out? Perhaps she'd been interested in Quint herself just as she had been years ago.

Lara shook her head. "Not a lot. It's all in a trust for when she turns forty. In the Grey family, you must prove your worth before Hiram will let a penny go to the next generation. He's a tyrant, and that's ultimately why my marriage to his son never worked out."

I sipped coffee and processed Lara's news. "Do you think Imogene told Paul that Quint asked her to get back together?"

"Paul is focused on his new role in shaping the future of Wharton County. He's loved her for a decade, but Quint coming back made him nervous. I asked Imogene if she confessed to her fiancé what Quint had requested of her, but she wouldn't tell me. Ever since Quint died, she's been a shell of her former self. As much as I didn't want him with my daughter, I could see how much she loved Quint. He made her feel like a queen among women." Lara's phone began to vibrate, and she took the call.

While she spoke to her boss at the station, I paid the bill. Could Lara have been worried about Quint hurting her daughter and taken matters into her own hands?

After she ended her call, she stood. "I need to go. My boss moved up a deadline, and I must interview someone today. Don't worry, it has nothing to do with what we spoke about."

"Lara, when did Imogene tell you that Quint asked her to break up with Paul?" If Lara had known before Quint died, it might give me cause to worry about her honesty.

"Ha! If you're angling to find a way if I killed the loser, you can stop right there. I didn't like Quint Crawford, and I sure as heck didn't want the man anywhere near Imogene. But I have my limits. I would've hired someone to beat the crap out of him if I'd been able to prove he was the one who'd attacked her in my home. I'm not gonna call people like your in-laws to permanently whack him, though." Lara leaned in to kiss my cheek, then smiled when she pulled away. "I leave that kinda stuff to your family, darling."

"You're a riot, Lara. Hold up, before you go," I said, preparing to leave with her. "Since we both believe Quint was the current thief, and it looks like someone might have intentionally electrocuted or killed him, who's at the top of your list?"

"I don't believe for a minute it was Paul. As I said, he's all about his life in politics now. Krissy Stanton has always been a thorn in my daughter's side, and her father was incredibly angry about Quint telling people he'd been stiffed by the Stantons for work he'd done. If I didn't have this other story, I'd be focusing on the Stantons and Nicky Endicott. Nicky only hired Quint because they were old friends, but Imogene said they fought all the time about the construction business."

After Lara left, I made some notes on my phone while waiting for the hostess to check if Eleanor was available. Her office door had been closed, and I didn't want to interrupt if she was meeting with someone. The waitress returned to the front counter and said, "She had to pick up a few things at the supply store that didn't come in on time this week. Eleanor won't be back until later this afternoon."

"Got it, thanks. I saw the door shut and thought she was on the phone."

"No, Chef Manny is on a break. He's inside with his wife," she noted and left to clear a table.

Wife? Had Eleanor spoken with him about the conversation I'd overheard? She never updated me, but knowing my sister, she'd endlessly berated him. I was curious myself about what was going on and decided to poke my head in to say hello. Emma adored Chef Manny, and if he was leaving town, I wanted to know.

"Who's there?" Manny said after I knocked on the door.

"It's Kellan. Just wanted to say hello."

When the door opened, I did a double take at the person standing next to Manny. "Raquel?" What was one of my students doing with Eleanor's chef?

Raquel stepped forward and draped her arm around Manny's waist. "Hi, Dr. Ayrwick. Have you met my husband, Manny Salvado?"

I stood stunned for a moment, then realized my mouth had hung open a few too many seconds. "I never expected to see you two together. I'm sorry. Just a brief state of confusion." He'd recently gotten married to someone from out of town. Raquel indicated she was new in town and waiting for her husband to figure out some things with his job. The conclusion made complete sense now. Except, was I about to lose a student and Eleanor a chef? "Congratulations to you both. I confess, Manny, I overheard you the other day talk about getting married and potentially moving to Las Vegas." I inhaled deeply and leaned against the doorjamb when they backed into the office. Could I ask about their future plans?

Raquel looked as if she realized she might have given too much away when we'd spoken. "Maybe I should leave you two alone. I have some errands to run." Raquel kissed Manny's cheek and told her husband she'd see him at home that evening.

Once she was gone, I turned to Manny. "So, has Eleanor confronted you? I mean... you have to do what's best for you, but she'd really miss you."

Manny waved me in and shut the door. "This marriage thing is new to me, Kellan. I really like her, but I might be in over my head. I don't know what to do." A few lines around the corner of Manny's mouth offered significant concern over the situation he'd found himself in. Earlier that spring, he and his buddies had taken a trip to Las Vegas after the previous owners of the diner had sold it to Eleanor. He was certain she would fire him and hire her own staff. He and his friends had hung out with a few girls at a club all night. Raquel was one of the girls, and they'd gotten together several times that week. On his last night, they hit the strip to party before returning home, and his friends had dared him to do shots most of the night. The next morning, he and Raquel woke up in bed with matching wedding rings.

"My friends were a little hazy on how it happened, but they were at the all-night chapel with us when we went through with the ceremony," he spit out, slapping his hand to his forehead with a pervasive thud I could feel across the room.

Wow! I thought what happened in Vegas was supposed to stay in Vegas. I guess not. "Do you love her?" His mixed nod and shrug told me he had no clue. "I assume if she's here, that means she's moved in with you. Is Raquel pressuring you to leave town?"

"Not exactly. She has bigger ideas about what she wants to accomplish in life. Raquel's been staying here for a few weeks, then heads home to visit her family and friends." He cracked his knuckles and looked at the ceiling in silent prayer. Then, he admitted that Eleanor still didn't know the truth.

"What do you plan to do?"

"For now, I guess, we're bicoastal until we decide the best solution. Raquel is trying to hook me up with some folks back home where I could get a job in one of the big restaurants. My family would kill me if I got a divorce. They're deeply religious." Manny explained that they've been chilly toward his wife because of the lack of a traditional wedding. "Can you talk to your sister?"

It wasn't my job, but the guy looked desperate. "I'll think about it. For now, don't say anything. If she asks you, though, you have to tell her the truth."

Once Manny acknowledged my advice and gave me a huge bear hug that almost cracked my ribs, I left Eleanor's office and grabbed my phone. I'd felt it buzzing in my pocket earlier but couldn't check while learning Manny's news.

When I listened to the voicemail, I felt the weight of doom lurking on my doorstep. Marcus had left me a message "Kellan, we need to discuss these jewelry thefts. I have proof that your brother has just stolen something from my family, and I am giving you the courtesy of a heads-up call before I turn this matter over to the police. I have a proposal to make, and if you're smart, you'll accept it without any questions. You have until five o'clock to return my call, or I'm contacting Sheriff Montague."

CHAPTER 16

"I completely forgot, thank you so much," I replied to the mother of one of Emma's friends. The girls had gymnastics practice at seven this evening, and we'd agreed to share transportation responsibilities. I called Woodland Warriors to let them know who would meet Emma at camp this afternoon since I'd be picking up the girls when they finished at eight thirty. As always, I was grateful when the school requested the secret codeword to prove who I was before they would agree to let Emma leave with someone else. Next, I texted Helena Roarke and her teacher to confirm release authorization. This day and age, one could never be *too* careful.

I agreed to meet Marcus at his house, which was next door to Nana D's farm, Danby Landing. Although his siblings lived in the family estate on Millionaire's Mile, he'd bought his own place years ago. I had no idea what the man wanted, but undoubtedly, it would be a dangerous meeting. He was on the warpath after his loss to Nana D in the election, and if he had something on Gabriel, it would be difficult to talk Marcus out of whatever cunning plan he'd concocted.

I pulled up to his house just as the cell phone Cristiano had given me began to ring. I couldn't ignore it, so I pressed accept and greeted him.

"It's Francesca," my wife said in a calm voice. "Cristiano thought you'd want to hear from me."

"Hi," I said with dire hesitancy in my voice as I stepped outside the SUV. "Is everything okay?"

"I'm fine. Cristiano set a time for the meeting. He'll release me unharmed, if my parents deliver everything he asks for in his next request: All the evidence of any past wrongdoing on the part of Las Vargas, a signed agreement officially turning over fifty-one percent of Castigliano International to his family, and a videotaped promise they will not seek any retribution or revenge." Francesca sounded as if she were negotiating a business deal and not the terms of her own release.

"Will your parents actually do that?" The volume of the concessions was astronomical. Of course, Francesca would be worth it to them, but something didn't feel right about this deal.

"They have no choice. Cristiano's father has made it clear that he expects his son to get rid of me permanently if my parents do not acquiesce." Francesca paused to speak with Cristiano, then returned to our call. "I haven't spoken with them in three months, Kellan. I need you to tell them how important it is that they do this. I don't want to suffer the consequences."

"I understand. Tell me where and when, and I'll make sure they show up." I couldn't let them harm my wife. I knew things had changed between us, but she didn't deserve to die because of what her parents had done over the years. "I'll protect you." Stress and fear plummeted inside me until they knocked my body out of balance and sent me careening against the stone pillar in the Stanton driveway.

"Cristiano wants to speak with you now," Francesca said, abandoning the call.

"I told you we were close to a solution, Kellan. If you listen carefully and obey every instruction I give you, this will all be done tomorrow night." Cristiano's smooth voice was not a comfort, despite his intentions. He told me that Francesca had left the room, so we could speak openly.

"Just tell me what to do, okay?" I refrained from letting my voice expose apprehension. The perspiration forming under my arms was enough of a reminder. "I'll drag the Castiglianos at gunpoint to your meeting spot, if I have to."

"That's just it, you won't need to worry about that. I've got a much simpler solution in mind." Cristiano explained that he wanted me to collect the evidence from the Castiglianos ahead of time. Most of it would be saved electronically on a storage device. Any physical copies, other than the agreement signing over their business, were to be destroyed.

"Then what?"

"Tomorrow evening at nine o'clock, you will meet me at a specific location for the exchange," Cristiano replied.

"Fine. That gives me just over twenty-four hours. Where do you want to meet?" I checked my calendar to confirm tomorrow's schedule and decided I'd ask my parents to watch Emma for the evening.

"I'll let you know thirty minutes before the meeting. I can't have you sharing that location with anyone in advance. I've seen how much time you've been spending with the sheriff lately. I wonder what your wife would think about that budding relationship." Cristiano must have smirked because a sinister sound emanated through the phone.

"It's not what you think. We're working on something else together—"

"I don't care to know the details. If you tell April Montague anything about this conversation, or any cops or FBI agents show up near the drop-off point, the deal is over. You, your wife, and your daughter will discover what it's like to swim in the middle of Crilly Lake with your feet and hands shackled together in iron cuffs and a plastic bag tied around each of your heads." Cristiano said nothing else and waited for me to respond.

"Your instructions are crystal clear, Cristiano. You're also the scum of the earth." I couldn't control my temper and pounded my fist against the stone pillar. "But I will do what you ask."

"I'm really not like my family. I've told you before that we could be friends in another life. I'm carrying out orders from my father, just as you're carrying them out for me. I'm the middleman in this predicament." Cristiano verified the timing of his plan and hung up the phone.

I stood at the end of the driveway absorbing the severity of the situation while blood trickled down my hands. My life had suddenly turned into one of the *Godfather* movies, but there was no character I could conjure in my mind that would assure me things would end up okay. I called the Castiglianos to relay the instructions. Vincenzo indicated he and Cecilia would have what I needed the following morning. We agreed to meet at noon for the first exchange.

I stared at my personal cell phone feeling desperate to call April with the details of the plan, but if I told her anything, Cristiano would kill Francesca. I wasn't sure which risk was the bigger one to take, but I had little time to decide. Marcus Stanton barreled down his driveway, anger in his voice.

"What took you so long? I have important things to do. Are you prepared to protect your little brother, Kellan?" Marcus, an early-sixty-something louse with a penchant for much younger women, had two features people ruthlessly gossiped about—eternally sweaty hands and a thinning pompadour that had seen better days. Neither short nor tall, thin nor fat, he was the preeminent plain and dull man except for those notable exceptions. Unfortunately, he thought much more highly of himself.

"Listen, Stanton. I've had a heck of a day already, and let me assure you," I blasted while stomping directly up to his face. "You are the least of my concerns right now. My brother hasn't done anything wrong, and if you've got any evidence, I'd bet my last dollar it's been manufactured by one of your lackeys. I'm getting close to throttling the next idiot that threatens me. You want to test my patience? Bring. It. On." The fury inside me must have been percolating for months. I knew better than to release it in a physical manner, but I could unleash a nasty verbal tirade on him if necessary.

Marcus stepped back with a genuine look of fear formulating in his demeanor. "I'm certain we can work out a mutually acceptable deal. There's no need to get agitated."

Noticing his retreat, I willed myself to calm down so that we could have a productive conversation. "What is this so-called evidence you have?" Yanking a tissue from my pocket, I pressed it to my bloody hand.

Marcus handed me a photograph of Gabriel from the Stanton home security system. "Look at the timestamp."

"It was taken at eight forty-seven this morning," I replied, studying the photo to understand was transpiring in the scene. "It looks like my brother is standing on your front doorstep. What about it?" I'd been wondering why Gabriel hadn't shown up for Nana D's inauguration ceremony, but I figured I could've missed him if he'd hung out somewhere else. I reminded myself to call my mother when I was done with Stanton to ask her to watch Emma the next night. My memory was shot lately.

"I left the house this morning at eight fifteen to attend Seraphina's little press conference. My daughter was with me, and Krissy can verify what I'm about to tell you." His face was reddening like a tomato as he spoke. Whether it was his temper, anxiety, or the warmer weather, I couldn't be sure. Nor did I care.

"Out with it, please. I don't have all day." I tapped my foot impatiently, waiting for him to get the point.

"Krissy got home at ten o'clock. She had a headache and couldn't be out in the sun. When she arrived, she found the safe unlocked and its door wide open. I'd kept cash and several pieces of my late wife's jewelry inside. It was all missing!" He threw his hands to his hips and glared at me.

"What does that prove? Gabriel must've stopped by to see Krissy, but she was with you downtown." My tolerance level was at its peak, and if he kept pushing me, he wouldn't like the results.

Marcus handed me a second picture. "Look at this one. It's from a side camera just three minutes later. Your brother was peering through my kitchen window."

"Okay, so he was persistent. How did he supposedly get inside?"

"When I got home to check for myself, I found a whole bunch of glass underneath the window in the mudroom around back. I don't have a camera there, so I can't show you another picture. But there are several footprints. Someone broke in during the two hours Krissy and I were gone."

"And you think it was my brother? This isn't proof. Let me see this glass," I said, marching past him up the driveway. His information didn't make sense unless the thief was breaking the nine-day pattern. The theft was supposed to have occurred yesterday. Gabriel may not have been with us at the inauguration, but I wasn't going to jump to any conclusions about his guilt. After our last conversation, he'd convinced me he was innocent.

Marcus came running after me. "I called you because we can work this out privately. If you get Gabriel to return what he stole, I won't press charges. But there's one more condition."

I walked around his house, ignoring his words. When I arrived at the broken window, I noticed all the glass was on the outside. Four large shards would fill ninety percent of the hole in the window. A few small pieces were scattered in the flowerbeds, but from what I could tell, the window had been broken by someone standing on the inside. Most of the glass wouldn't be on the ground outside. Either Marcus was trying to con me, or someone else with a key had stolen the items from his house, then broken the window to make it look like a robbery. Could Marcus have done it himself? Or was Krissy involved? Based on what I'd overheard, and what Lara had told me, either scenario was entirely possible.

Although I'd eventually call his bluff, I decided to play ball for a few more minutes. "Sure, we can keep this between us. What is it you want?"

"Convince your grandmother to step down from the mayor's office. She can recommend me as the replacement. I was the other candidate, and people won't want to wait for another election." Marcus smiled like a kid in a candy shop, only this kid wasn't one anybody should ever trust.

"How do you expect me to do that? No one will believe Nana D decided to quit after all the effort she put in to get this position. Seriously?" Was the man losing his mind?

Marcus kept urging me to consider his deal, threatening to call the cops without delay if I didn't agree. "It happens more than you think. Seraphina could claim she had a health scare, or maybe she has to leave town to visit one of your uncles wherever they're living these days."

Nana D's two sons, my interesting yet peculiar uncles, traveled for work. Zachary, a big-game and wildlife veterinarian, currently studied African elephant migration for the summer, and Campbell was on a covert humanitarian mission in the Amazon jungle. We hadn't heard from either in months, but that wasn't unusual due to their intense work and frequent isolation from society.

"I'm calling your bluff, Marcus. For one thing, you haven't mentioned anything about a calla lily. One had been left at all the previous crimes, so something doesn't feel right here. For another...." I explained the inaccuracy of the position of the glass, then told him I had a better deal to make.

His eyes darkened, and he kicked a pile of nearby dirt. "Don't try to mess with me, Kellan. I've still got pull in this town, and just because she's the mayor doesn't mean Sheriff Montague will listen to your nana. The sheriff follows the law, and if she thinks Gabriel is responsible, she'll arrest him. Especially since the last time we talked, the jewelry thefts were connected to the Crawford murder."

"That ship has sailed already. What I find most interesting is your family's potential role in Quint's death. How about you tell me where you were the night Quint electrocuted himself? Or how about Krissy? I overheard a conversation that leads me to believe she knows more than she's said." I shoved my sticky hands in my pocket and began to walk to the front of the house, knowing the rat would follow and beg for more information.

"I was in a late-night meeting with our former mayor. You can check with his assistant about it. I had nothing to do with Crawford's death," Marcus growled, chasing quickly behind me but unable to maintain my pace.

When I got to the SUV, I turned around and calmly asked, "Then, you weren't trying to get revenge for Quint telling people you never paid for his construction services? If that's the case, maybe April Montague will summon your daughter to the sheriff's office for a discussion."

"Nicholas Endicott was paid in full two days before the election. If I wanted to kill Quint, don't you think I would have done it sooner to stop him from spreading any negativity about me?" Marcus clamped a beefy hand on the SUV door so that I couldn't open it.

"It's time for me to leave. Get your hands off—"

"Krissy assuredly has an alibi for that night. Maybe she saw a calla lily today too. I'll discuss it with her, and we can close this matter. Don't you go thinking we're done with this negotiation. As soon as I confirm Krissy is in the clear, even though I know my daughter is innocent, I'll take these photos to the police. You have until tomorrow at noon to accept my terms, Kellan." Marcus waggled his finger inches from my nose and reiterated his point before plodding back up his driveway and pulling out his cell phone.

April was supposed to follow up on the feud between Quint, Nicky, and Marcus on the unpaid construction work, but I was certain Stanton wouldn't have lied to me. He had to know I could easily check his alibi, so I temporarily believed him when he said he had nothing to do with Quint's murder. I wasn't as convinced about his daughter's innocence and had to find a way to get her to talk to me in a public setting. Why had the thief waited an extra day to execute the last robbery?

I checked with Gabriel to understand what he'd been doing at the Stanton house that morning. When he answered on the first ring, I could hear shouting in the background. "Where are you? Some sports game?"

Gabriel asked me to hold on for a second, then reconnected twenty seconds later. "Sorry, I was just leaving Kirklands. I met Nicky for a drink after work."

My watch indicated it was already six o'clock. The day was going by way too quickly. Gabriel explained that Krissy had texted him the night before to ask for a ride to the inauguration ceremony because she had lent her car to Tiffany, who had sent hers to the shop for a seatbelt recall. "Did you notice any broken glass around one of the windows?"

Gabriel said he didn't, but he also had only looked at the front and side windows. "I thought it was strange that she asked me to pick her up at eight forty-five and wasn't around this morning. I waited in my car for a few minutes, but I didn't want to be late to Nana D's ceremony. Krissy never answered the doorbell or my calls, so I left."

"Okay, thanks. Listen, Marcus Stanton might be making trouble for you, so just be careful. How'd it go with the sheriff and Connor?" Why did Krissy ask Gabriel to pick her up, then go with her father instead? What was she up to?

"Fine. They haven't decided what to do about my involvement in the jewelry thefts from eight years ago, but the sheriff promised she wouldn't be letting it go easily. I'm not allowed to leave town or discuss it with anyone else except for you. What's up with that?"

"Another time, brother. I can't get into it." And I couldn't because even I didn't know anymore. "I'll call you tomorrow. I've got a lot of crazy stuff going on, and I need to find Krissy."

"Hold up. Krissy might still be here with Tiffany. They were drinking a few tables away from me. I was gonna confront her on my way out to ask why she blew me off this morning, but then you called. Want me to interrupt her?" Gabriel asked.

"No, I'll head over there. I don't need to pick up Emma for another couple of hours. Thanks." After I hung up, I drove to the bar. On the way, I called my mother to beg her to watch Emma the following night. She had just gotten home from work and was waiting for my father to get back with a pizza he'd gone to pick up. My mother hated waiting for the delivery folks to show up, as the food was always cold. Of course, she was excited to watch Emma. "I appreciate it, Mom. You're the best."

"I'll collect Emma at the bus stop at seven o'clock, but I have a late meeting with a prospective student at eight. Emma could hang out in the conference room for a bit. I don't expect it to go too long."

It would be better if Emma was concealed on campus with my mother while I was somewhere else meeting Cristiano and Francesca for the exchange. After we disconnected, I informed Woodland Warriors that Emma would take the late bus home tomorrow from day camp. By the time I reached Kirklands, I was starving. I walked into the bar and found Tiffany sitting by herself.

"Hey, I haven't seen you in a few days." I gestured a harried-looking bartender to order a burger with everything on it and a large ginger ale, then turned back to Tiffany. "Can I get you anything?"

She declined. "You just missed your brother. He was here with Nicky and some work colleagues, but they all took off. How's everything?"

"Not so good," I said, sipping from my glass and dropping a napkin on my lap. "I was told Krissy Stanton was here, and I need to speak with her."

"Good luck. She snuck out the back when your brother stepped outside. I think she's avoiding him. Besides, she's on her way out of town," Tiffany said with a hint of annoyance in her voice.

"Wait, what do you mean?"

"I met her for a drink and to return her car. She was going to let me borrow it for a few days, but something urgent popped up and she needed it back right away," Tiffany said, then hopped off the barstool and collected her purse from the undercounter hook. "Gotta head out. Take care."

"Before you go, do you know why she's leaving town?" I had my suspicions but wanted confirmation before taking any action. Things were starting to fall into place based on what had happened at the Stanton household today.

"I guess it doesn't matter if she's leaving town. I can tell you what she told me." Tiffany signaled the bartender for another drink and mentioned that it should go on my tab. "Krissy wanted to say goodbye before she hightailed it out of Braxton. She was worried about something, but I don't know exactly what it's all about. She dumped a lot of drama on me tonight."

"Did she give you any names or details you can share?"

"Krissy confessed that she'd been trying to snare Quint ever since he returned to Braxton a few months ago. His death had been a lot harder on her than she'd admitted last week."

If my assumptions were correct, Krissy must have figured out Quint had stolen all the jewelry and had taken it harshly. Could she have killed him in a struggle at the cable car trying to convince him to turn himself in? "Did she say anything about why she had to leave so quickly?"

"Just that no one understood her. I guess she was angry with Imogene too. Apparently, Quint was still in love with Imogene and wouldn't commit to Krissy. My guess is Krissy's tired of all the chaos in her life and needed a break." Tiffany explained that Krissy had a crush on Quint back in college, but he had been dating Imogene, so she'd backed away sophomore year. When Imogene had split up with Quint and chosen Paul, Krissy thought she had a chance. Then, Quint left town without telling anyone why. Krissy had always blamed Imogene for driving Quint away from Braxton. She didn't know that he'd been stealing all the jewelry and needed to escape based on his uncle's shenanigans and blackmail.

"It must have been hard on her. Do you think she's already skipped town, or can I catch her?"

Tiffany threw her hands in the air, extricating herself from the conversation. "Who knows? My Uber is outside. You might be able to catch her tomorrow. She mentioned something about a quick trip to the bank in the afternoon before she could head out of town."

As Tiffany left, my burger arrived. While I ate dinner, I ran through a number of theories. Bertha had said a girl showed up at the house and was in Quint's room. It was either Krissy or Imogene, but I couldn't be sure which one. Imogene could've wanted to say a permanent goodbye before she fully committed to Paul. Maybe Krissy found the jewels Quint had stolen and took them with her to the bank for safe keeping. What I wasn't certain about was whether she planned to turn them over to the police or to get rid of them, so Quint's memory wasn't further sullied with proof of his crimes. I just couldn't figure out how the latest situation with Marcus that morning fit in. Was he lying to me, or had something changed Krissy's plans to attend the inauguration with Gabriel? Either way, who'd broken into the Stanton house and taken the cash and jewelry from the safe?

I was flipping through my phone to call Krissy when Siobhan Walsh and Nicky Endicott gallivanted into the bar and grabbed a corner table. He pulled out her chair and kissed her on the lips before taking his own seat. Gabriel had said Nicky was always out with a new girl but seeing him with Siobhan was startling. What kind of scheme were those two cooking up together?

CHAPTER 17

I paid for my meal and sauntered over to Nicky and Siobhan's table, curious to find out for myself whether it had anything to do with Quint's death or the missing jewelry. I still didn't have confirmation about Siobhan's supposed visit to the doctor at the same time Quint was being murdered.

"What a surprise to see you two together. I stopped in for a drink and was just about to leave when you both sat down." I tucked the credit card receipt in my pocket and waited for their reply.

"Hey, Dr. Ayrwick," Siobhan began with a minute fluster and flash of panic. "We're on a date. I met Nicky when he came to stain some beadboard in my living room last week, and we hit it off."

"That dark stain you picked was perfect for the room." Nicky had a sneer forming on his face. "She's a delightful woman. I'm excited to spend more time with her," he said, reaching for her hand.

"As long as you don't cut yourself and bleed on my floor again," Siobhan quipped.

If what he'd just revealed was true, Nicky's fingers might not have been stained black from spray-painting a calla lily, and he hadn't gotten his injury from attacking Imogene and stealing the tiara at Lara's place. He might not be the secret accomplice. "I won't keep you guys, just wanted to ask a couple of questions." I turned to Siobhan and said, "My mother mentioned the twins have been sick a lot. She was worried when you had to go to the hospital last week. Everything okay?"

Siobhan nodded. "Yes, my son was fine, but my daughter had croup. It's common, but I couldn't get in to see the pediatrician. I was so glad the clinic remained open at that hour."

"Really? Which one did you go to? I'd love to have a back-up in case Emma is ever sick, and I don't want to go to the emergency room." It sounded like a logical statement, and in truth, I should have a better back-up than Nana D's old-fashioned remedies.

"Downtown, near the Pick-Me-Up Diner," Siobhan said, pulling her hand away from Nicky's.

"Kids. Always a worry, huh?" He seemed disinterested as he gazed around the room for a server.

"True, they get sick often. Does the clinic always stay open late? I guess it was busy, huh?"

Siobhan looked at Nicky and offered an apology for the interruption to their date, then grabbed her purse. "I think I still have the invoice. It wasn't that crowded," she said, then retrieved an envelope and pulled out the bill. "Says that I paid at twelve-thirty in the morning, and the hours of operation are... hold on, let me check... they closed for new patients by midnight. I was the last person to leave there."

Based on her timing, she was at the clinic and couldn't have been at the cable car confronting Quint. I supposed someone else could have taken the twins to the hospital and was covering for her, but I couldn't see Siobhan murdering a man for potentially leading her on. When I asked her about it, she acknowledged she'd been angry, but a few days later, she and Nicky had gone on their first date. "Aye, I got over Quint pretty quickly. I am not the kind of woman to go around killing men for being cads!"

After Nicky confirmed he had been near the cable car station and had dropped his running gloves the morning I'd found Quint's body, I realized he probably hadn't been the one to kill the man. I needed to be certain, so I asked about the unpaid bill with Marcus. "Do you think Quint's decision to go public had anything to do with Stanton losing the race? Was Marcus angry enough to seek revenge on Quint?"

He looked surprised at my inquiry but recuperated quickly. "Paul Dodd and I were talking about that earlier. Stanton was neck and neck with your grandmother for a while, but when Quint began telling people, Marcus did experience a shift in his numbers." While Nicky ordered drinks for him and Siobhan, I planned my next questions.

"Marcus was yelling about it this afternoon. Told me he paid the bill to you right away, that the confusion was on Quint's part because he didn't know you'd already taken care of it."

Nicky nodded. "Quint never was good with the accounting side of the business. He thought because he'd gotten Krissy to convince her father to use him as the contractor that he'd get the full amount from Stanton. It was through my company, and it took a few days to sort that all out."

"I guess once that was fixed, everything turned out okay, huh?" I wasn't sure what else to ask but felt like something obvious was at my fingertips.

"Yeah, Marcus tried to get a discount, as usual. Claimed that his daughter was helping Quint with all the work. Krissy was just interested in learning about the business, even followed me on a couple of jobs to understand how to do basic electrical work. She found the whole thing enthralling for some reason.

We good, man?" Nicky clearly wanted me to leave, so he could proceed with his date.

I wished them goodnight and headed back to my SUV. Everything was pointing to Krissy now. If she'd been knowledgeable about electrical work, was she savvy enough to cause a power issue in the cable car that knocked out Quint? When he didn't die from the initial injury, did she then decide to strangle him? It was looking more like I'd found the culprit, prompting me to chat with April as soon as possible to discuss our next steps.

After leaving Kirklands, I picked up Emma and her friend at the gymnastics facility, then dropped her friend off at home. Emma and I took the puppy for a walk and played with him for a few minutes. I was grateful one of Nana D's farmhands would stop by twice each day to walk Baxter while Emma and I were at work or camp. Once we were finished tiring out the adorable little beast, Emma complained that she was so exhausted, she could sleep for an eternity. My daughter climbed into bed and passed on our normal story time. It was okay to skip it occasionally, and I had an urgent call to make. April needed to know what had happened with Marcus and Cristiano earlier that day. And I deserved to talk to someone who was on my side for a change.

* * *

"Are you okay, Daddy? You look funny," Emma said while we waited for the bus to pick her up Wednesday morning. I'd considered driving her to camp but didn't want her to think there was anything out of the ordinary about today.

"Of course, sweetheart. It's just a really big day at work for me. You know how much I love you, right?" I cradled her warm cheek and kissed her forehead, silently willing the universe to protect her. "I'll do anything necessary to keep this amazing smile on your face."

"I know. You're the best. Sometimes I think about Mommy and get sad that she went to Heaven. I'll see her again one day." Emma gripped the back of my neck and held on tightly. "Way in the future because I'm gonna live forever."

"That's true. You're gonna be as old as Nana D one day, and promise me, you'll never forget that I tried to do the best things possible for you, okay?" I let Emma pull away from me as the bus arrived, then grabbed her for one final hug to give me the strength to do what needed to be done. If everything went according to plan that night, Francesca might be back in our lives. "Remember, Grandma will pick you up on the late bus today. She's gonna take you to her office at Admissions Hall."

Emma waved as she boarded the bus, then turned around giggling. "See ya tonight! Tell Baxter I love him."

Sixty seconds later, the yellow school bus was just a trailing vision in the distance. My eyes were brimming with the desire to cry, but I forced the tears back into their hidden state. Desperation clung to my soul for one of my grandmother's trademark hugs.

After finishing some work for an upcoming class, I arrived at the downtown administrative offices to update Nana D with Cristiano's plan.

"It'll work out, Kellan. God is looking out for this family, and you've been through the wringer more than enough for the Castigliano family. If there were ever someone who could negotiate terms to fix past mistakes, I believe it's you." Nana D had more strength in her arms than she had in her words that morning, and her message had been super loud, utterly clear, and difficult to top. "Don't do anything foolish. Trust your instincts."

"Scout's Honor," I said, as an aide knocked on the door to Nana D's new mayoral office to let us know that April had arrived.

As she entered the room, April jerked her head. "What are you doing here?"

When I'd called April the night before to strategize about the meeting with the Castiglianos and Las Vargas, I neglected to reveal my plan to attend her conference with Nana D. We'd focused on how to communicate today to ensure my safety and offer the best chances of Francesca's imminent return. I'd saved all the news I'd been collecting about Quint's death, including Krissy's potential guilt, for today's encounter. "I sent Emma to camp this morning and needed someone to tell me tonight would turn out fine," I replied, feeling guilty about the small lie. I had no strength to fight with April about anything else.

"I understand." April rubbed my shoulder. "Your family has your back, and that's a good thing."

Nana D narrowed her eyes at the discussion with April but wisely kept her thoughts to herself. "I'd like Kellan to stay while we discuss the jewelry thefts and Quint Crawford's murder. He's been instrumental in past investigations and knows the players. Any concerns, Sheriff Montague?"

April pursed her lips ready to disagree, then pulled up a chair and sat near the desk. "Not at all, Mayor Danby. I'm confident Kellan will keep anything we discuss in this room to himself. His intuitions have been helpful to date."

April wasn't backing down because she was afraid of Nana D. As two primary leaders protecting Wharton County, the women had a certain respect for each other. April was biding time to present objections at the right time. This conversation would do little harm regarding the open cases we were investigating.

Nana D asked April to summarize what she'd done to date. Once finished, we decided the scratches that the coroner had identified on Quint's body had come from Imogene's attack when he'd burglarized her mother's place. Based on the timing the coroner had specified, it was a perfect match. I'd been hoping they'd come from an accomplice, someone who might've then turned around and killed Quint two days later. I wasn't that lucky. Nana D then asked me to provide any working theories or new information I'd obtained since my last conversation with the sheriff. I said, "Based on everything we've heard to date, we know Quint stole the jewelry eight years ago. Gabriel might've helped him leave Braxton and hock some of the items at the San Francisco pawn shop, but he doesn't appear to have profited from it. Quint took all the money when they parted ways."

April nodded and folded her hands in her lap. "I believe Quint returned to town to take care of his sick mother and saw an opportunity to steal more jewelry. Based on his anger over mothers interfering in their daughters' lives, he recreated the crimes with the same families. I suspect there was an accomplice this time too, as security was more heightened and complicated to avoid."

"Krissy Stanton is probably that accomplice, and she seems resolute to leave town. Marcus might be involved too." I told Nana D and April about the blackmail attempt over Gabriel's visit to the Stanton house. "He gave me roughly twenty hours, and the deadline is coming up shortly. I expect him to contact the Wharton County Sheriff's Office by early afternoon."

"I don't have enough to do anything other than bring in Krissy for questions at this point. Yes, she has knowledge of electrical construction. Yes, she might've visited Quint's bedroom and taken something from it. Yes, you overheard that Imogene can place her near the cable car that night," April explained, the frustration in her voice clear and deep.

"Can you put a tail on her?" Nana D suggested, pacing the room. "Stop her from leaving town?"

"We have to do things in the right order, Mayor Danby. As soon as we're done here, I will speak with Detective Connor Hawkins about his previous interviews with Imogene and Krissy." April explained verification of Tiffany and Helena's attendance at a midnight movie while Quint was being killed.

With alibis for the time of Quint's murder confirmed for Siobhan, Nicky, Helena, and Tiffany, we were left with Gabriel, Krissy, Paul, and Imogene as the only other potential suspects. "We know Gabriel didn't do it even if no one can verify his whereabouts when Quint had been strangled. Paul and Imogene are a possibility even though it's not likely based on Lara Bouvier's input. I suppose if Paul had found out Quint was the one who accosted his fiancée, he might have sought revenge."

Nana D agreed to be more patient and wait until the following day before asking for an update. She knew April and I had to focus on the nine o'clock Castigliano trade-off. Once she left to meet with her staff, April and I finished chatting about the evening's approach.

"Cristiano will call at eight thirty to tell me where to meet him. He's watching, so you can't be anywhere near me," I said, worried that a slip could cause monumental failure in the plan.

"You're going to carry this tracking device." April handed me a new pair of glasses. "My FBI contact had a chip embedded in the frame."

"Wait! How did you get the details of my prescription? Oh... how clever, you stole my glasses the other day at The Big Beanery." My mouth dropped open in shock.

"Never underestimate me, Kellan. I'm a determined woman." April stood and removed my current pair of glasses. I could smell the new lavender body wash on her skin as her fingers brushed against my ears. "They're an identical match."

As April leaned back, I gently cradled her wrist. "I don't know how to thank you for doing this my way. You're not whom I expected, based on the day we first met."

"Neither are you," April replied, her hand quivering against mine. "You can be arrogant and stubborn sometimes, but there's also this incredibly ador—"

"Excuse me, are you two going to be leaving soon? I've got to clean up in here for Mayor Danby," a deep voice boomed from the doorway.

April turned around and told the assistant with inordinately bad timing that we were finished. While she was looking away, I closed my eyes and accepted the truth. I was developing feelings for the woman even with everything we'd been through together in the last few months. This was not a complication I could focus on until everything else calmed down in my life. I bolted from my chair and hurried to the other side of the room. "Sorry, we were working on a case together."

April and I left the office, pretending the moment never happened. An awkward and distant dance followed us from the silent office to the elevator, where we listened to light music and ignored each other. When we reached the lobby, she said, "I can track you wherever you are as long as you're wearing those glasses. Cristiano won't suspect we've done anything to them."

"I hope so," I mumbled, looking around the front entrance, certain a Vargas henchman followed me. "That's why we couldn't get the FBI involved or wire me. He'll check as soon as I show up. He's quite clever."

April opened an app on her phone and showed how she was able to track me via GPS. "It's extremely sensitive, so we'll be able to get to the address or building, but not specifically where inside. You'll need to drop breadcrumbs if you can, but don't be obvious."

"What about the fake storage device? You were creating false documents and files in case he checked the size of content." I waited for April to scan the lobby.

She slipped a large thumb drive into my coat pocket. "That's what you'll give them if they ask for something before I show up."

Our plan was straightforward, but there was little room for chance or error. There never was in a situation like this. Neither party trusted the other, and someone would always do something unpredictable. If I stayed the course, we had a solid chance of escaping unharmed.

I'd finish teaching my class tonight, then head home and wait for instructions from Cristiano. Once he told me where to meet them, I'd repeat it aloud on a recording device she'd already concealed in my living room. Someone from April's team would dial in to listen to the location as a fallback in case the GPS device in my new glasses failed to work. I'd drive to the meeting point and try to delay the handoff, assuming I could demand to see proof that Francesca was alive before handing over the storage device. Hopefully, it would give April's team enough time to surround the building and ensure a safe rescue. It could turn into a hostage situation if Cristiano checked specific files, but we expected that he would trust us once I handed over the signed agreement turning over fifty-one percent of Castigliano International to him. As he walked out of the building, April would nab him. If he sent Francesca and me out first, then the cops would enter the building for the capture.

"Call me after you get everything from the Castiglianos. I'm going to apprise Connor of what he needs to follow up on with the Quint Crawford case." April left me standing in the building with a dark cloud hanging over my future, and maybe the beginnings of a much brighter one down the line.

I headed to campus where the Castiglianos would be waiting. When I arrived at Diamond Hall, I found them sitting on a bench just outside the back entrance.

"You better not mess this up," Cecilia warned, a scathing look of judgment cast in my direction. "You've abandoned my daughter before, and I promise you, if that happens again tonight, you will suffer the consequences."

Vincenzo hushed his wife and suggested we recommence the conversation in my office behind a closed door. I let them sit first, then asked, "Why are you willing to hand over your company so easily? I've got a sneaky suspicion you're keeping information from me."

"You've got strong instincts, Kellan," Vincenzo said as he handed me the storage device and the folder with the signed agreement. "Some of the contents of this drive could get my company and family into trouble, but it's nothing my lawyers can't make go away. As for this so-called agreement—"

"It's not valid, and any court will throw it out the window. We've been coerced into signing the contract," Cecilia scowled in repugnance. "We're doing what we have to do to get our daughter back. Rest assured, we are not simply complying without our own equally injurious plan in place."

"You can't do anything to hurt her," I shouted, then soothed my voice so no one overheard us. All I needed was Myriam listening in and getting herself involved. "What kind of game are you playing?"

"Silence, Kellan," Cecilia replied, narrowing her gaze in my direction and forming an ominous smile I wouldn't soon forget. "Tonight will go as planned. You will turn over what Las Vargas has demanded. Meanwhile, Vincenzo and I have evidence of our own that we plan to disclose this evening. It might just convince Cristiano Vargas to release Francesca and return the storage device back to you."

"But he specifically said you cannot show up," I reminded them, thinking about his vicious threats and direction on how the evening would proceed. "How will you know where to find them?"

"We have our ways, Kellan. My wife will not do anything foolish, but I promise you that we will win this war." Vincenzo grabbed Cecilia's hand and led her through the hallway.

As they walked down the front staircase, Myriam poked her head out of her office. "Didn't we recently have a conversation about the type of visitors you've been having lately, Dr. Ayrwick?"

I wanted to rip into her, but I knew misplaced anger only exacerbated a problematic relationship. She'd also addressed me for the first time with a full title, something I hadn't expected. "You're one-hundred-percent right, Dr. Castle. This will be the last time you ever see those two again. I am done with this circus family and the self-absorbed drama they bring with it."

* * *

The end of my lecture arrived quickly. I spent most of it analyzing every decision I'd ever made since Francesca disappeared from my life over two-and-a-half years ago. In the first half of class, the students completed the pop quiz I'd designed. In the second half, they worked in pairs to compare and contrast distinctive styles of documentaries. Krissy Stanton never showed up, and Raquel was a little standoffish when I attempted to talk to her on break. Eventually, she admitted that she thought I was angry with her over Manny's potential relocation to Las Vegas. I assured her that I understood married couples needed to do what was best for their future and that I harbored no ill feelings. I cautioned her to be gentle when telling Eleanor of their final plan.

I collected my satchel and headed toward my office to drop off the quizzes. Before I reached the hallway, Imogene called out. When I looked back, she stood near the doorway with her fiancé.

"Dr. Ayrwick, I've been asked to introduce you to Paul. He was waiting for me outside Diamond Hall and wanted to meet you," Imogene said, holding his hand and resting her head against his shoulder. She stood several inches shorter than her fiancé, clutching her purse and tablet with reddened knuckles, embodying someone who'd rather be anywhere but right there.

Although I needed to check if April had located Krissy, a minor delay wouldn't impact my plans. I walked toward them with my hand stretched out to greet Town Councilman Dodd. "Good to make your acquaintance, Paul. I believe you and my brother, Gabriel, have been friends for a number of years."

"Yes, unless you count those eight years where we lost touch," he added with a brief but hearty laugh. Paul had jet black hair, broad shoulders, and a shiny complexion, one more polished than Nana D's silver collection. His duds must've cost more than my first car, and that was saying a lot since I'd saved up for three summers to buy a five-year-old Honda in prime condition.

"Congratulations on your new role. I'm confident you will be a stronger and more effective leader than your predecessor," I pointed out, throwing the strap of my satchel over my shoulder. "I'm also very sorry for the death of your friend, Quint Crawford."

"I'm still shocked we've lost him." Paul sighed and dipped his head toward Imogene. "Life must go on. Thank you for the praise. I'm excited to work with your grandmother for the benefit of Braxton."

While I had them both, I asked a few more questions. "From what I understand through Krissy, Quint's tirade against Marcus might've sunk his run for mayor. Have you heard anything like that?"

Paul leaned back on the heels of his feet and rocked back and forth. "Quint was a good guy, once upon a time. Ever since he returned to Braxton, he was a changed man. Darker. More troubled. I'm afraid to say, there's a rumor he might be the thief who attacked my poor Imogene."

Imogene made a small guttural sound. "Let's not speak ill of the deceased, Paul."

"You might want to be careful what you say, Councilman. The sheriff might ask where you were the night Quint died," I quipped, ensuring I laughed at my own statement to keep the conversation light.

"I'd like to see them try. I was at home with my fiancée. Besides, didn't Quint accidentally electrocute himself?" Paul asked, retrieving his phone and opening a new app. "In case you don't believe me, look through my photos from that day. I'm not even sure exactly what time he died."

"About midnight," I said, recalling Imogene claimed to be near the cable car an hour before then. If she'd been at the cable car, why would Paul say she was with him at home? Who was lying?

Imogene grabbed for the phone but missed. "Dr. Ayrwick doesn't need to. He trusts us, right?"

"Let him decide for himself. I'm working with his grandmother, so there can't be any doubt in his mind. I've heard how much of a snoop he can be," Paul replied, then turned to me. "I'm selling my house to find something bigger and better for Imogene. We took these for the real estate listing that night before we both went to bed. Imogene got home about eleven fifteen that evening, I believe."

I nodded hesitantly, took the phone from Paul, and shuffled through the photos, focusing on the timestamp as each one flew by my eyes. He had various shots of rooms in his house, starting shortly after eleven and ending at twelve fifty right about when Quint had been killed. Imogene was in many of the pictures too. While Paul or Imogene could've had something to do with the earlier electrocution attempt, neither could've gotten to the cable car station to strangle Quint and returned home to take those photos. Imogene had probably seen Krissy there at eleven, then gone home to Paul. I supposed the photos could've been a doctored alibi, but Lara was certain they were both innocent.

"Good luck with the sale, it's a beautiful home," I replied, hoping to keep the conversation flowing. "Have there been any updates on the burglary? I assume no one's returned your tiara."

Imogene shook her head. "It's missing, and I'm probably never going to get it back. Paul wants the sheriff to search the Crawford house, but they haven't gotten a warrant."

I convinced myself I could push harder, even prompt Imogene to reveal if she was the woman who'd gone to see Bertha earlier that week. "Why don't you visit Mrs. Crawford and see if you can find anything in his room? She'd love the company, I'm sure."

"We'll give it some thought. Thanks, Kellan." Paul wrapped his arm around

Imogene's shoulder. "We should be going, honey. You have to prepare for that dinner. Don't want to be late, do we?"

Imogene smiled sheepishly. "Krissy won't be there. I could use the break from that woman."

My ears perked up. "I notice she skipped class this evening. Are you two still not getting along?"

Paul replied, "They are not. Krissy was at the bank earlier today. I saw her in the room with the safety deposit boxes. I had to get added to the town's account to authorize future spending, so I stopped in after lunch but before Imogene's class started. Krissy must've skipped the lecture, and she's probably about to skip town. I say she should get a failing grade if nothing else, right?" He led his fiancée to the door with a sycophantic grin while wishing me a good evening.

CHAPTER 18

If Krissy had been in town earlier, she might not have left Braxton. I checked my watch to confirm I had more than enough time before Cristiano's call. I could stop at Marcus Stanton's house to convince Krissy to tell me what she knew about the jewelry thefts. If she was Quint's accomplice, I would appeal to her sense of friendship to protect Gabriel from any blowback. By the time I reached the parking lot, my cell phone rang. I jumped, thinking it was Cristiano calling earlier than he'd indicated. It wasn't the phone he'd assigned to me that was ringing. "This is Kellan."

"It's Connor. Sheriff Montague is here with me, and she asked me to give you a call."

"Everything on track for tonight?" I asked, uncertain if she'd told Connor anything about Francesca's return. We'd agreed to keep it between us, but if she needed help to coordinate, she might have enlisted him."

"What's tonight?" he asked.

"Never mind, I had my dates mixed up. What can I do for you?"

"Marcus Stanton showed up at the sheriff's office a few hours ago claiming Gabriel had broken into his house and stolen jewelry and cash. Your brother is in custody. We thought you'd want to know." Connor's voice was flat. I knew he hadn't wanted to deliver the news but figured I'd prefer to hear the unsettling information from him.

"He didn't do it. You can't believe that scoundrel Stanton," I shouted, feeling an increasing desire to drive to the man's house and harangue both him and his daughter.

"That's what we believe too. Only one problem, though."

"What now?" If my life didn't calm down, I'd be a prime candidate for an early heart attack.

"I visited your brother just over an hour ago to ask him some questions. We met in the parking lot at Braxton before he was heading out for the day. I'm not sure how to tell you this, Kellan," Connor began in a hesitant voice. There was something strange about how calm he was before finishing his statement. "Gabriel had some of the missing jewelry with him. Not everything, but a few pieces that had been stolen in the last month were in a backpack on the passenger seat of his car."

"You've got to be kidding me. This is a setup. Gabriel wouldn't be stupid enough to leave stolen jewelry in his car," I exclaimed. Paul saw Krissy at the bank; she must've been storing it there for safekeeping but realized we were closing in on her. How could I convince Connor?

"April and I talked about it. Unfortunately, she's busy on another case but told me to work directly with you on this one. She wants me to put your brother in jail for the night."

This nightmare was withering my last nerve. "Have you found Krissy? I'm driving to the Stanton's place to confront her. I'll make her admit what she's done." It had to be Krissy. There was no one else in the group who was still close with Quint and had been to his room to get the stolen items.

"Kellan, I need you to trust me. We have reasonable cause to put your brother in prison for twenty-four hours. April agrees, someone is setting him up to take a fall," Connor pleaded. He explained that the jewelry Marcus claimed Gabriel had stolen from him wasn't in the backpack. If Gabriel was trying to sneak out of town, he would have had all of it together.

"What are you going to do to stop it? He's my brother, Connor."

"Listen to me for a minute. If Krissy is the thief, she's trying to implicate Gabriel tonight. Then, she'll skip town with the jewelry she stole from her father's safe. I have no idea what's going through her head, but I'm convinced we've found Quint's killer." Connor begged me not to interfere with their plan. "If your brother is in jail, and we catch Krissy leaving with her father's money and jewelry, then we can prove Gabriel is innocent. I won't let anything bad happen to him." Connor paused to speak to someone else in the room. When he returned to the call, he said, "Gabriel says he's okay and to let me do what I have to do."

"Fine, but for the record, you're all gonna pay in spades for doing this to me!"

Connor laughed. "Why are you going to the Stanton house? I really think you should stay away."

I was stressed enough. I knew I should focus on one problem at a time. Waiting for Cristiano's call to meet him that night was my priority. "You've got a point. Okay, I'll let it go for tonight."

Connor assured me he'd update me as soon as they were able to get a warrant to search the Stanton house. Marcus had stopped them from getting inside earlier that afternoon without one, even though it was supposedly to obtain fingerprints from the break-in. Connor was already suspicious and had begun putting his case together for the judge. When we hung up, I drove to Danby Landing to prepare for Francesca's return.

After checking that my mother had picked up Emma at the bus stop, I quickly showered and attempted to relax. I had no desire to eat dinner, and I was unwilling to have a drink in case it clouded my judgment. I grabbed my shoes and tossed them on the floor next to the couch. It was too early to put them on. I sat in silence worrying over how things would go that night.

At precisely eight thirty, Cristiano called. "Do you have a package for me from the Castiglianos?"

"Yes, it's ready to go," I confirmed, patting the right pocket in my jeans. I'd hidden the real one in my shoe just in case I encountered any trouble with the fake one. While I didn't want to lose the only evidence we had against my in-laws, protecting Francesca came first. Would they find a way to show up tonight?

"Good, you follow instructions well. I like that about you." He paused to relay the news to someone nearby, probably my missing wife. "We'll convene at home plate on the Grey baseball field at Braxton. I thought it was a fitting location for Francesca's return home."

Outdoors might be a safe place. April could more easily track me with the GPS device without any interruption from walls or other barriers. It might also provide easier access for her team. As I thought about the plan, it worried me. Cristiano was smart, and this would open him up for potential danger. "Are you sure meeting on the baseball field near the Grey Sports Complex is the best place?"

"I hope that's not doubt in your voice, Kellan. Francesca assured me that you knew how to accept explicit directions," Cristiano replied.

"Okay, just checking. Don't lose your cool over it!" I repeated the location to be sure the recording device in my living room captured it, then stepped outside the front door of the cottage to check if anyone was watching from elsewhere on the property.

"We'll see you in thirty minutes. And please remember, Kellan, we know everything you are doing. Are you enjoying that lovely breeze across the front porch of your little cottage? It can be dangerous to walk around barefoot on a wooden surface. You might get splinters." Cristiano had someone scouting my every move. Where was this person? "You know the rules. No cops. No Castiglianos. No weapons. No funny business. We will be checking everything. Do not show until precisely nine o'clock."

When I confirmed his demands would be met, he hung up the phone. I had fifteen minutes before it made sense to leave Danby Landing. I desperately wanted to call April to verify everything was in place and that she'd heard the location. I paced the front porch with my ears intently focused on every strange noise. The recording machine beeped, and I knew April's team had dialed in to pick up the location. My confidence jumped one small notch higher on the already beaten-down scale.

Then I heard Krissy Stanton talking on her cell phone across the yard. I stepped closer to the fence and peered through a hole near one of the knots in the wooden gate. She was feverishly loading suitcases in the trunk of her car. I ran inside the cottage and stepped into my shoes. If I acted quickly, I could confront her before she took off. I sent a text message to Connor, letting him know I'd seen Krissy at the Stanton house.

I tiptoed down the gravel driveway and cut across the side lawn to the gate between our two properties. Within two minutes, I'd unlatched the lock and raced to her open front door. I stepped into the foyer and looked all around.

Krissy clomped around the corner almost crashing into me. "What are you doing here?" She backed up a few steps and dropped a bag to the floor. Her eyes were dark and distant.

"I know what you've done, Krissy. How could you do something so awful to one of your friends?" I put up an arm to stop her when she tried to barrel past. "We need to talk."

"I know trying to leave town is stupid, but I have to get away from my family. Gabriel will be fine, my father doesn't have a case against him," she said, tears forming in her eyes.

"You've got that right. Gabriel will survive, but you'll wind up in prison. You won't get the death penalty, but I'm confident you'll spend decades in prison for strangling Quint." I should've been more careful with my accusations, especially knowing she'd killed one person already and I could be next. Then what would happen to Francesca and the Castiglianos? I couldn't control my actions anymore. I suddenly understood how similar Nana D and I were. My body seethed with anger over reckless people who called themselves friends, people who would steal from you just as soon as murder you.

Krissy froze in place with tears streaming down her cheeks. "What are you talking about? Quint was electrocuted, not strangled. I never intended to kill him, just to scare him. It was an accident. I feel guilty enough already for what I've done. Don't make it any worse."

I paused to digest what she'd told me. The look of panic and shock on her face seemed genuine. "Didn't you strangle your boyfriend when your plan to electrocute him failed?"

"No, I didn't even know he'd been strangled. And according to him, he wasn't even my boyfriend." Krissy cocked her head and squinted. "Something doesn't make sense to me."

"Maybe you should start at the beginning. Tell me exactly what you did," I said, encouraging her to divulge her secrets as quickly as possible. "I have somewhere important to be soon, but I can give you ten more minutes."

"If you're telling me the truth, and someone strangled Quint, then I need to get out of here even quicker than I thought." Krissy tried to run past me, but I snatched her arm and pushed her toward the foyer wall.

"No, I want to understand what you know, what you did to him," I shouted, wanting to shake her until she agreed to talk. Even in my fury, I knew restraint was the optimal approach.

Krissy wiped her face dry and sat on the stairs opposite me. "Quint was the jewel thief. I didn't realize it at first. I told you that he helped me steal the brooch from the Paddingtons eight years ago, but evidently, he took the prank even further back then and was recreating the crimes again this year. He'd been secretly collecting information from everyone to identify the best times and places to rob them."

Krissy explained what she knew about the jewelry thefts. Shortly after Quint had stolen the brooch for her eight years ago, he'd seen Imogene and Paul kissing in Memorial Library. When Quint confronted Imogene, she told him that her family didn't approve of him and wanted her to marry someone better. Then, Lara tried to blackmail Quint with evidence of the bribes his uncle had taken. Imogene's mother had been trying to force Quint to leave town. He was enraged about not being accepted by the upper crust of Wharton County, so he planned revenge. Using the details from the story Imogene had told him about the sorority's calla lilies, Quint decided to target all the founding families in Alpha Iota Omega. She'd always suspected Gabriel was the thief because he'd been keeping secrets back then. Krissy had thought Quint was acting odd because Imogene had ended their relationship, so she tried to comfort him. Quint rejected her when she asked him on a date because he'd been angry and focused on getting revenge before leaving town.

Krissy had never known this until a few weeks ago when Quint returned to town. Krissy admitted to him she'd never stopped loving him. She tried to convince him to give her a chance, but Imogene flirted with Quint at Kirklands one night. When Quint was drunk, he revealed to Krissy he'd thought Imogene still loved him and that he still loved her. "I was so angry at Quint for hurting me again. I confronted Imogene and threatened to tell Paul if she didn't stay away. Imogene finally agreed to tell Quint she only loved Paul. Then, I had to deal with Siobhan."

"Huh?" I was perplexed at the change in direction.

"Siobhan and Quint slept together. He was devastated by Imogene's recent rejection. Instead of throwing himself at me, he hooked up with Siobhan. When Quint realized that he'd given her the wrong impression, he broke it off, but it was too late by then. I was angry about him always ignoring me, so I told Paul about Imogene secretly meeting Quint at Kirklands. I also told Quint that Imogene had taken the tiara to her mother's place that night. She'd bragged about it when I saw her on campus that day."

"Get to how Quint died." I was anxious to hear all the details but unable to stay much longer.

"Fine. When Imogene wouldn't end her engagement, Quint assumed she'd just been using him to make Paul jealous. He broke into her mother's house to steal the tiara, only he didn't know Imogene was sleeping there. He tried to escape, but she recognized him." Imogene never told Paul, and she didn't want to press charges because she was afraid the truth would come out about her feelings for Quint resurfacing. "When I confronted Quint, he confessed that he could never love me and that I was just a good friend. I was so livid with Quint, I wanted to hurt him in a monumental way."

"What did you do to the electrical panels inside the cable car?"

Krissy closed her eyes. "It was foolish. I just wanted to shock him. I'd been learning a lot by hanging around him, and Nicky had taught me basic electrical work, so I felt assured that I'd only scare Quint and teach him a lesson. Something went horribly wrong, and now I think I know why."

"Please hurry up, Krissy. Tell me what happened in the cable car." I wish I had that recording device now, but I could always update Connor and April after the meeting with Cristiano Vargas.

"Quint and I were meeting for a drink late that night. I'd already gone over to strip a few of the wires and turn on the main power supply at the station. We met up, then I begged him to show me the renovations." They'd stopped on campus to visit the cable car where Quint proceeded to boast about the work he'd been accomplishing. He thought the power had been off and flipped on his cell phone for some light. When he surveyed the panel, his hand had touched the wires, severely stunning him. "I wasn't thinking straight and turned off the power with my bare hands. I'd forgotten to wear gloves that time because I was nervous. Quint had been electrocuted, but he was still alive even though the shock had left him weak and hardly able to move. I'd gotten my revenge, but I also knew he would be fine. When I'd been at the Paddington estate earlier that day, I'd seen a bunch of black calla lilies and thought it'd be a perfect way to throw the entire disaster in his face. I'd retrieved them from my car after turning the power off, then tossed them near his unconscious body, so he'd know someone wanted revenge on him for what he'd done. I left him to sleep it off and went home. He never knew what I'd done to him."

"You're saying when you left, he was still alive?"

"He was. I swear," Krissy cried out. "When I learned he'd died the next day, I couldn't tell anyone. I was scared the cops would put me in jail for what was supposed to be evening the score." Krissy explained that she was the woman who'd confronted Helena at Woodland Warriors because Helena had known Quint was still interested in Imogene and only leading Krissy on. Krissy thought her supposed friend would've tried to protect her rather than let Quint hurt her.

While she had a point, I had five minutes to arrive at the baseball field. "Did you find the jewelry Quint had stolen and hide it in Gabriel's car today? He's been arrested, but he's not guilty."

"Quint was the thief, not me. I have no idea how it got in Gabriel's car." Krissy promised that she didn't try to set up Gabriel and had never known where Quint hid the jewelry. "But now, I'm scared someone else saw the whole thing happen at the cable car. I got a call earlier today from a disguised voice. This creep threatened me," Krissy said, beginning to hyperventilate.

"How?" I was getting more confused as she explained the situation.

"The caller taunted me about witnessing what I'd done to Quint. I thought it was Imogene because she'd threatened to tell the cops that she'd seen me near the cable car too."

"So, you no longer think it was Imogene calling you?" If Krissy hadn't gone into Quint's bedroom the other day, Imogene was the only other girl who could've visited Bertha's house. Who else would've taken the jewels from Quint's bedroom and put them in Gabriel's car?

"It was at two o'clock today when I got the call. Wasn't Imogene in class with you?" Krissy paced the foyer as if she wanted to stomp holes through the ceramic tiles.

Imogene had been with me at two o'clock today, but I had no time to linger right now. Hearing the rest would have to wait until after the Vargas meeting. "I have to go, but you need to speak with Detective Connor Hawkins. Maybe Paul Dodd was your blackmail caller. Could he and Imogene be conspiring together?"

"No, Kellan. Now that I'm piecing everything together, I know who it is. I saw someone following me the other day. When I confronted her, she had a valid explanation. I let it go at the time, but after today, I'm not sure anymore." Krissy froze in the foyer and faced the front of the house. My back was to the door. I couldn't see what was going on behind me. She gasped and pointed in my direction.

"What? Who do you think it was?" I implored, wondering what she was staring at and why she'd raised her finger at me.

A familiar voice answered, "Krissy must be dumbfounded to find me here. She's much smarter than I gave her credit for, and I'm guessing she's started to figure out a few things."

I turned around slowly as the trigger of a revolver cocked into place. When I came face to face with the woman holding the weapon, my mind had a meltdown in confusion and panic. Was I going to miss the meeting with Cristiano now? "What the hell is going on?"

"You might recognize me as Raquel Salvado, Chef Manny's new wife, but you'd probably know me a little better if I shared my maiden name. Allow me to properly introduce myself. Before I got married, my friends, family, business associates, and the government referred to me as Raquel Vargas. I believe you know my brother, Cristiano." Raquel waved the gun and instructed me to step backward, next to Krissy. "Maybe it's time I shared a little story about how well you all knew your friend, or shall I say foe, Quint Crawford."

CHAPTER 19

With a gun pointed at my chest, I had little time or focus to assemble what I was missing. Krissy clung to my arm as if it were a lifejacket. The color drained from her face like someone had wrathfully shaken an Etch-A-Sketch. My heart raced and breath quickened. "What about the meeting with Cristiano to exchange the storage device for Francesca?"

Krissy swallowed deeply. "Your wife? I thought she was dead."

Raquel laughed wildly. "Amateurs. Do you really think I'd let them meet in an open field where anyone could see them wandering around and call the police?" She glanced into the nearby living room to survey her surroundings. "The two of you need to sit on that sofa in front of the window. Pull the shade down first. The sun hasn't fully set."

While we complied, Raquel reached her hand toward me. "Give me the device now. Then we'll talk. I've sent Marcus Stanton on a wild goose chase about his missing jewelry, so he won't be home for at least an hour."

I clumsily patted down my pockets, uncertain which one I'd left it in earlier. When I found it, I second-guessed the decision to deliver a fake copy of the evidence that the Castiglianos had compiled, but it would look far worse if I admitted what I'd done earlier. I took a step forward before sitting on the couch, cautious not to move too quickly and risk having my arm shot off by a crazed mafia woman. "Here, this is what Cristiano is expecting. The signed contract is back at my house."

"We'll deal with that later. Let's talk about poor stupid Quint," Raquel began, leaning against a sideboard opposite us in the Stanton living room. She held the gun in her hand aimed directly at me, but her eyes occasionally darted back and forth to Krissy.

"You killed my boyfriend," Krissy snarled, her knees vibrating like the strings of an exquisite violin being stroked by a fine French bow. "You won't get away with this."

The irony of the situation seemed to have been lost on Krissy. She's the one who tried to electrocute him. My guess was if she hadn't stripped and loosened the wires to teach him a lesson, Quint would've been strong enough to fight off Raquel. "Let her talk, don't make things worse."

"Smart man, Kellan," she replied, then turned to Krissy. "Listen, girlfriend to girlfriend... Quint was a con artist. No woman should put up with a liar who doesn't treat her properly. I saved you from a life of misery." Raquel was proud of herself for ridding the world of a man who'd taken more from it than he'd given.

Krissy squirmed but refrained from opening her mouth. A clock on the far wall read nine-oh-seven. We were officially late, but April must have been able to track my location with the GPS tracking device embedded in my glasses. Would she send a patrol car to check on me?

"What's going on with the meeting at Grey Field? I'm not trying to distract you, but what happens next with Francesca?" I asked, hoping to divert her attention, in reality. As much as I worried for my safety, as well as Krissy's, my instincts told me to delay Raquel as long as possible.

"I spoke with my brother a few minutes ago. We've moved the meeting location. I don't trust you, and he's blinded by that vixen wife of yours." Raquel approached the sofa opposite us and sat with her elbows on her knees and the gun aimed at a very precious part of my body. "We'll be seeing our loved ones in a little while. Don't worry, everything's been taken care of."

Raquel was eager to share the story of how she'd easily integrated herself into the life of several people I knew. In animated fashion, she covered her arrival in Braxton four months earlier right before Francesca had been kidnapped. "My family knew the Castiglianos had faked your wife's death, but we could never prove it. They kept her well-hidden and paid their employees top dollar to keep it secret. When Francesca flew here to stop you from trying to relocate, we had undeniable proof. A security worker at the airport had taken a photo of her and sent it to us. We know how to take care of people on our payroll too."

"I get it. Vincenzo and Cecilia are awful people. I agree with you, but I had nothing to do with whatever vendetta your families have against each other. You have the documents from the Castiglianos; just let Francesca go, and everything can move forward," I said, hoping to find the rational side of Raquel. How had I missed picking up any clues while she'd been a student in my class?

"It's not that easy anymore, Kellan. Let me finish telling my story. You have a habit of talking too much, and I feel it's my duty to advise you that you'll do better in life if you shut up sometimes." Raquel told us that while Cristiano had focused on a plan to kidnap Francesca, she was responsible for collecting information and discovering secrets about the Ayrwicks and to blackmail people to do their bidding.

On an early stop at the Pick-Me-Up Diner, Raquel had overheard that Manny, Eleanor's chef, was planning to visit Las Vegas. She followed him out there and got him drunk one night, then convinced him to get married. It gave her an excuse to hang around the diner without people being suspicious. She'd begged Manny not to tell too many people that they were married until she could work out a few personal things with her family. He was happy to comply and openly talked about Eleanor, me, and any of our friends that visited the diner. "Honestly, Manny is a good husband. Except, of course, we're not legally married. We never filed with the state of Nevada, and the guy who married us never had a proper license. He owed a favor to the Vargas family, and well, now it's been repaid."

"You've collected all this data about us, that's brilliant. How does Quint Crawford fit in?" I hadn't brought my phone with me and had no way to notify anyone what was going on. I glanced sideward at Krissy who seemed frozen in a trance. Fear had taken over her ability to do anything or work with me on an escape plan.

"Quint liked to talk. I overheard him in the diner chatting to your brother, Gabriel. They were discussing all the jewelry Quint had stolen years ago, and Quint needed help to pay his mother's bills."

Raquel had offered money to Quint if he would spy on me and handle a few important tasks for her. Quint had watched Emma and me at the pet store, then purchased and delivered the puppy to the cottage the previous month. Apparently, Quint's slippery tentacles had invaded my entire life, and I'd been completely clueless for weeks. I had to hand it to Raquel; she was devious and cunning. I never realized Quint was pumping me for information the entire time I'd visited with him at the cable car. "Why did you kill him?"

"Quint started to get too big for his britches. When I'd gotten everything I needed from him, I gave him a nice bonus and told him to forget we'd ever met. He tried to blackmail me, but unfortunately he learned a lesson the hard way." Raquel tapped the gun against the coffee table when Krissy stirred and looked ready to bolt. "Stay where you are, sister. I'd prefer not to shoot you, but if I must, I must."

Raquel had known Quint was stealing jewelry again. She'd also discovered he was misleading Krissy and pining away for Imogene. Another of her goons had been following Quint to keep tabs on him. Raquel's henchman had seen Krissy sabotage the cable car renovation project and told his boss that someone might be trying to kill Quint. "When I went to the cable car station, Krissy had been running across the parking lot. I checked inside and saw Quint had passed out but was still alive. Krissy had placed a bouquet of black calla lilies she'd stolen while visiting the Paddington estate earlier that day near his unconscious body. After stealing one of the rubies from Quint, days earlier when he accidentally dropped one during our many secret meetings, I left it there in the cable car to implicate him and tie his death to all the robberies. I took immense pleasure in strangling my former snitch, watching the life and energy extinguish from a once supposedly clever and charming man. To hold something precious in your grip and be responsible for eliminating it from existence... there's nothing more I could ask for, to make my day complete. And voilà, my potential blackmail problem went away." Raquel grinned maniacally, watching Krissy's expression change from fear to shock and anger.

Krissy jumped across the table and punched Raquel. In the struggle, I tried to run, not because I didn't want to protect Krissy, but if I could escape, I might get to the phone to call 9-1-1. I didn't have enough time. Raquel swung the gun at Krissy and collided with her temple. Krissy flew to the floor and hit her head against the coffee table.

Raquel aimed the gun at me as I reached the hallway. "Stop, or I'll blow your ass to pieces, even if it's quite a fine—"

I backed into the room, turned around, and sheepishly said, "Okay. I think I'll stay put for now." Something dawned on me as I walked closer to her. "You complained to Myriam about me. Why?"

"Just causing trouble for you. I wanted you to feel attacked from all angles. It was my way to keep you off balance... unable to figure out what I was up to." A menacing smile formed on her lips.

"It almost worked." I hadn't trusted her but also wasn't able to pinpoint the exact reason.

Raquel instructed me to tie up Krissy with the wires from a piece of art that had been hanging on the wall—thick, coarse metal that was pliable but strong enough to hold someone at bay. I lifted Krissy, whispering in her ear that I'd do everything I could to save us. Raquel pointed to a nearby chair in the corner where I tied Krissy's hands to the back wooden rails and her ankles against its feet.

While I was directed to stand in the corner, Raquel inspected my work. "It'll do for now. Krissy looks like she's about to pass out anyway."

As I stood there, it hit me. Raquel had been the woman who went to Bertha Crawford's house under the deceptive guise of wanting to spend one last moment in Quint's bedroom before saying goodbye. "You took the jewelry Quint had stolen and implicated my brother earlier today."

"Guilty. Quint had sold a bunch to pay for his mother's expenses, so he only had a few pieces remaining in his bedroom. I worried you were getting too suspicious, so I decided to keep your meddlesome mind focused elsewhere," she confirmed, then waved the gun at me to march toward the front door. "Let's go. Someone else will come by soon to take care of Miss Stanton. We're due at the new meeting point in fifteen minutes."

"Wait," I stalled, noticing it was nine thirty. April had to be worried that I hadn't shown up at the baseball field. She'd come looking for me soon, finding the cottage empty and my SUV still onsite. "What made you think I was getting close? I had no clue you were involved."

"You had a crime show. You asked too many questions. I was sure you'd figure out the connections in no time at all. Besides, Krissy was catching on and might have discovered it herself. She knew I'd been following her the last few days. I had someone call earlier to try and get her off the scent, but she told you about it anyway. She'll suffer later tonight when she takes a nice, long swim."

"Where are we going?" I demanded as she pushed me out the door with one hand and jammed the gun into my shoulder with the other. While it was possible I could overpower her, I couldn't take a chance that—given her diabolical mindset—she'd shoot me.

"I found a lovely place that should be relatively quiet this evening. In fact, Cristiano is there with Francesca and a couple of our bodyguards," Raquel replied, directing me to shut the door. We walked across the lawn and through the gate as I had done earlier. Raquel truly had been watching my every move. "Oh, that's right," she said, stopping me once we reached my front door. "You're probably familiar with the location. Tell me, Kellan, have you visited your mother's office at Braxton recently?"

Emma! "No, please, we can't meet there." My stomach plummeted to the floor in anticipation of disastrous consequences.

"Go inside and get the signed contract. We can discuss it while you drive us there," Raquel insisted. The sun had set, but the front porch light shined across her face. It was then I knew only one of us would survive that night. No one threatened my daughter and got away with it.

I snatched the keys to my SUV and the agreement from the couch where I'd left it prior to rushing out of the cottage. I wanted to repeat the changed location aloud in case April's team had continued to listen in. "Does the new drop off point have to be Braxton's Admissions Hall? What about Diamond Hall in my office? No one's there, and it's even quieter."

"Aren't you cute? You should know my team destroyed that recording device Sheriff Montague planted earlier. Let me guess, when you heard that strange noise, you thought your little friend was obtaining the details?" Raquel took the key from me, shoved me out the front door, and followed closely behind.

I finally understood the far-reaching tentacles of Las Vargas. I had little hope left other than to believe they would keep their word and not harm my daughter, mother, or Francesca. At this point, I'd give my own life to ensure Emma's safety. "Please, I'll do anything."

"Good, then as soon as we park the car, you will remove your glasses. Unfortunately, you need them to drive, otherwise I would've smashed them by now." She waited, while I hopped into the SUV, before boarding and handing me the keys. "Yes, I know about the GPS device too. Drive."

Raquel ignored everything I said and held me at gunpoint while we drove to Braxton. I considered quickly jerking the steering wheel to throw her off balance, but the insane woman wouldn't think twice about taking control of the car and shooting me as soon as I made a sudden movement. I complied with her demands and parked in a nearby empty lot.

"Give me those," she said, thrusting my glasses to the street and crunching them with the heel of her red stilettos. "I'll be your eyes and navigate you to the building."

I thought I'd seen a dark car following us, but if I had, it was probably one of Raquel's bodyguards. Maybe campus security would drive by and wonder who was working late that night. Connor's replacement still hadn't been hired, and the college's security crew was lighter during summers, but I had hope someone would find us before long.

After we walked to Admissions Hall, Raquel called Cristiano. We stood outside the front entrance until he verified it wasn't a trap and checked me for wires or bugs. As I entered, I focused on remembering the layout of the office. It was eerily quiet. Where was everyone?

Raquel handed me over to Cristiano. "Kellan's been cooperating, but he's got quite an outlandish mouth on him. Are you sure I can't have a little fun teaching him a lesson tonight?"

"No, *hermana*. We only hurt those who hurt us. For all intents and purposes, Kellan is an innocent bystander." With his usual calm and collected tone, Cristiano addressed me next. "My sister tells me the only negative experience she's had these last few months on this mission was listening to you teach class. Raquel never was one for the movies; she much prefers being part of the action."

Without my glasses, my confidence was diminished. I felt disoriented from not knowing my surroundings, but I experienced adrenaline and fear coursing through my veins. "Where is my family?"

"I'm very sorry it's come to this, Kellan," Cristiano empathetically replied, then whispered something to Raquel, who quickly disappeared from the room. "Emma and your mother are currently sitting in an office with one of my employees. They're both fine, but I'll send him back for Krissy soon."

"And Francesca?"

Footsteps shuffled behind me. "I'm right here, Kellan."

I turned around and reached my hands in the direction of her voice. My vision was so impaired, I could only see something if it were a foot from my eyes. Everything around me was a blur, amorphous shapes and colors, no facial distinction or depth perception. "Are you okay? Have you seen Emma?"

"I'm fine. I saw them bring juice and cookies to her. Emma thinks it's a game. Your mother is with her, but they haven't seen me. I promise you," Francesca said, grabbing my hands, "I won't let them hurt her."

"I'd give you two a moment alone, but I'm afraid we might not have a lot of time," Cristiano said. His shadow crossed to the side of me, and he spoke to someone else. "Do you have the items he was supposed to deliver?"

Raquel replied, "Yes. The agreement has been signed, and it's in my back pocket. I haven't checked the storage device. He and the sheriff were fiddling with it earlier. Do you have a computer?"

"I'm sure Kellan's mother can help us with that," Cristiano replied and directed someone else in the room to bring her out of the office.

"I'm going to step away for a minute, Kellan. I don't want Emma to see me until we can talk to her together," Francesca whispered in my ear.

The room was beginning to feel hot, stealing the little oxygen I had remaining in my lungs. The air conditioning was always lowered at night, and there were too many of us standing in a small area without open windows and breezes. I felt grateful that Francesca was in a position to focus on protecting Emma, but what would occur when they checked the storage device? April was supposed to be here before that happened, but now, she had no idea where we were.

Cristiano said, "Violet, darling, I'm going to need your assistance. Can you please log on to a computer, so that I can read the contents of this drive?"

My mother managed to squeak out a yes before noticing me. "Kellan, Emma... Emma is okay. I can't believe Francesca—"

"It's okay, Mom. Just do what they want, and everything will work out." I wasn't sure whom I was convincing at that moment.

While my mother assisted Cristiano with the files, and Raquel shoved the gun against my back, I heard a sound coming from a nearby office.

"No, wait, you can't go out there," a raspy voice shouted.

Then, I heard Emma. "But I want to see Grandma. I don't understand this game anymore."

My panic intensified. I willed myself not to do anything rash. Emma must have seen me.

"Daddy's here." I heard tiny footsteps racing across the floor, but I couldn't do anything.

"Emma, I thought you were going to be a good girl and listen to me," Cristiano said.

I couldn't tell for sure, but it looked like he'd grabbed her arm as she ran by to stop her from reaching me.

"Who's that?" she asked, probably pointing at Raquel, given I didn't know everyone in the room.

At that moment, everything happened so fast, I could barely understand what was going on. Francesca stepped back into the room and walked toward us. She bent down in front of me, no more than ten feet away, saying, "My precious, Emma. It's—"

The door busted open, and two people rushed inside. I couldn't identify them at first, but I recognized their voices.

The fury behind Vincenzo's words was alarming. "Your lookout guard has been disarmed and knocked out. We've had enough drama for tonight, Cristiano. It's about time we had a little discussion."

Raquel grabbed me and aimed the gun at my forehead.

Emma and my mother both screamed. I saw a quick flurry of action in front of me and assumed either Cristiano or Francesca had picked up Emma.

"Listen, old man, your family started this game when you invaded our territory and killed several of our finest employees," Cristiano replied in a suave yet chilling voice. "You were not supposed to arrive here tonight. How did you find us?"

"We followed your sister and Kellan. We've been watching all night trying to figure out where the meetup was going to happen," Cecilia announced. She must've also held a gun because I could hear her racking the slide into position.

"Please, let me take Emma away from here," my mother begged.

"I'm frightened. I don't understand what's going on. Is that my mommy?" Emma's voice was strained. I knew my daughter. Her eyes were scrunched together as she clung to whoever held her, fighting to get free. Whenever she was scared, she ran and hid until I could protect her.

I'd always blamed it on the shock she'd gone through upon learning her mother had died. No one else could comfort my baby when she felt abandoned, except for me. "She's only seven years old. Please, don't hurt her."

Francesca whimpered, helpless while her worlds collided in one giant mixing bowl of miscalculated rage. She wanted to comfort our daughter but must not have thought she could do anything to safely break the tension.

"Kellan, nothing will happen to Emma. I'm holding and protecting her," Cristiano advised. He sounded sincere, but the room was a powder keg, and I could do nothing to stop the potential explosion. He addressed the Castiglianos. "You've handed over the evidence and your company. It's time for you to leave, and I'll let Francesca go."

"Not so fast," Cecilia sputtered, her words filled with an intense charge. She stood inches away from us. "There's one more piece of evidence we need to discuss."

"What's this all about?" Raquel's voice echoed in my ears, exponentially irritating me.

Vincenzo tossed something to my mother. "Would you mind bringing up this video on the monitor? As always, it's lovely to see you, Violet. You haven't aged a bit."

Her hands still trembling, my mother managed to insert the drive into the USB slot on the laptop. A window popped up on the screen with a single file available to select. She double-clicked it, and a new window came to the forefront. I couldn't make out the words, but I knew the shapes.

"Maximize it and raise the volume, will you, Violet?" Vincenzo requested with his gun still aimed at Cristiano. He'd never take a shot with his granddaughter in Cristiano's arms.

"I'm scared, Daddy," Emma cried and reached for me.

I'd lost track of where Francesca stood at that point. My heart broke into pieces at what was unfolding before me. Not being able to visualize any details made it even more tragic and haunting. "It's okay, baby, just a few more minutes."

Cristiano tried to comfort my daughter. "It's all a fun game, Emma. Just keep your eyes closed, and you'll be back to your daddy soon."

My mother must have enlarged the video. Someone began to speak on it, but I wasn't sure of his or her identity. I couldn't see details, given the loss of my glasses and not being close enough. By squinting and straining, I could make out only the bare minimum of actions.

"*Ah, Quint Crawford. You were once a valuable asset to my family. Now, you're nothing but an almost dead man,*" a cold and virulent voice from the video cautioned.

"*What are you planning to do, Raquel?*" another voice said on the recording.

"*We don't want his last moments to be a struggle. Life shouldn't be this diffi-cult for anyone. Turn that camera off and ensure no one's watching.*" It was Raquel's sadistic tone I clearly heard this time.

"*What are you doing to him, boss?*" the guy operating the camera questioned. A few moments of silence followed. "*You're gonna strangle him?*"

"*It was necessary. One more problem solved. As I told my brother, a woman will always save the day,*" Raquel replied on the video.

While my mother gasped across the room, Raquel screeched. "That's impossible. How did—"

"Perhaps you'd like to strike up a new deal," Cecilia suggested, then explained that the goon Raquel had following Quint had double-crossed the Vargas family and recorded Raquel while she strangled Quint to death. "It took me a while to track him down, but when I did, he was more than willing to sell me the video in exchange for a small sum of money to start a new life somewhere else."

Raquel released me and inched toward Cecilia. "He disappeared this afternoon. Now, I understand why. That arrogant son-of-a—"

"I'd rather not hear any foul language from you, young lady," Vincenzo replied, squaring off with her, still at least ten feet away. "You've done enough. About our deal, it's renegotiation time."

The next few minutes were a blur, and not just because I couldn't see what was happening. Raquel pushed past me and lunged for Vincenzo. I careened into a desk. After regaining my footing, I scanned the room to locate Cristiano and my daughter, trying to decipher their voices in the cacophony. My mother screamed bloody murder, and a burst of footsteps rushed by me from the front. I heard April yell, "This is the Wharton County Sheriff's Office. Drop your weapons and put your hands up!"

A few seconds later, several gunshots reverberated in the room, followed by an intense screech from my daughter. I covered my head and dived to the ground toward where I thought she was being held captive. I had no idea who'd been hit and cared little about protecting myself at that moment, only my daughter. "Emma," I cried out, begging for mercy from anyone who'd listen and promising my own life in return for her absolute safety.

CHAPTER 20

"I'm so sorry, Kellan. I can't imagine how you're feeling," April comforted me. We sat in my mother's office with the door closed. The gunshots from an hour ago still echoed in my head. I'd seen shoot-outs in the movies and through recreations for my former crime show, but to live through one in person was a whole different situation. To essentially watch someone be shot to death directly in front of you was something I'd never want to experience again.

"Have you ever killed someone before, April?" My weakened state of mind barely allowed me to respond, but I was beginning to come around.

"Unfortunately, tonight wasn't my first time. It's only happened on a handful of occasions, but it never gets any easier." April grabbed both my hands and covered them with hers. "In a situation like that, instincts kick in. I saw her raise the gun, but I didn't know who she was going to shoot."

"Raquel is definitely dead?"

April nodded. "They've loaded Vincenzo Castigliano into the ambulance. Raquel was able to get two shots in before *Old Betsy* took her down. He was hit in the chest. I'm not sure how it'll turn out." She brushed my hair out of my eyes and placed a pair of glasses on my face for the second time that day. "It's a good thing I kept your original ones from our breakfast this morning."

It felt good to be able to see again. "Thank you," I said, staring directly at the woman who'd just saved my entire family's life. My vision of April was now undeniably clear. "Where is everyone else?"

Once the earlier shots had been fired and April assumed control over Admissions Hall, I'd run to my daughter and grabbed her from Cristiano's arms. I'd lost all sense of what was happening in the room around me. I'd carried her to the closest office, shut and locked the door, only opening it again when my mother finished speaking to the cops and beseeched me to see her granddaughter. We'd comforted Emma for fifteen minutes before Connor let us know that it was safe to come out again.

"I'm allowing Cecilia and Francesca to go to the hospital with Vincenzo. They're both in handcuffs, and we'll deal with booking them later. If there's any chance Vincenzo won't make it, I wouldn't want to deprive his family of a last goodbye. There are several police officers with them, and both will be under scrutiny for the time being." April handed me a cup of water and urged me to drink some slowly.

"Emma is still with my mother?" I hadn't wanted to leave them alone but needed a few minutes by myself to process everything that had happened. I was ready to see them both again.

"Yes, she's asleep in your mother's arms. She'll be okay, you know. Kids are more resilient than we think," April assured with a knowing glance. "Let's talk for a few minutes about how this all happened. I want to be sure I understand everything while it's still fresh in your mind. I promise, just a brief summary, and then tomorrow or the next day, we can go through the details."

I stood and crossed to the other side of the office and updated April with everything that had happened after I'd returned home from class. "I hung up with Cristiano and heard Krissy's voice once I'd stepped outside again." When I said her name, I remembered that she'd been tied up in the Stanton house. "Oh, Krissy, she's—"

"Krissy's fine. At some point after you and Raquel had left, Marcus returned home early and found his daughter. She'd only passed out, and the head injury was minor. Krissy helped us track you down," April explained. Before losing consciousness, Krissy had heard me repeat the location of where Raquel planned to take me. "Marcus called the police. Connor heard the call details on dispatch, and he rushed over to the house. Krissy was worried about you, Kellan. She felt awful about everything that had happened, especially what her father had tried to pin on Gabriel. We also matched Krissy's fingerprints to the ones found on the electric supply box under the cable car platform. She claims she just wanted to hurt him, and knowing she hadn't wiped her prints from it, that's probably the truth. She's a smart girl. I doubt she'd intentionally attempt to kill him and purposely leave evidence behind."

"You're right. Did Marcus admit he lied about the stolen jewelry from his safe?"

"Not exactly. Krissy was the one who'd planned to flee with it. She broke the window to make it look like a regular burglary, assuming everyone would think it was the fifth robbery aligning with the previous string of jewelry thefts. When Marcus reported it to us a day after he spoke to you, he genuinely believed your brother was responsible." April explained that Marcus had confronted Krissy sometime after reporting it, and she confessed that she'd stolen the jewelry and cash, hidden it at the bank, and planned to leave Braxton. Her father had cut her off financially after losing the election because she'd been involved with Quint, the guy whom Marcus believed had cost him the win. Krissy and her father had fought for an hour earlier that afternoon after she arrived from the bank and began packing the car to leave. Marcus disappeared to find a way to stop her, but when he returned home, he'd found his daughter tied up in the living room.

"They're down at the sheriff's office with Connor sorting out that situation. As soon as Connor knew what had happened to you, he called me, and that's how I was able to track you guys down to Admissions Hall." April had proved tonight why she was the best person for the sheriff's role in Wharton County. Not only did her staff respect and trust her, but she was able to catch the criminal in the end.

"What about Cristiano? What will happen to him?" Through everything, as ruthless as his family had been, he kept promising that he never wanted to harm Emma. I'd believed him, but he was still partially responsible for everything that had transpired this evening.

"That's going to be tough. You knew I was investigating the Vargas and Castigliano families. Cristiano has managed to keep himself squeaky clean. Until I speak with your wife, I do not know what happened. He's outside with his sister." April opened the door to the office and let me peer into the main part of the room. Cristiano sat on the floor, cupping Raquel's hand.

"Can I speak to him?"

"I don't think that's a good idea, Kellan."

"Just for a minute. I want to thank him for something."

April agreed and walked over to them with me.

Cristiano looked at me, his expression unreadable. I could sense the devastation that surrounded him. He peered at Raquel, who lay peacefully at his side, and closed her eyelids. With a lengthy sigh, he rose. "Is Emma okay?"

I nodded. "I'm sure we'll have more to say to one another in the coming days, but there are two things I feel compelled to tell you before leaving."

"Yes?" He breathed deeply, likely waiting for me to rip him apart.

"Thank you for protecting Emma, and I'm truly sorry about what happened to your sister. I have little idea who she was outside of this event, but the woman I grew to know in class always felt like someone she'd wanted to be on the inside." I turned and began to step away.

Cristiano grabbed my arm. "Raquel was once a good person. As a child, she had a passion for the changing the world for the better. Our father is a tyrant, and he insisted she be part of the family business. It is his fault that she died tonight, not yours or anyone else's."

"Does that mean you won't seek revenge against the Castigliano family?" I asked, hoping the war would end so that we could all move on with our lives.

"Your friend, the sheriff here, will do her best to convict me of several crimes. None of them will stick. I've done many wrong things in my lifetime, Kellan, but after tonight, I'm a changed man." Cristiano released my arm and let an officer place a pair of handcuffs on him. "I didn't kidnap Francesca, and I'm confident she will tell you the truth soon."

Stunned by his response, I could barely move. As Officer Flatman led him away, I called out and asked them to stop. "Wait! If you didn't kidnap her, who did?"

"No one. Francesca came of her own volition. She knew the only way to end this war was to turn in her family. She blamed them for losing you and her daughter for all these years. Francesca insisted on working the negotiations through you, so that she wouldn't have to deal directly with her parents. Neither you nor Emma were ever at risk until Vincenzo and Cecilia showed up here tonight. They should've listened to us, and none of this would've occurred." Cristiano closed his eyes and mumbled a silent prayer. When he opened them, much of the pain that had been plastered across his face had disappeared. "I'm in love with your wife, Kellan. I believe she is in love with me too. I hope that's going to be okay because I plan to fight for her. No hard feelings, *mi amigo?*"

"Take him away, Officer Flatman," April demanded, gripping my shoulder and dragging me in the opposite direction. "There is another time and a place for you to address all that nonsense. Let's bring you back to Emma and your mother."

I watched Cristiano's snarky grin as he was led away. What he'd said hadn't bothered me at all. Too much had transpired since the last time Francesca and I had been happy together, perhaps we'd all find a win at the end of this conflict.

When the door to Admissions Hall opened, I saw my wife standing outside near the ambulance before it drove away. She and her mother were directed into the backseat of a squad car headed to the hospital to check on Vincenzo. "May I have one more favor, April? I need to speak with her."

"Yes, of course," she said as we walked to the car. "Keep it brief for now. Let her focus on her father, then you can deal with explaining her return to Emma."

April stayed behind while I approached Francesca. Cecilia was already in the squad car.

"Did you really let me think you'd been kidnapped this entire time?" I asked.

Francesca's face was red and blotchy. She wiped a few tears against her shoulder and sniffled. "I did what was necessary to protect Emma's future. When I left Braxton, I went to Vancouver to be somewhere that reminded me of you and our past together. You hurt me, Kellan, when you told me I couldn't see Emma anymore."

"That doesn't answer my question." I firmly held my ground.

"When Cristiano found me, I had no intention of doing anything harmful. We spent a few days together talking about our families. Although we'd known who each other was, even met as kids a few times, he was different than I expected. Cristiano understood what it was like to grow up in a house where people's lives were carelessly played with as if they were meaningless." She sighed and lifted her handcuffed hands to her heart. "Our life together was different. You helped me escape from that type of crazy, and I never wanted to go back to it. My parents forced me to live in hiding, and when Cristiano presented an opportunity to escape, I went for it."

"So, that's a *yes*. You knowingly let me worry a second time. First, I think you're killed in a drunk driving car accident. Then, I think you're kidnapped by a rival family. What's next?" I said, feeling only contempt for my wife at that moment.

"What's next is that I'm going to visit my father at the hospital and pray that he survives his injuries." She shook her head at me, and for the first time, I saw an entirely different side of the woman I'd once been deeply in love with. "And then, I'm going to work with Cristiano to ensure neither of us goes to prison over what has happened. We started out only wanting to end the war between our families, but we ended up falling in love."

"Does that mean we're over?" I asked, knowing in my heart it was true but needing to hear the words from Francesca. "What about Emma?"

"I think we've been through too much to fix anything between you and me. I'd like to be friends, but it depends on what you do next." Francesca nodded at the officer to open the door to the squad car.

"What does that mean?" My heart began to race again.

"Emma needs to know I'm alive, that I love her. Are you going to keep me from my daughter?"

I hadn't formulated a plan. All I knew was that I had to be honest with Emma. "I won't keep you from her, but I'll do anything necessary to protect her from something like this ever happening again."

"As I said, maybe you and I can be friends. Once Cristiano's lawyers ensure he and I are released from custody, I intend to find a compromise. I know you won't let me have custody of Emma, and no court in the world would grant it to me after today."

"I'm angry with you right now. Let's have that discussion when we have a better sense of the future." I needed time to think. Hopefully, Emma didn't ask too many questions when she woke up. I was certain she'd seen Francesca for at least a minute inside the building. "I'm sorry about your father."

"You'll hear from me soon." After Francesca stepped inside the car, the officer shut the door and jumped in the front passenger seat.

As they took off, April sidled up. "You okay?"

"Not right now, but I will be."

"What can I do to help you?"

When April stopped speaking, I turned toward her, smiling for the first time that evening. Despite the darkness surrounding us in the sky, there was a floodlight shining from behind her that gave her an unusual glow. I saw the soft-ened lime-green eyes of a woman who genuinely worried about me. I felt the consuming energy radiating from a huge heart that comforted me. "I have a wedding to attend on Friday. It's for my aunt and her fiancé, but it's a double wedding because two other people we know are getting married. After every-thing we've been through these last few months, I feel like I owe you something fun in return. How would you like to attend it with me?"

"Little Ayrwick," she teased with a curious voice. "Are you asking me on a date?"

"That all depends," I replied, shoving my hands in my pockets and lifting my chest. "Didn't you agree to stop calling me that awful, mean, absurd, rude name?"

"I suppose I did."

"Then I suppose I did too." I looked toward the sky and watched a few stars blazing down on us. "I'll call you tomorrow with all the details. For now, I need to take my daughter home."

April smiled merrily before slowly wandering away in search of an officer.

I felt a sudden change in the atmosphere and knew things were finally starting to move in a positive direction. As I stepped forward, I felt a pain shoot up my foot. "April, hold up," I called, jogging awkwardly to catch her. "I have a gift for you." I removed a shoe to retrieve the storage device containing the evidence the Castiglianos had originally provided.

Tilting her head, April looked at me with a peculiar expression. "Did you seriously just pull that out of your sweaty shoe and try to hand it to me as if it were a gift?"

"I don't know to give someone on a first date anymore. It's been a long time since I went on one of those. Besides, I showered three hours ago." I shrugged and rolled my eyes. "Should I just shut up?"

April leaned in really close, so that our lips were barely two inches apart. "If we weren't standing at a crime scene, and you hadn't just said what you said, I would have kissed you by now."

"That doesn't sound like a legitimate excuse to me. Go ahead, make my night," I replied, reducing the gap to only one inch and closing my eyes. We were breathing the same air at that very moment, and it felt like one shared breath could carry us through the whole night.

"I think I'll save that notion for our first legitimate date after the wedding. Or after you get divorced. I don't usually date married men." April stepped backward a few feet, and a charming and wicked smile formed on her lips when I opened my eyes again. "I have grand expectations of any man I date. You should know I'm hardly the type to be wooed easily."

I let her walk away claiming the final word this time. I never minded losing a small battle when I was absolutely certain I would win the entire war. I reflected on my interaction with Raquel earlier that evening when I promised myself only one of us would make it out alive tonight. At the time, I'd been scared it wouldn't be me. While I valued life way too much to feel good about what had ended up happening, I permitted myself to feel blessed that the good guys had won for a change. I returned to the Admissions Hall to be with my daughter and mother, uncertain what the next few days would bring but strong enough to handle it. When I walked through the main room, I saw a man kneeling beside Raquel's body. The forensics team was still addressing the scene, but they'd allowed Manny to visit before she was enclosed in a body bag.

Manny heard me approach. "I don't know what to say. How could I have been so foolish?"

I told Manny that we'd both been taken advantage of, so I knew how he felt.

"Raquel didn't deserve to die, but we can't change the past. We can only focus on your future. I understand what's on your mind and how you're feeling. Please know that I'm here to support you however you need."

"The police told me everything she did. Is it true, Kellan? Did my wife really kill your brother's friend, Quint? And maybe your father-in-law?" The grief over everything he'd potentially done by giving his wife information about my family had finally impacted Manny.

"Yes, but there's something else you should know," I said, hesitant to burden the weakened man on top of everything he'd just learned. "Raquel told me earlier that your wedding wasn't real. She never filed the papers with the state, and the guy who married you didn't have a license."

Manny let the news settle for a minute, then hugged me. "I have mixed feelings about what you've just told me, but you are right. I am sorry for the loss and the pain impacting Raquel's family, but it means I have my life back, and I don't need to leave your sister alone with the diner."

Manny and I chatted for a few more minutes, and when he left campus, I had an inkling that the reason he'd been acting so weird around my sister wasn't just because he was afraid of deserting the diner once he thought Raquel would force him to leave Braxton. He'd unexpectedly developed romantic feelings for my sister and wasn't sure how to tell her the truth.

The office door opened, and my mother waved me over. "Emma is awake."

I rushed into the room to check on my daughter. "Hey, baby girl. We can go home now. You need to get some sleep. Baxter will be so excited to see you, and I'll be home all day tomorrow with you. No camp until next week. How does that sound?"

Emma jumped into my arms and hugged me with more power than a seven-year-old girl should have. "That's awesome, but I have a question, Daddy."

I knew what it was, and I had no way of avoiding it. "What's that, sweet girl?" I said, looking toward my mother, who shuffled closer and kissed Emma's forehead.

"Was that Mommy I saw earlier, or was it just a dream?"

"Tell her the truth, Kellan. She's a strong little girl because of you. I have faith you will find the proper words," my mother whispered in my ear, shedding her own tears over the night's traumatic events. In an instant, my mother and I had grown closer once again. "You're both brilliant ones."

I replied to Emma, "Let's go home and have that discussion. I'll make you a cup of cocoa, we can climb into bed with Baxter, and Daddy will explain everything that happened to us tonight. Okay?"

CHAPTER 21

Thursday was the kind of bittersweet day that highlighted why I should be proud of my daughter and thrilled with the positive swing my life had taken upon returning home to Braxton. After a lengthy and difficult conversation the previous night, Emma understood that her mother had been taken by bad guys who'd wanted to hurt our family. We talked about the dangers of lies and secrets, remembered tons of precious moments she'd shared with her mother years earlier, and discussed how to move forward as a family once we sorted out the proper steps.

It was bittersweet because I had to tell Emma that her mother and I wouldn't be together in the future. I compared it to a divorce, which she understood, citing how her friend Shalini's parents had gotten divorced recently too. I realized that I'd need to think about filing formal separation papers in the future to officially announce my intent to divorce Francesca. Before we could do that, she'd have to be declared legally alive again, at least as far as I understood from my brief Internet search. I decided to focus on Emma for the long holiday weekend and deal with the repercussions of everything else the following Monday.

Fern postponed the cable car ribbon-cutting ceremony until the subsequent week, so I spent Thursday with my family. Nana D had mayoral responsibilities to assure the citizens of Wharton County that the drama unfolding that week was fully under control. Nana D had even partnered with April to show a united front against crime in our towns, discussing how it happened and what everyone could do to prevent it from occurring again in the future. Limited details were released to the public for now. The county's official position was that the Castigliano and Las Vargas families ignited a turf war that had begun in Los Angeles and worked its way to Braxton the last few years. Nana D explained that the erstwhile sheriff had done little to hold the jewel thief accountable for his actions eight years ago, and we continued to suffer because of his dubious and unethical actions.

She lobbied hard to tell the truth to the citizens, but the county's attorney and new town council members felt it would be better to collect all the facts before distributing inaccurate information. Ultimately, Nana D yielded, not because she wasn't holding up her campaign promises to be honest but to ensure she didn't misspeak. She also threatened her staff with vague notions of torture if they didn't assemble a press release with all the details by the middle of the next week at the cable car reopening.

Nana D stopped by to chat before checking on Bertha, who was nearing the end of her battle with cancer. "The news about her brother-in-law's secrets and Quint's death has taken its toll on the woman. I'm afraid she won't make it until the end of the month, Kellan."

Nana D and I exchanged sorrowful glances over peppermint tea. I sliced the banana bread she'd brought and handed her a hearty piece. "Bertha didn't deserve a family like those two, but she had a good life. Everyone loves her in spite of all the trouble those two men caused."

We agreed to visit her together that weekend before she was too sick to recognize us as well as to take responsibility for her funeral plans. "Is Emma doing okay today?" Nana D asked, looking down the hall as my daughter rolled a tennis ball away from Baxter, trying to teach him to fetch.

"She slept in fairly late, then Mom and Dad came by to eat lunch with her. Gabriel was here, even Eleanor and Aunt Deirdre brought a few toys and games. Emma's tough, she'll be okay."

"When are you going to let her talk to Francesca?" Nana D had never really liked my wife, but she knew not to say anything disparaging, even if I'd agree with the words.

"Her father passed away at the hospital early this morning. Vincenzo's injuries were too invasive. She wants to see Emma as soon as possible, but we have an agreement that I'm hoping she'll stick to." We'd spoken for a few minutes when Francesca called to tell me what had happened to her father and promised to fairly co-parent for the sake of our daughter.

I hadn't told Emma that her nonno had passed away, but once we had details of his funeral service, I'd have another difficult conversation with my daughter that weekend. Francesca was allowed to remain at the hospital overnight with her father. Two cops, hand-selected by Connor and April, had been assigned guard duty outside the room to ensure nothing shady occurred. Francesca was distraught over her father's death, but she had a meeting with her family lawyer, Cristiano and his lawyer, and Wharton County's district attorney that afternoon to discuss next steps. The state of California would ask for extradition for crimes related to faking her death, which meant anything illegal she'd done in Pennsylvania would follow suit. It was too early to tell what would happen, but until any decisions were made, we didn't want to connect her and Emma. For one thing, it was a holiday weekend and no judge would change his schedule to accommodate the situation. For another,

Francesca and Cecilia had a funeral to prepare, which might occur while they spent the weekend in prison.

"When does Emma think she'll see her mother again?" Nana D asked while stirring her tea.

"I told her that Nonno was hurt and in the hospital for a few days and that her mommy was taking care of him. I felt bad lying, but I will tell her the truth. Is it wrong to want her to have one happy moment at tomorrow's wedding before crushing her again?"

Nana D wrapped her arms around me and refused to let go. "It's not, brilliant one. You are the only one who knows what's best for her. I'll sit with you two when we get home from the wedding tomorrow night, and we can tell her together."

"Thanks, Nana D. She loves you so much, it'll be easier if she knows you're doing okay."

"I'm never gonna die. You've heard me say that ever since you were a small boy. I'm not letting my family get away with an easy life, not while I can live to a hundred-and-twenty and torture them every day," she replied with a waggish smile, then pulled out her phone to read an incoming text message.

"Urgent mayoral business?"

"Not exactly. It's your Uncle Zachary. He needs to speak with me as soon as possible," Nana D said, sitting back in the chair.

"Isn't he on a safari in Africa saving the elephants?" My uncle was an amazing veterinarian, but he'd taken off the previous summer while I'd still lived in Los Angeles. He'd been granted a one-year contract to save a rare breed from extinction and had jumped on the opportunity.

"Yep, hold on, let me call him quick," she replied, pulling up his number and dialing him. "Maybe he's getting married too!"

Uncle Zach had once been married. His wife died during childbirth many years ago. She'd been pregnant with twins, but unfortunately, only one of the babies had survived. My cousin, Ulan, was the boy who lived, and he'd been given that name because it meant *first born of twins* in Africa. Ulan was currently fifteen years old and had moved with his father to Africa for the school year.

"Zach, is that you? I can barely hear you," Nana said, then reprimanded him for not returning home for his sister's wedding.

While Nana D released a bunch of monotonous *uh huhs* and *ah hahs*, I checked on Emma. She and Baxter had cuddled up on her bed as she read a story about a little dog who'd gotten lost but found a new home. She looked at me and smiled when I poked my head further into her room. My own phone chimed as I shuffled down the hallway. It was a Los Angeles number, but I couldn't be sure who was calling. I hoped it wasn't a news outlet who'd gotten wind of Vincenzo's death and wanted an interview.

"Hello, this is Kellan Ayrwick."

"Hi, it's Gary Hill from the television network that owns the rights to your show, *Dark Reality*. I want to have a conversation with you about a few things."

Dark Reality technically wasn't my show. I'd been an assistant director on the last two episodes of the first season, but once it had been put on hold and the main director was fired, I was out of a job earlier that year. "Good to meet you. I guess you're the new executive producer who assumed control."

"Yes, that would be me. Do you have a minute to speak?"

"To be honest, it's not really a good time. I have a family emergency and a funeral to attend, but I could catch up in a few days." If I was about to be let go formally, I'd rather deal with more shocking news at a future date.

"I understand. That's not a problem. Listen, maybe you could fly out to see me next week. I've been doing some research on the show and your background. I've got a proposal for you to consider."

I guessed I wasn't being fired. "I thought that decision was on hold until early next year?"

"It was, but I move faster than my sluggish predecessors. I've read your files and the proposal you made to that former nimrod director who got canned. I want you back in Hollywood, and if you're up for it, we want to televise your idea to...."

I stopped listening to him at that point. I couldn't believe my ears. I'd just finished saying how being home in Braxton might've been the best decision I'd made all year long. Now, this happened. I agreed to a follow-up call next week and hung up with Gary to let the news settle.

I strolled into the kitchen in a daze, catching the very end of Nana D's phone call with my uncle.

"I'm not able to do that, Zach. If I could, I'd help you out, but I'm hardly at home anymore," she said to him as she looked up at me. A huge smile overtook her face before she responded again. "Actually, I have another idea in mind. Go ahead, book the flight. We'll make this work."

Nana D and my uncle talked for a few more minutes while I cleaned up the saucers and cups from our afternoon tea. What had she done to herself now? Nana D slammed her phone on the table and guffawed. "That boy of mine is absentminded and never plans ahead."

"What did he do now?" I shouted over the running water.

"He accepted an extension on that elephant project, and now he's gonna be in Africa for another year. I love my children to death, but they might actually stop me from reaching my goal of living another fifty years." Nana D grabbed her shawl from the back of the chair and tapped me on the shoulder.

I didn't like the wicked expression on her face. "I heard you tell him you couldn't do something, then you changed your mind. Spill it. You look like a cat who swallowed a canary."

"Now that the idea has sunk in, it's actually quite spectacular, brilliant one." She yanked my arm so I would bend down for her to kiss my cheek. "You won't be able to live here anymore, but we'll find you a new place."

"Huh?" I'd come to love living in the cottage. Why was she kicking me out? As Nana D walked toward the front door, I turned off the faucet, dried my hands, and raced to the living room. "What did you do?"

"Zach is gonna be too busy to pay attention to his son. He wants Ulan to stay with me for the next year. The schools are fine where he's working, but it's ostensibly not the same." Nana D pushed open the front door and sauntered onto the porch.

"What does that have to do with me moving out of the cottage?" If someone could lock my nana in a closet for the rest of her life, it would be the biggest blessing I'd ever receive.

"With my duties as the new mayor, I certainly won't have time to babysit Ulan. I'm done with raising kids, especially a hormonal teenager entering manhood. Your Uncle Campbell's still in the Amazon. Deirdre and Timothy will be newlyweds hopping back and forth across the Atlantic. That simply won't do." She stepped onto the main pathway and walked toward the driveway.

"Yeah, so?" I knew what was coming, but I didn't want to say it.

"Your parents have the room, but honestly, with the way some of your siblings turned out...." She swung open the car door, then spun, her hand cupping her chin and one finger tapping the side of her cheek.

"You. Did. Not."

"I did. Ulan will live with you for the next year while his father is trying to do something positive for the precious elephants. Emma will love having her cousin around. It'll be like an older brother." Nana D sat in her car, started the engine, and rolled down her window. "I guess you better start looking for a new place. With only two bedrooms, the three of you can't live here comfortably. Maybe Gabriel can take over the cottage now." Nana D waved at me and sped down the driveway to her next meeting.

I grunted. Twice. And then a third time because I realized I'd stepped in dog poop. "Emma, Baxter is not supposed to be out front unsupervised...."

* * *

On Friday, also Independence Day, we attended the much-anticipated double wedding. Aunt Deirdre asked me to escort her down the aisle since her father had passed away years ago, and her two brothers were out of town. She'd considered asking my father but quickly abandoned the idea. Nana D would be on one side of my aunt, and there was no way she'd share the role with Wesley Ayrwick.

Aunt Deirdre looked stunning in her vintage wedding gown when I met her in the dressing room. In just a few minutes, we'd walk down the path to a covered gazebo at Crilly Lake where she'd marry Timothy Paddington. Meanwhile, Timothy's sister, Jennifer Paddington, wore a beautiful but modern wedding gown that practically disguised her growing belly. Her Uncle Millard would escort her down the same aisle to marry Arthur Terry, Fern's son.

Friends and family of both couples were in attendance. Even my siblings, Penelope and Hampton, had returned for the weekend. Gabriel and his boyfriend, Sam Taft—Jennifer and Timothy's nephew—sat in the front row cheering them on. I saw them holding hands as I accompanied my aunt to the gazebo. On the opposite side of the seating area, Fern waved to me with tears flowing from her eyes. She'd never been so proud of her son and couldn't hold back her excitement about becoming a grandmother soon.

Eleanor had left the diner behind for the day, promoting Manny as her new manager, at least once Maggie, her mostly silent partner in the business, agreed with the change. He'd hold double duty as her chef in the meantime, but I was certain new things would blossom for them in the future. My sister might fight it at first, just as she struggled to deny everything until ultimately yielding to the truth. Perhaps she'd finally give up on my best friend, Connor, who was seated with Maggie in the far back making googly eyes at his date. Honestly, those two were meant for each other all along.

Emma was the flower girl, and she walked down the aisle leading Baxter at her side. She'd practiced with him several times, but no matter how hard she'd begged, he kept eating the cushion and swallowing the fake plastic rings that we'd strapped to his back. We weren't taking a chance that he'd eat the real ones on the wedding day, so Emma kept them safe in a small pocket in her dress. She told everyone how pretty she felt and that she couldn't wait until her wedding day in a few years. I explained that she would never be allowed to get married as long as I was alive. I won't share the inappropriate gesture Nana D taught her as an apt response—and at a wedding, no doubt!

Nana D shed another tear when the priest asked her who was giving away Aunt Deirdre. I handed her my handkerchief, but she brushed it aside, claiming her allergies were acting up from being outside near the lake. Grandpop Michael was with us in spirit; I could feel him at my side. I stepped off the gazebo and rushed to my seat, where April waited for me. I hadn't yet seen her that day. My attention had been occupied, keeping us on schedule and stopping others from bawling their eyes out.

When she came into view, my eyes bulged and my lips curled. She'd had her hair professionally styled into a chignon secured at the nape of her neck. A gorgeous green dress clung to her body, accentuating the shimmering lime pools that were her eyes. The perfect amount of cleavage peeked from the top of her dress, tempting me more than I desired, and a slit in the dress revealed two exquisite, shapely legs finished off with a pair of strappy heels. This was not the same sheriff I'd frequently seen wearing a tweed blazer, plain jeans, and boring boots.

"Who are you, and what have you done with April Montague?" I asked, sitting next to her and feeling my body react to the sudden hotness of my date.

"I assure you, Kellan... what you see is what you get with me. Everything is real, and there are many sides to me you've not been exposed to before." April grabbed my hand and shushed me. "There's a wedding going on here. Don't make me do something to shut you up." She opened her purse and showed me that *Old Betsy* was waiting inside, in case the need to make its appearance arose again.

When the ceremony ended, two new couples had become husband and wife. I reflected on my own wedding day—both the positives and the negatives that had since materialized. Despite a rough week, we had found our compromise, but my heart still panged for my wife's recent loss. I would visit her the next day to do whatever I could to help plan her father's funeral. She knew already, but I wanted to ensure they played a *Billy Joel* song to give Vincenzo a proper send-off.

The wedding reception was held at the country club not too far from Crilly Lake. After all the toasts, I turned to April. "This is probably an odd question, but have you ever been married before?" I knew she'd been engaged at one point, before her fiancé had been killed in a drive-by shooting.

"I feel like I know everything about your life. I guess I haven't shared much about mine other than what happened to my brother and my fiancé," she replied with a devilish gleam in her eyes.

"You didn't answer the question," I said, curious why she was avoiding the topic.

"No, I didn't answer it. Would you consider this our first date?" April countered, clinking our champagne glasses together. "Even though you are still married."

"Yes, I believe I would." I saw Nana D approaching and felt an urge to run for my life.

"We probably shouldn't cover all our history on a first date, right?" April said before swallowing half the contents of the glass. "Let's enjoy the process of getting to know one another."

What was she trying to tell me? Had she been married prior to the last fiancé? "Um, that's not fair. You know about Francesca. Shouldn't you be equally forthcoming about—"

"Your grandmother is almost here. We have time to discuss all that stuff, Kellan."

"Is it true?" Nana D asked, shifting her gaze from me to April, then back again a few times. "You understand my grandson is still a married man. And that I'm your boss based on our current jobs."

"Am I here with Kellan in an official capacity, you mean?" April offered as a response to Nana D.

Nana D crossed her arms. "Hmmm... I need a minute alone with my grandson, Sheriff. Would you mind refilling my glass?"

April took Nana D's flute. "Rest assured, Mayor Danby, I'm not the kind of woman to pry in another couple's marital woes. For the moment, I'm enjoying the company of a handsome guy who helped me solve a few investigations. What the future holds, I suppose we'll all find out." She winked at me, then seductively glided toward the bar on the other side of the room. Was that sashay for me?

My mouth hung agape until Nana D shut it with two fingers. "Maybe I misjudged that woman. You could do worse. You have done worse, actually, now that I think—"

"Please stay out of it. I have no idea what's going on, and my life is a mess, but I'm happy to be here with our family." I scanned the room to verify Emma still stood on my father's toes as he led her around the dance floor.

"That's fine. We have plenty of time to talk about it this weekend after we figure out how to welcome Ulan when he arrives next month," she complied, resting her head on my shoulder.

"Next month? I thought I had a few months before he flew here. How am I gonna find a new place to live?" I didn't dare bring up the phone call I'd gotten from Hollywood. Nana D might strangle me in front of everyone if I told her I had an offer to leave town again.

"Can it, or I'll slap your bottom silly in front of your new girlfriend." She tapped her foot against the floor, deep in thought. "You know, the old Grey place was on the market. I'm not sure it is anymore, at least if you believe the rumors."

Eleanor strode up just as Nana D mentioned the dilapidated house on the corner of Main Street near Millionaire's Mile that no one would buy. "The place that's been haunted for fifty years?"

Nana D smiled and slapped her thigh. "Yep, that one. The plumbing is leaking. The walls are falling. Just yesterday, a ceiling tile smashed into my shoulder and an angry spirit floated by me."

"I thought that place was ready to be demolished," I suggested meekly as my nerves prickled.

"It is," Eleanor said, tossing her head back and forth to the beat of the music. "Too many people claim they hear noises and voices emanating from it all the time."

"Ever since that woman vanished, there have been rumors about ghosts visiting the place. I blame it all on Hiram Grey," Nana D replied.

"What's he got to do with the woman's disappearance?" I asked.

"Don't you know anything about our town's history, big brother? His first wife went missing the day of that big fire in the old library. No one ever heard from her again." Eleanor shook her head repeatedly, reminding me of all the times she, Gabriel, and Nana D had ganged up on me in the past.

"That woman put a curse on their house before she skipped town. People always claim they see a spook haunting the place on the anniversary of the fire every year since it happened," Nana D said.

"Are you two pulling my leg?" My stomach sunk and my throat began to close.

Nana D was never one to tell ghost stories or believe in that sort of nonsense. Even though Eleanor claimed she was in touch with her psychic abilities, it was only something we joked about. "I don't know, Kellan. All I know is that's an historical home, and it would be a shame to let it go to waste."

"Are you proposing that I should buy the old Grey house, fix it up, and move into it?" I rolled my eyes at Nana D's foolish suggestion. "Nope, not happening. I will not deal with the paranormal or supernatural. I draw a line at the types of things I investigate when it comes to evaporating spooks!"

"You don't have to buy it. I already made an offer to the cantankerous old judge this morning. That restless tomcat couldn't wait to unload the place. You'll be able to afford it, trust me, brilliant one." Nana D accepted her refilled champagne flute from April, who'd returned in time to hear the news and toast my potential new home.

"I can handle dead people, but I'm not ready to live among a tribe of vengeful ghosts." Then, I hung my head and accepted Nana D would always run my life. What kind of adventure were we in store for next? It couldn't be worse than all the chaos and drama I'd stumbled upon so far this year. Could it?

Dear Reader,

Thank you for taking time to read *Braxton Campus Mysteries Collection*. Word of mouth is an author's best friend and much appreciated. If you enjoyed it, please consider supporting this author:

- Leave a book review on any book site you follow to help market and promote this book
- Tell your friends, family, and colleagues all about this author and his books
- Share brief posts on your social media platforms and tag the book (#BraxtonCampusMysteries) or author (#JamesJCudney)
- Suggest the book for book clubs, to bookstores, or to any libraries you know

ABOUT THE AUTHOR

 James is my given name, but most folks call me Jay. I live in New York City, grew up on Long Island, and graduated from Moravian College, an historic but small liberal arts school in Bethlehem, Pennsylvania, with a degree in English literature and minors in Education, Business and Spanish.

Writing has been a part of my life as much as my heart, my mind and my body. At some points, it was just a few poems or short stories; at others, it was full length novels and stories. My current focus is family drama fiction, cozy mystery novels and suspense thrillers.

* * *

To learn more about James J. Cudney and discover more Next Chapter authors, visit our website at www.nextchapter.pub.

Printed in Great Britain
by Amazon

24592498R00421